四海一家、天涯比邻

海外华人与中国梦

[美]谭中　[美]凌焕铭　主编

中央编译出版社
Central Compilation & Translation Press

图书在版编目（CIP）数据

四海一家、天涯比邻：海外华人与中国梦
汉、英／谭中，凌焕铭主编．
—北京：中央编译出版社，2015.8

ISBN 978-7-5117-2490-8

Ⅰ.①中… Ⅱ.①谭… ②凌… Ⅲ.①社会科学－文集－汉、英 Ⅳ.①C53

中国版本图书馆CIP数据核字（2015）第168806号

四海一家、天涯比邻：海外华人与中国梦

| 出 版 人：刘明清
| 责任编辑：邓　彤
| 责任印制：尹　珺
| 出版发行：中央编译出版社
| 地　　址：北京西城区车公庄大街乙5号鸿儒大厦B座（100044）
| 电　　话：（010）52612345（总编室）　　（010）52612335（编辑室）
| 　　　　　（010）52612316（发行部）　　（010）52612317（网络销售）
| 　　　　　（010）52612346（馆配部）　　（010）55626985（读者服务部）
| 传　　真：（010）66515838
| 经　　销：全国新华书店
| 印　　刷：北京京华虎彩印刷有限公司
| 开　　本：787毫米×1092毫米　1/16
| 字　　数：448千字
| 印　　张：29.25
| 版　　次：2015年8月第1版第1次印刷
| 定　　价：88.00元

网　　址：www.cctphome.com　　邮　　箱：cctp@cctphome.com
新浪微博：@中央编译出版社　　微　　信：中央编译出版社（ID：cctphome）
淘宝店铺：中央编译出版社直销店（http://shop108367160.taobao.com）
　　　　　（010）52612349

凡有印装质量问题，本社负责调换。电话：（010）55626985

目 录

序言（一） …………………………………………………… 谭　中（1）
序言（二） …………………………………………………… 凌焕铭（9）

一　路是践踏出来的

杆栏拍遍平生梦
　　——在美国教授西班牙语文学之低吟清唱 ………… 梁旭华（3）
凡我到处，就是中国
　　——"中国梦"在海外 …………………………………… 郁龙余（12）
愿将生命化彩虹
　　——第一个在西方创建东方艺术博物馆的中国人 ……… 朱新天（19）
愿中印两大文明永远昌盛
　　——我的中国梦 ………………………………………… 朱新天（26）
我的"中国梦"及父亲的教化 ………………………………… 袁　清（33）
谁解胡尘箫剑梦去留肝胆洒长城 …………………………… 陈咏智（41）
我的生活与环境健康之梦 …………………………………… 何淑薇（51）
乘剑漂洋世界入怀 …………………………………………… 斯蒂芬·陈（57）

二　"中国梦"与世界

我的中国梦
　　——东西方文明融会的伟大契机 ……………………… 林明雅（65）

美丽中国新纪元的曙光
　　——从郑观应到今天的"中国梦" ………………………… 郑国强（72）
世界进化的"中国力"升级版：
　　打造"命运共同体"世界的"中国梦" …………………… 黄枝连（80）
同族异梦怎同德？
　　——从关怀、思辨、和沟通方式看华人寻向 …………… 钟伦纳（88）

三　四海一家亲

世界大同：我家两代人的中国梦 ……………………………… 谭　中（101）
构建汉语桥　实现中国梦 ……………………………………… 顾利程（108）
我的中国梦：面向全民的高质量早期儿童教育 ……………… 陈杰琦（118）
梦绕东西文明：修辞与传播 …………………………………… 吕　行（128）
月亮船，带着希望和梦想 ……………………………………… 张四齐（134）
中印一家亲　共享富强梦 ……………………………………… 黄绮淑（142）

四　专题论坛（一）

化中国梦为世界梦 ……………………………………………… 王义桅（151）

四　专题论坛（二）

"中国梦"与"美国梦" ………………………………………… 熊　玠（177）
鉴别中国梦
　　——谁的"中国"，谁的"梦"？ ………………………… 凌焕铭（183）

序言（一）

谭 中

"背负起白人的包袱——
你繁衍的人种迸发——
流放你的子孙
去为你的俘虏服务。"

(Take up the White Man's burden—
Send forth the best ye breed—
Go send your sons to exile
To serve your captives' need)

这几句诗是英国诗人吉卜林（Rudyard Kipling）名诗《白种人的包袱》(The White Man's Burden)的第一炮，是西方征服全球梦想的呐喊。成诗时间是1899年，我出生的那年（1929年）正是《吉卜林诗集选定本》(Rudyard Kipling's Verse Definitive Edition) 初版在纽约问世，这首诗被认为帝国主义的时代灵魂。那时英国的世界"霸权"正在如日初升的"美国梦"中融化。"中国梦"呢？背着"东亚病夫"臭名的中国，还能谈什么"中国梦"，岂不让人讥笑！我三岁时在上海就看到日本兵在闸北的狰狞面貌。后来在老家湖南成长，那是抗日与逃难的岁月，从来听不到"中国梦"这三个字，却成天受爱国歌曲的熏陶。我还没成为少年（teenager）就爱上了一首歌，它的第一段是：

> "热血滔滔，热血滔滔，
> 像江里的浪，像海里的涛，
> 常在我心头环绕。
> 只因为耻辱未雪，愤恨难消，
> 四万万同胞啊，
> 洒着你的热血
> 去除强暴。"

这是一首悲壮的歌，虽然"中国梦"被压抑到人们心底，却仍有着强大的召唤力。每逢学校歌咏比赛，我就唱着这首歌参加。我一唱它，全身血液沸腾、满头大汗，有位老师看见对我说："别紧张，慢慢唱！"但我无法克制自己。现在把这首歌和上面引的吉卜林《白种人的包袱》第一段相比，也看出不同时代、不同国家的激动。

在"中国梦"唤醒人们抛头颅、洒热血的过程中，千千万万仁人志士倒下，中国却站起来了。我们这些海外华人没有亲自投身进去，却是这一历史进程的见证人。当今中国热情谈论"中国梦"，我们这些海外华人借这本书参加到谈论"中国梦"的热潮中来。在国内，中国人"热血滔滔"；在海外，中国人同样"热血滔滔"，这国内与海外的数不清的"热血滔滔"永远"像江里的浪，像海里的涛"，永远跟随时代的步伐向前。

"黄河落天走东海，万里写入胸怀间"，这李白的诗句每时每刻提醒我们，无论是国内中国人的"热血滔滔"，还是海外华人的"热血滔滔"，我们的胸怀间都有一幅"黄河落天走东海"的图画，是数千年文明智慧的结晶，是中华"文明国"与人类世界的交响共鸣。一千多年前李白有他的"中国梦"：锦绣山河、广袤大地、圣哲格言、诗人牢骚、国家命运、人生经历、今古变迁、阴晴圆缺统统收入李白的胸怀间与脑海内，怎么能不在他的生活现实与想象境界之间织成气象万千的丹青呢？！请听："安得倚天剑，跨海斩长鲸"、"长风破浪会有时，直挂云帆济沧海"！

我们今天的时代，比李白的生活环境不知要丰富多少倍，我们的"中国梦"想象力更是万花筒的灿烂多姿与千变万化。要看到，今天我们有李白做梦也想象不到的高速公路、高铁、汽车、火车、飞机、太空飞船、人造嫦娥、电脑、手机、互联网等等。也要看到，所有这些现代器具，没有一样是中国发明的，中国必须仿效别国来过现代生活。更要看到，发明这些现代器皿的国家却没有李白。它们一千多年前也没人写过"黄河落天走东海，万里写入胸怀间"。这就要求今天我们谈论"中国梦"，要把李白那手持"倚天剑"去"跨海斩长鲸"的想象力发挥出来，不使我们的头脑淹没于高速公路、高铁、汽车、火车、飞机、太空飞船、电脑、手机、互联网的世俗红尘之中而丧失中华数千年的文明智慧。只有这样，我们的"振兴中华梦"、"富强梦"、"全面小康梦"才有中国特色，才是真正的"中国梦"。

我们这本书作不了"中国梦"的权威性论述，因为"中国梦"并不是政治理论，论述"中国梦"也不是任何人的特权，没有什么"中国梦"的一家之言，也不可能对"中国梦"来一次百家争鸣。当今中国理论权威大谈"中国梦"，普通老百姓也大谈"中国梦"；国内与海外华人大谈"中国梦"，国际上"老外"也大谈"中国梦"。我们海外华人静观"老外"大谈"中国梦"，不免感觉他们有点隔靴搔痒，但承认他们和海外华人同样有权利大谈"中国梦"，有权利对"中国梦"作出这样或那样、近理或荒唐的结论。同样地，国内专家与知识精英可能感觉我们海外华人大谈"中国梦"不像他们那样深入透彻而切合实际国情，但是他们也应该承认我们海外华人有权利对"中国梦"作出这样或那样、近理或荒唐的结论。

我们这本书和国际上"老外"凑热闹来大谈"中国梦"是有本质区别的。我们是借"中国梦"来谈我们自己，也是借我们自己来谈"中国梦"，不是纸上谈兵，而是谈心底深处的感受。如果从来没有"中国梦"就不会有我们海外华人，如果没有我们海外华人，"中国梦"就不会这么甜蜜。

本书张四齐文章有一句："'游子的脚印，血泪斑斑'，自古以来华人离乡背井就有这样的形容。"马克思曾经描写新大陆铁路的"每一根枕木都躺着一具华人的尸体"，人们一谈起海外华人就不免回忆他们经历过的辛酸史。但是中国历史上也有怀着高尚理想去国外留学"求法"与"取经"的。七世纪到印度取经的著名高僧义净说："晋宋齐梁唐代间，高僧求法离长安；去人成百归无十，后者焉知前者难。"义净告诉我们虽然每次数百人成群结队去印度，生还回国的寥寥无几，求法高僧始终前赴后继。梁启超称之为中国古代的留学运动。参加本书写作的海外华人绝大多数都是现代留学运动中的成员，古代"求法高僧"的后继者，他们都是"中国梦"的圆梦者，是"中国梦"造成他们"四海一家、天涯比邻"的境遇。读者会发现他们谈"中国梦"是感性与理性的结合，具有参考价值。

读者从本书的文章中也可以看出海外华人的生存与处境和中国本身的发展与变迁有着密切的联系。新加坡佛学教授林明雅写道："我算是海外第三代华人"。他把"中国梦"提出的"为造福全人类，再创华夏辉煌"的"两个百年的宏伟目标"称之为"我这一海外华夏子民此时此刻最大的中国梦"。

本书作者中也有华人到海外创业的第二代，袁清教授从他父亲（著名图书馆长与图书学专家袁同礼）的"中国梦"写到他自己的"中国梦"，这自传式叙述两代海外华人在美国创业奋斗的故事也是整个"中国梦"故事的组成部分。我自己的拙文也以父亲谭云山1924年出国感怀的"异国远行我独去"开头。人称他为"现代玄奘"，但他最后一次回国是1959作为特邀政协委员，以后就再没有回国观光机会，最后于1983年在印度比哈尔邦菩提场的中国庙里被"平等王"召去。

回想起上世纪六十年代中期，我成为印度德里大学中文讲师，加入了该大学接受了美国福特基金会的援助的中国研究项目的开创，有机会与福特基金会派去指导工作的两位海外华人学术界前辈聚会、谈心。他们是四十年代去美国留学的、已故著名历史学家兼文学家、前纽约市立大学东亚系主任唐德刚教授与退休的哥伦比亚大学教育学专家胡昌度教授。唐德刚说，他本来对新中国是有隔阂的。但在美国公众场合经常受到白人侮辱，看见他就喊"僵泥Johnny"（和白人叫黑人"Nigger"一样具有贬义）。有一次他忍不住了，就理直气壮地在叫喊者面前站住大声说："Johnny现在有原子弹了！"那些白皮肤的侮辱者竟灰溜溜地走开了。

胡昌度（他是九旬寿星了，我祝他贵体康健）说，四十年代从中国去美国留学的都是些知识精英，他们发愤念书，读完硕士又读博士，五十年代初期一个个学业优异，就是找不到工作，许多人进了"三馆"（中餐馆、洗衣馆、图书馆），要到大学执教，难于上青天。新中国成立，特别是"抗美援朝"，使美国懂得中国厉害，于是大力加强对中国的研究，很多华人学者在大学找到好工作了，他们不管是亲共还是反共的，都从心底喊"毛主席万岁！"这两个例子很生动地勾画出海外华人没有强大的祖国支持是没有好日子过的，也道出海外华人对圆"中国梦"有切身的感性与理性经历。

我们在海外也能看到："人类只有一个地球"，一方面，地球日益变平、距离不断缩短；另一方面，与世界其他国家相比，中国的体积、重量、声望、责任一天比一天加大，海外华人又成了"中国梦"的客观缩影。"凡我到处，就是中国"，这是年轻海外华人郁秀为我们的书想出的杰出标题，由她父亲、深圳大学资深教授郁龙余成文，为本书添金。郁文说："中国是'国'，更是数千年的悠久文明。"每个海外华人都是数千年中华悠久文明的代表。海外华人对中国实现"朋友遍天下"作出了莫大贡献。

为我们书撰文的海外华人中有两位在中华人民共和国成长的女性知识分子，她们幼年时代心怀大志，后来在海外为自己、为祖国争一口气，创造出不凡的事迹。由外祖父母带大的梁旭华从才华横溢的舅舅阿姨那儿耳濡目染，承继了中华文明数千年的传统智慧与雄心壮志，在美国成为使人惊讶的"黑头发黄皮肤"的西班牙语言文学专家教授，为本书读者提供了一个动人的艰苦创业故事。在西方首创东方艺术博物馆的海外华人朱新天的故事说来话长，在本书中占了两篇文章的位置。本书所收的二十篇文章都有故事，请读者仔细去读、认真咀嚼其中的精神文明滋味，体会到海外华人"中国梦"的丰富内容。

梁旭华在美国有特别的经历。她那黑头发、黄皮肤无论是站在大学西班牙语文课教室的讲台上还是参加西班牙文学讨论会都会引起误会，迟到的学生一看见她就以为走错教室了，与会的专家一看见她就以为她走错会场了。最后的结果是美国西班牙语教育界服帖地接受了这位海外华人，美国西班牙文学研究群体热情地欢迎了这位海外华人。我们希望所有海外华人都像梁旭华一样打造黑头发、黄皮肤的可爱与可敬的形象，可惜现实并不如此。

"乱在内为宄，在外为奸"，自古皆然。海外华人良莠混杂，出了不少丢失国格、危害中华形象、甚至背叛炎黄老祖宗的败类，但绝大多数能为中华文明树立旗帜，在海外帮助祖国确定"和平崛起"的形象。本书写作班子的很多人都是在海外有建树的。除了上面谈到的梁旭华与朱新天外，何淑薇教授在医疗上与医学研究上的成可圈可点。陈咏智教授描述了周文中和他自己两位国际知名的音乐家的动人故事。还有将《红楼梦》译成法文的李治华教授的事迹为郁龙余文章收集。没想到本书问世竟超越了"海外华人与中国梦"的初衷，起了表彰海外华人为"中国梦"的奋斗成功事例的作用，是我们额外的收获。

澳门历史文物关注协会理事长郑国强先生为本书撰写郑观应和孙中山两位现代"中国梦"的急先锋的理想，帮我们把现代"中国梦"的来龙去脉理顺了。孙中山在一百多年前就自信"我们美丽的国家将会出现新纪元的曙光"，世界和平将随"中国的新生"而来。我们这些在孙中山这话的四分之一至半个世纪以后诞生的人，小时的中国仍然被困在内忧外患之中，谈不上"美丽的国家"，看不到"新纪元的曙光"。但有了孙中山的话，人们就有了"中国梦"，就开始等待"中国的新生"。1949年10月1日毛泽东在天安门城楼用浓重的湘潭口音说"中国人民站起来了"，的确是划时代的一刻。很明显，新中国诞生后，小时候经历过的那些受外国欺凌的"耻辱未雪"与"愤恨难消"都只能从小说与电影故事中去找了。

我听国内有些年轻人说，听国歌的"起来"、"起来"都听腻了。还记得，我这个从三十年代开始就喜欢唱《义勇军进行曲》的中国小学生，1959年在印度教书时从收音机（那时还没有电视）中听到容国团夺得世界乒乓单打冠军得奖时奏起《义勇军进行曲》，我的血沸腾了，眼泪夺眶而出，心中跟着唱"起来，不愿做奴隶的人们"来。七十年代末突然听到国歌的"我们万众一心，冒着敌人的炮火，前进"被华国锋等人修改成"我们千秋万代，高举毛泽东旗帜，前进"，真不知是什么滋味，我顿时对这首歌失去兴趣，也不想要它做我的国歌了。幸亏后来那修改的歌词遭到十一届三中全会否定。这一切又说明"中国梦"的历史背景不能篡改，谈论"中国梦"也不应和历史背景割裂开来。

这样，问题又来了，中国有数千年文明的历史背景，"中国梦"的来龙去脉究竟应该怎么理顺呢？前面我谈到了一千两百年前李白的"安得倚天剑，跨海斩长鲸"、"长风破浪会有时，直挂云帆济沧海"的梦想，难道不应该成为我们今天的"中国梦"灵感吗?

同是炎黄子孙,国内同胞"中国梦"比海外华人深刻,海外华人"中国梦"比国内同胞全面。本书最后一部分算是国内同胞与海外华人对"中国梦"的共同论坛。人民大学国际问题专家王义桅教授写了《化"中国梦"为"世界梦"》与国内外学者共同探讨,把宋儒张载的绝世名言"为天地立心,为生民立命,为往圣继绝学,为万世开太平"融入"中国梦"的灵感。

我写这些话的时候,看到6月23日印度《先锋报》(The Pioneer)一篇文章,是印度胜选当政的印度人民党BJP副主席、印度国会联邦院议员、时评家彭基(Balbir Punj)写的。它主张印度和俄国、中国、美国、英国、欧洲、孟加拉国、泰国、印尼等国联合起来结成全球反恐同盟以应付"伊拉克和叙利亚伊斯兰国ISIS"(也称"伊拉克和黎凡特伊斯兰国ISIL")的挑战。我们海外华人看得清楚,目前整个世界处于和平时代,美国不会想和中国开战,日本也不会想和中国开战,越南也不会想和中国开战,印度也不会想和中国开战,其他国家没有一个会想和中国开战的(只有一个还没正式成为国家的ISIS/ISIL发誓要使新疆演变成"东突厥帝国"),只要中国真正"和平崛起"、不逞强、不称霸,妥善处理涉外的问题与纠纷,在经济发展与贸易交往中不片面追求"对我生财",而是遵照"双赢"、"共富"的原则,甚至能做到《老子》所说的"既以为人己愈有,既以与人己愈多"那种与人为善而最终自己受益的开明聪炯,中国就不会再吃二遍苦,"中国梦"就会是真正的美梦。

编辑《化"中国梦"为"世界梦"》刚刚收尾,又听到2014年11月9日国家主席习近平出席2014年亚太经合组织(APEC)工商领导人峰会并作题为《谋求持久发展共筑亚太梦想》的主旨演讲,中国舆论的聚焦从"中国梦"转移到"亚太梦",这是极有意义的。北京APEC唱出"亚太梦"的理想之歌正是我们海外华人殷切巴望的化"中国梦"为"世界梦"的进程的开始,习近平提倡的"世界命运共同体"为这一进程打下坚实的基础。

读者可以看出,本书的每一篇文章都有一颗赤子之心,都希望"中国梦"圆满。文章中也有对中国的发展不同阶段进行评论,对某些不良现象进行批评的,都是些肺腑之言,提供中国政府与民间参考。

亲爱的读者们，本书是一本文集，每位作者见仁见智，我作为编者不能包办代替，只能把他们的肺腑之言奉献给大家，如果是有价值的，请大家欣赏；如果是不恰当的，请大家批评指正。

谭　中

2014 年 11 月美国芝加哥

序言（二）

我十分荣幸，出乎意料地受谭中教授邀请，合编这本书。我和谭教授幸会，是许多年前他到纽约新校大学（The New School）来讲演，讲演会由我主持。那天，恰巧是谭中教授的八十寿诞。现在回想起来，庆祝诞生的反而是我们。在讲演过后讨论时，冒出一位听众，看来四十岁左右，批评谭教授不是真正的历史家，由于历史研究方法"不正，"列举史实争辩。我心里烦想：这人大概是在德国受培训的，态度那么尖锐！谭中教授没有针锋相对，却和蔼地说："你我看法不同，无关紧要。可是我没说你不是历史学者，你为什么对我恰相反？"

这一插曲显示出学问与政治的交叉。谭中教授不像平常西方学术界常见的唇枪舌剑，也不想刁难企图贬抑学术界著名长者的小伙子而使他下不了台。相反地，谭教授却以中印两大古文明的智慧来反问提问者，好像在说：我们谁也不想高人一等，平起平坐地谈问题好吗？其实，在西方五个世纪的殖民与帝国思想支配下，这种智慧已被排挤到黑角，很多继承了中印文明遗产的人也融会贯通了西方学者的那一套而东施效颦。那个礼貌欠缺的提问者就是来自中国。

我们这本书正是为了发扬那天的启示，发扬"推己及人"之道，在西方的"己"的大环境中喊出东方文化的"人"的呼声。（本书作者绝大多数是在北美与欧洲工作的华人。）通过聚焦于所谓"海外华人"这一座人种与文化的桥梁，本书达到两个目的。第一个目的是打乱了那种以吉卜林（Rudyard Kipling）"白种人的包"自我"与"他人"的对立来显示一种"中道，"也是冲着一些海外华人（就像前面提到的那个礼貌欠缺的提问者）在他们的言行中早就把中华文明忘得一干二净迫使我们不得不这样做。第二个目的是通过我们海外华人梳理自己的"中国梦"而使大家看到个别国家的标志与经历不再是新枝嫩叶,它们相倚相缚、相辅相成,制造历史的成败悲欢,思念故乡与建造新居交织。这一"中道"使得人们学会运用—即使是片面地、逐渐地、尝试地—从单一方面(中国或是西方)获得的处世之道去到多元传统的多元处境适应环境。本书许多作者都强调了中国应该通过学习(或者再学习)而把自己当作众人之一,而不是以凤凰腾飞、鹤立鸡群的姿态,来在世界上长存。也许正是这样才能使世界、中国与我们自己复活转世。

凌焕铭

2014年12月美国纽约

一

路是践踏出来的

一 路是践踏出来的

出生于南国凤凰花开的鹭岛——厦门。"文革"期间她年幼时母亲因病去世，从小由外祖父母抚养。1977年以优异成绩考进北京外语学院（现北京外国语大学）西班牙语系，获得西班牙语学士学位。一度在北京外文出版社任翻译，之后考取北外拉美文学硕士专业为研究生。1986年赴美在纽约州立大学石溪分校攻读拉美文学专业，先后获得拉美文学硕士与博士学位。成为中国第一位女性西班牙语文博士。长期在美国从事西语语言文学教学与研究，曾先后在纽约州立大学及阿拉巴马州的私立大学教授西语语言文学。后移居美国首都华盛顿郊外的马里兰州。目前在Bethesda蒙哥马利公立学校教授西班牙语及大学拉美文学课程。

梁旭华

杆栏拍遍平生梦

——在美国教授西班牙语文学之浅唱低吟

在美国教授西班牙文学二十多年，每年九月学期开始时，我站在讲台上手执学生名单点名，教室大门总会被砰然推开，进来一位又一位神色慌张迟到的学生。他们看到我马上就向后转，都以为走错教室了。我赶紧用西班牙语叫住他们："您没走错，这是……西班牙语课。"学生做梦也想不到这个黑头发黄皮肤的中国女子竟是他们的西班牙语博士老师——从踏入美洲大陆的那一天起，这位东方女子日夜不息的工作就是教授西班牙语言文学。

在美国这片移民土地上，说西班牙语的拉丁美洲移民仅次于欧洲移民，占总人口17%。在这里千千万万美国人操着纯正的西班牙语。西班牙语已经成了他们非官方的第二语言。作为第一位在美国获得拉丁美洲文学博士学位、投身美国西语教育界20多年的中国人，这些年来我带出了一批批年轻的西语学生。他们有的是美国本土长大的各国移民后裔，有的是母语为西语的拉丁美洲移民子弟。这些出身美国精英家庭的年轻人，拉美外交官的儿女们，跟着我在西语文学里徜徉，一起吟咏聂鲁达（Pablo Neruda）的诗歌，为洛尔加（西班牙著名诗人 García Lorca）的吉卜赛之歌流泪。然而，这些学生大约想不到，他们这位可以用三种语言为他们演绎诗歌的西文老师是13亿中国人中的第一位西语女博士，她的身后藏着一段求梦追梦、与民族血脉相依相连的生命见证。

在中国，作为家中独女，我曾经有幸福的童年，纯真的梦。但红彤彤的"文革"中，身为资本家的外公外婆在阶级斗争的汪洋大海里受尽折磨。我跟着长辈亲身经历了民族的大劫难。幸亏舅舅阿姨才华横溢，使我从小耳濡目染，偷听音乐背诗词，一番天真的梦才悄悄播下：有朝一日成为一名博学的文学教授。因为跳班，我四年念完小学课程。上完初中后，不愿在学校浪费时光，又希望逃避被遣送农村服苦役的命运，我毅然辍学，终结了自己六年半的基础教育，到一所为2—6岁幼儿设置的寄宿幼儿园里当教师。

那是我鲜花一样的少女时代，但我的生活里没有歌声，也没有色彩，只有婴儿的啼哭和他们沾满屎尿的脏裤。我每天上课带孩子，充当保姆，洗刷厕所，寒风中坐在室外一件一件搓洗婴儿衣裤，还要种菜喂猪、运煤拉水。每天劳作时间长达16小时。园长以部队军事体制监管我们这些年轻女孩，每晚政治学习至十点。为了自给自足，养猪盖猪圈，我们拆掉山坡下的太平间，6个人用竹杠把一条条近2米半长、宽厚约25公分的花岗岩石条一步步抬到山顶。身材弱小的我榨干每一滴血也无法与那些农村来的大哥大姐同步。好心的大哥哥们用手把住麻绳不让它滑向矮小的我，即便如此，每一步重压下我仿佛都能听到哗啦啦一片片生命玻璃在我躯体内碎裂的声音。那一条条千斤重的花岗岩在我心灵烙下了千百道痕迹。它们日后终身陪伴着我，成了支撑我生命与意志坚不可摧的支架。

生活的磨难从未泯灭我儿时的梦想。然而，当1977年政府决定恢复人们巴望已久的高考时，摆在我面前的现实却带讽刺与残酷：我只有六年半残缺不全的学历。怎么可能报考大学？我想逃避现实、北上山东威海探望老家。离家前一天，工程师舅舅出差回来，夺走我的火车票，强迫我留下来报名高考。我遵从舅舅指示选报了西班牙语专业,尽管我连西班牙语有几个字母都不知道。当时的我,与千百万同龄人一样,只要有书读,哪怕是手抚驴臀的兽医专业也会令我欢呼雀跃。暴雨滂沱中我独自一人撑着一把破伞六进考场披荆斩棘。因为成绩优异,我被北京外国语学院西语系录取,儿时的梦终于实现。带着惊喜、忐忑,和一身新絮的棉衣,我北上京城,开始了四年寒窗岁月。

北京外语学院(现在的北京外国语大学)的前身是延安外国语学校,直属外交部,到 1980 年才回归教育部。已经是"改革开放"的 80 年代,一般大专院校外语系女生多姿多彩,但北外这个外交大本营里女生却红颜素裹,朴实无华,颇有延安女干部遗风。周六下午政治学习,雷打不动。学校实行严格的集体作息时间。每天清晨六点打铃,人人从热被窝翻身而起,冬冬跑到大操场排队集合。班长点名后全系围着校园长跑健身。出操解散后我们又纷纷冲上楼用冰冷刺骨的凉水擦一把脸,抱上书本讲义冲下楼晨读。四年下来,风雨无阻,几乎每个人都有自己习惯的角落:篮球架下,废弃的游泳池边,20 多种语言此起彼落。难怪北外的学生日后个个字正腔圆。

晨读后到食堂领取早餐。第一年包伙制,一天三张饭票,撕一张换一顿饭,早餐是一碗黄灿灿的苞米糊,一个发黄的蒸馒头和一小碟酱菜。中午有肉菜米饭,晚餐天天都是酱油熬大白菜粉丝。一月伙食费 15 元人民币(约当时 2 美金)。食堂有桌无椅,我们全是站着吃饭,因此也就演练出高效率的军队进膳作风。许多人一个月只有几块零用钱,但在寥寥无几的零用钱里每人都会想方设法省点钱买一二本心爱的书。甚至为买书而举债也在所不惜。

我庆幸自己苦尽甘来,对那种斯巴达式的生活毫无怨言。那个年代我们以胸前佩戴白色校徽为荣。戴上它似乎蓝天白云都漂浮在自己的脚下。图书馆每晚座无虚席。大家一天学习 15 小时以上。虽然物质极度贫乏,精神世界却是彩虹满天。我们憧憬着一个什么都可能发生、什么都可以实现的理想世界。我青春的梦里充满了色彩和音乐、诗歌与幻想。现在回想起来,那真是一个有心有梦、敢想敢为、不知天高地厚的年代。同学中有人宣称要在有生之年把红楼梦翻译成西语,有人立志要做世界一流的外交家,有人要撰写西语语言学大全。我比较胆小内敛，口中沉默，心里却豪情奔放。我的梦图案分明：立志要做一个第一流的中国西语专家。

那时大学里唯一的娱乐就是一周一次的广场电影。夜幕降临，学校在操场上扯起一块大白布，围上一根大麻绳，这就是同学们向往的电影院了。夏夜凉风习习，星空下是别有情调的露天电影院。有时狂风大作，银幕上的美女立时走样变形。严冬，每人包头裹脸，棉衣棉裤全副武装，坐在小板凳上，让心灵沉浸在艺术殿堂里。温度降到零度时，我们几乎冻僵。银幕上的激情对话刚落，全操场的同学就会不约而同地跺脚御寒，冬冬的跺脚声回应着青春激荡的心跳声，勇敢、纯真。当年那些跺脚流泪的青年男女中，日后不知道出了多少叱咤风云、独领风骚的大使、部长、文学专家和诗人！

我幸运地跻身于新中国第一代西班牙语学士之列，毕业后在北京外文出版社得到一份安逸稳定的工作。然而心灵深处的梦使我无法安定。两年后我再次苦读考进北外拉美文学研究生专业，师从柳小培教授与智利著名文学教授诺尔曼·科德斯（Norman Cortés）。当硕士文凭即将到手之际，我申请了美国拉美文学博士奖学金，幸运地获得六所学校的全额奖学金。在入学申请书上，我公开言志：好好钻研拉美文学，希望此生能用中文撰写一部西语文学史。真是初生牛犊不知畏也！

带着无限的梦想与憧憬，我负笈远涉重洋来到纽约州立大学石溪分校。我原以为中国名牌大学的西语佼佼者，在美国一定所向无敌。到了这里才发现当时的中国西语教学比国外落后30—50年。80年代石溪西葡语系荟萃了一批世界闻名的学者：时任世界西语协会会长的里瓦尔斯（Elías Rivers）教授是西班牙黄金时代研究泰斗。他的夫人杰尔吉娜·里瓦尔斯（Georgina Rivers）是巴洛克文学权威。我的导师拉斯特拉（Pedro Lastra）教授是拉美著名诗人，本科主任约尔丹诺（Jaime Jordano）教授也是智利诗人，研究生主任则是古巴革命英雄与国家领导卡斯特罗手下的外交官。另外还有日后蜚声全美的女性文学专家德伊施（Lou Deutsch）教授和现代文学专家德拉甘布教授（De la Campa）。这些教授不仅个个学问渊博、著作等身，还能从世界各地请来著名专家学者到系里开课。能在如此出类拔萃的学术乔木林里求学，沐浴名师恩泽，我倍感幸运。但名师的期待，同学们的出类拔萃，给来自地球另

一 路是践踏出来的

一端的我造成莫大的压力。时至今日，回想起当年那种"头悬梁、锥刺股"的艰苦学习，我的心还会隐隐抽痛。

中国的外语教学注重苦读死记，以语音纯正、语法严谨著称。外语本是一门最充满人性趣味的学科，竟变成数学一样的机械单调。课堂有时像军训，人人神经紧绷，人文趣味几乎消失殆尽。美国的外语教学虽然紧张严格、却不失风趣活泼。在中国我虽然经历了第一流的外语培训，但我的西语文学修养却几乎是初高中生的水平。北外四年本科，除了报刊文章及一些进步作家的短篇小说以外，学生并没认真研读过文学作品。现在跻身世界顶尖西语文学殿堂，我必须完成从中学向研究生阶段的飞跃。每周三堂文学课，阅读书目就是三大部作品（有的书近千页），同时还要兼职教授一门大二的西班牙语课。系里同学，有的已在拉美大学任教数年，来美只是为了赢得一张博士文凭。有的从西班牙本土跨洋来美，皮箱里装着已经写好一千多页咋咋作响的博士论文。身处如此严峻的环境，我竟然不懂得畏惧，因为在我们这代人的人生字典里没有"退却"二字。只要一想到当年读书无门，欲哭无泪的绝境，想到我们这一代人怀梦圆梦的艰难，我觉得自己是命运的宠儿，是苍天给了我在美国求学的机会。我是系里唯一角逐博士学位的中国人，只能逆流而上，勇往直前，别无选择。

入学一年就迎来了博士生入学资格考试（Ph.D Qualify Exam），这是美国博士学位中的第一道大难关。考试范围包括五本著作，哲学、诗歌、小说一应俱全。其中 Góngora 的晦涩诗歌几百年来曾经难倒过千千万万西语读者。我埋首苦读了一个月，顺利通过资格考试，而周围的美国同学却有好几位落选。在日后几年昏天黑地的学习拼搏里，我增长了学问，赢得了自信，更以自己的勤奋和领悟赢得了系里师生对我这位东方女研究生的尊重与厚爱。几位著名教授纷纷主动把他们的著作赠送予我。在里瓦尔斯教授的塞万提斯研讨课上，教授对我的期末论文大为赞赏，推荐我修改后送文学报刊发表。

寒窗苦读，三年后我再次面对拉美文学博士专业最难的一道关卡：精读150部文学作品，闭卷三天口试笔试。在我通过这场博士考试（Ph. D. Comprehensive Exam）之后，我成了正式的博士候选人，被纽约州立大学 Old Westbury 分校聘请，教授西班牙语和拉美文学，边教书边完成博士论文。当我第一次以讲师身份登上大学讲台讲授拉美文学通史时，我为梦想成真登上大学讲坛而高兴，同时内心也忐忑不安。我的三十几位学生全是拉美后裔，西语是他们的母语。这些学生个个都是沐浴美西文化陶冶长大的双语人才。我对他们讲堂吉诃德，讲西班牙的巴洛克与黄金时代，就有如一位美国教授驾临北京，用中文对中国学生剖析《红楼梦》、李白、杜甫诗句一样匪夷所思。然而，凭着自己多年的文史积累，更凭着一腔一丝不苟认真负责的教学态度，我赢得了这些青年学生的信任和爱戴。学期结束时我们成了朋友，学生们请我去他们家做客。而后当这些热血青年得知学校因经费缩减不能再为我续聘时，个个义愤填膺，准备集体到校方抗议。其实那时我已接受南部一所私立大学的聘书，但这些青年学子对我的爱戴与信任、及首次开课的成功始终温暖着我，让我在日后廿几年的教书生涯里无畏无惧、勇往直前。

在美国，黑头发黄皮肤常常会是一道偏见的门槛。我初到一处，人们"以貌取人"。一走进我的教室，总以为是中文系的课堂。有一次参加一个全美高级西语口语研讨会，主持人一看到我落座后就温和地提醒与会者这次会议不是 ESOL（英文为外语）的研讨会，会议全部使用西班牙语。我从容不迫地用纯正的西班牙语作了自我介绍、发表了自己的学术意见，从此会议主持人对我刮目相看，与会者也个个对我肃然起敬。这样的例子不胜枚举。凭着自己的努力与执著，这些年我在美国西班牙语界里逐渐赢得了许多尊敬。多年的奋斗与磨炼使得我学会既大方宽容又不退缩自卑，从不愧对自己海外华人学者的尊严。

只有学问扎实，待人宽厚仁慈，方能赢得学生的爱戴与信任。这是一个崇尚真理，不畏权威的国家。年轻学生钦佩的是你的学问为人，而不是你挂在名片上长长的职称。1992 年我在美国 Northeast Modern Language Association Annual Convention 上宣读关于西班牙 19 世纪小说家 Galdos 的学术论文。同年我远赴加拿大爱德华岛在加拿大西语专家 27 届年会上（XXVII Congreso de la Asociación Canadiense de Hispanistas）宣读我的另一篇以 Mikhail Bakhtin 理论解读塞万提斯小说的论文。我这个唯一的东方面孔敢于面对上百学者阐述对西语作家的一番见解，除了多年苦读铺垫的实力以外，最主要的是心中那团理想的火焰给了我胆与识。

这些年常常有学生想方设法调课表改到我的班上学习。2003 年我班上一位国家级体操队员进入斯坦福大学后提名我入选 2004—2005 年的美国"Who's Who Among America's Teachers"。我的学生们知道，这位东方老师对学生、对课业要求极其严格，学生因此可以学到许多别处学不到的知识。几十年教书生涯，我秉持祖先"知之为知之，不知为不知"和"教学相长"的训诲，细心备课、认真示范、循循善诱。记得有一次我的学生撰写 Quevedo（格瓦德，西班牙文艺复兴著名诗人）的诗歌评论时语法错误连篇，名词性数混淆无数，我一气之下连夜提笔，写了一篇以超现实主义手法，汇集学生错误、文情并茂的西文长诗赠送给学生。这首四十行的长诗引来了学生夹着泪水的笑声。他们一方面对自己的疏忽感到羞愧，另一方面也感佩老师的才华和对文学对学生锲而不舍的爱。

当 2014 年 9 月我为大华府地区专家学者介绍哥伦比亚作家，1982 年诺贝尔奖得主马尔克斯与魔幻现实主义文学时，许多人惊讶我能用自己的译文把如此艰深的作家与流派化为故事娓娓道来。当我的学生分别从美国布朗大学（Brown University）和加拿大麦吉尔大学（McGill University）写信向我讨教文学问题时，我发觉我对拉美文学的领悟有时比西方某些学者来得更为敏锐，因为我来自中国，我有别人所没有的生活感悟。中华五千年的文明浸泡过我的心、我的魂。我的血液里有屈原、李白、杜甫的基因，有吟起来令人落泪的诗句。

二十几年天涯孤旅，一路走来，我的耳畔常常回响着著名诗人安东尼·马查德的诗句：

"Caminante, son tus huellas
　　el camino, y nada mas;
　　caminante, no hay camino;
　　se hace camino al andar"

在这首西语世界里老幼皆知的诗篇里，伟大的西班牙诗人轻轻低吟：

"寂寞的行旅，你的脚印

你唯一的路；

孤独的行旅，人生本无路；

一步又一步，你，踏出了路！"

老柳枝探，轻拂慢顾。一步又一步，我踏出了自己的路。

从泥淖多难的童年，一步一个脚印，我跨出鹭岛，走进燕山脚下，最后飘来美国首都低吟浅唱，教授西班牙语文学。

怀梦难，追梦圆梦更难。回眸远望，唯以自慰的是在逆境中从未迷失一颗火热的怀梦诗心。这颗心，这个梦，化成点点音符，丝弦杂错，就像那八面湖水里一路挣扎，一路寻觅的青莲……

最后，在此谨籍拙诗一首祈愿我的同代人有如那高洁的菡萏，踏泥寻梦，一路高歌。撩开十里荷香，洒下一路芬芳。

詠蓮別韻

花衣轻舞

露珠密密地点

是吻？

是问？

是天地挥不去的浓雾？

老柳枝探

轻拂慢顾

似盼？

似慕？

似夏雷后一声声叹？

水香柔曼，

夏蕊初看，

玉珠滴滴含泪

艳阳里湖心上了岸，

一 路是践踏出来的

捡尽人间的爱与憾?

水边浮萍,
可闻浓绿粉妆下
深潭谷底含泪的清唱?
芙蓉幔下
吱吱行路的壮与寒?

水秀十面,
泥淖低处节节响,
丝弦杂错
撩开了十里荷香,
一路清凉。

Four seas to One Family: Overseas Chinese and Chinese dream
四海一家、天涯比邻：海外华人与中国梦

郁龙余

深圳大学印度研究中心教授、主任，1946年4月3日出生于上海，1965年9月考入北京大学东方语言文学系印地语专业学习，1970年3月毕业后留校教授印地语。1984年调入深圳大学中文系，历任深圳大学国际文化系副系主任、中国文化与传播系主任、文学院院长以及文学院学术委员会主任、留学生教学部主任等职务。

兼任北京大学东方文学研究中心（教育部普通高校人文社科重点研究基地）学术委员、研究员，中国印度文学研究会副会长，中国东方文学研究会副会长，中国比较文学学会常务理事，中国南亚学会常务理事，中国中外关系史学会副会长等。主要学术成果有：印度译著30多万字，在国内外期刊或媒体上发表学术论文80多篇，出版各类著作：《中印文学关系源流》《中国印度文学比较》《东方文学史》（主编）《梵典与华章：印度作家与中国文化》（教育部优秀成果二等奖）《中国印度诗学比较》（广东省优秀成果二等奖）、《印度文化论》（主编）《外国戏剧鉴赏辞典》（古代卷）（主编）《泰戈尔作品鉴赏辞典》（主编）《谭云山》（谭中、郁龙余主编）《天竺纪行》《中国印度文学交流史》（即出）等20多部。

凡我到处，就是中国

—— "中国梦" 在海外

我不是海外华人，但我和谭中教授是"四海一家、天涯比邻"的精神俱乐部成员，高兴为他编的"海外华人与中国梦"书写点感想。女儿郁秀给了我一个题目。她说：德国文豪汤玛士曼（Thomas Mann）好像说过："凡我到处，就是德国。"现在改动一个字，用"凡我到处，就是中国"来描写海外华人的"中国梦"。

一　路是践踏出来的

不禁想起 1993 年夏天，我应欧洲华人学会之邀，来到如诗如画般的维也纳，出席第七届"中西文化异同"国际学术研讨会。维也纳，欧洲名城，奥地利首都，曾经是奥匈帝国的王城，气宇轩昂，美轮美奂，令人叹为观止。也正是在这个会上，我有机会和"海外华人"进行交流，我也强烈地感觉到"中国梦"传布全球。

7 月 26 日上午开幕式，首先由李祥霆教授演奏古琴，使研讨会在东方优雅的气氛中揭幕，然后由奥地利—中国友好协会会长 Kaminski Gred 教授作主旨讲话。我有幸结识了名扬全球、从 60 年代开始已有四百多中外弟子的中国古琴第一名家李祥霆教授。

中国是"国"，但更是数千年的悠久文明。记得李祥霆当时弹奏的"九霄环佩"古琴就是 8 世纪唐朝开元年间的产品，在民间传了 1300 年的古物。在中国，李祥霆弹九霄环佩发出"天下第一声音"已经是家喻户晓的。会外和我李祥霆交谈，我问：这国宝级的古琴，怎么能带出来呢？他说：海关那些人不懂那么多，我说是我自己用的乐器，就带到英国来了（当时他在英国做访问学者）。我问他，你准备什么回去？他说，目前还不知道。

我当时亲睹李祥霆弹九霄环佩发出"天下第一声音"在维也纳外国听众中引起的热烈共鸣。只见李祥霆身着中式布褂，从容儒雅，张弛有度：忽而志在高山，峨峨兮若泰山；忽而志在流水，洋洋兮若江河。我们都听得如痴如醉。尤其是几位欧洲教授，对中国古曲之高雅动听，赞叹不已。听罢，他们意犹未尽，请求李教授多弹几曲。在整个会议期间，他又弹了《阳关三叠》等多首古曲。让我印象最深的是：李教授的即兴弹奏，只要给一个题目，或者一首诗，他即可抚琴弹出其意境。听者无不拍掌膺服。

李祥霆不但是音乐家，还是画家。1988 年参加中国美术家协会北京分会年展。1989 年在伦敦大学中国美术馆举行个人画展。1991 年在新西兰威灵顿维多利亚大学作《国画与古琴音乐的点线之美》演讲，传略载入《中国艺术家辞典》《中国当代艺术界名人录》，又被英国剑桥国际传记中心选为《二十世纪杰出人物》。1999 年以山水画《高山流水入梦频》获《世界华人艺术大奖》之《国际荣誉金奖》。

在私下闲聊时，李教授告诉我，他的演奏在欧洲很受欢迎，有人劝他留下来。但他身在欧洲，心在中国。他说，西方虽然有人喜欢古琴，但古琴的家乡毕竟在中国，中国才有更多的听众，才有真正的钟子期。那年回国后，我和李教授就再也没有联系。不记得是哪一年，我突然在电视上看到李教授。他依然是那样儒雅从容，依然抚弄着"九霄环佩"，依然弹奏《高山流水》，只是多了几许白发，也多了几许潇洒，更多了几位请益的学生。从那次之后，我又几次看见他出现在有关古琴的节目里。当然，我知道李祥霆和他那"九霄环佩"以及"天下第一声音"是伴随着"中国梦"不断在中国、在全球人们心中发出交响，数十年如一日。

在维也纳的研讨会上，给我印象最深刻的华人学者是翻译家李治华和太太雅歌（雅科琳）。李治华是开幕式之后的第一位发言者，论文题目是《中国文学在法国传播的历史及意义》。他当时已年近八旬，一头银发，但精神矍铄，还未走上台，就掌声四起。坐在我身旁的一位华人学者说，李教授是法国华人学者中最有名望的。

李治华1915年出生在北京，22岁从北京的中法大学毕业后，就来到法国里昂的中法大学。20岁的法国同学雅科琳主动提出与他"结对"，帮他补习法语。很快，这对"金童玉女"坠入爱河。他们喜结良缘到儿孙满堂，相濡以沫70多年。最值得骄傲的，是他用27年时间将《红楼梦》译成法文。李治华的博士论文是《中国元曲研究》《元曲的法文翻译》。正是他翻译中国古代文学的成就，引起联合国教科文组织《东方知识丛书》编委会主任艾琼伯的重视，希望他将《红楼梦》译成法文。从1954年动笔，到1981年封笔，李治华历时27载，终于将这部中国四大古典名著之首——《红楼梦》译成法文。雅科琳不仅是他的第一读者，而且常常和他切磋推敲译文。所以，李治华的法译《红楼梦》不但文采斐然，意境深邃，而且易于理解，大受法文读者欢迎。出版社用羊皮作封面，并列入著名的"七星文库"丛书。联合国教科文组织和中国驻法大使馆为他举行了出版庆贺酒会。此书一年出版数万册，居法国同类书籍发行量之冠，荣获法国文化部"法国文艺中级荣誉勋章"。

2002年9月，中国现代文学馆开设"李治华·雅歌文库"。李治华将全部《红楼梦》法译手稿，以及父母及亲朋好友数十年间写给他的全部书信，

一 路是践踏出来的

毫无保留地赠给了中国现代文学馆。李治华对此感到无比欣慰，说："这是我文化上的叶落归根。"

2014年4月，中国国家主席习近平访问法国，专门看望了99岁的李治华，引起了很大轰动。我想，李治华用毕生的精力在中法文化交流史上，写下了浓墨重彩的一页，最后又能做到"叶落归根"。这大概是圆了所有华人学者中最圆满的一个梦。

在维也纳的研讨会上，从德国来的关愚谦博士给我的印象特别深刻。他为大会提供的论文是《欧洲看中国的经济改革》，眼光犀利，见解独到。我和他初逢不是在会上，而是在汽车站。那天我看离报到时间还早，就在汽车站停留了一下。刚刚找到椅子坐下，看见对面长椅上躺着一个人，身材很长，脸上遮着一张德文报纸。我们到了研讨会上又重逢。以后在聊天中他告诉我：他父亲在抗战时曾任福建永泰县长。当日军从福州乘舰船在永泰湾边登陆时，曾率县保安大队到湾边抗击日寇。永泰紧挨着闽江，是我妻子的家乡。所以，关愚谦的名字以及他讲的故事，一直铭记在我心中。

最近，我突然在凤凰卫视上看到了他，正在分析德国各阶层对乌克兰局势的看法。我马上叫妻子来看，告诉她：这位穿红色上衣的学者就是关愚谦，他父亲曾在永泰抗击日寇。妻子说，永泰曾有一位姓管的县长，听父亲讲口碑很好。"关"与"管"会不会搞错？后来从网上一查果然如此。关愚谦的父亲关锡斌是中共党员，也是鸦片战争时期抗英名将关天培的后裔。解放初期，关愚谦在国内曾经担任过苏联顾问的俄语翻译。怪不得他在凤凰卫视台上对乌克兰那么熟悉。我想现在在海外的华人中，像关愚谦这样和鸦片战争以来中国的觉醒与成长有切身亲属关系的可能不少，是"中国梦"散布到世界各地的种子。

也是在这次欧华学会第七届国际学术研讨会上，我结识了海外华人朱新天博士和她的法国丈夫鲍思岱先生。7月29日下午，在参观了国会、市政厅和市容之后，便驱车来到维也纳森林用餐。在市区，见到的都是古色古香的宫殿式建筑，来到郊区山麓，一望无际的都是森林。好比来到了北京香山，就餐的餐厅是当地的农家乐。墙上挂着马车辘轳、车夫服饰等物件，吃的是地道的本地食品。我正和中山大学教授、广东省高教厅长许学强和他的学生陈镇雄博士，边吃边聊，朱新天向我招招手，让我到她和丈夫鲍思岱的桌子就餐。她又再要了几样食物，我们就海阔天空地谈了起来，但很快话题就转到了印度文化上。她向我打听金克木先生的情况，说金先生是他父亲的好朋友。

在维也纳我和鲍思岱、朱新天夫妇是第一次握手。第二次握手是在上个世纪末的深圳。中国一家企业要引进鲍思岱医药公司的一种治糖尿病的药，约好在深圳商谈协议。我和妻子郑亦麟一起去宾馆看望他们。之后，有着好一阵子的书信往来。但不知何时，就断了音讯。2009年11月突然接到她从印度孟买寄来的《印度教万神殿艺术》一书，顿觉眼前一亮。读了一遍，觉得回肠荡气，提笔给她回信，写了三点：您是印度艺术的恩人，您是朱家的荣光，您是我朋友中的骄傲。

通过阅读朱新天寄来的书和资料，我对她和夫婿鲍思岱有了全新的认识。鲍思岱，是法国反法西斯老战士，参加戴高乐将军的抗德部队，被选为美国飞行员。他功勋卓著，荣获法国国家骑士勋章。1949年开始，他一边在印度办制药公司，一边研究印度文化。六十年来，他将公司所得，一部分捐赠给印度医疗事业，一部分在拍卖市场收购包括印度在内的亚洲艺术品。1970年，在印度孟买成立印度文化研究所。1999年，倾其所有，在法国比亚里茨（Biarritz）市成立"东方艺术博物馆"（ASIATICA），成为与大英博物馆、巴黎吉美博物馆齐名的欧洲三大博物馆。经过数十年的田野调查、实物考证，鲍思岱出版了十几种学术著作，成了享誉国际的南亚艺术史研究大家。

朱新天出身杭州书香门第，是一位著名画家、摄影家。1986年以杭州大学文博专业教师身份赴法国深造，获巴黎第八大学比较美术国家硕士学位和巴黎大学著名的索邦分校（Sorboone）远东艺术与考古学国家博士学位。她的一系列学术论文及著作，在国际学术界获得高度评价。其中，博士论文《印度古代的神奇瑞兽研究》、硕士论文《中国扬州画派与法国印象派的比较研究》，被学术界喻为印度艺术研究及中法艺术比较的扛鼎之作。她用近20年时间，研究、宣传印度的王后井，终于促使这默默无闻的地下艺术宝库，于2009年1月入列联合国世界文化遗产名录。

有了以上认识，我就向学校打报告，希望学校能请鲍、朱夫妇来深作演讲，并聘请他们为名誉教授。深圳大学毕竟得改革开放风气之先，从章必功校长到人事处王恩堂处长，一路绿灯。章校长发出邀请信，请他们于2010年1月来深圳大学作客。1月6日下午，我在深圳蛇口码头接到他们夫妇，说：我们是第三次握手。朱新天用法语翻译给鲍思岱听，他那张经典的法国脸莞尔而笑。6日、7日晚，鲍思岱、朱新天夫妇为深大师生做了两场题为《印度王后井探秘》和《印度人的婚礼》的学术讲座，深受欢迎。

被人形容为"梅花香自苦寒来"的从小一直到巴黎从逆境中挣扎而取得成就的朱新天象征着"中国梦"的坚韧不拔，使我想起印度大文豪、百年前以第一位非白人获得诺贝尔文学奖的泰戈尔说的：

"古希腊文明之灯在它初点燃的土地上熄灭。罗马帝国的威力埋葬在广大帝国废墟之中。可是以社会与人类精神理想为基础的文明在中国和印度一直活着。虽然在现代物质威力眼光中看起来很弱小，但它会像饱含生命的小小种子那样在天空降下慈祥的雨水后发芽成长、伸展出有益的枝干、开花结果。"

泰戈尔这番话是1916年他在东京帝国大学讲演时说的，当时中国社会、政治、经济、文化按照"现代物质威力眼光"来看是很"弱小"的。但我1993年在维也纳所看到的（今天更不用说）国外对中国文化的印象，真可谓"发芽成长、伸展出有益的枝干、开花结果"。我由衷佩服泰戈尔的远见。

我们今天谈论"中国梦"可以通过李祥霆、李治华、关愚谦、朱新天以及许许多多本文没有涉及的海外华人的例子来证明"凡我到处，就是中国"。换句话说，哪儿有海外华人，那儿就会有中国文化，就会有"中国梦"的回响。国际文化人士在维也纳聆听李祥霆弹九霄环佩发出的"天下第一声音"，那就是中国。法国人阅读李治华翻译的《红楼梦》，那就是中国。关愚谦在德国治学理论，那就是中国。朱新天在比亚里茨设立"东方艺术博物馆"，那就是中国。

现在，全中国、全世界都在谈论"中国梦"，这是中国国泰民安的表现，也是中国人向世界各国的诉求。中国文化自古以来"气以实志，志以定言"；以"丹青之笔"，夺"造化之功"；丝竹金石，"感心动耳，荡气回肠"，实现"己之美"与"人之美"美美与共。这就是文化，这就是文学、美术、音乐。它没有国家、种族、语言、宗教的界限，能使人类走向世界和谐、天下大同。凡是有中国人的地方就必然有中国文化的体现，这就是"凡我到处，就是中国"。

当然，由于百余年来中国备受内忧外患困扰，贫穷落后，文化衰落。旧中国被人奚落为"鸦片鬼"与"东亚病夫"的国度，新中国百废俱兴，文化振兴尚未实现，华人把各种丑恶现象伸延国外。最近报载，有些华人在法国、西班牙不自爱，损害中国与华人的尊严名誉。中国暴发户出外旅游种种不文明行为也出了名。这种"凡我到处，就是中国"如果泛滥成灾，那"中国梦"就会是噩梦。"中国梦"就会无法实现。这样看来，要提倡"中国梦"，先要提倡中国文化振兴，先要在中国提倡"真善美"，把中国社会的"假恶丑"洗涤干净。

中国梦的最终实现，必然以世界大多数人民的拍手称好为成功标志。如何将中国梦和世界各国的梦相沟通，如何让世界上大多数人民了解、支持中国梦，海外华人是天然的桥梁，他们的中国梦离世界最近，他们的世界梦又离中国最近。海外华人，特别是华人学者，是沟通中外、推动世界进步的重要力量。一百年前，世界各地华侨、华人，支持中国的辛亥革命，孙中山称华侨、华人为"革命之母"。现在，实现中华民族伟大复兴的中国梦，华侨华人依然是一支不可或缺的巨大力量。

一 路是践踏出来的

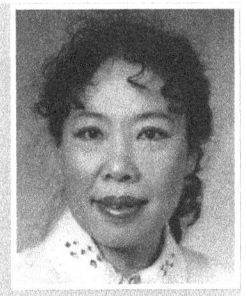

朱新天

画家、摄影家，80年代在杭州大学历史系任教。1986年到法国巴黎国立高等装饰艺术学院学习。1989以《中国扬州画派与法国印象派的比较研究》获巴黎第八大学硕士学位。1990年应聘为印度文化研究所研究员，在印度进行考古调查研究。1997以《印度古代的神奇瑞兽研究》获巴黎索邦大学远东艺术与考古学国家博士学位。1998年与世界著名考古学家、收藏家M. POSTEL共同创建法国东方艺术博物馆。现为法国东方艺术博物馆副馆长兼研究员、印度文化研究所研究员、联合国教科文所属国际博协（ICOM）会员、法国国家美术家协会（SNBA）会员、深圳大学特约教授，天津师范大学文学院兼职教授。著作有：《印度教万神殿艺术——印度王后井探秘》（中文版），《印度古代的神祇与神兽》（英、法文版）。

愿将生命化彩虹

——第一个在西方创建东方艺术博物馆的中国人

虹，对于我来说，是大自然赐予人类的最为绚丽的图景，是暴风雨交响乐中最具有光彩的和平乐章。虹，是阳光和雨雾的结晶，她将宇宙间无数的"元素"集合起来，在阳光下折射成一个七彩缤纷的梦境；虹，像苍穹里的一座宏伟无比的拱门，她变化万端，尽现大千世界的风采；虹，像一座跨越时空的桥梁，她凌驾于世间万物之上，将大地山河紧紧相连；虹，是希望与憧憬的象征，她宁静而辉煌，象征着未来美好的理想；虹，也是一座心灵的桥梁，她像画家手中多彩的画笔，在天地间挥洒出的一条神奇之路，让世界上不同种族的民众，超越一切地域和语言的障碍，在文化艺术的精神下相互沟通，相互理解……

四海一家、天涯比邻：海外华人与中国梦

我是一个画家。用自己的画笔来编织一条彩虹，是我的梦；用自己的生命，来构建这样一座横贯东西的桥梁，是我的理想。虹，对我来说，不是一个空幻的奇观，而是我研究和吸取东西方文化艺术后所形成的一种憧憬，是我深入和遨游于欧亚文明之中的一种精神象征。我愿用自己的生命来铺设这样一条道路，让中国和亚洲的文化艺术走向世界，也让世界文明的精华走向中国。

80年代初，作为杭州大学历史系文博专业教师的我，参加了中国博物馆协会举办的学术研讨会，并成为中国博物馆陈列艺术协会的发起人之一。那时候，国内博物馆的陈列设施还相当落后，各大博物馆基本上只是在展柜里摆放一些文物而已，照明设备也非常简单。带着将中国博物馆改变为代表华夏文明艺术殿堂的梦想，抱着改变中国博物馆陈列设计上落后状态的初衷，在父亲老友、著名红学家李治华先生的帮助下，我于1986年到法国自费留学，在巴黎国立高等装饰艺术学院专攻室内装饰和博物馆陈列设计艺术。

在这近三十年中，我不懈地在西方进行传播中华文化艺术的各种活动：我曾经在法国的巴黎、米鲁兹、里茂日、比雅利兹、盎格莱特、巴荣纳；在瑞士的日内瓦、德国的柏林、汉堡、纽伦堡、奥地利的维也纳、印度的新德里、孟买、阿默达巴德等地艺术画廊、大学和文化中心举办过许多画展和讲座，向人们介绍中国的文化艺术和哲学思想。我还在各种中外报刊杂志和学术研讨会上发表文章，除了向西方介绍中国，也向国内介绍世界的文化艺术。

1987年初，应巴黎野草书局的邀请，我举行了在国外的第一个中国书画艺术讲座。巴黎的报刊早早就刊登了消息，报名参加的人数已经爆满。不料就在讲座前几天，由于过度疲劳，我夜里提着两大包资料从十几层高的地铁台阶上摔了下去，造成右脚踝关节骨折。讲座无法取消，我是由一个同学背去的。两个多小时的讲座我一直用一条轻伤的左腿站立，骨折的右腿跪在凳子上，一边做书画演示，一边讲解。讲座受到了各界人士的欢迎，但讲座完我几乎晕倒。1987年4月5日，《中国青年报》刊登了我的文章《愿撒丹青化彩虹》。1988年，当我在巴黎接待了一百多人组成的台湾书法代表团之后，我在《欧洲时报》上大声疾呼："弘扬中国文化艺术的时代已经到来！"

一 路是践踏出来的

1989年，我以"中国扬州画派与法国印象派的比较研究"，顺利通过答辩，获巴黎第八大学国家硕士学位，并继续攻读博士学位。

1990年，我是唯一的中国人参加了印度千年以前的伟大历史遗迹"王后井"的考古发掘和拍摄工作。1992年，我放弃了已经准备了一半的博士论文，改变了我的学科和专长，转而攻读法国巴黎索邦大学（SORBONNE）远东艺术与考古学国家博士学位，并继续到印度去进行考古调查及古代艺术的研究。1997年，我的博士论文答辩得到了评审教授们的最高评价，获得巴黎索邦大学远东艺术与考古学国家博士学位。

1998年，我投入到创建法国东方艺术博物馆ASIATICA的工作。这是以法国国家电信局一个高科技工厂的旧址改建的艺术殿堂。在这样的建筑结构中，我们不可能按照文物收藏来制定展览空间；加上经费的原因，也不允许像通常博物馆那样按照文物定做专门的展柜。我们购买了巴黎吉美国立亚洲艺术博物馆和卢浮宫埃及艺术馆更新时撤下来的旧展柜，仅卢浮宫的展柜就有一百多年的历史。

博物馆陈列的主要是著名收藏家，艺术史家和考古学家鲍思岱先生（Michel POSTEL）的私人收藏。他热爱东方，潜心研究印度历史和文化艺术，出版了数本专著。他将一生的积蓄用于在西方古董市场和大型文物拍卖会上收集东方的文物艺术品。然而他并没有将这些艺术品藏之内府，仅供自己欣赏，而是用自己的资金创建了这座东方艺术博物馆，将这些人类文化的瑰宝公诸于世。让世界各地的观众能够欣赏到这些珍贵的人类文明的遗存，从而了解东方，热爱亚洲的文明，并从这些艺术品中获得灵感，得到智慧与知识，用东方的哲学思想和理念来丰富他们的人生哲理。

我们首先拆除了旧址中遗留的长达几百甚至上千公里的光纤电缆，重达数十吨的大型空调设备等。然后，我亲自动手制作：从西藏唐卡的双面镜框到印度首饰的特殊展柜，从中国鼻烟壶的博古架到西藏小型佛像的复杂展牌，从大小不同雕塑的基座到细密画、纪念邮票的专门陈列，从莫卧尔兵器刀鞘的制作到清代皇室家具的拆卸安装……我既是木工，又是漆工、钳工、机械工，制作、缝纫、装修等工作也都由我自己操作。

我们博物馆拥有不同国家、不同地区、不同历史时期和不同文化背景的文物，不仅包括中国与中国西藏、尼泊尔、印度、泰国、缅甸、印度尼西亚、日本、柬埔寨等国以及喜马拉雅地区和印度土著文化的艺术品，还有首饰、细密画、纪念邮票等等；时间的跨度长达数千年。错综复杂的藏品使博物馆陈列设计成为一项巨大而极其复杂的工作。在陈列艺术中，既要考虑到各个国家和地区的文化特色和文物特点，又要将整个层面的各个展厅赋予一种协调的气氛。在教育职能上，则需要按照历史、地理、文化背景和宗教特征来进行展示，让观众在参观时所看到的不仅是艺术品本身，而是从全方位来理解这件文物与人类文明的关系。

我别出心裁，打破了世界博物馆常规陈列设计中白色和象牙色的中性色调，采用了如同彩虹色谱中不同层次的色调，并运用这些色彩的象征意义来布置不同展厅的墙面。例如：中国的展厅采用红色调，西藏地区采用了象征喇嘛袈裟的橙黄色调；而自尼泊尔到喜马拉雅地区的色调则逐渐趋向冷色调并带有明显的神秘色彩……除了墙面，还要考虑到展牌、展柜及基座等各方面色彩的协调……这种陈列形式所造成的文化艺术和宗教氛围，使观众在参观时产生身临其境的感受。不计其数的观众在参观博物馆之后向我表示：在这里，不但让他们学习和增长了许多知识，更让他们有一种心灵洁净、远离尘世物欲横流之喧嚣的体验。他们认为这个博物馆不仅是一个学习和研究的场所，更是一个修行的好去处；参观博物馆，就像是一次世界性的旅行。我首创的这种色调陈列手法已经被法国的好几个博物馆采用。

2000年，坐落在法国西南部大西洋岸边的历史文化名城比雅利兹市（BIARRITZ）的东方艺术博物馆ASIATICA正式成立向观众开放，它是全欧洲最著名的三座收藏亚洲古代艺术品的博物馆之一，与伦敦的大英帝国博物馆和巴黎的吉美博物馆齐名。我也成为世界上第一个在西方创建东方艺术博物馆的中国人。

博物馆展厅内不但准备了详细的英、法、德、西班牙文和当地的巴斯克语解说资料，还专门配备了桌椅和台灯，以及各种有关的参考书籍，使观众在参观过程中可以坐下来进行更为深入的学习和研究。这在世界博物馆中是少有的。图书馆内收藏数千本有关于中国（西藏）、印度、日本、尼泊尔、柬埔寨等亚洲国家文化艺术的专著，也可以根据预约提供给专家们研究。

一 路是践踏出来的

创建这座博物馆已是难以想象地艰巨，运作这座博物馆更为困难。博物馆对外开放了，但我的工作并没有完。我希望将这座博物馆创办成一座东西方文化交流的桥梁。因为除巴黎之外，整个西南欧洲从法国西部到西班牙、葡萄牙、一直到希腊、意大利等国还没有一座真正具有规模和特色的亚洲艺术博物馆。

每年，我都举办以"约会亚洲"为题的绘画、雕塑、摄影展览和比赛，并用自己的工资为优秀的艺术家颁奖。我要求参展者必须从亚洲的文化、艺术、哲学、宗教及造型手段等方各面获得灵感，将他们的体会融入到艺术创作之中。这一活动不仅增加了中外艺术家之间的交往和友谊，更加深了西方艺术家对亚洲文化艺术的了解。2014 年是中法建交 50 周年的纪念，我将展览主题定为"约会中国"。参展艺术家们以中国为源泉，创作了不少优秀的作品。几年前，这个展览获得了市政府的支持，我们每年又多了一千欧元作为对优秀艺术家的奖励。15 年来，有上千的世界各国艺术家们满怀着对亚洲文化艺术的热爱来参加这个艺术交流的盛会，越来越多的中国艺术家也来参展。15 年来，我还为博物馆举办了一百几十个不同类型的展览和讲座。除了用自己的书画作品向西方观众介绍中国文化艺术，还邀请国内外的艺术家举行个展和联展，并进行当场演示和讲座。在我们举办的展览中，有中国剪纸展，中国陶瓷展，中国著名书画家作品展，中国和印度、泰国等国的刺绣和纺织品展，法国艺术家创作的中国画展，法国和日本艺术家们按照中国传统技术制造的瓷器展，法国艺术家制作的日本插花展，越南受中国影响的传统风俗画展，印度历代大王肖像展，19 世纪英国艺术家创作的关于中国风土人情的铜版画展，印度土著青铜艺术雕像展，还有表现中国、西藏、印度、尼泊尔、喜马拉雅山等地的风光、风土人情和考古艺术的摄影展览。我用自己多年来在印度及亚洲各国考古研究中拍摄的罕见文物古迹和摄影艺术作品举办了各种影展，向西方的观众介绍中国和亚洲伟大的历史文明。影展中有神秘的吴哥、圣城贝纳勒斯的祭祀、香港、印度都市里的村庄、万人空巷的象头神节、印度的婚礼、释迦牟尼佛的足迹、印度王后井探秘、一个新的吴哥古迹—阿图。印度驻法国大使曾多次专程到比雅丽兹，为我的展览剪彩并致辞。

多年的博物馆工作使我感到，博物馆的职能不仅仅是收藏、保护和展示，更重要的是教育。几年前，法国海关将他们缴获的一批走私的中国和日本牙雕交付给我们博物馆收藏，为此，我立即举办了一个展览。我的目的不仅是向观众介绍这些象牙艺术制品，更重要的是进行生态保护的教育。在展示这些被缴获牙雕的同时，我特别陈列了一批"植物象牙"雕刻的艺术品。让参观者亲眼目睹"植物象牙"雕刻的艺术品的欣赏价值丝毫不比真正的象牙逊色，以杜绝对大象的滥杀。

当前，法国政府将中国汉代和印度笈多王朝的历史作为法定教科书中的必修课程，我们博物馆的陈列正好为教科书的不足提供补充。让西方人了解中国和亚洲的文化艺术，一直是我梦寐以求的心愿。我们不可能要求法国每一个学校都能够将学生带到中国去看汉代的艺术品。故此，没有实物参照的教学只能是纸上谈兵。我们博物馆被政府批准为对少年儿童开放的亚洲历史与艺术的观摩场所。博物馆举办的文化活动，受到了法国教育部、文化部的赞扬和支持，更得到了当地群众和世界各国专家和参观者们的称誉。

每次回国讲学，媒体采访都向我询问关于博物馆及收藏的问题，关于"爱国热"和"收藏热"的问题。我认为，"热"是不正常的。"收藏热"导致了许多人对文物的私欲，也导致了对文物的非法盗掘和造假的活动。

去年7月，四个国际犯罪团伙的劫匪，正午时分持枪闯入我们博物馆，抢劫收藏的中国古代玉器。为了阻止劫匪，我与他们进行了殊死搏斗。我被劫匪多次打倒在地，并被拉住头发，从四层高的台阶上摔下来，打成重伤，至今未愈。但我坚持与他们斗争到底，直到他们逃走。当我与一个劫匪搏斗时，其他两个劫匪进入博物馆展厅，砸碎了两个陈列高古玉器的展柜，抢走了十余件珍贵文物。如今，被劫的十余件珍贵玉器仍然没有被查获。这便是"收藏热"在国际上出现的犯罪活动。根据警方调查，国内某些"收藏家"花钱指点国际犯罪团伙盗劫国外艺术博物馆的著名珍贵文物（使它们"回家"），英国几家博物馆收藏的中国文物已经被抢劫。事后我收到世界各地不少认识和不认识的朋友来信问候，他们认为即使这些文物价值连城，也不比生命宝贵，我不应该舍命拼搏。我感激他们的关怀。实际上，当时见到一支

一 路是践踏出来的

枪对准我的胸膛时,我既没有考虑文物的价值,也没有考虑我的生命,我只有一个信念:阻止劫匪进入博物馆,不能让恶人得逞。

文物是人类文明的财存,是人类历史的见证,是世界上各民族的精神财富而不仅仅是物质财富。我们的责任是把它们保存并传给后代。收藏家无论拥有怎样丰富精美的收藏,其归根结底只是一个历史的"过客"。收藏家可以为爱好而收藏,但不可为私欲而收藏。每一个收藏家必须注意道德底线,不可逾越,否则将成为千古罪人。

为了这座博物馆,为了东西方的文化交流,为了向西方世界介绍中国和亚洲的文化艺术,十几年来我们一直废寝忘食,呕心沥血地工作。鲍思岱先生以 88 岁的高龄,仍然为博物馆进行工作和研究。他以自己丰富的经验和知识,撰写了四部博物馆的图录,并免费提供 150 多件珍贵文物为 BIARRITZ 市举办《喜马拉雅之旅》大型文物展,撰写和出版展览的大型图录。

2000 年,我的论文《试论西方现代派绘画思潮与中国传统绘画理论的共性》获世界学术贡献奖论文金奖;2005 年,《人民画报》以整整四个版面,介绍了我在中外文化交流领域里所作出贡献;2007 年,法国的 E. E. D. C. M. 组织(L'ETOILE EUROPEENNE DU DEVOUEMENET CIVIL ET MILITAIRE)授予我"欧洲之星军民忠诚贡献金质勋章";2008 年,我的绘画作品在巴黎卢浮宫法国国家美术家协会举办的大展上获绘画类艺术银奖。我把这些当作人类对我的鼓励。

"生命对于我来说,不是一支短小的蜡烛,而是一支辉煌的火炬。我希望在我将它交出以前,为人类文明燃烧的更加绚烂一些!"我愿将生命化作彩虹,也让我的博物馆成为一支画笔,把人类文明这幅美丽的图画永远画下去……

愿中印两大文明永远昌盛

——我的中国梦

朱新天

1990年,当我作为唯一的中国人参加了印度千年以前的伟大历史遗迹"王后井"的考古发掘和拍摄工作以后,我被印度伟大的文明和无与伦比的艺术所震撼。

印度,是一个谜一样的国度:她悠久而又扑朔迷离的历史、她万分复杂而又密切相连的宗教体系、她无与伦比的智慧与哲学思想、她灿烂辉煌的神庙和宫殿建筑、她美轮美奂的雕塑和绘画艺术、她丰富多彩的语言文字、她包容万象的民俗民风,这一切无一不令人振奋,又无一不让人迷茫;无一不令人赞叹,又无一不让人困惑,她让几乎所有的人摸不着头脑。我曾经遇到过不少到过印度的人,其中包括在印度工作了好几年的外交官,只要谈到印度的神庙艺术,谈到印度的宗教神统,谈到印度古代艺术中的肖像学特征,所有的人都如坠云里雾中,无法理出一个清晰的脉络。

这就是印度。我深感,印度的历史文化与神话学就像是一本庞大的百科全书,研究它的人没有一个能够完全读懂它的含义和奥秘。

为了了解印度的民俗,我曾经冒着倾盆大雨,从中午到半夜,只身下到海里,在齐腰深的水中拍摄印度西部最盛大的节日,万人空巷的"象头神节"。在雨中,我披着塑料袋,身背三个相机,独自穿梭在那些虔诚的印度民众当中。我与他们一同唱诵,一同祈祷,一同接受祭司在额头点上吉祥的印记,一同分享大神赐予的供品……他们搂着我的肩膀,与我合影,不断地对我说"印度和中国是兄弟"。

为了向印度民众介绍中国的书画艺术,我曾经在不少专业画廊举办个人书画展览,介绍和展示中国传统的绘画、书法和诗词、哲理……有趣的是,当报纸上刊登出介绍我画展的文章时,我却连自己的名字都不认识。印度是

一　路是践踏出来的

世界上语言文字第一复杂的国家，光是钞票上使用的官方文字就有十五种之多。在我的展览期间，许多印度人从早到晚在画廊里与我畅谈，他们喜欢我的画作，也喜爱那些具有深刻哲学意味的中国题画诗，很多人带着笔记本，一字一句地抄写。后来，我将这些题画诗的英文翻译本打印出来，放在画廊里供大家参考。每天早上放下厚厚的一叠，到晚上就被拿得精光，第二天必须重新复印一批。

为了研究巴斯达土著艺术，我曾到散居在高山深谷中的不同部落，考察他们的图腾和生活习俗；到历经千年的"无字碑"中去找寻那些鲜为人知的过去；为了研究佛教艺术，我曾经沿着佛陀的足迹，参拜和考察释迦牟尼佛的历史遗迹；为了了解克拉拉山区充满魔幻般神奇色彩的宗教活动，我曾经度过多少个不眠之夜，从傍晚到清晨守候在燃烧的圣火前进行拍摄。

为了考证印度宗教艺术中的肖像学特征，我曾经到印度各地参拜那些著名的和被湮没的寺庙及古建筑遗址：卡珠拉俄、奥利萨、古吉拉特、拉贾斯坦、泰米尔……我参观考察过几百座印度古代的神庙，研究了从南到北、从东到西，从公元前1世纪到公元19世纪的几十座古代的神庙，拍摄了无数的第一手资料，描绘了几百幅神奇瑞兽的图像，绘制了几十座神庙建筑错综复杂的图纸。

到出版社校正书稿的那些日子，为了节省路上的时间，我尽量乘坐郊区火车。孟买上下班时候的火车拥挤不堪，就像人们在电视里看到的那样，许多人悬挂在车厢门口。为了避免拥挤，我只好购买头等车票。其实所谓的头等车厢与普通的二等车厢并没有什么两样，也是几条硬板凳而已，只是票价相差不少。

出版社的编辑室里有好多台电脑在进行各种书籍及图片的编辑制作工作。偶尔瞥上一眼，看到其他电脑里正在处理的图像，我会随口道出这些大神特殊形象的名字。在印度教神话中，被人们崇拜和信仰的神达三亿三千万之多。有些大神如湿婆、毗湿奴的名字就有一千个。编辑们听到我随口道出这些神祇的名字，甚至是一些鲜为人知的神祇，都大为惊讶。久而久之，他们感叹"她比我们知道的还多"。当我工作结束的时候，他们依依不舍，"非常希望继续与你一起工作"，对于一个能够深入了解他们宗教文化的外国人，满怀着友好和尊敬。

在印度，我参加过好几本考古学、人类学、宗教学和肖像学专著的研究和拍摄工作，并被聘任为印度文化研究所研究员。1997年，我研究印度艺术的博士论文答辩得到了评审教授们的最高评价，获得巴黎索邦大学远东艺术与考古学国家博士的学位。

印度的历史文化遗存十分丰富。在拉贾斯坦邦，我们印度文化研究所所长鲍思岱（M. POSTEL）先生曾经发现过一座公元九世纪坍塌的神庙。多年来，我所任职的印度文化研究所一直与印度考古监察部合作，对这座神庙的遗址进行勘察和研究。这是一座极具历史和艺术价值的建筑杰作。这天，我和鲍思岱先生及印度艺术史家K. MANKODI博士到达发掘现场，刚刚出土的四对神像展现在我们面前，虽然历经千年以上，仍然完好如初。我们都异常兴奋，希望进行拍照。但政府的负责人只允许一个人进行拍摄。大家都知道我是大学里教摄影的老师，故一致认为由我来拍摄最为合适。没想到我所拍摄的寺庙发掘现场和神像的特写，却在今后派上了用场。

为了保护和修复这一罕见的历史遗迹，为了呼吁世界和民众对这一文物古迹的重视，我在法国东方艺术博物馆举办了摄影展览，得到了许多新闻媒体的报导和支持。不料，这些神像出土半年多后，竟然被文物犯罪者盗劫。这一消息使我们彻夜难眠。几个月里我们查询了世界各国与印度文物出售有关的资料，发现被盗神像已被贩卖到美国的一家古董店。当即赶到巴黎，与印度驻法国大使联系。世界上只有我拍摄了发掘现场的第一手资料，这些图片成为追查失窃文物的铁证。在印度政府和国际警察总署的配合下，这些被盗文物终于归还故土。

位于古吉拉特邦巴坦的印度王后井也是鲍思岱先生于50年代发现的。王后井的发掘震惊了世界，可以说是20世纪最伟大的考古发现之一。为了拍摄那些千年以前的艺术杰作，我曾经攀援着抽取积水的管道，只身下到近30米的古井深处，仰卧在泥水里；或者将三脚架架在不足20公分宽的古井横梁上，悬在高达数米的空间。

18年里，我曾经多少次专程去那里考察和拍，我常常觉得对这座万神殿已经了如指掌。但每一次我都能在那里发现新的内容，揭示新的奥秘；每一次我到达它的面前,它给予我的仍然是一种震撼!王后井的考察与研究使我感受到的不仅是历史的沧桑和这座万神殿的伟大,也感觉到一种幸运与使命:能够在千年之后看到这一奇迹是一种幸福,能够尽自己的所能将它传递给大众是一种使命。

为了让世界和中国的读者了解这一历史奇迹,为了让更多的人分享我亲临这一世界奇迹的快乐,我花费了几年时间,撰写了《印度教万神殿艺术——印度王后井探秘》一书。其中包括我近20年的考古研究和对印度历史文化的了解,以及280多幅亲自拍摄、从未发表的图片资料。为了撰写此书,我每天在电脑上连续工作十五六个小时,导致急性青光眼发作,双目失明。

万神殿的研究给予我很多的启迪和思考:这神殿本身就代表着一个世界。世界是巨大的,但又十分窄小,特别是在今天;世界是渺小的,但又十分巨大,就像乌达雅玛蒂王后所建造的这座地下宫殿。

这是世界上第一部用中文撰写的印度考古学专著,涉及了历史、考古、宗教、建筑、艺术、神话学、肖像学、民俗学等各个领域的广泛内容,许多读者将它作为工具书使用。该书出版后,不少专家学者均为之振奋:中华书局编审、中国敦煌吐鲁番学会秘书长柴剑虹先生来信说"我感到王后井的万神殿艺术考古所展现出的历史文化瑰宝也将推动诸如敦煌学、中亚学这些学科研究的深入发展。";印度学家,深圳大学著名梵学教授、印度研究中心主任郁龙余教授来信说"您是印度艺术的恩人。花了近二十年的时间来研究、宣传王后井艺术。当年,这位被称为'朝阳之母'的王后,建造这座地下宫殿用了二十年。一千多年后,您已用了近二十年、以后还将用更多时间来关注她、弘扬她。她从默默无闻到进入世界人类文化遗产,无疑有您的一份功劳。您的这本中文著作,将她介绍给了13亿中国人和全世界的华人,功莫大焉。……"深圳大学国际文化交流学院教授、北京大学博士蔡枫写道:"这是一部令人震撼的专著。我自从2002年跟随郁教授研究印度文化,专攻印度艺术和印度艺术理论,阅读过不少中外印度艺术著作,但真正令人震撼的著作并不多。……您的作品应该在中国传播,让更多的中国人通过您的作品更好地了解印度文化……摆脱中国人言印度艺术只言佛教艺术的尴尬局面。"敦煌研究院杨富学教授写道:"内容丰富,研究独到,照片美轮美奂,我给博生、硕士生上《印度文化概论》课，艺术部分都利用此书"。

中印两国文化交流源远流长，但如今许多中国人除了知道佛教来自印度以外，对印度的了解相当肤浅。为此，我竭尽全力宣传和弘扬印度伟大的文明及灿烂的文化艺术，进行中印文化交流活动。该书出版后，中外很多报刊杂志都进行了专题报道，印度报刊将我称之为当代玄奘；印度驻法国大使亲自为我举办的《王后井》影展剪彩致辞；……在中印邦交55周年的时候，我作为中国唯一的民间代表，参加了政府邀请的官方庆典。

2012年，我的英法文专著《印度古代的神祇与神兽》[①]第一部出版，其中包括从印度河流域文明到笈多王朝时期三千年历史文明的研究，以翔实的考古实据证明了世界上许多历史学家考古学家争议多年悬而未决的问题，受到印度考古学研究领域和法国亚洲艺术及考古学领域的肯定和赞赏。

多年来，我为国内各大专院校举办印度文化艺术的专题讲座，从苏州职业大学到天津师范大学、外国语大学；从深圳大学到北京大学，我给他们讲授"王后井"的奇迹、"印度婚礼"的辉煌、桑琪大佛塔的珍奇、释迦牟尼佛足迹的历史意义……我希望用我在印度获得的知识和灵感，来启迪这一代年轻的大学生，让他们开阔视野，从不同的角度来看世界；许多外交官朋友在我的鼓励之下走出他们的圈子，去真正地认识印度，感受印度灿烂的文化，热爱印度精湛的艺术，体会那种深藏在外表之下的美，感悟那种不用心无法理解的真正的历史文明。

记得很小的时候，父母亲总是谈到他们的挚友金克木先生。那是一位才华出众的年轻人。抗日战争开始之后，父亲被选送到法国留学，而金克木先生则去了印度。尽管二战的烽火燃烧在亚洲和欧洲的土地上，但父母亲和克木先生却一直保持着书写来往。

---

① 此书的英文版是《THE FANTASTIC BEINGS OF ANCIENT INDIA》,From 2500 BC. to 6th Cent. AD. Vol. I. ;法文版是《LES ÊTRES FANTASTIQUES DE L' INDE ANCIENNE 》, De 2500 av. J. – C. au 6ème Siècle. Vol. I. ;Mumbai,Edition Franco-Indian Research 2012,文字252页,我亲自绘制的线描图像291幅,我亲自拍摄的第一手资料黑白和彩色图片307幅。

一　路是践踏出来的

克木伯伯得知我去了印度，立即给我写来长信，对我进行谆谆教导。他告诉我："你到印度的第一感受，是她强烈的对比度。"的确，很多到过印度的人，通常被她街头的贫困现象所迷惑，也被她无与伦比的复杂所困扰，或者对其逃避，或者妄加评论，最终无法去真正地认识印度这个伟大文明为世界所创建的精神和物质财富。

记得 1995 年 7 月，我在日记上写道：

> 前日，翻阅克木伯伯所著的《天竺旧事》，突然发现我曾经在扉页上写下了一些感想，现注录于下，作为一种纪念。此书的扉页上有克木伯伯的题记"赠老友锡候、小梵存念。金克木，1986"。十年以后，我在扉页上记道"读克木伯伯的《天竺旧事》，又给父亲通读了一遍，感触颇深。他文中写道的许多地方，都是我所去过的，只是岁月沧桑，仿佛往日那纯朴的民风已难以寻觅……最使我感动的是那位'鸟巢禅师'，他使我想起在鹿野苑遇到的玉清法师，从 9 岁时与众僧自青海塔尔寺走到印度取经，结果冻坏了一条腿成了残人。同是属于对佛教的虔诚和对真理的追求，不远万里来到天竺，而又有几人如唐玄奘功德圆满，名垂史册？"

以后每次回国，总要到北大朗润园克木伯伯的居所，与他畅谈。克木伯伯一直对印度所发生的一切极为关注，仔细地向我询问印度的现状，了解他当年所在地的一切发展与变化。他对印度的关注，更加强我为弘扬中印文化，进行中印文化交流而奋斗的信念。

如果说因与克木伯伯的友谊，保留在父母亲心里"印度"还只是一种文学和理念上的认知，那么，自从我去了印度，通过无数的书信、文章与照片，印度在他们的心里已经成为一种现实，一种憧憬，一种希望。我一直准备着接父母亲到印度来，看看他们所梦想的，然而，我没有能够实现自己的愿望。

父亲故世以后，我曾将母亲接到印度，去参拜著名的阿旃陀、埃罗拉石窟寺。在那里，85 岁高龄的母亲受到了印度民众与朝圣者的顶礼膜拜。

在印度进行考古研究多年的我，深感应该将自己的知识奉献给大众，让他们从中了解印度伟大的文明。为此，我撰写了《印度教万神殿艺术》一书，为父亲,也为天下的中国读者。我在前言中写道:"我谨将此书献给我亲爱的父亲:杭州大学(现浙江大学)心理学系的创始人之一,朱锡侯教授。他曾经是法国生理学和心理学的双博士,中国生理学会和心理学会的创始人之一。他曾是诗人,文学家和翻译家,是北京大学著名梵学教授金克木先生的挚友。他热爱印度的文化艺术,期望着能到印度来。然而他故去了,竟没能实现自己的愿望!"

"亲爱的父亲,你去了,未能到这里来;但愿你通过女儿的这本书,看到你所想看到的;你去了,未能到这里来;但愿你像这座王后井里的KALKIN,骑着白马再回来!我期待着与你相会,父亲!给予我生命,理想,人格和知识的人!"

我尽20多年的努力,学习、研究和传播印度的文化艺术,期望着让受印度文化影响匪浅的中国民众,能够更多地了解我们这个伟大的邻国,体会那一个与我们同样悠久的文明,让中印两国伟大的文明永远交融,永远昌盛。

一　路是践踏出来的

1949年11岁时到美国，曾攻读于乔治·华盛顿大学哈佛学院专修历史，1969年获宾州大学博士学位。曾在斯瓦特摩Swarthmore学院及赖特Wright州立大学任教并担任历史系主任。也曾在北京师范大学、俄亥俄州立大学任教，在南开大学、复旦大学、中山大学及其他大学讲演。发表过有关明清历史、中亚、海外华人及中日关系的论文。继唐德刚教授后任北美20世纪中国历史学会主席。

袁清

我的"中国梦"及父亲的教化

我的"中国梦"如何？是否有许多"中国梦"？请让我从头说起。日本侵略时我家逃难到内地，那时我做梦也希望中国强大，不再遭此灾难。我是卢沟桥事件两周后诞生于北京（当时叫"北平"）的，父亲袁同礼是国立北平图书馆馆长，被日本人列入黑名单。他在我出生前就离开北京南去，只剩母亲带着全家，我6个月襁褓期间，我们全家逃离日占北平，去到内地。抗战时期生活艰难，好不容易熬到1945年日本投降。

现在让我言归正传。在谈我自己不同时期的"中国梦"以前，先谈父亲的"中国梦"及其对我的影响。

我谈父亲的"中国梦"可能不太称职。从我历史学者的角度来看，他是梦想国富民强的。1895年他诞生于北京，童年亲历1900年八国联军占领北京，他看到外国军队在自己的城中横行当然会感到奇耻大辱。1916年，他和傅斯年同时毕业于北京大学。1920年，他获得奖学金去哥伦比亚大学读历史。他告诉我说，他最爱好的课程是著名民族主义历史学家海士（Carlton Hayes）开的课。1921—1922年华盛顿会议召开，他成为北京政府代表团顾问黄郛的秘书，又在夏天到美国国会图书馆见习。1922年他获得哥伦比亚大学学士学位后，决定专修当时中国稀罕的图书馆学。28岁时，他从"杜威十进制分类法"发明者杜威（Melville Dewey）创办的坐落于奥尔巴尼（Albany）的纽约州图书馆学院获得图书馆学学士，然后去英国在伦敦大学（University of London）历史研究所（Institute of Historical Research）进修一年，1924年回国在当时的"革命热床"广州的广东大学（中山大学的前身）担任图书馆长。

回顾父亲的事业，他的"中国梦"反映出几个方面。首先，他特别关注对图书馆与博物馆收藏的中国文化财产，进行专业性的管理与保存。1925年他30岁担任北京大学图书目录学教授兼图书馆长，成为李大钊的知己。1926年京师图书馆成立，梁启超任总务长，父亲担任馆长。1929年京师图书馆与旧国立图书馆合并成国立北平图书馆，（现在的中国国家图书馆），蔡元培担任馆长，父亲担任副馆长。蔡元培当时主掌许多文教机关，并兼中央研究院院长，国立北平图书馆实际上由父亲经管。

父亲也在故宫博物院的创始中起了作用，但把创建国立北平图书馆当作他的重要贡献。他帮助在北海公园旁设计并建筑一座中西合璧的图书馆。他主持编辑各种"联合目录"、"索引"、影印复制、建立图书馆联通借阅制度以及与国外交流资料。最重要的是他对国立图书馆学者、图书爱好者、研究生、实习生等年轻一代的培养，并保送他们出国深造，受惠者名单很长，重要人物有王重民、向达、谭其骧、孙楷弟、谢国桢、赵万里、傅振伦等人。

父亲从早年开始就注意追踪流散国外的典籍与文化财产。早在1927年就对日本收藏的《永乐大典》进行研究。后来把世界各图书馆收藏的永乐大典佚卷编成《永乐大典现存卷目》。他敦促助手王重民去美国国会图书馆与欧洲的各图书馆编制珍稀典籍、特别是敦煌文献的目录。他趁日军尚未占领北平就把国立图书馆的珍贵书籍迁移到后方避免丧失。

父亲"中国梦"的另一方面就是要摸清西方对中国了解（即汉学）的深度与精密性。我们于1949年离开中国时，父亲已经54岁，要负担五口之家，其中两人已进大学，另有一六年级小学生——就是我。他在获得美国国会图书馆的正式职务前好几年仰给于研究经费及临时职务。当时生活艰难，我们都懂得节俭。我们到美国的这些年月，他辛勤劳动，致力于编辑从1920年代

一 路是践踏出来的

到 1950 年代西方关于中国的书籍目录。在没有电脑的时代，他用手写，专心致志地把英文、法文、德文及葡萄牙文的一万八千册书本进行整理，1958 年由耶鲁大学远东出版社出版《西文汉学书目》(*China in Western Literature*)。这本书目的特点是外国作家的出生年以及中国作家的中文名与外文名都有了。他后来又出版了俄国作家论中国的书目。这本书也包括了俄国作家论蒙古与新疆以及中俄关系的课题。

父亲接受了国会图书馆一个相对次要的职务以后，继续不懈地从事许多重要研究项目。这说明他的"中国梦"是要加强中国的"智慧威力"。当时许多美籍华裔都从事洗衣与餐馆行业，他却决定编撰一个从 1905 年到 1960 年华裔获得美国博士学位的名单。我记得每天回家他都显得有点疲倦，但吃过晚饭就开始这项工作，1961 年出版了英文《美国的中国留学生博士论文指南（1905—1960）》(*A Guide to Doctoral Dissertations by Chinese Students in America 1905—1960*)，书中收集了 2789 篇论文的题目与作者的中英文名字、出生年、获得博士的机构与时间。他又再接再厉地编中国留学生在英国与欧洲大学获得博士学位的名单。1965 年他去世时还留下未编完的有关中国艺术与考古的书目。幸亏后来由芝加哥大学的范德本（Harrie A. Vanderstappen）教授完成，书名为《袁同礼的西文论中国艺术与考古的书目》(*The T. L. Yuan Bibliography of Western Writings on Chinese Art and Archaeology*)，1975 年由 Mansell 出版社出版。

什么是父亲的"中国梦"？在一次由家里走到国会图书馆时，他对我说中国需要和平，"有了五十年和平的日子中国就会强盛"，这是他说的话。诚然，从 1840 年起到他逝世为止，中国没有任何十年没有战争或叛变革命。父亲的"中国梦"也包括显示中国伟大文化与永久价值、增进外国及中国人民对它的赞赏。他一定也希望回国探亲、访故，但 1965 年他去世时，这个梦未能实现。

谈到我的"中国梦"，可以把我一生分为三个阶段来谈。一、50 年代我在大学学习期间，二、我在 80 年代的教书生涯，三、2010 年代我的退休年月。

1949 年我 11 岁时来到美国，一句英语也不会说。但我读过《三剑客》

《福尔摩斯》以及《汤姆叔叔的小屋》等西方小说的中文翻译。我也喜欢《三国演义》《西游记》《七侠五义》与《水浒传》。到达华盛顿并住在国会图书馆附近以后才开始读巴金、老舍、茅盾等人的现代小说，了解到新与旧的冲突、大家庭的紧张，以及中国资本主义社会中产业工人的痛苦。1954年我进哈佛大学时，我自认为对中国与中国文化很有见地，不必去听著名现代中国历史学权威费正清（John King Fairbank）教授的课。我当时的"中国梦"是去寻求在中国得不到的知识。

我在哈佛就读的头两年中，对职业的选择：究竟是当科学家/工程师还是当历史学家，决定不了。曾经一度我选了科学史专业，这样就涉足于两者之间。我选了物理、地质、历史课以后就决定了历史专业。我在大学二年级选修了梵文学家英格尔斯（Daniel Ingalls）的现代印度史课、沃尔夫（Robert Wolff）教授的俄帝国史课，以及福莱（Richard Frye）、兰格尔（William Langer）与富里昂尼斯（Speros Vryonis）合教的奥托曼帝国史课。虽然我得到哈佛大学奖学金，但仍然得问家里要钱。我也在周末到埃利奥特楼（Eliot House）宿舍图书馆服务，得点收入。我不敢说自己有"中国梦"，但我十分关心中国，我经常去哈佛—燕京图书馆阅读中国报纸。我最担心的是中国变成苏联的卫星国，苏联专家像老大哥控制中国。1956年，我参加"亚洲传统与改变"（Tradition and Change in Asia）作文比赛，我强调传统可使改变合法化，法律保护的重要性，以及在"民主"范围中的自由与平等。我以二年级学生得第三名，第一、二名都是博士研究生。还记得克鲁晓夫谴责斯大林的消息传到西方，我兴奋极了，马上写信给亲大陆的《华侨日报》，吁请编者把克鲁晓夫谴责的中文发表。虽然该报没有答应我的要求，不久后毛主席就发动了"百花齐放、百家争鸣"运动。我当时得到民主潮流的感染，认为自己回国的时机到了。那时我对职业（甚至对选修专业）还没打定主意，更加强回国的意图。我的生活环境也促使我朝这一方向倾斜。当有钱的同学假期去他们喜欢的地方度假，我却在周末干着最低工资六毛五分钱一小时的临时活。自私与无私的动机使我做着为祖国服务的"中国梦"。我的一个具体"梦"想就是中国每年钢铁产量能完成1800吨的目标。50年代我的"中国梦"就说到这里。

一 路是践踏出来的

我回中国的愿望一直到 1978 年才实现。80 年代我在俄亥俄州执教时，我的"中国梦"变了样。尼克松使中美关系解冻时"文化大革命"也告终，我访问中国的梦想实现。从香港到广州的火车，一路都是战斗音乐与阿尔巴尼亚的唱片。到了北京以后，能够在我们住的华侨大厦会见许多亲戚。那时北京马路上很少车辆，商店下午 5 点打烊，晚上街上看不到人。我们的亲戚缺少粮票、油票以及许多生活必需品。我们帮助他们从友谊商店购置一些东西。我们取得北京公安局许可去访问了西安、南京、上海、南昌、九江、庐山、桂林等地方。虽然有许多人用奇异的眼光看我们，但我们在各地遇见的人们都诚恳友好。他们一般不注重物质财富。

1982 年我所在的赖特州立大学与北京师范大学建立姐妹关系，我到北师大任教一个学期。这次访问使我对北京和中国人民了解更深。我更能使自己适应他们的生活方式，包括骑自行车去校园附近的地点。恰巧我的紧邻是政协委员，问我有什么好的建议他好在政协会上提出。我记得提供了三点当时属于我的"中国梦"的简单建议：建设高铁、减少抽烟、服务业取消 11 点半到 2 点的午睡，延长服务时间。去年是我最近一次访问中国，高兴地坐上高铁火车，也发现抽烟减少（至少在公共场合少了）。虽然许多机关午休时间仍然很长，但也有不午休的。

80 年代我的另一"中国梦"就是在大陆与台湾知识分子之间消除鸿沟。80 年代初期这样的学术交流是不受欢迎、很少举行的。1981 年，北美亚洲学会（Association for Asian Studies）年会上，两岸学者共聚一堂，专门讨论辛亥革命 70 周年，成为重要转折点。另外一个突破是几年后香槟伊大（伊利诺伊大学厄巴纳香槟分校）探讨 1936 年的西安事变。这两次探讨都是北美 20 世纪中国历史学会组织的。学会总部设在纽约，唐德刚教授是主要发起人，成员主要是哥伦比亚大学和纽约市立大学的教员。我参加后成为秘书长，又在 1989 年继任唐德刚为该会主席。

天安门学潮发生时我是该会主席。我组织了北美亚洲学会与美国历史学会（American Historical Association）联合举办的讨论会。尽管天安门事件引起感情冲动，我们尽量使讨论限于学术认识、平心静气。毫无疑问，许多亲华的美国新左派提出严厉批评。由于美国研究中国政治不断两极化，我觉得选择海外华人为我的研究领域更有益处与收获。

我特别热衷于研究东南亚的海外华人，他们许多人都是去海外圆"中国梦"而成为巨富。他们有些人融入本地文化，也有些人坚决保存中国语言文化。研究他们所在国家的情况也很有意思：例如印度尼西亚、马来西亚、文莱是伊斯兰教国家，泰国、缅甸、柬埔寨、老挝是佛教国家，菲律宾是基督教国家，越南是共产主义国家。多年来，我走遍所有东南亚国家。海外华人虽然有钱财，却在这些国家遭受不同程度的歧视与暴力。我一直以来的"中国梦"就是希望这些华人能在和平环境中生活，希望他们不在将来的反华暴乱中被迫害成凶手或代罪羔羊。

现在我退休了，值此2010年代我有什么"中国梦"呢？中国快速粗犷的工业化使河水、湖水污染，城市空气毒化。我的"中国梦"之一就是减少污染、限制车辆、关闭污染工厂。公共交通工具应该大增，自行车道与人们锻炼的跑道应该大增。事故累累的矿山应该关闭，太阳能的运用应该增加。城镇应该有更多的树木与公园。

我从父亲那里继承了对边缘地区的兴趣，特别是新疆。我去新疆旅行过四次，西藏一次，内蒙古三次，蒙古共和国两次。我的"中国梦"希望汉族与各种少数民族和谐和平相处。少数民族地区的汉人应该学习本地语言、风俗以及少数民族的宗教信仰与宗教生活。中国大学应该开维吾尔语、藏语、蒙语及其他少数民族语言文学课程，让它们像英语、德语、或俄语那样成为选修课。我的"中国梦"是希望有朝一日出个维吾尔人或者藏人的能源部长或外交部长。

我的"中国梦"也希望中国贫富差距缩小。现在是现代市场经济的受益者、贪污腐败官员以及他们的企业界友人窃据上层，下层是从农村来的劳工和女缝纫工流动人口。对城市的贫困者与许多农村居民来说，医疗与教育费用昂贵。最近几年城市大多数居民都感到看医生、买药以及教育费用飞涨。还有中国一般人民上有老、下有小，照顾老人的负担不轻。由于独生子女政策，老年中心大有扩充的必要。退休人员应该有机会参加到社会公益事业中去，不是专门玩麻将消磨时间。

中国军事上越来越强，经济上已成为世界"老二"，必然会有世界势力把中国当做威胁以及竞争对手。中国要维持友人又应付敌手不是易事。人之常情喜欢用武力解决问题。艾森豪威尔总统曾经提醒：像美国这样的国家庞大的军事工业不堪负担。现在美国因为预算赤字太大政府尽量节约军费，但国会议员不断作梗，使裁减军事开支无法实行。中国千万不要效法美国。为了军事开支必然宣扬战争，宣扬战争必有战争。我希望中国更多的钱用到教育、医疗与照顾穷人。战争孕育未来敌人却解决不了领土纠纷。我永远记得父亲对和平的评论："有了五十年和平的日子中国就会强盛"。中国与邻国发展友好关系并应付潜在敌手一个好办法就是利用中国出外旅客当作友谊使者。我在最近旅行中发现中国去泰国、斯里兰卡与尼泊尔的游客越来越多。他们的行为举止决定中国会受到尊重或者嘲笑。

我当今的"中国梦"包括中国人民的更大发展，成为有公德、负责任的"新公民"。百年前梁启超曾谈到改变中国民性。他提倡"新民"，每个人少顾自己与自家，多想国家与社会，应该改变抽烟赌博的恶习，少在婚丧上浪费钱财。我最近访问中国认为建立公民意识大有必要。中国驾驶汽车的人漠视行人的权利，肆意跨越行人的白色斑马线；行人闯红灯、穿马路。还有摩托车和电动自行车经常驶行人行道。许多年轻力壮的人在公共汽车上不给老人让座。中国公众需要发扬公德与礼貌，公安局应该惩罚违反交通规则的人。

中国应该有"民主"与"人权"说来容易。但"民主"的真正意思是什么？是自由还是平等？两者都是重要的，我们两者都要。中国不须模仿西方那种金钱能收买选举的民主。现在互联网在中国越来越普遍，政府越来越难对信息进行检查与封锁。中国中产阶级日益扩展，群众日益受教育，他们就会日益变得政治上敢讲话。中国共产党的任务就是团结中国最聪颖的精华。党本身必须避免任人唯亲及贪污腐败。我同意"社会稳定"最重要，但"社会稳定"现在越来越受威胁：维吾尔人搞武装袭击，藏人搞自焚，工人罢工等等，更不必说地震、洪水、雾霾等自然灾害。外交事务上中国正逢重新武装的日本耀武扬威，邻邦菲律宾与越南的不友好表现，更有搞"再平衡亚洲"的猜疑的美国设法遏制中国。台湾国民党民意低落，两年后主张"台独"的民进党又有可能赢得总统选举。虽然我殷切希望，但现在不是在中国开启西方"民主"的时刻。环顾全球，似乎只有斯堪的纳维亚国家既有自由、又有平等，然而也付出了高税率与物价为代价。

　　总而言之，我的"中国梦"很大部分是由父亲的典范形成。他生活在中国弱小与无权的时代。他的"中国梦"很平凡：保护中国文化财产与向全世界显示它的伟大。作为流亡国外的难民，他曾不懈努力地从事一个又一个研究项目。我的"中国梦"经过不同阶段。中国强了，我的"中国梦"也改变。因为童年在日本侵略中成长，主导我思想的是"我能帮中国做点什么？"我的情况和后"大屠杀"时代的犹太人希望帮助以色列相似。我少年时代是个理想家，怀着牺牲热忱。中年当教员时就只能提出忠告而别无能力。我是中国巨大变革的见证人，但也感到陋习难改。现在我退休了，在这古稀之年主要只关注自己的事务。我阅读有关中国的书，也阅读关于中东、南亚、甚至非洲的书。我的"中国梦"一方面希望中国实现理想，另一方面希望中国避免祸害。换句话说，中国应该获得好的，扬弃坏的。我最终希望中国繁荣、民主、和平，在当代以及未来受全世界尊敬。

乐界和诗界两栖的美国大学教授，美国诗人学院会员，美国交响乐团联会会员，美国绿山学院和沈阳音乐学院客座教授，华盛顿国际文化社 Washington Cultural International 总裁；曾任中国交响乐团、江苏演艺集团顾问，美国国家文艺基金会 National Endowment for the Arts、南卡州、新泽西州政府文化委员会以及华盛顿市府评委 consultant，华盛顿交响乐团副主席、华盛顿青年交响乐团发展总监、国家室乐团行政总监、华盛顿国家与社区服务委员会（National & Community Services Commissioner）委员。名列《美国名人录》及《全球名人录》。

陈咏智

陈咏智根据中国迴文诗与西方十二音列体，自辟英诗风格，其作品"A Fugue Of Tone Rhyming"入选2009年美国 Tom Howard 作诗比赛，风格得高度评价"Highly Recommended for Verse in All Styles and Genres"。

谁解胡尘箫剑梦　去留肝胆洒长城

好梦豪情40年：1973年我圆梦考入香港中文大学、住崇基学院。女辅导长庐慧卿博士以60高龄，带头在迎新营掘地劳动，锣鼓点卷起的欢呼在荷花池每一个角落回响！我通报应林堂宿生会港英特务探员 CID 没有法庭颁发的搜捕令擅闯大学，同学们豪言壮语要出动棒队捍卫校园。大丈夫当如斯，壮哉！

70年代的海外年轻人充满梦想，一个被标签为"放眼世界，认识祖国，关心社会，争取同学权益"，事实上又"吾将上下而求索"的火红年代，我们文科与社科同学遥对大陆的"文革"浩劫，无法忍受，屡屡在校内坚持反逆流的言论。青春如此多娇，强哉矫！我课后自己分析勃拉姆斯的第一交响乐，暑假磨透了《史记》"乐书"、吉联抗译的《乐记》、丘琼逊的《历代乐律志校释》、康熙御编的《律吕正义》上编、嵇康的《声无哀乐论》、《毛泽东选集》第五卷、《共产党人宣言》，还涉猎钱宾四、王健民、李定一、费孝通、劳思光、杨阴浏、麦啸霞、欧阳予倩等人的部分著述。修崇基学院 IBS 课程时，钻研了柏拉图的 The Republic。课余与知己在校园内展开对《李一哲大字报》、杨小凯的《中国往何处去》和张春桥的《论资产阶级法权》等著作的评论，指点源流，不枉少白头！

1976 年初周恩来总理逝世，电视转播其追悼会那晚，每一个宿舍的大厅都挤满了沉痛的同学，大家泣不成声。九月初至十月中旬，由于"四人帮"被捕的消息隐不公布，在那群情汹涌的黑夜，我与三两位知己向往"周（恩来）"、"邓（小平）"的务实政策方针，误以为江青快要登基了，就在中大学生会代表会截止干事会内阁报名的前十分钟，拼凑出一份 12 人的名单参与竞选第七届中大学生会，依据学生会健全的普选体制而高票当选。

1977 年 11 月，新选的学生会成功举办了"中大开放日"，招待了 20 多万市民到校园各院系参观，晚间在林荫大道摆了两千人的露天盛宴，为"百万大道"的大学广场弹出绝响。一周后，马临候任校长指示我在年底筹办一场具有外交派头的"中大十五周年餐舞会"，在 12 月 30 日加座当时能容纳二百余餐桌，最够气派的香港会议中心的大舞厅，邀请了时任辅政司的 Sir Dennis Roberts 及全港主要外交使节出席，拉来了两大电视台与数十位中英报界记者到场采访。席上李卓敏校长及我分别公开以外交辞令，高姿态地坚持中大的四年学制不得被殖民地政府硬改为三年，全场中大师生沸腾的掌声触发翌日 South China Morning Post、《华侨日报》等媒体广泛评论。奈何 80 年代末，阴谋深算的殖民地政府抢在香港回归前，迫使当时全港唯一本科四年制的中大改成三年制，赤裸裸地埋下导致九七后学额膨胀、连锁性思维萎缩的深层社会病根，学术界由是偏向追求市场效应，争相巧取豪夺。翻阅 70 年代香港大学生报，印证当年不少本科生所发表的文章之深度和广度，比起时下两岸在职学者的手笔，诚然更能表现出知识分子应有之风骨与灵魂，确是情何以堪？

1980 年，我在美国北伊利诺伊州大学念研究院。除夕，我搭同学的便车在雪花纷飞下自芝加哥直闯纽约，途中翻车，幸而无恙。到了哥伦比亚大学

一　路是践踏出来的

拜见著名音乐家周文中教授，报上师门，他笑道："张世彬先生的书我看过了，很有才华，我第一次访问香港中文大学时就想见他，可惜他英年早逝。"打开了艺文的话匣子，他慷慨地邀请我参与他与家人的除夕餐宴，饭后再请我翌日晚上到他位于 Soho 的古宅详谈。

文中先生祖籍江苏常州，1923 年出生于山东曲阜（孔夫子的故乡），其族谱溯源到宋儒周敦颐。尊翁周淼先生号仲洁，年轻时投身辛亥革命，民国初年代表北洋政府交涉接收日占青岛市时，为捍卫民族主权，不惜与日寇拔枪相向、寸土不让。文中先生 6 岁染肾疾危殆，幸蒙国医陆仲安大夫妙手回春。1937 年"七七事变"，周氏阖府从南京迁至上海租界，周淼先生时任内政部总务司，殿后随政府辗转撤退至后方。长子文晋稍前已赴美国麻省理工学院研修，日后主持盟军战斗机与美国洲际弹道系统科研项目，功勋彪炳。1938 年初，周家府内三子皆罹染日寇生化武器所导致的伤寒病毒。最小的弟弟文正最早痊愈。老二文禾是家中最赋音乐天聪、能无师自通、贵为金陵中学乐团提琴手，不幸夭折。文中先生由留美返沪之西医陆锦文大夫诊断，危急万分。护士为其擦酒精时不慎起火，早已四肢无力的幼年文中，以其坚强的求生意志，从床上挣扎坠地，体内毒素呕吐一空，奇迹逃脱鬼门关。

1941 年珍珠港事变后，日寇占领上海租界。文中先生弱冠，誓不作亡国奴。尊慈周富守女士典当资产，资之自从浙江冲破日寇封锁线，到达抗日后方，先到衡阳再去桂林，出生入死。在此期间周淼先生冒险返沪去接家眷潜赴后方，竟然因文中之成功出逃而被日寇羁囚数月。文中先生之姑母在常州清凉寺戴发修行，掩护救治游击队伤员，被日寇拘捕，迫供不屈，惨烈牺牲。未逾两年，桂林失守，文中先生出走重庆，再度死里逃生，见证民族血泪交织之湘桂大劫难！

抗战胜利后，周文中获全额奖学金，到耶鲁大学修读建筑，抵美随即改习音乐。1955 年，其管弦乐曲《花落知多少》被路斯威交响乐团委约、首次公开演出，其抵美后十年寒窗之刻苦励进与战乱浩劫余生之多年情感压抑，化为激昂慷慨音乐，震撼美国乐坛，为华人作曲家在西方音乐史上竖立里程碑。此后周文中被誉为西方史册上首位通晓东西文化语汇之现代作曲家，为

Four seas to One Family: Overseas Chinese and Chinese dream
四海一家、天涯比邻：海外华人与中国梦

首位华人学者出任常春藤学府哥伦比亚大学之艺术学院执行副院长与作曲系系主任，首位华人作曲家被授美国人文学院院士，且曾被委任为美中关系全国委员会之常委逾 16 年，并在欧洲、美洲、亚洲许多国家作了百多场学术讲演与音乐演奏。

1977 年，文中先生推荐由管平湖弹奏的古琴曲《流水》录音为美国政府采纳，经"旅行者"号太空飞船发射到各卫星站，再转播人间，蔚为美谈。这时"美中艺术交流中心"成立，忙于帮助大陆重振文化，安排 Arthur Miller，Isaac Stern，曹禺、沈从文、阴法鲁、谭抒真、陈纲等中美文化人士互访。30 年来，文中先生与我鱼雁不辍，是我终生的良师益友。

1985 年，我再怀梦被聘任为华盛顿青年交响乐团发展主任，策划该团 108 位师生到青岛、济南、北京、上海、香港、台北、台南及高雄演出。老美上司数次去函首都市长求援拨款不果。我与市府一位女士午餐取得锦囊妙计，草拟一信交给十多位学生联署上书市长夫人，申诉贫穷子弟无法推销"彩券"（Raffle Tickets）苦况，未几，市长从 Escheat Fund 拨来数万元，并 endorsed 背书公函予华府区内所有与中国有贸易往来的财团，呼吁它们赞助。一下子"发梦啦"，青年交响乐团不单那次风光出征，而且还有了数十万元的预算积蓄。

乐团出发前一月，突然接到韩叙大使秘书乐爱妹小姐杨洁篪夫人电话，要求安排一次记者招待会，让韩大使与乐团师生及家长欢聚。虽然适值中国驱逐了一位美籍记者出境，但我排除了各种困难，此次文化活动更是两岸竞赛式同时对乐团发出邀请，我一周内拼老命，动员了各大电视及报界媒体云集华府重庆酒楼；韩大使风度翩翩地推崇青少年担任"文化使者"（Cultural Envoy）的积极意义。历史的吊诡是，台北经文署文化组长李庆平在招待会前两日来电话，要求安排他在会上发言。我答道："我绝对欢迎您与韩大使同场发言，但此事对您在官场上的影响，可得由您自己决定。"庆平结果没有来，五年后，他出任海基会副秘书长，成功主办"汪辜会谈"，定案了两岸"一中各表"的历史性坐标！

在北京民族宫演出那晚，陈昊苏副市长接见我，指示我要对祖国的统一作出"贡献"。我说："两岸若能同台交响合奏，那是和谐，不需要统一！"

一　路是践踏出来的

谁叫我的"河蟹论"喊早了20年呀?! 演出后，美国大使 Winston Lord 邀请乐团到他官邸餐宴，《华盛顿邮报》驻北京特派员 Dan Sutherland 问我为什么昨天当我在台上宣布演出曲目为贝多芬"第五命运交响乐"之际全场掌声如雷。我解释道："'文革'十年，批贝多芬和西方文化，斗臭老九知识分子，如今都被解放了，这是惨痛命运的交响。"

1988年，我被美国国家艺术基金会 National Endowment for the Arts 委派到纽约唐人街现场评审（on-site visit）某华人乐社，我对其行政总监说：你们行政人员全不支薪，如果把不支薪项纳入 In-Kind Support 预算内，重新要求加大拨款，再附一页描述唐人街人口剪影（social demographics）和"市内少数民族"（inner-city minority）历史沿革，我乐于推荐。该乐社按照我的主意得到 NEA 拨款，聘任作曲家周龙为艺术总监。22年后，周龙被授予美国艺术最高荣誉 Pulitzer 奖。

2000年，我又怀梦被北京中国交响乐团聘为顾问，介绍美国乐团"分权分责分工"的不牟利董事会制度（501c3式 Corporate Structure）。事后大陆一位退休干部兴高采烈地问："成立董事会可以发股票分红吧!"唉，怪不得香港人要被骂"不懂闷声发大财了"。2004年，哥伦比亚大学250周年校庆，我被邀发表论文《阴阳际合再生缘—周文中跨界限的泛音》，与温汉璋先生，胡昌度教授（首任中大研究院院长）欢聚一堂。晚宴上，哥大校董胡应洲教授安排我致词，我引述1968年哥大学运时的流行电影 Strawberry Statement （烈火暴潮），参加晚会的两岸学人都不熟悉这一典故而毫无反应，当时我想，香港长期的新闻自由太可贵了!

2007年，我圆梦被委任为南京大屠杀七十周年音乐会合唱指挥，率领十二位美国声乐家参与演出。途中，我撰七绝《金陵祭》：

　　天涯咫尺祭金陵　箫管压弦倾挽情　起板招魂冤不息　落红离岸觅凄声

12月13日音乐会演奏完毕那一刻，台上台下的热泪交织，荡气回肠……我竟夜不眠，撰了英文诗《南京祭》：

MASS FOR NANKING'S 1937

Stanza II

Japan in years of memorization for nineteen thirty-seven,

pounding wave over wave of bombs/stones on lives.

In name of Emperor, under de flag,

sun turned wrinkle and dark.

Bone, after butcher's hand,

flipping.

Weeping

blood upon ruptured land,

gun overturned each single park,

framed as Messiah, thunder of mad.

Wounding cave after cave, combed bones by knives,

pen it a year off civilization, mini-civilized be irrelevant.

Recalling lines of devil page:

Hundreds of thousands,

females, even minors,

weeks for seven,

gang raped—

under de killers' chilled katana.

……

Global integrity torched against sin in two thousand seven.

By emotion, wrap up such map being harked of rape,

weep with peers for rings of passion underground.

A country atoned bad long by cold moon,

saddened past never make thy pain

alone.

Tone,

heartened pick thou an ever-main,

toned each entry of sad song off old wound.

Rip, with no fears, strings in lotion of extra-sound.

Of a nation, lapping over gap marked among shape,

vocal sincerity with torch accompanied de dignity in heaven.

Unrusted thou dears——

We do hear: May our tone, peel the stone, seal thy tear.

Be rested, dears.

《南京祭》（第二段）
回忆日寇三七年，
滥炸生灵顶皇天，
红日旗压黯乌烟。
屠夫斩肉不眨眼，
血流成河江山虚。
魔王自称救世主，
毒焰燎原成地狱。
伤残堆山尸成坑，
刺刀丛中无生还。
蓬莱小岛何须有？
文明倒退轮后转。
如今重阅阎王册，
七周残暴鬼神泣。
妇女不分老和孺，
尽遭鬼子性暴虐。
中华妻女遭轮奸，
兽行外加武士剑。
……

二零零七全球化

南京屠杀全球骂。

奸淫烧杀记忆新，

耻辱未雪泪未干，

欲盖弥彰遮羞难。

寒月岂能藏旧孽，

拒不忏悔永遭责。

唯我中华国难深

但愿生灵永安息！

——谭中译

7年来，尝试据回文诗与十二音列体，自擀英文诗风格—终能有幸梦圆。拙作 A Fugue Of Tone Rhyming 入选2009年美国 Tom Howard 作诗比赛的"高评"（Highly Recommended for Verse in All Styles and Genres）。我撰写新或旧诗时，力求贯彻"声、韵、情、境"的同步规范（synchronization profile）。以下举几个例子：

《旋相甲子情—时年陆拾》

不负胡尘箫剑情　　披肝沥胆赋流形

旋相甲子斯夫逝　　敢有狂歌照汗青

《春夏秋冬北西南东咏》（仿高启《梅花》原韵）

春溪点滴漱亭台　　夏雨连珠柳浪栽　　秋月印潭擎酒卧　　冬虫傲雪待莺来

北征沿路寻幽竹　　西渡横戈嚼苦苔　　南下他乡箫剑咏　　东招故里紫阳开

《殇忌》（仿龚自珍《咏史》原韵）

鱼肉生民泛九州　　歌台舞榭欲横流　　自肥银锭斤斤算　　钦定脂腔靡靡游

江姐芳留渣滓狱　　林昭殉为芷兰谋　　刑场烈女冤灵在　　魂斥楚翘封爵侯

一　路是践踏出来的

《卅七年后重游西湖》
初吻三潭桨影空　残堤冷月照枭雄　再游花港观秋煞　谁识鉴湖埋落红

《望道天涯海角魂》
涉重洋闯异方　披星追腊月　霹雳飙白尘　去留肝胆雨潇潇
固予弹铗横戈　袖卷莽莽天涯网
沿浅涧依星斗　踏雪采寒梅　氤霜淼银鬓　登落岳岩风淡淡
何妨抚弦望道　襟悬氲氲海角魂

民国初期，中国知识精英因应民族危机而梦醒于必须普及教育，1917 年胡适发表《改良文学刍议》，怀梦新文学运动，言文一体，以话面语取代僵化的文言文，并为传情表意，解放了格律、对仗、用典对诗文的束缚。徐悲鸿和林风眠在 30 年代，怀梦融汇水墨抹骨法和西方素描透视，各领风骚。同期，中国引入西方作曲、记谱、乐器、演奏法为主要媒介，新时代音乐家亦怀梦创作出各类优秀的歌曲。从 1905 无声电影片《定军山》到 1933 年首部取得国际大奖的有声电影《渔光曲》，进展长足，一直至 1949 年，怀梦经典电影源源不绝！受到电影《风云儿女》主题歌《义勇军进行曲》和这时代的严肃文艺所鞭策鼓舞，音乐驱使中国仁人志士凭"血肉长城"来抗击日寇凶恶枪炮，怀梦为民族奋斗不懈，进而建立新中国！

《论语》："据于德、依于仁、游于艺"。早在 1983 年 10 月，我与上海音乐院院长丁善德教授于香港对话，题为《欣赏严肃音乐必须要有高度文化水平》，全文载于《明报月刊》。若要广泛有效启发国民的高度原创性科学思维，又怎可不圆梦于深层文化艺术素养的滋润？

近 20 年来，祖国固得益于全球经济一体化、发达国家"外包"的来料加工，建成"世界工厂"，从而把 GDP 提升到国际前茅。与此同时，淫赌毒泛滥，庸俗煽情，格调委靡之夜总会式文化全面膨胀，甚至被纳入高等教育课程！？《乐书》："审音知政"！从功能角度而言，此类庸俗演艺文化充斥于学府和市场，反映出在体制上国家长期陷入贪污腐败的危机，思维价值早已罹患人情道义沦落与品味低劣的民族沉疴！"入则无法家拂士，出则无敌国外患者,国恒亡!"仰望十四年抗日战争而至上甘岭之役,英烈长啸的悲壮国魂,再环顾 时下国家公民意识与社会文化素养所积陷的思维雾霾:诡诈阴狠、敛鬻成风,文官武将,济私假公;谋权逐色,臭味相同,仁人志士无不义愤填膺,劲草拦风,笔诛虎熊,歌啸苍穹!

壮哉!衷心怀梦祝福习近平主席团队早日除贪铲腐,内外廉清,充公罪赃,兵凶莫惊,平权刑政,司法透明,启通言路,审冤秉诚,四维彰显,正文育英,庠序移俗,抑倡郑声;荷戈守土,两岸情倾,共和重建,诏谕生灵,九韶四区,邦国中兴!

神州海内外炎黄子孙同舟共济,全民并肩拔棘斩荆,圆了凌霄好梦豪情!

一　路是践踏出来的

美国辛辛那提大学环境健康系史密立讲座教授兼系主任，兼任辛大医学院副院长和辛辛那提癌症中心主任。曾担任美国国立健康所和国防部科研审查和政策委员会主席、国家科学院新兴科学委员会委员。培养出百余位来自各国的研究生、博士后、专科医生、和年轻教授。曾被选为美国泌尿科基础研究学会会长。组织过美国及国际大型会议，多次担任大会主席或特邀主讲人。所获荣誉包括美国泌尿科基础研究2007年度女性科学家、俄亥俄州杰出公民、和2014年列腺癌协会首届导师奖。

何淑薇

我的生活与环境健康之梦

在香港殖民地统治下生长的我，对中国和华人的看法比较复杂。在我幼年的心灵中，对作为一个国家的"中国"印象模糊，我所接触到的新闻传媒与信息来源也不能产生我作为华人的自豪感。更因为在教会中学念书，政治理念极少。中国历史课程只到清末为止。老师和父母只教我们好好做人、助人为乐，大家都不谈政治。我们大部分生活在真空的世界观中。我想为人群服务，但除了发愤读书以外，不知如何入手。我们没有多大梦想，只是按着长辈的指导：愈学得多，本领愈大。于是我发愤读书，考进了亚洲著名的香港大学。

大学生活使我政治启蒙，让我开始对中国大陆、台湾和世界产生一些看法。70年代初期的香港社会充满动荡和学生运动。中国知识分子有个关心世事的传统。我参加了多种学生活动、走过台峡两岸一些大小城镇、在英国东北一个叫作"可怜我"（Pity Me，以西方标准来说是个很穷）的小镇待了一个夏天、并背着行囊在欧洲数国转了一圈。通过这些经验，我感觉到中国需要大规模现代化，才能把民众生活提升至西方水平。除了内部改革，中国还需要大量外来的财务和科技支援，需求量之大，难以想象。

1974年，香港大学选我为该年度最出色的毕业生，并给我颁发奖学金，进修博士学位。我努力了三年，完成了所有博士学位的要求，才发现除非再到海外进修，很难开始教职生涯，我作为女性就业机会更少。带着一个破碎的梦，我远赴波士顿大学进行博士后深造，满以为一两年后会有机会回港任教，却料不到竟然被达傅思大学聘任。达傅思长期被列为全美国最佳的三十名大学之一。我在那里待了18年，每周7天、每天14小时工作．我的事业从此腾飞。

我开始不断地争取到联邦级的研究基金，年资虽浅，却获邀去评审联邦研究经费申请书和学报论文。达傅思大学比较快地把我升为正教授、并聘任我为副院长，负责研究事务、研究院、和持续教育等方面的工作。当时我的研究已趋向临床和理论结合，便转职往麻州大学医学中心，主持泌尿科和理论跟实践结合两方面的研究工作。在升任外科系副主任后，我得到多所机构邀约，决定接受辛辛那提大学医学中心环境健康系系主任一职。

辛大环境健康系是全美最佳学系之一，有大约五十名全职教授、250名研究生、还有为国内外专科医生和专业人员提供的生物统计学、生物讯息学、流行病学、分子毒理学、职业安全和医学、工业卫生、公共健康、环境和遗传等方面的不同期限的训练课程。在我任内，环境健康系每年获得两千万美元左右的研究经费和发表大约150篇论文。稍后，我被聘任为辛辛辛那提大学医学院副院长职务，最近又增添辛辛那提癌症中心主任职务。这所中心的三个成员是辛大医学院、辛大医疗系统、和辛辛那提儿童医学中心（其儿童癌症科现居全美之首）。我有幸不断得到多项研究经费，包括最近来自美国环境健康科研所的环境遗传学中心这份涉及百多名学者的多年合约。由于有了这个项目，我更被聘兼任基因组学和表观基因组测序核心的主任。

我长期从事对由激素和内分泌失常导致前列腺癌、卵巢癌、子宫内膜癌、乳腺癌等癌变的研究。我采用大量基因组学、转录组学、蛋白质组学、表观基因组学、和信息学等前沿研究科技，探索重金属、氧化应激、和发炎等对癌变、生物标志物用于癌症检测、病人分类、及以机制为基础的药物开发等多方面的作用，最后能研究出对疾病的预测与预防。

近年来，我的研究领域扩展到对疾病易感性根源的发掘，通过将表观遗传学应用到流行病学，揭示环境曝露对健康影响过程中面临的两项难题—即在不同成长阶段中多次曝露对健康的影响特别是对下一代健康的影响。我们的研究揭露了内分泌干扰合成物（EDC）的（例如双酚A）如何影响健康，如何触发婴儿出生前重编易感组织的表观遗传景观，如何影响老年期的疾病发展。这些研究引起社会各界对食品和饮水作用的关注，并促成加利福尼亚州通过其"有毒玩具法案"、及国家毒理学项目对双酚A风险的重新审查。我们又初步证实了空气污染物（柴油机排气颗粒和多环芳香烃）如何透过表观遗传失调而成为哮喘等敏感病的根源。这些研究又针对了消防员和处理有机溶剂人员易患癌症和生殖能力受影响的情况使他们注意提防。其他研究成果还包括发现转录调控的表观遗传失调成为多环芳烃（PAHs）相关疾病基源的证据。这些在目前属于世界上最前沿的环境卫生研究，都对中国有极大的参考价值。

在科学界，服务范围越大责任也越重大，身临其境也等于荣耀与奖励。我除了自己的研究项目外，还参与多项前沿科学的集体活动之中，包括担任美国国家科学院关于应用新兴科学于环境健康决策的常务委员会委员，以及美国毒物学高通量科技发展蓝图委员会的主席。我经常主持或参加许多美国国家健康研究所和国防部的科学评审和政策委员会的会议，例如膳食补充剂办公室、对雄激素和抗雄激素小组委员会、国家毒理学计划和全国性关于环境因素破坏女性生殖系统的关键性科学文献调查等。此外，我曾充任英国、加拿大、以色列、台湾和香港等地的研究经费申请书评审委员会的主席或成员。我也是数份学术期刊的常务编辑，并替数十份期刊当专题评审员。

我重视跟其他大学建立合作网络，籍此熟悉其他复杂的学府运作，从而受邀主持或参与数十所其他大学，例如约翰斯霍健斯大学、宾州大学、加州大学伯克莱分校、MD安特臣癌症中心、和密歇根大学等数十所机构组织的专家咨询小组定期会议。

我积极参与专业学会活动，例如美国泌尿学会、内分泌学会、泌尿科基础研究学会（我是前任会长）、前列腺癌研究计划、毒理学协会、及全美癌症研究协会等的各项活动。我在美国组织过多次全国性和国际性会议，也曾担任大会主席或主讲人，包括美国环境健康科研所的2002年度主讲者和加州环保署前观遗传学和环境疾病讲座系列的开讲人。

作为一名女性研究员经常处于以男性为主体的泌尿科研场合既有利也有弊。我们少数女性在男性占压倒多数的圈子中表现出强大的凝聚力，互相帮助鼓励。2007年，由于发现早期接触双酚A会增加前列腺癌的几率及其他研究成果，我获得美国泌尿科基础研究学会和和女性泌尿科学家联会授予该年度女性科学家称号。又由于于对辛大和省市的贡献，我在2007年获得俄亥俄州参议院授予杰出公民的荣衔。我也数次获颁教师和服务奖，最近一次是2013年前列腺癌基金会最佳导师奖。

我深深懂得工作需要同事的大力支持，尤其在跨科研究与新学科研究中更需要群策群力。由于这篇文章篇幅太小，我无法对帮助过我的人们一一致谢（这我在别处做了）。但我对两位早期恩师特别难忘，他们除了把科学知识传授给我外，还指导我的学术成长。我永远忘不了香港大学的博士学位导师陈启安教授的殷殷教诲，他常说："单靠勤力不成，还须精灵！"我也得特别感激波士顿大学的博士后导师卡勒德教授经常推对我的鼓励，他屡屡敦促我发表研究成果，使我建立起自信。

我为在我实验室工作过的百多位来自五大洲的中学生、本科生、研究生、博士后、专科医生、年轻教授、和访问学人感到骄傲，也庆幸有和他们共事的机会。现在他们大多数都有了自己的学术事业，在约翰斯霍健斯和华盛顿等大学、国家健康研究所、生物医药企业、和美国政府机构中起着栋梁的作用。

职业女性要兼顾自己的学术事业并在家庭生活中尽贤妻良母的责任真不容易，我所认识的科系中有相当比例的女性教授都单身或离婚。我自己也经过三趟"无形产子"（工作至临盆那天、不告假产、孩子病了也不缺席会议）！虽然生活紧张，当母亲也是最大的乐趣，也是生命中最大的成就。我在跟孩子相处时每分每秒都认真尽母亲的职责，却也有失职的时候。有一天接

一 路是践踏出来的

近黄昏的时刻，我匆忙从办公室出来突然恐慌起来，因为忘了那天早上把孩子送到那一位保姆家去（孩子生病那天不能进托儿所，要送往特约保姆家，以保证无虞），这样的情况时有发生。所幸的是：在达傅思大学，有非常关注女性工作人员需要的女性领导，许多问题迎刃而解。我也幸运全家充满恩爱，从公婆到小孩三代人都能互敬互爱，相互体谅。

美国大学都是世界不同民族、国籍师生同聚一堂。人们经常以为我是来自中国大陆或台湾。我的实验室简直是个联合国，却以华人居多。我经常跟来自两岸的学者交流，愈来愈多学人来自中国国内，不少已经回国并且卓有所成。我创业初期曾经得到多位来自台湾的前辈指导帮助，他们对年轻一辈的华人学者特别热情慷慨照顾。我发扬了他们开创的这一传统，尽量多方协助华人学者，帮助他们申请经费与建立合作关系，扩展他们的联络范围，提名他们担任职务，支持他们角逐及当选，以及提升他们接掌重要位置。

我曾为香港的大学研究拨款委员会和台湾的国家健康研究所基因组医学评审申请书，也当过香港中文大学的荣誉生物化学教授和理工大学创新产品和科技研究所的校外顾问。最近我们获得美国政府医疗卫生机构的拨款到中国东南部一个城市进行电子废料的研究，初步报告已经引起国际注目。

作为一所世界有名的环境健康和职业安全教研中心，我们可以对中国的发展提供许多帮助。我们从世界各地吸引人才，也愿意为世界各地服务。在中国最近的五年计划中，环境保护和健康得到优先关注，可惜医疗卫生专业和环境保护专业的研究人员缺乏。我们这个系可以提供多种训练以及建立合作项目来帮助中国解决空气污染、水质污染、改善居住环境和保证食物和消费品安全等问题。伦敦花了几十年功夫才清除历史文物的煤渍，洛杉矶用了17年时间降低雾霾，中国现在已经有足够的资金和组织能力去推行大型环境改善工作。除了政府以外，中国的富豪也应该行善参加这些公益事业。

我不能说自己有什么宏伟或完善的中国梦。我在大学念书时关怀政治，对中国的发展怀有比较热忱的梦想。时过境迁，作为从事科研医疗、服务于人类健康幸福的工作者，我的中国梦又扩大到世界人类的范围。作为一名科学人员，我惯于归纳性观察。我会先从个别问题开始，进而探索相关的问题而扩大视线与关怀。科学人员的角色是观察、提问、理解然后提出解决问题的建议、并预先估计建议的期望和意外效果。我相信如果每一位科学人员都能这样做，中国和世界任何社会都可以作出理性决策。

作为环境科学家，我们希望一般国民都能呼吸清洁的空气，有卫生安全的饮水和食物，并保持健康的生活方式。人们普遍的梦想是得到高薪与利润，可是个人致富不能把环境损坏或以下一代的健康作代价。经济繁荣国家社会富足、人们生活水平提高以后，应该注意保持卫生健康的生活习惯：不过食、多运动、不浪费资源、注意保护环境卫生。如果不这样做，人口特别多的中国以及消费量特别大的中国就会加重世界的负担。我希望中国发展成保护地球自然环境的先锋，养生养性的世界模范。

一 路是践踏出来的

曾经两次担任伦敦大学亚非学院院长，也在世界许多大学担任过访问教授或者被授予名誉教授头衔。2010年因"非洲及高等教育的贡献"由英国伊丽莎白女王授予"大英帝国勋章"（Order of the British Empire）。国际研究学会（International Studies Association）授予"杰出学者"（'Eminent Scholar）荣誉。出版了29本学术书籍、5本诗集与两本小说。作为"国际公务员"，经常被邀请参加国际外交活动。他也在几个非洲国家的贫民窟设立教育与武术项目吸收数百青年参加。

斯蒂芬·陈

乘剑漂洋世界入怀

（一）

我没有中国梦，只有中国幻想。我没有过去中国的经历，只有对未来中国的希望。我访问中国总是遭人误解。人们看我像中国人，也像日本人。他们在我背后悄悄议论，肯定我是日本人，对我鄙视。有人说，我像个歌星，留长头发，不像教授，有点中国人"味道"，应该对新中国多些了解，多些调和。我要求新中国了解我所居住的外边世界。在我所居住的世界我可以任意说话与打扮，不必适合某种定型。我觉得中国看世界总是用定型的眼光。五湖四海的世界却没有任何定型。

我生于1949年。我父母从小来到新西兰，是抗日战争时期逃出来的难民。母亲回忆起她那时跨越满地死尸的原野，目击我外祖母向中国军人塞钱而平安出国。父亲全家乘着最后第二条船在日本占领前逃离香港。恰巧那是一条撤退新西兰军队的船。当时的难民对新西兰全然无知。但母亲的先人曾在那个遥远的国度当过金矿工人，听说过白人对有色人种的歧视以及毛利土著武士的故事。在这个新的国度至少没有战争。

他们到达新西兰时当然受过种族歧视，甚至得忍受压迫华人的法律。我父母还未成年就让家庭包办成亲。我是长子，生下来父母才18岁。1949年新西兰工党执政，鉴于共产党在中国胜利，允许中国难民居留。第一代华侨每次选举都投票给工党以示感激，后来在70年代从越南来了第二波华裔难民，以后又有香港来的难民，情况就不同了。但新西兰从来没有华裔国会议员，没有华裔被封为爵士，没有华裔当政府大官。虽然压迫华裔的法令取消，但华裔只不过是受包容的贱民，难民们世世代代在贫困中生活。我的最初人生记忆就是贫困，似乎一切都带着棕褐颜色。棕褐色组成我对一切事物的记忆。那就是我喜欢树的原因。树是棕褐色，但顶上有绿叶覆盖，叶子中间有喜欢唱歌的鸟。因此我最早的美好记忆就是绿叶与小鸟。直到今天，我在非洲漫游时总是寻找鸟儿。

为白种人的新西兰说句公道话，他们在第二次世界大战中参加同盟国，很大比率的年轻人丧生，战后逐渐恢复元气。我刚生下来配给制度仍未取消。白种人同样贫困。气息粗俗的人们倒注意行为端正。最大城市奥克兰开始发展出郊区，年轻退役军人盖起木房，没有下水道，拾粪在新西兰像第三世界国家一样普遍。从许多方面来看这是一个发展中国家（或者说是重新发展中国家），无暇注意把中国难民吸纳到社会主流。

华裔人口也散布于郊区，他们经常在市中心格雷斯大道（Greys Avenue）的小小唐人街聚会。这唐人街实际上只有两家饭馆和两爿杂货店。我们全家星期天常去那家叫"重庆"（抗战时期的陪都）的饭馆打牙祭。那也是新西兰华裔的凝聚点。他们支持工党，也支持台湾国民党政权。新西兰人粗俗，华裔也一样，一口土里土气的广东话，随地吐痰，缺乏文化修养，很少洗澡。我活到7岁才第一次洗澡，那时我们家已经搬进郊区的木房，有洗澡间与抽水马桶。我从小上学，拼命念书，立志要比同班同学英文说得更好，因此有意识地停止说中国话。我当时大概不像个中国人，连个广东人都不像。我专心致志想当个有出息的新西兰人。那以后不久，也不知何故，我在梦中认同欧洲与非洲，梦见翁布里亚（Umbria）的松柏。起初我并不知道翁布里亚有

一 路是践踏出来的

松柏,成年以后我去翁布里亚看到山上的松柏,与我梦中相同。至于非洲,我梦见的是贫困,那贫困是棕褐色。1960年美国《生活》画报刊载南非联邦夏普(Sharpeville)市大屠杀的著名照片,用两个版面刊登白人警察殴打并枪杀黑人,画报6星期后到达新西兰,我看了异常愤怒。当时我只有13岁,已经决定一定要去非洲。我发展为立志离开新西兰的新西兰人。老师们早已教我像英国人一样说英语,我立志去欧洲上著名的大学,在绿树下念书,然后去非洲。

我一面念书,一面写作。20余岁在国内已经成为有名的诗人与知识分子。还有个小小出版社。60年代末至70年代初我参加街头游行示威,反对越南战争,反对与种族歧视的南非联邦保持外交关系,基本上反对任何压迫人民的行径。我和友人占领了美国领事馆。我们被警察拘禁,到法院受审。我们毫不畏惧,大学的法律教授们挺身而出支持我们。1973年我当选全国学生会主席,我为新西兰承认中华人民共和国开路—华裔亲台湾的年月一去不复返。我开始留长发,戴长的丝围巾,穿长上衣与长皮鞋,活像个17世纪的英国绿林好汉。我和漂亮女人(她们中没有一个华人)的绯闻臭名昭著。我的事迹变成加州大学伯克利分校的博士论文题目。这对新西兰容纳华裔的迟缓是当头棒喝。我成为著名的报纸编辑。27岁时,我离开新西兰,以后就再未回去过。整整十年我拒绝访问新西兰。以后我变成非洲历史的行家。

我的非洲奇遇始于罗德西亚的末年,1980年1至3月它开始独立成为津巴布韦。我在执行和平条约中起了作用,监督停火及选举进程以及四个被承认的军队的士兵行为。我们不带武器旅行。从那时开始我一直如此,自己不带枪,也不要带枪的卫队。别人用枪对准我的心脏与头脑的次数比大多数人用早餐的次数还多。和我打交道的人是中校级别。我遇见罗伯·穆加贝部队的中校们时,他们不但带枪,还带了别的东西。看见我是中国人,他们马上拿出筷子来说:"你们的人在我们急需的时候来帮助我们,谁也没这样做的,今天我们就用你们的方式吃饭。"那一刻,我为自己是华人而自豪。

我的非洲奇遇已有33年之久,其间也去过中东与世界其他地方。我的非洲奇遇最重要的是80年代初在推翻了伊迪·阿明的灾难性统治后的广大受难地区重建乌干达，90年代初在推翻了斯大林式独裁者马里亚姆（Mengistu Haile Mariam）以后重建厄立特里亚与埃塞俄比亚的田园寥落与骨肉分离的大地。21世纪初，津巴布韦分裂，2010年南苏丹在艰难中独立，我都前往帮助。最近，我为似乎拒绝重建的利比亚的重建尽力。我也参加到许多协商中去，参加了美国、中国与非洲的高层谈判。中国人看到我坐在非洲代表团方面有点困惑。我曾经在释放曼德拉（Nelson Mandela）的首次（1984）与末次（1989）协商中扮演次要的角色。在南苏丹有过一次有趣的遭遇。

我被派到莱克斯省（Lakes Province），要到仍在骚乱中的伦拜克（Rumbek）城活动。由于那儿是解放运动的发祥地，对当地选举的国际观察就显得重要。我带领的观察员缺乏经验、本不应派去的。我们在那儿找不到住宿，晚间戒严又将开始。我找到联合国维和部队的营地，分别由加拿大与乌克兰军人、肯尼亚军人与中国军人驻扎。我前去询问："能有地方让我们的队员住宿一晚吗？"乌克兰军人爽快地腾出了地方，我根本没去问中国军人，我想我自己和本文读者会知道他们会如何回答的。第二天清早5点钟我起床去看士兵们早操。中国军人在跑步，他们看见我就像看见从太空飞来的外星人。我穿的是很脏的白衬衫，没刮胡子。太阳初升我的长发飘动。我大概像功夫电影中的角色。中国军人们瞅着我，我也瞅着他们。很多人太肥胖，他们不像，实际上也不是前线作战部队。苏丹的中国部队是技术方面的后备。我真希望他们能赶快锻炼得坚强些以应付困难处境。

在那三年前我曾为达尔富尔（Darfur）问题去过北京。许多美国电影明星责备中国为了买他的石油而包容苏丹总统巴希尔（Bashir）屠杀老百姓。我会见的许多高层人士对这种谴责表示费解。"我们能做什么？"他们解释说。我说："真丢人，你们可以做很多事，不必公开谴责，中国总统可以在私下和苏丹总统谈话时把话说得强硬些，只有中国能对苏丹总统施压。"我在一次大会上重复了这番话。我说："中国说正在帮助非洲，这不假。但也帮助许多非洲的坏总统。很多中国经商者太腐败，种族性太强。过去非洲解放军告诉我他们感激中国人，现在我为自己是中国人感到羞耻。"

一 路是践踏出来的

（二）

今天的中国人过得比过去任何时期都好。虽然还有不足之处，但比历史上任何时候都幸福、自由。他们不再像十九二十世纪那样受帝国主义欺侮。中国重新在许多科技领域领先。中国的音乐家与艺术家受人敬仰。最近两位中国作家荣获诺贝尔奖。在未来的岁月里谨慎的政府行为与越来越自由的国际秩序更难取得平衡。我对此无言可陈，但只想说中国应该更好地了解世界。

中国外交官员把自己关在使馆内，他们到公众中讲话只念官方的讲稿，不和听众打成一片。中文电视新闻节目仍然只报道对中国政府友好的新闻。在这一点上，它们比 BBC，CNN，以及 Al Jazeera 电视台更糟糕，甚至不如伊朗电视台。今天世界上只有俄国像他们一样播送自我偏袒的节目。这不是一个成熟的国家的所作所为，因为成熟的国家知道广大观众不会相信广播。如果中国电视有时能批评中国，广大观众会更欣赏的。那样中国就显得成熟、诚实与善于自省，不害怕暴露另一面。

我也希望中国能任意发扬过去的优点，那就是她的哲学与诗歌。

我在新西兰决定不再做华人，因为我觉得海外华裔并不代表我所知道的中国历史与文化。我所读过的大量哲学家与玄学是人们难以想象的。在自己读过的中国哲学与玄学基础上我想看到怎么样的中国呢？我的中国幻想是什么呢？我在什么地方对中国抱有希望呢？

（三）

中国道家真人与波斯诗人有令人惊讶的相似之处。他们都装出长醉不醒，也利用这长醉不醒当作脱离顾前顾后的世俗的比喻。我的了解是他们想把这个照顾严谨的世界规章改变成信仰上的严谨，在正正式式的体制中发展出不同的形式来。圣贤们从来不脱离世界。他们必须吃饭、买酒、得到船和牛去周游世界。他们在世界上不需要停泊。他们不拘泥于某个中心点。对他们来说，"中国"失去意义。他们走向世界毫无畏惧—因为他们兴致勃勃、随遇而安，没有任何定型。

过去有一位道家真人爱上了海洋，因为海洋把他带到许多新的大地。他最喜欢漂海，但没有船，只有一口剑。他一到新的地方就成为和平使者，对自己在新地方的存亡全不在意。每次登陆以前，他直立于剑上，乘风破浪，狂笑不止。他的头发在空中飘扬，也经常与海豚及信天翁鸟交谈，它们从水底与海空为他引路。这样一种"天人合一"成为他的处世方式，使他漂流四海。他每到一处都是和平使者，他的剑在漂海中锈得不成武器。在生人面前他只有笑容，生人拿出筷子来请他吃饭。

我并不以为任何民族可以这样生存。因此孔夫子的伦理哲学必须问世。但每个民族都可以像这样悠闲，以悠闲交往使得世界拜倒。

应该在非洲与中国多栽些树。

我幻想中的中国，我期望的中国未来，是一个不当拼命三郎的中国，她认识具有巨大差异及个性的世界—包括非洲，那54个国家的大洲甚至可以吞没中国。我期望一个真正国际主义的中国，真正了解国际主义。我住到那样的中国不成问题，那就要求中国进入我的幻想而不强为其难地硬要我做中国人。

在国际主义的中国，我希望她是哲学与诗歌的振兴，少强调物质的奢华。唐朝是个伟大的时代。我父亲与母亲的祖先都发迹于唐代。那是个黄金时代。我为那个黄金时代自豪。当然，每个民族都有黄金时代。欧洲的文艺复兴运动使画家能发现透视的景象—绘出眼睛看到的远景与近景以及远近之间的各点。用透视法回顾与前瞻是所有文化与文明的共性。中国当然可以做到，可以和别国对话——和美国、和非洲对话，在享用一切食物时可以有所嗜好。那样才是成熟。我为那样成熟的中国自豪。

二

"中国梦"与世界

二 "中国梦"与世界

出生于新加坡一佛教家庭,早年毕业于新加坡南洋大学经济学系,后负笈加拿大约克大学完成经济学硕士学位,毕业后在大中华地区经商二十多年。曾在新加坡佛学院教《佛教生态学》,在新加坡佛教总会教《中国佛教史》及研读佛学。现为新加坡佛教总会高级文化研究员。

林明雅

我的中国梦

——东西方文明融会的伟大契机

梦,包罗万象。有别于动物,人类除了会做梦,还会解梦,原始宗教由此产生。如古埃及人会通过各种仪式来寻梦,甚至会跑到"待梦神殿"里去被托梦,然后经由祭师来解梦以指点迷津,趋吉避凶。宗教文明是与整个人类文明同步产生与发展,用马克思的话说:"宗教是整个世界总的理论,它是包罗万象的纲领。"

在说文解字里,"宗"表示对人类祖先鬼神的尊崇和敬拜,"教"有教导、培育、训诲的意思。受西方宗教学的影响,中文的"宗教"与西方的 Religion 画上了等号。

我出生于战后第三年,祖父母一百多年前来自中国厦门市,祖母一生茹素,在家修行,我算是海外第三代华人。出世时的身份是英国海峡殖民地子民,之后又经历过自治子民,马来亚公民,马来西亚公民,新加坡公民等;唯一始终没有被人为改变的身份是血浓于水的华夏子民。

祖母没受过教育却能唱诵佛经,父母所受教育不多,对孔孟之道知之甚少;之所以自称是华夏子民,那是因为家中供奉着佛菩萨与祖先的牌位,过的是中国传统节日。族人从生、老、婚嫁、病、死之丧葬彩礼节,乃至节日到庙堂祭拜的也都是孔子、老子、佛陀以及中华的各路鬼道（如盂兰盛会、中元法会）与神明（从轩辕黄帝、关帝爷到妈祖）。

这些都是海外华人祖先，从祖籍地虔诚请到落籍地供奉起来的诸神明，才能与祖籍国长期维系着不离不弃的文化脐带。能够继承华夏文明，靠的就是释、儒、道文化这一缕缕不灭的香火。

2010年9月，著名现代理论物理学家霍金与伦纳德·姆沃迪瑙合著出版的科普著作 The Grand Design（我译成《大因缘》）面世，书中提出了 Model Dependent Realism（我译为"模型相即相入实相论"），说明宇宙与生命生成的实相，是依不同模型逻辑理性的相即相入，"不需要造物主"，自然没有造物主的设计，才为我们对宗教的定义作了有科学依据的厘清。

原来，西方认为宗教是与一个全智、全能、至高无上的造物神祇有关；并认为宗教是对现象的"诠释"（interpretation）而不是"解释"（explanation）。很显然，这与东方的宗教观有很大的区别。

儒家信"四时行焉，万物生焉"、道家信"三生万物"，而释家信的是"因缘和合"，"实相无相"，一切都有其自作自受的因果（业 Karma）解释与充足理由，都不信有一个造物主。我以下谈到东西方的文化与宗教一词时，就包含这样不同的含义，请看官注意。

不厘清这一点，我们就无法与西方文明作有效的对话，即使对话，也只是各说各话。或大而化之地说所有宗教都是"教人做好事"；要不，就说着一些诸如"爱"、"良知"、"和平"、"平等"、"人权"等一些既抽象又无法交接的概念。

西方长期以来把这些抽象的概念提升到所谓的"普世价值"观，由此来掌控对文化、"宗教"与"普世价值"的话语权，形成西方的文化霸权。

中华文化要复兴，首先就必须要拿回对宗教文明与人类普世价值观解释的话语权，而非本末倒置地拿起香来跟着对拜。把孔子、老子、佛陀等与西方耶和华神明等同起来，把具体的孔子仁爱、老子的无为以及佛陀的慈悲思想与抽象的"神爱世人"等同起来。

更要命的是，自新中国成立以来，只对封建文化与殖民地主义抨击，而不作彻底的反思，造成中国各传媒至今依然不知反省地以洋为圣，对海外华

二 "中国梦"与世界

人的大声疾呼，充耳不闻；这不单会混淆包括基督教在内所有各宗教信徒的思想，也不利于中华文明的伟大复兴。

上个世纪 50 年代中叶，伯父参加由周恩来总理邀请，陈嘉庚号召组团的第一届广州中国进出口商品交易会，我家族就此成为新加坡，马来亚西亚第一家长期代理中国成药的进口商。记得小时候，经常要到货舱帮忙处理由于运输所造成的破碎药瓶，而划破手指，从而对中国有了血的认识。

我自小受华文教育，那时海外排华事件频频发生，就在中国宣布改革开放之际，海外唯一的华文大学被令关闭，所有华校一夕之间被英化，华人的方言母语被禁，中华文化惨遭摧残。

中学时代，适逢中国发生大动乱，常随父辈们在晚膳时间，收听中央人民广播电台的厦门话新闻，与中国的时局同呼吸共脉搏。当时就梦想中国能够赶英超美，中华民族能够早日屹立于世界民族之林，海外华侨（当时我们还是被称为华侨）不被人欺负，文化不被消灭。

大学第一年《农业经济学》的最后一堂课里，谢教授讲的就是《马克思主义经济学》，下课之后就到书店买了一整套的《资本论》来读。毕业之后留学加拿大，更有机会加深对中国当代文化的学习与了解，当时就化梦想为行动，到中国去！去实地了解那梦萦牵绕，风起云涌的神州大地。

在两个多月的时间里，背着行囊，独自畅游了沿海十几个城市，还处理了祖母在中国银行厦门分行遗留的存款，将之分派给厦门的两位表舅。沿途看到百业凋零，物资匮乏，被广州普通市民请到家中用餐，但见他用清水炒菜。

在难得一见的国营商店里买了一瓶茅台酒，才花了 8 元人民币。我用的是外汇券，虽然身上带有全国粮票，但基本上都在旅店用餐，所以很少用到；友谊商店卖的都是一些国外常见的日用品，可是不让国内人进入。

八达岭长城外竖起一块告示牌，写着"外国人止步"，虽然我身上带着"中国人通行证"，背枪的解放军一看到我，就知道我是"外国人"。此行结束，就梦想中国能够早日走向现代化，国强民富。

在加拿大学成之后，很快便赶上了中国改革开放的这一趟列车，20 多年的商尘滚滚，既无终生遗憾，也未遗憾终生。在千禧年一过不久，在把女儿送入北大上本科班后，便归去来兮，延续祖母衣钵，参研伟大浩瀚的中华佛家文化思想。

除了上课、参禅、到处讲课、发表论文之外，还参加了新加坡、中国、美国、香港等地好几个国际文化论坛、会议与世界佛学研讨会。尤其是在美国认识了好多佛客，更目睹了佛教网站与禅修道场如雨后春笋般地在美国各地出现，佛教信仰已成为美国宗教信仰的新趋势。

美国的垮掉一代从1950年代开始，前有著名诗人加里·史耐德，后有苹果企业创办人乔布斯等人，开始了拜师参禅寻求真理的东方之行。在与我对话的新一代美国禅修者，他们通过将佛教与科技相结合，开拓了西方新型的禅修之路。

由于有越来越多的美国人不再上教堂，他们自称为"nones"，我把它译为"赧（读音为 nǎn）士"，意思有不再上教堂感到羞惭。随着前美国卡特总统在2009年发表《为了平等而失去我的宗教信仰》一文后，相信这种羞惭的感觉会随之消失。

据《纽约时报》2012年12月22日引用美国著名皮尤研究中心调查的资料显示，从2008年开始，美国"赧士"的人数已从占美国人口的16%上升到2012年底的20%，以每年约三百多万之数增长，成为继中国之后的第二大无神论国家。

一些教堂如我所参访的科罗拉多第四基督教堂，由于无人再上教堂而改为禅堂，像这一类把教堂改为禅修中心的事例，在美国各地已经是屡见不鲜，最著名的有纽约市的盖瑞森学院，原为圣洁玛琍修道院。

由于全球化的原因，造成中国人热衷于西方宗教，而西方人却向往于禅宗修行。西方人借助脑神经科学以及科技的发达，使修行更趋向科学化、科技化、现代化、自由化、可量化与可实现化，驱使西方人士对禅修趋之若鹜。

见此情景，我就梦想如能趁此良机，通过佛教文明，契合科技的学展，来达成融会贯通东西方文明，将有利于东西方的文化交流，更有利于港、澳、台地区与东亚以及中南半岛的佛教国家交流。

这种融会与交流的契机是有其历史的脉络可寻，良性的有如古印度智慧，通过牟子把释迦穆尼的思想与中国的儒、道思想相融会，发展出中国的禅宗思想，形成中国化的汉传佛教，传播到东亚，最终影响了宋明理学。

恶性的如民国初五四运动时期，受西方排他性文化冲击，使中国的传统文化遭到前所未有过的灾难与摧残。如早期的毛泽东就曾沉迷于当时的白话文运动，而以"学任"为笔名来仿效梁任公的"新民体"进行写作，幸被其恩师袁吉六（又名袁仲谦）发现，嘲笑其作文有如"新闻记者的手笔。…认为梁启超文章半通不通。"

老师对"新民体"一针见血的批判，促使聪明的毛泽东"只得改变文风，钻研韩愈的文章，学了古文体，"毛泽东曾说："多亏袁大胡子，今天我在必要时仍然能写出一篇过得去的文言文。"中国也才能出这样一位伟大的诗人。

毛泽东当时的"多亏"深刻反思，是值得今日有心致力中华文化伟大复兴的有识之士，好好地去反省；今天还有多少中国大学生，能够写出一篇过得去的文言文？

而佛教就在当时，经由太虚法师从"人生佛教"到"群众的佛教"，在后来大陆基本的缺席之下，通过海外佛教界的努力，发展了"人间佛教"；为中华文化的伟大复兴，为世界文明点燃了心灯，开辟了新的智慧法门。

另一契机是经由西方哲学家叔本华的意志哲学，他用欧洲的哲学来阐述佛教这一远古的印度智慧。在其博士论文《充足理由律的四重根》里提出了因果律，阐明了发生学的根源；解释为什么现象世界必须通过充足理由律来了解，即任何事物都有它之所以如此的理由，皆可被解释。

用佛教的语言来说，就是事物的存在必有其缘由与条件性。佛教就是假借事物存在的条件性，来净空事物存在的真实性，就在净空事物的那一刹那或当下间，还事物本来的真面目。说明事物的发展，除了有其逻辑理性规律，还有更为重要的悟性道德因果规律。东西方文明的最高智慧，可谓是殊途同归，可相互融会。

在苏格拉底、孔子、老子、释迦穆尼等圣哲出现的时代，被德国哲学家卡尔．雅斯贝尔斯，冠以"轴心时代"的称谓。他说在这一段时期，中国、印度与西方，涌现了革命性的思潮，目前世界上主要宗教背后的哲学都同时发展起来。人类每在复兴之时，总要向轴心时代作回顾。

雅斯贝尔斯的这一番话,说明人类在轴心时代出现的革命思潮,到今天依然是人类思想回顾的依归,正说明人类的精神文明发展有其必然的科学性。释迦穆尼在菩提树下顿悟到缘起论时说道:"奇哉!奇哉!一切众生,皆具如来智慧德相,只因妄想与执着,不能证得。"这一段话足以说明,意识流与物质流是一样,都是可以通过科学的实证来获取到的。

综观人类历史,科技进步改造了客观世界,直接推动了物质文明的发展,却也造成对人类外部生态环境的巨大破坏,进而对人类精神内部道德观念的荼毒,使人逐渐远离具有悟性的"高贵野蛮人",成为"野蛮的理性人"。

自17世纪莱布尼茨和牛顿两人几乎同时发明了微积分学以来,人类进入了一个研究"无常"刹那间变化、研究"当下"的新时代。到19世纪,叔本华的意志哲学,为我们提供了因果律的理论根据,并由此夯实了唯实论的基础,把佛学从形而上的出世间拉回到器世间来。

进入20世纪,爱因斯坦的广义相对论,使人类了解时空是弯曲的无限性,为佛教的"无始观"提供了科学的依据,使人类不必再迷信于世界有创始必有末日到来的神话。量子论的出现,使人类了解"我"(即观察者observer)才是世间万物真正的主宰,即"天上天下,唯我独尊"。

进入21世纪,尤其是世纪转换的前后20年,哈勃望远镜的升空,使人类不需依赖数学逻辑的计算,也不需要语言作累赘的阐述,第一次通过肉眼,就可以直接凝视到137亿年来我们这大千世界的无常演变。

至2010年9月,霍金的"模型相即相入实相论",在理论物理学的研究与实践上,向"缘起论"迈进了重要的一步。这些进步,将为人类揭开宇宙、神学、形而上学等神秘学科的面纱,有助人类除魅的思想。

这三百年多年来科学的发展,改变了人类的思维方式,颠覆了人类的逻辑线性"理性"思维。伴随着近10年来全球在社会、政治、经济、金融、气候、环境等的进一步恶化,人类有必要开始重新定义21世纪之前所有熟悉的东西。当然包括由西方"理性"所产生出来的自由、民主、人权与社会制度。

正值中国成为世界第二大经济体之际,我们有必要再一次地对轴心文化作回顾,以中华伦理的圆融、宽厚与包容,必将会成为东西方文明融会的伟大契机。

二　"中国梦"与世界

综合以上所述，在中华文明伟大复兴的这一关键时刻，中华伦理如能结合过去这三百年来人类的科学思想发展观，必将能总结出一条有别于西方的执政理论依据，为当代社会、政治、经济、文化等各领域亟待解决的问题，提出具有科学性、先进民族性的解决方案，这些都是有助于中华文明的复兴。

其实，早在1954年，爱因斯坦就曾为文艺复兴、宗教改革、启蒙运动以来的思想发展，作了一次具有前瞻性的回顾。他说："未来的宗教将是一种宇宙宗教。它将是一种超越人格化神，远离一切教条和神学的宗教。这种宗教，包容自然和精神两个方面，作为一个有意义的统一体，必定是建立在由对事物的——无论是精神，还是自然的——实践与体验而产生的宗教观念之上的。佛教符合这种特征。"

恩格斯也曾在《自然辩证法》中说过："只有辩证思维才是有效的。只有东方的佛教徒和希腊人处在人类辩证思维的较高发展阶段上。人类到了释迦牟尼佛时代，辩证思维才成熟了。"

受韦伯《新教伦理与资本主义精神》的影响，上个世纪八十年代，"儒家资本主义"曾风行一时，直至亚洲金融危机之后，儒家因素就此沉寂。今天，社会主义中国的贸易总量已经超越美国，成为世界经济发展的主要引擎；马克思主义也会像轴心文化一样，"每当人类社会发展面临重大问题或面临重大转折时，马克思主义理论的影响都会引起人们格外的关注。"

2010年底，中央编译局局长在回答记者时说，该局"已利用历史考证版对《马克思恩格斯全集》进行修订"，以便能更全面来理解马克思主义。中国第一代马克思主义者，通过将马克思主义中国化，最终成为全体中国人民所拥戴的执政党。

值此中华文化伟大的复兴之际，企望当代的中国马克思主义者，能够通过全面认识马克思主义的主要精髓，来与中华文化的辩证思维做有效的融会，进一步深化马克思主义的中国化；从而夯实"中华伦理"的"社会主义精神"建设的理论基础，引领全体中国人民大踏步地迈向两个百年的宏伟目标，为造福全人类，再创华夏辉煌。

这正是我这一海外华夏子民此时此刻最大的中国梦。

Four seas to One Family: Overseas Chinese and Chinese dream
四海一家、天涯比邻：海外华人与中国梦

郑国强

1947年3月出生于澳门，祖籍中山三乡。1966年起在澳门参加新闻工作，具近半个世纪多种媒体工作经验，历任澳门日报编辑副主任、市民日报董事总编辑、澳门电台特约评论员、澳亚卫视、莲花卫视评论员；长期参与文化产业推动工作，对历史文化承传、文物保育、影视传播推广，以及"一国两制"下地区合作领域，均有深入研究，并致力海峡两岸文化交流。现任澳门环球文化传播有限公司总经理、澳门历史文物关注协会理事长、澳门影视传播协进会理事长、澳门学者同盟副会长、澳门文化传媒联合会副会长、澳门地区中国和平统一促进会副秘书长、国情教育（澳门）协会监事长、澳门历史学会副理事长、郑观应研究中心副主任。长期以来，对推动郑观应《盛世危言》成书处澳门郑家大屋保护、孙中山中西医局遗址及澳门成功申报世界文化遗产、保护文化遗产，作出贡献。他还是中国国家历史文化名城委员会常务委员、广东南方软实力研究院副院长、广东省社会科学院副理事长、客座研究员、中山市文化顾问、孙中山故居纪念馆学术委员、西安市海外联谊会常务理事、河南荥阳振兴郑氏祖籍研究顾问。

美丽中国新纪元的曙光

——从郑观应到今天的"中国梦"

"一旦我们革新中国的伟大目标得以完成，不但在我们的美丽的国家将会出现新纪元的曙光，整个人类也将得以共用更为光明的前景。普遍和平必将随中国的新生接踵而至，一个从来也梦想不到的宏伟场所，将要向文明世界的社会经济活动而敞开。"

——孙中山《中国问题的真解决》（1904年）

二 "中国梦"与世界

"有国者苟欲攘外,亟须自强;欲自强,必先致富;欲致富,必首在振工商;欲振工商,必先讲求学校、速立宪法、尊重道德、改良政治。盖宪法乃国家之基础,道德为学问之根柢,学校为人才之本源。政治关系实业之盛衰;政治不改良,实业万难兴盛。"

——郑观应《盛世危言后篇》自序(1909年)

梦是什么?梦是人的意识潜在的萌发。所谓:日有所思,夜有所梦。

中国梦是什么?是国家富强的复兴梦,追求人民安康,生活幸福快乐的梦,是理想生活的理性追求。

中国,这个曾昏睡百年的睡狮,唤醒迷梦、独立自主,艰苦奋斗,百折不回,实干苦干,经过几代人百年奋斗,终于今天成为世界名列前茅的经济实体,有独立意志的政治大国。这只"已经睡醒了的可爱狮子",重振雄风,正在和平崛起。

近代史上,在中国帝制夕阳走向垂死的黑暗,昏昏沉沉的睡梦中,两位晚清勇立潮头、在澳门建立起师承关系的香山双杰:甲午战争前夕开始撰述初刻《盛世危言》,为国人指点迷津,以危言惊醒皇朝盛世梦的郑观应(1842—1922);以振兴中华梦作为毕生追求的孙中山(1866—1925),为唤醒国民,奔走呼唤,成为开创中国历史新篇章,连绵百年改造中国革命运动的先行者。

珠江口伶仃洋香山地区的子民,那些深受海洋文明浸染,"得风气之先,敢为天下先",视通中外的饱学之士,对现代世界理解最深,同时充满文化自信。

郑观应身为商人心牵政治、不在其位偏谋其政,研究富国强兵开之道,1892年成书于郑家大屋的《盛世危言》初刊自序中写道:

"六十年来,万国通商,中外汲汲,然言维新、言守旧、言洋务、言海防,或是古而非今、或逐末而忘本,求其洞见本原、深明大略者,有几人哉?孙子曰知己知彼,百战百胜,此言虽小,可以喻大。应虽不敏,……乃知其治乱之源、富强之本,不尽在船坚炮利,而在议院上下同心、教养得法。兴学校、广书院、重技艺、别考课,使人尽其才;讲农学、利水道、化瘠土为良田，使地尽其利；造铁路、设电线、薄税敛、保商务，使物畅其流。"

"议院上下同心、教养得法"，这是民主政治雏形，是郑观应的中国梦。

郑观应这位一生坚信"国非富不足以致强，亦非强不足以保富"，大力提倡"商战为本，兵战为末"提倡实业救国的中国最早的宪政主义者，一百多年前是怎样描绘他穷半生寻找的中国富强梦？

宣统元年（1909年）的中秋圆之夜，在甲午战争失败后的第十五个年头，在澳门郑家大屋，时年68岁的郑观应对月抒怀，写下他中国富强之道名篇：

"有国者苟欲攘外，亟须自强；欲自强，必先致富；欲致富，必首在振工商；欲振工商，必先讲求学校、速立宪法、尊重道德、改良政治。盖宪法乃国家之基础，道德为学问之根柢，学校为人才之本源。政治关系实业之盛衰；政治不改良，实业万难兴盛。"

一百年后，再重读这篇文章，仿佛笔墨犹温，似乎为今天中国而写。

前人的梦，今人不会忘记！

2010年11月，时任国务院总理温家宝视察澳门，发表公开谈话提到："百年前，著名思想家郑观应就在这里，写下了唤醒千百万中华儿女的《盛世危言》。他一针见血地指出：欲强国，先富国；欲富国，先富民。富强之本不尽在船坚炮利，而在使人尽其才。这些振聋发聩的真知灼见，使无数怀抱富国救民理想的仁人志士在沮丧和迷茫中看到了希望，至今仍闪耀着真理的光芒。"

奈何一个多世纪前腐败清廷，此路不通！

继之而起的孙中山，在自述《伦敦被难记》中说明了他的振兴中华救国梦与澳门的关系："予在澳门，始知有一种政治运动，其宗旨在改造中国，故名之曰'兴中会'。其党有见于中国之政体不合时势之所需，故欲以和平手段、渐进方法，请愿朝廷，倡行新政。其最要者，则在改行立宪政体，以代专制及腐败的政治。予当时深表同情，即投身为党员，自信因为国利民福计耳。中国睡梦至此，维新之机，苟非发之自上，殆无可望，此兴中会之所由设也。"

"时则日本正以雄师进逼北京，在吾党固欲利用此时机，而在朝廷亦恐以

二 "中国梦"与世界

惩治新党,失全国之心,遂暂搁不报。但中日战争既息,和议告成,而朝廷即悻然下诏,不特对于上书请愿者加以叱责,且云此等陈请变法条陈,以后不得擅上云云。"

"吾党于是抚然长欷,知和平方法无可复施。然望治之心愈坚、要求之念愈切,积渐而知和平之手段,不得不稍易以强迫。且同志之人,所在皆是,其上等社会,多不满意于海陆军人之腐败贪贼,平时骄奢淫逸,外患既逼,则一败涂地。因此人民怨望之心,愈推愈远、愈积愈深,多有慷慨自矢,徐图所以倾覆而变更之者"。

1879年,13岁的少年孙中山从澳门出发,前往当时尚未成为美国一个州的檀香山求学。"始见轮舟之奇,沧海之阔,自有慕西学之心,穷天地之想",萌发少年救国梦。因为,当时的中国太落后了!对比参照物,是同处珠江口,落在洋人手上,治理得远比家乡井井有条的澳门和香港是也。这是当时中华帝国黑屋子里透光的破洞。

孙中山的青春梦很简单,他还未成为一个革命者前,通过郑观应引荐,上书李鸿章,要求拿护照看世界,目的只是干实事,要求朝中大老关顾众生,使:"人尽其才、地尽其利、物尽其用、货畅其流"。这也是郑观应在《盛世危言》自序中使用的共同语言。

《盛世危言》的爱国情怀和兴利除弊建言,数十年后也感染了少年毛泽东,使他成为"指点江山"、"到中流击水"的第二波中国自强梦的追求者。这是后话。

孙中山认为清朝的管治令国家衰败,提出要"驱除鞑虏,恢复中华,建立民国,平均地权"。这位香山地区农家子,对土地感情最深,潜意识中最早提出均享地权,是解决民生吃饭问题的首义,民生、民族、民权的三民主义理念交织成振兴中国梦。

当然,当他其后踏足英格兰、前往美利坚时,百年前美国新大陆上先进文明之国的繁荣景象,构建了他的美国梦。

决心拿革命主义救中国的追梦者,孙中山致力谋求中华民族万世兴旺,要把美国梦化成中国梦。

这位善于游说,用两张嘴唇皮鼓动潮流最终赢得一场革命的做梦者,在

Four seas to One Family: Overseas Chinese and Chinese dream
四海一家、天涯比邻：海外华人与中国梦

20世纪的新曙光初照中华大地时，显得如此自信。他在1894年檀香山成立兴中会十周年前夕的1904年8月，也就是辛亥革命成功前七年，发表《中国问题的真解决》谈话，描绘他的宏伟中国梦：

"一旦我们革新中国的伟大目标得以完成，不但在我们的美丽的国家将会出现新纪元的曙光，整个人类也将得以共用更为光明的前景。普遍和平必将随中国的新生接踵而至，一个从来也梦想不到的宏伟场所，将要向文明世界的社会经济活动而敞开。"

"拯救中国完完全全是我们自己的责任，但由于这个问题近来已涉及全世界的利害关系，因此，为了确保我们的成功、便利我们的运动、避免不必要的牺牲、防止列强各国的误解与干涉，我们必须普遍地向文明世界的人民、特别是向美国的人民呼籲，要求你们在道义上与物质上给以同情和支援。"①

"全世界大公无私的人们将会逐渐理解，占世界人口四分之一的国家的复兴，将是全人类的福音。"②

回首历史前尘，百多年前孙中山的中国梦，是如此的可爱！这位有梦的一代伟人，对中华民族立下的不朽功勋，在于推翻封建帝制，将中国向现代文明推进，开始了振兴中华富强梦的奋斗！

百年奋斗，由民国而人民共和国，一个甲子以来，在中国内地的土地上，经历过急风暴雨殊死斗争、大锅饭均贫阶段、改革开放让一部分人先富起来的阶段，如今，经济发展了，国家富强了，该如何走下去？均贫容易共富难，13亿人口，如何有序进入小康社会，可以共富吗？面对关系国计民生和政权稳定的大难题，我们可以回想一下孙中山先生。

孙中山一生书赠友好最多的两个题词是"博爱"和"天下为公"。

"天下为公"来自公元前551年出生的老祖宗儒家始祖至圣先师孔子的《礼运大同篇》：

"大道之行也，天下为公。选贤与能，讲信修睦。故人不独亲其亲，不独子其子。使老有所终，壮有所用，幼有所长。鳏寡孤独废疾者，皆有所养。

---

① 《孙中山全集》第1卷，第255页。
② 1906年11月8日《致鲁赛尔函》，见《孙中山全集》第1卷，第319页。

二 "中国梦"与世界

男有分,女有归。货恶其弃于地也,不必藏于己。力恶其不出于身也,不必为己。是故谋闭而不兴,盗窃乱贼而不作。故外户而不闭。是谓大同。"

《礼运大同篇》是世界上最早的民主社会主义思想话语。提到的价值包括民主选举、诚信社会、社会福利和教育普及、就业机会等大同世界理想。儒家学说精粹,深深烙刻在炎黄子孙灵魂深处,两千多年来,传颂不衰。是理想王国中华梦之源。由此可见,中华民族是天生的社会主义理想追求者。

《礼运大同篇》"讲信修睦"从人际关系构建出发,推及国与国之间和平外交原则,是对人类和平事业的贡献。

1945年联合国成立,联合国大厦落成后,孙中山先生手书的《礼运大同篇》碑记礼物曾恭立在日内瓦联合国大厦前。

《礼运大同篇》的民主理念和大同世界思想也融入了《人权宣言》走向世界。1948年,联合国颁布世界第一部《联合国人权宣言》,当时,罗斯福总统夫人任宣言委员会主席,起草人之一的委员会副主席中国学者张彭春,将《礼运大同篇》的精神融入宣言中。所以,尊重人权的崇高精神也源自古老的优秀中华文化,并不是西方的专利!

两千多年后,1863年,美国林肯总统提出"民治、民有、民享"的思想,与《礼运大同篇》精神对接。可以说,儒家学说的古老中国梦,化为新大陆美国梦的一个组成部分。

孙中山在西方三权理论基础上提出中国特色的"五权宪法论",以中华智慧开科取士考试权的定制,开通民间人才进入政府架构,防止官员营私舞弊的监察权,这不正是现今富起来了的中国,因特权作怪、分配不公,最大的腐败是教育腐败,新领道人要打击贪污所下重药相关吗?

今之中国梦与上升期的美国梦本来是相通的。可是如今,"已经睡醒了的可爱狮子"梦醒时分,睁眼看世界,感受到的却是来自太平洋彼岸金融资本狼吞天下超霸国家鼓起的恶浪威胁。

美国社会财富分配极度不公,百分之九十三的财富落在百分之一的最高收入人士口袋,美国越来越远离立国先贤的立国精神,变成一个由超级富豪与特权阶层金融寡头管治超级大国,利用科技军事优势,要掌控全球,霸道十足。

美国布控全球的策略："如果你控制了石油，你就控制了所有国家；如果你控制了粮食，你就控制了所有的人；如果你控制了货币，你就控制了全世界"！在全球一体化的时代，美国政府将经济金融政策筹码，视为控制别国和维护霸权的战略武器。利用先进网络技术，窃听监控全世界。这个"老大哥"由扬言反恐开始频频对外用兵，赶尽杀绝，与策动颜色革命交替运作，顺我者生、逆我者亡，成为世界新的不稳定因素。

中国梦不是不着边际的春秋大梦。奉行社会主义的中国，经过左摇右摆、上下求索百年奋斗，经过全民艰苦奋斗，找对了大国发展之路，成为世界第二大经济实体。但如今中国，面对难题一大堆，社会制衡力弱，长期权钱交易劣习成风，上下交征利。社会危机隐患遍布社会不同角落。

令国人稍感安慰的是，执政党现正雷厉风行推行反贪腐，反滥权、反垄断、反竭泽而渔式发展经济、反恐、反暴。以清醒的头脑认识到：尽管中国的经济总量位居世界第二，但人均所有仍是排列在全球百强榜尾，地区发展机会不平衡，不同处境的人群收入有天渊之别。

实际上，中国至今还只是中等发达水平的小康之国。按国民人均产值计算，2013年生产总值为16.2万亿美元的美国，排名全球11；9.1万亿美元的中国，排名全球第86。预测中国人均GDP从2011年到2060年有可能增加近7倍，从8387美元飞跃到6万美元，却依然难以超越美国。

从英国工业革命开始，英国花费了逾150年时间使人均GDP翻了一番，从1300美元涨至2600美元；120年后的美国，实现同样倍增所花费时间（约53年）约为英国的三分之一；中国从1300美元的人均收入水准涨至2600美元的水准，所花时间是英国的十分之一，仅为12年。

增速预测资料显示，仅需7年，中国就能将人均GDP从目前的8400美元翻倍增长，突破一万美元大关，届时将步入"高等收入国家"。

中国有梦，帝国无眠。

在中国稳步发展势头面前，美国难道会袖手旁观，甘心让潜在对手有出头之日吗？超霸睡榻之旁，岂容他人安枕寻梦？

美国兵临太平洋，插手亚洲事务，纠集众多小伙伴包围中国，以海权之争，能源之夺，要挫折中国！面对美日同盟，中俄走近合契、亚洲战云密布，

二　"中国梦"与世界

有山雨欲来风满楼之势。

中国梦美梦未圆,面对的可能是狂风恶浪刮起飞沙走石一场噩梦!

回顾前文引述孙中山先生百年前一段话,总结甲午战争输给日本的原因:"多不满意于海陆军人之腐败贪赎,平时骄奢淫逸,外患既逼,则一败涂地。因此人民怨望之心,愈推愈远、愈积愈深"。用这段话对照一下今日中国大陆雷厉风行反贪赃枉法所揭露的种种怪现象,可见当外敌进逼时,整党强军,整固内部,上下整合,以振民心,是必须的。

如何破解内外交困之局,不战而克敌?中国人五千年文明智慧,要有足够的文化自信与制度创新精神,善于因应。不要忘记由《礼运大同篇》开始的理念、处世原则和郑观应、孙中山的阐述。

"我欲因之梦吴越"(唐·李白),"铁马冰河入梦来"(宋·陆游)!中国梦,梦醒何处?杨柳岸晓风残月!

为实现伟大中华民族复兴中国梦,我们的国家还需要几代人充满文化自信、以开放心态对现代文明兼收并蓄,与世界平等待我之民族共同奋斗的过程!

祝福中国!

2014年6月5日于澳门

Four seas to One Family: Overseas Chinese and Chinese dream
四海一家、天涯比邻：海外华人与中国梦

黄枝连

黄枝连出生于马来亚，在那里接受中学教育；后到香港新亚院主修历史副修哲学。他到哈佛大学文理学院深造；回香港中文大学崇基和联合等学院开始大学教书与研究的生活，到过新加坡南洋大学；主持东南亚华人史的教学与口述计划，倒回香港，入浸会学院；主要的教授课程中西社会思想，社会制度及社会发展．故进行有关"天朝礼体系研究"，中国未来，台港澳未来的教研；有大量的相关著作；他刚完成"中华文明的未来史论"；并准备在今后三几年进行有关"美式文明未来史论"的钻研与撰述，他是香港亚太二十一学会的创办会长。

世界进化的中国力升级版：打造命运共同体世界的中国梦

1964年秋，我从美国哈佛大学留学回香港到刚成立的中文大学崇基学院任教，讲授"近三百年中国社会思想史"，备课时细读从明末清初一直到新中国成立后思想家的著作，可以说是对近现代"中国梦"的一个探索。不久后我去伦敦参加一个讨论中国发展模式的国际研讨会，提出《中国发展模式与毛泽东思想中的群众路线》的论文。毛泽东是中国有史以来伟大梦想者之一，我也受到他的梦想的感染。我那篇论文变成对"中国梦"的首次探讨。

其实，1960年代，由于中国内地的无产阶级"文化大革命"和反越战运动，西方世界有不少年轻学者十分"左倾"，我也受到影响。因此，我们便认为"文革"是对"美国模式"的挑战，也是对"苏俄模式"的一种否定，认为毛泽东思想提供了一个崭新的发展范式，正在逐渐完善。

在伦敦会议上，我们也谈到印度的发展；除了印度学者外，各方学者多半对印度独立采取一种否定态度，认为它是和平演变，没有走出西方模式的范畴，不能从复杂的历史和现实中，迈开步子走向发展。

二 "中国梦"与世界

半个世纪过后再回过头来看，当时人们的思维过于幼稚。如今的世界形势比当年复杂得多，中国和印度这两个全球唯一的人口在十亿以上的既有数千年古老历史，又有长足的发展潜力的新兴国家在全世界面前展现出既相似又不同的"中国梦"与"印度梦"。我们今天探讨"中国梦"，绝对不要以"井蛙"的眼光来看它，而应把它放到世界的大局来做文章。中国和印度这两个未来巨人为全球提供两种不同发展模式，当然，它们之间相辅相成、取长补短的潜力是很大的。

我在香港浸会学院/大学长期任教期间（1972—2002），有半年时间，在林华生教授协助安排下，到日本早稻田大学亚太研究生院做访问教授，和他共同开了一门"经济中华"课程，探讨两岸四地的四个不同中华经济体及其同世界华人经济网络的交流协作，其中也牵涉到"中国梦"。

其后，应廖泽云博士之邀，到澳门科技大学创办并主持可持续发展研究所任职四年（2002—2006）。由于教研与行政需要，研读大量同"澳门研究"有关的书刊，加深了对中国采取"一国两制"、带领港澳共同发展的透视。

几十年来，我一直是把中国和印度的发展范式相提并论并做比较研究。我认为"美国梦"和"中国梦"之外，"印度梦"也伟大。对这三大梦的比较研究，便是一部人类文明史的重要内容。

经济发展是天时、地利、人和三结合，人和是重中之重。我认为"中国梦"与"印度梦"之所以重要，是因为两国是世界上唯一的十亿以上人口超级大国，人口总和占人类三成以上。过去印度是铁路交通运输最发达的国家，每天都有许多百万乘客。现在中国超过印度，每年几个黄金节日成千上亿人大流动，中国人几千年来不敢梦想的事，现在居然变成现实。哈佛大学美籍印裔经济学教授坎纳（Tarun Khanna）2007 年出书，正书名是"数十亿企业家"（Billions of Entrepreneurs），副书名是"中国与印度如何重建它们和你们的未来"（How China and India Are Reshaping Their Futures and Yours）。我认为他没有夸大其词，中印两个人口超级大国人人竞相致富而成为企业家，不但世界会多了"数十亿企业家"，也必然改变全世界所有人的"未来"。这样看来，实现"中国梦"就是打造"中国力"的升级版。

去年10月以来，我同上海市立外国语大学国际关系与外交服务学院副院长武心波和中共广东省委党校教授周峰交流协作，提出了一个"打造'#3.0版'的全球化"概念。我把全球发展分成三个阶段：在公元1500年以前的许多个500年间是第一阶段，我称之为"#1.0版"世界；从1500年到1999年的500年是第二阶段，我称之为"#2.0版"世界；从2000年到2499年的500年是第三阶段，我称之为"#3.0版"世界。

为了方便起见，这三个阶段从1500年开始，那时西方刚步入现代化进程，中国处于明朝，在经济发展上也比前朝进步。我的每版世界以500年为期，也只是根据世界进化的大致进程。"#2.0版"世界比它以前的500年的"#1.0版"相比，当然进步得多，但这"#2.0版"世界也是地球上各方面发展天翻地覆的时代，新旧事物与东西文明之间的交融与碰撞也是史无前例的。现在再把从2000年到2499年的500年界定为"#3.0版"世界是对未来世界的洞察与期望。

我对世界形势的分析是：美国是在南北战争后，全面进入"#2.0版"世界，并成为其佼佼者，持续地兴旺了一百多年。今后三几十年，它必须走出"#2.0版"世界，走进"#3.0版"世界，才能返老还童，恢复生气和竞争力。可以说，欧盟也正在走出"#2.0版"世界，走进"#3.0版"世界。日本的情况也一样。新生的印度共和国有赖其大国文明的建设，也正在进入"#3.0版"世界。东盟积极推动10+1/10+3/10+3+3 FTA等等，也可以算是走出"#2.0版"世界，走进"#3.0版"世界的一个范例。

现在回过头来看中国的发展。在过去走出"#1.0版"世界，走进"#2.0版"世界的转变过程中，中国人的表现十分差劲。我把中华文明数千年的发展总结成"天朝礼治体系"，是辩证性看问题。从好的方面来看，中华文明能够合理地处理个人的"内心世界"、人际关系的"社会世界"、人物关系的"自然世界"和宇宙等四个层次的种种矛盾，从而获得暂时的和谐宁静，这就是所谓的"秩序"——是一个庞杂的巨大系统。在19世纪之前，在西方文化、西方国家、西方殖民帝国主义兴起直到扩张之前，在亚洲大陆这个地区，突出的区域秩序可是说是由中国封建王朝为中心而以礼仪、礼义、礼治及礼治主义为其运作形式；对中国和它的周边国家地区之间，周边国家之间的双边

二 "中国梦"与世界

和多边关系,起着维系和稳定作用的体系,就是"天朝礼治体系"。我在1992年由北京中国人民大学出版社出版的《天朝礼治体系研究》三卷中详细讨论了这一点,特别是中国文化对朝鲜与琉球的影响。从坏的方面来看,"中华帝国—中华文明"及其"天朝礼治体系"未能及时有效地对西方挑战做出有力的反应,故在鸦片战争后,遭遇到摧毁性的打击—挫折—耻辱;对境内外—国内外的群体—文明的安全,它根本未能提供保护,丧失其存在的效益性—合理性—合法性。

自1840年以来,中国是对世界各个文明及其发展范式做过最多探索–引用–失败的国家。1950—1970年代,中共领道下的新中国对马列主义及"苏俄模式—苏东模式"效法模仿、有得有失,最后掉过头来。

由于被内忧外患困扰,中国现代化发展长期原地踏步,走不出"#1.0版"世界,只有在中华人民共和国成立后才插翅高飞。我们可以对1949年以来追求"中国梦"所走过的曲折路程,概括出三个"三十年"的台阶,新中国现代化沿着这三台阶前进,交出昂贵学费,不断从纠偏中学乖,保持着朝前的步伐。

从1950到1979年,中国处于"毛泽东模式"的第一个"三十年"台阶,它先是参照斯大林的"苏联模式",喊出"今天的苏联就是明天的中国"。但是毛泽东"草根性"强,决不搞"全盘苏化",不让莫斯科牵着鼻子走。在国内,新中国以党政强势领道进行农工和国防工业的高速建设,突出思想意识,开展群众运动,政治和政府对社会组织和社会生活实行直接的严密的领道与控制,所谓"政治挂帅",社会主义改革力度大于社会主义建设力度,对于个人"五理(生理、心理、群理、物理、天理)系统"的开发有很大程度的介入。由于急切求成,搞"大跃进"与"全民炼钢"等运动,不惜违反自然法则与经济发展规律,滥肆开发自然资源,破坏生态体系,近乎竭泽而渔,引发自然灾害。外交政策走极端,先是对苏俄"一边倒",联苏制美,后来又转到"一条线"战略联美制苏。内地政府同港澳有所往来;但把台湾置于敌对面。新中国和海外华人的正常关系受国际形势—大国抗争的制约,两者之间的交流协作难以展开,东南亚国家中反共反华的势头强劲。

从 1980 到 2009 年的第二个"三十年"是"邓小平模式",从"政治挂帅"大转变到"经济挂帅",从"四人帮"的"宁要社会主义的草,不要资本主义的苗"到邓小平的"贫穷不是社会主义","筑巢引凤"(筑巢就是基础建设现代化去吸引外资凤凰飞来),"要致富先修路",搞好基础建设,产业多样化,引进外资以及外国人、台港澳及海外华人企业,鼓励民间企业,政府与个人及社会群体之间逐渐形成宽松的空气。开展境内外与国内外的交流,变蔽塞为沟通。

特别值得一提的是利用香港与澳门和西方经济的紧密联系而在其旁建立深圳与珠海两个经济开发特区,可谓邓小平的一大发明创造。我那时住在香港新界沙田,亲眼看到新出现的世界最繁忙的运输大动脉—从广东生产基地把货物运到香港码头转销全球。中国加入世贸组织 WTO 以后正式成为"世界工厂",这又是千余年来向往"世外桃源"的中华文明做梦也想象不到的。大陆的民众和台港澳以及外国加强人文交流,台港澳人士自由进入内地,参与不同的社会发展。中美关系解冻后,大陆主动同台港澳改善关系;"叶九条"和"港澳回归——一国两制"逐步推出,对台关系亦然,有了 CEPA 和 ECFA 等机制。

国际观察家、特别印度朋友、注意到改革开放以来的中国发展模式,由于吸引了大量外资而能高速发展工业,积极涌入中国内地的外资中很大一部分是海外华人(包括台港澳同胞)的投资,既是"血浓于水"的原因,又有"一个中华"的因素,印裔在海外也有大量资金,却不如华裔向国内投资踊跃。后来印度效法中国,实行改革开放,注重吸引海外印资回国建设,在信息技术革命中起过重要作用的海外印裔对印度变成软件超级大国、变成"世界办公室"作出巨大贡献。这也说明"中国梦"和"印度梦"起了呼应与交响的效应。

我从 1980 年开始提倡打造"中国人共同体"与"中华经济协作系统",二十余年来振臂高呼,得到国内外许多学者响应。我高兴地从《中国网》上看到一篇南开大学台湾经济研究所副所长曹小衡教授的《海峡两岸经济一体化的选择与定位》的文章,其中提到世界银行也从 1993 年开始附和我的理论,把大陆、台湾、香港、澳门四个中国人地区统称为"中华经济区"。世界

二 "中国梦"与世界

银行也从1993年开始附和我的理论,把大陆、台湾、香港、澳门四个中国人地区统称为"中华经济区"。(www.china.com.cn/chinese/TCC/haixia/50151.htm)

中共十一届三中全会后,海外华人积极参与改革开放与建设发展,国内和海外炎黄子孙多元化交流协作。世界华人的"华人经济"开始同两岸四地"中华经济"交流,形成一个所谓"经济中华"。我曾经以"香港亚太21学会"的机构与四川社会科学院、云南社会科学院、重庆社会科学院、贵州社会科学院合作组织"欧亚大陆桥"研讨会,推动大西南各地与东南亚、南亚、中亚地区交流协作。我高兴看到云南社会科学院两届院长何耀华和任佳坚持不懈地推动"昆明倡议"建立"中印缅孟经济走廊",现在开始有了眉目,写入了2013年5月中国总理李克强与印度总理曼莫汉·辛格在新德里发表的《联合声明》。

从1980到2009年的第二个"三十年"间,不但香港与澳门都回归祖国,台湾海峡两岸关系也化戾气为和谐。炎黄子孙四海一家的传统文明精神不断发扬。从2010年开始,中国进入第三个"三十年",开始走出"#2.0版"世界,走进"#3.0版"世界。现在人们的"中国梦"比起世界现代化潮流第二波冲击中国、唤醒国人"自强"时代的"中国梦"不知要丰富多少千万倍了!

我一贯呼吁两岸四地与海外华人集中的东南亚国家之间深化交流合作。现在习近平主席提出"周边国家命运共同体",我举双手赞成。习主席关于"建设好丝绸之路经济带、21世纪海上丝绸之路"的意见正是我多年的思路。我二十多年前提出的"中国人共同体"可以在现在习近平提倡的"周边国家命运共同体"中起骨干作用。

我再查一查,习近平2012年12月就对外宾说出"我们的事业是同世界各国合作共赢的事业。国际社会日益成为一个你中有我、我中有你的命运共同体"(见《人民日报》2012年12月6日第一版)。"你中有我、我中有你"是禅宗思想,是中华文明(也可以说是"中印文明")的传统精神。这就标志着中国进入第三个"三十年"是发扬"中华文明/中印文明"的传统精神走出"#2.0版"世界,走进"#3.0版"世界的。我看到大陆专家诠释习近平的思维时，总括出"一个国家要谋求自身发展，必须也让别人发展；要谋求自身安全，必须也让别人安全；要谋求自身过得好，必须也让别人过得好"这样的道理，这就大大超越受到地缘政治范式支配的"#2.0版"世界的国际精神了。这也是我所说的"中国力的升级版"的精神面貌。

读者可能觉得我在用禅宗思想探讨"你中有我、我中有你"，这与我文章的从"#1.0版"到"#2.0版"再到"#3.0版"的直线发展进化理论结构不相调和。我承认我的理论受到直线发展思维的西方论者的启示。但读者已经可以发现我非常器重中国传统对时空的思维——其中佛教起了重大作用。我特别欣赏七世纪唐朝诗人王勃的"天高地迥，觉宇宙之无穷"的观察。我们可以突出中国，但不能把它从无穷的宇宙中孤立开来。是因为无穷的宇宙使我们觉得世界"命运共同体"的存在。

全世界都关注当今中国提倡的"中国特色社会主义"，它已经超越所谓姓"社"姓"资"的争论，填平了"资本主义"与"社会主义"之间的鸿沟。中国共产党是坚信社会主义的政党，那是毋庸置疑的；中国现在靠资本主义"市场经济"发展，那也是毋庸置疑的。中国出了吴仁宝、吴协恩、郭凤莲、鲁冠球、梁稳根、王健林等千千万万个"红色企业家"，中国各地有许多融资巨万的既属于资本主义性质又是共同致富的"小康村"，这也是中国正在走出"#2.0版"世界，走进"#3.0版"世界的重大标志。这样的"中国梦"是其他国家不可想象与难以效法的。

我是"进化论"的信徒，坚信"#3.0版"世界会胜过"#2.0版"世界，就像"#2.0版"世界胜过"#1.0版"世界那样。《纽约时报》著名专栏作家弗里德曼（Thomas Friedman）在他2014年7月31日专栏中写道，现在有两个世界，一个是"治世"（world of order），另一个是"乱世"（world of disorder）。中国、美国、欧盟、日本、印度、东南亚国家都属于"治世"，形势一天比一天好。具体来说，是这些国家发展成"#3.0版"世界样板，会出现美国的"#3.0版"、欧盟的"#3.0版"、中国的"#3.0版"世界、印度的"#3.0版"、日本的"#3.0版"世界、东南亚国家的"#3.0版"世界，各有各的特色。但我认为，"中华经济体"的"#3.0版"世界会具有"中华"特色，那就是说中华文明的数千年传统智慧会有所发扬。

二 "中国梦"与世界

当今中国习李领导班子在国内加强亲民、勤俭、反腐败,在国际上试图与美国建立"新型大国关系",和俄国与欧盟国家加强往来,再加打造"周边国家命运共同体",这也明显地展示中国走出"#2.0版"以及走进"#3.0版"世界的路线图。

时下中国热烈讨论的"中国梦"是两个"百年"理想:一是2021年中国共产党成立百周年时中国全面进入"小康"社会,二是2049年中华人民共和国成立百周年时中国变成名副其实的世界"强国"。所以我觉得"中国梦"就是"中国力"的升级版。中国回到世界舞台中心并不是回到"天朝礼治体系"的"#1.0版",并不是要用"王道"式的作风取代美国"霸道"式的"老大"地位,而是要提倡中华文明"天下大同"的精神,把一个你中有我、我中有你的"命运共同体"世界建设起来。

Four seas to One Family: Overseas Chinese and Chinese dream
四海一家、天涯比邻：海外华人与中国梦

辛辛那提大学中国事务主任钟伦纳教授是香港中文大学学士、波士顿大学博士。曾任辛大医学院副教授、辛市生物医学教研基金主任、麻州老人部研究主任、大辛市中国商会主任、兼创办了华/亚裔研究/训练所和达傅斯大学国际领袖训练所，长期参与了老年政策的研究、评估、立法、和策划工作。义务工作包括香港专上学生联会会长、美国国家健康所研究申请书评审员、辛市理性思考会会长、俄亥俄州长亚太裔顾问。中文著作有华夏文化辨析、华夏历史重构、美国社会分析、社会研究法、会议规则等书、及在中港台美报刊上关于中港欧美社会和文化的诗文。

钟伦纳

同族異梦怎同德？

—— 从关怀、思辨和沟通方式看华人寻向

一

我的中国美梦有多方面，由于自己的梦想不断发展，也跟别人的不常一致，因而感到最重要的梦想，是愈来愈多华人关心中国的持久发展，愈来愈多华人去梦想中国美好的将来并学懂不断以理性态度去探讨、沟通、和合作，以实现这些梦想。我的总体美梦不是一晚之间一气呵成的，而是把长期众多的梦交织而成，不像写生那样依定点和比例出发，不像油画那样塗满画面，而像中国山水画那样，游神多处后，既擷选各处特性集成整体，又保留多处空白，让观者想象。

梦的内容多属个人化，这里只谈带有集体期望的梦。有集体期望的梦可分两类：一类是反抗性的梦，有具体的反对对象，少提具体的建设内容，较易在短期内集结力量，也较易道致暴力解决。但即使得胜，由于欠缺对新方

二　"中国梦"与世界

向的讨论，难以达成新共识。虽或可以打倒个别的反对对象，替换的运作系统却免不了要受军方或情报机关左右，至少在几十年间，军法和严刑统治的可能性增加，社会经济很易退回原来轨迹，这种演变，以往在中国并不罕见。

另一类是建设性的梦：提出一些新的做法或方向，但具体建设的蓝图可能很分歧。这类梦还会在不同阶段遇上各种反对意见，需要用多些时间去说服各方和聚集共识。但望新的共同纲领愈多共鸣和弹性，愈可能避免暴力。周初第二次封建和宋初数度大规模改革是少有获得实践的大型建设梦，但都是从上而下，挟带王权或军事优势才可推动的。

从下而上、可以避免大规模暴力而成功的反抗性梦的典型，是美国民权领袖马丁路德·金博士的梦。这个反歧视的运动口号简单，在黑人中很易振动共鸣，虽然对如何建设的讨论尚嫌不足，但美国社会已经有了建设新生事物的程序和文化。民权运动在数十年间除了推动立法、司法、和行政手段，还透过各地的学校、教堂、和传媒进行教化，来预防和制裁违权举动，这些做法后来被其他人群援引和推广，甚至扩展到国外去。

建设性梦牵涉范围比反抗性梦较为广深。尤其是中国人多地杂、变动快，做梦者既多又杂，似乎更难糅合出共同期望。加上中国缺乏立法传统，长期以来，建立新制度的程序多出于行政决策，朝野皆未习惯依据既定的立法程序。权宜激进的行政决策较易立竿见影，成败和代价的起跌幅度却也较大（北宋数次变革的反复是最明显的例子）。中国知识分子即持异议，大多仍限于发表宏阔的评论，民间对异见的表达，每每流于情绪性的谩骂，整个社会不善于提供和商讨细致可行的新意，不惯于共同寻梦、解梦、和沟通梦，忽略了混含的梦境和口号必须翻译为共识，才可提炼成可行的操作方式。

最能和平地带出持久效果的建设性梦，似乎最可能在文化层次找到。人类社会各个部门的发展步伐难以齐一，改变是迟早发生的事。心急者欲毕全功于一役，军事行动似乎可以快刀斩乱麻，却也易引起武力反弹。行政手段要靠权势积聚，权宜决策也不能久恃。依据立法程序来除旧立新是目前地球上最稳定的做法，但大部分选民投了票后便不再理事，议员为求选票而以近利来讨好选民，往往牺牲了少数派的福利，或忽略了整体的长期利害，西方民主历程从希腊到美国都陷入了这条穷巷，轻则政党相持不下，道至政府失能，重则政府倒台，为了先使未来钱而致国策被债权国压制。考虑及此，民主的出路，应该由"当选一派作主宰"改为"全民主动关怀整体的长短期利害"。这种想法，在西方虽已在环保界显现，尚未汇成全民风气，在中国却已有了长期实践的经验，成了华夏文化持续之气，可惜由于狭义的理解和应用，一些传统观念反成了现代化的绊脚石。我的中国梦中一个很重要的环节，便是从传统文化中发掘出可以和平地由下而上养成的主动建设文化，方便除旧立新。有了诚意和责任感，异见者才易达成共识，立法和行政决策才易水到渠成。

我生长于香港，长期以来，它兼有殖民地、全球经商者与冒险家聚集地与大陆人士避难地的不同性质。我自幼对于中华民族如何振兴很模糊。1960年代香港人口和经济急剧转型，社会问题尖锐化（例如危楼、拆迁、工资、残疾人士的生计等）。当时制度措手不及，传媒既散又弱（一城日报数十家，各有背景，但皆怕开罪港府），弱民求救无门，在传统中国知识分子以天下为己任的心态驱使下，有些大专学生开始走出校园，从修桥、铺路、赈灾、到为了中文合法化、反贪污、保卫钓鱼台等目标而参与或组织示威。

我从初中起便参与学生活动，大学时当选香港专上学生联会的会长，毕业后继续参与社会活动，接触到多种梦想的交锋。当时港府和多派政治力量都监视和企图渗透学生组织，一件本来很纯朴的工潮可以发展为多派争夺的阵地，哪种方法最宜解决问题？谁的背景和企图如何？肩负当时社会运动主力的大学生入世未深却成了廖化，何去何从？有没有理论可作指引？这些问题迫得我要边干边想。

传统中国智慧被"五四"运动冲激后，只能在日常生活作些规范。国共长期互骂以后，大部分稍作思考者都难以继续盲忠，何况还有各派红卫兵和汪精衞等旧部的叫屈和控诉，加上"文革"时流出港海的浮尸，令更有理想的真诚思索者都必须考虑社会行动的代价。

希望从外国取经者的观点更分歧，单是极左派便有托派和无政府主义者的公开介入、有没有人仿效日本赤军派的残暴尚未知、泰国式学生运动可以长期发生正面作用吗？英国在欧洲共同市场对香港产品的打压，露出殖民主义的真面目。美国民间的反越战和民权运动，显示出最稳定的政治体制也免不了

二 "中国梦"与世界

要受冲激才愿改变……

为了进一步了解各种理论，我选择了社会理论作主修，但为了避免走火入魔，同时兼修研究方法论，对理论的探索步步为营。大体上说，西方理论从带有明显价值取向的社学哲学，走向要求例证的宏观分析；不满宏观架构过度抽象者改往建构中规模理论，虽然没那么耀目，却把探讨的范围落实到一时一地的分析和归纳，例如对各地现代化过程的研究，带来一些比较清晰的评估架构，更易显示任何理论都有局限。

我的结论是理论可以提供讨论发展方向的大纲，却因为过于抽象而不足成为实践的具体指道；但理论中不少经过严格界定和检验的概念，则可能直接改善现状，例如不少物理学的大理论已被挑战或推翻，但许多物理学概念则对工程和建筑等产生了莫大作用。社会理论中即使一度成为指道一切的意识形态也纷纷退潮，但不少可发展出科学假设的个别概念，则已可帮助决策者踏实地制定政策，例如人口学和经济学里不少概念，一旦成为决策的基石，便可产生立竿见影的效果。

在组织社会运动和参加议论纷纷的辩论时，我养成一种不预设成见的态度，对任何理论都要找出用于分析当时事件时的优劣之处，提取可以援引或改造后有助于实践的概念。最后方案最好是最接近现实、最能以小代价获得大收获的概念组合，不管来自那方理论，也许正是这种开诚的态度，我成为多方面皆可沟通的桥梁、学习到多方面的关怀、扩展了我的织梦范围。

我不会梦想那些可以解决一切的理论，但希望能够多些发掘和修葺任何来自事实和相应理论的概念．念博士班时我不再搅理论，转向较能结合实践的医疗社会学和社区研究。我的"正职"，从中文大学社会研究中心、香港社会服务联会、麻州老人部、辛辛那提大学医学院、辛辛那提生物医学教研基金会、大辛城华商会，以及自创的华/亚裔研究和训练所，都环绕着如何提供和应用最能解决问题的资讯。无论在数所大学教授研究方法、在达傅思大学国际领袖训练所、纽英伦中华公所侨领和波士顿年轻亚裔领袖训练课程中，我都提倡采用多种方法，从事实中找出主要和所有矛盾，并集合各方角度来汇成解决方案。在麻州，我主持过在351城镇的抽样调查，以量化不同背景老人的需要。在辛大医学院，我研究糖尿病尤其是在亚裔美国人中的预防、诊断和治疗方法。在"业余"时间中，我在麻州和俄亥俄州等地作出十多项华亚裔社区研究报告。这些工作，都不依成见、集思广益，因而偶有新发现，也有助于制订解决问题的踏实方法，一些概念和研究方法还可以推广。

多年来隔洋远望，深感中国人谈"赛先生"（科学）和"德"先生（民主）已经个多世纪、谈现代化也已经半个多世纪、对华夏文化更辩论了多个世纪，误解仍多，信心仍少。鉴于这几方面题材对华夏社会的重要性，我于是不昧于业余勤修，抱着削肉还母的情怀，用中文写成几本书、数十篇在大陆、港、台、美国期刊和书报上的报道、议论、和诗作，尽量客观和精简地介绍科学精神和方法、会议规则和组织技术、美国社会如何现代化、及如何从传统文化中提鍊出可为时用的元素。

从传统文化中提鍊出可为今用的元素，在我美梦中占上最重要的内容，对中国的政治、经济、和科技前途的梦想和建议已经很多，对一般民众道德或日常生活规范方面的争论也不少，至于能够促进高效率思考和沟通方法的梦想则颇为少见，由于篇幅已过所限，思考和沟通方法只在第5节稍为提及第3节和第4节则是本文重心。

近30多年来，无论在大陆、港澳、或海外生活的华人，都经历著急速的社会经济变化，一般都幸得享温饱，在各个社会的上进机会也增加了，但精神生活却反而逐渐迷茫失从，除了讲究实际的态度跟西方的个人理性化模式相接，其他行为则愈来愈随波逐流。很多华人，无论是任何国家的居民或游客，无论认识到多少外国文化，都表现过不少惹人侧目的陋习：打尖、随地吐痰、弄脏公共设备、拿走过量的供应、过度拣择而捏坏蔬果、伪造证书、虚报技能、抄袭别人作品、只拿居留权或公民权而逃避当地事务、瞒税、申请不符资格的福利……等等，在外国不少地区已经渐渐被称作"丑陋的中国人"。在国内，对不道德行为的报道既广又频，这些情况能否尽诿作社会经济急剧转型期的自然伴生现象？如何培养适合新时代的道德意识，成了急务。

新时代的道德意识可以依全新的时空背景而营造，也不妨从传统伦理中提取可为今用的养分。若果新道德可以全盘"理性化"地营造，则华人和欧美非洲人迟早可能不再存分别，若果新道德可从传统伦理中提取，则可借文化承传的惯性更有效率地建立，何法更可取，不妨辩论。

二 "中国梦"与世界

在日出而作、日入而息的时代,勿须强求迟到不可超过五分钟.但不违农时地下种和收割,则是农业经济的保障,也是华夏民族延续的要诀.我们今天不宜以昔日时辰钟不普遍而否定当时也有守时观念。指出传统中的守时观念和应用场合,有助于凝聚集体认同;以表面上的差异来否决所有传统,是自外的鲁莽态度。

关于传统文化应否保留的辩论,一直很简单化和情绪化.赞成和反对者皆习用笼统含混的观念,例如不少反对儒家仁爱观者坚持它会促进裙带关系,而鼓吹仁爱观者的对策主要是强调亲属的重要性,没提出仁爱观未必会促进裙带关系来直接反驳,也忽视了今天亲属分居的情况愈来愈普遍,缩窄了狭义仁义观的应用范围。在第3和4节,我提出从"仁"和"德"这两个核心传统道德观念中提取可为今用的方法,以实现梦想的尝试。

二

每个人都有多种梦,如何把各人梦中关于集体的期望汇成共同行动的动源?从中国文明的悠久和远播看来,华夏民族其实已经累积了许多经验.追溯这些经验的一个途径,是检讨"德"字的演变,德作为"德行"或"道德"的意思是后起的[①]。先秦文献常见"同心同德"的说法,这些德字主要代表"德征"。"征"源于饰物,在战场上凭着共同的配饰来辨别敌我,同德者同心,异德者非我族类.德字也可代表同地、同俗等的认同表征,皆具有胜利的依赖、安危的保障之意。

到了商末,德字的表面指谓从辨族的具体外征延至"德政"这种抽象的政治号召。周族领袖为了解释小邦周何以能取代大邑商,举出文王的德政来对照纣王的暴行。"德政"成了更换统治权的天意根据.作为长保天下的凭借,周初领道遂以德政作为后代教育的主要内容,要求贵族不断爱民克己。后来孔子把教育推广到平民阶层,以个人修养的"德行"来代替贵族才可接受的德政教育。至此,德字从具体的外征延伸至宏观的德政,再内化为个人

[①] 请见拙著《华夏文化辨析》第二章。

进修的德行．但儒家自修的本意并不离群，而是以集体福利的马首是瞻。

"德"字的表面意涵虽从人类学（德征）发展到政治学（德政）以至伦理学和心理学（德行）的范畴内，本质上却保持着一个可以历久常新的核心意义和概念架构——要不断检讨跟目标相配的手段/工具/凭借在不同场合下的目标可以不同（战胜、统治、内圣外王），需要釐清，并配合每个目标，不断改进手段（例如不断地维系共识、施行善政、修齐治平），是谓"敬德"。

可惜秦代统一以后，集体目标和手段之间的关系渐远．由于中国规模渐增，参政机会有限，内圣外王变得陈义过高，两千多年来，常人能实践的机会和意愿有限．集体目标渐成空谈，连带至相对于个人目标的手段也得过且过。华人是勤力的，但不惯于釐定目标、有时甚至忘记或逃避对目标的界定．不尊重原订目标，便难认真检讨手段，不易真正敬业，中文字彙中不乏对这种态度和后果的贬语：舍本逐末、买椟还珠、形式主义、虚与委蛇等等，都是华人自己觉察到行动不符目标的写照。

因此，在目前这历史关键时刻，恢复敬德的首务，是把努力的目标跟切身可及的内容拉近。每个人做好所有自己能做的事：个人的身心理健康、人际关系、学业、职业、和各种集体工作，都可以是努力的对象．敬德既可由敬征发展至敬政、敬性，也可以发展为敬己、敬人、敬学、敬业、和敬集体，这些态度可以统称为"敬生"。至此，德字更适合用作动词，可说就等于"敬"。"敬"的策略，就在于不断辨认和检讨配对的目标，并不断改善相应的讨论手段，这策略看似抽象，却有三套现成的元素可用：源自孔子的仁念和源自西方的科学方法及理性讨论的态度结合起来、推广出去，可以不断建构和实现华夏的美梦。

敬德的目标在不同时期有不同的努力对象，在德征期的对象是部族、德政期的是王国、德行期的是自身/家族/国家（诸侯国）/天下（天子关注所及的范围）。今天，天下是全球、国变成了现代国家制度、这两层组织对个人的影响比以往都直接和深刻多了。加上家族弱了，家国之间出现了愈来愈多被儒家忽略了的人群和组织，关系的深浅也复杂多了。怎样处理各种关系？欧美的处理准则是鼓吹国内人人平等、个体权利不可侵犯、个人可以自由参与政治或不参与（除了缴税，对其他公务尤其是对其他可能分享或竞争共同资源

二 "中国梦"与世界

者的权利,可以不闻不问)、可以透过选举或集体行动来争取权益、可以透过金钱和国家权势在国内外享受特殊待遇和额外消费。这种生活方式可取吗?可以持久吗?应该无条件地追随吗?

肯定个人权利已成全球趋势,现代国家愈来愈难凭借戒条来阻吓违规行为,欧美法制不但是套昂贵的系统,也需数百年的立法和司法实践,才能积聚多种法例和判例,供裁决者援引,发展中国家不能单望积累到足够的案例才去维持秩序,儒家以教化来减少诉讼仍可以是一种有效的策略。教什么?与其仓猝颁发无数规条,最直接有效的策略,很可能就是培养人们去爱,以爱为教的策略颇多,孔子提倡的"仁"最简易可行,其真义却一直被曲解。

多种对仁字的解释并不算错,却几乎尽属一些同义重复或过度抽象的儒门字汇,说法并不清晰透彻,又跟其他涉及美德的字眼缠绕不休,令人无所适从。我认为若从孔子原意探索,可以得出一个简洁可行的概念。

孔子亟欲解决的问题,是周初透过拟血缘关系建立起来的宗子制,经过多个世代的疏远,已经无法纯用礼制来维持,侯国内外篡夺不止,民生痛苦。他提出的解决方法是向封建侯国内外体制灌进一种真挚的感情,以恢复秩序,"仁"就是他冀图恢复亲爱关系的一种真挚的感情和责任感。"仁"并非一个天马腾空地创造出来的理想化观念,而是基于孔子成长的东夷社会里一种具体的母系风习——也就是称为"悌"或"仁"的兄弟关系。后儒不明白或不愿接受仁的来源和原意,硬性地把仁的感情和责任感捆绑到父系架构上,限制了仁在其他社会关系的展现。

孔子并非粗率地把仁移植进当时社会的,父系层级化社会的功能和结构远较母系的复杂,兄弟间之仁不足以直接推广往多种关系去,是以在《论语》的记载中,孔子透过多种具体情况和各种特殊关系来阐释仁的多种实践方式。孔子也不会无条件地接受宗子制,对于宗子制的流弊,他认得比周公清楚。孔子提出来的"仁",除了在简单社会中自然发展出来的感情和无条件的责任,还包括在认清个人在复杂社会架构中每一种角色后,主动营造的亲爱感情及相对责任。

现代社会又比周代远为复杂,个人常须在多种社会架构下,在不同角色之间跳跃,单凭宗主制一个拟血缘架构的行为准则,不足指道亲属以外的生活，若完全接受现代西方强调所有人地位平等的处理方式，在理论上虽然简单易行，实则把人际关系草率化，各种架构的要求不易平衡，各种日常关系的分寸不易把握，细致的、破格的关系唯有留给文学、电影、和心理学家去探讨交代，跟这两套准则比较，孔子的仁道，很可以在复杂社会中处理多重关系时，提供最贴身的应对准则。

追溯出仁字的源流后，我把仁的真谛从父系架构中抽离出来，提纯为一种可以普遍化的真挚感情和责任心，可以使现代生活更和谐、尽责、及持久，我们勿须墨守于那种基于先天血缘的差序格局来践仁，因为即使远离亲族，每个人仍可对朋友、邻居、同事、或任何一位发展出真情的人士，主动地建立起互爱互助的关系。

近年西方政治多集中于选举这一环节和用选票争取权利这些手段，却忘了对目标的检视，忽视了不投票者（包括后代）和少数派的代价，这种不重视整体责任的做法难以持久，中国若能提倡仁教，让选民接受到公民的责任不止于投票求胜，还在保障整体和环境的长久利益．让旅行者认识到游客的责任不止于花钱，还包括尊重当地的文化和生活条件，则礼义之邦，可以真正实现。

"一视同仁"的原则能被推广到的范围其实很有限，对所有人都同样地爱的想法并不切实际．"仁"则只要求顺着自然而生的爱意和责任感去实践，仁的实践虽然有层次之分，但也要求爱及万物，（孔子的爱普及到鸟兽，孟子以人们见到别人孩子跌下井时油然而生的恻隐之心作仁端的证据，可见儒家祖师的仁爱对象不限于亲属，民间"远亲不如近邻"的说法同样普遍），把仁扩展到其他可以发展出自然情感的对象的做法，不但已被传统社会接受，其实更适用于现代生活，现代人迁徙多，子女散居各方，坚持把仁局限于亲属之间的做法，只会剥夺行仁的机会，因此，如果我们能把践仁的对象从直系亲属推广至华人、族人、同乡、国民、所有人类和万物，华人便可望把家里和同事邻居之间的纠纷淡化、在国内降低地区间和收入上的歧义带来的怨怼、在国际间避免憎厌和敌意、及对各种生物和环境关心起来。

三

华人修德可以跟英美的专业运作互补，西方职业团体透过标准化的训练、标榜高品质的自律服务程序来建立同行的声望，他们既依仗立法途径去垄断生意和争取权利，又透过自行决定执业的内容和责任范围来维持专业自主（例如美国医学会鼓吹不计成本去救护每一名病人，不论病者、家庭、其他病人、社会的负担），总体来说，这种有限责任的设计，注重对同业者的保障多于对服务对象的关心。

修德者也可以从西专业精神那里学到系统化的训练和不歧视任何病人/顾客/服务对象的服务态度，但专业运作的目标和手段都受制于制度，训练和提供服务都涉及不少资源，专业圈子排斥了外界参与，修德的目标和手段则可由个人自订，不必制度化，预备和实践不必涉及资源，践仁者虽然重点在照顾主要对象，却不会漠视其他可能间接受影响者，目前西方的医、商、工、和法律等专业都开始注重专业德育（professional ethics），但针对的主要是执业者个人，对整行利害的保障，依然高于一切，美国医学会若接受仁的观念，会多些考虑应否把远高于人口比率的医疗卫生资源，用于一个月内去世的病人身上。

华人思考方式中有不少障碍发展的陋习，常见的是：以常变观来否定定义的作用（认为"定"义会固化变动中的状态）、以比附代替逻辑、照顾多方混沌的关系多于追探特殊的因果关系、解释惯于含糊马虎、强不知为知、以权威主义和神秘化来制止追问和辩论等（拙著《华夏文化辨析》中有些关于《易经》和《诗经》注释对传统华人思考和教育影响的探索）。

西方人在严谨定义之上，发展出逻辑和统计来作推论，以验证作为判断的根据，华人逻辑松懈的一个文化基因，是不习惯采用严谨的定义（例如历代的度量衡单位多不一致，官方和民间即有记载，亦多出入，学界却绝大多数是搬字过纸），除了墨子和名家，传统学界多任意延展用词，甚至互相袭用（例如仁义道德等核心观念），定义不稳，思想便流于蔓延，无怪华人往往宁愿凭类比代替逻辑作推论，又常草率地处理必须条件和充分条件。

中国大学生一个常见弱点是不习惯处理从多种角度（包括对手的角度）来分析和综合事象，中国大学长期执行的严格限制跨科系活动的制度，助长了师门权威，单一角度容易保持共识，代价是窒息辩论和创新。

除了闭门自修和秘方保密这些保守作风，传统的讨论方式也有不少障碍，谦逊婉转，有时绕大弯子，会令对方摸不着轻重，但客气习惯克服不了上下有别的沟通格局，华人并不善于以平等地位和多角度的态度聆听不同意见，又事先假设了不同道便不相为谋的心理，往往排除了在某一事项中持异议者在其他事件上也可以同心的期望，矛盾公开化后的交涉，往往假设了双方立场不能改变，言论集中于抨击对方的背景和动机，而非冷静地发掘和分析一些彼此可以接受的提议，练习会议规则，有助于培养存异求同的态度、和推广省时实用的沟通方法。

中国的前途受很多长短期因素影响，摸着石头可以帮助过江，却不足以道行深海，这需要更多人的远望、专识、钻研、沟通和精诚合作，是以我的中国梦做得很大：希望华人不单要做各种美梦（多角度），还要扩展自然的爱心和责任感（行仁）、辨清行事的目标和不断改良手段（敬德）、一起多学习和采用点金之指（科学方法）、与及实习有效的沟通方法（会议规则），行仁和敬德是传统文化已有的元素（先周的敬德实践和孔子旳推广东夷仁俗，已生实效），只需稍加提炼，并结合西方跨越东方时依赖的科学和议决方法，便会踏上把集体梦想变为事实的稳健路途，这个大梦若得实现，则华人不但能延续优良的传统，凝聚别的社会难得的文化认同，还可突破一些不良传统的局限；中国社会不但能推广西方的点金术，还可补救西方偏重个人、忘记程序背后最终目标的倾向。

三

四海一家亲

谭中

1929年生，历史学硕士、博士，在印度大学教书40年，曾任德里大学副教授兼中日系主任（1971—1978），尼赫鲁大学教授兼亚非语言系主任（1980年代）及东亚语言系主任（1990年代）直至1994年退休。复任新德里英迪拉甘地国立艺术中心教授顾问兼东亚部主任（1990—1999）。为德里中国研究所创始主席（1990—2003）。现定居美国芝加哥。2010年获得印度政府颁发的二等莲花奖，是继季羡林以后获得此奖的第二个中国学者。2013年获得泰戈尔创办的印度国际大学最高荣誉学位，是继周恩来、谭云山、巫白慧以后获得此荣誉的第四个中国学者。2013年受聘为云南社会科学院荣誉院士。

世界大同：我家两代人的中国梦

"异国远行我独去，如何能分好友手？……国事已不堪，乡事更勿云，造乡与造国，责任在吾人。……造福固当在人类，但须造乡造国始。……大难已来责不缓，愿我好友同努力。"

这是26岁的谭云山（我的父亲）1924年5月15日即将出国下"南洋"前夕写的《长沙临别赠茶陵学社诸友》（文载1925年12月28日《叻报》副刊《星光》23期）。那时正与长沙第一师范学校高班校友毛泽东同作"中国富强与民族振兴"梦的谭云山很想跟随李富春、蔡畅等人去法国"勤工俭学"，学了西方那一套现代革命理论再回国"振兴中华"。但一时路费难筹，于是先去东南亚帮华侨办报、办教育，打算以后去欧洲、甚至去参观共产主义革命发祥地苏联。可是到了"南洋"、于1927年在新加坡拜会了印度大文豪泰戈尔以后，他的人生道路完全改变。

湖南茶陵农村泥土中滚出来的谭云山走出国门后志行万里，在《叻报》《星光》副刊（1925年11月13日）发表《赤道上的呼声：致意》说："凡是有志的青年，要大家联合起来，……以我们底热烈的感情，使这冷酷的世界温暖，以我们底优美的人格使这堕落的世界超拔。"谭云山是个超越现实、满脑梦想的炎黄子孙的典型。

法国著名作家罗曼·罗兰说印度是地球上唯一的"人类从古到今梦者的家园"，我认为印度是"梦文化"的祖国，人类第一个最伟大的梦就是佛陀在梦中诞生。中国最早的伟大的梦，不是孔子梦周公（《论语·述而篇第七》说："久矣，吾不复梦见周公！"），而是汉明帝梦金人。印度的佛陀梦使得佛教传入中国，汉明帝的"金人"梦象征中国自上而下欢迎佛教。两个伟大的梦使中国成为梦文化繁盛的大地。

谭云山自幼熟读佛经，学生时代特别敬仰现代印度两大伟人：甘地与泰戈尔。这两人是好友，甘地给泰戈尔取名"Gurudeva/师尊"，泰戈尔给甘地取名"Mahatma/圣雄"。甘地是印度独立、民族振兴的象征，泰戈尔是印度现代文艺复兴的始祖。1924年泰戈尔访华，谭云山恰好出国，错过拜会机会。1927年泰戈尔在东南亚各国讲演，谭云山亲自找到他新加坡的客舍去求教，两人一见如故，泰戈尔邀请谭云山去他的"国际大学"教书，谭云山就于次年冬到了印度。

印度文明的中心思想是"vasudhaiva kutumbakam/天下一家"。泰戈尔办学，把学校取名"Visva-Bharati"实际意思是："世界在这个鸟巢相会"（我们现在称它为"国际大学"，按原文的意思应该是"世界鸟巢大学"）。1920年泰戈尔写给中国作家许地山的信中说："对我们来说只有一个国家——那就是世界。我们只有一个民族，那就是人类。"（这话和中共十八大"政治报告"说的"人类只有一个地球"异曲同工。）泰戈尔信中又说，在"国际大学"没有地理障碍的幻念。谭云山一到"国际大学"就把泰戈尔这一理想与中国传统的"大同思想"等同起来，决定为实现泰戈尔的"中印大同"梦想献出力量。

被泰戈尔的梦想陶醉后，谭云山马上行动起来。他知道泰戈尔渴望在"国际大学"建立一所"中国学院"，就穿梭于中印两国成立了"中印学会"，

三 四海一家亲

然后筹款、筹书于 1937 年使"中国学院"建成。泰戈尔在开幕式上激动地说:"这是大喜的吉日,我盼望已久。我现在可以代表我的同胞把我们过去暗中的诺言付诸实践,维持我们和中国人民之间的文化交流和友好相处。"这番话道出了谭云山帮助了泰戈尔实现他的"世界在这个鸟巢相会"的梦想,帮助他实现了恢复历史上中印"文化交流和友好相处"的梦想。谭云山担任了"中国学院"创办院长,从 1937 年一直到 1967 年退休为止。

中国和印度这两大文明,可谓喜马拉雅圈内背靠背的两姐妹,交往起来,正像泰戈尔所说,根本没有地理障碍的幻念,是边界盲。4 世纪 20 年代印度高僧慧理到杭州西湖畔山上,很有感触地说,这座山是从"中天竺"飞来的灵鹫山,当地人相信了,在山上建了"灵隐寺",意思是"印度飞来的灵鹫在庙中隐居",那座山得名"飞来峰",附近有"上天竺"、"中天竺"、"下天竺"等名胜,中国地图上有了象征中印友好的印度领土,千余年来没人发出怨声。

古代出了"飞来峰"这样的佳话,现代谭云山竭力促成的"中印学会"帮助泰戈尔的"国际大学"建立了"中国学院",实现了中国对印度以德报德,"中国学院"实质上是从中国飞到印度的"飞回峰",与杭州"飞来峰"形成文明交响。

一方面,谭云山毕生梦想"中印大同",他那中印"兄弟国家"的信念从不动摇;另一方面,我们这个被西方"民族国"的"地缘政治范式"蒙蔽的世界把中印关系推向竞争防范、互为对手的方向。1962 年中印边境战争后,印度民情视中国人为敌。对印度最忠诚、对泰戈尔最崇拜的谭云山长女谭文在"国际大学"博士生导师家遇见许多客人,导师介绍她说:"她与那些(中国)坏蛋不同",她听了十分伤心,"种族盲"的泰戈尔理想在她心中动摇。

但数千年中印两大"文明国"的传统是永存的。边境战争两周后印度总理尼赫鲁在"国际大学"年会上看见听众中端坐着坚信"中印友好"从不动摇的谭云山,他心中那股对中国的强烈怒气顿时消失,临时改变了腹中的讲稿,没骂中国一句,却以谭云山与"中国学院"为例强调"印度不与中国的文化或者伟大开战",使谭云山热泪盈眶。

四海一家、天涯比邻：海外华人与中国梦

谭云山过世后被人誉为"现代玄奘"，他和7世纪的著名高僧玄奘有相同也有不同之处。玄奘周游印度以后又像大雁一样飞回中国讲道译经（现在西安"大雁塔"就是他的象征符号）。1928年飞到印度的谭云山，先是在泰戈尔的"世界鸟巢大学"引了一大群中国鸟使它成为名副其实的"国际大学"，退休后又想到印度菩提场建立"世界佛学苑"而于1983年不幸在当地"中华佛寺"圆寂。他毕生研究著述、不断奔波，促进泰戈尔的"中印大同"理想实现，无私地为"中华文明梦"、"印度文明梦"、"中印大同梦"奋斗终生。

我作为谭云山的长子，1929年4月诞生于马来西亚的峇株巴辖（两个月时由父母抱到印度"国际大学"拜见泰戈尔，承泰翁起名"Asoka/阿输迦"，小住两周后又返回峇株巴辖），2岁回到中国成长，1955年开年时到印度与父母弟妹团聚，一直到1999年夏天离开印度到美国芝加哥定居。泰戈尔给的印度名字"Asoka/阿输迦"从来没有用上，但我的毕生事业却在这个名字注定的轨道上运行。"Asoka/阿输迦"与秦始皇同时，是佛教运动的大力推动者，把"喜马拉雅圈"内背靠背的两姐妹——中印两大文明——连成一片。谭云山就是这中印两大文明的结晶，"Asoka/阿输迦"象征着这个结晶成为我体内遗传的基因。

我到了印度于1958年开始教中文，一直到1994年（满65岁）从大学退休为止。古训曰："教学相长"，我对这话深有体验。在印度当教员（主要教中文，曾经将近十年兼教中国历史）最感幸福的是以一个懂点中华文明的放射体和千万要求了解中华文明的年轻思想感情放射体亲密神交，使我永远"长青不老"，我的莘莘学子始终把我当作亲人、甚至家长。有时学生家长来大学找我，要我做学生的思想工作，或者对学生的婚姻对象进行咨询。我觉得自己变成印度社会文化的组成部分。由于我的讲解，学生们对中国的许多"不解"与"误解"逐渐融化，我的潜移默化使他们把爱我的情感扩展到爱中国。

毛泽东主席于1951年（出席印度大使馆国庆招待会上）及1970年"五一节"（在天安门城楼和印度代办米什拉握手时）两次说印度是"伟大的民族/国家""很好/伟大的人民"，我在印度对这些话深有体验。父亲和我两代及家人80余年来爱中国、也爱印度，觉得自己既是中国人、又是印度人，从

来没有民族与国家的差异与隔阂。"中印大同"对谭云山和我不是空洞的词汇,而是真实的生活经验、理想与情感。

日新月异的中国不断受到国际注视,印度统治精英却把中国当做最重要的国家、对中国的发展最为关怀。我和德里大学与尼赫鲁大学"中国通"组成的小集体,从60年代开始每周聚会一次讨论中国发展经常有政府人员参加,好几年是在印度前驻华大使苏杰生的父亲、印度国防研究所创办所长苏伯(Krishnaswamy Subrahmanyam)的办公室举行。小集体于九十年代正式变为印度中国研究所(经费由印度政府外交部赞助)。

我和老伴黄绮淑是这个中印一家的小集体的创办成员,许多至友都过世了,只剩下现任中国研究所主席莫汉蒂(Manoranjan Mohanty)。我们不但在生活上像亲生兄弟姐妹,思想上也志同道合,坚决主张中印两大文明紧密团结。我们各自在印度报刊发表文章,成为印度有关中国言论的主流。已故好友白蜜雅(Mira Sinha Bhattacharjea)对中印边界纠纷谈论得特别多,她从70年代就提出必须"政治解决",现在已被两国政府接受。

1994年印度外交部请我于"和平共处五项原则"提出40周年为其公开刊物 Indian Horizons("印度地平线")编"印度与中国"特刊,出了一本555页的厚书,发行后加印了两次,共出了9000册,由全世界印度各驻外使馆及其他机构分发全球。90年代我在英迪拉甘地国立艺术中心组织"India and China Looking at Each Other"(印度与中国相互注视)讨论会,编了 Across the Himalayan Gap: An Indian Quest for Understanding China("跨越喜马拉雅鸿沟:印度寻求了解中国"),继而把张敏秋编的《跨越喜马拉雅障碍:中国寻求了解印度》改动内容译成英文,有了 Across the Himalayan Gap: A Chinese Quest for Understanding India("跨越喜马拉雅鸿沟:中国寻求了解印度")。我又和北京大学好友耿引曾合写了《印度与中国——两大文明的交往和激荡》,中文版于2006年由商务印书馆出版,英文版成为《印度文明中的科学、哲学文化历史丛书》的第三卷第六部分。我就是以写书、编书去踏着父亲谭云山的足迹走上了实现"中国梦"、"印度梦"与"中印大同梦"的征途。

我在印度教学研究45年和印度知识精英朝夕相处,对中印两大文明之间交流与共鸣深有感触,印度朋友至今仍然不断鼓励我去发掘那些久久被人遗忘的信息。他们支持我大力提倡"地缘文明范式"来帮助增进中印了解与友谊，改造被"文明冲突"论毒焰熏得令人窒息的当今国际秩序。印度的"天下一家"和中国的"天下大同"是"喜马拉雅圈"文明数千年的"梦"的追求。正是有了这种"梦"的追求，中印两大古文明才是古文明中唯一没有变成古邱废墟的伟大典范。

中国和印度不但是两大历史悠久的文明，而且在18世纪以前领先全球，两国人口与财富总和约占世界40%—50%。现在两国同做"富强梦"，中国要在2030年经济超过美国，印度要在那时候变成"第二个中国"（这是2013年12月29日美国CNN"全球公众广场/Global Public Square"国际时事节目的中心议题）。印度"富强梦"的另一个内容就是到那时中印两国人口与财富总和又回复到世界40%—50%，这是"印度梦"，也是"中国梦"。"印度梦"中可以有"中国梦"，实现"中国梦"也可以包括实现"印度梦"—体现禅文化的"你中有我、我中有你"。

印度教徒每天拜神念的"Satyam, Shivam, Sundaram"一千多年前就传到中国，起初叫"真善妙色"，后来叫"真善美"，这样"印度梦"和"中国梦"实际上早已融合在一起了。泰戈尔的文学与文化就是在现代社会实现"真善美"的梦想。泰戈尔获诺贝尔文学奖已经一百年，这一百年间中国文学界与文化界出现多次"泰戈尔"热。泰戈尔主要是孟加拉文作家，中国过去已经出过《泰戈尔全集》，现在又直接从孟加拉文翻译出版新的《泰戈尔全集》。将来书出全以后，中文就超过英文而成为泰戈尔作品的最大外国语表达形式，使得印度"真善美"精神在中国语文中发出灿烂光彩。

1921年郭沫若从日本回国，船在上海进入黄浦江时，他看到阔别的祖国心情特别激动，即兴在《黄浦江口》诗中吟出："平和之乡哟！我的父母之邦！"他那时一心敬仰泰戈尔的"Santiniketan/和平乡"而在思想感情上打破中印界限。"Santi/和平"是印度文明的灵魂，正与"和为贵"是中华文明的灵魂一样。如今，"和为贵"这金光闪闪的三字经已经像嫦娥飞到月亮上去了。她在"明月"上回望我们这戾气万丈的"民族国"地球是不愿意回来的。"中国梦"中不但有正在成功实现的"嫦娥探月/登月"计划，还有嫦娥载人登月的意图，要是一面让中国人登月，一面让"和为贵"从月亮上回归

三 四海一家亲

地球,那"中国梦"就会更加功德圆满,也圆了"印度梦"。

大量海外华人的祖先都是由于祖国缺乏和平安宁而离乡背井的。数千万对局势动乱感触最深的海外华人最大的"梦"就是"和平梦"。和谐与冲突就像人世的"阴"与"阳","中国梦"应该大力发扬"中国精神",在"中国道路"上向世界辐射,使和谐的"阳"压倒冲突的"阴"。"中国梦"必然能把中印两个伟大"文明国"团结起来,把世界变成天伦之乐的温暖大家庭。

"风霜何事偏伤物,天地无情亦爱人"这是唐朝诗人刘长卿诗句。"中国梦"就是天地爱人类、政府爱人民的表现。"中国梦"就是"世界梦"。中国数千年来是一个"天无私覆,地无私载,日月无私照"的天下,是一个"大道之行也天下为公"的天下,是一个"推己及人"与"普度众生"的天下。父亲谭云山和我两代人在中印两大文明之间的最大的"梦"就是让这种"大同世界"实现。

谭云山为自己、家人与学生制定《中印箴铭》,开头八个字是"立德立言、救人救世",前半部是中国数千年教诲从帝王到庶人的"三不朽",后半部是印度传到中国的"菩萨精神",从小受到这八个字教诲的我不敢说把它们身体力行,但我无论走到世界任何角落都被这八个字跟随而感受鼓舞。我真希望"中国梦"不是一个狭隘的民族梦、不是一个东施效颦的"霸权梦",而是一个"救人救世"的"菩萨梦"。

Four seas to One Family: Overseas Chinese and Chinese dream
四海一家、天涯比邻：海外华人与中国梦

顾利程

博士、美国西北大学亚洲语言文化系教授、西北大学在华（北京大学）暑期训练班主任。生长于北京，酷爱乒乓球与戏曲。顾利程教授在北京第二外国语学院获得学士学位，在澳大利亚堪培拉高等教育学院获得硕士学位，在美国俄勒冈大学获得博士学位。顾利程教授曾经在美国的明德大学、普林斯顿大学任教，并且教授过各个级别的汉语课程及中国文学课程，对华裔汉语的教学更有独特的见解。除了相关论文以外，顾利程教授发表的专著有 Learning Chinese Characters through Pictures《古字新说》及 Learning Chinese with Lulu and Maomao《跟露露、毛毛学汉语》。主要研究方向为对外汉语教学法及华裔移民美国史等。

构建汉语桥，实现中国梦

桥能够使两岸人民畅通往来，顺利从此岸到达彼岸，没有乘船时的风急浪险之虞。梦是一个人的远大理想，是一个人一步一个脚印，踏踏实实终生奋斗的目标。作为一名移居美国的华人，笔者的桥就是汉语桥，即世界大学生汉语演讲比赛，笔者的梦就是帮助架设这座汉语桥，使之成为中美两国人民沟通的桥梁。希望通过这座汉语桥，中国人民和美国人民在文化上密切往来，贸易上互惠互利，经济上通力合作。希望这座汉语桥能够增进两国人民的相互理解和信任，从而促进世界和平。

《圣经》里有一个通天塔的故事。据说很久以前，地球上不同国家的人们都使用同一种语言，享有同一种文化。整个世界是一个和谐安定，没有误解，没有争端的人间天堂。但是人类希望瞻仰天庭的上帝，亲耳聆听上帝的教诲，从而取得真经，所以计划建造一座通天塔与上帝沟通。他们绘制了图纸，分

三　四海一家亲

配了工作，开始了人类的登天计划。

不同国家的人们顺畅沟通，通力合作，有条不紊地建设着通天塔。没过多久，一座雄伟高大的通天塔已经拔地而起。它高耸入云，直逼天庭。人类很快就可以见到上帝，与上帝面对面通话了。每个人都在为此兴奋无比。

但是人类的这一通力合作惹恼了上帝。他担心一旦人们把通天塔建成，就会天天把他们的凡人琐事向他诉说，使他永无宁日。为了自己的清净，上帝想出来一个办法，使人类无法继续齐心合力完成通天塔。他悄悄改变了人类的语言，让不同的国家使用不同的语言，发展不同的文化，从而导致国家与国家之间无法沟通，无法合作。从此以后，人类再也不能共同建塔了。这个国家的人怀疑那个国家的人出工不出力，那个国家的人怀疑这个国家的人把通天塔建在了自家门口，以图己便。双方说也说不清，讲也讲不明，最后只好各奔东西，不欢而散。从此那座通天塔变成了一座烂尾楼，矗立在那里向人们诉说着自己的无奈。

这虽然只是一个神话故事，但是却蕴含着深远的意义。不同的语言和不同的文化可以给人类顺畅沟通带来巨大的麻烦。隔阂、误解、甚至战争有时竟会由此而生。如今世界上有70多亿人口，使用大小不同5600多种语言。学习其他种族的语言，了解其他国家的文化，成了世界人民共同面临的挑战。

在世界众多语言当中，中文和英文是两种常用的语言。在世界范围内，以汉语为母语的人口为12亿，以英语为母语的人口为四亿（能说英语的人口总共有10亿以上）。为了走向世界，成为世界公民，许多人在学习这两种语言。中国人为了了解世界，有一亿多人在学习英文。美国人为了了解中国，有十万多人在学习中文。自然也有很多人投身于教外语这一行业。笔者就是千千万万个普通外语教师之一。

早在1976笔者于北京市外国语学校毕业以后就成了一个英文教师，从此在中国教英文教了12年。1992年在俄勒冈大学获得教育学博士以后，笔者在美国成了一名中文教师，至今教中文已经教了22年了。回头看来，自信在中国教不少中国人学会了英文，帮助他们走向了世界；在美国教不少美国人学会了中文，帮助他们走向了中国。笔者的梦想是能够帮助更多的中国人走向世界，帮助更多的美国人走向中国。这就是笔者的中国梦。

笔者如今的中国梦有如下三个组成部分。

1. 在美国大学里推广汉语教学，发展中文项目，给美国学生提供不同级别的汉语课程及中国文化课程，让更多的美国学生学习汉语，了解中国。

2. 组织美国暑期在华中文项目，带领美国学生来中国学习汉语及中国文化，让学生有机会真正深入了解中国，与中国百姓交朋友。

3. 在美国大学组织初级汉语桥演讲比赛，从中选出金牌得主，送到中国参加世界大学生汉语桥演讲比赛的复赛及决赛。希望汉语桥比赛能扩大影响，反过来吸引更多的美国人学习汉语。

1993年起笔者在美国西北大学教汉语至今，已经把一个当初只有60名学生三名教师的中文项目发展到今天拥有300名学生，十名教师的中文项目。我们给美国学生开设了一至四年级常规汉语课程。我们还给华裔学生开设了一至四年级的华裔汉语课程。每门课每周三至五个课时不等。

一年级的汉语课程是打基础的关键阶段。我们注重汉语拼音，笔画顺序和掌握四声。我们非常注意学生的发音，有错必改，直到学生能够字正腔圆地说好每一个句子，保证让学生打下一个良好的基础。二年级则是帮助学生掌握中文句法，扩大中文词汇量，培养学生养成用中文沟通的习惯。我们训练他们用简单的句子与别人交流，同时尽可能地做到听说读写齐头并进。二年级我们还让学生看一些中文的小品和影视节目，提高学生的听力水平。三年级主要培养学生通过阅读及写作培养语感。通过阅读不同题材的课文，丰富学生的知识面，提高学生快速阅读的速度，感受中国文化的博大精深。三年级的学生还会看中国电影，讨论电影的主题，并且写出影评。四年级的阅读及写作则侧重于经典文学作品，特别是古典文学作品。通过模仿一些文学短篇，帮助学生提高写作水平，特别是典雅度。总体来说，四年的中文训练可以使一个零起点的学生从无到有，逐步提高，稳步前进，为将来的突飞猛进打下良好的基础。

我们的华裔班也有四个年级的课程。华裔班学生指在华人家庭里面长大的美籍华人子弟。他们生长在美国的华人家庭，从小接受中华文化的熏陶。他们在家里吃中国饭，跟爸爸妈妈说中国话。但是一出了家门进了学校，他们跟美国老师和朋友都是用英文交流。相当一部分美国的中学都没有中文课，所以他们没有机会从小学习中文阅读和写作。虽然每到周末父母都会送他们去中文学校，但是每周才上一次中文课，远远不能切实学好中文。往往是上一个周末刚刚学了一点东西，一个星期以后，早已忘光了。笔者曾经做过八年的中文学校的校长，深知其中的问题。所以我们大学的华裔中文课程基本上与正常班一样，也是从零开始，逐步提高学生听说读写的四项技能。与正常班不同的地方是我们的华裔班主要强调培养学生的阅读与写作及与中华文化的认同。

除此以外，西北大学还开设了许多中国文化课，如中国文学、中国历史、中国哲学、中国宗教、中国艺术等等。越来越多的美国学生上汉语课，上中国文化课，选修中文专业和副专业。我们非常清楚，要真正帮助学生学好中文，了解中国文化，仅仅在美国学校是远远不够的。就像当年的玄奘一样，只有到了西天，才能取得真经。所以我们鼓励、帮助学生们到中国去留学一段时间。为此我们为他们做好了准备，组织好了暑期赴华汉语项目。

自从2000年以来，笔者每年夏天组织美国学生来来中国留学两个月。2000年至2010年的十年，我们西北大学在华暑期班与清华大学合作举办。2011年至今，我们的暑期班与北京大学合作举办。上午学生们学习汉语，中午跟中国老师和学生一起共进午餐。下午他们学习中国文化课，课程包括中国历史、政治经济、公共卫生、中医中药、环境保护、绿色能源。晚上学生们准备功课，或者参加当地学生的各种课外活动。周末学生们到北京各地游览参观，欣赏京剧、杂技、魔术表演。长周末学生们还到外地长途旅游，领略中国的大好河山，体会中国不同地域的风土习俗。在过去的十几年里，笔者组织学生们去过千岛湖、杭州、上海、西安、桂林、重庆、内蒙古、长沙、泰山、九寨沟、海南三亚等地。我们曾经在黄山上看日出，在长江三峡看日落，在野长城上采集中草药，在蒙古草原策马扬鞭。我们也曾经在太阳能电厂参加劳动，在老人院为老人服务，给孤儿院的孩子送去礼物并帮孤儿们学习英文。我们也曾在公社卫生院做义工，帮助卫生院的医务人员照顾患者。

我们的美国学生也曾在中国城市的大街小巷做社会调查。有的采访出租车司机，了解中国城市交通的衍变；有的尾随乞讨人员，观察中国人的施舍行为规律；有的帮助小商小贩卖东西，熟悉城市居民的购买习惯；有的跟踪观察城管的工作方式,分析他们的初衷与实际效果。有的华裔学生甚至混迹于农民工当中,在建筑工地上绑钢筋,浇水泥,并且和农民工一起吃大锅饭,睡大通铺,从而体会城市底层社会的艰辛。美国学生在课上跟中国老师学习中国的语言与文化,在课余时间与当地的中国民众深层接触,在生活中了解真正的中国。通过社会实践,我们的美国学生丰富了阅历,一步步走向成熟,写出了一篇篇具有独特见解的社会调查报告。他们用自己的双眼在观察中国,了解中国,不再轻易受任何媒体不客观的报道所左右。

通过社会实践,美国学生与中国普通百姓交上了朋友。从他们身上学到了很多课本里学不到的东西。下面是西北大学的学生黄大伟（David Harris）与农民工周大力的一段故事。

去年夏天大伟在北京学习。一天大伟去后海玩儿,逛到中午有些饿了。正想买些东西吃,突然从旁边小胡同里飘来了一阵轻快的歌声和一股特别的香味。大伟走近一看,原来是一个煎饼摊儿。只见那个摊煎饼的浑身是汗地忙活着,煎饼摊前还有五六个人排队等着。虽然他在高温里烘烤着,可是兴致还很高。一边摊煎饼,一边唱歌。好像是在娱乐他的顾客,更像是在娱乐他自己。排队买煎饼的人似乎也失去了往日北京人的那种焦躁,而是悠闲地站在那里闻着摊煎饼的香味,享受这他那有一句,没一句的歌声,等着自己的煎饼。大伟被这情景吸引住了,也身不由己地排在队后,准备买一个煎饼尝尝。

排到大伟了,摊煎饼的问,

"小伙子,你要几个？"

"我要一个。"

"几个鸡蛋？"

"两个。"

"要不要辣酱？"

"当然要。"

这个人一边问着,一边熟练地摊着煎饼。只见他潇洒地把面糊舀到饼铛上,灵巧地一划,推出了一个圆圆的煎饼。稍后用铲子一挑,煎饼在空中翻了一个个儿,平稳地落在饼铛上。接着他一丝不苟地加上鸡蛋、辣酱、香菜、

三　四海一家亲

葱花、薄脆。不到两分钟，一套香喷喷、热腾腾的煎饼果子已经送到了大伟的手上。大伟咬了一口，嘿，内焦外嫩，香辣可口，好吃极了。因为后边暂时没有别的顾客，大伟就边吃边和摊煎饼的攀谈了起来。

原来他叫周大力，是个农民工。家里有一个孩子叫兰兰，却不幸患有癌症。兰兰不到5岁，就已经做了四次手术，十二次化疗。为了给兰兰治病，大力拼命地工作。他一个人每天打两份工。白天在胡同里摊煎饼，晚上给一所学校做保安。日子虽然很辛苦，但是大力仍然对生活充满了热情。他没有恨天怨地，没有自暴自弃，更没有去向别人乞求同情或者施舍。他每天勤恳地工作，愉快地生活。一有时间，他就给兰兰唱歌，给她欢乐和希望，同时也以此来鼓励自己。

大伟被大力积极的生活态度感动了，主动跟他交上了朋友。大力教大伟说中文，摊煎饼；大伟教大力唱歌，弹吉他。

大力是个好师傅。大伟摊煎饼的手艺越来越好。大家亲切地称大力为"中国煎饼哥"，称大伟为"美国煎饼弟"。他们每次在胡同里摊煎饼时，总能吸引很多顾客。最忙的时候，一天就摊了800多个煎饼。他们虽然很辛苦，但是很愉快，因为他们又给兰兰挣了一些医药费。

大力也是个好学生。他很有音乐天赋。歌儿越唱越好，吉他也越弹越棒。去年，大力和大伟联袂唱到了北京电视台，做了"北京客"节目的嘉宾。今年，他们又一起唱到了中央电视台，走上了"星光大道"。相信他们的歌声会给人们带来音乐的享受，他们的友谊故事一定能够打动众多的中美百姓。

跟大力在一起，大伟不仅提高了中文水平，同时也学会了怎样克服困难，面对人生。大力积极的生活态度会激励大伟及所有的人勇敢地面对困境，勇于承担，永不言退。

当然，大伟也从大力那里学会了摊煎饼。在今年的汉语桥演讲比赛上，大伟准备的演讲题目是"中国煎饼哥，美国煎饼弟"。而他的才艺表演是边摊煎饼，边唱"煎饼歌"。相信观众届时不但会一饱耳福，也会一饱口福。

为了帮助美国学生尽快走进中国人的生活，笔者给每一个学生配备了一个中国学生作为语伴。这些语伴都是清华大学或者北京大学学生会给我们组织的志愿者。美国学生和中国语伴用中英文互相介绍，互相了解。笔者要求中国学生把他们的美国语伴带到他们的生活当中去。去中国学生的课堂，看他们的学生宿舍，参加他们的各类活动，跟他们出去游玩，甚至跟语伴一起回家乡参观访问。同样笔者也要求美国学生把美国的情况，特别是美国大学的情况一一向中国学生介绍，了解美国大学的申请程序，帮助他们学习英文，将来在美国接待他们的中国语伴。总而言之，笔者要求他们互相了解，互相学习，互相帮助。

首次见面的时候，笔者给他们安排好餐厅，用中英文两种文字准备好40个问题，供中美语伴们边吃喝、边交流。然后组织他们定期或者不定期举办活动。比如7月4日美国的独立日，农历七月初七的中国情人节都是中美学生举办活动的好机会。笔者的工作就是给这些中国学生和美国学生牵线搭桥。而这座桥十几年来已经帮助不少中国学生和美国学生顺利地到达了彼岸。以往这座桥还没有一个正式的名字。后来这座桥有名字了。这就是如今众所周知的"汉语桥"。

为了进一步促进中国人民与世界其他国家的人民顺畅交流，鼓励外国学生学习汉语，中国国家汉语推广办公室自2002年以来，已经举办了八届世界大学生"汉语桥"演讲比赛。每年七八月间，中国政府会邀请来自世界各地的100名学习汉语的大学生来中国参加汉语演讲比赛。他们每人做5分钟汉语演讲，以展示他们标准的语音语调，地道的选词造句，以及引人入胜的演讲内容。选手们还会选答关于中国语言与文化的一些问题，展示他们对中华文化知识的理解与掌握。除此之外，他们还要比赛他们掌握的中华才艺，比如书法、绘画、歌曲、舞蹈、烹饪、小品等等。

2002年是汉语桥诞生的第一年。作为一名评委，笔者有幸见到了众多酷爱汉语的莘莘学子。他们来自五湖四海，携手跨过汉语桥，来到中国。记得那一年美国西北大学的姚家舜同学不仅演讲做得很好，他的才艺表演更是一鸣惊人。别的参赛选手的中华才艺是唱中国歌，跳中国舞，写毛笔字，或者演奏中国乐器。而家舜的才艺表演竟然是——抻面。当别的参赛选手展示高雅中国文化的时候，家舜却在央视的舞台上和面、揉面、抻面。在不长的时间里，家舜不用擀面杖，不用切菜刀，竟然用双手抻出了细细长长的面条。当家舜举起那细如盘丝的抻面时，全场爆发出了雷鸣般的掌声。十几年过去

三　四海一家亲

了。相信家舜一定给他的家人和亲朋好友做过多次中国的抻面。相信他的抻面一定会把更多的美国朋友带的中国。

对于中方推广汉语，建设汉语桥的举动，美方也作出了积极的反应。奥巴马总统于 2009 年 11 月宣布启动"十万强计划"，预计数年内安排十万名美国学生到中国学习。中方对此非常支持，立即宣布将向美方提供一万个汉语桥奖学金名额，帮助美国学生来华学习。当时的胡锦涛主席亲自过问，中国的企业家慷慨解囊。十万强项目启动以来，进展顺利。在众多的企业当中，中国万象集团是较为突出的一个。在过去的两年里，在中国万象集团的资助下，仅芝加哥地区就已经有六批 100 名学生到中国学习。他们是芝加哥公立学校系统的高中生，西北大学的学生，及芝加哥大学的学生。2012 年夏天，胡锦涛主席还在中南海亲切接见了来华学习的"十万强计划"的高中生。足见中方对"十万强计划"的大力支持。而"十万强计划"也进一步促进了美国各个地区汉语教学的发展，提高了参加汉语桥比赛的热忱。

美国中西部地区是汉语教学的重镇。曾任芝加哥市市长多年的戴利先生非常热衷于发展美中友谊，推广汉语教学。中国驻芝加哥总领馆教育组也大力支持，国家汉办也出人出力，所以本地区的中小学及大学的汉语教学突飞猛进，发展迅速。越来越多的中小学开始开设汉语课，给大学培养了不少后备人才，各个大学中文项目的注册人数不断增加。所以各个大学里面有不少学生有志于到中国参加汉语桥演讲比赛。而中国汉语桥组委会也希望美国中西部地区能够选派优秀选手参赛。

为了满足双方的要求，帮助建好这座意义非凡的汉语桥，笔者自 2004 年开始组织美国中西部地区大学生汉语桥演讲比赛。为了及时把汉语桥选手送到中国参加 7 月份的汉语桥演讲比赛，中西部地区的预赛每年定期在五月份举行。作为主要的发起人和组织者，我们西北大学主办了六次。另外两次轮流由普渡大学和明尼苏达大学主办。在国家汉办与总领馆教育组的大力支持下，每年都有来自美国中西部九个州 20 多所大学的 60 名选手来参加比赛。

为了鼓励更多的选手参加比赛，逐步培养学生比赛的经验，我们给所有级别的学生提供锻炼的机会，允许低年级组的学生参加比赛。根据学生选修中文课的班级，我们把选手分在六个不同级别的比赛场地。初学者一年级学生参加一年级组的比赛。中文二年级的学生参加二年级组的比赛。中文三年级的学生参加三年级组的比赛。中文四年级的学生参加高级组的比赛。华裔学生分在华裔组里面比赛。如此所有参赛选手只可以跟自己同样年级的选手比赛。华裔与非华裔组截然分开。让所有的选手都能够充分发挥自己的水平。

根据规定，每一个参赛选手在听众及评委面前做一个5分钟的脱稿演讲。然后选手还要做一个中华才艺表演。根据各自的条件，选手可以唱中国歌，跳中国舞，或者任何与中华文化艺术有关系的才艺。评委根据选手的语音语调、句法结构、演讲内容、演讲效果，及才艺表演水平当场打分。其中演讲占50分，才艺占10分。二者加起来就是参赛选手的最终成绩。

最后，组委会从最高年级组，四年级组里面选出两名一等奖选手，派送他们代表美国去中国参加世界大学生汉语桥演讲比赛。在过去的十年里，西北大学、明尼苏达大学、芝加哥大学、威斯康辛大学共有12名学生当选。他们在历次世界大学汉语桥演讲比赛中都获得了好成绩。最重要的是，他们在中国开阔了眼界，增长了阅历，跟当地的中国人交了朋友，还跟来自世界各地学中文的学生交了朋友，使他们受益匪浅。这是对我们中西部地区汉语教学的一个承认，是对我们汉语教师的最大的褒奖。

自从2002年以后，在国家汉办及海内外学者专家的帮助下，汉语桥成了一个品牌。其比赛程序和规则越来越规范化、正规化、趣味化。汉语桥每年7月中旬都会在中国举办一次。经过初赛、复赛、及最后的决赛，评选出金牌、银牌、铜牌得主。虽然选手们取得的成绩不同，但是每一位来中国参加汉语桥比赛的选手都会被命名为中华文化传播使者。参赛选手们不仅参加汉语桥比赛，他们还有机会到中国各地参观旅游，甚至住在中国寻常百姓家中，和不同层次的中国人交流，交朋友。最后他们满带着中国人民的深情厚谊回到各自的祖国。相信我们的学生会通过汉语桥，穿梭于中美两国人民中间，增进两国人民的了解，切实起到了民间使者的作用。

由于语言不通，文化不同，人类最终没有能够建成通天塔，也没有机会抵达天庭，直接从上帝那里取得真经。但是今天，在中美双方的配合下，在众多建桥者、寻梦人的辛勤劳动下，我们建成了汉语桥。通过这座汉语桥，众多的美国学生开始学习中文，并来中国取经。如今汉语桥已经成为中美两国人民之间友谊的纽带,沟通的桥梁。随着时代的发展,这座桥必将越来越畅通,越来越宽广。通过这座汉语桥,越来越多的美国人会学习中文,会到中国来,会了解中国,会宣传中国。这就是我在帮助构建的汉语桥,这就是我要实现的中国梦。

愿连接中美两国人民的汉语桥坚实永固,愿中美两国人民的友谊地久天长,愿海内外华人的中国梦早日实现!

Four seas to One Family: Overseas Chinese and Chinese dream
四海一家、天涯比邻：海外华人与中国梦

陈杰琦

1982年毕业于北师大教育系，现任美国芝加哥埃里克森儿童发展研究院终身教授，博士生项目主任，国际合作项目执行主任及儿童数学教育项目首席主持。她的研究领域包括儿童认知发展，儿童数学教育，教师专业成长，课堂教学评价及多元智力理论的教育运用。她在美国所获得的教育干预和研究基金达1千多万美元。她出版过八部中英文专著，发表过多篇学术论文，被世界许多国家和地区的儿童教育机构邀请讲学。作为联合国儿童基金会咨询顾问，她参与了中国教育部国家幼儿教师培训计划的评价。

我的中国梦：面向全民的高质量早期儿童教育

中国梦的实现，包括高水平的人民道德、政治秩序，健康绿色的经济增长，及和谐的人际关系。教育，是实现这一梦想的关键之一。没有针对全民的基本教育，任何国家都不可能真正发展，而全部教育的基础与优先部分是儿童早期教育。早期儿童教育，是指针对0到8岁儿童的养育、教育。我在这个领域从事学习、教学、和研究已经有40多年了。人常说，三句话不离本行。我的本行是幼儿教育，我的中国梦是让全中国的幼儿，不分城乡、贫富、出生背景，都能普遍享有较高质量的早期教育。

我的中国梦由来已久。"文革"中，在农村插队，我就做过小学教师。文革恢复后，我是第一批儿童早期教育专业的大学生。在这之前的30年，幼儿教育领域一直比较沉寂。自中苏决裂以后，这个领域的大学本科教育就处于中断状态。结果，懂行的人越来越少。记得那时听到的、亲友们问得最多的问题是："哎哟，你怎么上了这么个专业？看孩子还要一个大学本科学位吗？"

今天，问这种问题的人已经不多了。脑科学与大量实证性研究早已表明，高质量的早期儿童教育十分关键，影响深远。适宜儿童身心发展的，合理的早期教育，可以有效地助进幼儿发展健康的身体、积极的情绪、语言能力、与认知水平。

幼儿阶段受到的有益的教养，会持续影响至成人阶段。大量长期追踪性研究表明，高质量的早期教育还有减少犯罪、提高学习成绩、增加个人收入等效果。事实上，很多教育家，经济学家，政治家等都认为，一个社会、一个家庭、一对父母，在一个孩子身上的最佳"投资"，就是向孩子提供高质量的早期教育。

中国政府了解儿童教育的重要性。国家2010到2020年的十年战略规划中规定：到2020年，全体学龄前儿童都应该享受至少一年的学前教育。在较为发达的地区，则应该普及两年到三年的早期教育。将早期教育作为国家战略规划的一部分足以表明中国政府对其的重视程度，中国幼儿教育工作者们对此感到欣慰鼓舞。

然而，我们必须清醒地认识到，目前有关早期教育的发展还非常初步。例如，投入到早期教育中的各类中央及地方政府资金，大多仅限于启动阶段的项目，如房舍的基本建设和教养人员的雇用等等。没有基础设施与教养人员当然不行，但是要使全中国的幼儿，尤其是边远贫穷乡镇的幼儿，都能普遍享有较高质量的早期教育，我们还有大量的工作要做。以下就三个具有紧迫性的领域谈谈自己的看法。这三个领域分别为：关注贫穷和留守儿童的需要，教师的专业成长或职业培训，以及提供有针对性的家长教育。

关注贫穷及留守儿童

自改革开放以来，中国的儿童教育无论是数量，还是质量都有了前所未有的提高。然而许许多多生活在边远、贫穷、少数民族地区的儿童依然得不到最基本的教育。最近几年我在与中国教育部以及华东师大同行合作工作时，有机会访问过若干边远贫穷地区的幼儿园。那里的所见所闻常令人心酸。

在一所农村幼儿园，我看到超过40多名3到6岁的孩子，挤在一间教室里，一排排坐着。房间窗户很小，天花板很低，室内光线很暗。教室里虽然有灯，却没有开，原因是为了节约电钱。

一位年轻的老师在带领孩子们背诵儿歌。有些孩子在听，另一些孩子在左顾右盼，还有些孩子在打瞌睡。教室门外，贴着每一个星期的日程表。上面列着一节接一节的 30 到 40 分钟的课程，例如数学课，语文课，书写课，图画课与音乐课，完全是小学化的教学形式。我真不知道这类教育实践在多大程度上有益于儿童的发展。

幼儿是需要在活动中和游戏玩乐中学习的。由于农村地区空间一般不大成问题，孩子们可以在室外探索、观察、试验、和谈论周围事物中学到很多东西。那样要比连续几个小时坐在室内，死记硬背一些与孩子们自己有兴趣的东西或自己的生活很难联系起来的东西强得多。

当被问到最主要的困难有哪些时，我们访问的幼儿中心主任说，"是小孩子不守规矩"。换句话说，主要问题在于孩子们很难几个小时、老老实实地在室内坐着，并且集中注意力。如果这位主任受过一点有关儿童发展知识的训练，那么她就会明白，3—6 岁的孩子们被要求那样地坐在室内，以及主任对孩子们的期望—希望他们听话—都是不符合儿童身心发展的基本规律的。

在这所幼儿园里，许多孩子是所谓"留守儿童"。这些孩子的农民工父母，为了生存远出在外打工赚钱，只能把他们留给爷爷奶奶或亲戚照看，父母自己往往一年只能在春节期间探家一次。当我向园长了解孩子们关于与父母分离所表现的情绪情感心理问题时，我听到回答十分意外："孩子还小，他们不懂这些。"幼教人员如果连最基本的有关儿童的社会发展、情感心理学知识都没有，那么他们就很容易误解和误导孩子们的教育、照料，而犯下各种各样的玩忽职守错误。这不仅是遗憾，而且还有一定的危险。

在另外一所幼儿中心，我所见到的情景更加令人吃惊，难以接受。一位老师在教孩子们唱歌，唱得是电视剧《黑猫警长》的插曲。但是，这位老师实际上是在用孩子们唱这首歌的办法，去羞辱一个不守纪律的孩子。老师让同学们围成一个圈，每一个人的手指都指着那个犯错的孩子，大家一齐成为黑猫警长，而同声高唱"你就要受罚！你就要受罚！"那个受罚的孩子，双手捂着脸，蹲在屋子的角落里。当我们质疑这种做法时，那个老师理直气壮地说，"这是纠正孩子纪律错误最有效的办法！"

是的，这种办法能够向那个孩子表明，整个班的孩子都不喜欢他。然而大量研究表明，这类惩罚并不能有效地改变孩子的行为，并且这种羞辱和欺负，会对孩子的自尊心与自信心，乃至对孩子的心理健康和自我看法，产生长期的消极影响。

获得良好的教育，受到别人带尊重性的对待，是我们现代生活中每一个人都具备的基本人权。贫穷和留守儿童经常缺乏最为基本的照料，例如食物，营养，以及他人的情感安慰。他们常常无法得到基本，而必要的智力发展刺激。遗憾的是，我们社会为这些孩子所作的呼吁，通常声音微弱而偶然。我们社会给他们的关注和实质性的帮助太少太偏。

如果我们的社会不去积极地满足这些孩子的需要，我们在这些孩子成年之后将会吞下苦果。他们成长起来很可能会有反社会情绪，会有比较多的困难与人交往。他们没有知识好能力来适应各种不同的、21 世纪性质的工作及其要求。美国的例子可以证明。我在波士顿，芝加哥的少数族裔及贫穷地区工作了 20 多年，亲身经历告诉我：幼儿阶段得不到正常的身心照料，智力发展的儿童，在成人之后更有可能成为无工作，无家，无朋友的流浪者，更有可能成为社会救济者，更有可能贩毒，犯罪。前车之鉴，后须记取。

中国梦不应该只是精英们才能做。中国梦也不应该只是到了成人阶段才能开始做。中国梦是每一个孩子，包括贫穷，边远地区的孩子都可以很早就能开始做的梦。换句话说，中国梦的实现，应该是每一个人都能实现从其童年就开始做的那样一种梦。这里，特别重要的就是不能忘记，有相当大一批中国孩子，他们目前拥有的最少，需要的最多。任何人，无论身处什么地位，都应该时刻把这些孩子的迫切需要放在心头。

关注教师职业培训

众所周知，教师的学养是决定幼儿教育质量的根本性因素。然而许多中国学前教师的职业修养，目前仍嫌不足。一方面，绝大多数幼儿教师的教育水平有限。在边远乡镇农村，受过幼儿师范专业训练的老师寥寥无几。另一方面，职前教育，无论是大学本科的幼儿教育专业还是幼儿师范，都是有限，短期的。职后或在职教育才是长期，不断的。因此，在岗培训是教师质量，也是幼儿教育质量提高的必要和主要手段。

近年我与联合国儿童基金会的专家合作，参与了中国教育部教师工作司，学前教育司，以及华东师大关于学前教师职业培训的项目活动。在这个过程中，我走访了中国不少城市和社区，了解了国内幼儿教师培训中的挑战，看到了目前在这方面还存在许多有待解决的认识与实践性问题。

从培训时间来看，幼儿职业培训不够经常，密度很低。每一次的专业发展培训时间过短。职业培训后，很少有必要继续支持。从受培训的人员看，通常仅仅限于少数负责的教师或教师带头人。从培训的内容看，往往比较单一，很难适应参与培训的大量教师们的不同需求、五花八门的疑难。从培训的形式看，多以专家讲，老师听，参与性培训水平较低，职业培训的质量参差不齐，效果有限。

我在美国参与制订计划并且组织实施学前教师的职业培训，已经超过20年。我的经验以及大量的研究证明，有效的职业培训涉及下列几个方面：培训框架的正确；培训内容的适当；培训方式的有效，和培训时间的合理。

首先，教师本人的改变提高，是一个动态而多元的过程。这个过程涉及教师自己的信念、所教的知识，以及课堂教学实施。教师的在岗职业培训，如果仅仅关注这三者中之一，而不能同时兼顾另外两个方面，就很难有效地改变教师。

其次，职业培训的内容，如果能够起到最大的作用或影响，那么它一定要与课堂教学实践紧密相连。培训内容，需要专门联系于教师们所教的课程，并且提供充分的工具，或者参考资料。同时需要注意，单一的尺寸，无法适合众人。不同的专业水平，需要不同水平的职业培训经验。与不同的儿童群体相联系的教师，需要不同的职业培训。

就培训方式而言，教师职业培训必须包含师生互动，动手参与，以及全神投入。只有让教师们参与到积极的培训活动中来，面对挑战，用批评性思考解决具体问题，他们才会真正学到东西。

就培训的时间而言，有效的培训必须是系统的，经常的，并且有后继支持，追踪措施。那种一次性的、简单的工作坊，很难对教师改变产生延续性作用。

三 四海一家亲

幼儿教师的培训质量的提高取决于培训者本身的素质,而这方面他们所得到的各种支持也十分缺乏,例如,国内没有专门培训培训者的机构,培训者本身的受训经常不够,或者不够经常,不够及时。这里,国外的某些经验,值得参考。下面我举一个亲身经历的案例,来说明培训者需要什么样的支持,以便其有效地为教师服务。

我目前参与美国教育部支持的一个旨在提高美国儿童教育质量的项目,其中包括教师职业培训。为了保证我们培训者能够向教师们提供高质量的职业培训,美国教育部首先向我们这些培训者们提供了大量的支持,资源,及训练。

例如,我们需要一年两次到华盛顿受训,学习自身领域新近的发展与趋势,了解联邦的教育新政策,讨论各自的难题及其解决办法,以及分享各自实践中已经证明为有效的方法和有用的信息。此外,每一个项目都有一个指定的联络教育部官员,有一支技术支援的专业队伍,以便为我们提供个别的,有针对性的援助。所有项目成员,都能参与分享一个共同的网站,里面的信息资源可以说应有尽有。

美国教育部并不直接评价我们的工作,但是它制订了十分严格的评定标准。每一个项目都有一个第三评价机构对其工作的有效性进行评价。在我的项目里,我每星期都和我的评价团队要进行一小时的电话会议,相互了解工作进程,讨论评价结果。

与我的中国同事相比,我在执行美国教育部的教师培训项目过程中,得到更多、更直接的来自上面的支持和帮助。这种充分的支持,在很大程度上保证了我的项目的有效性,包括教师教学的变化和学生学业的进步。

大量研究表明,决定学生学什么的关键是他们的老师知道什么。教师们若想与其学生有效地互动,持续的职业培训必不可少。然而教师职业发展,与早期儿童教育一样,又是一个要求有专业知识的特殊领域。这意味着培训培训者的必要性。这里,我们需要有关的专家。同时,在执行之前,必须有周到的计划。在这方面,中国才刚刚起步。如果我们不能有效解决上面提到的这些重要的困难与挑战,学前教师的职业培训只会始终基础薄弱,不尽如人意;同时将危及国家在此一重要事业上的成败。

很清楚，贯彻职业培训，需要不可动摇的努力，包括来自中央，地方政府，企业事业单位，以及团体基金会等的资金支持。此类投入，会有丰厚的回报。当高水平的教师在我们的教室里影响孩子们的时候，我们的学校将更有可能培养出未来能够实现中国梦的一批批人才。

关注针对家长的教育

父母是孩子最早的老师。儿童幼年与父母一起相处的时间最多。父母的信念、态度、习惯、与价值观，以及与人交往的方式，潜移默化或者直截了当地影响着孩子成长的方式与类型。父母对孩子发展的正面影响，就像阳光与空气之于植物一样，必不可少而助益良多。

中国文化的特点是特别强调学习与教育。然而目前学习教育中经常聚焦的内容，是获得知识与掌握技术性技巧。这类技巧包括，熟悉汉语词汇，能够数数，引用古典诗文，以及演奏传统乐器。许多父母重视这些技巧，因为它们可见可摸，实实在在，能够让人感到对它们的掌握，能够让父母向旁人显要其孩子的聪明才能。

许多中国人羡慕犹太人取得的成就。犹太人很像中国人，也强调学习与教育。然而犹太人不同于中国人的是，他们更注意培养孩子的批判性思考能力，来发展孩子的心灵。对这一点我个人有亲身体会。我的学术导师，是一位德裔犹太人，曾经获得过麦克阿瑟天才奖。他把自己获得的成就，在很大程度上归功于幼年成长时父母经常问的两个问题。

他的父母在他开始上学以后，几乎天天晚上问他："今天你的老师问过你们什么问题？"，"今天你问过你的老师什么问题。" 我在研究生期间的一位犹太人同学，现在已经成为一位杰出的大学教授。她告诉我，质疑与辩论，也是她成长过程中贯穿始终的一部分家庭生活的内容。"我的成长一直伴随着辩论。任何题目，任何假定、事实、理论、断言、或假说，都会成为我家里辩论的题目。" 应该说，这类养育孩子的方式，在中国人中还是不多见的。问题是，在21世纪里，只有能够独立思考的孩子，才会变成能够实现中国梦的创造者。

三　四海一家亲

我多年来养成了一个职业习惯，喜欢观察幼儿与成人间的互动。我在美国的住所，离开芝加哥大学附属实验学校大约步行十来分钟远。于是经常能看到孩子及其护送长辈走在上学或放学的路上。我看到，无论年龄大小，欧裔美国人的孩子，总是自己背着书包。有一次，看到一个身高体壮的父亲走在前边，他的学龄前孩子跟在身后。孩子弯着腰在走，因为他背的书包太重了。他爸爸显然不在乎孩子的背包很重，而指望他自己背着它。

我儿子的一个朋友家里是做医生的，同时也是芝加哥大学医学院的教授。有好几个暑假，这位教授、医生父亲，带上两个儿子，作长途越野跋涉。这两个十几岁的男孩，需要背负非常沉重的背包，跟随父亲沿着美国、加拿大边界的森林、湖泊穿行。三个人携带着全部野外生活的装备，包括一只用来渡河的小艇。他们每天长途行进，晚上在野外露营。我佩服这位父亲。他给了孩子激动人心和十分艰苦的经验，途中充满发现与挑战。在那个时刻，我自叹不如，感到惭愧。

形成对照的是，我看到很多中国父母对孩子的教育缺乏让他们艰苦锻炼的部分。过去4年，我每年都要到华东师大短期工作一个月。同样，我的住所离一所大学附属幼儿园大约有十分钟步行的距离。每天早上，我都看到大量父母或爷爷奶奶送孩子上幼儿园。根据我不严格的统计，大约有70%的家长，替孩子背着书包。在幼儿园里，那里的老师告诉我，园方不得不取消一些大型器械的户外活动，因为家长太担心他们孩子的身体安全。

这些表面上的小事，实际上会导致儿童发展上的重大后果。中国家长的过度保护，削弱了孩子们发展强壮体质、发展自己在面临挑战时锻炼意志的机会。现在，大量中国学生在海外留学。就我个人的观察、经历，以及与大学同事们的交流中了解到的情况看，绝大多数中国学生学习努力而成绩优良。然而另一方面，有许多中国学生都显示出自我中心意识较强，责任感较差，缺少社会交往技巧，不习惯也不善于帮助别人。必须指出，这里列举的性格特征，并不是生而具有的，而是后天教养形成的，是由不适当的儿童养育方式导致的。

中国教育界大力提倡素质教育已经有很多年了。但是效果看起来似乎仍然不尽如人意。素质发展是一个长期过程，其中父母教养孩子的方式与类型，起着决定性的作用。除非家长们提供有益的，合适的支持，家外的早期儿童教养，只能达成至多一半的效果。父母只有本身接受一些关于早期教育的教育，才会变成有效的父母。由此可见，实现关于幼儿教育的中国梦，必须强化对幼儿及其家长两方面的教育和培养。

结束语

幼儿期是人生发展最关键的阶段。这个人生的最早阶段，提供了一个独一无二的教养孩子的良机，能够将孩子身上的潜力加以最佳的调动。各种儿童发展研究反复证明，社会向高质量的早期教育中投资，仅从经济回报看，便能获得大大高于股票与通常经济发展所能带来的回报。例如，最近美国一项长期追踪研究表明，社会向贫穷孩子身上每投下一美元，用于早期教养和发展，就能够在日后回收近两美元的回报。

向早期教育中的这种投资，是长期、长效的投资，要求人们有长远眼光，清晰的政策，充足的基金，官方的支持，以及足够的耐心。它要求有关各方都能充分参与，各尽其责。这个事业，考虑到中国巨大的幅员，和参差不齐的经济发展水平，当然充满挑战。然而，它却能够保证中国梦有一个肯定能够实现的途径。

作为富布赖特儿童教育专家，我曾经访问过许多不同的国家，见识过不同的儿童教育，教养系统。我能够充满信心和自豪感地说，无论是从硬件还是软件来看，不少中国的幼教机构，可以列入世界一流。但是总体来看，这类一流的机构仍然偏少。大量的孩子们目前仍然只能得到平均水平、乃至低于平均水平的早期教养教育。

确保所有的中国儿童都能得到有质量保证的教养，是我的梦想。这一梦想的实现有赖于目前做好三件最基本的事情：第一是特别关注那些贫穷，落后，各方面条件较差的孩子的教养工作。第二是要求具有高水平、达到高标准的幼儿教师的职业培训；第三是要求能够对家长进行必要的教育，以便强化孩子的全面的正常的发展。

三　四海一家亲

我也希望与其他中国人，包括海外华人一起，统统分享这一梦想。实现这个梦想，取决于我们能够提供给祖国的幼小一代以多少支持。如果我们能够容许千百万孩子去构想他们自己的梦想，能去追求他们自己的梦想，充分动员出他们自身的潜力，为他们创造有关光明的前景，我们就离实现整个中华文明的复兴梦想不远了。

1982年在北京第二外国语学院获英语学士学位，1984年在澳大利亚堪培拉高等教育学院获TESOL硕士学位，1991年在美国俄勒冈大学获修辞与传播学（Rhetoric and Communication）博士学位。自1992起在美国迪堡大学（DePaul University）任教并从事研究工作，1998年被评为终身教授，2004年被评为正教授。研究方向包括：东西方修辞学比较，政治话语分析，跨文化沟通，华裔文化认同。专著英文书两本，合编书两本，还在美国传播学学术刊物上和书中发表了20多篇学术论文。她担任过在美国的中国传播学研究学会会长，曾在2005—2008年被聘任为厦门大学新闻传播系讲座教授。

吕行

梦绕东西文明：修辞与传播

我1987年来美国攻读修辞与传播学博士学位，在校所读的书籍和学术文章都是西方的修辞说辩历史和实践。这门专业给我打开了一扇知识的大门。我对古希腊和古罗马的说辩理论着迷，被西方的雄辩，逻辑，和丰富悠久的修辞历史与实践震撼。我还被柏拉图，亚里士多德的修辞理论吸引，对自古希腊以来在修辞方面著书的西方学者无比佩服。我当时认为"苏格拉底的对话"是探讨和发现真理的最好渠道。亚里士多德的三个说服诉求（伦理诉求，情感诉求，逻辑诉求）是说辩学的最大亮点。西方政客，律师，和社区领袖们的精彩演说是无与伦比的。2013年我去罗马时，特意在西塞罗当年演讲的讲坛前徘徊良久，想象着两千多年前他在这里舌战群儒的情景。因为语言犀利，西塞罗得罪了很多政敌，最后被处死并被割掉舌头。

可是当我读博士学位的第二年时，突然意识到美国修辞学历史的课本里没有中国修辞和说辩的历史。虽然也有少数西方学者研究中国古代修辞实践，但这些零散的研究没有受到重视。不但如此，有些学者还对东方修辞历史和理论抱有偏见。有人竟直截了当地声称中国根本就没有修辞历史和实践，修辞的研究是西方的专利。有的学者则认为东方即使有修辞传统也是不系统，不完整，没有逻辑，没有理论支撑的。由此他们得出结论：东西方的修辞学没有可比性。

　　我被这些对东方文化的贬低话语和西方文化至上的傲慢刺痛了。我开始问自己"难道中国就真的没有修辞历史、理论与实践吗？"我不相信拥有五千年文化传统的中国没有修辞学历史。我开始考虑去考证和研究中国古代修辞学，从而改变西方这种对中国文化的偏见和误识。法国学者福柯认为历史的鉴定和文化的影响力是由话语权决定的。由此看来，当一个民族对文明的某一方面贡献被否定和淹没了，并由所谓的学术权威认同，这个民族在世界的地位就降低了，甚至销声匿迹了。这也就是为什么西方文明总居于霸权地位的原因之一。他们掌握话语权，可以任意评价非西方文化。作为华夏子孙，我觉得我有义务来纠正西方学者对中国修辞传统的偏见；有责任向他们传授华夏灿烂多彩的说辩理论和实践。我要挑战西方对中国的认识；我要在海外传递华夏文明的香火。现在想起来，这就是我的中国梦！

　　一位社会心理学家曾经说过"对一个社会和它的主要价值观的了解是可以通过研究它是怎样制造梦想而得到的"（Herbert Kelman）。梦想不是现实，但是只有通过梦想，才能达到现实。习近平主席提出的中国梦有两个要点。第一是目的；第二是途径。目的是国家富强，民族振兴，人民幸福。途径是走中国道路，弘扬中国精神，凝聚中国力量。中国自改革开放 30 年以来经济上取得了世人瞩目，令人惊叹的显著成就。毛泽东时代站起来的中国人在后毛泽东时代富裕了起来。但是由于多年来的"东方主义"和"冷战"思维的影响，这个世界，尤其是西方世界对中国的认识还有很多误区，甚至无知。我刚来美国时发现个别美国教授居然认为所有从中国大陆来的亚洲学生都是共产党员，一直有提防心理。个别美国同学以为中国男人还梳着清朝时的辫子。还有的同学如果丢了东西找不到就说，"一定是丢在中国了。"意思是中国充满了神秘，东西丢在那种地方是绝对找不回来的。看到听到这些现象后，我立志要研究中国的修辞传统并把它介绍给西方。为弘扬中国精神，为民族复兴尽微薄之力。

　　我是"文革"当中长大的。在中小学没有学过中国的古典作品，没有经过古文训练。我所在的美国大学的图书馆里没有中文原版的学术读物。当时国内正在热播《西游记》电视连续剧，我给我女儿买了一套录像带和她一起看，帮助她学习中文。剧中的插曲歌词"敢问路在何方，路在脚下。"激励了我。习主席在他的许多讲话了曾引用过《尚书》里的一句话"功崇惟志，业广惟勤。"这句话表达了我当时的决心。在读博士学位的第三年我确定了我的论文题目为"中国先秦辩学思想研究与古希腊辩学思想的比较。"我回国买了一大箱子中国古典书籍。我找老师补习古汉语。我开始认真阅读《尚书》，《诗经》，《论语》，《孟子》，《老子》，《庄子》，《墨子》，《韩非子》，《史记》，《国语》，《左传》，《战国策》等古典原文书籍。通过阅读，我发现先秦哲人学者的修辞理论丰富有内涵，孔子与孟子的伦理思想可与柏拉图的伦理学相提并论；名家的认知观点与古希腊的智者观点相似；墨家的逻辑公式与亚里士多德的逻辑系统雷同。辩士们的观点和游说活动生动多彩，也与古希腊的智者们大同小异。双方都非常重视说辩者的道德人格，都对象征符号在心理说服和认识世界的作用上有精辟的观察和论述；都强调了理性和情感在说服他人的过程中所起到的巨大作用。但道家的"无为"和"不争"的理念与古希腊强调争辩和取胜的目的却截然不同。我被中华民族文化的深厚底蕴震撼并为此而骄傲。我给自己找到一个新的研究题目：中西方修辞学与名辩学比较。

　　通过阅读和认真做笔记，我发现中华文明的修辞理论溶解和分散在中国的哲学，伦理学，文学和逻辑学之中。我需要把它的精髓提炼整理出来并进行分析和研究它的历史与现实意义。以春秋战国时期为历史背景，我认真地研究了名家，儒家，道家，墨家，和法家的修辞理论和名辩思想。于1991年夏天写完了论文并顺利通过答辩，取得博士学位。后来我又用了7年时间改写补充完善内容，终于在1998年完成书稿由南卡大学出版社出版。书名为《中国公元前3—5世纪古典修辞与古希腊古典修辞的比较》。因为此书填补了西方对中国修辞学研究的空白，挑战了权威，次年这本书获得了修辞与传播界的优秀图书奖。现在这本书被世界许多修辞学界的同仁们认可和引用，还

三 四海一家亲

被美国一些大学采用为中国语言,修辞与文化方面的教材。我本人也为能够传播中华文化而骄傲。

我在海外学习工作生活了近30年。我深深地体会到祖国的强大对海外华人的深刻意义。这个意义不仅是物质生活方面的提高,还有对中国人和中华文明的尊重,摆脱西方人对中国"东亚病夫"和"疯狂共产"的认识。这就得让西方人了解我们丰富灿烂的文化和承认中华文明对世界文明的贡献。上个世纪的著名学者如辜鸿铭、谭云山、林语堂等都在向西方介绍中国文化方面做出了杰出的贡献。在他的《中国人的精神》一书中,辜鸿铭先生向西方人介绍了中国人的三大精神:深沉,博大,纯朴。他还最早把《论语》,《中庸》,《大学》翻译成英文。谭云山先生旅居印度心向祖国,用毕生精力向世界介绍了中国的宗教,文学,语言和文化。林语堂先生向世人展示了中国人的幽默和生活艺术。他们是我的楷模。弘扬中国精神,传播中华文化是我最大的心愿。具体说就是 用西方能够接受的语言传递东方的文明,智慧,学识和经验。促进中西方的沟通和了解,减少偏见,误解和刻板印象。

我已经在美国芝加哥的迪堡大学从事教学科研22个春秋了。这期间我开设了20多门课程。其中有四门课的内容是与中国文化和亚洲文化有关的。还有一门课是我22年来每年都教的课。题目是"跨文化交流。"我之所以坚持上这门课就是为了达到我上边陈述的心愿和目的。我生长在中国大陆,又接受了些西方教育,有在中美两国多年生活的经历和视野。我有担当文化桥梁的优势和平台(我的课堂)。我可以为中美文化交流,为促进世界和平做些点滴贡献。

美国学生对中国的了解甚少。美国的媒体很少对中国有正面报道。在美国学生的眼里,中国是个专制独裁的国家。老百姓虽然生活好了,但没有言论自由和人权保障。中国官员给他们的印象也是呆板,正统,不会自如表达。他们认为中国人的沟通方式太含蓄;中国人的一些生活方式(比如人情往来,请客送礼,爱管别人的事)更让他们不可理喻。在我的课堂里,我尽量让美国学生认识一个多元化的中国,向他们解释由于特殊历史环境和因素造成的各项国家政策。比如独生子女政策。我向美国学生们解释中国传统文化重视孝悌,多子多福,可是人口膨胀给中国和世界都带来很大的资源短缺和生存危机。这个政策是中国人不得不做出的文化牺牲，而且也是暂时的国策。这样讲学生就理解了。对许多类似的文化差异问题，我都精心准备教材，尽量不用大道理而是用具体事例和数据讲述和解释。

文化习惯的不同反映了价值观的不同。中国文化注重亲情，讲究孝道和信义，群族观念强，更情感化一些。美国文化注重个人自由，个人选择。人与人之间的关系建立在法律和契约上，更理性化一些。中美两种文化有许多不同，但可以互相包容，互相补充，互相学习。这在当今国际化的大背景下尤为重要。

作为一名修辞学教授，我现在的中国梦是希望能够用我的专长帮助我们的政府官员用一种更自然、更亲和、更直接、更有说服力的方式在公共场合下与受众交流。中国的官方语言很大程度上受前苏联政治语言的影响，在句子形式和语言修辞方面过于冗长、枯燥、死板、平庸、抽象、含蓄、重复。经常听到的是官话、套话、空话。这种政治修辞方式对当代中国人和外国人都失去吸引力，影响力和说服力。我经常听到一些党员干部在开会时发送短信或传递笑话，这种现象很说明问题。在我们华夏文明的宝库里，有着丰富的语言表达形式和修辞方法。春秋战国时期，诸子百家著书立传，游说各国，用高超的智慧的口才，展示了中国语言的魅力和魔力。中国历史上记载了无数能言善辩的人物和故事。在中国的近代史上，梁启超，孙中三，毛泽东都是赫赫有名的演说家。他们通过公共演讲，阐述革命理论，动员参与意识，改变人们的思想，最终推动了中国历史的进步。

20世纪的伟人之一，中华人民共和国的缔造者毛泽东主席就是政治修辞的大师。在他的演讲和文章里，他用巧妙丰富的语言表达形式，睿智的修辞手段，比如叙事，比喻，格言，引经据典来传播他的治国理念和做人标准。他用简单朴素的语言说服了中国老百姓和他的战友们走社会主义道路，坚持独立自主，赢得了中外人民的拥护和崇敬。毛泽东曾说过打江山不仅要靠枪杆子，还要靠笔杆子。他憎恨"党八股"，称它是"懒婆娘的裹脚，又臭又长。"

最近两年来习近平主席的讲话体现出了其修辞风格。在他的许多讲话里，习主席都使用比喻、引证、叙事的手法阐述对党员的要求和对外政策。"中国梦"的提法就是一个非常好的比喻。比通常的政治口号更具体、更形象、更容易与受众产生共鸣。中国梦的实现需要发扬中国精神，凝聚中国力量，就要挖掘和利用我们的文明宝库。用更生动，形象，具体，幽默的语言展现我们的国家形象，传播中国人的智慧，运用中国的文化符号。

为了实现我的中国梦，我在2005—2008年三年间利用寒暑假的时间到厦门大学给硕士和博士研究生开设了六门修辞沟通学课程，帮助他们建立了言语传播学专业，设立了奖学金，捐赠了书籍，为学生和老师撰写了《言语沟通学概论》的教科书。此外，我还在北京航空航天大学、哈尔滨工业大学英语系和外交协会做过介绍西方修辞学的讲座。我真诚地希望中国的大学里也能培养出既有远见卓识，又有演讲魅力的政治人才。总之，作为海外学者，我衷心地祝愿我们国家富强，民族振兴，人民幸福。中国梦是几代国人的梦，是全世界华人的梦。它激励我们无论是为了一个长远目标还是为了一个小小的愿望都要不断努力、不断改进、不断提高。中华文化底蕴雄厚，是我们取之不尽的文化宝库和心灵深处的精神家园。Max Weber说的好"人类若不是通过一次次地追逐不可能性是不会得到可能性的"。中国自改革开放以来已经创造了经济发展的奇迹，如果我们真正发扬中国精神，凝聚中国力量，中国梦就一定能实现。

四海一家、天涯比邻：海外华人与中国梦
Four seas to One Family: Overseas Chinese and Chinese dream

张四齐

祖籍湖北省通城县，国籍中华人民共和国，北京大学博士。2001年起，先后在中国现代国际关系研究院、北京大学从事南亚地区，特别是印度问题的研究。2008年起移居日本，开始关注日本社会和中日关系，并致力于推动中日两国人民间的友好往来和在日华人间的互助合作。2010年6月，在日本科学城创立筑波竹园友好互助会。

月亮船，带着希望和梦想

> 白发书生神州泪
>
> 尽凄凉
>
> 不向牛山滴
>
> ——刘克庄《贺新郎·九日》

  日本民族很单一。这个单一的民族用制度、语言、文化、社会组织等扎起一道道篱笆，把本国人围在里头，把外国人挡在外面。外国人，无论是欧美人还是亚洲人，到这里后，都会感觉到自己是局外人，很难融入这个社会。而对我们中国人而言，虽然也有"同文同种"这一说，但受两国间遗留的历史问题和当前高度紧张的政治关系的影响，这种此处是他乡的疏离感、漂泊感更明显，希望与自己同胞加强交流和往来的动机更强烈。

  科学城筑波集中了日本近60%左右的科研机构，这里的中国青年科研工作者也较集中，人数近两千。他们有的在日本取得学位，情况较熟，生活方面比较得心应手；更多的是从国内或别国取得博士学位来这里做博士后，只懂英语不懂日语，又逢结婚生子的年龄，上有老下有小地带着，租房、签证、

三 四海一家亲

医疗、保险、教育等必须处理的问题更多也更复杂。

2010年6月，以华人居住较集中的筑波竹园510栋为中心，部分中国人发起成立了筑波竹园友好互助会（以下简称"互助会"），建立了自己的网站和邮件群。互助会的成员包括在筑波的科研工作者及其家属，其总数难以准确统计，但可知的邮件群中有近160人——这160人多数都有3人以上的家庭，他们也非常积极地参加互助会组织的各种活动。

互助会自成立至今一直都较活跃：每逢中国传统节日和国家重大节假日都会组织形式不同、规模不一的聚会活动；日本的节假日会也会开展植树、烧烤、采摘等近郊活动和组织滑雪、观光等长途旅行。它还针对不同的群体开展有针对性的活动：对希望回国工作者开展人才供需洽谈会，数十次地接待国内人才招聘团，还和深圳驻日经贸代表所等在日单位进行联谊会；为摄影爱好者举行摄影展和组织摄影沙龙；为初来者开办日语学习班；组织孕产妇、主妇间的生育经验交流会……多种形式和内容的活动旨在加强小区域内华人的人际交往和信息交流，鼓励成员间提供力所能及的帮助，互慰乡情，敦睦友谊，一定程度缓解大家的孤独感和压抑感。

互助会由刘雪峰任会长、张四齐任副会长，日本友人矢部健担任顾问，来自台湾的小MIU贡献了很多有意义的创意，为互助会制作了月亮船[1]，设计了会徽。

从下面这封写给小MIU的信中，可以窥见互助会成立之初的活动点滴，中国人的爱国团结友的精神，更有大陆台湾同胞间亲密无间的友好互助。

亲爱的小MIU：

你好！又是一年春节到。互助会正筹备第五个"春晚"。谁来负责会场设计布置呢？真让人愁。有你在，我们就万事不愁了：因为你总能把场面搞得热热闹闹，而且能搞出品位和档次。你走后，互助会逢年过节

---

[1] 中秋之夜，中国很多地方有燃灯以助月色的习俗。灯的种类有差异：如湖广一带用瓦片叠塔于塔上燃灯；江南一带则有制灯船的习俗……现代很多利用声光电技术制造的供中秋节或平日投放在水上的各种形状和图案的浮漂物也被称为"月亮船"，还有一些像弯月样的船或船模也被称为"月亮船"。

也搞活动，但都不如你搞得那么精彩和轰动。也许这方面的负责人是新手，不像你那么能理解互助会的精神，照顾各个年龄阶段的需求；有时是如我一样的"老人"，又没有你的才气和投入。

说起你这个投入，每每让我感佩不已。记得在2010年的中秋晚会筹备会上，我突发奇想，提议在品尝月饼、唱卡拉OK之外，给孩子们增加个月亮船节目：大人小孩合唱《月亮船》歌，去竹东公园投放月亮船。大家都说"很好、很好"。但月亮船从哪里来呢？我们又犯愁了。你在旁边轻轻地说："可以试着做做看。我以前好像有做过类似的东西。"我像抓住了救命稻草似的，把这事托给了你，还给你派了两个助手。

第一次和你共事，不太知道你的风格。过了两天，没见动静，我悄悄地向你的助手打听下进展情况，她们回答说："小MIU好像不用我们帮忙。"听了这话，我心里直犯嘀咕：你一个人带着孩子，能行吗？我的这么"好"的提议会不会被黄掉？没想到第三天的深夜两三点，你将你亲手制作的、由你老公拍摄的月亮船照片通发给了中秋晚会筹备委员会的全体成员。你不知道我刚见它时的撼动：太美了，太恰当了。一叶扁舟，有些许的寂寞和冷清。不过，船首的那支蜡烛，小而不冷；船尾的那轮紫红秋菊，美而不言。画面很有崔涂所谓的"孤独异乡人"的意境，但昏黄的蜡烛和紫色的菊花一反前者的消极，带来了点点温暖和浪漫。后来，你的这张照片成了互助会主页图片，至今被大家喜爱着。

2010年的中秋节晚会，大家最大的期待食的方面是品尝来自中国内地的月饼，晚上就是参加月亮船节目了。还记得那晚你提着一大袋月亮船和老公孩子一起站上舞台时引起的轰动：响哨和惊呼响彻510一层的集合室。大家这么亢奋，我想，一是因为你们全家打扮得太漂亮了，另外就是因为大家期待已久的月亮船终于要露面了。不过，当你把一只只用粽叶做的月亮船摆出来时，大家都有点失望和怀疑：就这么简单吗？月亮船，月亮船，这是照片中的那只美丽的月亮船吗？它真能下水吗？它能承托起大家的心愿吗？这时，主持人李红芳全家招呼大家有家庭的以家庭为单位，单身的朋友以个人为单位，把自己的蜡烛摆好在船头，把菊花摆在船尾。然后，大家又在主持人的带领下，小心地捧着自己的

三 四海一家亲

月亮船，列队走向竹东公园。

这晚月色并不好，黑云浮动，凉气习习，秋虫在草丛中深深浅浅地吟唱，垂枝樱在路边高高低低地摇摆。一路上，大家都没敢说话，生怕打破这份神圣和美好。小湖是我们经常搞聚会和带孩子们玩水的地方，百米来长，二三十米宽，石头镶岸，湖边悄无人声，湖面微波荡漾。我们站好后，依次点亮手中的月亮船，许下自己的心愿，轻轻地护在胸前，沿着台阶，送到湖里。一只、两只、三只……越来越多的月亮船下水了，湖面顿时亮堂起来，人声开始鼎沸，大家都急忙把自己的月亮船送下水，急切为自己的月亮船加油，热切盼望自己的月亮船冲第一，大人小孩一起大惊小怪。这时，主持人李红芳全家打断大家，领唱起《月亮船》的歌来：

> 月亮船呀月亮船
> 载着妈妈的歌谣
> 飘进了我的摇篮
> 淡淡清辉 荧荧照
> 好像妈妈 望着我 笑眼弯弯
> ……

月亮船啊，在这中秋月圆之夜，请把我们的问候和祝福捎给祖国的家人和朋友，请保佑我们的大人小孩平平安安，请让我们的努力和梦想变成现实。

月亮船点亮了我们压抑已久的热情，《月亮船》歌唱出了我们内心的温情，大家的脸都变得红扑扑的，眼睛也亮晶晶的——这在日本这个严肃社会是少有的激情绽放。大家都希望把月亮船项目作为中秋节的保留项目。我则乘机请你帮助互助会设计会徽，大家都鼓掌赞成。

一个寒冷的冬日下午，互助会在筑波CAPIO为李茂举办摄影展结束后，你向与会者展示了你的会徽设计初稿，从月亮船的灵感开始一直讲到成像的全过程，有抽象概念，更有心路历程，给我很大的冲击：外表柔柔弱弱的你还有这么深的功力；做出这么高难的工作不知有多少灯下的苦思和筹划。会徽，沿袭了月亮船的主色调黄和黑，很对我们炎黄子孙们的胃口，很容易让人想起九曲黄河和它滋润着的肥厚的土地。……

总觉得你无偿付出背后的巨大动力来自台湾。记得有次聊天，我说你总在小君睡后偷时间为互助会做事，好让人佩服，我在这方面真是自叹弗如。你在一阵谦虚后，玩笑地来了句"我是台湾的唯一代表"。不过，实际情况也的确是这样，当时互助会因你的加入，把名字改来又改去，最后改成"筑波竹园友好互助会"。它就这么模糊着，似乎不属于大陆，不属于台湾，也不属于任何别的人，但我们都知道它就是我们大家的，是我们大陆的朋友专为台湾的你而改的。顺便说一句，你走后互助会又有新的台湾朋友加入，是个搞研究的漂亮女生。有次她告诉我说，在互助会里她学会了包饺子。

2011年互助会的"春晚"，你主动挑大梁，工作做得好细致：会场的每个角落你踏勘了又踏勘（写到这里，忍不住要打个小报告：刘雪峰会长过后告诉我说你太挑剔，害得他好几求管理员给你开门看场子），务求装饰得合理到位；筑波的很多店你都和老公一起跑了好多遍，为的是采购到与中国春节类似的材料；晚会的每个环节你都跟相关负责人沟通交流，为的是不要出差错。实在地说，虽然是玩，但我们这些大陆人从你身上学到了很多东西，特别是做事态度认真投入方面，我们以前重视得很不够。

你这么努力，是为自己为台湾"建构形象"吗？的确，你负责的这次春晚是目前为止互助会春晚的最高水平，为你也为台湾赢得了掌声。记得那晚，100多中外人士慕名而至，把二の宫HOUSE一层挤得水泄不通。……一些老外在吃完饺子后围着你问中国艺术的方方面面；而最有趣的是大家都把你设计的会徽剪纸带回家，贴在门窗上，迎春接福。

中国有句话俗话说"没有不散的筵席"。我们这些女人却想天天延续这种热闹和快乐。这不，元宵节，我们又在二の宫HOUSE添酒回灯重开宴，把春晚剩下的装饰品抖出来，整一整重新挂上，化为三用：过元宵节；为回国的朋友开欢送会；还首次搞了亲子会。

平时被埋没在油盐酱醋茶的主妇们，终于有了个放松机会，大家一个个拿起话筒，个个倾心露胆，抒发生平之怀，讲述理想与现实的落差，回忆自己在异文化和语言下的遇到的一些囧事。开始大家都嘻嘻哈哈，但当有个人说到自己和孩子因为没朋友，到处都一片死寂，她们每天不希望太阳升起只

三　四海一家亲

盼着太阳落下时，说者无言，听者有泪，大家惺惺相惜，想着自己初到日本的孤寂，唏嘘不已。而你，是第一个走上去给演讲者递纸巾的人。然后，你接过话筒，讲你初到日本摸不到北的感觉，然后讲在510、在互助会所感受到来自内地同胞方面的温暖。你还说，加入互助会后你改变了对内地人不团结、一盘散沙的印象，发现"新大陆人"很抱团，经常一起交流学术方面和生活中的信息；你在仙台的台湾朋友也与你有同感。你的落落大方和讲故事的能力又把大家折服得五体投地。我提议搞个互助会的亲子会，由你来主持和协调，不定期地搞文期酒会，多方结交诗朋酒侣，大家一起来为自己为朋友减压，共同来为我们单调无味的生活加油加盐，也让孩子们从小生活在友爱的中国大家庭里，学会讲中文，避免形成孤僻自闭等性格缺陷。

2011年3月11日的下午2点半左右，你和小君、我和端端，还有几个中国朋友正在510楼下广场聚会时，日本史上最强的地震突然来袭。天昏地暗中，震天撼地的震波接二连三传来，510和周边的楼群在我们面前猛烈摇晃，门窗砰砰作响，我们一个个被吓得狂叫，谁都没有过这种经历，谁都不知道怎么办，但大家始终站在广场中央，围成一个小圆圈，手拉手、肩抱肩，一刻都不曾分开过。这种抱团取暖让我们很快消除了地震的恐惧。但几天后从福岛飘来的那团核乌云，让我们再度陷入无边的恐怖和浮躁。在匆忙和慌乱中：你飞回了台湾，而大多数的我们则转道日本各地飞回了中国内地。

当我再次回到竹园，在510楼下聚会，带孩子们到我们放月亮船的竹园东公园玩，翻出你设计的互助会会徽准备搞活动时，你已不在我们身边，互助会好多一起玩的朋友也已离开了筑波。"聚散苦匆匆，此恨无穷。今年花胜去年红。可惜明年花更好，知与谁同？"这种感觉每每袭击着我，让我感觉好无奈好无力。你从台北寄来的、自己设计的明信片是不是也传达着和我类似的感情？看着你们一家三口深情守望的背影，看着中间位置鲜明地放置的互助会会徽，看着你对510情感记忆化成的一个个视觉符号……真的忍不住泪下：为互助会失去你这样有才气的朋友，为我们共同经历的岁月，更为分隔两地难得再聚的尴尬。不过，还有网络，我们可以在孩子们睡着后聊聊；还有你为我们设计的月亮船和会徽，那是互助会的诺亚方舟，大家看着都会感到很安全。特别是船中那团小小的火焰，那是你的心火，也是互助会全体成员的心火，温暖着我们孤独的心，点亮着我们前进的路。

……末了，我要再次谢谢你为互助会的无私付出！祝福你们全家新春佳节快快乐乐、幸福满满！

张四齐

2014年1月23日

这个"小MIU"，这个中国人的筑波竹园友好互助会，这个平凡而又不平凡的故事，这个海外华人"斩不断、理还乱"的比海洋更深的炎黄子孙、同胞手足的情谊，这块被海洋惊涛骇浪切断与外界心灵沟通的民族土壤，这一切……使我的心飞到久违的祖国，飞回那未名湖旁"高谈阔论"、"指点江山"的校园。是"中国梦"在拨弄人们心中的吉他吧！我又何尝没有中国梦呢？虽然梦已没有年少时如风般的轻狂，却朴实坚实得如一株落地生根的蒲公英，快乐地开着漂亮的小黄花，满足地看着孩子们在风中轻舞飞扬。

"游子的脚印，血泪斑斑"，自古以来华人离乡背井就有这样的形容。改革开放后，出国留学叫"镀金"，出国工作经商叫"淘金"……但"外面的世界很精彩，外面的世界很无奈"。进入21世纪后特别是在中华民族在加速走向伟大复兴的过程中，中国与外界的交流和往来越来越频繁，人员的流动越来越多。除了短期的旅游和会议外，13亿人的中国将有无数人为实现自己的"中国梦"到世界各地学习、经商、工作、定居。由于祖国经济的发展，我们的腰包鼓起来了，腰杆也挺直了，但地球仍然不是一个"村"，语言、文化、制度等方面的障碍还需要跨越，到一个陌生的环境后还会想念祖国、思念家乡、眷念亲友，而国内的各种组织系统、关系网络都难以覆盖到国外来。"位卑未敢忘忧国"，我愿意继续努力，动员长期在日本定居的华人华侨科学家及其家属参加到互助会来，把它建成一个成功的海外华人华侨互助合作模式，让大家在国外也生活得很好，变四海为我们的家。

我的"中国梦"是中日永远成为"一衣带水"的睦邻；我的"中国梦"是中日两国梦里相通，中国人爱日本，日本人爱中国；我的"中国梦"是中国、日本与世界人民都把全部精力灌输到社会安宁、生态美好上来；我的

三　四海一家亲

"中国梦"是"小我"、"大我"、个人、家庭、社会、国家、全球都能美满，化戾气为祥和；我的"中国梦"是现实就是梦想，梦想就是现实……已经写得太多了！我的母亲、我的孩子，我的祝福！

■■ Four seas to One Family: Overseas Chinese and Chinese dream
■■ 四海一家、天涯比邻：海外华人与中国梦

祖籍上海，1955 至 1999 年在印度任教，1997 年从德里大学副教授岗位退休。是印度中国研究所（Institute of Chinese Studies）的创办人之一及终身研究员。曾翻译过印度文学作品在中文报刊上发表。曾在新加坡《联合早报》以及香港中文报刊上发表过数百篇时事评论。她教出的中文学生中出过很多印度外交官以及印度政府高官。

黄绮淑

中印一家亲　共享富强梦

2014 年 2 月 18 日，习近平主席在北京会见以连战（国民党荣誉主席）为首的台湾友好代表团时道出"两岸一家亲"，在台海两岸产生强大的共鸣。我现在引用他的话来谈我的第一故乡中国和第二故乡印度之间的情谊与未来展望：中印一家亲、共享富强梦。

80 年代我和谭中在出国 30 年后回国访问，人们听说我们长住印度都非常诧异："你们怎么能在印度生活下去的?"对许多中国人来说，印度是一个陌生的、也许还是不友好的国家，像我这样把印度当作"家"的华人令他们费解。

我从 1955 年到印度，一直到 1999 年离开到美国芝加哥定居，在印度生活了 45 年。谭中是我丈夫，谭云山是我公公。谭家是一个完全融入印度社会的家庭，我是这家长媳，尽我孝媳、贤妻、良母的责任，还在德里大学教了 33 年中文，为这个家庭的中印文化融合贡献一点微薄力量。

曾受泰戈尔尊重的谭云山在西孟加拉邦和平乡（Santiniketan）"国际大学"校园里是文化一景，我一到达就受到热烈欢迎注视。泰戈尔的侄女、著名音乐家 Indira devi 女士给了我印度名字"Shubha"（意思是"贤淑"），一时

这"Shubhadi 淑姐"、"Shubhaboudi 淑嫂"、"Shubhama 淑妈"的称呼在校园内叫响了。谭云山的印度挚友钱达（Anil Kumar Chanda）先生，独立前是泰戈尔的秘书及国际大学教授，印度共和国成立后当了副部长，我们住在新德里常常见面。他和夫人把谭中和我当作儿媳。钱达夫人每次见到我就"Shubhama 淑妈"长、"Shubhama 淑妈"短（孟加拉人情味极浓，婆婆叫媳妇也用"ma 妈"字），和我亲切拥抱，这种经历在中国从未有过。我心中热乎乎，思想感情上也把自己当作印度大家庭一员了。

印度需要我的中文学问，需要我在中国成长的感性知识。印度德里大学东亚系将于2014年举行金庆，这是追溯到创系的最初阶段，1964年秋大学在获得美国福特基金会的赞助下决定开展中国研究。建系还没被教育部批下来就成立"中国研究中心"（Centre for Chinese Studies），放在佛学系内，后来得到教育部批准有了系的名义但系主任还没有到位，许多教员还在美国进修，"中心"由文学院院长直接领导。这"中心"实际上只有两个教员和一个中文课节目，两个教员就是谭中和我。

转瞬50年过去，回想起当初我们夫妇两人把中文业余班办起来（起初几年还得到福特基金会从国外短期聘来的访问教员襄助），学生特别多，热闹得很。大学本科的许多学生来学中文，因为印度政府文官考试外国语试卷可以选择中文，中文试卷得分比其他科目容易。许多中文学生后来考上印度外交官或行政官，其中最著名的是梅农（Shivshankar Menon），当过印度驻华大使、外交秘书（等于外交部常务副部长）、国家安全顾问。也有"左倾"学生为了思想意识来学中文。谭中后来当上系主任又兼教历史（随后又转去尼赫鲁大学），我成为专职中文教员唯一的华人。系里开展博士与副博士研究后，研究生在学完中文课程后继续找我解读中文材料，大学研究中国的同事也经常为此找我咨询，我成了一本中文活字典，成为中华文明的讲解员。

大学特别建了文学院新楼给四个系，二楼由中国研究系（当时已经扩展成中日研究系）与语言学系共有，语言系教员学生少，我们占了多半房间。我分到一间相当宽敞的房子当办公室兼教室（我多半教中文高班及研究生，学生少，地方够用）。我每天一到大学、打开房门坐下就没闲空，不是上课就是有人来咨询。我把茶叫到房里，和印度知识精英谈中文也谈中印两国关系，我房里的思想活动促进印度朋友认识、理解与同情中国，从 1971 年开始，一直到 1997 年退休离开为止。

汉字何等巧妙！非拼音、论笔划，既是汉语的视觉音符，又是中国文化的表意形体，印度人初学有点难，学了觉得有意思。我解释"仁"字时告诉学生"仁"从"二"、从"人"，阐明社会是由两个人组成：一个是自己，另一个是别人。我趁机向他们介绍孔孟关于"推己及人"、"己所不欲勿施于人"、"己欲立而立人"、"己欲达而达人"的思想，学生听了对中华文明很有体会。许多时候，他们会举出和中国成语相似的印度成语来，我的中文课变成中印两大文明的交流对话。

中印同为东方文明，重和谐、轻逞强、重集体、轻个人。"atma／我"这个观念在印度吃不开。冯友兰在《中国哲学史》书中总结佛教精神是崇仰"法执／dharmagraha"、压抑"我执／atmagraha"，这是对印度文明的深刻认识。印度教的观念中，"atma／我"绝对从属于"paramatma／神我"，这种认识传到中国就有了"牺牲小我为大我"的文化。中印文化都是反对"我执"的推己及人文化，这一点我在印度的生活中体会特别深。人说印度人"argumentative／好辩论"，他们勇于表达己见，但也认真听取别人，面红耳赤争论后最终握手言和、取得共识。中国有些人貌似谦逊、实际不然。他们不争辩不等于虚心接受别人意见，只是当面不说出来而已。有些中国知识分子在美国学习了一阵更不得了，因为感染上美国人的"唯我独尊"恶习而特别目中无人，他们看不起发展中国家的学者、尤其不能接受没有"洋化"的传统智慧观点。我一碰到这样的人就不禁想起《阿Q正传》中的"假洋鬼子"。

我和谭中与印度朋友结成一个小圈子，不但每周定期聚会讨论中国和中印关系，而且在生活上打成一片。我到印度之前从来没进厨房做过饭，在印度社会应酬却变成中国菜高手。这其实是一种假象，因为我根本没时间研究烹饪，只是到中国饭馆与华侨家中吃了饭以后取了经，自己来点创造而已。我得此虚名也因为印度朋友很"迷信"，以为我是中国家庭主妇必然是中餐名厨，他们平常吃中国饭的机会不多，我也想办法迎合他们的口味。吃过我的中国饭的印度朋友宣传开来，就经常有朋友主动要求到我家来吃饭，当然这是有来有往的，我们经常成为印度朋友家应酬活动的座上客。

三　四海一家亲

谈到印度朋友迷信中国人一定会做饭使我想起一件事。80年代我申请到一笔研究经费独自去中国调查研究，过了一个月回家在晚会上听到大家赞扬谭中会做饭，我心中纳闷：我这位"茶来张手、饭来张口"的外子怎么会变成做饭能手呢？原来他独自在家无聊，常去挚友戴辛格（Giri Deshingar）家摆龙门阵。有一天，戴辛格突然建议由他做饭大家好好吃一顿，谭中当仁不让，戴辛格就打电话请了很多朋友来家，谭中打开戴辛格家厨房的柜子，里面塞满了中国罐头与大包小包香菇、木耳、虾米、干贝等，戴辛格平时舍不得吃或者不知道怎么做，谭中结果做出一顿丰盛的中国饭来。

中国人好面子（甚至打肿脸充胖子）。每次我们请印度朋友吃饭，打扫与装饰屋子的时间比买菜与做饭的时间更多、更累。印度朋友却不这么认真。有两次印度朋友在我家吃完饭后作出反应令。一位新交的朋友问道："你们每天都吃这么多、这么好的菜吗？"我当然不会说"是"，却不好意思说出平常我们只有蔬菜淡饭，请客才这么铺张讲究。另外一位是我们"中国通"小圈子里朋友的丈夫，他说："你请客这么丰盛，我们怎么能请还呢？"

印度人不像中国人那么"内外分明"，朋友间相处，真有点"你的就是我的，我的就是你的"那种气派。我分到德里大学教员宿舍，隔壁住着一位单身英语系同事由他老母照顾。邻居老太太来我家用电话，我热情接待。我有时从大学回来太晚临时发现没盐了，有时来了客人要做印度牛奶茶而没牛奶了，我就去找邻居老太太"借"。她说："借什么！都是一家人，尽管来拿。"她经常对我说："我们只不过隔了一垛墙，把墙推倒我们就是一家人。"人们说习近平谈"两岸一家亲"时很有感情，我想我谈"中印一家亲"感情更深，这五个字不是出于我的脑袋，而是发自我的内心。

我和邻居、学生、同仁以及所有熟识的印度朋友结成相亲相爱的群体，这个群体"亲华"主要因为我"亲印"，如果我不"亲印"或者"反印"就不会形成周围"亲华"群体的。我想国与国之间也是同样道理。中国"不亲印"就莫想印度"亲华"。我开始懂得《老子》说的"既以为人己愈有，既以与人己愈多"。一切都应该从自己开始。中国不应该疏于责己、律己而勤于责怪印度人"不亲华"或者"反华"。我希望当今中国年轻人热情去印度留学、定居，在民间把"中印一家亲"的情谊建设起来。中国带头去把中印两国之间的墙推倒，中印就变成一家人了。

我看到《环球时报》2014年1月17日刊载的吴楚克《邻国民间的对华无知令人震惊》文章说："印度编造中印边境战争史，也是极大地影响印度人民对华正确认识"，这正是我刚才谈到的不从责己开始而一味责怪印度的典型态度。中印之间缺乏"正确认识"并不是印度单方面的现象。我经常关注中国民间对印度的言论，我想中国人民对印度的"正确认识"比印度人民对中国更少。

谭云山、谭中和我都有自己的"中国梦"。我白天生活在外国环境中，晚上进入睡乡常常飞回抚养我成长的祖国，久违数十年的亲朋好友的面孔在"梦"中栩栩如生。这是朴实而真切的"中国梦"，没有渲染色彩的"中国梦"。印度是我"第二故乡"，我在美国又经常在"梦"中飞回印度。我的"中国梦"和"印度梦"紧紧连接，拆不散了。

中印边境1962年一场战争，谭云山心里难过，钱达副部长来家看他，他吐出心中苦痛说："怎么会这样？中印两国是兄弟呀！"钱达素来达观、幽默，他说："那又怎么样？兄弟不也打架吗？"钱达对中国一直很友好，曾经于1956年带领一个庞大的印度友好代表团访华，他从中国回来后，大大赞扬中国，还说周恩来总理比尼赫鲁英明得多。1962战后，早已回国述职的印度驻华大使帕塔萨拉蒂（G. Partasarathi）再没回北京，中国驻印大使潘自力也不得不离开新德里。潘自力离印前，请了钱达副部长到官邸单独晚宴，两人都伤感，那顿饭吃得很沉闷。中印关系好像被一只黑手绑架，谁也奈何不得。

那只黑手至今仍把中印关系绳捆索绑，那就是西方文明"民族国"之间的地缘政治范式的黑手，它的字典中找不到"兄弟"的概念，邻国只能是竞争对手与潜在敌人，这不符合中印两大文明的基本精神，却伤害了这世界上唯一两大"文明国"之间的和睦。当然不能只怪西方，中印两国本身也犯错误。一方面，两国在某些问题上有看法有分歧，另一方面，在分歧的争执上，中印两国传统的推己及人与设身处地的精神不翼而飞。论起理来，中国认为错误全在印度那边，印度认为错误全在中国这边。这样自以为是的心态里出得了睦邻关系吗？！中国怪印度不互谅互让，印度认为中国铁板一块毫不妥协，这样怎么能解决边界纠纷呢？！

三　四海一家亲

对印度来说，中国是世界上最重要的国家、搞好对华关系也最重要，因为中国不但是紧邻，历史上与印度有长期交往，而且未来发展前途无量。尼赫鲁1950年3月17日写给各邦首席部长的信中说："中国是我最钦佩的国家"。当时尼赫鲁的通信都是国家机密，他这话不是外交辞令，而是发自内心。已故印度总统纳拉亚南曾是外交部东亚司副司长、印度驻华大使、谭中教书的尼赫鲁大学的校长，对谭中特别亲热。我们经常去总统府晚宴，其他客人都是大人物或外国使节，我们是唯一自己驾车开进总统住处天井停泊的寒酸学者。不管两国关系热不热，纳拉亚南总是从内心喜欢中国，这点我们熟知。

俗话说："邻居好，无价宝"，希望中国政府在实现"新型大国关系"的同时也实现"新型睦邻关系"。我在印度和上层精英经常接触，深知印度从内心想和中国睦邻友好，他们并不妒忌中国强大（有些人还为中国敢于挑战西方霸权感到骄傲、经常公开喝彩）。但中国是印度的紧邻，1962年那场战争对印度的自尊、自信打击极大。如果说印度在发愤图强时对中国带点竞争与敌对的情调，这是客观形势逼使的。

中国进步比印度快、中国实力比印度强大，而且差距越来越大。中国人专门注视印度政治欠团结、行政效率差，环境脏乱。中国不重视印度就免不了轻视印度、免不了盛气凌人。中国人的通病是"崇洋媚外"，但这"洋"却没有印度的份。人们却看不到：12亿人的印度文化高、智慧高，人才济济，很多印裔在西方世界享有盛誉（他们很多人还极力宣传"中国崛起"），中国人望尘莫及。印度的国际关系也比中国好。

如果中国和印度同享"富强梦"，"中国梦"就会是"印度梦"，"中国梦"和"印度梦"都会甜蜜。如果"中国梦"排斥"印度梦"，中印两大邻国同床异梦，"中国梦"就甜蜜不起来。印度和中国不和睦，西藏就不会稳定，这正是当今的政治写照。

古人有"天涯若比邻"和"千里共婵娟"的诗境，现在我们的思想境界难道退化了吗？！对中国来说，印度不在"天涯"，而是"比邻"，中印更应该共享"富强梦"的"婵娟"明月。中国人躺在床上做"中国梦"也要像李白一样看到"床前明月光"，也要看到"白云千里万里，明月前溪后溪"。中国和印度是地球"第三极"喜马拉雅拥抱着的"前溪后溪"，那也是共享"中印富强梦"的"前床后床"，只应同床共梦，不应同床异梦。中印和睦是人类历史与未来进化的必然规律，当前中印之间的非战非和、爱恨兼存只是"狂云妒佳月，怒飞千里黑"，不会长久的。

"中国梦"的"梦"是由挚爱（爱生活、爱人类）、追求（追求真理、追求光明、追求未来）与共富（神州共富、印度共富、中印共富、世界共富）的金线、银线、丝线织成的灿烂愿景。我作为海外华人对它抱有无限希望。我坚信"中国梦"不会让我失望。

四

专题论坛（一）

四 专题论坛（一）

中国人民大学国际关系学院教授，博士生导师，欧盟研究中心主任，国际事务研究所所长。先后担任天津联合化学有限公司助理工程师、复旦大学美国研究中心教授、中国驻欧盟使团外交官、同济大学特聘教授。出版专著《海殇？——欧洲文明启示录》（中英文版）等6部；译著《大国政治的悲剧》等3部；编著《全球视野下的中欧关系》等3部；主编"中国北约研究丛书"（10卷本）。在12个国家的学术刊物发表学术论文150余篇。

王义桅

化"中国梦"为"世界梦"

探讨"中国梦"牵涉到最容易引起有待厘清的关于中华民族复兴的三大问题：

其一，复兴到何种程度算够？有没有汉唐盛世的哪个年代做一指标呢？最关键的，复兴之后就不发展了吗？要讲清楚中国持续发展是为了人类文明永续发展的逻辑，让世人信服"中国梦"的合理性。

其二，中国为何要复兴？中华民族伟大复兴的前提是中国近代被西方打败了，于是在探寻一条自立、自强、自尊的道路。但是，被西方打败的国家多的是，其中还不乏文明古国，它们就不复兴了吗？要讲清楚只有复兴的中国才能包容西方，而非重复二元对立的悲剧，让世界心悦诚服"中国梦"的合法性。

其三，如何对待他国的复兴？除了近代被西方打败的国家外，西方国家本身要不要复兴呢？如果大家都复兴，地球能承受得了吗？要讲清楚中国复兴是为了帮助他国复兴而回馈世界，让国际社会欣慰"中国梦"的目的性。

Four seas to One Family: Overseas Chinese and Chinese dream
四海一家、天涯比邻：海外华人与中国梦

中国不是现代诞生的国家，而是持续了数千年的历史悠久的文明，今天探讨"中国梦"不能忽视这一点。中国自古有梦：从人与自然关系的天人合一梦，从人与社会关系的天下为公梦，从国与国关系的天下大同梦，不一而足。灵感来自五千年文明，激情来自万里河山。中华民族向来是会做梦、敢做梦、做好梦的民族。

我认为"中国梦"就是解答现时代社会主义运动的"张载命题"：

"为天地立心"就是去挖掘中华文明与中国价值的世界意义，探寻人类共同价值体系。

"为生民立命"就是全面建成小康社会，彰显中国的人权、国权。

"为往圣继绝学"就是实现人类永续发展，各种文明、发展模式相得益彰、美美与共。

"为万世开太平"就是推动建立持久和平、共同繁荣的和谐世界，实现全球化时代的"天下大同"。

我们根据梁启超确定的中国三重身份：中国的中国、亚洲的中国、世界的中国来看，① 中国梦就是实现"传统中国"、"现代中国"、"全球中国"身份的三位一体，也就是对内建设"和谐社会"，对外追求"和平发展"与"和谐世界"理想追求的三位一体。

今天，"中国的中国"指的是具有中国特色的社会主义，"亚洲的中国"讲的是东方文明（东亚文明）。"世界的中国"则更加突出中国作为一个发展中国家和新兴大国的身份。中国的多重身份，折射出中国梦的多重内涵：

1. 社会主义梦：中国的中国。中国梦作为社会主义梦的主要表征是国内追求共同富裕、国际追求公平正义，这与欧洲梦殊途而同归，共同服务于人类的可持续发展事业。

2. 东方文明复兴梦：亚洲的中国。中国梦在复兴中华文明的同时，也宣告了所谓普世价值只是西方的话语霸权，终结了东方从属于西方的历史。

3. 发展中国家的发展梦：世界的中国（Ⅰ）。中国梦的成功实现，必然

---

① 梁启超："中国史叙论"（1901），载《梁启超全集》，北京出版社1999年版第1卷，第11—12页。

鼓励其他发展中国家走符合自身国情的发展道路,破除了西方发展模式、制度与价值为普世发展模式、制度、价值的神话,激励发达资本主义国家内的社会主义信念,鼓舞世界各国走社会主义道路的自信、选择社会主义制度的自信、坚定社会主义理念的自信。

4. 新兴大国(现代化模式)梦:世界的中国(Ⅱ)。中国是最大的新兴国家。中国梦是新兴大国梦的典型体现,必将鼓舞新兴大国群体崛起势头,鼓励中国与其他新兴大国一道,推进国际关系民主化,推动国际秩序朝向更公平、合理和包容的方向发展。

根子在近代西方的入侵。鸦片战争以来,中华民族梦被西方的普世价值梦打断了,切割为国家梦、民族梦:中华之崛起、民族之振兴,成为洋务运动、民主革命、社会改良人士孜孜以求的梦想,概括起来就是民族独立、国家富强、社会现代化三个层面,实现动力就是德先生(民主)、赛先生(科学)。赶超、接轨成为实现中国梦的主要逻辑;中学为体、西学为用,甚至西学为体、中学为用成为实现中国梦的路线之争。然而,那本不是中华民族梦——民族独立、国家富强原本不是个问题,只是被西方打败了的反弹;现代化其实是西方梦。

为何现在才提倡中国梦呢?

经过一百多年和西方的碰撞,现在中国跟西方很多方面第一次处于同一起跑线上,面临的很多问题是一样的或类似的——发展的可持续问题、生态环境问题等。以前是西方着眼于解决"西方的问题",中国着眼于解决"中国的问题"——国家统一、改革任务未完成,现在各国都在改革,处在改革变动的时代。在这一时代背景下,中国梦应运而生,不仅要探讨中华文明的伟大复兴,而且要探讨中华民族如何"为人类做出较大的贡献"。中国的发展不只是解决中国的现代化问题,不只是为其他发展中国家、新兴国家提供借鉴(当然是"桃李不言下自成蹊"),也为西方走出危机提供启示,为解决人类的可持续发展提供中国式答案和另一种选择,为国际社会提供"源于中国而属于世界"的器物、制度、精神各层面的公共产品。这,就是中国梦的文明担当。

中国不做自己的梦,就会做美国梦,做普世价值梦。奥巴马总统 2010 年

Four seas to One Family: Overseas Chinese and Chinese dream
四海一家、天涯比邻：海外华人与中国梦

4月15日在接受澳大利亚电视台采访时说道，如果超过十亿的中国居民也像澳大利亚人、美国人现在这样生活，世界所有人都将陷入十分悲惨的境地，因为那是这个星球所无法承受的。他认为中国领导人会理解这一点。他们会采取新的、更可持续的模式，在追求经济增长的同时，能应对经济发展给环境带来的挑战①。

因此，中国梦的合理性不在于近代西方的入侵，而在于时代的需要，不仅在理论上、而且会在实际上，为人类永续发展之所需，为世界各国之所期，为国际社会之所爱。它不仅是对中华民族五千年文明复兴之梦的超越，更是对世界和平与发展这一潮流的有力回应。一句话，中国梦不仅是自己的，也必定会是世界的。

中国梦的提出，宣告"历史终结"的终结。中国梦的实现过程，也就是世界社会主义运动从历史低谷逐步走向复兴的过程。这是由中国梦的多重意义决定的。

（一）崛起之后：中国梦的时代意义

实现中华民族伟大复兴的中国梦，实现了从中国崛起的他者表述向自我定位的转变。其宗旨，就是让中国百姓从国家崛起中普遍受益，让中国崛起有了精神支柱，让世界明了中国的追求。这，就是中国梦的时代意义。

让中国百姓从国家崛起中普遍受益，就是让中国崛起带来全体中国人的全面幸福感、成就感，而不是以牺牲中国人的健康权、发展权等为代价的崛起。从这个意义上讲，中国梦，也就是中国人的梦，是中国人追求美好生活的梦。

让中国崛起有了精神支柱，就是在器物、制度贡献外，追求与展示中国精神与软实力，增强中国崛起的底气，阐明中华文明复兴对于人类文明发展史的伟大意义。从这个意义上讲，中国梦，也就是中华文明复兴梦。

让世界明了中国的追求，就是从回答崛起过程中"我不是什么"、"我不

---

① Interview with Barack Obama,15 Apr 2010. http://www.news.com.au/national/president - barack - obama - says - prime - minister - kevin - rudd - is - smart - humble/story - e6frfkvr - 1225854306896

做什么"，向崛起之后"我是什么"、"我要什么"转化，关键是实现"中国，让世界更美好"的承诺。中国在追求现"中国梦"的同时，也在推动其他国家的人民实现自己的梦，这些"梦"共同汇聚成"世界梦"，实现"各美其美，美人之美，美美与共，天下大同"（费孝通语）。从这个意义上讲，中国梦，也就是世界梦。这是由中国梦作为社会主义梦的属性决定的，因为社会主义并非民族国家的使命，而是全人类的共同事业。

（二）从特色到普遍：中国梦的世界意义

自鸦片战争以来，中华崛起之梦想集中于国强民富的目标，自强不息是崛起梦的主题词，赶超逻辑是实现崛起梦的主要路径。当今中国梦，以中华民族的伟大复兴为内涵，超越了民与国的层面而提升为文明关怀与人类意识，厚德载物是复兴梦的主题词，文明转型是实现复兴梦的主要路径。

过去，我们强调特色，是马克思主义中国化、坚定走自己道路的自信表现，另一方面也是中国传统文化低调、务实的风格所致，本质上讲，也是基于在中国国情、党情、世情下实现13亿中国人梦想、五千年文明复兴无先例可循、无退路可走的清醒认识。

这样，中国梦的世界意义有三：中国人的梦，丰富了人权的内涵，人的幸福、价值与权利从此打上了中国的鲜明印记而非西方的普世折射；中国发展模式与道路选择，丰富了大国崛起的内涵，鼓励其他国家走符合自身国情的发展道路，现代化、全球化从此打上了中国的鲜明印记而非西方的话语垄断；中国梦也是和平梦、发展梦、合作梦、共赢梦，这就丰富了国际关系内涵，国际体系、国际规范从此打上了中国的鲜明印记而非西方规范的延伸。这是中国梦作为社会主义梦在国际层面的集中体现。

实现中华民族伟大复兴的中国梦，实现了从中国崛起的他者表述向自我定位的转变。其宗旨，就是让中国百姓从国家崛起中普遍受益，让中国崛起有了精神支柱，让世界明了中国的追求。这，就是中国梦的时代意义。

（三）从单向接轨到双向建构：中国梦的历史意义

中国崛起，是近代大国崛起进程中唯一非宗教国家的崛起，不以西化为目标，且是非基督教国家的崛起；中国的崛起，是唯一未被西方殖民的文明国家崛起；中国的崛起，是唯一既要复兴古老文明，又复兴西方另类意识形态——社会主义思潮的崛起。种种中国崛起的特殊性决定了中国崛起的复杂性、艰巨性，也预示着中国崛起的历史使命。

实现中华民族伟大复兴的中国梦，实现了从中国崛起的他者表述向自我定位的转变。其宗旨，就是让中国百姓从国家崛起中普遍受益，让中国崛起有了精神支柱，让世界明了中国的追求。这，就是中国梦的时代意义。

中华民族的伟大复兴，不是"复古"——复古解决不了今天中国面临的问题，也不能应对世界挑战；更非"接轨"——西方难言先进，且自顾不暇，一些国家还希望中国创出一条崭新的道路来与中国接轨；而是复兴、包容、创新的三位一体：合理地复兴我们的原生文明——催生中华文明中海洋/工业/全球文明的种子而走向海洋/工业/全球，合法地包容西方文明——通过相互包容，既包容西方价值、同时又为西方价值所包容——而塑造人类共同价值体系；通过引领"海洋时代2.0"、第三次工业革命、全球化2.0而实现人类永续发展，从根本上确立中国作为世界领导型国家的道统。

这样，中国在变，世界也在变。没有离开世界的中国，也没有离开中国的世界。中国不断在适应世界的变化，世界也在不断适应中国的变化。我们因此提出中美致力于建立新型大国关系。

中国梦在吹响中华文明复兴号角的同时，也在开启全新世界梦的时代。

张四齐评论：

粗读了下王教授的文章，总体感觉不错，我赞同他的以下思想："中国梦"的提出实现了中国崛起的他者表述向自我定位的转变，让中国在世界面前更有底气；中国在实现"中国梦"的过程中，与世界的关系将由"单向接轨转变为双向建构"；中国梦就是要创造出一种既有益于自身、也有益于地区和世界的文明,"美美与共"。但有些问题还有待指教。

首先,有关文明转型的问题。王教授提出,"文明转型是实现复兴梦的主要路径"。什么是"文明转型"?如何实现这种转型?王教授并没有提出具体可操作性的建议,他只提到"是复兴、包容、创新的三位一体:合理地复兴我们的原生文明——催生中华文明中海洋/工业/全球文明的种子而走向海洋/工业/全球,合法地包容西方文明——通过相互包容,既包容西方价值、同时又为西方价值所包容——而塑造人类共同价值体系;通过引领'海洋时代2.0'、第三次工业革命、全球化2.0而实现人类永续发展"。这些说法比较漂亮有趣,但进一步推敲很有必要。比如,什么是"复兴我们的原生文明——催生中华文明中海洋/工业/全球文明的种子"?虽然中国拥有近300万公里的领海国土,有3.2万公里的海岸线,但我们的文明本质上是大陆文明,我们怎么改变这一特性而催生出海洋文明?"海洋时代2.0"哪些方面超出了1.0版?海洋文明的扩张主义、重商主义、自由主义、物质享受主义我们能复制得出吗?

中国如何引领第三次科技和产业革命?中国的产学研体制、创新人才准备好了吗?中国有实力把西方科技烂熟于胸而推陈出新吗?西方技术文明涉及环境、生态、道德的悖论我们能克服吗?中华文明要注入什么样的新价值和因素?

还有,"全球化2.0"指的是什么?

如果就搞这些2.0版的话,是不是说就实现了文明转型?

其次,有关接轨和赶超的问题。王教授一再强调实现"中国梦"不是西化,不是接轨。上面提到的这些"海洋/工业/全球"不都是西方现代化走过的路吗?而"海洋时代2.0"、第三次工业革命、全球化2.0,不是在与西方接轨,在西方"海洋时代1.0"、"全球化1.0"的基础上搞2.0版吗?中国要实现民族复兴不是在空中建楼阁,必须在地上埋锅造饭,必须吸收人类文明,也包括西方文明,先进成果。我们曾经落后了,挨打了;这落后不是我们的错,被打的耻辱却烙在我们的心里。我们以何来雪耻?当然不是以暴易暴,中国古老的智慧启示我们:"以暴易暴兮,不知其非矣";也不是简单拒绝,还必须向曾经的敌人学习、模仿、创新从而实现超越。中国上世纪50年代就提出"超英赶美",也许现在还没有过时。从 GDP 总量来讲,英国早就被超过了,但在制度层面,我们还有些方面没有超过,比如医疗制度:英国全民及境内的外国人看病是不要钱的。而且,英国的软实力往往在世界排第一第二。"赶美"也不是那么容易。到目前为止,美国依然处于较大的领先优势。上世纪 80 年代末,日本曾经对美国"说不",但很快,日本陷入 20 年的经济萧条而泄了气。中国不会重复日本的老路,但在可量化的经济指标上,在可见的技术创新层面,如果连美国都没有超越的话,如何引领世界、做"世界领导型国家"?

第三,是复兴东方文明的问题。王教授提到,实现中国梦的过程也是复兴东方文明的过程。面对西方文明,我们不能妄自菲薄,因为西方文明如王教授所言,"难言先进"。但是,我们也不能盲目自大,因为近代史的发展证明了东方文明有落后性。复兴东方文明,是复兴哪些东西?要做要什么程度?我们可以从日本韩国这些实现了崛起的东方文明国家借鉴哪些经验?东方文明的哪些东西可以拿来和西方价值结合,共同"塑造人类共同价值体系"?

第四,不知道王教授是不是把题目中的"世界梦"与文中谈到的"世界的中国Ⅰ"(即"发展中国家的发展梦")与"世界的中国Ⅱ"(即"新兴大国/现代化模式梦")等同起来?如果"是",那就把"世界梦"简单化,如果"不是",那就值得说明:如何把后者扩展到前者的宽度与复杂程度?

总之,王教授的想法很好,但要"化'中国梦'为'世界梦'"的话,这个"化"字很重要,希望在这方面听到更多高见。

谭中评论:

我本想王义桅的文章会从"中国梦"的文明渊源谈起,不想他开门见山,直指"中华民族伟大复兴"的主题,这当然是当今掀起"中国梦"热潮的实质,应该突出。但突出这一主题后他再把"中国梦"纳入"持续了数千年的历史悠久的文明"就有点勉强。我很欣赏他所说的"中华民族向来是会做梦、敢做梦、做好梦的民族",那就要求我们从"梦文化"的角度来探讨今天的"中国梦"课题。

"梦"是生活的一部分,所谓"日有所思,夜有所梦",指的是人的头脑不断与生活实践交响,凡是与现实结合得比较密切的想象就是"思",凡是远离现实的想象就是"梦",这是传统的看法。传统看法又把"理想"和"梦想"区别开来,也是以想象力的实践程度来界定的("梦想"不能或者较难实践)。今天我们突出"中国梦"的课题是进入一种新的思维,不受传统看法的束缚。"中国梦"成为一种思潮就是鼓励人们想象力超越生活实践的限制,使人们想象力登高望远(我们不叫它"好高骛远"),使生活实践精神焕发、发愤图强。

我在本书拙文中谈到印度是"梦文化"的祖国,人类第一个最伟大的梦是佛陀在梦中诞生。中国最早的伟大的梦是汉明帝梦金人。针对现在中国政府与民间大力推动"一带一路"的国际发展,我想告诉读者最早的"丝绸之路"应该是丝绸从"古蜀国"四川经过云南、缅甸从孟加拉湾进入印度,从而古代印度政治家考底利耶(Kautilya)创造了"cinabhumi/丝绸之地/丝国"这个概念,使全世界两千多年都知道"cina/China"。这条四川-云南-缅甸-孟加拉"丝绸之路"大概是两三千年前民间最值钱的国际通道,从而衍生出古印度的"金地/Suvarnabhumi/Golden Land"梦。我是从"cinabhumi/丝绸之地/丝国"概念发展到"金地/Suvarnabhumi/Golden Land"概念来得出这一结论的,也可援引一个旁证。古希腊人不但到印度去买中国丝绸,还把"丝国"的概念带去。古希腊地理学家克罗狄斯·托勒密(Claudius Ptolemy)说从孟加拉到中国有个"金地"(*Aurea Regio*),这一定是传达古印度的文化信息。印度人作"金地/Suvarnabhumi/Golden Land"梦,一直到现代大文豪泰戈尔作《我的金孟加拉》(*Amar Shonar Bangla*)诗(现在是孟加拉国国歌),等于是对"丝绸之路"能使国际经济繁荣的一种理想,可以和中国"一带一路"的口号联系起来,把它的精神内涵提高到世界"命运共同体"的精神境界。这也属于"化中国梦为世界梦"的范畴。

我想趁此机会谈谈毛泽东时代建立起来的"古为今用,洋为中用"的思维框架,我们大家都深受其束缚。这其中有个西方法国大革命创造又为马克思主义继承的推翻"旧世界"(ancien regime)的心结。我们是推翻了"旧世界"以后再喊出"古为今用",这个"今"就是去"古"以后的西方世界，我们是站在"洋"的立场来喊"古为今用"的，这就矛盾了，不真实了。既然"古"是旧的、坏的，怎么样来"古为今用"就成问题了。印度哲学家、比方说泰戈尔、就不接受推翻"旧世界"的观点，认为文明像一条不断进化的长河，就像《汤之盘铭》说的："苟日新、日日新、又日新"。泰戈尔称赞李白的诗比现代诗人作品更"现代"，认为"新"与"旧"不能按照日历来排队。我不知道王义桅的思维是被"古为今用，洋为中用"的框架所束缚还是像泰戈尔那样的文明整体观念？如果是后者的话，那他说的"传统中国"、"现代中国"、"全球中国"身份的三位一体就有点把文明割裂开来了。

王义桅文章谈的"解答现时代社会主义运动的张载命题"很有新意。张载的"为天地立心，为生民立命，为往圣继绝学，为万世开太平"是我几十年的思想灵感。我认为张载的"立心"，立的是"菩提心"（bodhicitta），是中印合璧；张载"开太平"的"平"是佛教提倡的"平等"（upeksa），又是中印合璧。这样看来，张载说的"往圣"是包括孔孟和佛陀的，王义桅把"为往圣继绝学"诠释为"实现人类永续发展，各种文明、发展模式相得益彰、美美与共"，我认为是恰当的。但是他说"'为天地立心'就是去挖掘中华文明与中国价值的世界意义，探寻人类共同价值体系"，可能与张载的原意有点出入。张载的意思是：文明离不开一颗"菩提心"（孔孟的"仁爱"加佛教的"慈悲"），这和泰戈尔一直强调的东方文明提倡"Love"（爱心），西方文明提倡"Power"（强力）的命题有关。如果我们今天的"中国梦"是"解答现时代社会主义运动的张载命题"，那就应该特别注意发扬东方文明对"Love"（爱心）的推广，摒弃西方文明对"Power"（强力）的追求。说得更具体一点，现在很多人的"中国梦"中"逞强"的成分太多，这就使得中国在全世界、特别邻国之间、受人"敬畏"，而不是"敬爱"。我的意思是请王义桅呼吁一下，我们做"中国梦"要"为天地立心"，要使"仁爱"心和"慈悲"心在全世界推广，中国首先以身作则，这样来"解答现时代社会主义运动的张载命题"。

再回过头来谈"古为今用，洋为中用"，两千多年中华文明做的是"天下大同"梦（这一点王义桅也提到），不是什么"富强梦"。这"富强梦"可以称之为"洋梦"(或者说是受"洋人"压迫而引起的"中国梦")。今天我们做"富强梦"那就不完全是"古为今用,洋为中用",而有很大的"去古顺今"与"离中从洋"的成分。我并不是说这样做是不应该的,但从理论上来说是把中华文明数千年的智慧矮化到西洋文明的低度。

百余年前中国仁人志士提出"振兴中华"的口号是因为中国在世界上一蹶不振,当时要达到"振兴"目的颇不容易,因此也是"梦想",这不等于"中国梦"只是要"振兴中华"而已。这"振兴中华"和"富强梦"一样是针对当时中国不景气的情况提出的,从今天来看就不是怎么样的"梦想"了。当然,由于"振兴中华"是响亮的口号、富有爱国激情,百年来号召力不减。但我们今天讨论"振兴中华"就失去具体的参数。王义桅提出中华民族复兴要"复兴到何种程度算够?有没有汉唐盛世的哪个年代做一指标呢"的问题似乎想把抽象具体化,反而不切实际了。今天我们做"中国梦",不是乘飞机或太空飞船去到哪个世外桃源,而是使中国发展达到某种物质上与精神上的高度。我们现在还没有达到,但希望将来有一天世界人民和中国人民一样,谈起"中国梦"来都津津乐道,憧憬着一种胜景,不是"谈虎色变"而是"谈梦色颐",那样的话,就是真正化"中国梦"为"世界梦"了。

上世纪50年代初期我在中国,很欣赏一个国际发展理论:第一次世界大战打出一个社会主义的苏联,第二次世界大战打出一个社会主义的中国,如果第三次世界大战爆发,全世界都会变成社会主义。后来中苏交恶,这一理论的热忱小事。我们可以把二战后的"冷战"视为第三次世界大战(欧美很多学者都是如此看法),苏联与"共产主义集团"从地球上消失,这个理论的逻辑寿终正寝。所幸的是:"社会主义的中国"经过剧烈震荡考验变成全球一枝独秀,为这一理论挽回一点说服力。今年中国与其他国家热烈庆祝"二战"70周年,人们关注日本军国主义复活的问题,日本似乎也有人幻想在将来亚太争夺领导地位的中美冲突中又有机遇,能够充当"四战"的马前小卒。我认为这不是日本所能梦寐以求的。我们要让"热"或"冷"的"四战"胎死腹中,不让日本军国主义复活,主要决定于中国今后崛起。第一,中国必须妥善处理与美国的"新型大国关系",在美国出现下一位"鹰派"总统前把亚太发展旋律写进"和为贵"的谱曲。第二,中国必须振兴以"天下大同"

为基调的数千年"中华文明国",与"唯我独尊"的"民族国"意识划清界限。我看这也是王义桅"化中国梦为世界梦"课题值得我们大谈特谈的重要原因。

马加力评论①:

一个时期以来,中国媒体上乃至不少国际媒体上"话梦"的文章越来越多。本来,人们传统上对"话梦"者往往嗤之以鼻,甚至讽之为痴人说梦。但是中国领导人却化腐朽为神奇,创造性地将"中国梦"定义为中国未来的目标追求,此刻梦想则成为中国人民为之奋斗的理想代称。甚至不少类似的说法也都得到广泛认可,诸如"印度梦"、"巴西梦",等等,更有甚者演化出"世界梦"的说法。

王义桅教授如今又提出来应该化"中国梦"为"世界梦"的命题,笔者认为王教授的想法很有创意,在国际社会对"中国梦"进行不同解读的情况下,尝试用一种新的思维去阐释中国梦的内涵,并用一种新的方法去推动外界对中国梦的理解,应该被看作是一种有益的尝试。

第一个问题,我们首先应该厘清"中国梦"的内涵。只有清楚表达中国梦的具体含义,至少是清楚描绘中国梦的基本轮廓,才能够探讨是否能将其化为"世界梦"的问题。当然,在自然人的活动中,梦往往是潜意识的表达方式,是模糊不清的意象呈现。另外,科学家也告诉我们,梦想是没有边际的,梦境是没有色彩的。但是,在当今中国乃至国际社会的语境中,中国梦应该是相对清醒的思想意识、比较清晰的远景图画和坚定不移的理想信念。

笔者认为,不论国际社会如何解读"中国梦",我们自己必须对梦寐以求的境界即"中国梦"的轮廓进行一番描述。中国梦的基本内核应该是在努力构建公正合理的世界经济和政治秩序的过程当中,将中国建设成为一个具有

---

① 吉林大学历史系毕业,曾为中印交换学者在新德里尼赫鲁大学进修一年,曾在中国现代国际关系研究院担任研究员,为增进中印关系献策。现任中国改革开放论坛战略研究中心常务副主任,高级研究员,著述有4本关于印度的书,并发表论文250余篇。他是中印名人论坛中方成员,中国南亚学会顾问。

清明政治、发达经济、繁荣文化、和谐社会和文明公民的大国，同时成为一个能够对世界和平与繁荣做出较多贡献，为促进各国间的和平共处做出必要贡献的强国。笔者认为，中国梦的基本含义首先是把自己的事情做好，使自己的国家强盛起来，使自己的人民富裕起来，使自己的同胞文明起来。这样，占世界人口五分之一的中国人就是对世界的最大贡献。当然，我们还要尽己所能地为那些发展中国家的人们做出一些贡献，也要坚持国际正义，为建立公平合理的世界政治经济新秩序做出贡献。

第二个问题，我们能否将中国梦化为世界梦。每一个自然人都有自己的个人梦想，每一个国家也都有自己的国家梦想。只要都是从善良和正义的角度做梦，不管梦境如何迥异，基本的内容是相通的，至少是相近的。在这个意义上可以说将中国梦化为世界梦是没有问题的。例如，中国国务委员杨洁篪和外交部长王毅在访问印度时都提出来中国梦与印度梦想通的命题，我十分赞赏这样的提法。但是并不是所有国家的梦想都是相通的，有些甚至还有巨大的矛盾和冲突。这个世界是一个多维的世界，这个世界是一个多样的世界。在这个世界上，并不是每个人都很善良，并不是每一个国家都很正义。因此，要让世界接受中国梦的概念，真正做到环球同此凉热是十分艰难的。例如，当今世界国际政治经济秩序还差强人意，霸权主义和强权政治还大范围地存在，不少国家间的矛盾还大裂度地存在，南北差距和贫困落后的现象仍然大面积地存在，人类的内心纠结还大尺度地存在。所以，在相当长的历史时期中，中国梦很难成为世界梦。

王义桅教授将"张载命题"纳入对"中国梦"的阐释，即"为天地立心、为生民立命、为往事继绝学、为天下开太平"，显示出道义的高企、视野的开阔和胸怀的广大，表明了中国的时代担当和历史责任，大有"一点浩然气，千里快哉风"的气概。但是，张载所论似乎有一种居高临下的感觉，有一种拯救世界和人类的感觉。另外，用这样一种充满豪气的语言能否真正为外界所接受，恐怕是一个问题。当然，我们在表达中国的正当利益和合理诉求时无需唯诺，无需心虚，但是需要在豪气与理性、张扬与隐忍之间寻找理性的平衡，否则就会出现"知我者谓我心忧，不知我者谓我何求"的局面。正如中国近两年提出对邻国实行"亲诚惠容"政策，在很大程度上加深了邻国对中国外交政策的理解，但是有些文章在表达上是否带有一种居高临下的味道，使一些邻国产生疑虑和不快，也是值得考虑的。于右任先生有联云：气平更事久，心旷得春多。我们是否可以从中得到一些启示，使得外界更多地理解，使得自己更好地被理解。如果我们能够更平和地用容易被接受的语言阐述中国的战略目标，能够更谦虚地认识到自身的诸多弱点，能够更理性地处理与有关国家麻烦，将会大大有助于中国形象的建立，大大缩短实现中国梦的距离。

过去 30 多年来，随着中国的快速崛起，中国的综合国力在相对较短的历史时期急剧增强，国家财富迅速膨胀，人民生活明显改善，国际地位不断上升。这种情况确实引起了广大发展中国家的羡慕，但是也引起了不少国家的疑虑。中国对中国梦的阐释恐怕还是要更谦恭一些，这是一个值得研究的问题。中国对邻国以及对其他一些国家确实做了大量工作，也花费了不少精力和资源，收到了明显的效果，但也反映出一些问题。我们如何确实避免重复历史上某些大国崛起过程中的弊端，如何避免国际社会特别是周边邻国对中国崛起的担心，恐怕是我们在自我定位、对外宣传过程中特别需要注意的问题。笔者十分期待王义桅教授在这方面进行更有价值的学术研究并做出更有价值的贡献。

钟伦纳评论：

王义桅教授的中国梦不但联系到世界梦，也不忘个人梦（"全体中国人的幸福感、成就感、健康权、和发展权等"）。把国家兴盛联系到人类活动最大的脉络和最基本的单元，王教授明白宣示出国家至上主义的不足。他要为西方走出危机提供启示的倡言，显示出中国人开始摆脱源自百多年国耻的自卑情结，开始踏实地接受和思考国家运作的客观环境。对此我想在他"个人—国家—全球"这个从最小至最大的人类生活框架上，加上家庭和次层组织这两层梦的需要。

家庭是人类从脱离氏族生活后最坚韧的社会单位，是柏拉图、斯巴达、资本主义、马克思、和文革都打不破的人际生活圈，漂洋过海的华侨往往依靠家庭的经济和精神维系。即使在个人主义膨胀、离婚率高、同性爱者争取平权的社会里，家庭仍是大多数人的最后归宿。可是，家庭的传统生育、教育、经济、和照顾功能在西方工业化以来便不断被其他组织取代，在当代中国，不但子女数目减少，代间年龄、教育、职业、娱乐、和获取资讯方式等种种分歧也渐增。家庭如果解体，人类社会的动荡势必增加。

相对于家庭之一直广受传统力量维系，次层组织在中国素来不受重视，甚或被国家视作威胁，在儒家的修身齐家治国平天下构想中，最大的漏洞便是疏忽了家国之间的次层组织（专业职团、工会、市场机掣、教会、志愿团体等等）。现代世界复杂，国家事务千头万绪、开支庞大，很难适时而充分地照顾到全民所有福利。组织有效的次层群体则可在地方性、专业性、机动性、时间性、延续性等多方面补充政府之短。个人可以透过在次层团体的参与认识家务和国政之间的事物，锻炼集体议决的过程，当然，次层团体也有发育不全和尾大不掉的情况，需要其他各层来帮助及监督，是以中国梦的实现，要兼顾"个人—家庭—次层群体—国家—全球"的健全发展。

王教授希望国家内外皆追求和谐。但既分层，即不能排除各层之间出现利害冲突的可能性：有些个人渴望消费、有些家庭要储蓄、有些次层团体希望多些自主、有些政府在国际竞争之际还须救急……各层之间的理性思行难免出现矛盾，例如目前各国遇上经济不振时，无论当时推行那种主义，祭出的主要板斧都是要刺激国内外的消费，此法跟保存全球资源和家庭储蓄的期望逆向而行。想避免过度生产、降低消费欲望、控制人口、推动环保、为了疏导洪水而须选择决堤地点等等，着着免不了冲突，各层各单位都有权伸张其利益。如何促进理性讨论和讨价还价，令受决策损害者不致情绪化地反对，如何善待冲突，需要更具远见的政治智慧。

西方民主偏向于强调个体权利，策略上惯于先发制人，政客常以短期之利投选民之好，终致国债高筑（如希腊）、地方利害冲突（如泰国和土耳其的城乡之别和西班牙北水南运之争）、地方闹独立（如苏格兰从英国、魁北克从加拿大、比士克和加特隆尼亚从西班牙）。推广孔子原意的"仁"（克己、爱、和责任感，请阅本书拙文，详见拙著《华夏文化辨析》第 2 章），会有助于调协个体和整体的利害冲突。

王教授提出一个极重要的问题:"复兴到何种程度算够?"我建议用"发展"来代替"复兴",因为"复"字隐预"兴"的规模不超越以往最盛的阶段,而且世界梦应包括未曾大盛的国家,还有两点更重要的,一是"全盛时期"可能只属片面的盛(例如军事或农业),笼统的"复兴"提法会把目光导向和局限于该方面,二是"复兴"把眼界扯向以往,今天我们除了承先,还须启后,要立足现世,放眼将来。

世界梦若要顾及所有大小国家,不能以个别大国鹤立鸡群的国际模式作衡量标准,最能持续共荣的发展,不必预设上限,但下面四项原则,应该成为各国尊重的下限标准:

1. 不受其他国家或机构欺负,也尊重别国主权和文化;
2. 不采用违背国际公义的手段来扩展利益;
3. 不滥用不可复用的自然资源;
4. 减少破坏环境的生产和消费。

中国和各国都可以在这些原则之上广结外盟,透过学习及和平竞争,来发展本国持续和新增的优势。

为了从历史中借取"复兴程度"作参照,王教授举出很多中国人都可能举出的指标:"汉唐盛世"。但对汉唐的重视,会有意无意地强调了武功.这两朝的确曾保卫和扩张过国土,也打过多场败仗.打开唐代前后期的地图稍作比较,读者便会惊讶于唐代版图不单面积时涨时缩,形状变迁也大,反映出武力并不稳固.合况无论胜负,人民皆受苦。汉唐内部问题甚多,唐代武将割据,汉代几乎经历过所有朝代的人祸.在经济方面,汉唐皆曾有远胜于外国的工商业,却因过度依赖农业而局限了多元发展。

跟中国当前情况比较,宋代其实可以提供更多启发,在一般人印象中,宋是个最弱的朝代,这错觉来自它表面上的军事被动,没留意到宋也曾数度主动出击,蒙古铁蹄践踏欧亚各国时,不出数月便摧枯拉朽,灭南宋却用上44年(从窝阔台决定攻宋起计)。

尤应指出的是:宋代立国时不像汉唐那么在国际间鹤立鸡群,而且虽然强邻环伺,宋代却仍坚持消除武人干政的策略;在国土难再扩展情况下开发南方;在外来思想冲激下检讨旧思想、重整新思维、发展技艺和经济、树立新的文艺标准、提拔儒士和稳定基层社会,填补了门第和豪门消除后朝野的真空。

魏楚雄评论[①]:

王义桅《化"中国梦"为"世界梦"》的论述,为我们对"中国梦"的讨论开启了一个很好的先端。王文对"中国梦"的描绘,充满了历来先哲"天下大同"的精神,这也是古往今来成千上万中国杰出人士为之奔走呼告、前赴后继地追求的目标。然而,这样对"中国梦"笼统的、大而化之的概括,容易引起许多误读、误解、甚至误用,轻则会把社会主义的"梦"与传统中华帝国的"梦"混为一谈,重则会把化"中国梦"为"世界梦"的说法误解为中国欲一霸天下之美丽话语。所以,我们还应该对"中国梦"作出比较准确细致的定义。

首先,我们必须明确的是:我们这里所讲的梦,当然不是一种完全脱离现实、无法实现、只能在虚幻境界中才能充分享受的白日梦。我们这里所说的梦,应该是一种终究能实现的、阳光灿烂的美丽远境。它虽然遥不可及,若隐若现,但只要我们持之以恒、不断努力,有朝一日我们最终是能抵达这彼岸之梦境的。换言之,我们这里所谈的梦,实际上是远大、美好而且可以变成现实的理想。这种梦之所以美好,因为它不是以损人利己为基础的,是同时有益于个人、群体、社会、民族和世界的。任何只求一己、一家、一方、一团体、一社会、一民族之利益而不顾他人、他家、他方、他团体、他社会和他民族利益的目标,我们都不能称之为"梦"。

其次,梦想是有其时间性和空间性的。有各种时代的梦,有各种层次的梦,有各种类型的梦。如果我们排除时间与空间以及各种范域的界定来谈梦、来寻求一种普天之梦,那是不可能的,那真是白日做梦。比如,在时间层面上,从国家的角度来说,洋务运动的梦跟"五四"时期新文化运

---

① 中国河南大学(1982)及美国圣路易市华盛顿大学(1991)历史硕士,圣路易市华盛顿大学(1996)历史博士,澳门大学历史教授(曾三次担任历史系主任),兼是上海社会科学院历史研究所及犹太研究中心客座教授。著述有英文书8种异己无数学术与报刊文章。

动的梦是南辕北辙；同治中兴的梦跟大跃进的梦也是失之千里。从社会的层次来说，红楼梦时代林妹妹们渴望同心上人终成眷恋的梦与当今剩女们的事业梦是不可同类而语的。晚清北京居民筹划扩建四合院以扩建家族的梦与当今北京青年拼命赚钱以另立家门的梦也是无法比拟的。从个人的层次上来说，40年代兰攷农民期望一日三餐有白面的梦与现时兰考农民羡盼苹果机和摩托车的梦是属于不同生活水准的。当年钱学森急切从美国回归投报新中国的梦与如今海归派融入中国改革浪潮的梦也是尽然不同的。再如，在空间层面上，辛亥革命后北洋政府的梦与南方孙中山的梦也是南辕北辙的。晚清到香港和上海寻找生路的葡属澳门人所怀的移民梦跟晚清下南洋寻求发财之道的广东华侨所怀的移民梦是很不一样的。上世纪60年代上海小市民的"上海人之上海"的梦与北京大爷"中国人之北京"的梦是产自于不同情怀的。即使在同一时间和同一空间，不同的人也会拥有不同的梦。当年同赴延安的爱国青年，有的是满怀壮志报国之梦的，有的却是怀抱共产主义梦想的。同样立志为共产主义奋斗终生的中共第一代领道人，毛泽东发动了"文化大革命"来实现其共产主义梦想，刘少奇却想通过包产到户来实现其共产主义梦想。上世纪60年代上山下乡的知识青年，有的是心怀扎根农村一辈子的雄心壮志和梦想而奔赴农村的，但有的却是誓言一定要重返故乡而挥泪告别父母的。

所以，我赞同钟伦纳的话："以中国梦的实现，要兼顾'个人—家庭—次层群体—国家—全球'的健全发展"，不能以一概全、以一概偏。那么，怎么样的"梦"才能成为最大公约数，为普世之众都能接受呢？我认为，一个真正能为普世都接受的"中国梦"，就一定要具备一条原则，哪怕它是遥不可及的。这个"中国梦"的原则，就是要让每个人或至少大多数人都拥有其做梦的权利和机会、追求其梦的权利和机会、实现其梦的权利和机会。我们绝不能以"中国梦"的口号，剥夺在中国大多数人做梦的权利和机会，或者在"中国梦"的口号下，把国家的梦替代了个人或群体的梦。过去大跃进年代那种令人丧失理性的疯狂的"梦"，过去文革时期那种扼杀大多数人做梦权利的专制的梦，绝对不能重演了。让大多数人拥有做梦的权利和机会之原则，也意味着不允许任何个人或团体做有损于他人或他团体之利益的梦。这一原则,其实也蕴含在历来先哲以及社会主义者追求世界大同的梦想之中。

但是,恰恰在这一点上,是说起来容易做起来难。王文对此就做出自相矛盾的论述。一方面,王文指出,"中国梦"就是让"各种文明、发展模式相得益彰、美美与共。"但另一方面,王文又说,"中国不做自己的梦,就会做美国梦,做普世价值梦。"中国应该"从根本上确立中国作为世界领道型国家的道统。"这样的论述,是否会让人认为中国梦就是要跟美国和西方抗衡的梦?中国梦是否就是要将中国的模式强加于世界、让中国领道世界的梦?如今,中国还没有好好展开对"中国梦"的宣传和阐述,中国的崛起就已经让邻边的几个国家忐忑不安。在美国的纵容支持下,它们已经开始肆意挑战中国实现其和平崛起的梦想了。假如中国一旦公开宣称其力图作为世界领道型国家的梦,这些国家岂非可以获得更多借以挑战中国的口实?

所以,我们一定要对"中国梦"作出很精到无误的具体诠释。描绘一个要让十亿多人都为之雀跃欢呼的梦想,是一项非常艰巨而具有挑战性的工程。但是,也许讨论"中国梦"过程的本身,就是一件非常有意义的事情,因为它可以是一个总结历史、理清是非、敞开群言、调整思路、凝聚共识、重建思想意识的过程。自改革开放以来,中国最缺乏的不是精明的经济政策、出色的市场手段以及卓越的发展战略等等;中国目前最缺乏的,是一种能够凝聚民心、引领民意、聚集民气的中国价值观。所以,"中国梦"的核心层面,应该不是物质层面的,而是精神层面的,它应该是一种指道人类去怎样生活、怎样追求生活和怎样管理人类生活的价值体系。王文中所提到的"复兴"、"国权"、"人权"等,其实都是某种价值观的物化层面。我们更需要关注的,是作为这些物化层面之核心的精神层面。"中国梦"所体现的精神层面,应该能够把个人的价值观、家庭的价值观、社会的价值观以及民族的价值观都融为一体、把它们一致起来,同时它也能融入世界的价值观、兼顾到世界各民族的梦。"中国梦"不仅应该像一座灯塔一样,照亮大多数中国人的心扉、指引他们欢欣鼓舞地朝此梦境前进;同时,它还应该像一座巨大的磁场一样,把世界上绝大多数民众吸引过来,让他们感受到"中国梦"的美好与温暖。

只有这样一个能为中国大多数人和世界大多数人所理解与接受的，才是真正的"中国梦"。

王义桅答复：

拙文"化中国梦为世界梦"能得到众多大家的批评指正，是晚辈的福分。这些批评切中要害，是必须回答好的。我尽己所能，试图答复，未尽事宜，还望海涵。

马加力教授提出，"在当今中国乃至国际社会的语境中，中国梦应该是相对清醒的思想意识、比较清晰的远景图画和坚定不移的理想信念。"的确，思想意识—远景图画—思想信念，就是分析中国梦的三大维度。

思想意识，中国梦超越了"古今中外"的思维定势；远景图画，中国梦是实现"两个一百年"的形象表述；思想信念，中国梦与世界梦相通。

一、中国梦的历史意义

中国梦的提出，实现了三大超越：

其一是超越"古今中外"思维定势。鸦片战争以来，中—西、体—用的思维定势，严重束缚了国民心态；甲午战争后，中华民族更一度走向全盘西化的邪路。文化自信与文化自觉，只有落实到"三个自信"——道路自信、理论自信、制度自信，才真正得以体现。中国梦的提出，就是中国作为国民、民族和国家自信、自觉的最终体现。在今天的中国，仍然纠缠于中国特色－普世价值的二元对立。为超越这"中学为体、西学为用"的思维定势，告别东西方，关注大南北，恢复中国本为世界领导型国家的道统，就是中国梦的应有之义。

其二是超越"百年国耻"。170年来的现代化梦，造成中国"超英赶美"的狭隘与躁动。中国梦的提出，超越了西方梦、美国梦、现代化梦，开始做真正属于中国、也只有中国配做的光荣与梦想。张四齐提出的中国是否重复西方走向海洋的扩张之路等问题，笔者在"中国海洋强国梦不走西方老路"，(《人民日报》海外版"望海楼"2013年1月11日) 已经回答。中国梦不仅不排斥西方，而且主张中欧携手，开创新人文主义 (参见拙著《海殇？——欧洲文明启示录》第九章)。当然，应然与实然总是有差距。张四齐的诘问仍待现实检验,但是认识上的超越是迈出的最关键一步,接下来是如何做到知行合一。

其三是超越了"复兴"。中华民族伟大复兴的中国梦,尽管冠以复兴——所谓复兴,一是强盛,二是威望——其实超越了5000年中华文明,正在实现三大文明转型:从农耕向工业(信息)文明转型,从内陆向海洋文明转型,从区域向全球型文明转型。之所以说转型,是因为"天人合一"、"量入为出"等理念在今天空手套白狼的虚拟时代需要确立新的价值规范;是因为"上善若水"的思维局限于淡水——海水夹杂的血腥味深深烙在西方列强入侵中国的记忆里;是因为"四海一家"的时代已经让位于"四洋一体"的时代;是因为"天下"观需要升级为全球观。当然,文明转型并非否定传统文明特质,而是传统中国、现代中国、全球中国的三位一体。

总之,中国梦的提出及其实现,表明中国真正走出近代,超越国家心态、崛起冲动、复兴情结。中国梦不仅属于中国人,也属于世界人民。真所谓天下无外,中国梦也无外。正如魏楚雄教授所说的,"中国梦"不仅应该像一座灯塔一样,照亮大多数中国人的心扉、指引他们欢欣鼓舞地朝此梦境前进;同时,它还应该像一座巨大的磁场一样,把世界上绝大多数民众吸引过来,让他们感受到"中国梦"的美好与温暖。只有这样一个能为中国大多数人和世界大多数人所理解与接受的,才是真正的"中国梦"。

二、中国梦与"两个一百年"

此梦非彼梦。中国梦并非虚无缥缈,而是有明确的愿景、现实的路径和可靠的条件的,正在靠中国人踏踏实实去实现。还是魏楚雄教授说得好,"我们这里所说的梦,应该是一种终究能实现的、阳光灿烂的美丽远境。"

"两个一百年"目标,即到中国共产党成立100年时(2021年)全面建成小康社会;到新中国成立100年时(2049年),实现中华民族伟大复兴,就是中国梦的现实表述,是国家梦、民族梦、社会梦的有机统一。

要实现"两个一百年"目标,须处理好以下几对辩证关系:

一是整体性——个体性:中国梦属于全体中国人民,也属于每一个中国人。如何处理个体——整体的关系?换言之,如果一些中国人的梦与另一些中国人的梦矛盾,怎么办呢?这就要既注重同等机会,也追求整体效果。

二是同时性——差序性：钟伦纳教授提出："中国梦的实现，要兼顾'个人——家庭——次层群体——国家——全球'的健全发展。"这一点，笔者非常赞同。中国梦的实现进程有先后，是层次性实现共同富裕、共同美好生活。

三是和谐性——特色性：如果所有中国人的梦一样的，则太单调了。梦想本身也是五彩缤纷又各具特色、总体和谐的。中国梦，不仅不扼杀个人的梦，反而通过包容、提炼，是各种梦想的集大成者。

三、化中国梦为世界梦的途径

近代以来"改变自己，影响世界"的逻辑，正在朝向"塑造世界，塑造自己"的逻辑转变；把中国自己的事情办好，就是对国际社会的最大贡献，让位于积极参与全球治理、地区治理过程中实现治理能力与治理体系的现代化。实现中国梦，离不开世界梦。

化中国梦为世界梦的途径关键有三条：

其一，己欲立而立人。中国是发展中国家的佼佼者，中国梦对广大发展中国家产生强大吸引力。中国要实现中国梦，也要帮助其他发展中国家脱贫致富、提升国际地位的共同梦想。为此，中国秉承真、实、亲、诚理念，倡导正确的义利观，着力打造命运共同体，就是化中国梦为发展梦。所谓命运共同体，通俗的说，就是同甘共苦，最终追求共同的归宿和身份。共同利益，只是同甘；共同安全，才是共苦。

其二，己欲达而达人。中国是新兴国家的领头羊，对其他新兴国家产生极大的示范、鼓励。中国梦也是新兴国家的发达梦。发展中国家和新兴国家在中国外交中地位越来越重要，因为随着中国在全球产业链中从低端迈向高端，与发达国家竞争性一面上升，而与发展中国家、新兴国家互补性增强——发展中国家承接中国产业转移的后方市场，新兴国家则承接中端市场，与发展中国家中的新兴大国合作具有推动国际关系民主化、法制化方向发展的战略意义。

其三，己所不欲勿施于人。中国梦是东方文明复兴梦。对周边国家，中国秉承亲、诚、惠、容理念，着力打造责任共同体；对发达国家，秉承互利共赢、相互尊重理念，着力打造利益共同体。中国不会重复国强必霸的历史循环，不会将自己的意志强加于人，正在展示传统文化的忠恕之道，努力开创新兴国家关系，提出亚洲新安全观，倡导和谐地区、和谐世界。亚洲是中国和周边国家的共同家园，各方有责任共同维护好和平繁荣稳定的局面。要做到这一点，关键是实现中国与周边国家的"政策沟通、道路联通、贸易畅通、货币流通和民心相通"这五通。中国与发达国家的竞争性有所上升，但合作性仍有待发掘。中国提出与美国建立新型大国关系，并倡导与欧洲国家共同开发第三方市场，就是避免零和博弈，实现中国梦与美国梦、欧洲梦的共赢。

化中国梦为世界梦有无指标？谭中教授指出，"我们现在还没有达到，但希望将来有一天世界人民和中国人民一样，谈起'中国梦'来都津津乐道，憧憬着一种胜景，不是'谈虎色变'而是'谈梦色颐'，那样的话，就是真正化'中国梦'为'世界梦'了。"

总之，化中国梦为世界梦，既是意愿，也是必然。中国梦与世界各国追求美好生活的梦是相通的，其理念就是——用我的梦托起你的梦。中国梦，让世界更美好。

四

专题论坛（二）

四 专题论坛（二）

美籍华人。美国哥伦比亚大学博士。除在哥大及其他大学任教外，连续于纽约大学执教40余年迄今。为该校政治学系资深终身正教授。香港回归期间，任香港岭南大学访问讲座教授兼政治系主任两年（1997—1999）。著有22种英文书籍及无数篇中英文学术论文。1987年7月底曾有幸蒙邓公小平之邀请，以火车专列由北京载至北戴河，与邓公辟室面谈天下与国家大事近6小时之久，包括共进晚餐。

熊玠

比较"中国梦"与"美国梦"

中国文化史上，庄子的"蝴蝶梦"首先为"梦"添上罗曼蒂克色彩，也使"梦"变得虚无缥缈。"梦"并无标准定义。习近平总书记上任伊始就提出"中国梦"的号召，国际媒体注意到这是中国共产党最高领导人首创先例用"梦"的符号凝聚全国勇往直前的能动力，因此值得我们特别重视与推敲。中国民间习俗有梦必找先生"说梦"。这也是我"解说"中美两国"梦"的意图。

"中国梦"有双重意义：第一，是指国家的梦；第二，是指个人的梦。两种"梦"境均代表一种憧憬（英文称为"vision"）。全世界有史以来曾有四大憧憬，三个外国的，一个中国的。这四大憧憬是：（一）古希腊柏拉图（Plato）的"哲学王胄"（philosopher king）之理想；（二）英国霍布斯（Hobbes）"绝对王权"（人们如要脱离森林法则必须有强大政府作为后盾）的学说；（三）马克思的"无产阶级专政"论；（四）中国礼运大同篇的"天下大同"观念。

"国家梦"与"个人梦"之间的视角差异，可以用一个简单比喻来表明。从中央银行的视角来看物价与从个别消费者视角来看物价迥然不同。消费者都希望物价下跌，越低越好。可是，中央银行要保证全民经济健康发展，就担心物价过分下降会导致通货紧缩，导致全民受损。同样的，"个人梦"难免偏重一己之私利与自由。从国家角度看"中国梦"，则须兼顾全体人民整体利益与宏观社会秩序以及国家机构之权能与实力之健全。俗谚云："风调雨顺、国泰民安"。

大家常听到的"美国梦"，虽然也有国家梦（维持美国霸权）与个人梦之别，但平常多半是指个人梦。譬如，对一般移民美国的人来说，"美国梦"的含义即是个人有充分发展的自由以及成功享受在社会上出人头地的机会；再加上拥有某些物质上的满足，包括自己的住房（甚至豪宅），以及其他物质的享受（甚至酒醉金迷的生活）。最有名美国梦的版本，可以马丁路德·金的"我有一个梦"（I have a dream）为代表。他理直气壮地引述美国宪法保证所有国民都有不可剥夺的权利，申述了自己的希望：即有朝一日美国昔日黑人奴隶的子孙能和白人奴隶主的子孙济济一堂、平起平坐。他希望有那么一天他自己的后辈不再因为皮肤的黝黑色而被白人淘汰，而是以他们内在的素质赢得白人的尊重与一视同仁。马丁路德·金的"我有一个梦"是1963年喊出的，他自己随后不久就被人刺杀，没有看到他那崇高的"美国梦"引发出的巨大影响。45年后（2008）美国居然选出第一位黑人当选总统。这说明马丁路德·金那堪称美国"第一梦"显灵了，这也无形证明了"美国梦"主要是"个人梦"的定律。

习近平总书记的"中国梦"和他自十八大以来的新政有直接关联。这次十八大政治报告，对中国特色的社会主义提出了许多新论述与新观点，皆以振兴中华作为目的，既要坚持以经济建设为中心，又要全面推进政治建设、社会建设、文化建设、生态文明建设以及其他各方面建设。除此之外，习总还加以引申复兴中华盛世的最终任务。习总在参观《复兴之路》展览以后的讲话，透露了他的心声。他语重心长地道出了"中华民族的昨天，正可谓雄关漫道真如铁"，而"近代以后，遭受苦难之深重，付出牺牲之巨大，这在世界历史上都是罕见的，但是中国人民从不屈服"。继而他提醒大家："我们现在比历史的任何时期，都更有能力实现这民族伟大复兴这个目标"。他宣告"实现中华民族的伟大复兴，就是中华民族近代最伟大的中国梦"。

习总的复兴伟业是要经过两个过程。首先，他希望在中华人民共和国成立100周年（即2049）时，把中国建成"富强、民主、文明、和谐的社会"。再由此达到"复兴"中华盛世的阶段。虽然他并没有明确说出复兴到相当于中国以往什么时候的"盛世"。但既然他提起中华民族近世的苦难是在1840鸦片战争以后开始，所以按照他的语气，应该是1840以前的盛世。我个人自命对中华盛世略有研究，我想时间应该是公元713（即唐朝开元盛世之始）延至1820的一千多年。根据英国权威经济历史学家麦迪逊（Angus Maddison）所整理的世界经济历史数据（再配合其他数据之佐证），中国在这一千多年中，曾经是世界上第一大强国。其经济总产量（GDP）一直是比欧洲全部加起来都要大得多。加之，中国在11世纪已有大量生产（mass production）的技术；在13世纪更有机械化生产（mechanized production）的能力。这两项进展在西方只有到18世纪工业革命以后才开始出现的。又根据英国海军历史学家孟希斯（Gavin Menzies），明朝的郑和在1421年（即早于哥伦布71年）已经发现了美洲大陆。所谓中国盛世，正是指这713-1820的一千多年的第一次兴起。

我们讨论"中国梦"与盛世复兴时，一定有人会问是否涉及西方"普世价值"的问题，故必须先对西方的文化根源与中国的文化根源作一简短而有意义的阐释与比较。中西文化有很多不同，我在这儿只谈两点：一、中西方原始祖先的宇宙观，二、中西文化中有关"救赎"的信仰。

第一，我们所谓的西方文化，主要孕育自犹太教与基督教的教义，也反映了他们原始祖先游牧民族的人生观。游牧民族在一个地区的水草资源耗尽时，必须放弃原有居住地（第一个排他）迁至新的绿草地。如果发现那个新的绿草地已有别人占领，就必须将他们驱逐出去（第二个排他）方能谋自己的生存。这样的生活经历，自然而然地形成了一个习惯于"排他"而没有安全感的文化与人生观。反观我们中华文化的原始祖先本是定居性农民。农业社会是"安土重迁"的。因为这些农民生活中经历大自然有节奏地日月更替与四时循环，故对事物的重复、持续与永恒习以为常。再因为他们在土地上生根并且对万物来之不拒的习惯，故显示在文化上的是兼容包涵而不排他之习性。

第二，游牧民族因随时水草资源都可能告罄而被迫迁徙，故游牧民族非常没有安全感；而在寻找与迁徙至另一新绿草原的途中，随时须与别的族群搏斗。而别的族群也可能随时侵犯过来抢夺自己的土地，因而深感人性之邪恶。正巧犹太教与基督教的教会均传扬"原罪"之教条，附和了这人性本恶之说。故在西方性恶之说为一切处世、治理社会、与统治政体方针之大前提。在中世纪以后的主要有关治国理论的名家（包括马基维利、卢梭以及霍布斯等）均认为：第一，人与人之间（由于性恶）之尔虞我诈，个人无法保护自己，故必须借助政府力量以克服之；第二，政府既然也是由人所组成，那么将何以保证这些人（有原罪而免不了邪恶倾向的官员们）不致徇私罔民以至误国？所以既需要法律约束对个人的保障、又需要政府的分权。简而言之，这就是西方民主、法治以及人权（即所谓西方"普世价值"）的肇始点与理论基础。

再看我中华文化。它受儒家性善思想之熏陶，而认为人性原善，而其恶化只不过是受了后天环境（包括愚昧与物资缺乏）之影响。故自古以来中华文化对政府的功能有两项要求：

1. 政府有教化与培育天下子民的责任。是故自汉朝以来国家实施开课取士的科举制度，以达到选择贤能之士用以治国之目的。自此，知识与德育代替了资本钱财作为社会精英升迁之标准与依据。（1949年以后，以党来选拔干部治国，其用意庶几可相比拟。）

2. 中华文化孕育下政府的第二功能，就是参与民生大计，以辅佐生产，俾使全民经济得以发展无误。所谓经济者，经世济用也，政府难免其责。自秦汉以来的政府盐铁酒烟专卖以至清朝开拓工业的官督商办，均为政府参与民生大计之事例。当下中国式的社会主义市场经济，虽是规模比往任何时代均庞大与复杂，然其精神与学理基础，可说是按照古代沿革。

自从2007华尔街金融危机以来，"美国梦"已在很多人心目中起了莫大疑惑。一位英国研究社会病理的教授魏恳荪（Richard Wilkenson）首先在电视上发难，公开宣称"如果美国人还要享受'美国梦'的话，他们应该移居丹麦（或芬兰）。"一时竟引起很多美国政论家的热烈响应。造成他们如此悲观有几点原因：美国近年来贫富不均愈趋严重；譬如美联储的宽松量化政策只照顾了华尔街金融机构所需，而非为选民或政府服务。金融危机 5 年以来美国新增财富 95% 尽归华尔街为首的极少数富人手中。再加人与人之间严重缺乏互信与安全感，人民习惯与政府唱反调也愈见显著。譬如奥巴马政府施舍给穷人（绝大多数是黑人）粮票的经费上升了四倍。可是为了支付这些直线上升的开支，据说政府部门考虑削减一般（包括白人在内）社会保障福利的开支，引起了一般白人对奥巴马的高度不信任。这一切都是丹麦（或其他北欧国家）所没有的毛病。当然，中国在这方面已有警觉。如果能克服贫富不均以及贪腐泛滥的问题，应当不至于沦落到有人同样揶揄地说：凡是要作中国梦的人（像美国人一样），均须搬去丹麦！

我年前曾写过一篇短文，指出美国人之没有安全感表现在个人"富不知足"与国家"强不能安"之病症上。文中亦提供此种病症之文化根源，乃因西方商业文化强调进取竞争以至不择手段，导致贪婪永无止境。其宗教"救赎在外"教条之影响，益发导致对自己毫无自信。中国近年来，虽然亦遭受外来商业文化拜金主义之冲击，几乎一时泛滥成灾，但习总实行新政，首先着手整肃贪腐：既打苍蝇也打老虎。这也是实现中国梦之必要途径。归根结底，无论中外，根治贪婪与霸道之解药无他，须靠中华文化"内圣外王"之教诲。

"内圣"乃指内在精神之修养，以臻内心完善。中华文化相信克服人间无安全感之道（救赎）不在求诸外，而在反躬自问。设若心灵完善不再空虚，则没有必要再靠夺取外来物资财富（或强权）以填补心灵之空虚。"外王"则是力行外在的功业建树，以完善外部世界。按照孔子教导，以个人言，君子不独善其身，而须己立立人。以一个国家而言，则须行王道而远避争夺霸权。美国于苏联崩溃 23 年后之今日，以其超强仅存之地位，富甲天下之财力，犹不能安。美国 6820 亿（美元）的国防开销比美国之后的十大国防预算国加起来的 6520 亿总和还要多，却见中国日渐兴起而忧坐愁城。此无他，只知霸权而不行王道也。

"内圣外王"观念出自庄子，最终成为儒道法三家思想共有的产物。可见它不只是儒家着重的仁人君子之专业，而是芸芸众生俱可奉为内以修身、外以建树的圭臬。社会成员若俱有这种抱负与决心，则何愁世人仅知争夺与无止境扩张以填补其无安全感之需耶。

中国自改革开放以来，30多年持续突飞猛进，已于2011超过日本，成为世界上仅次于美国的第二大经济体。总部设在巴黎的OECD（经济合作与发展组织）不久以前作了一个预测，认为中国不出2017年将赶上美国。美国的"国家情报委员会"（NIC）前年（2012）底的一个报告估计该时间当在2030年。美国的高盛（投资）公司则认为在2027年中国在经济上将会超过美国。同时认为在此以前，中国的消费市场，在2015年也将跃居全球第二。事实上，去年（2013）中国已是全球最大的贸易国。其4.1万亿的贸易额，已超过美国的3.8万亿。

无论根据以上任何一个预估，中国盛世之来临，不是会不会发生，而是何时发生——究竟是早至2017年，还是"晚"到2030年？所以，习近平的复兴中国盛世之"中国梦"的实现，决非梦呓之言，而是指日可待。希望由于习总的呼唤，更多国人对自己国家信心更能大幅增强，俾使这中国盛世复兴早日来临。

综上所言，中国（国家）梦之最终含义乃在顺应21世纪潮流时恢复以往中华盛世之辉煌显要，并为世界树立一个崭新的"内圣外王"国际秩序规范，俾使"内圣外王"作为新一代的"普世价值"。当然，先决条件是中国在国内先要彻底发扬孕育"内圣外王"的中华优良伟大文化，再向国外推广，成为全世界典范。

以上所言加以引申，我们可说"中国梦"绝非霸权梦。由于它的到来世界将为一个完全崭新的文化所笼罩。这个文化将揭橥讲信修睦之教，而"内圣外王"将成为新一代的普世价值让人效法。如果美国文化能采纳"内圣外王"，美国上下均能恢复自我信心，从而使目前"富不知足、强不能安"之痼疾得到根治。

四 专题论坛（二）

凌焕铭，美籍华人。美国麻省理工学院（MIT）博士。自2002年在纽约的新校大学（The New School）任教。她是副教授兼任副院长。她的著述有英文书4本及无数篇英文学术论文。她于2002年出版英文书《后殖民时代国际关系：西方与亚洲之间的征服与愿望》(Postcolonial International Relations: Conquest and Desire between Asia and the West)；于2009年与阿加坦格娄（A. M. Agathangelou）合著《转变世界政治：从帝国到多元世界》(Transforming World Politics: From Empire to Multiple Worlds)；2014年出了《世界政治的道：朝向后威斯特伐利亚世界秩序的发展》(The Dao of World Politics: Towards a Post-Westphalian, Worldist International Relations)与《想象世界政治：时代的寓言》(Imagining World Politics: Sihar & Shenya, A Fable for Our Times)。她正在编的新书除了本书外尚有《印度—中国：把古代辩证法运用到当代世界政治》(India-China: An Ancient Dialectic for Contemporary World Politics)，《印度与中国：对边界与安全的新思维》等。

凌焕铭

鉴别中国梦

——谁的"中国"，谁的"梦"？

30年一瞬而过！那是1985年春，我去台北探亲，作了这样一个梦：

那儿有一座破旧不堪的大家宅，一阵寒风把枯叶吹落在它往昔的豪华大理石地板上。大宅左边的深蓝色水中有一只小船，船上有个6岁左右的儿童弹着钢琴，奏出悦耳的音乐，却看不清究竟是男孩还是女孩。大宅前面右角上有另外一个小孩—肯定是男孩—，年龄较大，可能十来岁，身着白色汗衫、短裤，脚上是塑料拖鞋。他坐在临时搭起的桌子前的凳子上。桌子凳子都是乌木做的，边上有些磨损。小孩手持毛笔写作业，一笔一画地练习正楷。

梦中醒后，我顿时感到："这座大家宅还有希望！"它虽然破旧，但儿童继续弹奏钢琴、练习书法，说明前途光明。很可能，这座旧宅象征了当时我生命中的许多心事。那时我是穷困的研究生，即将结婚。[①] 我和家人为父亲癌症复发而忧心忡忡。[②] 台湾又面临各种挑战。[③] 这一切都像是那座大家宅的对照。可是我觉得不对。那座大家宅正是"中国"——不是国家的"中国，"而是文明与人民的"中华。"况且，梦中的各种形象引起"中华"的纵横画面。那"一阵寒风"与"枯叶"代表北方，身着汗衫、短裤与拖鞋的男孩代表南方，左边的船代表西方，生气勃勃的深蓝色水代表东方。这个梦显示无论身在何方的华人，如果都能发扬悠久文明遗产，"中华"那古老破旧的大家宅是可以振兴的。

令人惊讶的是，我的梦中没有食物。谈到中国文化难免以中国佳肴作代表。中餐烹调方式与美味是有口皆碑的，更不必说它对全球的影响。在中国历史上，"食"又是个政治代号，是人民幸福的象征。能使庶民丰衣足食的政府就能保持"天命。"正如《孟子》所言，"天下之本在国，国之本在家，家之本在身。"[④]

诚然，自从19世纪以来，所有中国领导都得为民生福祉犯愁。最后的清朝被腐败无能困扰。清廷无法抵挡以贸易平等为借口的英帝国侵略，尤其是英国东印度公司强迫中国输入鸦片为商品。正如阿米塔卜·高施（Amitav Ghosh）在他的小说《罂粟海》（*Sea of Poppies*）和《烟河》（*River of Smoke*）中生动描述的：大英帝国企图在印度的旧殖民地生产毒品来崩溃中国以便建立新殖民地。钦差大臣林则徐在虎门销毁237万斤违禁的毒品后，大英借以"国家主权"（sovereignty）的口号向清朝发动战争，宣扬"现代"国际关系最

---

① 一个月后我在美国波士顿结婚。
② 梦后两年父亲病故于台北。
③ 当年国际贸易与投资抛弃台湾，转向大陆。
④ 《孟子·离娄上》。

响亮的原则。以后的发展，熟为人知：中国遭受百年外侮的羞辱，同时发生国内动乱与革命。

正是这段历史，导致习近平的"中国梦。"他的意识形态、①爱国精神②与国家统一，③三合一的"中国梦，"是要建设一个强大的中国。对中国共产党或者绝大多数中国人来说，建立强大的中国是回应历史的必然结果。有了强大的中国才不会再吃19世纪末与20世纪初外国侵略的二遍苦。

大众评论者，闻风而至。他们把"中国梦"看成中国新兴中产阶级的愿景，④或者剖析习近平提出"中国梦"的政治背景。⑤更有人采用解释学方法把"中国梦"解读为政治、社会、文化和知识环境的产物。⑥

我不禁要问：强大的"中华，"一定要按照西方的意识来建立吗？无法否认，中国人可受尽了苦头。从前的中国必须整顿。可是现在的中国，这座大家宅，基础已牢固，难道还要重建帝国主义列强既僵硬又缺乏想象力的建筑吗？为什么我们一定要东施效颦，模仿西方的一切？难道我们没法子来设定自己的"力量"与"国家"吗？为什么一定要走上西方的老路，依靠石化燃料工业化而承继其污染、堵塞、颠沛与异化等恶果？现在人们所料到的"中国梦，"是否已经背离"中国"与"梦"的原意而像过去，又上瘾西方列强的毒品？

新闻标题经常报导："国家调查发现，中国五分之一的农田受到污染，"

---

① 习近平2013年3月17日在第十二届全国人民代表大会第一次会议上的讲话谈到"中国特色社会主义道路"。参见 http://theory.people.com.cn/n/2013/0619/c40531-21891787-2.html，2014年4月23日查阅。

② "爱国主义为核心的民族精神"。（同上）

③ "各族人民大团结，凝聚中国力量"。（同上）

④ 古德曼 David S. G. Goodman："中产阶级的中国：梦想与愿景"（Middle Class China: Dreams and Aspirations），美国《中国政治学刊》（*Journal of Chinese Political Science*）2014年19期，49—67页。

⑤ 汪铮 Zheng Wang："中国梦的概念与背景"（The Chinese Dream: Concept and Context），同上，第1—13页。

⑥ 约瑟夫·玛哈尼 Josef Gregory Mahoney："用解释学诠释中国梦"（Interpreting the Chinese Dream: An Exercise of Political Hermeneutics），同上，第15—34页。

Four seas to One Family: Overseas Chinese and Chinese dream
四海一家、天涯比邻：海外华人与中国梦

"中国的生态环境：经济发展的死刑宣判，"①"调查发现，中国向美国输出污染。"②西方论者，暗指中国有自我陶醉与自我损伤行为的痼疾。哈佛大学历史学家尼尔·弗格森（Niall Ferguson）在2011年的书上有这段话，把鸦片战争的罪恶压缩成文化癖好，类似于"幸运"：

英国人服用麻醉品同样幸运。先是酗酒成习，17世纪染上美洲烟草、阿拉伯咖啡与中国茶，从此咖啡馆兴起——又是饮料室、又是股票市场、又是闲聊处所。中国人则到鸦片烟馆磨蹭，烟枪里却装满了英国东印度公司的毒品。③

文中，弗格森继承西方人对亚洲人的偏见。④黑格尔（Hegel）认为，"东方"人民、社会与国家像女人一样，永远一成不变，需要极阳至刚的西方，从外闯入，才能使他们惊醒。⑤黑格尔认为，中国人无能、落后，没有自我意识："早在欧洲之前，中国人就有很多发明，但不会进一步运用自己的发明，罗盘与印刷术就是例子……还有火药，他们宣称比欧洲人发明得早，却是耶稣会的神父为他们创造出第一尊大炮。"⑥黑格尔显然认为火药的杀伤力高于它的艺术与娱乐价值。他还贬抑亚洲另一古老文明。他认为印度人在"迷梦"

---

① 裴敏欣 Minxin Pei："中国的生态环境：经济发展的死刑宣判"（China's Environment: An Economic Death Sentence），《财富》（Fortune）杂志，2013年1月28日。参见 http://management.fortune.cnn.com/2013/01/28/china-environment-economic-fallout/，2014年4月22日查阅。

② 黄安伟 Edward Wong，"调查发现，中国向美国输出污染"（China Exports Pollution to the US, Study Finds），《纽约时报》（New York Times），20 January 2014年1月20日。参见 http://www.nytimes.com/2014/01/21/world/asia/china-also-exports-pollution-to-western-us-study-finds.html?ref=environment，2014年4月22日查阅。

③ 尼尔·弗格森 Niall Ferguson：《文明：西方与全球对照》（Civilization: The West vs The Rest），2011年，纽约：企鹅 Penguin 出版社，第46页。

④ 关于这一点，请看潘成鑫 Chengxin Pan 著：《全球政治中的知识、欲望与强力：西方对中国崛起的介绍》（Knowledge, Desire and Power in Global Politics: Western Representations of China's Rise）2012年，英国切尔滕汉 Cheltenham：埃德加 Edward Elgar 出版社。

⑤ 黑格尔 G. W. F. Hegel：《历史的哲学》（Philosophy of History），参见 http://plato.stanford.edu/entries/history/#HegHis，2013年1月15日查阅。

⑥ 黑格尔 G. W. F. Hegel：《历史的哲学》（Philosophy of History），参见 http://plato.stanford.edu/entries/history/#HegHis，2013年1月15日查阅。

中流浪。①"从印度人那儿找不到我们称之为历史的真理与诚信—对事物明智地了解与真实地表达…"②在讨论亚洲时,马克思(Marx)一丝不苟地师从黑格尔。他认为印度与中国本身不能现代化,必须靠有害的英国殖民主义与帝国主义迫使他们才能行动起来。③ 同样的,韦伯(Weber)在1915年出版的《中国的宗教:儒教与道教》(*The Religion of China: Confucianism and Taoism*)书中,认为中国之所以与西方不同,在于中国文化缺乏欧洲的新教伦理,因而发展不出资本主义。

以西方观点塑造中国形象已成痼疾。国关学者巴里·布赞(Barry Buzan)说,中国要站到国际舞台就"必须遵循该制度的深层规则。"④当然,他并未说明这些"规则"是西方强加于世界的。从15世纪,哥伦布(Columbus)的"征服号"帆船在"成熟大地"(*abya yala*)⑤登陆—欧洲人随后把这个本地名称改为"新大陆,"掠夺当地居民的领土为西班牙国王费迪南(King Ferdinand)以及丽莎贝拉皇后(Queen Isabella)的殖民属地。6个世纪已过,

---

① 黑格尔 G. W. F. Hegel:《历史的哲学》(*Philosophy of History*),参见 http://plato.stanford.edu/entries/history/#HegHis,2013年1月15日查阅。

② 黑格尔 G. W. F. Hegel:《历史的哲学》(*Philosophy of History*),参见 http://plato.stanford.edu/entries/history/#HegHis,2013年1月15日查阅。

③ 可以参阅马克思写的"帝国主义在印度"(On Imperialism in India)的散文。参见罗伯特·塔克 Robert C. Tucker 编:《马克思与恩格斯读物》(*The Marx-Engels Reader*),第二版,1978年,纽约:诺尔桐 W. W. Norton 出版社,第653—654页;又见托尔 Dona Torr 编:《马克思论中国:一八五三年至一八六〇年纽约每日论坛报文集》(*Marx on China, 1853—1860: Articles from the New York Daily Tribune*),1951年,伦敦:Lawrence & Wishart 出版。参见 http://www.marxists.org/archive/marx/works/1853/china/index.htm,2013年1月17日查阅。

④ 巴里·布赞 Barry Buzan:"中国在国际社会:'和平崛起'可能吗?"(China in International Society: Is 'Peaceful Rise' Possible?),《中国国际政治期刊》(*The Chinese Journal of International Politics*),2010年第3期,第6—7页。

⑤ 按照今天巴拿马的库纳(kuna)语,"*Abya yala*"应该译成"深远美洲"或"我们生活的富饶大地"。参见 约瑟夫·伊斯特曼 Josef Estermann 文章:"以安第斯哲学为质疑异议:对西方大男子主义与种族主义的跨文化批判"(Andean Philosophy as a Questioning Alterity: An Intercultural Criticism of Western Andro - and Ethnocentrism),参见尼廓尔·诺特 Nicole Note 等人编:《世界观与文化:夸文化角度的哲学思考》(*Worldviews and Culture: Philosophical Reflections from an Intercultural Perspective*),2009年,荷兰多德雷赫特 Dordrecht: Springer Science + Business Media BV 出版,第130页,注2。

人们仍然信仰与宣传国际政治中的欧洲极阳至刚精神。请注意高龙江（John Garver）对中国的劝告，他认为只有仿效西方，中国才能取得世界强国的地位：

中国必须出现一个像当年排开俄、法、英干扰而统一德国的俾斯麦（Bismarck），不然就不会有光明前途，不会避免后冷战时代中—印—美三角僵化。①

反对这种政策上、思维上的独霸大有人在。成功范例有1998年的马来西亚与2002年的阿根廷，在面对金融与经济危机时，抵制了西方压力而没有把政体转变为自由主义民主制度。②同样的，从亚洲到非洲、从拉丁美洲到中东，后殖民主义思潮影响了人们对殖民主义与帝国主义的分析与认识。台湾社会理论家陈光兴（Chen Kuan-hsing）认为亚洲需要"去殖民"化与"去冷战"化，③不但政治、经济上如此，思想上也应如此。西方有些学者同意他的观点。例如，国关学者约翰·霍布森（John Hobson）批评国际关系研究在经过三个世纪的争辩后仍然受到"欧洲中心主义"（Eurocentrism）的思维、方法、理论与实践的主宰。④我在自己的研究中用道家的辩证法重新理解国际关系为"西方"的阳与"非西方"的阴，两方相互作用，使世界政治疏远霸权与暴

---

① 高龙江 John W. Garver："中—印—美三角：后冷战时代的战略关系"（The China - India - U.S Triangle: Strategic Relations in the Post - cold War Era），《亚洲研究分析》（*NBR Analysis*）13卷5期，（2002年10月），参见 http://unpan1.un.org/intradoc/groups/public/documents/APCITY/UNPAN015790.pdf，2013年1月15日查阅。

② 凌焕铭 L. H. M. Ling："文化沙文主义与自由主义国际秩序：亚洲金融危机中的'西方与非西方'针锋相对"（Cultural Chauvinism and the Liberal International Order: 'West versus Rest' in Asia's Financial Crisis），见乔杜里 Geeta Chowdhry 与纳雅尔 Sheila Nair 编：《强权、后殖民主义与国际关系：种族、性别及阶级的解读》（*Power, Postcolonialism, and International Relations: Reading Race, Gender, Class*），2002年，伦敦：Routledge出版社，第115—141页。

③ 陈光兴 Kuan-hsing Chen：《以亚洲为研究方法：去帝国主义化展望》（*Asia as Method: Toward Deimperialization*），2010年，美国杜伦 Durham：杜克大学 Duke University 出版社。

④ 约翰·霍布森 John M. Hobson：《世界政治中的欧洲中心论概念：西方国际关系理论，1760—2010》（*The Eurocentric Conception of World Politics: Western International Relations Theory, 1760—2010*），2012年，英国剑桥：剑桥大学出版社。

力，而趋向平衡与接触。①再有，路特雷奇（Routledge）出版社2007年出版了"跨越西方看世界"（Worlding Beyond the West）系列书籍。②罗曼和利特尔菲尔德（Rowman & Littlefield）出版公司2014年也出版了两个书籍系列来"对伸延学术领域到地球南方作出贡献。"终于，国际关系学术界体会到，世界政治是西方与非西方相互组成的。③

正像新当选的国际研究学会主席阿米塔卜·阿查利亚（Amitav Acharya）于2014年3月所宣布的："老爷与仆从的时代已经过去。"阿查利亚在接受国际研究学会主席位置讲演时，举了一个加尔各答19世纪的学院的例子。那个学院的英国教授被人称为"老爷"（*sahib*），把他们的学术地位捧上天；印度教师却被称为"仆从"（*munshee*），表明他们是说本地话的教员，欧洲人的助理。阿查利亚强调，国际关系学术界再也不能这样来反映殖民时代的知识产物了。坐在我后面的一位听众说："国际研究学会，再也不是前辈子所想象的了。"

中国内部也出现新思维。国关学者秦亚青建议用另一方式来认识中国"崛起。"与要求中国遵循权威的规则相反，秦亚青用中国的辩证法来诠释中国参入"国际社会"之中：

社会不是自我封闭与孤独单干的领域，而是复杂社会关系不断发展的进程。规则、权威与机构不是为了统治或限制社会的个体角色的行为，而是为了保证社会成员之间的和谐关系。这种对社会的认识是建筑在源于中国哲学

---

① 凌焕铭 L. H. M. Ling：《世界政治的道：朝向后威斯特伐利亚世界秩序的发展》（*The Dao of World Politics: Towards a Post-Westphalian, Worldist International Relations*），2014年，伦敦：Routledge出版社。

② 参见 http://www.taylorandfrancis.com/books/series/WBW/, 2014年6月13日查阅。

③ 这两个书籍系列，一是"理想国：国际关系与殖民主义问题"（Kilombo: International Relations and Colonial Questions），参见（http://www.rowmaninternational.com/news/intro-kilombo-ir-colonial-questions）；另一是"全球对话"（Global Dialogues），因为刚出笼，尚无网址。

与思想传统的关系思维过程与相辅相成的辩证方法的基础上的。①

秦亚青进一步阐明，中国辩证传统重融会变通，因此不提倡中国或者任何国家称霸。②中国传统辩证法与黑格尔－马克思的辩证法迥异，强调变通与包容，形成"以非察是、以是察非"的正反相通灵活性。他借用黑格尔－马克思逻辑论的"正题"（thesis）、"反题"（antithesis）与"合题"（synthesis）的表达形式得出"合正题相辅相成"（co-thesis complementation）或者"正题间相辅相成"（inter-thesis complementation）的命题。③从这一基点引申，中国是否和平崛起不是单靠中国独自决定的，也不能与是否遵守或适应当今国际社会的原则、规则与做法同言而语。他认为国际社会折射出"关系网络的复杂性，"因而中国崛起的性质必然牵涉到"中国与国际社会、即美国与其他国家的交往与相互响应."④ 总而言之，中国的崛起呈现出一种总形势。是中国与这一总形势相互作用才能决定未来全球政治的议程，那种所谓的一成不变的"国际社会"的"深刻持久的现实"和中国的崛起是对不上号的。

中国社会历史学家汪晖也发挥出新思维。他质疑西方学术、特别是社会科学、强加于其他社会与文化的一些基本理论。他认为"亚洲"（Asia）的标志需要重新认识。汪晖说，亚洲不仅是一个自在的地理与文化概念，更是由外来力量作用而形成的永恒的能动力，亚洲"既是殖民主义的也是反殖民主义的，既保守又革命，既提倡民族主义又提倡国际主义，既发源于欧洲又反过来形成欧洲的形象。"⑤

---

① 秦亚青 Qin Yaqing："作为过程的国际社会:机构、标志与中国和平崛起"（International Society as a Process: Institutions, Identities, and China's Peaceful Rise），《中国国际政治期刊》，2010 年第 3 期，第 138 页。*The Chinese Journal of International Politics* (3) 2010:138. For more on his views, see a recent interview, 《网上谈理论》（*Theory Talks online forum*）2011 年 11 月 30 日有他的观点的更详细报道。参见 http://www.theory-talks.org/2011/11/theory-talk-45.html,2012 年 2 月 1 日查阅。

② 同上书，第 139 页。

③ 同上书，第 139 页。

④ 同上书，第 138、130—131 页。

⑤ 汪晖 Wang Hui:《亚洲形象的政治》（*The Politics of Imagining Asia*），胡志德 Theodore Huters 编辑，2011 年，哈佛大学出版社，第 59 页。

北京清华大学公共管理学院的崔志远教授举出习近平改革战略的例子。①习近平为了实践有中国特色的社会主义"总目标"提出60项重点。②崔志远认为这是目前的指导思想,以"架框目标"来使"总目标"明确化、具体化,同时也使国家与地方的关系更为宽松、更富活力,让地方对国有企业、农村发展中的土地信托以及党政关系有更大创新。我听崔志远讲演时,不禁想起公元前139年,以道家为本的《淮南子》,探讨"帝王之术,"来引导初登基的15岁的汉武帝。其中心思想是建立稳固的统治中心又使权力下放以赢得民心。③

一位西方论者,把这称为"自相矛盾"(oxymoronic)。英国伦敦政治经济学院教授柯岚安(William Callahan)写道,引申孔孟经典等于"把中国注意力转向远古的黄金时代而不是未来的理想境界。"④ 他同时宣称,实际上是美国梦引导中国梦,"至今强调中国本土论者仍然被美国所陶醉。"⑤ 不过,柯岚安很方便的忽略到,西方学者通常引用西方的古老哲学。正如著名哲学家,玛尔塔·纳丝苯(Martha Nussbaum),广采亚里士多德(Aristotle,公元前382—322)的原理来评论现代法治。⑥印度政治活动家,从《薄伽梵歌》等经

---

① 崔志远 Cui Zhiyuan 2014 年 4 月 29 日在纽约新校大学(New School)印度—中国研究所(India China Institute)以"诠释习近平的伟大改革战略"(Understanding Xi Jingping's Grand Reform Strategy)为题所作的讲演。崔教授代表了在自己领域内与政府合作的学人。2010—2011 年他从大学请假去担任重庆直辖市政府国有资产管理委员会的助理主任。

② 《中共中央关于全面深化改革若干重大问题的决定》,参见 http://news.xinhuanet.com/politics/2013-11/15/c_118164235.htm,2014 年 5 月 1 日查阅。

③ 梅觉尔 John S. Major、奎恩 Sarah A. Queen、麦雅尔 Andrew S. Meyer 与洛特 Harold D. Roth 合编与翻译:《淮南子:汉朝初期执政的理论与实践指南》(*The Huainanzi: A Guide to the Theory and Practice of Government in Early Han China*),2010 年,纽约:哥伦比亚大学出版 New York: Columbia University Press。

④ 柯岚安 William A. Callahan:《中国梦:对未来的20愿景》(*China Dreams: 20 Visions of the Future*),2013 年,英国牛津大学出版 Oxford University Press,第 9—10 页。

⑤ 同上书,第 10 页。

⑥ 玛尔塔·纳丝苯 Martha Nussbaum:《性别与社会法治》(*Sex and Social Justice*),1999 年,牛津大学出版社。

典中，不断地汲取灵感。①

柯岚安说什么中国梦是美国梦的观点，说什么虽然中国已经转到"内向"但中国将永远仿效美国，中国梦永远将是美国梦的回光返照，更是荒唐。很明显，中国对自己的历史、文化与政治的大量文献重新重视与研究将会增进并打造新的中国梦的内容与目的。

也许我30年前的那个梦，显示出中国人民与中国文化对"复兴"的观念，有所更新。诚然，我梦中出现的音乐与书法，印证了古代的"礼乐"概念。有人评论说：

从周朝流传下来的是"礼乐论，"这是一个封建社会（在宽泛的意义上）的视野，它要求政治统治通过"礼乐"来展开，而礼乐是一个有机和稳定的道德秩序的组织性原则。在这里"礼乐"不能从字面上理解，它们是那些具有直接道德目的的制度的名称，包括了封地、朝贡、田制、学制等等。由于道德本来就内在于这些制度，其结果是，外在秩序的准则就可以直接作为道德评判的标准。在礼乐论的视野中，经学—对一系列儒学经典的仔细研究—成为知识的主干。在《兴起》中，礼乐论相当于第一卷的前史，而这一卷的主要内容是探讨礼乐论如何崩溃，以及出现了何种替代物。②

请注意：我并非提倡中国复古。我也不赞成北京奥运会的简单化口号："同一个世界，同一个梦想"。我认为"礼乐"具有深藏的涵义。就是说，一个"有机和稳定的道德秩序"必须统治社会政治机构，使得伦理成为道德评判的标准。这种伦理又必须接触现实，与当地的行为、习俗、愿望与追求相呼应。以古论今，指的当然是走出中国古典传统去交流与适应。如何结合古今、中外、东西文化必然是一场挑战。我们说的中国人民与中国文化对"复

---

① 卡彼拉 Shruti Kapila 与德武济 Faisal Devji："薄伽梵歌与现代思想：简介"（The *Baghavad Gita and Modern Thought*: Introduction），参见《现代思想史》（*Modern Intellectual History*）杂志，2010 年第7期（2），第269—273页。

② 章永乐 Zhang Yongle："过去之未来—评汪晖《现代中国思想的兴起》"（The Future of the Past: On Wang Hui's *Rise of Modern Chinese Thought*），参见《新左派评论》（*New Left Review*），62期（2010年3-4月），57页。中文翻译录自 www.jingluecn.com/spdp/duping/2013-10.../768.html，2014年12月19日查阅。

兴"的态度是指大陆的发展，大陆的态度与海外的态度大有相互学习的天地，可以被认为新的"经学。"

我也不主张拒绝、驱逐或推翻"西方"。这种刚愎自用的思维正是西方殖民主义精英与他们在全球的应声虫强加到世界各地人民的"知识。"换句话说，"威斯特伐利亚西方"（Westphalia's West）① 并不是"西方"的全部。国际关系专家阿尔克（Hayward Alker）认为把西方文明自我关闭、与外界脱节并且相互害怕，等于把西方文明的多样性与复杂性清除。②

同样的，美国不是个单一文化。其国内纵然有奴隶、贫穷与萧条，但是美国的老百姓，经过各种的奋斗，才片面的获得自由，这一强烈的斗争传统在美国文化心脏中跳动。二十世纪 30 年代到纽约避难的德国犹太人汉娜·阿伦特（Hannah Arendt）认为只有通过与别人合作而培养出宽恕精神，人类才得到解放，虽然认识到有些事物是无法宽恕的。这和佛家与道家思想相似。③

关于这点，我特别欣赏道家关于创造的观点，庄子说的"圣人无己，"从精神上超脱一切自然和社会的限制，泯灭物我的对立，使得创造成为个人与集体的事业。④这种洞察不限于道家，其他传统，例如伊斯兰的苏菲主义，也发挥出这一智慧。12 世纪的波斯诗歌《鸟的语言》（*Mantiq-ut-Tayr*）中有这样一段：

一个声音说：我们都是镜子，
我们照着他物，他物照着我们，

---

① 国际学术界常用"威斯特伐利权威"（Westphalian regime）来形容西方通过物质与思想上的殖民主义扩张把"威斯特伐利和约"后的欧洲国际秩序强加到整个世界。
② 阿尔克 Hayward R. Alker："不是亨廷顿的文明又是谁的？"（If Not Huntington's Civilizations, then Whose?），参看《评论》（*Review*）杂志，18 卷第 4 期（1995 年秋季），第 533—562 页。
③ 汉娜·阿伦特 Hannah Arendt：《人的境况》（*The Human Condition*），1958 年初版，1998 年再版，芝加哥大学出版社。
④ 参见安乐哲 Roger T. Ames 编：《庄子的逍遥游》（*Wandering at Ease in the Zhuangzi*）1998 年，美国奥尔巴尼 Albany：纽约州立大学出版社。

Four seas to One Family: Overseas Chinese and Chinese dream
四海一家、天涯比邻：海外华人与中国梦

你中有我，我中有你。①

总之，中国梦不应该被当做一种带有意料中自我毁灭的令人淌汗的雾霾的舶来毒瘾。中国人民的古今中外充满丰富内容，能够作出巨大贡献，充满梦得更美更好的豪壮与想象。

谭中评论：

我们特别把这两篇海外华人的文章：熊玠教授的《比较"中国梦"与"美国梦"》和凌焕铭教授的《鉴别中国梦——谁的"中国"，谁的"梦"？》抽出来，放在北京人民大学王义桅教授的《化"中国梦"为"世界梦"》后面作进一步深化对"中国梦"性质的论坛探讨，也请了国内专家参加，这样就使本书对"中国梦"的诠释能作出一点贡献。

我们从中国舆论可以听到两种声音，一种是中国要"多！高！快！强！"，另一种是国际合作、世界共荣，打造"命运共同体"，可以看成"中国梦"的梦呓，也说明"中国梦"中思想感情复杂矛盾。这两篇文章可以说是在习近平提出的弘扬"中国精神"，遵循"中国道路"，凝聚"中国力量"的大框架中发挥自由思想来增进对"中国梦"的洞察。熊玠文更多聚焦于中西文化的差异来把"中国梦"与"美国梦"划清界限。凌焕铭文却是从后殖民主义的思维来进一步明确"中国梦"指引的既不要被西方思维操纵而东施效颦，又不要把中国未来发展从全人类相依为命的世界潮流中孤立开来。这两篇见仁见智的文章也是相辅相成的，它们的共同点在于对中国数千年文明传统智慧的高度自信，想要使中国知识界摆脱几百年来西方影响的误导，但它们本身是否完全摆脱西方影响却未能盖棺论定，这是我的看法，熊、凌两位可能不同意的。我这也是故意激励这两位好友，起抛砖引玉的作用。

熊玠文章把"梦境"说成"憧憬"（vision），这和我们平常对"vision"（愿景）的解释不同，合编者凌焕铭认为熊玠说的"憧憬"是"yearning"。熊

---

① 阿塔尔 Farid Ud-Din Attar：《鸟的语言诗集选译》(*The Simurgh and the Birds*, a selection from *Mantiq-ut-Tayr*)（里雅兹 Fahmida Riaz 选译），2014 年，巴基斯坦卡拉奇：牛津大学出版社，第 94 页。

珌列举了"全世界有史以来"四大"憧憬",又形容庄子的"蝴蝶梦"有"罗曼蒂克色彩",似乎觉得不能与柏拉图(Plato)、霍布斯(Hobbes)与马克思的"梦境"相比。如果我们换一个角度来看,"庄周梦蝴蝶"与"蝴蝶梦庄周"正是人类"梦境"的一种飞跃,因为它超越了人世规律约束,达到自己与蝴蝶、人与其他生命的转化境界。其实熊玠教授说的那四大"憧憬"都不过是一种政治行为的伸延,远不能与庄子的"蝴蝶梦",更不能与佛教企图超越"生、老、病、死"的人世规律约束的那种"憧憬"相比。

我在本书拙文中提到,"人类第一个最伟大的梦就是佛陀在梦中诞生",中国最早的伟大的梦就是汉明帝梦金人。正是这两个"梦"使得中华文明在精神修养上更上一层楼,出现了范仲淹的"先天下之忧而忧,后天下之乐而乐","居庙堂之上则忧其民,处江湖之远则忧其君"这样的中印合璧的伟大思想,出现了禅宗"你中有我,我中有你"的至高人际逻辑,出现了"牺牲小我为大我"的个人与整体合一的美德。我高兴地看到凌焕铭文中引的12世纪的波斯诗歌《鸟的语言》(*Mantiq-ut-Tayr*)中也有"你中有我,我中有你"的话,这真是"普世价值"(或者说:"共同价值")。

我对农业文化与游牧文化的看法不是那么绝对的。我们这些"海外华人"似乎都是背叛了"安土重迁"传统而变成现代"游牧人"了。我基本上认为中国的形成有些特别。地球第三大河长江与第五大河黄河发源于青藏高原唐古拉山与巴颜喀拉山(两个发源地近在咫尺),这两条同源大河却流向相反方向。黄河向北,流经四川、甘肃、宁夏、内蒙古、陕西、山西、河南、山东入海;长江向南,流经四川、西藏、云南、湖北、湖南、江西、安徽、江苏入海。更奇特的是,它们在入海前又被淮河连接起来。这两条大河先是分道扬镳、一南一北,然后在中国沿海合拢,在欧亚大陆东端画出一个欧洲那么大的中国版图。这以后,动植物与人类在这一版图内逐渐诞生与发展,先是游牧文化,再有农业文化。到孔子的时代,游牧文化仍旧盛行。孔子和孟子都像游牧人,喜欢旅行,不注重"安土重迁"。秦始皇兵马俑描绘的是当时许多不同游牧民族组成一支统一的军队,比今天美国的军队更多元化。中华文明发展的旋律是:居住在两河流域的不同民族部落慢慢把民族的"原始"(primordial)属性与分歧清除,逐渐发展成一个文明与一个国家,我们可以称它为"文明国"。

游牧文化对印度的影响比中国更大。印度大文豪泰戈尔形容印度文化有"行僧"（wandering ascetic）与"家园主"（householder）两大因素，前者代表游牧文化，后者代表农业文化。我把它引申，得出古代佛教传入中国、中印两大文明数世纪内在神州大地交流与激荡，正是这"行僧"与"家园主"两大能动力的有益结合而使中华文明稳固繁荣。古代有千百印度佛教高僧来中国传道，也有千百中国佛教高僧去印度取经。印度高僧从不想家，绝大多数死于中国，中国高僧只要有可能就争取回国，西安有"大雁塔"与"小雁塔"象征他们荣归故里。再有，中国出现许多"安国寺"、"兴国寺"、"隆国寺"、"清国寺"、"护国寺"、"保国寺"、"宁国寺"、"报国寺"（这"国"是中国，不是印度），象征印度高僧不但使中国佛教繁荣，也使中国繁荣、安定。相比之下，游牧文化的因素比农业文化高尚、伟大。

凌焕铭文从她自己三十年前"破旧大家宅还有希望"的梦开始，影射中华文明像那破旧大家宅而现在被"中国梦"鼓舞，致力于"复兴"。她围绕着这一课题进行了有关中外学者新旧思维的探讨。问题是：2014年已经结束，人们正在谈论"2015年是中国世纪元年"的问题，中国已经出现如何在这美国"霸权之治"理想破灭的时刻成为国际新秩序的创造者与维持者的问题，有人甚至喊出"中国外交更加硬朗"、"中国外交更加主动"、"中国外交更加灵活"、"中国外交更有担当"的近乎超级大国姿态的口号。也许这一切正是熊玠文所强调的，使凌焕铭文显得跟不上形势发展。我这是又一次为了抛砖引玉而激励好友。

凌焕铭谈到"中国"时在"作为国家的中国"与代表"文明与人民的中华"之间画上楚河汉界，使我想起外国朋友中存在的"China"与"Chinese"的二元论。凡是和海外华人有所接触的西方外国人几乎毫无例外地觉得"Chinese"可亲可爱，但它们一提起"China"，不但这一感觉消失，还产生其他复杂的感性与理性知识，小自疑虑，大至恐惧（拿破仑与马克思都有这种心理）。在这一点上中国和美国似乎情况相同。我认为这是违反逻辑的现象。"中国"作为"国家"或者"人民"的象征符号只应该有统一的精神放射。如果这象征符号出现精神分裂症，那样的"中国梦"是做不好的。不知道凌

四 专题论坛（二）

焕铭是否想说明这一点？

刚才我强调"你中有我，我中有你，"这虽是佛教传入中国后的思潮，但《老子》与《庄子》都有这样的思路。凌焕铭文引了《庄子·逍遥游》的"圣人无己，"从精神上超脱一切自然和社会的限制，泯灭物我的对立，使得创造成为个人与集体的事业。她也提到当代国际关系研究仍然受到"欧洲中心主义"（Eurocentrism）影响，使东西文化之间的鸿沟不能消失。从这一角度来看熊玠文强调的"内圣外王"就难以顺应。

再回过去谈中华文化在黄河与长江画出的轮廓中逐渐发展起来，也发展出强大的向心力与"天下大同"概念。另一方面，中国成为世界上空前持续的"大一统"帝国，也像今天的美国一样"胜利主义"旺盛，对邻近国家态度不免傲慢。"天下大同"概念与鹤立鸡群式的傲慢组成中国传统智慧的正负两面。

熊玠文说："无论中外，根治贪婪与霸道之解药无他，须靠中华文化'内圣外王'之教诲，"我数十年研究中国文明偏偏错过这只在《庄子·天下篇》中昙花一现的四个字，也看不到古代名家的诠释。我只知道近几十年来香港、台湾掀起的儒家传统中有莫须有的这一精髓，被人蹩脚地译成"inside the saint outside the king"的"内圣外王"，颇有莫名其妙的感觉。与此相关的，美国国际关系研究中——包括好友芝加哥大学著名"进攻现实派"（offensive realism）国际关系专家米尔商牟（John Mearsheimer）教授在内—可能由于中国（特别是台湾）知识分子不全面的投入而聚焦于中国的《孙子兵法》，外加"远交近攻"与"内圣外王"等语录，认为中国的国际关系传统完全和美国一样。使我不禁担心，如果将来崛起的中国在国际战略上贯彻"内圣外王"的精神是否会变相地在世界上捧出另一个美国式的超级大国呢？这和中国最近强调的要对周边国家"亲诚惠容"的原则是否水火不相容呢？我不知道为什么熊玠文却以它来为"中国梦"画龙点睛？我这是再一次抛砖引玉而激励好友！

我主动参加到评论这两篇文章的论坛中来既是为了出书，也是为了求教。我没有提出自己的论点，因此不存在胜辩的动机。我想，读者看了两位学者对我的回应可以加深对"中国梦"的认识。

197

Four seas to One Family: Overseas Chinese and Chinese dream
四海一家、天涯比邻：海外华人与中国梦

王义桅评论：

熊玠教授的《比较"中国梦"与"美国梦"》和凌焕铭教授的《鉴别中国梦—谁的"中国"，谁的"梦"？》涉及中国梦的两大话题：一是中国梦如何超越美国梦？二是如何超越西方话语体系看中国梦？

先说中国梦如何超越美国梦。中国梦的提出，一方面受到美国梦的启发，另一方面也是对其超越，表明中国人开始做自己的梦，而非追逐美国梦。美国梦（American Dream）诞生于大萧条时期，强调每一个移民来到美国这片希望之土，都能通过个人奋斗实现自身价值。然而，美国梦的实现也造成大量的资源、能源浪费。在可持续发展约束的时代，美国梦在褪色，欧洲梦受推崇。在欧债危机的当下，欧洲梦也在褪色。这样，中国梦的提出，自然给外界加强了中国软实力威胁的口实。尤其是，在将中美关系定位为老二－老大关系的错误理念下，担心中国梦要取代美国梦。其实，这是对中国包容性文化的误解。中国并非主张一神论的宗教国家，不会妨碍其他国家实现其梦想。但简单以"中国梦与世界各国人民追求美好生活的梦是相通的"概括之，无法说服世界。如何相通？不相通又如何？中国梦是否意味着中国的世界雄心？

其实，中国不做自己的梦，就会做美国梦，做普世价值梦。美国梦关注机会平等，不太计较结果；关心效率，不太计较可持续。泱泱大国、巍巍中华，沦为与美国一般见识，将带给世界不可承受之重。正如美国总统奥巴马2010年4月15日在接受澳大利亚电视台采访时所言，"如果超过十亿的中国居民也像澳大利亚人、美国人现在这样生活，那么我们所有人都将陷入十分悲惨的境地，因为那是这个星球所无法承受的。所以中国领导人会理解，他们不得不做出决定去采取一个新的、更可持续的模式，使得他们在追求他们想要的经济增长的同时，能应对经济发展给环境带来的挑战"。而中国做到这一点的结果，便是开创了人类可持续发展的新文明，成为世界领导型国家。这一点，自然是奥巴马所未能意识到的。当然，美国梦有其宗教逻辑、立国之本，也有其可贵可爱之处，最大的迷惑性就是淡化国家关怀，倡导普世成功，将美国优越论蕴于人类先进逻辑。至于一些人笃信的普世价值，将价值的普世性包装为普世价值，如今连西方面临的问题都解决不了，遑论中国式

问题?!

再说"谁的中国,谁的梦?"中国梦具有与别国梦的相通性,也具有特色性。理解中国特色的时代内涵,非常有必要。"特色"之特,特在哪儿?

第一,中国并非民族国家,而是文明型国家。中华文明不仅连续不断,未被殖民,更重要的,是一种世俗文明。中国崛起是世俗文明的崛起,这是最大的特色。今天,中国共产党的领导,就是这种世俗文明在政体上的体现。

第二,中国是社会主义国家。坚持社会主义制度,是中国政治的鲜明特色。故此,我们强调社会主义核心价值观,自由、民主等是社会主义理解的自由、民主,不能等同于西方的自由、民主。尽管自由、民主具有普世性,但并非普世价值。以所谓的普世价值,反对中国特色,是政治意识形态斗争的焦点。

第三,中国是超大规模社会、具有超长历史,正在走出一条有别于历史上其他国家的独特的现代化与民族复兴之路。中国崛起本身因而丰富了现代化与民族复兴的内涵,也在鼓励其他国家走符合自身国情的现代化与民族复兴之路。

当今世界乃至人类历史上,能有资格称自己为特色的国家不多;同样,能够有资格做梦的国家也不多。中国特色、中国梦超越了一般国家的个性,具有鲜明的中国内涵与时代色彩;强调中国特色,倡导中国梦,体现了中国的自信、自觉、担当。

先说自信。中国特色的中国梦充分表明"三个自信"——中国特色社会主义道路能走通、中国特色社会主义理论能管用、中国特色社会主义制度能不断焕发活力。三个自信,折射的是文明自信。历史上,中华文明成功将外来的佛教包容为佛学、禅宗,近代又将马克思主义中国化,这就是中华文明的包容特色与包容能力,现在完全能够以第五个现代化——治理能力与治理体系的现代化,将西方普世价值包容为人类共同价值。

再说自觉。现在的中国,颇似一百七十年前的美国。当时,美国开启了脱欧洲化进程。美国诗人爱默生1837年在哈佛演讲时说,"我们依赖的日子,我们向外国学习的漫长学徒期,就要结束。我们周遭那千百万冲向生活的人不可能总是靠外国果实的干枯残核来喂养。"爱默生说的外国指的是欧洲,表明美国自独立战争以来迈入精神立国阶段。现在的中国,强调中国特色的中国梦,正是表明告别鸦片战争以来中—西、体—用的二元思维与接轨、转型的迷思,自觉践行社会主义,在国内外倡导公平正义,并结合传统"公天下"思想,实现中国的精神立国。

再说担当。我们讲的中国特色,绝非排他,恰恰相反,是强调和而不同、和谐共生。兼收并蓄、融会贯通,是中华文明之所以长盛不衰的原因。中国特色是源于中国而属于世界。因此,中国梦必须从人类文明史来理解,将中国从文明型国家来看待。中华文明不是简单复兴、转型,更面临创新的伟大使命,即为人类文明的可持续发展做出中华文明应有的贡献。

越来越多的事实表明,全球治理不能只是指望技术、制度,越来越多有赖文明的转型与创新,也就是要在吸取人类一切优秀文明成果基础上,走出一条包容西方、兼顾南北的"新人文主义"。笔者在《海殇?——欧洲文明启示录》一书中指出,这种"新人文主义"有三个维度:推动人类可持续发展以证实其合理性;推动国际社会的包容性,尤其是西方包容东方,北方包容南方,实现持久和平、共同繁荣,以证实其合法性;推动各种文明成为自己,追求和而不同,推动国际关系民主化,从根本上消除海洋文明对内民主、对外专制,对内多元、对外普世的对立,真正还原世界的多样性,以证实其合目的性。

反思今天,起源于西方的资本主义文明在全球的扩张,产生并日益加剧着三种紧张关系:人与社会关系紧张——后冷战时代的冲突和危机还在显示,随资本主义工业化而来的现代性矛盾,并未因冷战的结束而消除;人与自然关系紧张——现代工业文明彻底打破了自然的和谐与宁静,人类成了自然的主人和敌人;人与人关系紧张——现代化带来了"迷心逐物"的现代病,席卷世界的金融危机,就起源于华尔街从金融衍生品追逐超额利润的过度贪婪(叶小文语)。

因此,中华民族的伟大复兴的中国梦,不是"复古"——复古解决不了今天中国面临的问题,也不能应对世界挑战;更非"接轨"——西方难言先进,且自顾不暇,一些国家还希望中国创出一条崭新的道路来与中国接轨;而是复兴、包容、创新的三位一体:通过合理地复兴我们的原生文明——催生中华文明中海洋文明的种子而走向海洋，合法地包容西方文明——通过摈弃西方普世价值神话而塑造人类共同价值体系，合目的地创新人类文明——通过引领"海洋时代2.0"以实现人类文明永续发展，从根本上确立中国作为世界领导型国家的道统。

总之，中华文明面临复兴、转型、创新三位一体的历史使命与时代担当。中国梦不是单纯的现代化梦，更不是西方梦、美国梦，而是文明梦—通过开创人类新文明而复兴、转型中华文明的文明梦。既要从中华五千年文明发展历程，也要从人类文明史视角，才得以看清中国梦的历史意义与世界价值。

王德华评论①：

读了熊玠《"中国梦"、"美国梦"与"普世价值"》和凌博士《鉴别中国梦——谁的"中国"，谁的"梦"？》两篇文章，我的大致印象如下：

熊文在介绍何为美国梦和中国梦之后，着重了讨论"中国梦"与"盛世复兴"的问题。他文章的亮点在于：以其独到视角，强调"中西方原始祖先的宇宙观"和中西文化中有关"救赎"的信仰。熊文提出：个人"富不知足"与国家"强不能安"之此种病症之文化根源，乃因西方商业文化强调进取竞争以至不择手段，导致贪婪永无止境。其宗教"救赎在外"教条之影响，益发导致对自己毫无自信；而中国近年来，虽然亦遭受外来商业文化拜金主义之冲击，几乎一时泛滥成灾，但自习总实行新政，首先着手整肃贪腐：既打苍蝇也打老虎。这也是实现中国梦之必要途径。熊文指出"中国梦"绝非霸权梦，西方应效仿中国搞"内圣外王"。

凌文用道教的辩证法重新理解国际关系为"西方"的阳与"非西方"的阴两个能动性的相互作用使世界政治疏远霸权与暴力而趋向平衡与接触，提到"中国人民与中国文化对'复兴'的观念有所更新"。我很欣赏它强调

---

① 上海国际问题研究中心南亚中亚研究所所长、研究员；上海同济大学南亚研究中心主任、研究员；上海社会科学院中国–印度比较研究中心副主任、研究员；中华能源基金委员会研究员；主要著作有：《话说知识经济》《列国争雄与亚太安全》《龙象共舞—对中国和印度两个复兴大国的比较研究》《高油价时代的中华民族复兴》《南海诸岛主权与国际争端》等10余部著作。

"礼乐论"。我辈在孩提就吟诵过：子曰："兴于诗，立于礼，成于乐"。懂得礼的价值在于规范人民的行为，培养一种吃苦耐劳精神，这能够使人们放弃眼前的享乐而追求长远的幸福和快乐，乐的价值在于能够引领人们走向人生最高境界。

两位大家由于长期生活在美国，对美国梦有深刻理解；同时他俩是华人，文章流露"爱我中华"的情怀，都对习总提的中国梦进行了充分肯定，深信"中国盛世复兴"会早日来临。

应该说，首先，中国梦是中国人民的理想信念，就是中国理想。正如习近平同志指出"中国梦是历史的，现实的也是未来的"，我们的民族是一个善于追梦的民族。从后羿射日，嫦娥奔月等神话故事就可以看出我们是一个有理想有梦的民族，只是我们"中国梦"概念的提出较晚。熊文和凌文引文，大部来自西方和古代经典，而直接引用习近平同志著作（比如：《习近平谈治国理政》[①] 等）和系列讲话不够。从党的十八大以来，习近平同志提出并深刻阐述了实现中华民族伟大复兴的中国梦，内容极为丰富。我粗略地聚焦于五点。一、中国梦是和平、发展、合作、共赢的梦，不仅造福中国人民，而且造福世界人民。历史告诉我们，每个人的前途命运都与国家和民族的前途命运紧密相连：国家好，民族好，大家才会好。[②] 二、中国梦归根到底是人民的梦，必须紧紧依靠人民来实现，必须不断为人民造福。[③] 三、实现中国梦必须走中国道路。中国特色社会主义，承载着几代中国共产党人的理想和探索，寄托着无数仁人志士的意愿和期盼，凝聚着千千万万革命先烈的奋斗和牺牲，凝聚着全国各族人民的奋斗和实践，是近代以来中国社会发展的必然选择，是历史和人民的选择。[④] 四、实现中国梦必须弘扬中国精神。中国传统文化博

[①] 习近平：《习近平谈治国理政》，北京，外文出版社，2014年10月第1版。

[②] 习近平：在参观《复兴之路》展览时的讲话（2012年11月29日），参见习近平：《习近平谈治国理政》第35页。

[③] 习近平：《在第十二届全国人民代表大会第一次会议上的讲话》（2013年3月17日），见习近平：《习近平谈治国理政》第38页。

[④] 习近平：《全面贯彻落实党的十八大精神要突出抓好六个方面工作》（2012年11月15日），习近平2012年11月15日，在党的十八届一中全会上讲话，引自《求是》2013年第1期，第1—3页。

大精深，学习和掌握其中的各种思想精华，对树立正确的世界观、人生观、价值观很有益处。① 五、共圆中华民族伟大复兴的中国梦。团结统一的中华民族是海内外中华儿女共同的根，博大精深的中华文化是海内外中华儿女共同的魂，实现中华民族伟大复兴是海内外中华儿女共同的梦。②

第二，我想指出，熊、凌两文对中国梦与美国梦本质区别阐发不够。中国社会科学院中国特色社会主义理论体系研究中心专职副主任夏春涛指出，中国梦和美国梦是两个国家自己的梦想，但是这两个国家自己的梦想在本质上的区别，表现在四个主要方面。从主体性上来讲，美国梦是美国人的梦，中国梦属于中国，是中国人的梦；从路径选从路径选择上讲，美国走的是资本主义道路。我们走的是中国特色社会主义道路，弘扬中国精神，凝聚中国力量，具有鲜明的中国特色中国风格中国气派。从概念内涵上讲，"美国梦"主要以自由、繁荣为标签，宣称一个人无论什么背景，只要来到北美新大陆，通过个人奋斗，就可以实现自己的梦想。

中华民族伟大复兴的"中国梦"包括国家富强、民族振兴、人民幸福三个层面，落脚点是"人民幸福"。全国各族人民是实现"中国梦"的主体力量，也是实现"中国梦"的直接受益者。因此，"中国梦"归根到底是人民的梦，是社会主义的强国富民之梦，是对"美国梦"的超越。提出"中国梦"的概念，是自信和实力的体现，吹响了民族复兴伟大征程上新的进军号角，令人心潮激荡豪情满怀。从动态或趋势上讲，"美国梦"早已褪去其耀眼光环，缺少新内涵和活力，缺乏可持续性。我国则持续保持着强劲发展势头，中国社会充满生机和活力。③

第三，我觉得熊文关于普世价值观点值得商榷。目前，大多数中国学者并不赞同西化的"普世价值"概念，从这个概念在国内出现一直到现在，他

---

① 习近平：《在接受拉美三国媒体联合采访时的答问》（2013年5月），北京《人民日报》6月1日。

② 习近平：《实现中华民族伟大复兴是海内外中华儿女共同的梦》（2014年6月6日），见习近平：《习近平谈治国理政》第63页。

③ 夏春涛：中美两国"梦想"的四个本质区别，人民网记者 万鹏/文，2013年03月28日，来源：人民网，http://theory.people.com.cn/n/2013/0328/c148980-20950853.html。

们都是在学术的意义上用它来指称人类的共同价值。但是，考虑到这个词的起源、词面意义和现在国内外一些人对它的使用，笔者认为应该用一个较少争议的概念取代它，以免造成不必要的混乱。

在中国多数学者认为，"普世价值"这个概念经历了从宗教的普世主义，到神学家倡导的普世伦理，再到今天代表西方强势话语、专指西方政治理念和制度模式。"普世文明"的概念就是塞缪尔·亨廷顿的"文明冲突论"的理论基础。[1] 人类文明的发展是一个不断累积和进步的过程，每一代人都在前人的基础上进行创造。文明的积累、进步既包括同一种文明纵向上的继承，也包括不同文明之间横向上的借鉴、吸收和融合。特别是伴随着经济全球化的进程，不同国家、不同文明之间的交流、交往日益频繁，各民族的历史正逐渐成为"世界历史"，人类面对的许多挑战超越了国界的限制，都需要团结合作、共同应对，从而需要确立一些超越国家、民族和社会制度的共同行为准则或价值准则。经济全球化愈发展，价值领域的共同性也愈发展。

但是，共同价值却不是绝对的"普世价值"。有放之四海而皆准的真理，没有放之四海而皆准的价值。共同价值反映的是人类的共同需要、共同利益、共同追求，是人的社会性和相互依存性，是不同的人、民族、国家之间的共性。共同价值不可能适用于一切时代、一切国家和民族，只能适用于特定时期、地域，只能存在于具体的价值关系中。共同价值也不是特定价值比如西方价值的普世化。

第四，熊、凌两文对中国梦、美国梦和世界梦交流互鉴战略思想理解有失偏颇。2014年，习近平同志在访问欧洲期间，围绕东方文明与西方文明在当代的交往，阐释了世界文明交流互鉴的重要理念，提出了"中国世界文明观"，以此作为构建和谐世界的新理念、新思想、新方法。[2]

我赞同凌教授"礼乐"具有深藏的涵义论述，但不赞成她否定："同一个世界，同一个梦想"口号，因为这是对中国梦与其他梦能和平共处缺乏信心。

---

[1]《文明的冲突与世界秩序的重建》，新华出版社2010年，第45页。
[2] 张雷：习近平关于推进世界文明交流互鉴的战略思想，参见《文化论苑》，总第492期，第30页。

我想凌博士之所以不认同"世界梦",也许她看到目前国际上对中国梦认同的现实困境,由于国家利益、文化传统、价值观念以及竞争等因素的影响,中国梦的国际认同也遇到诸多困难。比如:国际社会对中国梦能否实现存在疑问,对中国梦的目的存在疑问,由此有关"中国威胁论"、"中国未来霸权"的提法应运而生了;再就是国际社会对中国梦与个人梦关系存在疑问,因此不认同"同一个世界,同一个梦想"的口号是不足为奇的。

黄绮淑评论:

我想先谈一下我的直觉:"中国梦"所包含的主要主要是一种感情、一种对中国的热爱,缺少了它什么豪言壮语、什么理论逻辑都不会变成对"中国梦"的理解。现在我们开辟了这样一个"中国梦"的专题论坛,如果尽是些没有"中国感情"的空空洞洞的高深理论是浪费时间的。孔子说:"智者乐水,仁者乐山",毛泽东说:"江山如此多娇,引无数英雄尽折腰"就是说明只有像唐朝伟大诗人李白等人那样尽情在神州大地游山玩水才能迸发出最为丰满的"中国梦"。那些不能像李白等人游山玩水的中国人读了李白等人的诗也会使他们对"中国梦"的浓厚感情潜移默化到自己的精神细胞里来。当然,感性认识还必须有理性认识支持才能巩固。一个人如果对中华文明有深刻的理解与感受也会积累对"中国梦"的深厚感情。许多海外华人就是这样热衷于"中国梦"的。

读了熊玠与凌焕铭两篇大作及谭中、王义桅、王德华三篇评论,我对"中国梦"的认识有所加深。凌焕铭文章的结语是:"中国人民的古今中外充满丰富内容,能够作出巨大贡献,充满梦得更美更好的豪壮与想象"。熊玠文章的结论是:"我们可说'中国梦'绝非霸权梦。由于它的到来世界将为一个完全崭新的文化所笼罩。这个文化将揭橥讲信修睦之教"。王义桅的评论对此产生共鸣,说出:"历史上,中华文明成功将外来的佛教包容为佛学、禅宗,近代又将马克思主义中国化,这就是中华文明的包容特色与包容能力,现在完全能够以第五个现代化——治理能力与治理体系的现代化,将西方普世价值包容为人类共同价值"。王德华评论则把中国梦提得高得不能再高。可以这样说,凌、熊与两王四篇文章把我们书的"中国梦"的探讨提升到空前的

"文明"高度。

我们有幸请到国内两"王"来谈中国梦。北京的王义桅教授当过中国政府驻欧盟外交官，他对中国领导提出"中国梦"理想的了解可能是我们书的所有作者中最权威的。他说："中国梦的提出受到美国梦的启发"这一信息证明凌焕铭的疑虑是有根据的。上海的王德华教授更令人佩服，他把出版不久的《习近平谈治国理政》都消化了，在我们海外华人面前大谈"习近平同志"怎么怎么说的，我看本书的海外作者都还没见到该书英文版 *Xi Jinping of Governance* 的影子呢？

王义桅说："中国并非民族国家，而是文明型国家"，这就印证了我们在海外（特别是在印度）看到的当今世界有"民族国"和"文明国"两大类，可是我们比王义桅在国内更清楚地看到："民族国"的沙漠包围"文明国"的绿洲，不断对它们进行腐蚀，要将它们沙漠化的严重形势。

我特别欣赏王义桅在评论中说的"将中美关系定位为老二－老大关系"是一种"错误理念"。他指出了中国领导人提出"中国梦"并不是要把中国摆到怎么样的巅峰，而是有一个"开创人类可持续发展的新文明"的新意图。不幸的是：他马上补上一句中国想要"成为世界领导型国家"，这样又把我们的探讨拉回到"民族国"世界的政治形势中来了。

我同意两位王教授认为"中国梦"不是"复古"，不是复兴到"中华盛世的阶段"。生活在"盛唐"时期的伟大诗人杜甫对当时社会的评论是："朱门酒肉臭，路有冻死骨"。他的名著生动地反映出在那兵荒马乱之年，"石壕吏"抓老妇人去充军，老百姓"被驱不异犬与鸡"，"新鬼烦冤旧鬼哭"，"古来白骨无人收"。杜甫的时代人们短命，"人生七十古来稀"。现在的中国有2亿多身强力壮的60岁以上的老人，超过杜甫时代唐朝总人口数。我从《环球网》上看到，2011年中国人均寿命已经达到76岁（只比美国少3岁），神州大地"百岁老翁"毫不稀奇。难道"习总的复兴伟业"是到2049年以后回复到杜甫所诅咒、所哀伤的那个时段中去吗？！我没看到习近平自己这样说过，也没有其他领导权威这样暗示过。

国内专家参加到海外华人议论"中国梦"的论坛中来帮助我们集思广益是件好事，但是国内与海外对中国梦认识的差距是无法填平的。我不是国际关系专家（只把评论国际形势当作嗜好而已），王义桅评论中的一句话使我既觉得新鲜，又难以理解。他说："美国梦有其宗教逻辑、立国之本，也有其可贵可爱之处，最大的迷惑性就是淡化国家关怀，倡导普世成功，将美国优越论蕴于人类先进逻辑。"我想他在突出美国提倡的"小政府、大社会"，把它当作一种普世价值。如果王义桅认为两千多年来中国的政治一直是围绕着提倡"大政府"、考虑如何完善国家权力机关的功能，我是完全同意的。具体地说，中国的政治二元论是"国"与"民"两大要素。中国梦绝对不会抛弃"人民"。我想这也就是凌焕铭文章尖锐地提出必须弄清梦"谁的梦"的问题的用意。王德华评论也提到中国梦"必须不断为人民造福"；他又说："中国梦归根到底是人民的梦，必须紧紧依靠人民来实现"。我想，只要说"中国梦"就是"民"梦（中国人民的梦），凌焕铭的问题就有了答案。

今年2月1日公布的"中央一号文件"（即中共中央与国务院联合颁发的《关于加大改革创新力度加快农业现代化建设的若干意见》）似乎对凌焕铭提出的"谁的中国，谁的梦？"有所交代，它突出了习近平2013年在中央农村工作会议上说的"中国要强，农业必须强"、"中国要富，农民必须富"、"中国要美，农村必须美"，作为今后发展目标，象征着从汉文帝开始的"重农"与"亲农"口号两千余年延续发出火花。谭中评论引了中华文明对"中国梦"的"国"与"民"的二元论最光辉灿烂的总结—宋儒范仲淹名言："居庙堂之高则忧其民，处江湖之远则忧其君"，但历代帝王统治时代对"居庙堂之高则忧其民"的具体政绩阙如。毛泽东时代，中南海的"庙堂之高"的确为"农民"办了事，很多农民变成"解放军"、变成国家干部、变成新一代知识分子、变成各行各业的工人、店员，绝大多数摘掉"农民"的帽子，变成人民公社"社员"。我想补充一句，全世界所有国家中，只有中国是这么一个做"农民梦"的国家。但毛泽东越俎代庖，那"农民梦"只是毛泽东的"梦"，不是农民自己的"梦"。邓小平时代解散了人民公社，他选择的是一条发展城市、发展工业的西方梦，毛泽东式的"农民梦"被人遗忘。改革开放30余年，中国农民"一分为二"，变成"农民工"和"留守农民"，两者都艰辛奋斗而道路坎坷。政府也一直想办法为他们谋点福利（中国政府每年颁发的"中央一号文件"总是念念不忘"三农"问题）。我曾经长住印度，印度的农民问题和中国一样突出，但新德里居庙堂之高的人们却从来没有突出"农民梦"。王义桅评论大谈中国发展"特色之特"，要是能提一提这"农民梦"之"特"就好了。我认为千讨论万讨论都没有意思，只有使"中国梦"变成农民的"美梦"而去实现它才能功德圆满。这也是我特别欣赏习近平强农业之强、富农民之富、美农村之美的思路。

与此同时，我对王义桅评论所说的"中国不做自己的梦，就会做美国梦，做普世价值梦"有些不解。依我的陋见，中国梦的只能是自己的梦，只能是"中国梦"，中国想做美国梦是做不成的。我想日本的情况很可以解释这一点。明治维新以后，日本做"脱亚"梦，想把太阳旗的东瀛三岛潜移默化成主宰"日不落帝国"的英伦三岛，从"脱亚"梦发展到"脱亚入欧"梦，后来又变成"脱亚入美"梦，结果落得个东施效颦的结局，日本既没"入欧"，也没"入美"，它不愿意"入亚"，亚洲也不一定欢迎它。这就是"日本梦"的下场。

王义桅说："中国梦不是单纯的现代化梦，更不是西方梦、美国梦，而是文明梦"。这是一个相当宏伟的结论。顾名思义，他说的这个"文明梦"必须是超越了"民族国"思维框架的，同时发扬了"文明国"精神文明精髓的一种"柳暗花明又一村"的新想象境界。可是我从他的整篇评论中（以及国内许许多多对中国梦的权威论述中）却看不到它"柳暗花明又一村"的新想象境界。这也说明"中国梦"仍然是一种发展中的概念，远远没有盖棺论定。

谭中再评论：

本来不预备再次进入讨论的，但是读了王义桅、王德华和黄绮淑三篇评论以后就无法克制了。一方面，我必须感谢人民大学的王义桅教授和上海社会科学院的王德华教授在极短的期限内特别为我们撰文，评论熊玠与凌焕铭探讨"中国梦"的高水平文章，使我们这本书的"压轴戏"热闹而生动，造成一场颇为不凡的有关中国梦的学术讨论。我还得向他们两位道歉，他们是下了工夫写出对熊玠与凌焕铭文章的评论，两人评论的长度都超过熊、凌的文章，不符合我们论坛的规格，我只能割爱，删掉了两王许多精彩内容，特此道歉。最后，我也想针对两篇评论谈两个观点。

四　专题论坛（二）

感谢王义桅帮助本书提出"民族国"和"文明国"两种截然不同的观点来讨论中国梦，这是我在其他地方特别强调的。（请读者参阅 2015 年 3 月问世的由美国与新加坡世界科技出版公司 World Scientific Publishing Company 出版的谭中 Tan Chung 的英文新书《喜马拉雅在呼唤：中国与印度的起源》*Himalaya Calling：The Origins of China and India*。）我根据印度大文豪泰戈尔的基本思维把"仁爱"（泰戈尔说的"Love/爱心"）定为"文明国"的价值观念，把泰戈尔说的"Power/强力"定为"民族国"的价值观念。关于这"Power/强力"的思维，哈佛大学教授约瑟夫·奈（Joseph Nye）是个权威，所谓"hard power/强力"、"soft power/软强力"与"smart power/巧强力"就是他的"魔术"。我称这些为"魔术"是因为它们的欺骗力很大。约瑟夫·奈在他自己各种著述中都清楚地说明"Power/强力"是一种"制约别人的力量"（the ability to coerce others）而不是自卫、自强的力量。因此我觉得中文不是把"soft power"翻译成"软强力"，而是翻译成"软实力"是受约瑟夫·奈"魔术"的误导。像约瑟夫·奈这种"民族国"的宣传大师，对"文明国"的"中国精神"一窍不通的人，居然会在中国特别吃香，简直成为中国"智囊"了，这是令人不解的。

我这么说并不是反对约瑟夫·奈（他如果对中国外交提出好的意见应该接受），而是觉得人们把"民族国"提倡"soft power/软强力"的价值观念当作建设中国综合实力的"软实力"实际上是背离了"文明国"的"仁爱"价值观念，这就会使世界对中国只"敬畏"，不"敬爱"。黄绮淑评论希望能从王义桅评论中看到超越了"民族国"思维框架并且发扬了"文明国"精神文明精髓的那样一种对中国梦的探讨就是从这一点出发的。

为了确立"文明国"与"民族国"的区别，我必须重复前面说过的中国的诞生先是由黄河与长江在地球上画出中国版图，然后居住在两河流域的不同民族部落发展出中华文明，把民族的"原始"（primordial）属性与分歧清除，是这样变成"文明国"的。《大学》的"修身—齐家—治国—平天下"实际上简明地勾出中华"文明国"的"个人"、"家"、"国"、"天下"即"文明"的四个结构性的层次。"民族"在这一结构中并无立锥之地。费孝通是中国"人类学"的创始者，他生前想用现代西方观念讨论中国的"民族"

问题，毫无建树。

我从小在比较保守的湖南中小学受教育，每天朝会念《总理遗嘱》，受到的有关"国父"孙中山的灌输不亚于台湾的知识精英。但我必须指出，孙中山提倡的"中华民族"不但理论性不强，而且使得近现代中国思维受到"民族国"地缘政治范式的毒害。王德华评论并不一定宣扬"民族国"思维，却那么强调"中华民族伟大复兴的中国梦"。他说："中华民族伟大复兴的'中国梦'包括国家富强、民族振兴、人民幸福三个层面，落脚点是'人民幸福'"。他又说：中国梦归根到底是"社会主义的强国富民之梦"，等于把"民族振兴"那个层面省略了，也使他的"民族复兴伟大征程"悬空而虚。我想他心目中的所谓"中华民族"实际上指的是"中国"或者"中华文明"，也许他想以"中华民族"来在精神上把"大陆"和"台湾"统一起来。难道"中华文明"不是地球上所有华人的统一机制吗？

王义桅评论在结尾时说中国梦要"合理地复兴我们的原生文明"，我想具有"包容特色与包容能力"（王义桅语）的中华文明是还原不出"原生文明"的。如果硬要"复兴我们的原生文明"，那就等于把数千年不断清除民族的"原始"（primordial）属性与分歧的"文明国"进化过程解体。再有，这样的还原过程必然接触历史上那些"反满"、"反元"、"反胡"的不愉快经历而损害民族团结。我们强调发扬"文明国"精神来做中国梦，与"民族国"文化划清界限也正是为了增进中华文明以"整体"包容"局部"、以"大我"压倒"小我"的精神文明，让"中华"无限发扬光大，让"维吾尔"、"西藏"、"朝鲜"、"蒙古"、"港人"、"台湾"等狭隘的意识消失。那样才能打造王义桅提倡的具有"新人文主义"精神的"人类新文明"。

王德华答复：

谭中教授在评论中说："王德华评论并不一定宣扬'民族国'思维，却那么强调'中华民族伟大复兴的中国梦'。"他的评论我完全赞同。我想请他和各位读一读"习近平会见第七届世界华侨华人社团联谊大会代表"的报道。习近平说：

团结统一的中华民族是海内外中华儿女共同的根,博大精深的中华文化是海内外中华儿女共同的魂,实现中华民族伟大复兴是海内外中华儿女共同的梦。共同的根让我们情深意长,共同的魂让我们心心相印,共同的梦让我们同心同德,我们一定能够共同书写中华民族发展的时代新篇章。

老乡见老乡,两眼泪汪汪,见到大家感到特别亲切。习近平代表中共中央、国务院,向第七届世界华侨华人社团联谊大会的召开表示衷心的祝贺,向与会的侨胞朋友们表示热烈的欢迎,向世界各地的华侨华人表示诚挚的问候。

在世界各地有几千万海外侨胞,大家都是中华大家庭的成员。长期以来,一代又一代海外侨胞,秉承中华民族优秀传统,不忘祖国,不忘祖籍,不忘身上流淌的中华民族血液,热情支持中国革命、建设、改革事业,为中华民族发展壮大、促进祖国和平统一大业、增进中国人民同各国人民的友好合作作出了重要贡献。祖国人民将永远铭记广大海外侨胞的功绩。

当前,中国人民正在为实现"两个一百年"奋斗目标、实现中华民族伟大复兴的中国梦而奋斗。在这个伟大进程中,广大海外侨胞一定能够发挥不可替代的重要作用。中国梦是国家梦、民族梦,也是每个中华儿女的梦。广大海外侨胞有着赤忱的爱国情怀、雄厚的经济实力、丰富的智力资源、广泛的商业人脉,是实现中国梦的重要力量。只要海内外中华儿女紧密团结起来,有力出力,有智出智,团结一心奋斗,就一定能够汇聚起实现梦想的强大力量。

中华文明有着5000多年的悠久历史,是中华民族自强不息、发展壮大的强大精神力量。我们的同胞无论生活在哪里,身上都有鲜明的中华文化烙印,中华文化是中华儿女共同的精神基因。希望大家继续弘扬中华文化,不仅自己要从中汲取精神力量,而且要积极推动中外文明交流互鉴,讲述好中国故事、传播好中国声音,促进中外民众相互了解和理解,为实现中国梦营造良好环境。

中国梦既是中国人民追求幸福的梦,也同各国人民追求幸福的梦想相通。国家好、民族好,大家才会好。世界好,中国才会好。中国坚持走和平发展道路,是世界繁荣发展的正能量。广大海外侨胞要运用自身优势和条件,积

Four seas to One Family: Overseas Chinese and Chinese dream
四海一家、天涯比邻：海外华人与中国梦

极为住在国同中国各领域交流合作牵线搭桥，更好融入和回馈当地社会，为促进世界和平与发展不断作出新贡献。"①

我想促请读者注意：报道第一段说到的习近平同志强调"团结统一的中华民族是海内外中华儿女共同的根"，这里，"团结统一的中华民族"是针对着百余年来西方殖民主义与帝国主义蚕食中国领土，并且在世界舆论中制造出中国分裂的现象，以至现在台湾、香港等地仍有炎黄子孙不认自己是"中国人"的现象。这样"中华民族"一词就有力地反击分裂了。我想我强调"中华民族伟大复兴的中国梦"并没有受到"民族国"地缘政治范式的毒害，这一点谭中也已经谅解了。

习近平去年 6 月 6 日在北京会见第七届世界华侨华人社团联谊大会代表时的讲话似乎和我们这本书进行交流对话，我们这本书的丰富内容也似乎是对习近平语重心长讲话的反馈。

---

① 参见《习近平谈治国理政》，北京：外文出版社，第 63 页；www.chinanews.com/.../6254229....

'China' or 'Chinese civilization'. Perhaps, he thinks the term 'Chinese nation' can spiritually unite Mainland China and Taiwan. We might ask him: is not the 'Chinese civilization' an effective institution to unite all Chinese on the globe?

Towards the end of his comment, Wang Yiwei suggested that China should '*helidi fuxing womende yuansheng wenming* (合理地复兴我们的原生文明)' (reasonable rejuvenate our primordial civilization). In my opinion, the Chinese civilization that shows the 'idiosyncrasy and capability of internalization' (包容特色与包容能力), to quote Wang Yiwei's words, would not be able to 'rejuvenate its primordial civilization'. In case we want to do it by coercion it would start a process of negating the progress of the 'civilization state' that had millennial hard work in eliminating the 'primordial' natures and differences of nationalities. Moreover, such a rejuvenation process would inevitably refresh the unhappy experiences of Chinese history that manifested xenophobic anti-'Hu (胡)', anti-Mongol and anti-Manchu sentiments which would be detrimental to the unity among nationalities of China. It is utterly important that we cherish the 'Chinese dream' in the spirit of civilization state and stand clear from the culture of the 'nation states', making the 'whole' inclusive of all 'parts' while all the '*xiaowo* (小我)/atma/micro-selves' are prevailed by the '*dawo* (大我)/paramatma/macro-self' and all the marrow-minded percepts and concepts of the 'Uighur', 'Tibet', 'Korea', 'Mongol', 'Hong Kong' and 'Taiwan' going out of sight and mind. Only then can we create the 'new human civilization' (人类新文明) with the spirit of 'new humanism' (新人文主义) as advocated by Wang Yiwei.

popular in China—simply like China's 'think tank'.

I have no personal animosity towards Joseph Nye (China should willingly accept his suggestions if they are really good for China's foreign policies). My anguish lies in China's accepting the advocacy of 'soft power' of the 'nation states' as a means of construction of China's comprehensive strength which is tantamount to abandoning the virtue of 'Love' of the 'civilization states'. This has resulted in China's being feared, not loved, by the world. Thus the comment of Ishu Huang longing to see the Chinese mindset carrying forward the quintessential culture of the civilization states and stay clear from the thinking of the nation states is worthy of serious consideration.

In order to distinguish the civilization state from the nation state, I would like to reiterate what I have said in my first comment that it was Huanghe and Yangtse having carved out 'the contours of a country as big as Europe' that had enable different nationalities and tribes within China to cleanse their internal 'primordial' natures and differences to create the civilization state of China. The classic equation of '*xiushen* (修身)/cultivation of the character of the individual'—'*qijia* (齐家)/harmony in the family'—'*zhiguo* (治国)/law and order of the state'—'*pingtianxia* (平天下)/pacification of all-under-Heave' propounded by '*Daxue* (大学)/The Great Learning' has actually marked precisely the four layers of Chinese civilization from the individual to the entire civilization ('*tianxia* (天下)/all-under-Heave') through '*jia* (家)/family' and '*guo* (国)/state' in between. The category of ethnic 'nation' has had no place in such a civilization state. We have seen how Fei Xiaotong (费孝通), the founding father of anthropology of China had tried to discuss without success China's issue of '*minzu* (民族)/nationalities' in his life time.

I grew up from conservative primary and middle schools in Hunan, chanting '*Zongli yizhu* (总理遗嘱)/Will of Sun Yat-sen' everyday in the morning gatherings. I consider myself no less indoctrinated about the 'Father of the Nation' (国父) that was Sun Yat-sen than the intellectual elite of Taiwan. However, I should point out that the concept of '*Zhonghua minzu* (中华民族)/Chinese nation' propounded by Sun Yat-sen is not only theoretically unsound, but has also led the modern thinking of China to the garden path, getting it poisoned by the geopolitical paradigm of the nation states. I see Wang Dehua's comment obsessed with the idea of "Chinese dream' of realizing the great rejuvenation of the Chinese nation' (中华民族伟大复兴的中国梦) although he may not be consciously demonstrating the mindset of the nation states. Wang Dehua also observes: 'The 'Chinese dream' of realizing the great rejuvenation of the Chinese nation covers the three layers of enriching the country, rejuvenating the nation, and bringing happiness to the people. Happiness for the people is the foundation.' He also observes that 'in the final analysis, the 'Chinese dream' is the people's dream'. These observations have glossed over the 'rejuvenation of the Chinese nation'. I think, by 'Chinese nation' he actually means quintessential culture of the 'civilization states' and leads us to a brand new arena beyond the dark horizon we see all round in our world. Nevertheless, I miss such a new arena in the overview of Wang Yiwei's comment. Nor do I see it in the innumerable authoritative discourses on the 'Chinese dream' in China. All this shows that the 'Chinese dream' is still a developing concept without a firm definition and conclusion.

Tan Chung's second comment:

I had no plan to join in again, but could not restrain myself from this second intervention after reading the three comments by Wang Yiwei, Wang Dehua and Ishu Huang. Moreover, I should express my thanks to Professor Wang Yiwei of Renmin University of China, Beijing, and Professor Wang Dehua of the Shanghai Academy of Social Sciences, Shanghai, for their special comments on the essays of Professors Hsiung and Ling at very short notice. Their comments of high academic standard have added glitters to this finale of our book—making it a very unusual academic discourse on the Chinese dream. Both of the two Wangs have given their best in their comments creating a situation that the length and contents of the comments have surpassed those of the essays that they are supposed to comment. I must apologize to the two Wangs that we cannot allow our forum to have weightier comments than the principal essays. I am compelled to delete many valuable and substantial parts of these two comments. Since I have jumped into the fray once again, I would also say something particularly about these two comments.

It is gratifying that Wang Yiwei has extended his hand in helping our book distinguish the two different sets of mind of 'nation states' and 'civilization states' in viewing the 'Chinese dream'. I have particularly reiterated this distinction elsewhere and readers can see my book, *Himalaya Calling: The Origins of China and India*, which has been brought out in March 2015 by the World Scientific Publishing Company of the USA and Singapore. Based on the great Indian writer, Rabindranath Tagore's basic understanding I conceive that the 'nation states' are obsessed with the pursuit of 'Power' in contrast with the 'civilization states' embracing 'Love'. Professor Joseph Nye of Harvard University is definitely an authority of the concept of 'Power'. He is the magician of the so-called 'hard power', 'soft power' and 'smart power'. I describe them as 'magic' because of their tremendous deceptive power. In his books and various writings, Joseph Nye has clearly defined 'power' as 'the ability to coerce others' instead of the strength of self-defence and self-strengthening. Thus, I have my eternal regret that the term 'soft power' is being translated into Chinese as '*ruan shili* (软实力)/soft strength' instead of '*ruan qiangli* (软强力)/soft power' which is the proof of China's being overpowered by Joseph Nye's deception. I am always puzzled that such a mighty protagonist of the values of 'nation states' like Joseph Nye should have been so cadres of the administration, new intellectuals and worker of factories and shops. The majority of them were no longer 'peasants', but members of the People's Communes. I must add that among all countries of the world, only China has been such a country cherishing the 'peasants' dream'. Nevertheless, Mao Zedong had overreached himself by walking the walk for the peasants, and that his 'peasants' dream' was only Mao's dream, not the peasants' own dream. During the post-Mao Deng Xiaoping Era the People's Communes were largely disbanded and China's Mao-style 'peasants' dream' forgotten as China pursued the Western dream of prioritizing the development of industry and urban centres. For three decades and more since the inception of Reform and Opening Up, Chinese peasants have been divided into '*nongmin gong* (农民工)' (peasant workers in urban centres) and '*liushou nongmin* (留守农民)' (peasants left behind in the countryside), both have had their travail and ordeal. The government has never stopped, it seems, its caring for the welfare of the peasants (every year, the 'Number One document of the Centre' has been chanting the mantras of the '*san nong* (三农)/triple "nong"' (agriculture, peasants and countryside). I had a four-decade sojourn in India and knew that India, too, had a prominent problem of 'peasants' like China. However, those sitting at 'the height of imperial court' in New Delhi had never highlighted the 'peasants' dream'. If Wang Yiwei had mentioned the 'peasants' dream' while illuminating his 'Chinese idiosyncrasy' it could have been perfect. It would be meaningless for us to discuss the 'Chinese dream' if it is not the Chinese 'peasants' dream'. All this has enhanced my appreciation of Xi Jinping's ideas that 'to make China strong means a strong agriculture', 'to make China rich means the prosperous peasants' and 'to make China beautiful means the pretty countryside'.

Meanwhile, I am somewhat puzzled by Wang Yiwei's observation: 'If China does not dream its own dream, it would dream the American dream, or the dream of universal values.' In my humble opinion, the 'Chinese dream' can only be China's own dream. Even if China wants to dream the American dream it would not succeed. The experience of Japan provides a footnote to this. After the Meiji Reformation, Japan was dreaming of going 'out of Asia' (脱亚). It had cherished the 'vision' of transforming the three Japanese islands under the flag of the rising sun into the three British Isles that was the 'Empire on which the sun never sets'. This ended in disastrous failure. Japan first failed to become a part of Europe, and then failed to become a part of America. It does not like to be a part of Asia while Asia might say 'good riddance' to it. This is a lesson for China that it would not succeed if it wants to 'dream the American dream, or the dream of universal values'.

Wang Yiwei also observes: 'The 'Chinese dream' is not a simple dream of modernization. It is not a Western dream or American dream. It is a civilization dream'. This is rather grandiloquent. It would mean that such a 'civilization dream' goes beyond the mindset of the 'nation states', but carries forward the

Part V
Symposium II: Delving into All Aspects of the Chinese Dream

people within China and overseas. I am no expert of international relations (only occasionally writing international comments as a pastime). I find a sentence in Wang Yiwei's comment refreshing but puzzling. He observes: 'The American dream is charming by its religious tenets and founding principles. Its greatest captivating power lies in its minimal state concern by highlighting the universal success, predicating the American superiority on the advanced logics of humanity.' I should imagine that he is highlighting on the American mantra of 'small government and big society' and treating it as a 'universal value'. I would agree with him totally if he thinks that for two millennia the Chinese political thinking has hinged on the 'great government' in perfecting the functions of the state authorities. In concrete terms, '*guo* (国)/state' and '*min* (民)/people' are the two essential elements of Chinese politics. The 'Chinese dream' will never abandon the '*min* (民)/people' element. I think this is the issue that has made L.H.M. Ling sharply raise the question of 'whose dream'. In his comment, Wang Dehua observes: 'in the final analysis, the 'Chinese dream' is the people's dream. Only by closely relying on the people can it be realized'. To my mind, this dual scenario of '*guo* (国)/state' and '*min* (民)/people' is the answer to L.H.M. Ling's question.

The 'Number One document of the Centre' (中央一号文件) issued on 1 February, 2015 entitled 'Opinions on deepen reform and innovation to accelerate the modernization of agriculture' (关于加大改革创新力度加快农业现代化建设的若干意见) seems to be an answer to L.H.M. Ling's 'Whose "Chinese"? Whose "Dream"?' It highlights as the goal of China's agricultural development the observation of Xi Jinping at the Centre's Conference on Agriculture in 2013: 'to make China strong means a strong agriculture' (中国要强，农业必须强), 'to make China rich means the prosperous peasants' (中国要富，农民必须富) and 'to make China beautiful means the pretty countryside' (中国要美，农村必须美). This observation symbolizes the sparks of the Han Emperor Wen's policies of 'prioritizing agriculture' (重农) and his 'personal participation in agriculture' (亲农) which have vigorously survived after two millennia. In Tan Chung's comment to Hsiung and Ling's essays, he has quoted the famous adage of the Song Dynasty scholar, Fan Zhongyan (范仲淹) of Caring for the people from the height of imperial court, and caring for the ruler from the remoteness of rivers and lakes. (居庙堂之高则忧其民，处江湖之远则忧其君)

I regard this observation as the most brilliant summary of the '*guo* (国)/state'-'*min* 民/people' dualism of Chinese civilization and of the 'Chinese dream'. However, we don't see concrete results of 'caring for the people from the height of imperial court' on the part of the emperors of various dynasties in China. During the Mao Zedong Era, those who sat at 'the height of' Zhongnanhai (the erstwhile imperial palace) did, indeed, care for the Chinese 'peasants' many of whom were elevated to the status of PLA (People's Liberation Army) soldiers,

235

Four seas to One Family:
Overseas Chinese and Chinese dream

The great poems of Du Fu give a vivid account of the chaos and insecurity of his times. He gave a remarkable eye-witness account in his masterpiece, '*Shihao li* (石壕吏)/Official of Shihao' that the government officials raided the home of veterans and took away an old woman for military service. He also described, in one of his great poems '*Bingche xing* (兵车行)' (Troops marching), the common people's being 'chased like dogs and chicks' (被驱不异犬与鸡) and:

> Their spirits crying to complain
> fighters on the battlefields slain
> those of the olden times and these days
> (新鬼烦冤旧鬼哭)
> In addition to:
> The skeletons white
> of the braves
> lying in the battlefields
> from olden days ...
> (古来白骨无人收)

Chinese did not live long during Du Fu's time, thus lamented Du Fu in his second poem of '*Qujiang* (曲江)' (The river Qu):

> From olden days till today
> rarely anybody
> live at seventy.
> (人生七十古来稀)

In our 'today' we have more than 200 million healthy and robust senior citizens (on the wrong side of 60 years) in China—more than the entire population of the Tang Dynasty. I saw from the website of 'Global Times' (环球网) that the expectancy of Chinese population has reached 76 in 2011[1], just three years shorter than that of the USA. Centenarians are no longer a rarity in Mainland China today. I don't think Xi Jinping has wanted China to return after 2049 to the times which Du Fu had lamented and cursed?! I have not seen Xi Jinping made such a statement, nor other Chinese leaders hinting to that effect.

It is a good thing that experts within China have participated in our discourse of overseas Chinese on the 'Chinese dream' which helps enrich our thought albeit there is an unbridgeable gap of understanding the 'Chinese dream' between

---

1 See the report of the *Global Times* (环球时报) dated May 17, 2013 from world.huanqiu.com (Downloaded: 31 January 2015).

Symposium II: Delving into All Aspects of the Chinese Dream

unprecedented high cultural pedestal.

We are fortunate to have the two Wangs from China to talk about the 'Chinese dream'. Professor Wang Yiwei of Beijing came back to the academic circles from an assignment in the Chinese embassy to the European Union at Brussels. His understanding of the motivations of Chinese leadership in advocating the 'Chinese dream' may be the most authoritative among all authors of our book. His allusion that 'it is the inspiration of the American dream that the 'Chinese dream' is conceived' is a valuable piece of information which shows that L.H.M. Ling's apprehension is not groundless. Professor Wang Dehua is even greater. He has already digested the four-month old new book of '*Xi Jinping tan zhiguo lizheng* (习近平谈治国理政)' (literally, 'Xi Jinping talks of governance') and flaunts before us, overseas Chinese, how 'Comrade Xi' has conceived the 'Chinese dream' in Xi's own words while, perhaps, no overseas author of our book has even seen its English version, *Xi Jinping: The Governance of China*.

Wang Yiwei comments: 'China is not a nation state, but a civilization-type of state' which upholds our impressions overseas, especially in India, that we have two main categories of 'nation states' and 'civilization states' in the modern world. However, we see more clearly overseas than Wang Yiwei can see inside China that the desert of the 'nation states' is encircling the oases of the 'civilization states' and eroding the latter continually—there is the serious situation of the 'civilization states' (like China and India) being desertified.

I appreciate especially Wang Yiwei's considering it a 'misleading concept' in making the 'Sino-American equation as the world's Number Two versus Number One'. Unfortunately, Wang immediately reiterated after this observation that China would like to become 'a leader country of the world' thus dragging our discourse back to the political situation of the 'nation states' world.

I agree with the two Wangs' opinion that the 'Chinese dream' is not a 'return of the past glory'. The great Tang poet, Du Fu (杜甫), who lived in 'High Tang of the Kaiyuan Era' famously describe his society as:

> Wine and meat decay
> Inside the red gate,
> Skeletons on the roadside
> Those who died of frostbite.[1]
> (朱门酒肉臭，路有冻死骨)

---

[1] Du Fu's extraordinarily long poem of 500 characters entitled '*Zi jing fu Fengxian xian yonghuai* (自京赴奉先县咏怀)' (Rhyming my inner feelings in my journey from the imperial capital to Fengxian County).

pompous words and pedantic theories can contribute to the understanding of the 'Chinese dream'. Now that we have this 'symposium' section of our book, we shall be wasting time if it is filled with verbality sans the 'Chinese sentiments'. Confucius said: '*zhizhe le shui, rezhe le shan* (智者乐水，仁者乐山)' (The sagacious loves the river while the humanist loves the mountain) while Mao Zedong rhymed:

> Rivers and mountains
> What a charming bride!
> Countless braves have vied
> For her with ravenous eyes.

Only people like the great Tang poet, Li Bai, who had toured the length and breadth of China would have the richest 'Chinese dream'. Those who cannot tour China so much like Li Bai and others can transpose the profound affection for 'Chinese dream' of Li Bai and others into the DNA of their own feelings by reading Li Bai and others' great poems. Of course, perceptual understanding must be firmed up by conceptual understanding. Anyone who has a profound comprehension of the Chinese civilization can also accumulate rich affection for 'Chinese dream'. Many overseas Chinese have become ardent lovers of 'Chinese dream' in this way.

I have deepened my understanding of the 'Chinese dream' after reading the two essays of James C. Hsiung's 'The "Chinese Dream," in Comparison with the American Dream' and L.H.M. Ling's 'The 'Chinese dream': Whose "Chinese"? Whose "Dream"?' in addition to the three comments on them by Tan Chung, Wang Yiwei and Wang Dehua. The concluding remark of L.H.M. Ling reads: 'The experience of the Chinese people, in all its richness between past-present- and future, on the mainland and elsewhere, with the West and the rest of the world, has much to offer. There is no lack of spirit or imagination to dream better dreams.' James C. Hsiung's final words are: 'The 'Chinese dream' is absolutely no dream of the hegemon.' 'The world will be prevailed by a totally new culture because of the advent of the 'Chinese dream', and this culture will propound trust, confidence and harmony.' Wang Yiwei echoes these sentiments by saying, in his comment, 'In historical times, Chinese civilization internalized the imported Buddhism and created Buddhist studies and Chan. In modern times, Chinese civilization has Sinified Marxism. We see the special internalization-capability of Chinese civilization. Now, China can demonstrate its fifth modernization, i.e., the modernization of governing ability and system, to transform the Western universal values into the shared value of humanity.' Wang Dehua's comment discusses the 'Chinese dream' at a cultural height that cannot be higher. Thus, we can say that the four essays have raised the discourse of the 'Chinese dream' to an systems and behaviour norms that are cross-boundary and international. We see more commonality of values develop along with the intensification of economic globalization.

However, the common values are absolutely different from 'universal values'. We have the universal truth applicable all over the earth, but not universal values. What the common values reflect are the common needs, interests and aspirations of humanity. They are the sociality and interdependence of humanity and the commonality between various people, nations and countries. The common values are not valid in all times and among all countries and nations. They are applicable to only specific durations and areas. They exist only within specific value equations. The common values are not specific as the universalism of the Western values.

Fourthly, both Hsiung and Ling do not have a comprehensive and symmetric understanding of the strategic thinking about the interactions and mutual emulations between the 'Chinese dream' and the American dream as well as the world dream. When he was in his European trip in 2014, Comrade Xi Jinping propounded an important concept about the interactions and mutual emulations among world civilizations. He put forward the '*Zhongguo shijie wenming guan*中国世界文明观' (Chinese world view of civilization) to be the new concept, new idea and new method for the construction of a harmonious world.[1]

I am in agreement with Professor Ling about the profound meaning of '*li yue*' (rituals and music), but I disagree with her negation of the 'One World, One Dream' slogan which betrays her want of confidence in the 'Chinese dream' and China's ability in peaceful coexistence with other dreams. Perhaps, Dr. Ling is seeing the practical difficulties of the international community in appreciating the 'Chinese dream' because of the factors of divergent national interests, cultural traditions, value systems and competition. It is the apprehension of the international community towards the realization and the purpose of the 'Chinese dream' that the bogeys of 'Chinese threat' and 'future Chinese hegemony' are floated. Or else, the international community has doubts about the relations between the 'Chinese dream' and the individuals, hence it is not surprising that people disagree with the 'One World, One Dream' slogan.

Ishu Huang's (黄绮淑) comment:

Allow me to state my intuition at the outset. I think what is latent inside the 'Chinese dream' is the sentiment, the ardent love for China without which no

---

[1] Zhang Lei (张雷), 'Xi Jinping guanyu tuijin shijie wenming jiaoliu hujiande zhanlue sixiang (习近平关于推进世界文明交流互鉴的战略思想)' (The strategic thinking of Xi Jinping about promoting the interactions and mutual-emulation aong the civilizations of the world), see *Wenhua lunyuan* (文化论苑) (Forum on culture), No. 492, p. 30.

dream'. They are also the direct beneficiaries of the 'Chinese dream'. Thus, in the final analysis, the 'Chinese dream' is the people's dream. It is the dream of a strong country and rich people in the socialist spirit. It is beyond the American dream. The enunciation of the 'Chinese dream' is the manifestation of China's self-confidence and strength. It makes us excited, proud and enthusiastic to hear the bugle for starting the march of the great rejuvenation of Chinese nation. From the perspective of dynamism and development, the halo of the American dream has long faded sans the refill of new contents and new energy, wanting sustainability. On the other hand, China is maintaining a robust developing dynamics and the Chinese society is vibrant with life and strength.[1]

Thirdly, there is the problem about the concept of universal values. Today, the majority of scholars in China are opposed to the 'universal values' concept of Westernization. The concept, from its appearance in China till date, has meant to be the common values of humanity academically. However, I think we should avoid unnecessary confusions and replace it by a less controversial concept considering its origin as well as the pro-Western connotations in the manner it has been used by certain people.

The majority of Chinese scholars feel this term of 'universal values' has travelled a long way from its original religious universalism to the universal social norms as advocated by the theologians and further to the expression of Western hegemony highlighting the Western political theories and systems as models. The concept of 'universal civilization' is the theoretical foundation of Samuel Huntington's theory of the 'Clash of civilizations'.[2] He invented a pronoun of 'Davos Culture' for it and thought it dominated the world development.[3] The development of human civilization is an on-going process of accumulation of experiences and progress, and every generation contributes to its creation on the basis of their forefathers. The accumulation and progress of human civilization include the vertical succession of every civilization as well as the horizontal emulation, absorption and internalization from other civilizations. The development of globalization promotes increasing interactions between various countries and civilizations, and the history of various nations is gradually becoming the 'world history'. The challenges faced by humanity have broken the boundaries between countries. We need to unite and collaborate to face these challenges. Thus, it is necessary to identify certain societal

---

1 Xia Chuntao (夏春涛) on the four basic differences of the 'Chinese dream' from the American dream. See Wan Peng's (万鹏) report on March 28, 2013. Chinese website of *Renminwang* (人民网), *theory.people.com.cn › cn/n/2013/0328/c148980–20950853.html* (Downloaded: 21 January 2015).
2 Sanuel Huntington, *The Clash of Civilizations and the Remaking of Woels Order*, paper backs, Penguin publication, 1996, pp. 56–59.
3 Ibid, p. 57.

Part V
Symposium II: Delving into All Aspects of the Chinese Dream

communists of China. It sustains the will and visions of innumerable patriotic and enlightened Chinese of modern times. It coagulates the sweat and blood of millions of revolutionary heroes and martyrs. It crystallizes the struggle and practices of all nationalities of China. It is the inevitable development of Chinese society in modern times and the choice of history and the people.[1] Four, we have to carry forward the 'spirit of China' in order to realize the 'Chinese dream'. The traditional Chinese culture is enormous and profound and it is beneficial for us to study and grasp its quintessential ideas and ideals so that we have a correct world view, living philosophy and value system.[2] Five, the 'Chinese dream' marks the great rejuvenation of the comity of Chinese nation. A unified and closely united Chinese nation is the common root of the sons and daughters of China within and outside China. The enormous and profound Chinese culture is the common soul of the sons and daughters of China within and outside China. The great rejuvenation of Chinese nation is the common dream of the sons and daughters of China within and outside China.[3]

Secondly, both Hsiung and Ling's articles have not said enough about the basic differences between the Chinese and American dreams. Xia Chuntao (夏春涛), who is the whole-time vice-director of the Centre for the theory and system of socialism of Chinese characteristics of the Chinese Academy of Social Sciences, points out that the 'Chinese dream' and American dream are

the respective dreams of two different countries, and their basic differences are reflected on four facets. From the subjective perspective, the American dream is that of the American people while the 'Chinese dream' is that of the Chinese people. From the perspective of the choice of the onward journey, the US travels along the capitalist path while we (in China) travel along the socialist road. We carry forward the Chinese spirit, gather the Chinese strength, and show the Chinese characteristics and Chinese style. From the perspective of the inner concept, the American dream brags freedom and prosperity as its signature, and claims the capability of making anybody, whatsoever background he or she may come from live his or her dream through individual struggle in the new continent.

The 'Chinese dream' of realizing the great rejuvenation of the Chinese nation covers the three layers of enriching the country, rejuvenating the nation, and bringing happiness to the people. Happiness for the people is the foundation. People of all nationalities of entire China are the main force to realize the 'Chinese

---

1 Xi Jinping: 'The full implementation of the party's eighteen Spirit must focus on six aspects of the work', talk at the first plenum of the 18th Party Congress on November 15, 2012. See *Qiushi* (求是) journal, 2013, No. 1, pp.1–3.
2 Xi Jinping's talks with the media people of three Latin American countries in May 2013. See *People's Daily* (人民日报), June 1, 2013.
3 See *Xi Jinping talk of Governance*, p.63.

"rejuvenation" (*fuxing*) from the state to the Chinese people and Chinese culture'. I commend her reiteration on '*liyue lun* (礼乐论)' (discourse on rituals and music). I belong to the generation who recited the Confucian adage of '*xingyu shi, liyu li, chengyu yue* (兴于诗，立于礼，成于乐)' (rise from poetry, stand on ritual, and accomplished by music)—the generation who understand the value of the ritual of remoulding people's behaviour, creating a culture of hardship-bearing to encourage people to pursue long-term happiness and good fortune rather than indulging in immediate merry-making. The value of music lies in its leading people towards the highest state of life.

The two great scholars have lived in the US for long and conceived a deep understanding of the American dream. They are also Chinese, and their writings have revealed their sentiments of 'I love China'. Both of them have firmly appreciated the 'Chinese dream' enunciated by General Secretary Xi Jinping. They firmly believe that the rejuvenation of golden days of China will appear soon.

To begin with, the 'Chinese dream' is the rational concept of Chinese people. It is the Chinese idealism. Just as Comrade Xi Jinping said that 'The 'Chinese dream' is historical, realistic and futuristic', ours is a nation that has shown its penchant in pursuing dreams. Ancient fairy tales like Houyi's (后羿) shooting down nine extra suns and Chang'e's (嫦娥) fleeing her husband on earth to the moon reveal a nation of idealism and dream. Unfortunately, we have been a little late in propounding the concept of the 'Chinese dream'. Both James C. Hsiung's and L.H.M. Ling's articles have quoted chapter and verse mainly from ancient and Western sources, deficient in their quotations directly from Comrade Xi Jinping's writings (such as '*Xi Jinping tan zhiguo lizheng* (习近平谈治国理政)/Xi Jinping Talk of Governance' by Foreign Languages Press, Beijing, October 2014) and a series of talks.

Since the 18th Party Congress Comrade Xi has succinctly unfolded the 'Chinese dream' narrative which is meant to realize the great rejuvenation of the Chinese nation. I shall just abstract 5 points from the richness of his thought. One, the 'Chinese dream' is a dream of peace, development, cooperate and win-win not only for the Chinese people, but also for the people of the world. History tells us that the future and destiny of every individual are interconnected with those of the state and the nation. Only when the state and the nation are in good shape can we all have a nice time.[1] Two, in the final analysis, the 'Chinese dream' is the people's dream. Only by closely relying on the people can it be realized, thus we must continually strive for the happiness of the people.[2] Three, only along the 'Chinese road' can we live the 'Chinese dream'. Our choice is socialism with the Chinese characteristics. It bears the ideal and quest of several generations of the

---

1 See *Xi Jinping talk of Governance*, Beijing: Foreign Languages Press, 2014, p. 35.
2 Ibid, p. 38.

traditions in addition to new inclusions and innovations. The 'Chinese dream' is not a simple dream of modernization. It is not a Western dream or American dream. It is a civilization dream—to create the new human civilization to rejuvenate and transform Chinese civilization. The historical significance and world value of 'Chinese dream' can only be clearly visualized from the perspective of history of human civilization.

Wang Dehua's (王德华) comment:

Director and Researcher of the Institute of South Asia and Central Asia of the Shanghai Center for International Studies, and concurrently the Director and Researcher of the Center for South Asia of Tongji University, Shanghai, Vice Director and Researcher of the Center for China-India Comparative Studies of the Shanghai Academy of Social Sciences with more than ten books in Chinese to his credit.

Below is my general impressions after reading the two articles of 'The "Chinese Dream," in Comparison with the American Dream' by James C. Hsiung and 'The 'Chinese dream': Whose "Chinese"? Whose "Dream"?' by L.H.M. Ling.

James Hsiung's article has its focus on the 'Chinese dream' and China's national revival after a general introduction of the American dream and 'Chinese dream'. The bright spot of his piece lies in his highlighting 'the earliest world view, or weltanschauung, held by the ancient forefathers' of China and the West as well as their different views on 'salvation'. It traces the cultural origins of the West where individuals are insatiably avaricious while the states are restive in pursuing power to the prioritization of progress and competition by hook or by crook on the part of the Western commercial culture, carrying voraciousness to infinity. The Western religious belief in 'salvation lying outside oneself' makes the Western world further demoralized. Though China has been widely hit by epidemic waves of mammonism of foreign commercial culture in recent years, the new leadership of General Secretary Xi Jinping has taken measures in dealing with corruption with an iron hand—killing both tigers and flies mercilessly. This is also the essential path in realizing the 'Chinese dream'. Hsiung's article distinguishes 'Chinese dream' from the inspiration of hegemony and advises the West to emulate China's spirit of 'neisheng waiwang (内圣外王)' which he translates as 'be a saint to yourself, and a magnanimous patron to others'.

L.H.M. Ling's article defines the 'Chinese dream' with her creative application of the Taoist/Daoist dialectics to conceive international relations as the interaction between the two dynamics of the *yang* of the West and the *yin* of the 'non-West' so that world politics moves away from hegemony and violence and towards balance and engagement. Her article alludes to 'a shift of the concept and goal of *lu* (Elegy of the ocean—A realization from the European civilization) that this 'new humanism' has three dimensions: (a) to prove its rationality by pushing the sustainable development of humanity; (b) to prove its eligibility by becoming all-inclusive to all international societies, especially with the West embracing the East, the North embracing the South, to realize a lasting peace and shared prosperity; and (c) to prove its purposefulness by eliminating the dichotomy of the maritime civilizations of maintaining democracy internally and autocracy externally, of allowing diversity within and pursuing universality abroad so that the world can return to its divergent self.

The genesis of the troubles of the world today can be traced from the global expansion of Western capitalist civilization which generates three increasing tensions. These are: (a) tension between the individual and the society—the modern contradictions created by the capitalist industrialization has not been eliminated by the end of the Cold War while the post-Cold War conflict and crisis are showing up; (b) tension between humans and their natural environment—humans have become both masters and enemies of Nature as its harmony and tranquility have been thoroughly devastated by the modern industrial civilization; and (c) tension between humans and humans—modernization is the creator of modern malaise of the 'pursuance of greed and materialism', the financial crisis that has engulfed the entire world was resultant from the scramble for financial derivatives and super profit and all the excessive greed that went into them.

Thus, the great 'Chinese dream' about China's rejuvenation is not 'a return of the past glory'. Such a 'return of the past glory' neither resolves China's problems today, nor enables it to effectively respond to the serious challenges of the world. It is even more misleading to conceive the 'Chinese dream' as meeting the international advancement at the frontier level. We wound not concede that the West means advancement. The West is too seriously bogged down by its own troubles to even 'lead from behind'. Some Western countries are hoping to blaze a new trail to meet China's advancement. The great 'Chinese dream' of rejuvenation is a three-in-one realization of the return of the best traditions in addition to new inclusions and innovations. We must germinate the seed of the maritime civilizations within Chinese civilization after optimally restoring our native civilization so that the Western civilization becomes a part of Chinese civilization. We must discard the myth of the so-call universal values of the West so that we can create the shared value systems of humanity and further create a new human civilization. We must lead the world into the '2.0' version of the maritime era to realize the sustainable development of human civilization which will create the leading role of China as a state.

In short, Chinese civilization is shouldering a historical mission and the responsibility of our era of a three-in-one realization of the return of the best system with Chinese idiosyncrasy. All the three manifestations are reflections of China's self-confidence in culture. In historical times, Chinese civilization internalized the imported Buddhism and created Buddhist studies and Chan. In modern times, Chinese civilization has Sinified Marxism. We see the special internalization-capability of Chinese civilization. Now, China can demonstrate its fifth modernization, i.e., the modernization of governing ability and system, transforming the Western universal values into the shared value of humanity.

About China's self-realization, China today is rather identical with the United States 170 years ago when it started its de-Europeanization. The American poet, Ralph Waldo Emerson, said in his speech at Harvard University in 1837 thus: 'Our day of dependence, our long apprenticeship to the learning of other lands, draws to a close. The millions, that around us are rushing into life, cannot always be fed on the sere remains of foreign harvests.'[1] By 'other lands', Emerson meant Europe. This observation shows the arrival of the USA at a new stage of independent spirit after the War of Independence. China today highlights the Chinese idiosyncrasy of the 'Chinese dream' to mark its departure from the post-Opium War ideological confusions of the dualistic fusion and transformation of the roles of traditional Chinese wisdom and Western learning. China is self-consciously implementing socialism, championing justice and righteousness within and outside China, establishing China's national spirit on the tradition of 'all for the public good under Heaven'.

About China's responsibility, it is important to note that we highlight the Chinese idiosyncrasy sans xenophobia. On the contrary, what we reiterate is harmony, not uniformity, a harmonious coexistence of divergence. Absorbing the best from divergent sources and internalizing external inspirations and influences have been the cause of the sustainable development of Chinese civilization. The Chinese idiosyncrasy has a world origin via Chinese acculturation. People should understand the 'Chinese dream' from the history of human civilization and to treat China as a civilization-type of state. We are not seeing a simplistic rejuvenation or transformation of the Chinese civilization. We are seeing the Chinese civilization facing a great mission of innovation—to contribute to the sustainability of human civilization.

More and more facts indicate that only technology and institution cannot put the world in order, it will have to depend increasingly on the change and innovation of civilization. We have to create a 'new humanism' that encompasses the West, North and South, that is built on the foundations of all the excellent civilizations of humanity. I have pointed out in my book, *Haishang?—Ouzhou wenming qishi*

---

1 From '*An Oration delivered before the Phi Beta Kappa Society, at Cambridge, August 31, 1837*', www.emersoncentral.com/amscholar.htm *accessed on 6 February, 2015.*

their economic growth. When China does this it opens a new leaf for the culture of sustainable development and it becomes a leader country of the world. This is, of course, what Obama had not realized. The American dream is charming by its religious tenets and founding principles. Its greatest captivating power lies in its minimal state concern by highlighting the universal success, predicating the American superiority on the advanced logics of humanity. There is the issue of universal values that some people are so obsessed with. The so-called 'universal values' are nothing but the packaging of some wide-spread values which provide no solutions to the problems faced by the West, let alone China.

Let us turn to 'whose China, whose dream?', we see in the 'Chinese dream' a convergence with the dreams of other countries, but also its idiosyncrasy. It is vitally important to comprehend the temporal contents of this Chinese idiosyncrasy. What is it?

In the first place, China is not a nation state, but a civilization-type of state. There has been uninterrupted continuity of development of the Chinese civilization which has never been colonized by any other civilization. More important is its worldly nature. The rise of China has been that of a worldly civilization. This is the greatest idiosyncrasy. Today, the leadership of the Communist Party of China is the manifestation of this worldly civilization in the political arena.

Second, China is a socialist country. Persevering with the socialist system is refreshingly special of Chinese politics. We reiterate the value system with socialism as its core. We pursue freedom and democracy as they are understood by socialism, not to be confused with the Western freedom and democracy. Though freedom and democracy are universal phenomena, they are not universal values. Those who are opposed to the Chinese idiosyncrasy by invoking the so-called universal values actually pursue an ideological struggle.

Third, China is an extra-large society, having an extra-lengthy history. It is embarking on an extraordinary historical odyssey of modernization and rejuvenation. The rise of China has not only enriched its own modernization and rejuvenation but also encouraged other countries to embark on the journey of modernization and rejuvenation according to their own circumstances.

Among all countries, past and present, few can blow their own horns of idiosyncrasy, and few can dream their own dreams. The 'Chinese dream' has surpassed the identity of an ordinary country to reflect China's own contents and the rays of the times. When we propound the 'Chinese dream' by highlighting the Chinese idiosyncrasy, we are showing China's self-confidence, self-realization and responsibility.

About China's self-confidence, there are three manifestations of the 'Chinese dream' with Chinese idiosyncrasy, namely, the socialist road with Chinese idiosyncrasy, the socialist theory with Chinese idiosyncrasy, and the socialist the book and also for my own enlightenment. I'm not here to score debating points. Perhaps, readers will deepen their understanding of the 'Chinese dream' after reading the two scholars' reply to my provocation.

Wang Yiwei's (王义桅) comment:

Professor James C. Hsiung's article 'The "Chinese Dream," in Comparison with the American Dream' and Professor L.H.M. Ling's article 'The 'Chinese dream': Whose "Chinese"? Whose "Dream"?' do encompass two scenarios of the 'Chinese dream': (a) how would the 'Chinese dream' go beyond the American dream, and (b) how do we go beyond the Western narrative when we view and discuss the 'Chinese dream'?

Let us first see how the 'Chinese dream' can go beyond the American dream. In fact, it is the inspiration of the American dream that the 'Chinese dream' is conceived, but the enunciation of the 'Chinese dream' itself is a step beyond the American dream. It shows that China has started its own dream instead of pursuing the American dream. The American dream was born during the Great Depression. It highlighted the USA as the land of hope for every immigrant who could supposedly realize his or her values through hard work after landing on American soil. Nevertheless, the realization of the American dream resulted in tremendous waste in resources, especially energy. In our era of constrictive sustainable development the American dream is fading while the European dream is being commended albeit the latter also starts to fade along with the rising European debt crisis. All this has provided validations for playing up the Chinese threat. The misleading concept of Sino-American equation as the world's Number Two versus Number One all the more creates an anxiety of the American dream being supplanted by the 'Chinese dream'. The misunderstanding lies in the lack of realization of China's all-inclusive culture. China is not a monolithic religious country, thus does not handicap other countries in realizing their dreams. We cannot convince the world by saying 'the 'Chinese dream' echoes the dreams of all other peoples in pursuing a better life'. How does it echo? What happens if it doesn't echo? Does the 'Chinese dream' mean China's world ambition?

If China does not dream its own dream, it would dream the American dream, or the dream of universal values. The American dream cares for equal opportunities rather than results. It cares for efficacy rather than sustainability. China's super size would bring an unbearable burden upon the world if it emulates everything American. President Obama said when he was interviewed by the Australian Television on April 15, 2010 that if all the one odd billion Chinese lived like Australians and Americans the globe would not be able to sustain it, and all people on earth would become miserable. He thought the Chinese leadership would understand this and pursue a new and more sustainable model for pursuing

'Chinese'—until 'China' is mentioned. Then their feelings of endearment vanish. A complex of feelings and perceptions emerges, ranging from apprehension to fear. (Both Napoleon and Marx shared this fear.) On this point, China seems to fall into the company of the USA. I think such a phenomenon is contrary to reason. Whether 'state' or 'people', China should be considered a uniform spirit. How could there be a good 'Chinese dream' if China is understood in schizophrenic terms? I wonder whether this is the thrust of Ling's article?

I have just now reiterated 'you in me and I in you'. Buddhism introduced the concept but it was present also in *Laozi* (老子) and *Zhuangzi* (庄子). Ling's article quotes Zhuangzi's 'there is no self in the sage' (圣人无己) as elucidated in the section, 'Wandering at Ease' (逍遥游), in the *Zhuangzi*. It highlights 'the self's relations with others such that creativity is both an individual and a collective enterprise'. Here, Ling alludes to the grip of 'Eurocentrism' on modern studies in international relations, creating a yawning gulf between Eastern and Western cultures. Hsiung's reference to the spirit of *neisheng waiwang*—which he translates as 'be a saint to yourself, and a magnanimous patron to others'—seems difficult to establish in this context.

Hsiung presents *neisheng waiwang* as a means of addressing Chinese corruption *and* US hegemony. However, in all my decades of studying Chinese civilization, I have yet to notice this phrase, especially regarding the notion of 'All under Heaven' (天下). Nor have I come across any commentary on this motto from ancient Chinese masters. What I know is that in recent decades, there has been a vogue in Hong Kong and Taiwan to play up *neisheng waiwang* as the quintessence of Confucian thought. This all the more puzzles me: what is the substance in this four-syllabic phrase ridiculously translated by some as 'inside the saint and outside the king'? On this point, some circles in US international relations—including my good friend, Professor John Mearsheimer, champion of 'offensive realism' at the Chicago University—have been partially misled by Chinese intellectuals into focusing on Sunzi's (Sun Tzu) *The Art of War* (孙子兵法), in addition to the Chinese slogans of *yuanjiao jingong* (远交近攻, alliance with those distant and attacking those close by) and *neisheng waiwang*, thereby drawing a conclusion that China's tradition of international relations is no different from that of the US. This makes me worry whether there would not emerge another, US-style superpower if China were to adopt the spirit of *neisheng waiwang*. Would this not conflict with emphases in Chinese diplomacy on the principles of 'closeness, sincerity, sharing in prosperity and inclusiveness' (亲诚惠容) for regional neighbors? All this makes me wonder why Hsiung would so prominently focus on *neisheng waiwang* when discussing the 'Chinese dream'. Once again, I am provoking my friend for the purpose of 'getting a gem by throwing a brick'.

My active participation in the symposium for these two articles is for the good of eliminated the identities and differences of the 'primordial' idiosyncrasies of the nations and gradually developed into one civilization and one state. We can call it a 'civilization state'.

Nomadic culture exercised an even greater influence on India than China. Rabindranath Tagore, the great Indian writer, spoke of two major features in Indian culture—the 'wandering ascetic' and the 'householder'. The former represents nomadic culture; the latter, agriculture. With the advent of Buddhism in China, the Indian 'wandering ascetic' merged with the Chinese 'householder'. Their millennial interaction and vibrations stabilized and flourished Chinese civilization. Hundreds of Indian monks went to China to preach Buddhism while hundreds of Chinese monks went to India to learn about Buddhism. The Indian monks suffered no nostalgia and a majority of them breathed their last on Chinese soil; while the Chinese monks tried their level best to return home. Today, we have the Dayanta (大雁塔/Great Swan Tower) and the Xiaoyanta (小雁塔/Small Swan Tower) in Xi'an to symbolize their triumphant return to the homeland. Indeed, many such Buddhist temples dot the Chinese landscape: Anguosi (安国寺, Temple pacifying the state), Xingguosi (兴国寺, Temple rejuvenating the state), Longguosi (隆国寺, Temple enriching the state), Qingguosi (清国寺, Temple purifying the state), Huguosi (护国寺, Temple protecting the state), Baoguosi (保国寺, Temple safeguarding the state), Ningguosi (宁国寺, Temple tranquillizing the state), Baoguosi (报国寺, Temple of redeeming gratitude to the state), and so on. The *guo* (国/nation) in these names referred to China, not India. The Indian monks not only wanted Buddhism to thrive, but they also had dedicated themselves to the prosperity and security of China. This comparison demonstrates that nomadic culture could be nobler and greater than its agricultural counterpart.

Ling's article begins with her own dream thirty years ago about a dilapidated grand, old mansion. Yet it still showed signs of hope given allusions to China's age-old civilization and its ability to 'rejuvenate' (复兴). With this theme she dwells on a discourse of old and new ideas among Chinese and foreign scholars. The problem, however, is that at the end of 2014, people have started talking about 2015 as being 'the first year of the Chinese century'. We see people in China raising the issue of how to create and maintain a new international order at the moment when US hegemony seems in decline. There is even a cry for 'harder'" 'more proactive,' and 'more sophisticated' Chinese diplomacy in addition to 'Chinese diplomacy shouldering greater responsibilities'. Perhaps, Hsiung's essay makes Ling's appear to lag behind the times. I make this remark only in the spirit of 'getting a gem by throwing a brick'.

In Ling's article, a boundary is drawn between 'the state of China' （中国） and 'the Chinese people and civilization' (中华). I am reminded of the distinction— 'China' vs 'Chinese'—made by foreign friends. They seem to embrace all things

Four seas to One Family:
Overseas Chinese and Chinese dream

In my essay for this book, I posit that 'Humanity's first great dream was the one that gave birth to the Buddha.' I also consider Han Emperor Ming's (汉明帝) dream of a golden Buddha flying over his palace as China's earliest great dream. I think these two great dreams have greatly contributed to the spiritual cultivation of Chinese civilization. As a consequence, China features such great *Chindia* thought voiced by the 11th–century, Song Dynasty scholar-cum-minister, Fan Zhongyan (范仲淹): 'Be the first to worry about the worries of the world, and the last to enjoy the enjoyment of the world' (先天下之忧而忧，后天下之乐而乐) and 'Caring for the people from the height of the imperial court, and caring for the ruler from the remoteness of rivers and lakes' (居庙堂之高则忧其民，处江湖之远则忧其君). Chinese civilization has also reached one of the greatest insights into human relations: that is, 'you in me and I in you' (你中有我，我中有你). It relates to the virtue of merging the individual with state (the part with the whole) as expressed in the saying: 'sacrifice the *micro*-me for the *macro*-me' (牺牲小我为大我)—the '*micro*-me' (小我) actually transposes into the Indian concept of '*atma*'; the '*macro*-me' (大我) into '*paramatma*'. I am glad to see this sense echoed in Ling's piece whereby she quotes the line, "you in me and I in you," from the 12th–century Persian poem, 'Conference of the Birds' (*Mantiq-ut-Tayr*). This is, indeed, a 'universal value'.

I don't see a sharp contrast between nomadic and agricultural cultures. It seems, we overseas Chinese have betrayed China's 'reluctant-to-move' or 'rooted-to-the-soil' tradition and become nomads of sorts in modern times. Basically, I find the creation of China quite unique. The third greatest river on earth, the Yangzi, and the fifth greatest, the Huanghe, start their journey from almost the same area in the Qinghai-Tibetan Plateau, i.e., the mountain ranges of the Tangula (唐古拉山) and the Bayanhar/*Bayankela* (巴颜喀拉山). The Huanghe flows from Qinghai mostly in the northern half of China through eight provinces.[1] The Yangzi flows across China's southern half, again through eight provinces.[2] In the lower streams, the Huai River connects the Huanghe and Yangzi before it flows into the sea. Such a unique layout of the two great rivers carves out the contours of a country as big as Europe in the eastern end of Eurasia. Flora and fauna, as well as humans, developed along these rivers to form a nomadic culture before the onset of agriculture. Even during Confucius' time, nomadic culture was still thriving. Both Confucius and Mencius were nomads fond of traveling, not reluctant to move. We see the Shaanxi terracotta archaeological finds providing a group image of Emperor Qin Shihuangdi's army. It consists of members of various nomadic tribes, rendering this ancient army more diverse than today's US military. The rhythm of the development of Chinese civilization is: innumerable ethnic tribes slowly

---

1 Sichuan, Gansu, Ningxia, Inner Mongolia, Shaanxi, Shanxi, Henan and Shandong.
2 Sichuan, Tibet, Yunnan, Hubei, Hunan, Jiangxi, Anhui and Jiangsu.

'Chinese dream': A Comparison with the American Dream' and Professor L.H.M.Ling's 'The 'Chinese dream': Whose "Chinese"? Whose "Dream"?, and placed them after the article, 'Transform the 'Chinese dream' into a World Dream', written by Professor Wang Yiwei of the Chinese Renmin University of Beijing. We do so to make our discourse on the nature of the 'Chinese dream' more penetrating. We have also invited Chinese experts to comment on these articles and join the discourse so that our book can make a small contribution to further understanding the "Chinese dream."

We hear two voices from the Chinese media: one calls for 'more, higher, faster, and stronger' while the other seeks international cooperation and co-prosperity with the world in order to create a 'shared destiny'. These reflect the complexities of thinking about the "Chinese dream." Hsiung and Ling represent two sources of insight from overseas Chinese into the "Chinese dream," as articulated by Xi Jinping in terms of carrying forward the 'Chinese spirit', traveling along the 'Chinese road', and consolidating 'Chinese power'. Hsiung's piece focuses more on the difference between Chinese and Western cultures, drawing a clear division between the 'Chinese dream' and the 'American dream'. Ling's piece is an elucidation guided by her post-colonial perspective with a clear vision that the 'Chinese dream' is neither a copycat of the Western dream, nor is it isolated from a world of common destiny. Yet these two, seemingly divergent essays are mutually complementary. Both of them are highly confident in China's millennial civilizational wisdom, and both urge Chinese intellectuals to free themselves from centuries-old Western mis-guidance. My skepticism lies in whether these two scholars have liberated themselves from Western influence. This view may not be shared by them, but it serves my purpose to provoke them into further clarification. I look forward to, as the Chinese saying goes, 'getting a gem by throwing a brick'(抛砖引玉).

Hsiung's article defines a 'dream' as a visionary paradigm. He draws on four, great visionary paradigms: Plato's philosopher king, Hobbes' Leviathan, Marx's dictatorship of the proletariat, and the *Liji*'s (礼记, Book of Rites) 'Grand Harmony' (大同). Hsiung sees the ancient Chinese philosopher, Zhuangzi (庄子), and his 'butterfly dream' (蝴蝶梦) as too romantic to reach the height of these four visionary paradigms. But we can view this claim from another angle. We could regard Zhuangzi's 'butterfly dream' as achieving a kind of spiritual metamorphosis between the philosopher and the butterfly that transcends the bounds of worldliness. Such a perspective overshadows the four, previous visionary paradigms (which merely extend ideas and ideals from the political world). These do not measure up to Zhuangzi's 'butterfly dream', much less the great visionary paradigm of the Buddha who transcended the bonds of human life as epitomized by 'birth', 'decay', 'sickness', and 'death'.

and complexity from the West itself.[1] We fail to register that various strains of history—and its contending interpretations—have always swirled within the West. For Alker, the 'conceptions of our common, multi-layered history' may be 'incomplete and uneven',[2] but it offers greater emancipatory potential for world politics than the conventional, closed, and singular story of humankind.

The US, too, is not just a global superpower intent on policing the world. There beats within American culture a strong tradition of struggle and solidarity to attain freedom despite conditions of slavery, poverty, and depression. Hannah Arendt, a German Jew who found refuge in New York in the 1930s, sounds very Buddhist and Daoist when she theorized that humanity's emancipation lies in forgiveness fostered through cooperation with others—even while recognizing that some things cannot be forgiven.[3]

Here, I find Daoism's take on creativity especially helpful. It arises, the *Zhuangzi* notes, from the self's relations with others such that creativity is both an individual and a collective enterprise.[4] This insight, however, does not belong to Daoism alone. Other ancient traditions, like Sufi Islam, also teach such wisdom. Note this stanza from the 12th–century Persian poem, 'Conference of the Birds':

> And a voice said to them, 'We are mirrors all.
> All are reflected and reflecting, see,
> It is "*Me*" in "*You*" and "*You*" in "*Me*".'[5]

The 'Chinese dream', in conclusion, doesn't have to be an imported addiction, producing a sweaty haze of predictable self-destruction. The experience of the Chinese people, in all its richness between past-present-and future, on the mainland and elsewhere, with the West and the rest of the world, has much to offer. There is no lack of spirit or imagination to dream better dreams.

Tan Chung's (谭中) comment:

We have taken out two contributions, i.e., Professor James C. Hsiung's 'The

---

1 Hayward R. Alker, 'If Not Huntington's Civilizations, then Whose?' *Review* 18 (4) Fall 1995: 533–562.
2 *Ibid.*, 560.
3 Hannah Arendt, *The Human Condition*, 2nd Edition (Chicago: The University of Chicago Press, [1958] 1998).
4 See, for example, Roger T. Ames (ed.), *Wandering at Ease in the Zhuangzi* (Albany: State University of New York Press, 1998).
5 Farid Ud-Din Attar, The Simurgh and the Birds, a selection from Mantiq-ut-Tayr (Conference of the Birds), translated and simplified by Fahmida Riaz (Karachi: Oxford University Press, 2014), p. 94.

Part V
Symposium II: Delving into All Aspects of the Chinese Dream

politics will affect the content and purpose of the 'Chinese dream'. The former invariably transforms the latter.

Perhaps my dream from thirty years ago was telling. It suggests a shift of the concept and goal of 'rejuvenation' (*fuxing*复兴) from the state to the Chinese people and Chinese culture. Indeed, my dream's focus on music and writing evokes the ancient notion of *liyue*礼乐 (rituals and music):

> Descending from Zhou times (11th–3rd centuries BC), there prevailed *liyue lun* [discourse on rituals and music], the vision of a feudal society (in the most general sense) in which political rule was supposed to be conducted mainly through 'rituals and music', as the governing principles of an organic and stable moral order. Here 'rituals and music' should not be understood literally. They are the name for institutions with a direct moral purpose, including the systems for fief and tribute, land, education, etc. Since morality was intrinsic to these institutions, the norms of the external order could serve as criteria of ethical evaluation. In the horizon of *liyue lun*, textual study or *jingxue*—scrutiny of a series of Confucian classics—came to be the major branch of learning.[1]

Let me be clear: I am not suggesting a 'back to the future' scenario for China. Nor do I support the Beijing Olympic's simplistic slogan of 'One World, One Dream' (*tong yige shijie, tong yige mengxiang*同一个世界，同一个梦想). The meaning of *liyue* lies deeper. That is, an 'organic and stable moral order' must govern social and political institutions such that *ethics* become a major criterion of evaluation and judgment. And these ethics must be grounded in what resonates with *local* practices, customs, desires, and aspirations. These now reflect, of course, exchanges with and adaptations from learning that come from outside China's classical traditions. The challenge remains how to integrate the old and the new, the native and the foreign, the East and the West. Here, 'rejuvenation' (*fuxing*) for the Chinese people and culture need not refer only to what happens on the mainland. Rather, much can be learned between those on the mainland and those 'overseas' (*hai wai*海外), constituting a new kind of 'classic' knowledge (*jingxue*经学).

Nor am I advocating a rejection or expulsion or overthrow of the 'West'. This kind of linear, categorical, and uncompromising thinking is precisely what colonial elites in the West and their acolytes in the Rest have imposed on peoples everywhere as 'knowledge.' Westphalia's West, in other words, is not the entire West. Rendering Western civilization as self-enclosed, mutually exclusive, and fearful of the Other, IR scholar Hayward Alker had pointed out, exiles diversity

---

1 Zhang Yongle, 'The Future of the Past: On Wang Hui's *Rise of Modern Chinese Thought*,' *New Left Review* 62 (March/April 2010): 57.

Chinese characteristics further clarified by 60 points.¹ The latter, Cui explains, serve as provisional guidelines to the overall goal. To Cui, this delineation of an 'overall goal' supplemented by what he calls 'framework goals' (*jia kuang mu biao* 架框目标) suggests a greater loosening of and creativity in state-local relations, thereby allowing for more local experimentation with key assets like state-owned enterprises, land trust in rural development, and the party-state relationship. While listening to Cui's deep analysis of Xi's reform strategy, I couldn't help but think of the *Huainanzi* (淮南子) (Master of Huainan, 139 BCE), an exemplar of Daoist politics.² A treatise on proper governance, the *Huainanzi* was presented to the newly ascendant, 15–year–old Emperor Wu of the Han Dynasty to educate him on 'the entire body of knowledge required for a contemporary monarch to rule successfully and well.'³ And a crucial feature of such knowledge focused on how to maintain a stable, imperial center while enabling, at the same time, strong, active local sources of power, thereby ensuring their loyalty.

One analyst in the West considers this inward focus 'oxymoronic'. Resorting to Confucian classics, William Callahan writes, turns the Chinese 'gaze back to an ancient golden age rather than to a future utopia'.⁴ At the same time, he claims, the American Dream *really* drives the 'Chinese dream'. '[E]ven China's nativists are still fascinated by America.'⁵

Callahan's first observation, however, simply defies history. Scholars in the West like Martha Nussbaum, for example, have garnered widespread acclaim for drawing on Aristotelian philosophy (382–322 BCE) to theorize about justice under modernity,⁶ and political activists in India have long mobilized support for various movements, including independence from Britain, by invoking the ancient scripture, *Baghavad Gita* (2nd–4th century BCE).⁷ And Callahan's second observation makes an invalid assumption: that is, the 'Chinese dream' will remain forever reactive to and emulative of the American Dream *despite* China's 'inward' turn. Clearly, a re-appreciation of China's own archives of history, culture, and

---

1 'Decision of the Chinese Communist Party Central Committee on Several Major Questions About Deepening Reform' (中共中央关于全面深化改革若干重大问题的决定), available in Chinese at (http://news.xinhuanet.com/politics/2013–11/15/c_118164235.htm) (Downloaded: 1 May 2014).
2 An Liu, *The Huainanzi: A Guide to the Theory and Practice of Government in Early Han China*, in John S. Major, Sarah A. Queen, Andrew S. Meyer, and Harold D. Roth (eds and translators) (New York: Columbia University Press, 2010).
3 *Ibid.*, p. 1.
4 William A. Callahan, "*Chinese Dreams*": *20 Visions of the Future* (Oxford: Oxford University Press, 2013), pp. 9–10.
5 Callahan, "*Chinese Dreams*", *op.cit.*, p. 10.
6 Martha Nussbaum, *Sex and Social Justice* (Oxford: Oxford University Press, 1999).
7 Shruti Kapila and Faisal Devji, 'The *Baghavad Gita* and Modern Thought: Introduction', Forum, *Modern Intellectual History* 7 (2) July 2010: 269–273.

Part V
Symposium II: Delving into All Aspects of the Chinese Dream

and intellectual traditions.¹

Because the tradition of Chinese dialectics 'does not seek certainty', Qin explains, it could not sanction hegemony for China or any other state.² *Contra* Hegelian/Marxian dialectics, Chinese dialectics 'stresses change and inclusiveness,' leading to a dynamic co-production of identity or what Qin calls 'co-thesis or inter-thesis complementation'.³ From this basis, the peacefulness of China's rise will not depend on China alone. Nor does it necessitate conformity or adaptation to the norms, rules, and practices of today's international society. Rather, international society reflects 'a complexity of relational networks'; consequently, the nature of China's rise will involve an 'interaction between China and international society, the United States, and other members of the international community.'⁴ In short, China's rise unfolds in a context. And it is China's engagement with this context that will shape the agenda for global politics, not an unchanging set of 'deep and durable practices' that emanate from a fixed 'international society'.

Another source of new thinking comes from the social historian Wang Hui. He questions some of the basic assumptions and categories that Western knowledge, especially social science, has perpetrated onto other societies and cultures. Even the category of Asia, he notes, requires re-imagining. To capture 'the idea [of Asia]', Wang suggests, we need to see it not only as a piece of geography with a specific culture and history but also as a constant dynamic of creation empowered through seemingly opposite forces. That is, Asia 'is at once colonialist and anticolonialist, conservative and revolutionary, nationalist and internationalist, originating in Europe and, alternatively, shaping Europe's image of itself.'⁵

Cui Zhiyuan, a professor of public policy and management at Tsinghua University, provides an example in Xi Jinping's reform strategy for China.⁶ In it, Xi outlined the 'overall goal' (*zong mu biao*) of implementing socialism with

---

1 Qin Yaqing, 'International Society as a Process: Institutions, Identities, and China's Peaceful Rise,' *The Chinese Journal of International Politics* (3) 2010: 138. For more on his views, see a recent interview, *Theory Talks* (online forum), 30 November 2011 (http://www.theory-talks.org/2011/11/theory-talk–45.html) (Downloaded: 1 February 2012).
2 *Ibid.*, 139.
3 *Ibid.*
4 *Ibid.*, 138, 130–131.
5 Wang Hui, *The Politics of Imagining Asia*, edited by Theodore Huters (Cambridge: Harvard University Press, 2011), p. 59.
6 Cui Zhiyuan, 'Understanding Xi Jinping's Grand Reform Strategy', public talk at the India China Institute, The New School, 29 April 2014. Professor Cui represents a new breed of Chinese academic who also works with government in the field. From 2010–2011, he took a leave of absence from Tsinghua University to work as Assistant Director of the State Asset Management Committee of the Chongqing Government.

of Eurocentric ideas, methods, theories, and practices in the field of International Relations (IR), even after three centuries of discourse and debate.[1] In my own work, I draw on Daoist dialectics to re-envision IR as a dynamic between the *yang*-'West' and the *yin*-'Rest' as a means of turning world politics away from hegemony and violence and towards balance and engagement.[2] In 2007, Routledge launched the book series, 'Worlding Beyond the West';[3] in 2014, Rowman & Littlefield added two other book series that aim to 'contribute to debates in the field which extend beyond Western academic constituencies to include [those] from the Global South' such that we can finally realize how the 'West' and the 'Rest' *co-constitute* world politics.[4]

'The time of *sahibs* and *munshees* is over!' Amitav Acharya declared, as incoming President of the International Studies Association (ISA) in March 2014. In his acceptance speech, Acharya analogized the ISA, the world's largest organization for the study of world politics, to a British college established in 19th–century Calcutta. The college referred to the British professors as *sahib*, given their status as lordly purveyors of knowledge. The Indian instructors, by contrast, were called *munshee*, to designate their status as native language teachers or secretaries to Europeans. IR will no longer mirror this kind of colonial knowledge production, Acharya underscored. IR will globalize. 'It's no longer your mentor's ISA', someone remarked behind me in the audience.

New thinking is emerging from within China as well. Qin Yaqing, an IR theorist, suggests another way to understand China's 'rise'. Instead of requiring China to assimilate into pre-established 'rules of the game', Qin draws on Chinese dialectics to redefine what it means to participate in and constitute an 'international society':

> Society is not a self-enclosed, self-contained entity. Rather, it is a process, an open process of complex social relations in motion. Rules, regimes, and institutions are not established to govern or restrain the behavior of individual actors in society, but to harmonize relations among members of society. This understanding of society is based upon the relational thought process and the complementary dialectic, both of which originate in the Chinese philosophical

---

1 John M. Hobson, *The Eurocentric Conception of World Politics: Western International Relations Theory, 1760–2010* (Cambridge: Cambridge University Press, 2012).
2 L.H.M. Ling, *The Dao of World Politics: Towards a Post-Westphalian, Worldist International Relations* (London: Routledge, 2014).
3 See: (http://www.taylorandfrancis.com/books/series/WBW/) (Downloaded: 13 June 2014).
4 These are the book series, 'Kilombo: International Relations and Colonial Questions' (http://www.rowmaninternational.com/news/intro-kilombo-ir-colonial-questions) and 'Global Dialogues,' at Rowman & Littlefield. (The latter doesn't have a webpage yet since it's brand new.)

the deep rules of the game'.[1] Unmentioned, of course, is that the West imposed these "rules of the game' on the rest of the world. It started in the 15th century when *conquistadores* first landed on *abya yala*[2]—the indigenous name for what Europeans later dubbed the New World—and staked it for King Ferdinand and Queen Isabella of Spain, completely disregarding all those who already lived there. Six centuries later, many still believe in and propagate such Euro-hypermasculinity in world politics. Note John Garver's advice to China. To achieve great power status, he writes, China must emulate the West:

> Unless China can produce a statesman closer to the caliber of Otto von Bismark, the *sine qua non* of whose diplomacy was to keep Russia, France, and Britain from uniting against Germany, the future may be gloomy, or to return to the narrower theme of this essay, alignments within the new post-Cold War Triangle may become rigid.[3]

Not all accept such hegemony in policy or thought. Most notably, two states in recent decades—Malaysia in 1998 and Argentina in 2002—have defied the West's demand that they convert to neoliberal policies during periods of financial and economic crisis, and both to positive effect.[4] Similarly, postcolonial thought from Asia to Africa, Latin America to the Middle East has contributed significantly to our analyses and understandings of colonialism and imperialism. Asia needs to 'de-colonize' (*qu zhi min*去殖民), 'de-imperialize' (*qu di guo*去帝国), and 'de-Cold War' (*qu leng zhan*去冷战), advocates Chen Kuan-hsing, a social theorist from Taiwan.[5] And it must occur not just politically or economically but intellectually as well. Some scholars in the West agree. For example, John Hobson exposes the dominance

---

1 Barry Buzan, 'China in International Society: Is "Peaceful Rise" Possible?' *The Chinese Journal of International Politics* 3 (2010): 6–7.
2 *Abya yala* translates into 'Profound America' or 'the fertile earth in which we live', in the *kuna* language from today's Panama. Josef Estermann, 'Andean Philosophy as a Questioning Alterity: An Intercultural Criticism of Western Andro- and Ethnocentrism,' in Nicole Note *et.al.* (eds), *Worldviews and Culture: Philosophical Reflections from an Intercultural Perspective* (Dordrecht: Springer Science + Business Media BV, 2009), p. 130 (footnote 2).
3 John W. Garver, 'The China-India-U.S Triangle: Strategic Relations in the Post-cold War Era', NBR Analysis. 13(5) October 2002. PDF version online: http://unpan1.un.org/intradoc/groups/public/documents/APCITY/UNPAN015790.pdf
4 L.H.M. Ling, 'Cultural Chauvinism and the Liberal International Order: "West versus Rest" in Asia's Financial Crisis', in Geeta Chowdhry and Sheila Nair (eds), Power, Postcolonialism, and International Relations: Reading Race, Gender, Class, 115–141 (London: Routledge, 2002); Michael A. Cohen, Argentina's Economic Growth and Recovery: The Economy in a Time of Default (London: Routledge 2012).
5 Kuan-hsing Chen, *Asia as Method: Toward Deimperialization* (Durham: Duke University Press, 2010).

tea. They got the stimulation of the coffee house, part café, part stock exchange, part chatroom; the Chinese ended up with the lethargy of the opium den, their pipes filled by none other than the British East India Company.[1]

Here, Ferguson is merely continuing a longstanding tradition in the West on Asia.[2] For Hegel, the peoples, societies, and states of the 'Orient,' like women, wallow in stagnation until an outside agent (the hypermasculinized West) stirs them awake.[3] Hegel judged the Chinese, for instance, as incompetent, backward, and incapable of realizing their worth: 'The Chinese...knew many things at a time when Europeans had not discovered them, but they have not understood how to apply their knowledge: as *e.g.* the Magnet, and the Art of Printing... Gunpowder, too, they pretended to have invented before the Europeans; but the Jesuits were obliged to found their first cannon.'[4] Clearly, for Hegel, the killing capacity of gunpowder mattered more than the aesthetic value and fun of fireworks. He disparaged Asia's other ancient civilization, as well. The Indians, he dismissed, wander in 'confused dreams'.[5] 'What we call historical truth and veracity—intelligent, thoughtful comprehension of events, and fidelity in representing them,' Hegel declared, 'nothing of this sort can be looked for among the Hindoos....'[6] And Marx followed Hegel like an obedient student when it came to Asia. Neither India nor China, Marx wrote, have what it takes to modernize on its own. They deserve something as noxious as British colonialism and imperialism to goad them to act.[7] Similarly, Max Weber in *The Religion of China: Confucianism and Taoism* (1915) identified China's difference as a lack: that is, China couldn't develop capitalism, as in Europe, due to the absence of a Protestant ethic.

Attempts to re-make China into the Western image continue unabated today. If China wants to play on the international stage, Barry Buzan states, it must 'accept

---

1 Niall Ferguson, *Civilization: The West vs The Rest* (New York: Penguin Press, 2011), p. 46.
2 For a comprehensive review of Western representations of post-Mao China, see Chengxin Pan, *Knowledge, Desire and Power in Global Politics: Western Representations of China's Rise* (Cheltenham: Edward Elgar, 2012).
3 G.W.F. Hegel, *Philosophy of History* (http://plato.stanford.edu/entries/history/#HegHis) (Downloaded: 15 January 2013).
4 *Ibid.*
5 *Ibid.*
6 *Ibid.*
7 See, for example, Marx's essay 'On Imperialism in India', in Robert C. Tucker (ed.), *The Marx-Engels Reader*, 2nd Edition (New York: W.W. Norton & Co., 1978 [1972]), 653–654. See also, Dona Torr (ed.), *Marx on China, 1853–1860: Articles from the New York Daily Tribune* (London: Lawrence & Wishart, 1951) (http://www.marxists.org/archive/marx/works/1853/china/index.htm) (Downloaded: 17 January 2013).

Part V
Symposium II: Delving into All Aspects of the Chinese Dream

politics behind Xi's 'Chinese dream'.[1] Others propose a hermeneutic method to understand the 'Chinese dream', given the political, social, and intellectual environment that produced it.[2]

Still, I ask: does a strong China *always* have to mean a strong state, defined in Western terms? I honor the history of the 19th–20th centuries. The Chinese people suffered famines and floods, civil wars and long marches, family separations and other communal tragedies due to a disintegration of social order previously maintained by a centralized administration. There was a need to re-organize and re-order the House of China. But now that the foundations of the house are strong, does China need to keep the same, unyielding, and unimaginative architecture forced upon the nation by foreign, imperial powers? Do we all need to look and dress, work and play, think and behave in the same ways? Could not 'strength' and 'state' be defined differently from what the West says they are? Must we abide by the same kind of 'development' based on fossil-fueled industrialization with the same legacy of problems like pollution, congestion, displacement, alienation, and so on? Could it be that the 'Chinese dream', as currently defined, neither represents what is organically 'Chinese' nor a natural 'dream' but a Western-imposed addiction, like opium smoking, now turned by the West into something irrevocably, derisively 'Chinese'?

Headlines blare daily: 'One Fifth of China's Farmland is Polluted, State Study Finds',[3] 'China's Environment: An Economic Death Sentence',[4] 'China Exports Pollution to the US, Study Finds'.[5] Self-delusional, self-destructive behavior, analysts in the West imply, is nothing new to China. Note, for example, this passage from a book published by Harvard historian Niall Ferguson in 2011. It condenses the abomination of the Opium War into a cultural predilection shaped, no less, by 'luck':

> The English were luckier in their drugs, too: long habituated to alcohol, they were roused from inebriation in the seventeenth century by American tobacco, Arabian coffee and Chinese

---

1 Zheng Wang, 'The 'Chinese dream': Concept and Context', Journal of Chinese Political Science 2014 (19): 1–13.
2 Josef Gregory Mahoney, 'Interpreting the 'Chinese dream': An Exercise of Political Hermeneutics', Journal of Chinese Political Science 2014 (19): 15–34.
3 Edward Wong, 'One-Fifth of China's Farmland is Polluted, State Study Finds', *New York Times* 17 April 2014 (http://www.nytimes.com/2014/04/18/world/asia/one-fifth-of-chinas-farmland-is-polluted-state-report-finds.html?_r=0) (Downloaded: 22 April 2014).
4 Minxin Pei, 'China's Environment: An Economic Death Sentence', *Fortune* 28 January 2013 (http://management.fortune.cnn.com/2013/01/28/china-environment-economic-fallout/) (Downloaded: 22 April 2014).
5 Edward Wong, 'China Exports Pollution to the US, Study Finds', *New York Times* 20 January 2014 (http://www.nytimes.com/2014/01/21/world/asia/china-also-exports-pollution-to-western-us-study-finds.html?ref=environment) (Downloaded: 22 April 2014).

material well-being of the nation. And it stands to reason. Corruption and incompetence riddled the last dynasty. The Qing could not withstand England's aggressive demands for trade and equality, especially after the British East India Company forced opium as a commodity onto China's economy and society.[1] As Amitav Ghosh has described so vividly in his novels, *Sea of Poppies* (2008) and *River of Smoke* (2011), mighty Britannia harvested the drug from one colony, India, hoping to establish another, China. And when Commissioner Lin tried to end the opium trade, England chose to interpret Lin's act of sovereignty as an act of war—despite trumpeting sovereignty as the new, 'modern' principle to international relations. What followed is familiar history: a Century of Humiliation from external powers in tandem with chaos and revolution from internal powers.

This history accounts for Xi Jinping's 'Chinese dream'. It aims to produce a strong China as a state (*zhong guo*) with three, key components: (1) ideology,[2] (2) patriotism,[3] and (3) unity.[4] For the Chinese Communist Party (CCP)—and perhaps the majority of the Chinese people—a strong state is a logical response to history. Only a strong state can defend the nation against future encroachments by foreign powers as experienced in the 19th and early part of the 20th centuries.

Commentators tend to follow suit. They analyze the 'Chinese dream' as a reflection of China's rising middle class and its aspirations,[5] or they decipher the

---

[1] Opium as a medicinal herb was well-known in China since the 8th century. Due to its ability to alleviate 'diarrhea, coughing, pain and fever', opium was used routinely to treat the 'symptoms and aftereffects of infectious and epidemic diseases, including what biomedicine would identify as dysentery, malaria, smallpox, and cholera' (Yi-Li Wu, 'The Qing Period,' in T.J. Hinrichs and Linda L. Barnes (eds), *Chinese Medicine and Healing: An Illustrated History* [Cambridge: Harvard University Press, 2013], p. 188). Opium smoking emerged only in the 19th century from Southeast Asia, transmitted primarily through Dutch traders. The British East India Company subsequently manufactured opium in India to export to China on a mass-scale. The Company sought intentionally to addict the Chinese population to rebalance England's payment deficits in trade with the Qing court. By 1838, two years before the first Opium War, the Company was selling more than 34,000 chests of 'foreign mud' per year (*Ibid.*)

[2] That is: a 'socialist path with Chinese characteristics' (*zhongguo tese shehui zhuyi daolu*). Xi Jinping, "Zai di shierjie quanguorenming daibiaodahui diyici huiyishang de jianghua (zhe lu) 2013 nian 3 yue 17 ri (Speech Given at the First Meeting of the 12th Party Congress on 17 March 2013) (http://theory.people.com.cn/n/2013/0619/c405–31–21891787–2.html) (Downloaded: 23 April 2014). Author's own translation.

[3] That is: a 'national spirit with patriotism at its core' (*aiguo zhuyi wei hexin de minzu jingshen*) (*Ibid.*).

[4] That is: a 'consolidation of Chinese strength' (*ningju zhongguo li liang*) through a 'great unity of all ethnic groups' (*ge zu renmin datuanjie*) (*Ibid.*).

[5] David S.G. Goodman, 'Middle Class China: Dreams and Aspirations', Journal of Chinese Political Science 2014 (19): 49–67.

waters. A child of about six years of age was playing a piano on the boat. I couldn't tell whether the child was a girl or a boy. The music tinkled pleasantly. In front of the mansion, to the bottom right of my vision, was another child—this time clearly a boy. He seemed slightly older, perhaps ten years old. Dressed in a white undershirt and shorts with plastic sandals loosely on his feet, he was sitting on a stool before a makeshift desk. Made of dark wood, both the desk and stool were slightly chipped on the sides. He was writing large characters with a brush and ink, stroke by stroke in the traditional style, as if practicing calligraphy for school.

Then I woke up. My first thought was: 'There is hope yet for this old house!' That children continued to play music and write calligraphy despite the ruins before them suggested an optimistic future. Of course, the mansion could have symbolized many things in my life at the time: I was a struggling graduate student and about to get married;[1] my father's cancer had relapsed and we were frantic with worry;[2] and Taiwan was facing several challenges on several fronts.[3] Each of these references could have applied. But I knew the mansion stood for 'China'—not the state of China (*zhong guo* 中国) but the Chinese people and civilization (*zhong hua* 中华), as a whole. The dream referred to the length and breadth (*zong heng* 纵横) of this 'China' both physically and metaphorically: the North, with its 'lonely, cold wind' and 'withered leaves'; the South, with the young boy in shorts and sandals; the West, with the boat on the left; and the East, with the vibrant blue waters. The ancient, dilapidated House of China could revitalize, the dream suggested, as long as the Chinese people, wherever they are, do not forget their ancient cultural heritage.

Surprisingly, food played no role in the dream. Yet most representations of Chinese culture would list its cuisine as a major feature. All acknowledge the distinctive tastes and cooking style of Chinese food, not to mention its influence across the globe. Food has been, also, a major *political* marker in Chinese history: it signals the well-being of a people. If a regime is able to keep the people well-fed, sheltered, and clothed, then it cannot lose the 'mandate of heaven' (*tian ming* 天命). 'The essence of all under heaven (*tianxia* 天下)', Mencius declared, 'issues from the state (*guo* 国); the essence of the state issues from the family (*jia* 家); and the essence of the family issues from oneself (*shen* 身).'[4] Here, the character for 'oneself' (*shen* 身) also connotes 'the body'.

Indeed, all Chinese leaders since the 19th–century have agonized over the

---

1 I got married a month later in Boston.
2 He passed two years after this dream.
3 Investments and businesses from the international community were increasingly directed towards the People's Republic, leaving the Republic of China behind.
4 天下之本在国，国之本在家，家之本在身 (*Mencius*, Book 4, A:5).

Four seas to One Family:
Overseas Chinese and Chinese dream

The 'Chinese dream'

—Whose 'Chinese'? Whose 'Dream'?

L.H.M. Ling 凌焕铭

She is Associate Dean for Faculty Affairs, New School for Public Engagement (NSPE) and Associate Professor, Milano School of International Affairs, Management, and Urban Policy, The New School. She has authored four books: *Postcolonial International Relations: Conquest and Desire between Asia and the West* (2002), *Transforming World Politics: From Empire to Multiple Worlds* (co-authored with A.M. Agathangelou, York University, 2009); *The Dao of World Politics: Towards a Post-Westphalian, Worldist International Relations* (2014); and *Imagining World Politics: Sihar & Shenya, A Fable for Our Times* (2014). Forthcoming is a co-authored volume with Payal Banerjee (Smith College) titled, *India-China: An Ancient Dialectic for Contemporary World Politics*. In addition to this volume, Dr. Ling is also editing or co-editing three other anthologies: *India and China: Rethinking Borders and Security* (University of Michigan Press); *International Relations Theory: Views Beyond the West* (with Nizar Messari and Arlene B. Tickner, Routledge); and *Decolonizing "Asia"? Unlearning Colonial/Imperial Power Relations* (with Pinar Bilgin, forthcoming). Dr. Ling's articles have appeared in *International Studies Quarterly, Review in International Studies, Millennium: Journal of International Studies, International Feminist Journal of Politics, International Relations of the Asia-Pacific, positions: east asia cultures critiques*, among others. In 2014–2015, Dr. Ling is Program Chair (along with Pinar Bilgin, Bilkent University) of the International Studies Association (ISA). As of 2014, she is co-editor, with John M. Hobson (University of Sheffield), of *Global Dialogues: Developing Non-Eurocentric IR and IPE* (Rowman & Littlefield International). Dr. Ling is currently developing a research hub at SGPIA/Milano/NSPE titled, "OASIS: A Holistic Paradigm to Healing Our Worlds."

Almost thirty years to the time of this writing, I had a dream about China. It was Spring 1985 and I was in Taipei, visiting my parents. The dream went like this:

> I saw a grand, old mansion now dilapidated. A lonely, cold wind blew withered leaves across its once expansive, marble floor. To the left of the mansion bobbed a small boat in deep-blue

acquiring a still bigger arsenal by the government, is the updated equivalent of garnering still another oasis for the survival of the nomadic ancestor.

By contrast, the way of life of the agrarian forefathers in ancient China had conditioned them to look for salvation (or solution to challenges to survival) within their own habitat and by resorting to their own means. Hence, the Confucian motto, which confirmed this notion, called for *neisheng waiwang* (内圣外王), which loosely translates into English as 'be a saint to yourself, and a magnanimous patron to others'. The unsaid part is that if one lives by this motto, one need not worry about having no self-confidence. And as the progression in the motto suggests, confidence radiates from the self to the others. From the spread of confidence as such will come a restoration of mutual trust, including trust of each other and trust of the government.

It is not hard to detect that just as the Dengist Great Leap Outward has brought on enormous success due to a partially marketized economy, an unprecedented commercial culture has crept in and taken grip of an ever-growing sector of the Chinese nation. The *neisheng waiwang* motto would be a timely antidote to the moral laxity associated with the corrupting influences of this nascent materialistic culture. Hence, national revival such as President Xi Jinping has called for may commence with a cultural revival that will regenerate a commitment to the motto of *neisheng waiwang*.

Once *neisheng waiwang* is society's buzz word and serves as the guiding light for its members, it will enable China to stand in good stead as a trust-worthy nation. The same will be true for America if the same motto should disseminate to and take hold in the American society, whereby Americans in search of the American Dream will no longer have to go to Denmark, as the critics above have facetiously asserted. The reasons why this Confucian virtue will bring rectification to both countries are not far to seek. First, for the Chinese, it will help fill the vacuum created by both the decline in ideology in post-Mao China—and the discipline it brought—and the additional uncertainty in the moral rearmament called for by changes in the work place, when the former planned economy gives way to partial marketization with its corrupting commercial culture in tow. Second, it will bail out the American society by ridding it of its creed of greed at the individual level and the deep-seated insecurity complex at the nation-state level.

Thus viewed, the 'Chinese dream', if it is ultimately aimed at a national revival, as is in President Xi's lexicon, would require a prior revival of the best in traditional Chinese culture that places a premium on moral armament, known as *neisheng waiwang* in Confucian virtues. Furthermore, as we have seen, to the extent it can regenerate a much needed self-confidence, this moral rearmament likewise is something that could help reverse the loss of the American Dream for the Americans.

program.[1]

While nobody has yet articulated a 'looking for the 'Chinese dream', go to America (or Canada)' refrain, these reported capital flights from China should be serious enough to alert Beijing's leaders to take remedial action in order to stem the tides. But the question is how?

In view of what has caused the Americans to lose the American Dream, as noted above, the way to preclude a similar loss by the Chinese of the 'Chinese dream', obviously, is to ensure that like the Danes, the Chinese will not lose their trust in their government, as well as trust among each other. And, the way to do it, I think, is to bring back in full the best traditional values vaunted in Chinese culture, including Confucian teachings.

Elsewhere I have dealt with what I diagnosed as America's deep-seated problems, at both the individual and the national levels.[2] At the individual level, the root problem is an insatiable greed that knows of no end, as typified by the Bernard Madeoff investment scandal on Wall Street, which broke out in 2009. Using an elaborate Ponzi scheme, Madeoff swindled some $65 billion out of 4,800 clients over five decades. The same creed of greed that led to the Madeoff scandal was likewise the primogenitor of a series of fraudulent big-firm bankruptcies starting from Enron (2001), WorldCom (2002), to the Lehman Brothers (2008), etc., in which, as it became known only much later, the principals pocketed billions of dollars at the cost of the investors.[3] At the nation-state level, the U.S. government never ceases to fear for America's national insecurity, a fear not assuaged by the collapse of Soviet power or by spending more money on national defense than the rest of the world combined.

The root cause for both the personal creed of greed and the government's perennial sense of insecurity, as such, likewise lies in Western culture, which sees salvation (include the key to security, at both individual and nation-state levels) as lying outside oneself. This, too, derived from the ancient nomadic origins of Western culture. The perpetual search for new oases by the nomadic forefathers instilled in their psyche the instinctive belief that one's survival depended on still another oasis lying somewhere out there. And, the Abrahamic religions, with their teaching that one cannot save oneself, certainly confirmed this notion. The upshot, for our purpose here, is that this inherited creed deprives one of one's self-confidence. Hence, amassing still more material goods for the individual, or

---

1 World Journal (New York), 2/18/2014, p. A1.
2 James C. Hsiung, 'Cultural Roots of the American Insatiable Greed and Uncle Sam's Sense of National Insecurity Despite Wielding Hegemonic Power', unpublished paper given at the Nishan Conference on Confucian Culture, summer Of 2012.
3 In the Enron case, it was not immediately known that it filed for bankruptcy while it had an unreported $63.4 billion in assets.The Lehman Brothers bankruptcy, as it became known much later, followed Enron's path in that its executives benefited from $691 billion in hidden assets.

one's pioneer bootstraps –all the way to the Wall Street, even the White House. But, after the financial tsunami that followed the melt-down of Wall Street, a period that coincided with the Barak Obama era, this New World fairy tale is fast dissipating. A recent report from Pew Charitable Trust's Project on Economic Mobility confirms what early studies showed: If you are born into the underclass, you are likely to die there, as stuck in your station as a Victorian housemaid. The same Pew study also shows that two thirds of all Americans think social inequality is more damaging to the nation than racism. Most Americans think the habitual American Dream's promise of social mobility is broken. The Europeans, it seems to most Americans, now have more opportunity to improve their lot.[1]

Although the idea seems to have first originated from Richard Wilkinson, a British professor of social epidemiology, that one would now look for the 'American Dream' in Denmark, it soon caught on among American critics. In addition to Denmark's legendary income equality and strong social safety net, the Forbes magazine recently cited another factor, namely: the high levels of trust among the Danes. They trust each other, they trust outsiders, and they even trust their government. These qualities, especially the last mentioned, about trusting the government, are not found in America.[2]

However, despite these scares about the Americans losing the American Dream, many wealthy Chinese seem to believe differently. By the estimate of the Boston Consulting Group, wealthy Chinese had moved their assets overseas (supposedly most of them to America), to the order of $450 billion. And it anticipated a 300% increase in the next three years. However, a higher estimate given by Wealth Insight, a financial consulting firm in London, showed that the total assets sneaked out of China by wealthy individuals (including officials) —obviously much of it running away from China's relentless anti-corruption campaign—exceeded $658 billion (or RMB4.80 trillion), approximately 30% of China's total annual revenue. This vast capital flight from China to America (and elsewhere) has impacted, for example, on the real-estate market in metropolises like Los Angeles, Chicago, and New York.[3] The casino effect created by this massive inflow of Chinese hot money has so caused concerns about their economic stability that the United States and Canada, each at its own initiative, decided to put a stop to the investment-for-immigrant quota program, a measure that has kept off an aggregate of over 60,000 Chinese immigrant applicants trying to benefit from the quota offered by the

---

1 As cited in Diane Roberts, 'Want to Get Ahead? Move to Denmark', carried by theguardian.com, January 17, 2012.
2 Cf. 'If Amercans Want to Live the American Dream, They Should Go to Denmark', <www.twitter.com/kerytrueman>.
3 As reported in World Journal (New York), 2/15/2014, p. 3.

for new oases, they may come into conflict with other competing nomadic groups and, indeed, may have to chase them out from the new oasis they were occupying.[1] As such, the nomads' way of life was marked by periodic bouts with relocation, exclusionism, and conflict.

If we carry this generalization one step further, we may find a connection between the two variants of weltanschauung, on the one hand, and the respective views of the two contrasting ancient peoples regarding human nature, on the other. With the ancient Chinese continental farmers, their habituation to a largely non-conflictual and non-exclusivist way of life may have yielded an intuition about human nature as being inherently disposed toward good, but contaminated only by post-natal circumstances, such as scarcity and deprivation. Confucianism simply confirmed this interpretation. Hence, the government's functions, in the consequential Chinese political culture, are essentially twofold: (a) to ensure the provision of a social environment that keeps contaminating influences to a minimum; and (b) to make sure that, with government intervention, the economy will forestall a deterioration of the problems of scarcity and deprivation. The combination of these two functions may result in an all-powerful government. But, the inherent social-rationality focus, over and above the private interests of individuals can be likened to the concern of the proverbial central banker lest the falling prices damage the larger economy, as noted above.

With the ancient nomadic forefathers who shaped the Western culture, their habitual conflictual and exclusivist way of life may have led to their intuition that human nature was inherently evil, a view certainly confirmed by the Abrahamic religions. From this evil human nature premise, Western political thinkers from Hobbes to Montesquieu believed that individuals will be unable to protect themselves from the anti-social behavior of other individuals, imbued as they were with their innate evil nature. Hence, the remedies are (a) that society be strictly governed by the rule of law, to be enforced with organized coercion by an efficient government; and (b) to prevent (potentially evil-natured) government officials from abusing power, government must have built-in safeguards ensured by the separation of powers. In this legally and institutionally fortified environment, freedom in the sense of emancipation from its rigidity is depicted as 'dreams' of individual citizens. Hence, in the Western political ambience, the kind of 'dream' as used in Martin Luther King, Jr.'s 'I have a dream', or as in an immigrant's dream in America, is a micro-level expression of self-oriented personal aspirations.

It used to be that the American Dream implies what a land of plenty can offer the rugged individual, in which one could overcome poverty and pull oneself up by

---

1 Cf. Gary N. Knoppers and Kenneth A. Pistau, eds., Community Identification in Judean Histography (2009), esp. 1–26; and 119–146.

Part V
Symposium II: Delving into All Aspects of the Chinese Dream

revival is the greatest 'Chinese dream' for the contemporary Chinese.'¹

Thus, it is clear that Xi's 'Chinese dream' envisages a national rejuvenation, or a return of past glory. But, it is unclear what exactly is the period in China's long history that he had in mind as holding the ideal goal for the re-rising China to aspire to. From his dating of China's modern decline from the Opium War of 1840 on, we may infer that the high point of past glory fascinating him was somewhere in the pre–1840 era. Based on my own study of China's first rise, documented by statistics kept by, among others, Angus Maddison, the eminent British global economic historian, it should be the millennium from 713 through 1820, A.D., when China's GDP consistently topped that of East and West Europe combined.² Furthermore, during its first rise, China already had mass production by the 11th century and mechanized production by the 13th century, two features known to the West only after the Industrial Revolution of the 18th century. According to the study of Gavin Menzies, a British submarine commander-turned historian, China's Zheng He (Cheng Ho) had discovered the Americas in 1421, or 71 years before Columbus set his foot in the New World.

That feat, too, fell well within the period of China's first rise (713–1820). Hence, the millennium of China's first rise rightfully held the fascination of Xi Jinping in his aspirations for a national revival. As such, his call for a national revival is no nostalgia, but a try at achieving a new headway in the world today, comparable to China's lead during its first rise.

We have noted above the difference between macro-and micro-dreams, as captured respectively in Xi Jinping's 'Chinese dream' and Martin Luther King, Jr.'s American Dream. If there is any way to account for the difference, it probably is inherent in each of the two cultures. And, if a culture's roots can be traced back to the earliest world view, or weltanschauung, held by its ancient forefathers, then a generalization can be made on the essential differences between the two cultures. The forefathers of the ancient Chinese, for one, were farmers living in a continental agrarian economy. Hence, their weltanschauung reflected their exposure to the physical world around them and, to be more exact, their habituation to a way of life that was sedentary, non-conflictual, and non-exclusivist.³ The Western civilization, in contrast, began with the ancient nomads in today's Middle East, who had to roam the land in search of new oases after depleting the water and other resources in their previous pasturing ground that they had to abandon. And, in their search

---

1 Xi Jinping, 'The Road to National Rejuvenation' (12/1/2012), text available at:<wenku.baidu.com/link?url=z0-raYq8ULFDTbGBuyuchdP>.
2 James C. Hsiung, *China into Its Second Rise, Myths, Puzzles, Paradoxes, and Challenge to Theory* (Singapore: World Scientific, 2012). Chapter 3, on China's first rise, employed the data provided by Angus Maddison, *Contours of the World Economy, 1–2030 A.D.* (Oxford University Press, 2007).
3 Cf. FUNG Yu-lan, *Zhongguo zhexue shi (A History of Chinese Philosophy)* (1968 edition).

may simply be an accommodation of an individual's fond aspirations, hence a self-oriented personal dream. At either level, a dream boils down to a visionary thought of some sorts. Throughout human history, we know of four most distinctive visions for a good society, including three of foreign origin, namely: (a) Plato's vision of a philosopher king, (b) the Hobbesian expose of absolute monarchy as a necessary assurance of the individual's emancipation from the law of the jungle; and (c) Marx's ideology of the dictatorship of the proletariat. The fourth vision, of Chinese origin, inhered in the parable of the land of Great Harmony, extolled in the classical Book of Rites (礼运大同篇). All four partake of a macro-level visioning.

By contrast, a micro vision is often implicit, for example, in the piped American Dream, as typified in Martin Luther King, Jr.'s oft-quoted 'I have a dream'. King's dream, aired in 1963, was for his children's generation not to be judged by the color of their skin, but by the quality of their character. Even if his life had not been cut short by an assassin's (a white man) bullet, King could not have lived long enough to see the day some 45 years later, in 2008, when the first black man ever was elected to occupy the White House. But, King's dream, in a way, did seem to have come true, for a black individual.

A cogent illustration of the difference between a macro and a micro dream may be found in the contrast in attitude between a central banker and a consumer toward the falling market prices. For the consumer, the lower the prices fall the better for him. But, for the central banker, he is concerned lest the prices fall so precipitously low as to trigger a deflation to foredoom the economy. At the risk of over-generalization, a similar divide can be found between the 'Chinese dream' as floated in Xi Jinping's call and the American Dream as expressed by Martin Luther King, Jr.

On closer examination, we discern in Xi's 'Chinese dream' exhortation the implications of a macro imagery of what ideally should prevail at the national level, or what the Chinese nation should be striving for. At the time of the 18th Party Congress, November 2013, he expressed a wish for China to metamorphose by 2049, the centenary of the founding of the People's Republic, to be a powerful, wealthy, democratic, and environmentally-sound modern country. He called on the nation not only to sustain its miraculous economic growth, but also to launch political, social, cultural, and environmental rebuilding efforts, toward the ultimate direction of a Chinese national rejuvenation. On another occasion, he actually went further, and explicitly recalled that for all its past glory, China met with harrying and un-foretold discomfitures in modern times. And the sacrifices the Chinese nation had to endure, as a result, defy comparisons in human history, he lamented, adding: 'we are better equipped today than at any juncture before, to embark on the task of a national revival.' And, he concluded, 'to realize China's national

Part V
Symposium II: Delving into All Aspects of the Chinese Dream

The 'Chinese dream': In Comparison with the American Dream

James C. Hsiung 熊玠

He is Professor of Politics and international law at New York University, His broad interests extend to East Asian politics (China and Japan), and Asian international relations. He is author and editor of 21 books, including his Anarchy and Order: The Interplay of Politics and Law in International Relations (1997); and China into Its Second Rise (2012). His forthcoming 22nd book is an in-depth analysis of the Sino-Japanese disputes as seen from both history and international law.

He was specially invited to Beidaihe traveling in the special train from Beijing in July 1987 to talk with Deng Xiaoping for six hours including dining together.

Due to its name, the celebrated 'Butterfly Dream' (胡蝶梦) by the ancient philosopher Zhuangzi (also Chuang Tzu, (庄子), circa 369–286 B.C,) may have imparted a romantic ring in the very idea of a 'dream'. In Chinese folklore, however, a dream is often viewed as possibly containing a hidden message like an omen worth looking into. From early on, the Chinese have acquired the habit of having one's dream deciphered by a guru versed in dreams, in search of its hidden meaning. In our time, Xi Jinping held up a 'Chinese dream' (中国梦) as his rallying call for the nation to scale greater heights in the time ahead. He did so as he assumed the stewardship of the Chinese Communist Party in November 2012 before becoming President of the People's Republic four months later. Foreign media immediately spotted that this was the first time ever since 1949 when a top Chinese leader used 'dream' in a clarion call to action issued to his fellow countrymen. Thus, what President Xi had in mind for a 'Chinese dream' well merits our close attention, and an attempt at its explication.

Indeed, the idea of a 'Chinese dream' may have different meanings. At the macro level, it may well serve to conjure up the imagery of what the Chinese nation should aim for, hence a national dream. At the micro level, on the other hand, it

Part V

Symposium II:
Delving into All Aspects of the 'Chinese dream'

the rejuvenation of Eastern civilization. China is adopting 'affectionate, sincere, benedictory, broad-minded (亲诚惠容) towards neighbouring countries to forge a commonwealth with shared responsibilities. China is also forging a community with the developed countries in the spirit of mutual-benefit and win-win as well as mutual respect. Never will China replicate the historical rhythm of a strong country degenerating into hegemony. Never to impose its own will on others, China is carrying forward and demonstrating the spirit of 'truthfulness and empathy' (忠恕之道) of its cultural tradition and create a emerging international relationship, advocating a 'new security concept for Asia' (亚洲新安全观) and creating 'harmonious regions' (和谐地区) and a 'harmonious world' (和谐世界). Asia is the common home for China and its neighbouring countries, and safeguarding its peace, prosperity and stability is the responsibility of all concerned. The crux of the issue lies in the 'five interconnectivity' (五通) encompassing 'knowing each other's political mind' (政策沟通), 'connecting each other with good roads' (道路联通), 'free flow of trade' (贸易畅通), 'circulation of currency' (货币流通), 'people-to-people understanding' (民心相通). Though with enhanced intensity of competition, China and the developed countries can expand their potential of cooperation. China has raised the issue of forging a 'new-type relationship' (新型大国关系) with USA. China has proposed to the European countries of joint development of the third-party market. All this is to avoid the zero-sum game and enable the 'Chinese dream', American dream and European dream to thrive together.

Is there a target of transforming the 'Chinese dream' into a world dream? This is pointed out by Professor Tan Chung: 'We are not there yet, but look forward to the day when all the people of the world would join the Chinese people in relishing the pleasure of 'Chinese dream', and when other peoples are not turning pale instantly as if the tiger is there, but feel relaxed and happy in the discourse of 'Chinese dream'. That would be the real transformation of the 'Chinese dream' into the world dream.'

In conclusion, transforming the 'Chinese dream' into a world dream is both a vision and a corollary. There is echo between the 'Chinese dream' and the dreaming of good life of all countries of the world. The underlying idea is: I raise your dream by my dream. O, 'Chinese dream', create a better and prettier world.

dream' would not smother various individual dreams, but it would be the total collection of all the individual dreams through the process of integration and sublimation.

III. The Path of transforming 'Chinese dream' into World Dream

The logic of 'impacting the world through self-transformation' (改变自己，影响世界) which has prevailed in China in modern times is changing into that of 'moulding the world through self-recast' (塑造世界，塑造自己), i.e., making the greatest contribution to the international society by tidying up things in China. There is the proposition of earnestly participating in the global and regional administrations to enable China modernize its own system and capability of administration. To live the 'Chinese dream' means to live the world dream.

Three things are crucial in the process of transforming the 'Chinese dream' into a world dream.

First, there is the motto of '*ji yu li er li ren* 己欲立而立人/establishing others in order to establish oneself'. China's eminent position among the developing countries has given the 'Chinese dream' enormous attraction to them. China has to help other developing countries to abandon poverty and get rich as well as elevating their international status so that the 'Chinese dream' can be fulfilled. China must be 'true, real, intimate and honest' (真、实、亲、诚) towards other countries and judiciously balance righteousness and self-interest so that a 'common destiny' (命运共同体) is forged. This is transforming the 'Chinese dream' into a world dream. The concept of 'common destiny' (命运共同体) can be plainly interpreted as the pursuit of a common identity and goal through thick and thin. We share our common interest through the 'thick' and we enjoy our common security through the 'thin'.

Second, there is the motto of '*ji yu da er da ren* (己欲达而达人)/making others in order to make oneself thriving'. As the leader of the new-emergent countries others regard China as a model and encouragement. 'Chinese dream' is that of the new-emergent countries. There is increasing importance of the developing and emerging countries in China's diplomatic schemes. When China is moving from the low-end towards the high-end in the international production chain there is increasing competition with the developed countries while the complementarity with the developing and emerging countries get enhanced. The developing countries become the rear markets of China's industrial transformation while the emerging countries interconnect the markets in the middle section. China's solidarity with the developing and emerging countries is strategically significant in making the world order more democratic and law-abiding.

Third, there is the motto of '*ji suobuyu wu shiyu ren* (己所不欲勿施于人)/don't do onto others what you don't want others do onto you'. The 'Chinese dream' marks manifestation of China's getting free from the 'modern times', getting rid of the feelings about the country, and getting the excitement of rising and rejuvenating. The 'Chinese dream' is not just the dream of the Chinese, but also the dream of the people of the world. As *tianxia* (天下)/all under Heaven' is all inclusive, the 'Chinese dream' is all inclusive. Just as Professor Wei Chuxing observes, the 'Chinese dream' should not only be like a lighthouse illuminating the hearts of most Chinese people and direct and elate them in spirits moving toward the dreamland, but it should also serve as a powerful magnet to attract most people of the world, letting them feel the beauty and warmness of it. Only such a dream that could be understood and accepted by most people in China as well as in the world is a real 'Chinese dream'.

II. The 'Chinese dream' and the 'Two Centenaries'

No two dreams are alike. There is nothing mystic and illusory about the 'Chinese dream'. It has a clear vision and realistic path as well as reliable circumstances for its fulfillment. More important, the Chinese people are taking concrete steps to make it materialize. I appreciate the observation of Professor Wei Chuxiong: 'The dream we talk about here should be the shining, beautiful, promising and reachable future, though which appears looming far away.'

The goal of 'two centenaries' (两个一百年) are: In 2021 when the Communist Party of China celebrates its centenary China becomes a society of universally moderate prosperous while in 2049 when the People's Republic of China celebrates its centenary China realizes its great national rejuvenation. All this is the narrative of the 'Chinese dream' which is a three-in-one entity of the state's dream, the nation's dream and the societal dream.

The fulfillment of the goal of 'two centenaries' is predicated on the proper tackling of three dialectic relationships. First, the relationship between each and every singularity and entirety. The 'Chinese dream' belongs to every and all Chinese, hence this relationship is there. In case some Chinese have different dreams from those of other Chinese we have to settle it. That would mandate us to pay attention to equal opportunities and to emphasize on the overall effect.

Second, the relationship between simultaneity and sequentiality. Professor Tom Lun-nap Chung thinks 'the realization of the 'Chinese dream' should take into account of the healthy development in all layers of the "individual-family-secondary organizations-state-global" framework.' I totally agree with it. There will be difference in time for the materialization of 'Chinese dream' for different people. It will be sharing prosperity and happiness at various levels in the country.

Third, the relationship between harmony and idiosyncrasy. All Chinese would not have the same dream which would be boring. Dream itself is multi-colour and divergent though maintaining harmony on the whole. Not only the 'Chinese

China playing a leading role in the world.

Second, it outshines and leaves far behind the humiliation of '*bainian guochi* (百年国耻)/a century of national ignominy'. China's dreaming of modernization for 170 years created a narrow-minded and impatient momentum of '*chao Ying gan Mei* (超英赶美)/surpassing Britain and catching up with America'. The advocacy of the 'Chinese dream' outshines the Western dream, American dream and modernization dream; it dreams what belongs to China and what only China is qualified to dream. In her comment, Zhang Siqi expresses her apprehension whether China would replicate the expansionism, mercantilism, liberalism and hedonism of the maritime civilizations. My article in the column of '*Wanghai lou* (望海楼)/Overseas Sites' of 'People's Daily, overseas edition' (人民日报海外版) on January 11, 2013 has given reply to this. In my opinion, the 'Chinese dream' is not anti-West, but would result in a Sino-European solidarity to create a 'new humanism' (新人文主义). (This is thoroughly dealt with in Chapter 9 of my book '*Haishang?—Ouzhou wenming qishi lu* (海殇？—欧洲文明启示录)/Elegy of the ocean—A realization from the European civilization.) Of course, there is always a gap between illusion and reality. We have to see how things turn out in answering to Zhang Siqi's apprehension. We have already advanced a crucial step in our thinking which would have to be followed up by concrete actions.

Third, it outshines '*fuxing* (复兴)/rejuvenation', the combination of '*qiangsheng* (强盛)/power and prowess' and '*weiwang* (威望)/veneration and awe'. Though there is '*fuxing* (复兴)/rejuvenation' in the advocacy of the 'great rejuvenation of Chinese nation' (中华民族伟大复兴), the 'Chinese dream' signifies the totality of three 'model-transformations of civilization' (文明转型): from agricultural civilization into industrial and information civilization, from inland civilization into maritime civilization, and from regional civilization into global civilization. We need to inject new values and norms into the traditional conceptions of '*tian-ren heyi* (天人合一)/integration of Nature and humanity' as well as '*liangru wei chu* (量入为出)/cut the coat according to the available cloth' in our unreal modern world dominated by *sleight-of-hand* tricks. We had conceived '*shangshan ruo shui* (上善若水)/water as superior perfection' which was limited within fresh water, but the sea water with the smell of blood which was stirred by the aggressions of umpteen Western powers against China has been ingrained in our memory. Our era is no longer '*sihai yijia* (四海一家)/four seas to one family', but long replaced by '*siyang yiti* (四洋一体)/the integration of four oceans'. Our notion of '*tianxia* (天下)/all under Heaven' has to be raised to the global perspective. All this requires 'model-transformations'. Of course, 'model-transformations of civilization' does not mean the negation of civilizational idiosyncrasy. It is the creation of a triad of traditional China, modern China and global China.

In sum, the advocacy and implementation of the 'Chinese dream' is the dreams of other nations into consideration. The 'Chinese dream' should not only be like a lighthouse illuminating the hearts of most Chinese people and direct and elate them in spirits moving toward the dreamland, but it should also serve as a powerful magnet to attract most people of the world, letting them feel the beauty and warmness of the 'Chinese dream'. Only such a dream that could be understood and accepted by most people in China as well as in the world is a real one.

Wang Yiwei's reply:

I consider it a great privilege that my article has been commented by so many academic seniors. All the criticisms are on target and have to be carefully replied. I shall try my level best to do it, and would beg the indulgence of my critics in case I fail to do so.

Professor Ma Jiali is right for saying that amidst divergent international interpretations we must have the clear contours of, and unswerving confidence in the 'Chinese dream'. Indeed, ideology, long-term vision and conviction are the three innate dimensions in analyzing the 'Chinese dream'.

About ideology, the 'Chinese dream' outshines the mindset of 'past and present, Chinese and international' (古今中外). About long-term vision, the 'Chinese dream' is the manifestation of the fulfillment of 'two centenaries' (两个一百年). About conviction, the 'Chinese dream' interconnects the world dream.

I. The historical Significance of 'Chinese dream'

The advocacy of the 'Chinese dream' has outshined things in three arenas. First, it outshines the mindset of 'past and present, Chinese and international' (古今中外). The Chinese mindset was severely constricted during the post-Opium War (1840–42) period by the dualistic formula of '*Zhongxue wei ti, xixue wei yong* (中学为体，西学为用)/Chinese culture as the substance while taking advantage of the utility of Western culture'. During the post-Sino-Japanese War (1894–95) period, China deviated further into whole-hearted Westernization. We must restore self-confidence concretely in our own 'road' (道路), our own 'theory' (理论), and our own 'system' (制度) so that 'we trust our own culture' (文化自信) and are 'culturally self-conscious' (文化自觉). The advocacy of the 'Chinese dream' epitomizes the cultural self-confidence and self-consciousness of the Chinese people and nation. We are still bogged down in China today by the antagonism between the Chinese idiosyncrasy and universal values. The 'Chinese dream' should be able to get beyond the mindset of the dualistic formula of '*Zhongxue wei ti, xixue wei yong* (中学为体，西学为用)/Chinese culture as the substance while taking advantage of the utility of Western culture', getting away from 'East is East and West is West', focussing on the North-South equations and resuming the conventional status of most people have the right and opportunity to make their own dreams means not to allow any individual or community to achieve their dream through hurting the interests of other people or communities. This is also a principle included in the 'grand harmony under heaven' dreamed by the sages of old and socialists.

Yet, just at this point, it's easier said than done, and the relevant point made in the article by Wang Yiwei seems self-contradictory. On the one hand, the article pointed out that the 'Chinese dream' is to 'sustain the eternal development of humanity so that all civilizations and development models benefit each other and share the beauty and joy of the comity of nations'. On the other hand, however, it claims that the 'Chinese dream' for 'laying the foundation for China to act as a leading country'. Won't this kind of statement mislead people to thinking that China attempts to impose its model for development on the rest of the world and challenge the leadership of the United States and the West? Right now, the rise of China has already made its neighboring states nervous, which, ignited and supported by the U.S., have begun to audaciously challenge against the 'Chinese dream' for a peaceful rise. If China keeps its announcement of 'the Chinese Dream' unclear and poorly defined, even openly announces that its dream is to become the world leader, won't it give these countries more excuses for their challenge against China?

Thus, we must offer an accurate definition of the 'Chinese dream' and no chance for its misinterpretation. It will be a very difficult and challenging task to describe a dream that can make ten billions of people excited and joyful about that. Yet, the process discussing the 'Chinese dream' and trying to define the 'Chinese dream' itself is already a very exciting and significant event because through this process we can from the past, tell the right from the wrong, provide a platform for the public opinions, clarify our thoughts, form collective ideas and reconstruct the national ideology. Since China started reform and opened door in the 1970s, it has never lacked smart economic policies, effective means for market economy and great strategies for development; what China has not found is a new Chinese ideology and value system that could make Chinese people's hearts cohered, their minds guided, and their morale aroused. Thus, the core of the 'Chinese dream' is not in the physical but spiritual dimension. It should be based on a value system that could tell people how to live, pursue and manage a good life of the human being. The 'resurgence', 'national rights', 'human rights' and so on mentioned in Wang's article all belong to the physical dimension of certain values, which are actually products of the spiritual core beneath them, which we pay more attention. The spiritual core displayed by the 'Chinese dream' ought to be able to accommodate the individual values, family values, social values and national values and integrate all of them into one harmonious entity, which could then be further incorporated into the values of the world, taking the students studied abroad after China started reform in 1980s and later came back to China, with a dream to ride on the wave of China's reform, but this kind of dream is quite different from that Qian Xuesen (钱学森) had, who eagerly returned from the United States to China after 1949 for the purpose to assist the development of new China.

In term of space, the Beiyang Government in Beijing after the 1911 Revolution had a dream differing from what the former Provisional President Sun Yat-sen dreamed at the same time in the south. Many Macanese people of Macao went to Hong Kong and Shanghai in Late Qing with a dream for finding a new path for survival, which differed from that of the Cantonese who migrated to Southeast Asia for making fortunes. In the 1960s, the dream of the urban pretty bourgeois in Shanghai that 'Shanghai is for Shanghainese' was made from a sentiment different from that of the Beijing Uncles expected that 'Beijing is for all the Chinese'. Even at the same time and space, different people will have different dreams. When many patriotic youths went to Yan'an (延安) during the Second Sino-Japanese War, some of them were aspirated by a spirit to sacrifice their life for saving the nation, but others by the dream of achieving the Communist goal. Belonging to the same first generation of the Chinese Communist Party and determined to fight for the Communist cause for the life time, Mao Zedong launched the Cultural Revolution in order to accomplish his interpretation of the Communist dream, but Liu Shaoqi (刘少奇) attempted to carry out the policy of 'fixing farm output quotas for each household' as the means of achieving the Communist goal. Among the educated youth who went to the countryside in the 1960s were not only those who departed for the countryside with the great aspiration, ambition and determination to settle down in the remote area for lifetime, but also others who said good bye to their parents with tears and resolution to return to their hometown as soon as possible.

Thus, I agree with what Tom Lun-nap Chung said: 'the realization of the 'Chinese dream' should take into account of the healthy development in all layers of the "individual-family-secondary organizations-state-global" framework.' Indeed, we should not make one 'Chinese dream' for all and use one 'Chinese dream' to represent all. Then, what kind of 'dream' could serve as the denominator to be accepted by most people in the world? I think, a 'Chinese dream' that can be truly accepted universally must follow a principle, no matter how remote it may be. That is: let everyone or most people have the right and opportunity to make, pursue and achieve their own dreams. We shall not deprive most Chinese people of the right and opportunity to make their own dreams under the slogan of the 'Chinese dream', or replace the dreams of individuals and communities with the 'Chinese dream' of state. The crazy and irrational 'dreams' of the Great Leap Forward Movement and the Great Cultural Revolution that strangled the dreams of most people should not be allowed to happen anymore. The principle letting that has ever since been pursued and advocated by hundreds and thousands prominent Chinese people one after another. Yet, this kind of broad and unspecific generalization of 'Chinese dream' may lead to much misreading and many misunderstandings and even misuses. It may result in, at least, mixing up the dream of socialist China with the ambitious dream of the traditional Chinese empire. Or, at most, the advocate for turning the 'Chinese dream' into a world dream may be viewed as the pretty words to cover China's ambition for the hegemony power over the world. Thus, we should accurately and carefully define 'Chinese dream'.

First of all, we must be clear that the dream we are talking about is not an unfeasible day dream, out of touch of the reality and to be an illusionary enjoyment. The dream we talk about here should be the shining, beautiful, promising and reachable future, though which appears looming far away. As long as we are persistently trying our best, we will achieve this dream and arrived the dreamed other side sooner or later. In other words, our dream is a broad and long-ranged one that would eventually become true. It is beautiful because it won't gain one's own benefit yet hurt other's interest. Rather, its realization will benefit not only individuals but also communities, societies, nations and the world. Any goal that seeks only for the interest of one person, one family, one side, one community, one society or one nation while ignoring the interests of another person, another family, another side, another community, another society or another nation won't be called as the 'dream' that we are talking about.

Moreover, any dream is confined by time and space. Every era has its dream, and every dream is expressed on different levels and has with various types. If we seek a universal dream without taking into account of its specific era, location and dimension, it will be impossible, like day dreaming. For example, in term of time, in the aspect of politics and state, the purpose of the Self-Strengthening Movement just runs against that of the Cultural Movement during the period of the May Fourth Movement; the aim of the Tongzhi Restoration (同治中兴) is completely diverging from that of the Great Forward Movement. In the aspect of society, what all the 'Lin sisters' of the Red Chamber era dreamed, namely to find and be married to a sweetheart, is not comparable to the ideal life that nowadays an independent career woman has. Neither can the dream of many Beijing residents in Late Qing, who wanted to enlarge their conventional home compound in order to accommodate the newly established family of their clan members, be comparable to that a Beijing youth who hopes to earn enough money to set up a new home independent out of the old family. On the individual level, a peasant in Lankao (兰考) County in the 1960s just dreamed to have wheat-made buns every day has a living standard entirely different from that a Lankao peasant in the twenty-first century who instead dreams to buy an Apple cell phone and motorbike. Many Chinese in early and late Tang, one would be surprised to find that not only the total area of China's territory had expanded and shrunk, even the shape of the territory changed significantly. This is an indication of Tang's inconsistent military power. Whether victory or failure, people suffered. Han and Tang also suffered from serious internal turmoil. The generals' separatist tendencies directly led to Tang's fatal decline, whereas Han suffered almost all kinds of man-made disasters other dynasties encountered. In the economic sphere, despite their advantage in industry and commerce, Han's and Tang's over-reliance upon agriculture restricted their evolvement into a pluralistic economy.

The Song experiences are actually more relevant to China today. Despite a common impression that Song was the weakest dynasty in China due to its lack of military initiatives, Song actually did launch several expeditions. Compared with all of the Asian and European sovereignties whom were overcome by the Mongols within merely a few months of attack, the Song defense against Mongol invasion lasted 44 years (starting from the date Ogadai decided to invade China.)

We should also be aware of the fact that Song emerged at a period when China no longer dominated its neighbors like Hang and Tan did. And despite the threat of foreign invasion, Song persistently carried on its policy of preventing generals from interfering government operation. It decided to develop Southern China rather than to expand its territory. In response to the challenge from foreign ideas, the Song people reviewed traditional thoughts, integrated tradition with new ideas, developed technology and economy, established new standards for literature and arts. After being recruited in larger numbers and treated generously, Confucians staffed government posts and helped stabilizing the grass root communities, thereby filled the leadership vacuum after eliminating the wealthy houses that dominated the government and local communities.

C.X. George Wei's (Chuxiong Wei) (魏楚雄) comment:

He is Professor of History of Macau University (having been Head of Department of History three times) having obtained double MA degree from Henan University, China (1982) and Washington University, St. Louis, USA (1991) and Ph D from the latter (1996). He is also guest professor of the Institute of Historical Research and Center for Jewish Studies of the Shanghai Academy of Social Sciences for nearly two decades. Published 8 books in English and innumerable academic and newspaper articles.

With his article 'Transform the 'Chinese dream' into a world dream', Wang Yiwei has made a very good start for our discussion on 'Chinese dream'. Wang's description of 'Chinese dream', which is fulfilled with the spirit of 'the grand harmony under heaven' and shared by all the sages of the past, is the goal competition. Rational thinking and behaviors within each layer will sooner or later be found at odd with those in other layers. For instance, whenever the economy becomes stagnant, all governments nowadays, regardless of their ideological inclination, would resort to stimulating the economy by encouraging consumption inside and outside of the country. This strategy is at odd with the family's desire to save and the global need to conserve resources. The intention to avoid overproduction, reduce consumption, promote environmental protection, select a village to let the flood burst off, … any of these moves would create conflict. Every player at each level has a right to state their interest. How to promote rational discussion and negotiation, how to avoid emotional opposition from those who are being or going to be hurt, how to handle conflict carefully, … all require additional wisdom in modern politics.

Western democracies place a heavy emphasis on individual rights. They are accustomed to preempting the oppositions. Politicians often appeal to voters with short-term benefits that could lead to huge national debts (like in Greece), regional conflicts (such as the urban-rural division in Thailand and Turkey, the dispute on channeling water from rivers in the northern Spain to the south), independence movement (like Scotland from Britain, Quebec from Canada, Basque and Catalonia from Spain). Promoting Confucius' original idea of 'Ren' .

Professor Wang raises a very important question: 'when is resurgence enough?' I suggest to replace the term 'resurgence' with 'development' because the former presumes certain highest stage/s in the past that cannot be surpassed. The World Dream cannot ignore countries without a particularly thriving period. There are two more important points. First, when people talk about 'heydays' they usually mean the period of thriving in only a specific aspect such as in military or agriculture, rather than thriving in all or most aspects. The term resurgence risks restricting attention to a certain specific direction. Secondly, 'resurgence' pulls our view back to the past. However marvelous the Chinese history was, the role for Chinese now is to not only inherit and extend the best from the past, but also to visualize the best path toward the future on the basis of sustainable development in the contemporary world.

If the World Dream takes all countries big or small into account, it should not be assessed under an international framework dominated by only one or a few countries. There is no need to set an upper limit for sustainable mutual development.

In search of historic reference for the proper extent of 'resurgence', Professor Wang brought up the 'Golden Period in the Han or Tang Dynasty' as examples, like most Chinese would do. The emphasis on Han or Tang, however, intentionally or not, stresses upon military power. While Han and Tang indeed protected and extended China's territory, they also suffered multiple defeats. Compare the maps interpretation of the 'Chinese dream' which, I think, deserves an in-depth study. True that much efforts have been put in for the sake of neighbouring and some other countries which have yielded positive results but also encountered certain problems. In our external exposition we must sincerely avoid repeating the wrong doings of some great powers in history. We must be modest in our self-placement and in our narrative. I look forward to Professor Wang Yiwei's undertaking more profound studies on the 'Chinese dream' and making more valuable contributions.

Tom Lun-nap Chung's (钟伦纳) comment:

Professor Wang Yiwei's 'Chinese dream' is linked not only to his 'World Dream' but also to his dream for individual citizens. Linking a country's dream to both of the largest context and the most basic unit of human action is a declaration of the inadequacy of state supremacy. Meanwhile, Professor Wang's advocacy for offering the Western world with inspiration on dealing with crises indicates that the Chinese are shaking off the inferiority complex stemmed from over a century's national humiliation, and are beginning to recognize and assess the objective environment in which the state operates. In this regard, I want to add two more layers to complete the 'individual-state-global' framework: family and secondary organizations.

Whereas the family has been supported by plenty of traditional forces in China, secondary organizations have not. In the Confucian scheme of layer-specific dedication efforts, the duties of secondary organizations (such as professional associations, labor unions, the market mechanism, churches, and voluntary organizations) are conspicuously absent. Contemporary affairs are getting complicated. As the state has to deal with a huge amount of tasks with limited budgets, it could hardly take care of everything for everyone in a timely and sufficient manner. Well-organized secondary organizations could supplement the state administration with its local accessibility, professionalism, flexibility, timing, and continuity. Through participation in secondary organizations, individuals learn more about what is going on between family affairs and national politics, and practice more of the collective decision making process. Of course, secondary organizations can be hypoplasia or too independent. They do need support and monitoring from other layers. Therefore, the realization of 'Chinese dream' should take into account of the healthy development in all layers of the 'individual-family-secondary organizations-state-global' framework.

Professor Wang wants to see harmony inside and outside of China. Yet, as long as there is a need to separate layers for consideration, there can be no denial of potential conflict across layers: some individuals want to consume more, some families want to save more, some secondary organizations want more autonomy, some governments need to prepare for disasters while engaging in international thin. Think of it, with the murky world order, the control of hegemony and great powers in large parts of the world, the schism among many countries, the North-South disparity and wide-spread poverty and backwardness, how can people be at ease and worry-free? I don't think the 'Chinese dream' can transform into a world dream in any foreseeable future.

Professor Wang Yiwei's interpretation of the 'Chinese dream' through the 'Zhang Zai Adage' detailing 'Develop a heart for Heaven and Earth', 'Ensure good life for all people', 'Rejuvenate the forgotten wisdom of past sages', and 'Establish peace for all eternity', is a demonstration of the high spiritual plinth, expansive vision and great munificence as well as China's historical responsibility in the new era. It reminds us Su Dongpo's (苏东坡) famous lines of 'unbounded sweeping bliss kindled by a spark of righteousness at heart' (一点浩然气，千里快哉风). However, Zhang Zai's discourse betrays a sentiment of becoming the saviour of the world and humanity with a superiority complex. Moreover, such a pompous narrative may not be appreciated by other peoples.

Of course, we are not obliged to be passive and modest when we claim China's legitimate rights and reasonable entreat, yet maintaining a rational balance between self confidence and reasonableness, between bravado and reserve so that we avoid the embarrassment of 'those who know me express pity while those who don't know me are perplexed' (知我者谓我心忧，不知我者谓我何求) as famously depicted in the verse of 'Exuberant millet plants' (黍离) in the *Book of Odes*. We have the experience (if not lesson) of some Chinese articles interpreting the expressed Chinese government policy of '*qin, cheng, hui, rong* (亲诚惠容)' (generally indirectly translated as 'mutual trust, mutual benefit, equality and cooperation' while we might render them as 'affectionate, sincere, benedictory, broad-minded) towards neighbouring countries with a patronizing tone provoking disagreeable and apprehensible feedback from some neighbouring countries. This reminds me about a couplet by Yu Youren (于右任): 'quietude begets prolonged harmony while broad-mindedness is rich Spring warmth' (气平更事久，心旷得春多). We can benefit from such a mood and win more appreciation and understanding from others. There is the need for us to calmly and mildly spell out our strategic goals in widely acceptable expressions, to be modest in seeing our innumerable shortcomings, to tackle the trouble spots between us and the neighbours with more rational mindset so that we create an image of China and double up in our materialization of the 'Chinese dream'.

In the past 30 odd years, the rise of China has rapidly enhanced its comprehensive national strength within a relatively short period, expanded its national wealth, improved people's living standard and elevated the country's world standing. Such a development evoked the envy of the vast developing countries as well as the apprehension of other nations. I would like a more modest dream' a quest for China's future goal. At the moment, dream is the pronoun of strife for idealism, making it commendable for similar discourses like 'Indian dream', 'Brazilian dream' and so on, even the 'world dream'.

Professor Wang Yiwei has advocated 'transform the 'Chinese dream' into a world dream' which, according to this writer, is refreshing, and an innovative attempt to unpack the myth of 'Chinese dream' and get to its inner meaning amidst divergent interpretations among international communities. This attempt is commendable.

The first question: We should be crystal clear about the inner meaning of the 'Chinese dream'. Only with a clear understanding (at least knowing the gist) can we talk about transforming it into a 'world dream'. I don't rule out the ambiguity since all subconscious ideas have to be like this. Scientists have informed us that dream is unbounded and clourless. However, the 'Chinese dream' should maintain its relative clarity in the Chinese and international narratives. It should be a precise vision and reflect a firm conviction and idealism.

To me, whatever the international public may interpret we ourselves have to sketch out the clear contours of the 'Chinese dream'. The core of 'Chinese dream' is the creation of a great country of clean politics, thriving economy, harmonious society and civil citizenry while it is striving for a just and reasonable world politico-economic order. China should also become a powerful country that can make greater contributions to world peace and prosperity and is ready to give necessary input to the peaceful coexistence internationally. I think the crux of the 'Chinese dream' is to do a good job in China, enabling its strength, enriching its people, and enhancing the civility of its people. Achieving all this will be the greatest contribution to the world on the part of the Chinese who make up one fifth of humanity. Of course, this is not mutually exclusive with China's devotion to the developing countries, to adhering to international justice, and to the establishment of a just and reasonable politico-economic order in the world.

The second question: Can we transform the 'Chinese dream' into a world dream? People dream their own dreams, countries dream their own dreams. All virtuous and righteous dreams echo with one another in spite of their divergent environments. In this way there won't be any problem. For instance, Yang Jiechi (杨洁篪), Member of the State Council, and Wang Yi (王毅), Foreign Minister, have both talked about the echo between 'Chinese dream' and Indian dream during their visit to India. I quite appreciate such talks. However, not the dreams of all countries echo with one another, some of them might have great potentials of contradiction and conflict. Our world is a multi-facet world, a variegated world. Not everyone in this world is kind hearted, not every country in this world is righteous. Under such circumstances, it would be rather difficult for the world to see eye to eye with the 'Chinese dream', and to forge a solidarity through thick and

I was quite impressed by a theory which I came across in the early 1950s when I was in China: The result of World War I was the birth of socialist Soviet Union, the result of World War II was the birth of socialist China; if World War III broke out, socialism would prevail all over the world. The theory lost its enthusiasm when there was schism between the two socialist giants, USSR and China. We can regard the post-war 'cold war' as World War III (many European and American scholars actually takes this view), which resulted in the disappearance of the Soviet Union and the world communist bloc and destroyed the logic of this theory. Fortunately, there is the saving grace of 'socialist China' overcoming its shock and challenge and emerging as a lone bright spot. This year, China and other countries are warmly celebrating the 70th anniversary of the victory of World War II and people are anxious about the possibility of the revival of Japanese militarism. In Japan, there is also a 'dream' to get another opportunity in the future Sino-US tussle for leadership in the Asia-Pacific region so that Japan can again play the role of the underling of World War IV. I see this an undoable Japanese illusion. Let us nip the *hot-or-cold* World War IV in the bud to prevent the revival of Japanese militarism. It all depends on how China is *rising*. First, China must properly foster the Sino-US 'new-type great power relationship' and fine-tune the rhythm of development of Asia-Pacific in the melody of '*he wei gui* (和为贵)/harmony be precious' before the emergence of a forthcoming hawkish US president. Second, we must rejuvenate the millennial 'Chinese civilization state' that was predicated on '*tianxia datong* (天下大同)/grand harmony all under Heaven' and bid farewell to the *triumphalism* mentality of the nation state. This, to my mind, is the very reason that we undertake this discourse on Wang Yiwei's 'Transform the 'Chinese dream' into a world dream'.

Ma Jiali's (马加力) Comment:

He graduated from the Department of History, Jilin University in 1975 and studied in Jawaharlal Nehru University, New Delhi for one year in early 1990s as a China-India exchange scholar. He was a Senior Researcher of China Institute of Contemporary International Relations during 1981–2010 and is Executive Deputy Director of the Centre for Strategic Studies of China Reform Forum. He published 4 books on India and 250 odd research articles. He is a Member of China-India Eminent Persons' Group Forum and adviser of China Society for South Asian Studies.

For quite some time there has been an increasing number of articles on 'dream' in Chinese media, even in international media. Conventionally, people sneer at such discourse to the extent of mocking it as idiotic. The Chinese leadership has turned the putrid stuff into celebrated brilliance, creatively making the 'Chinese to Wang Yiwei to call upon fellow-Chinese to 'develop a heart for Heaven and Earth/(为天地立心)' in their Chinese dream so that the spirit of 'ren'ai (仁爱)/love and benevolence' and 'cibei (慈悲)/compassion' is prevailing all over the world with China showing the way. Only in this way can the Chinese dream become, in Wang's words, the 'modern socialism's response to the "Zhang Zai Adage"'.

Let us return to the adage of 'gu wei jin yong, yang wei Zhong yong (古为今用，洋为中用)' (serving the present with historical experience, and serving China with foreign experience), we see China dreaming of 'tianxia datong (天下大同)' (grand harmony all under Heaven) for more than two thousand years (which Wang Yiwei has also alluded to), instead of 'fu qiang meng (富强梦)' (dream of prosperity and power). We see also that the 'fu qiang meng (富强梦)' (dream of prosperity and power) is the penchant of the 'foreigners' while many Chinese have been hypnotized by it as a result of 'foreign repression'. When we 'dream of prosperity and power' (富强梦) in China today it is not exactly 'gu wei jin yong, yang wei Zhong yong (古为今用，洋为中用)' (serving the present with historical experience, and serving China with foreign experience), but 'qu gu shun jin (去古顺今)' (abandoning history to suit the present) and 'li Zhong cong yang (离中从洋)' (abandoning Chinese tradition to ape foreign practices). I don't see anything fundamentally wrong. However, in theory, this only means to debase the millennial wisdom of Chinese civilization to the low level of Western civilization.

It was China's miserable conditions and performance in the world that Chinese patriotic heroes have trumpeted the slogan of 'zhenxing Zhonghua (振兴中华)/rejuvenation of China' for more than a century. It was too high an order in the past to rejuvenate China hence it was a 'dream'. Yet, this does not mean the 'Chinese dream' is satisfied with the 'rejuvenation of China' (振兴中华). Both the rejuvenation of China and China's dream of prosperity and power were in vogue when China was not in good shape. They are not much a '*dream*' now that China has had a facelift. Surely rejuvenating China is a thunderous slogan highly charged with patriotic passion which has been forever appealing for a hundred years. Yet, its parameter has disappeared in today's discourse. Wang Yiwei has raised the question of any target year/period of rejuvenation of China whether the 'golden period of the Han or Tang Dynasties' could be the target. I think such attempt of concretizing the abstract dream is counterproductive. The 'Chinese dream' today is not flying to any illusory 'Land of Peach Blossom' by plane or spacecraft, but to elevate China to a certain height materially and spiritually. We are not there yet, but look forward to the day when all the people of the world would join the Chinese people in relishing the pleasure of 'Chinese dream', and when other peoples are not turning pale instantly as if the tiger is there, but feel relaxed and happy in the discourse of 'Chinese dream'. That would be the real transformation of the 'Chinese dream' into a world dream.

Part IV
Symposium I: Transform the Chinese Dream into a World Dream

'serve the present with historical experience'. The Indian philosophers like Tagore have regarded civilization as a long river forever progressing which echoes with the motto that was engraved on the bathtub of the great Tang of Shang Dynasty, i.e., '*gou ri xin, riri xin, you rin xin* (苟日新、日日新、又日新)' (we should go on renew, everyday is newer than yesterday, renew daily and renew). They disagreed with the theory of overthrowing the 'ancien regime'. Tagore admired the works of Li Bai and thought his poems more modern than the works of modern poets, and he was opposed to evaluating modernity according to the sequence of the calendar. I do not know whether Wang Yiwei's mindset is constricted by the framework of '*gu wei jin yong, yang wei Zhong yong* (古为今用，洋为中用)' (serving the present with historical experience, and serving China with foreign experience) or he adopts a holistic view about civilization. From a holistic perspective, we cannot divide China into 'traditional China', 'modern China' and 'China of the World'.

It is refreshing to read Wang Yiwei's 'modern socialism's response to the "Zhang Zai Adage"'. The 'Zhang Zai Adage' of 'Develop a heart for Heaven and Earth' (为天地立心), 'Ensure good life for all people' (为生民立命), 'Rejuvenate the forgotten wisdom of past sages' (为往圣继绝学), and 'Establish peace for all eternity' (为万世开太平) have inspired my thinking for many decades. To me, his advocacy of '*lixin* 立心/establishment of *xin*/heart/mind' is the advocacy of '*putixin* (菩提心)/bodhicitta/the mind of enlightenment' which is a Chindian synthesis. His '*kai taiping* (开太平)' is the Buddhist advocacy of '*pingdeng* (平等)/upeksa' which is a Chindian synthesis once again. In this way, Zhang Zai's '*wangsheng* (往圣) past sages/(往圣)' includes Confucius and Mencius as well as Buddha. Thus, I commend Wang's interpretation that the 'Chinese dream' propounds 'all civilizations and development models benefit each other and share the beauty and joy of the comity of nations'. However, Wang Yiwei interprets 'Develop a heart for Heaven and Earth/(为天地立心)' as a quest for 'exploring how Chinese civilization may resonate with universal values in order to establish common values for all peoples' may not be what Zhang Zai had originally meant. I think Zhang Zai highlighted the '*putixin* (菩提心)/bodhicitta/the mind of enlightenment' of civilization which is the '*renai* (仁爱)/love and benevolence' of Confucius and Mencius as well as the Buddhist '*cibei* (慈悲)/compassion'. This is resonant with Tagore's emphasis on the Eastern civilizational value of 'Love' contrasting with the Western civilizational obsession with 'Power'. If our 'Chinese dream' today is the 'modern socialism's response to the "Zhang Zai Adage"', we must pay special attention to the universal application of the value of 'Love' of Eastern civilization and the abandonment of the Western pursuit of 'Power'. To be more precise, there is an excessive demonstration of 'Power' in the 'Chinese dream' of many people making China '*jingwei* (敬畏)' (respected and feared), instead of '*jingai* (敬爱)' (respected and loved) by the entire world, particularly among China's neighbours. I am appealing regard the dream of the birth of the Buddha as the first great dream of humanity. I also think the first great Chinese dream was that of Han Emperor Ming seeing the golden Buddha flying over the imperial palace. Today, both the government and people of China are promoting '*yidai yilu* (一带一路)/along the way/one zone and one road' as a happy international development. I want to tell the readers that the earliest 'silk road' started at the ancient Shu state (古蜀国), i.e., Sichuan, through Yunnan and Myanmar, and enter India from the Bay of Bengal. This enabled the ancient Indian statesman, Kautilya/Chanakya to create the concept of 'cinabhumi/land of silk/country of silk' which has been an important information for the world about 'Cina/China' for more than two thousand years. This Sichuan-Yunnan-Myanmar-Bengal 'silk road' was probably the richest international highway 2–3000 years ago. It created the ancient Indian dream of the 'Suvarnabhumi/Golden Land/金地'. I arrive at this conclusion by guessing the possibility of the derivation of the 'cinabhumi/land of silk/country of silk' into the 'Suvarnabhumi/Golden Land/金地'. I can cite the Greek evidence for it. Ancient Greeks went to India to buy Chinese silk and carried the concept of 'cinabhumi/land of silk/country of silk' to the West. Claudius Ptolemy, the great ancient geographer, conceived the existence of 'Aurea Regio/golden land' on earth which he located between Bengal and China. Doubtlessly, his 'Aurea Regio/golden land' originated from the Indian dream of the 'Suvarnabhumi/Golden Land/金地'. And this Indian dream has been long cherished till modern times and getting reiterated by the great writer, Rabindranath Tagore's verse of '*Amar Shonar Bangla*' (My golden Bengal) which is now the national anthem of Bangladesh. All this shows that the 'silk road' is already an idealism symbolizing international economic prosperity. It can interconnect with the slogan of '*yidai yilu* (一带一路)/along the way/one zone and one road' and elevate its spiritual height into embracing the world 'common destiny' (命运共同体). We have here something supporting Wang Yiwei's '*Transform the 'Chinese dream' into a world dream*'.

I wish to get into the framework of an adage of Mao Zedong Era, '*gu wei jin yong, yang wei Zhong yong* (古为今用，洋为中用)' (serving the present with historical experience, and serving China with foreign experience). I think many of us (especially the Chinese who grew up with Chinese revolution and Mao Zedong Era) have been impacted by it. There is the heart sore about overthrowing the 'ancien regime' which was first unearthed during the French Revolution and then inherited by Marxism. We raised the slogan of '*gu wei jin yong* (古为今用)' (serving the present with historical experience) after overthrowing the 'ancien regime'. Thus, this '*jin* (今)/present' is the Western world sans historical tradition and wisdom. We are standing on the 'foreign' stand to call out '*gu wei jin yong* (古为今用)' (serving the present with historical experience) which is controversial and unreal. Since the 'ancien regime' is outdated and bad, it would be a problem to of modern times does prove the drawbacks of the East. Then, what are the things to be rejuvenated in our endeavour of rejuvenating the Eastern civilization? To what extent should we rejuvenate? What can we learn from the experiences of Japan and South Korea—the rising stars among countries of the Eastern civilization? What aspects of the Eastern civilization can infuse with the Western values in order to create the 'common value system of humanity'?

Fourthly, I wander whether Professor Wang has equated his 'world dream' with his two categories of 'the China of the World (1)' (the development dream of the developing countries) and 'the China of the World (2)' (the modern model dream of the new-emergent countries)? If the answer is 'yes' it is tantamount to oversimplify the 'world dream'. If the answer is 'no', then he has to spell out the wide range and complexity involved in extending these two categories into the world dream.

In short, the idea of Professor Wang is wonderful. Since the title is *Transform the 'Chinese dream' into a world dream*, how to *transform* is the most important, and I look forward to more enlightenment on this.

Tan Chung's (谭中) Comment:

I had expected Wang Yiwei to discuss the civilizational origin of the 'Chinese dream', but throughout his article he focusses on the theme of China's great resurgence which, of course, is the crux of the issue for the rage of 'Chinese dream' today. He should highlight on it. His first highlighting the resurgence of China then juxtaposing it with China's millennial old civilization looks rather unnatural. I like very much what Wang has said about 'The Chinese people have historically been capable of and dared to dream great dreams.' This will demand that we tackle the topic of 'Chinese dream' from the perspective of 'dream culture'.

'Dream' is a part of life. There is the Chinese saying '*ri you suosi, ye you suomeng* (日有所思，夜有所梦)' (In daytime we think, at night we dream). This shows that the human brain constantly reverberates with the living reality. When the two are close, we say the imagination is '*si* (思)/thinking', and when they are far apart, we say the imagination is '*meng* (梦)/dream'. This is a conventional perspective. Conventional wisdom again distinguishes '*lixiang* (理想)/ideal' from '*mengxiang* (梦想)/dream' to be defined by the degree of the feasibility of the imagination (that which is difficult or impossible to materialize is 'dream'). Today, we highlight the topic of 'Chinese dream' with a new perspective, no longer constrained by conventional wisdom. Making the 'Chinese dream' a new tide is to encourage people to imagine beyond the confines of their living reality, enabling them to stand high and look far (which is different from '*hao gao wu yuan* (好高骛远)/over-ambitious to the extent of unpractical'), lead an energetic life striving for constant excellence.

In my essay in the book, I call India the motherland of 'dream culture', and technology? Are the research structure of production as well as the talents for innovation in China ready and fully prepared for it? Has China fully digested the Western science and technology, and is it in a position to give a facelift to it? Can we overcome the mistaken and misleading theories of the Western modern civilization on ecology and morality? What will be the new elements which we have to inject into Chinese civilization?

Furthermore, what is the 'globalization 2.0'? Is the quest for the '2.0' version the real transformation of civilization?

Secondly, there is the question of 'interconnecting' or developing beyond the West. Professor Wang repeatedly reiterates that the Chinese dream does not mean China's westernization or interconnecting the West though what he has initiated in the discourse is all about the western road of development. How can China's embracing the 'Ocean Epoch 2.0', the 'globalization 2.0', and the third industrial revolution not be 'interconnecting' the West? How can we advance into the '2.0' version without establishing the foundation of 'Ocean Epoch 1.0' and 'globalization 1.0' of the western civilization? Realizing China's great resurgence does not mean building castles in thin air, and we have to create our kitchen on the ground taking advantage of the merits of world civilizations, including the western civilization. We were lagging behind and given a heavy beating. It is not our fault for lagging behind, but the humiliation of being beaten has a deep imprint in our heart. How do we cleanse the humiliation? Replying violence to violence is surely not an alternative as we have been enlightened by the ancient Chinese wisdom that 'We won't distinguish right from wrong if we exchange violence with violence' (以暴易暴兮，不知其非矣). Nor should we boycott the West in a simplistic manner. We have to emulate our enemies, find our new path and surpass them. China's slogan of '*chao Ying gan Mei* (超英赶美)' (surpassing Britain and catching up with America) raised during the 1950s is not outdated yet perhaps. In terms of GDP, China has gone ahead of Britain, but is still lagging behind in some aspects structurally. For instance, the entire population including foreigners in Britain enjoys universal health insurance. The soft power of Britain ranks the world's top or second. Catching up with America is easily said than done. America still has a huge superiority. During the 1980s, Japan tried to be defiant to America. Two decades of economic depression has made Japan lose heart. Of course, China does not follow the beaten tracks of Japan. However, China is still unable to surpass American at the levels of quantitative indexes and technological outlooks, how would China be able 'to act as a leading country' of the world?

Thirdly, there is the question of rejuvenating the Eastern civilization. Professor Wang confidently mentions that living the Chinese dream is a process of rejuvenating the Eastern civilization. Of course, just as he says, we may not have our inferior complex in the face of Western civilization now that the West has paled in advancement. Nevertheless, we cannot be bigheaded blindly. The development

While blowing the trumpet of the renaissance of Chinese civilization, the 'Chinese dream' also sounds a clarion-call of reinvigoration for humanity's socialist movement, creating a new epoch of a brand new world dream. ∎

DISCOURSE:

Zhang Siqi's (张四齐) Comment:

At the first glance, Professor Wang Yiwei's article *'Transform the 'Chinese dream' into a world dream'* makes fascinating reading. I agree with him that the realization of the 'Chinese dream' is meant for the resurgence of the Chinese nation. It transforms China's resurgence from a third person's expression into a first person's identification. I also agree that China's relations with the world changes from a mono-track of development toward a two-way structure. I also agree that Chinese dream aims at creating a new civilization not only for its own good but also for the good of other regions as well as the whole world—beauty amidst beauty, bliss amidst bliss. However, I would like to raise a few questions for deepening my own understanding.

The first question is about the renewal of civilization as he observes: 'the reinvention of civilization is the main avenue of the Chinese dream'. He talks about *'wenming zhuanxing* (文明转型)' (transforming the pattern of civilization) without defining it, and without proposing concrete measures to realize it. His observation of China's great resurgence being 'rejuvenation, all-embracing and renovation rolled in one' is grandiloquence. He also has this to say:

> '…reasonably restores our primordial civilization—expediting the germination of the seeds of ocean/industry/global civilization within the Chinese civilization so that China marches towards the ocean/industry/globe, thereby legitimately embracing Western civilization. Through this, a common value-system of humanity is created. Through ushering in the "Ocean Epoch 2.0", the third industrial revolution, and "Globalization 2.0", a sustained development of humanity becomes reality…'.

All this sounds a little pompous and refreshing yet must be thoroughly analyzed before we go further. For instance, what is China's 'primordial civilization', and how do we 'expedite the germination of the seeds of ocean/industry/global civilization within the Chinese civilization'? Though China is a country having three million square kilometers of maritime territory and a 32000 kilometer coastal line, Chinese civilization is basically continental in nature. How can we transform it into a maritime civilization? What is the 'Ocean Epoch 2.0', and in what way is it superior to 'Ocean Epoch 1.0'? Can we (should we) replicate the expansionism, mercantilism, liberalism and hedonism of the maritime civilizations?

How would China lead the third revolution of industry and science and is changing. There cannot be a China without the world, and a world without China. China is increasingly adapting itself to the changing world, and the world is adapting to a changing China. That is why we propose a 'New Model of Great Power Relations' between China and the US.

Now that China has the capability, it must have its own dream.

China is empowered to dream its own dream, despite the passage of time. After a century of clashes with the West, China is now on the same starting line with the West in a number of realms with the West. China is encountering identical problems like other countries—sustainable development, environmental challenges, and so on. Earlier, the West used to solve the 'Western problems' while China solved 'Chinese problems'—the unfinished tasks of unification and reformation. Now, all countries are embarking on reforms as we live in an epoch of conversions and transformations. The 'Chinese dream' is born of such an epoch. It not only has to deal with the great resurgence of Chinese civilization, but also attempt to 'make a greater contribution to humanity'. The development of China is not just for China's modernization, not just for providing a mirror to the developing and new-emergent countries (like a poem describes: 'Though peach and plum trees speak not, a path is worn beneath them'), but also a message for the West to come out of its crisis. The 'Chinese dream' brings in an alternative, Chinese answer to humanity for sustainable development. It supplies a public good with gadgets, institutions and spirit 'originated in China but belonging to the world'. This is the cultural responsibility of the 'Chinese dream'.

China must dream its own dream lest it dreams the American dream, or the universal dream. Just as President Obama said on April 15, 2010 to Television Australia: if over one billion Chinese lived like Australians and Americans then everyone would fall into a terrible situation because the globe could not sustain it. He thought that the leaders of China would understand this. They must adopt a new sustainable model so that economic growth could also deal with environmental challenges.[1]

Thus, the rationality of the 'Chinese dream' lies in the demand of the times, rendering Western aggression irrelevant. The demand of the times is not just a matter of theory, but also, in reality, a part of humanity's sustainable development to live up to the expectations of other countries of the world, and loved by a comity of nations. The 'Chinese dream' is not just transcending the dreams of five millennia of Chinese resurgence, but also a powerful response to the world tide for peace and development. In a word, the 'Chinese dream' is not only China's own, but also destined for the world.

---

1 Interview with Barack Obama, 15 Apr 2010.http://www.news.com.au/national/president-barack-obama-says-prime-minister-kevin-rudd-is-smart-humble/story–e6frfkvr–1225854306896

Part IV
Symposium I: Transform the Chinese Dream into a World Dream

conditions, overthrowing the Western monopoly of world opinions; c) the 'Chinese dream' being the dream of peace, development, cooperation, Win-Win thus enriching the international relations and discarding the extension and interference of the paradigm of the Western civilization.

3. The historical significance of the 'Chinese dream' from a mono-track interconnection toward a two-way structure:

The rise of China is that of the only non-religious country in modern times—neither Westernized, nor Christian. The rise of China is that of the only civilization-state not colonized by the West. The rise of China is that of the only case of not only rejuvenating an ancient civilization but also reinvigorating the alternative Western ideology of socialism. All this reveals the historical mission of the rise of China.

The great resurgence of China is not revivalism which neither resolves the problems encountered by China today, nor helps respond to the world challenges. The great resurgence of China is not, all the more, 'interconnecting' the West which is hardly advanced, nor trouble-free—some countries even want to interconnect China that has chalked out a brand new road of development. The great resurgence of China is rejuvenation, all-embracing and renovation rolled in one. It reasonably restores our primordial civilization—expediting the germination of the seeds of ocean/industry/global civilization within the Chinese civilization so that China marches towards the ocean/industry/globe which legitimately embraces the Western civilization. Through China's embracing the Western values and being embraced by the Western values a common value-system of humanity is created. Through ushering in the 'Ocean Epoch 2.0', the third industrial revolution, and 'Globalization 2.0' the sustained development of humanity becomes reality, laying the foundation for China to act as a leading country.

China's great resurgence today is not a return to the past. Returning to the past cannot resolve China's problems today nor can it help with contemporary world challenges. China's great resurgence is not, all the more, 'taking over'. One cannot say without qualification that the West is 'advanced' or 'trouble-free'. Some countries want to China to chart forward a brand new road of development. China's great resurgence lies in rejuvenation. It is all-embracing and renovative rolled in one. It reasonably restores our primordial civilization—expediting the germination of the seeds of ocean/industry/global civilization within the Chinese civilization so that China marches towards the ocean/industry/globe, thereby legitimately embracing Western civilization. Through this, a common value-system of humanity is created. Through ushering in the 'Ocean Epoch 2.0', the third industrial revolution, and 'Globalization 2.0', a sustained development of humanity becomes reality, laying the foundation for China to act as a leading country.

In this way, the China's relations with the world will develop from a mono-track of development toward a two-way structure. China changes just as the world

Thus, the process of realizing the 'Chinese dream' is also the process of pushing other people to realize their own dreams. All these 'dreams' merge into one 'world dream'. This is to translate into reality what the famous scholar Fei Xiaotong (费孝通) said so beautifully: 'beauty for all, beauty for others, beauty amidst beauty, and grand harmony for the world'. In this way, the 'Chinese dream' is the dream of the world.

2. The world significance of the 'Chinese dream', from specificity toward universality:

China's resurgence dream after the Opium War focused on the goal of a strong country and rich nation. The broad caption of the resurgence was 'non-ending self-strengthening' (*ziqiang buxi*, 自强不息). The main avenue of resurgence was the logics of catching-up and surpassing the Western powers. Today, we have a 'Chinese dream' predicated on the grand rejuvenation of China that exceeds the limits of the country and people with enhanced civilizational concerns and humanist empathy. 'Profound virtue bearing all on earth' (*houde zai wu*, 厚德载物) is the broad caption of the 'Chinese dream', and the reinvention of civilization is the main avenue of the Chinese dream.

Earlier, our accent was on Chinese characteristics—Marxism of Chinese characteristics which was an expression of self-confidence in marching with firm steps along one's own developing path. This typified a low-profile cultural expression and a down-to-earth style. Basically, it was because of a clear-headed realization that realizing the dream of 1.3 billion Chinese under the present conditions of the country, the Communist Party and the society had to go ahead, but it could not take advantage of a ready roadmap from 5000 years of civilization.

However, this perspective of Chinese characteristics often caused misunderstanding, being branded by certain countries as 'Chinese exceptionalism', 'Chinese threat', 'Chinese hard approach', 'Chinese responsibility' and so on, driving a wedge between China and the world. We must firmly refute all this. Confucius taught: 'order in oneself requires order in others' (*ji yu li er liren*, 己欲立而立人), 'prosperity for oneself requires prosperity for others' (*ji yu da er daren*, 己欲达而达人). Being a big country and ancient civilization, China intends to modernize itself and also help other late-comer states to modernize; China intends to become a world power and also help other world powers abandon the zero-sum game of world politics and find a way to uphold their own status, living standard and dignity. Such an all-inclusive resurgence is the Chinese expression of universal concerns, i.e., the world significance of China's peaceful development.

We see the three aspects of the world significance of the 'Chinese dream': a) it is the dream of the Chinese people with a prominent Chinese imprint, not the reflection of the universal values of the West; b) the choice of Chinese model and road that makes all countries of the world march along the path befitting their own

Part IV
Symposium I: Transform the Chinese Dream into a World Dream

Australia: if over one billion Chinese lived like Australians and Americans then everyone would fall into a terrible situation because the globe could not sustain it. He thought that the leaders of China would understand this. They must adopt a new sustainable model so that economic growth could also deal with environmental challenges.[1]

Thus, the rationality of the 'Chinese dream' lies in the demand of the times, rendering Western aggression irrelevant. The demand of the times is not just a matter of theory, but also, in reality, a part of humanity's sustainable development to live up to the expectations of other countries of the world, and loved by a comity of nations. The 'Chinese dream' is not just transcending the dreams of five millennia of Chinese resurgence, but also a powerful response to the world tide for peace and development. In a word, the 'Chinese dream' is not only China's own, but also destined for the world.

The 'Chinese dream' ends 'the end of history'. The process of realizing the 'Chinese dream' epitomizes the rejuvenation of the world socialist movement from its present nadir. This brings us to the multiple significance of the 'Chinese dream'.

1. The relevance of the 'Chinese dream' after the rise of China:

The realization of the 'Chinese dream' is meant for the resurgence of the Chinese nation. It transforms China's resurgence from a third person's expression into a first person's identification. The aim of such resurgence is to benefit the common people of China, to spiritually prop up the resurgence of China, and to make clear to the world what China seeks to achieve. This is the relevance of the 'Chinese dream'.

By benefiting the common people, China's resurgence brings a sense of happiness and achievement to the entire Chinese nation but not at the expense of the right to good health and the right to development. In this way, the 'Chinese dream' is the dream of Chinese people, of their quest for a happy life.

By spiritually propping up the resurgence of China, there is the display of the Chinese spirit and soft power in addition to Chinese contributions in terms of gadgets and commodities as well as institutions. The 'Chinese dream' makes the resurgence of China robust. It spells out the great significance of the rejuvenation of Chinese civilization in the annals of human civilization. In this way, the 'Chinese dream' is the dream of renaissance for Chinese civilization.

By making clear to the world what China is in pursuit of, China announces 'what I am not' and 'what I won't do' during the course of the Chinese resurgence, and 'what I am' and 'what I will do' after the Chinese resurgence. The crux lies in fulfilling the promise of 'China, making the world happier and more enchanting'.

---

1 Interview with Barack Obama, 15 Apr 2010.http://www.news.com.au/national/president-barack-obama-says-prime-minister-kevin-rudd-is-smart-humble/story–e6frfkvr–1225854306896

up to the expectations of other countries of the world, and loved by the comity of nations. The 'Chinese dream' is not just transcending the dreams of five millennia of resurgence of China, but also a powerful response to the world tide for peace and development. In a word, the 'Chinese dream' is not only China's own, but also destined to be that of the world.

Why is there is a push for the 'Chinese dream' today?

Its genesis may be traced to the aggression of the modern West. From the Opium War onwards, the dreams of China as a state and as a nation were broken by the West's dream of universalism. China's resurgence, in turn, has inspired various movements like that of the 'self-strengtheners' (Westernization), democratic revolutionaries, and social reformers. Their dreams included the three levels of national independence, a rich-and-strong country, and social modernization with 'Mr. D' (for Democracy) and 'Mr. S' (for Science) as motivation. The main logic was to catch up, even surpass, the Western countries. There was the vogue of 'Chinese learning as substance' (*zhongxue wei ti*, 中学为体) and 'Western learning as utility' (*xixue wei yong*, 西学为用) or *vice versa*. They became a two-line struggle in the realization of the 'Chinese dream'. These, however, were alien to the dreams of China as there had never been any problem of national independence and a rich-and-strong China. These were just the reflexes of a defeated China at the hands of the West. Modernization has always been a Western dream.

Now that China has the capability, it must have its own dream.

China is empowered to dream its own dream, despite the passage of time. After a century of clashes with the West, China is now on the same starting line with the West in a number of realms with the West. China is encountering identical problems like other countries—sustainable development, environmental challenges, and so on. Earlier, the West used to solve the 'Western problems' while China solved 'Chinese problems'—the unfinished tasks of unification and reformation. Now, all countries are embarking on reforms as we live in an epoch of conversions and transformations. The 'Chinese dream' is born of such an epoch. It not only has to deal with the great resurgence of Chinese civilization, but also attempt to 'make a greater contribution to humanity'. The development of China is not just for China's modernization, not just for providing a mirror to the developing and new-emergent countries (like a poem describes: 'Though peach and plum trees speak not, a path is worn beneath them'), but also a message for the West to come out of its crisis. The 'Chinese dream' brings in an alternative, Chinese answer to humanity for sustainable development. It supplies a public good with gadgets, institutions and spirit 'originated in China but belonging to the world'. This is the cultural responsibility of the 'Chinese dream'.

China must dream its own dream lest it dreams the American dream, or the universal dream. Just as President Obama said on April 15, 2010 to Television the China of Asia speaks of an Asian (or East Asian) civilization. As for the China of the World, it straddles between a developing country and a newly-emergent sense of greatness. These multiple identities of China reflect the many faceted aspects of the 'Chinese dream':

1. A Socialist Dream for the China of China. This dream aims for general prosperity domestically and justice with equity internationally. This dream may seem to diverge from the European dream but they still arrive at the same destination. They unite in seeking greater sustainability for humanity.

2. A Renaissance Dream for the China of Asia. In revitalizing Chinese civilization, this version of the 'Chinese dream' exposes the hegemony of the West perpetrated in the guise of so-called 'universal values'. The Renaissance Dream thus ends Asia's subservience to the West.

3. A Development Dream for the China of the World I. Successful realization of the 'Chinese dream' invariably will encourage other developing countries to follow a similar path according to their specific conditions. This will expose the myth of the Western model, its system and values, as the universal standard for all. In this way, the 'Chinese dream' reinforces the socialist convictions of developed capitalist countries, and inspires various countries of the world to embark on the socialist road, adopt the socialist system, and believe in the socialist ideology.

4. A Dream of Grand Resurgence for the China of the World II. China is the biggest country to newly emerge. The 'Chinese dream', accordingly, serves as an icon for all newly-emergent great countries, inspiring their collective rise. China would inspire other new-emergent great states to follow suit, so China and others could walk together, injecting democracy in international relations to develop a more equitable, reasonable and inclusive world order.

Why is there a push for the 'Chinese dream' today?

If China doesn't follow its own dream, then the universal Western dream is the only alternative. Just as President Obama said on April 15, 2010 to Television Australia: if the over-one-billion Chinese lived like Australians and Americans then everyone would fall into a terrible situation because the globe could not sustain it. He thought that the leaders of China would understand this. They had to adopt a new sustainable model so that while pursuing economic growth China could also deal with the challenges of the environment.[1]

Thus, the rationality of the 'Chinese dream' lies in the demand of the times, that makes the Western aggression irrelevant. The demand of the times is not just a matter of theory but, in reality, a part of the sustainable development of humanity

---

1 Interview with Barack Obama, 15 Apr 2010.http://www.news.com.au/national/president-barack-obama-says-prime-minister-kevin-rudd-is-smart-humble/story-e6frfkvr-1225854306896

I emphasize: China's resurgence aims to help others resurge, thereby giving back to the world. Hence, the world should feel assured of the purpose of the 'Chinese dream'.

China is not a country born today but a millennial-old civilization. We cannot overlook this aspect when discussing the 'Chinese dream'. The ancients of China also had dreams. They dreamed of an integration between Heaven and Humans ('*tianren heyi*', 天人合一)—an ideal interconnectivity of humanity with its natural environment. They dreamed also of the concept of justice under Heaven ('*tianxia wei gong*', 天下为公)—an ideal relationship between the individual and society. And they dreamed of a grand harmony under Heaven ('*tianxia datong*', 天下大同)—an ideal order among all states. All these and other 'Chinese dreams' come from five millennia of civilization; they are motivated also from the country's vast landscape. The Chinese people have historically been capable of and dared to dream great dreams.

To my mind, the 'Chinese dream' is modern socialism's response to the 'Zhang Zai Adage' (*zhang zai ming ti*, 张载命题):

1. 'Develop a heart for Heaven and Earth' (为天地立心), meaning to explore how Chinese civilization may resonate with universal values, in order to establish common values for all peoples.

2. 'Ensure good life for all people' (为生民立命), meaning to build a society in which everyone enjoys a well-to-do living, thereby instantiating China's human rights and national rights.

3. 'Rejuvenate the forgotten wisdom of past sages' (为往圣继绝学), meaning to sustain the eternal development of humanity so that all civilizations and development models benefit each other and share the beauty and joy of the comity of nations.

4. 'Establish peace for all eternity' (为万世开太平), meaning to promote and create a harmonious world of enduring peace and shared prosperity, and usher in a grand harmony under Heaven (*tianxia datong*, 天下大同) for contemporary times.

We draw on Liang Qichao (梁启超) to identify a triple status for China: the China of China, the China of Asia, and the China of the World.[1] The 'Chinese dream' fuses these three identities. In other words, the 'Chinese dream' enables China's internal creation of a 'harmonious society' to align with external pursuits of 'peaceful development' in a 'harmonious world'.

Today, the China of China points to a socialist China with Chinese characteristics;

---

1 Liang Qichao (梁启超), 'Zhongguoshi xulun' (中国史叙论/On Chinese history) (1901), in *Liang Qichao Quanji* (梁启超全集/The Collected Works of Liang Qichao), Beijing: Beijing Press, 1999, vol. 1, pp. 11–12.

Transform the 'Chinese dream' into a World Dream

Wang Yiwei 王义桅

Currently, Professor of International Relations, Director of the Centre for the Study of European Union and Director of Centre for the Study of International Relations, Renmin University of China, Beijing. Previous experiences include Assistant Engineer of the United Chemical Company, Tianjin, Professor in the Centre for American Studies of Fudan University, Shanghai, Diplomat in China's Mission for the European Union, Brussels, and Visiting Professor of special assignment of Tongji University, Shanghai. Published nearly ten books in Chinese and one in English, and 150 research papers in 12 countries. He is now the chief editor of the 10 volume Chinese series of NATO studies.

Exploring the 'Chinese dream' invariably involves clarifying three perplexing questions relating to the 'resurgence' of China:

First, when is resurgence enough? Do we refer to any particular time, say, during the golden period of the Han or Tang Dynasties, as an indicator? More important is: after China resurges to the level expected, does it—should it—stop? We must clarify: China's continuing development is based on the logic of sustaining human civilizational development. Hence, the world should believe that the 'Chinese dream' is a rational dream.

Second, why should China resurge? It is well known that China was defeated by the West in modern times, and was forced to find its way towards self-reliance, self-strengthening and self-respect. However, the West defeated many states, including ancient civilizations. Do they not resurge? Again, let's be clear: only a resurgent China can embrace the West, thereby avoiding the tragic repetition of a China vs West rivalry. Hence, the world over should rejoice in the legitimacy of the 'Chinese dream'.

Third, how should China regard the resurgence of other states? Should the West itself also resurge? If every state resurges, can the Earth take it? Once more,

Part IV

Symposium I: Transform the Chinese Dream into a World Dream

neighbours dream differently on the same bed the 'Chinese dream' cannot be sweet. When India does not live with China cordially, the Tibetan situation is not stable. This is the real political picture today.

The ancients had the lyric vision of 'world-wide separation is as close as the next-door neighbourhood' (天涯若比邻) and 'sharing the moonshine between a thousand miles' (千里共婵娟). Where are such visions now? How are we degenerated?! To China India does not lie in 'world-wide separation' (天涯), but is a 'next-door neighbour' (比邻)—China and India are entitled to share the 'moonshine' of the 'rich-and-strong' dream. When Chinese lie on the bed and live the 'Chinese dream' they should see 'the bright moon shines by my bed' (床前明月光)—as Li Bai (李白) saw it—and should see 'the white clouds covering thousands of miles, the bright moon shines upon the front and rear streams' (白云千里万里，明月前溪后溪). China and India are the 'front and rear streams' embraced by the 'third pole' of the earth, the Himalaya. This is also the 'front and rear beds' (前床后床) to share the 'rich-and-strong' dream. China and India should be in the same bed and share the same dream, not in the same bed sharing varying dreams. Cordial neighbourliness between China and India is the inviolable law of human history and future evolution. The present no-war-no-peace situation and love-hate sentiments are like 'mad clouds envy the good moon, flying furiously and blackening a thousand miles' (狂云妒佳月，怒飞千里黑)—this won't last.

The 'dream' of the 'Chinese dream' is a magnificent vision woven by the gold, silver and silk threads of Love (loving life and humans), Pursuit (pursuing truth, brightness and future) and Co-richness (of China, India, Chindia, and the world). As an overseas Chinese, I look forward to the 'Chinese dream' with unbounded expectations. I am confident that it would not let me down.

resolve the border dispute?!

For India, China is the most important country of the world, and it is most important to maintain cordial relations with China. This is because China is a close neighbour, a country that had long contacts with India in the past and one that has infinite future. Nehru wrote on March 17, 1950 to the chief ministers of the Indian states that 'China is the country for which I have the greatest admirations'. At that time all Nehru's correspondence was state secret. His words were not diplomatic gesture, but from the heart. Late Indian President, Kocheril Raman Narayanan, was Director of the East Asian Division of the Ministry of External Affairs, Indian Ambassador to China, Vice-Chancellor of Jawaharlal Nehru University (where Tan Chung was teaching), and showed special warmth to Tan Chung. We were often invited to the Rashtrapati Bhavan (the President's House) for banquet. Other guests were big shots or foreign ambassadors. We were the only miserably poor scholars driving our own car and parking it at the courtyard outside the president's residence. President Narayanan liked China from his inner heart. This we know clearly.

'A good neighbour is a priceless jewel' (邻居好，无价宝) as the Chinese saying goes. I hope the Chinese government construct a 'special good neighbourliness (新型睦邻关系)' as it is working hard in constructing a 'special (China-U.S.) great power relationship (新型大国关系)'. When I was in India I had regular contacts with the ruling elite, and I knew that India heartily wished to be China's good neighbour. They were not jealous of China's increasing power (some of them even felt proud that China dared challenge the Western hegemons, and often openly commended it). However, China is India's next-door neighbour. The 1962 war hits hard India's self-respect and self-confidence. If India shows a little competitive and rivalry mood vis-à-vis China it is a bi-product of objective circumstances.

China progresses faster than India. China is more powerful than India. The leeway between China and India is increasing. Chinese attention concentrates on India's lack of unity, dysfunction, and dirty and chaotic environment. China which does not prioritize relations with India cannot but despise India, cannot but putting on airs. Chinese generally suffer 'reverence and servitude to *yang*/ocean-foreignness (崇洋媚外)' but India is not a part of this '*yang* (洋)/ocean-foreignness'. People in China don't see the high quality of culture and intelligence of the 1.2 billion Indians. They don't see the large number of Indian talents and many of them enjoy high reputation in the Western world (some even earnestly advocate 'the rise of China') while Chinese are far behind. India's foreign relations are better than China's.

If China and India share the 'rich-and-strong' dream, the 'Chinese dream' also becomes the 'Indian dream', both the 'Chinese dream' and the 'Indian dream' will be sweet. If the 'Chinese dream' excludes the 'Indian dream' and the two great

India greatly prevents the Indian people from a correct perspective about China'. This is the typical attitude of putting the blame on others without self scrutiny that I have talked above. The want of a 'correct perspective' between China and India is not just a unilateral phenomenon on the Indian side. I constantly watch the popular Chinese pronouncements on India. The Chinese deficiency of a 'correct perspective' on India is even more serious than vice versa.

Tan Yun-shan, Tan Chung, and I have had our respective 'Chinese dream'. I have lived in a foreign environment in day time, but when I fell in sleep I often flew to the motherland that had brought me up. The faces of near and dear I have left behind for decades appeared in my 'dream' vividly. This was my simple and real 'Chinese dream', the 'Chinese dream' sans colouring. India is my second motherland, and I often fly to India in my 'dream' now that I live in the U.S.A. My 'Chinese dream' and 'Indian dream' are closely connected—inseparable.

Tan Yun-shan never recovered from his agony about the 1962 Sino-Indian border war. When Deputy Minister Chanda came home to see him, he lamented: 'How would this happen? Are not China and India brothers?!' Chanda was always up beat and witty. He replied: 'What's wrong? Brothers also fight.' Chanda led a huge friendship delegation to visit China in 1956. On returning, he praised China enormously. He observed that Premier Zhou Enlai was a much greater leader than Nehru. After the 1962 war, the Indian Ambassador to China, G. Partasarthi, who had earlier been on duty leave in India never returned to Beijing. Pan Zili (潘自力), the Chinese Ambassador to India, could not but leave New Delhi. Before his departure, he invited Deputy Minister Chnada to his official residence alone for dinner. Both of them felt sad, and the dinner immersed in a gloomy atmosphere. It looked like that there was an evil hand that had kidnapped Sino-Indian relations. Everyone was helpless.

That evil hand still holds Sino-Indian relations to ransom. It is the evil hand of the geopolitical paradigm of the 'nation states' of Western civilization. In its dictionary there is no concept of 'fraternity'. Neighbouring states can only be rivals and potential enemies—not 'brothers'. This does not agree with the basic values of the two great civilizations of China and India. It hurts the harmony between these two only 'civilization states' of the world. Of course, we should not just put the blame on the West and overlook what China and India have erred. On one hand, there have been differences in opinion while, on the other, the great traditional spirit of China and India of 'putting oneself in the other's situation' disappears when both sides quarrel over their differences. During argument, China feels all mistakes are on the Indian side while India feels all mistakes are on the Chinese side. How could such egotist mentality create good neighbourliness?! China blames India for not coming round to mutual understanding and mutual accommodation while India feels China like a piece of iron unyielding. How could such attitudes produced a sumptuous Chinese meal.

Chinese are face-conscious (even becoming generous beyond their means). Every time when we invited people for dinner we spent more time and energy in cleaning and decorating the house than shopping and cooking. Indian friends were not so serious. But two friends made comments after having food with us. A new friend asked: 'Do you eat so many dishes and such good food every day?' I could not say 'yes' but felt shy to tell him that we generally ate very simple, only became extravagant when we asked people to eat with us. Another time, the husband of a member of our 'China experts' gang said to me: 'You have invited us for such lavish food, how can we return your hospitality?'

Unlike the Chinese, Indians generally don't draw a clear distinction between *us* and *them*. Among friends, it is somewhat like 'yours is mine, and mine yours'. I lived in a University-quarter and was the neighbour of a bachelor colleague of the English Department looking after by his old mother. The old lady came to my house to use the telephone, and I welcomed her warmly. Sometimes, when I returned late from the University and discovered I was out of salt. Sometimes, unexpected guests turned up and there was no milk to make the Indian tea. I dashed to the neighbour to 'borrow' from the old lady. She would say: 'Take it! We are in one family, no question of borrowing.' She always said to me: 'We are only separated by a wall. If we pull down the wall, we become one family.' People say that Xi Jinping talked about 'Both sides on the Taiwan Strait are in one intimate family' with passion. I think, I am more passionate when I talk of 'China and India are in one intimate family'. These words don't appear from my brain, they emerge from my heart.

I and my neighbour, my students, my colleagues, and all my Indian acquaintances formed a community of mutual love. The community was 'pro-China' mainly because I was 'pro-India'. If I were 'not pro-India' or 'anti-India' I would not have formed this 'pro-China' community. The same is with the states, I think. A China that is not 'pro-India' would not wish India 'pro-China'. I began to understand what *Laozi* observed: 'One who does for other gets richer and richer. After giving away to others one possesses even more.' (既以为人己愈有，既以与人己愈多). Everything begins from oneself. China should not eschew from self-scrutiny and busy itself in blaming Indians for 'not pro-China' or 'anti-China'. I wish young Chinese go merrily to India to study and settle down, thus establishing the relationship of 'China and India in one intimate family' at the grass root level. When China takes initiative to pull down the wall between the two countries, China and India will become one family.

I read in *Global Times* on January 17, 2014, Wu Chuke's (吴楚克) article on 'The shocking ignorance about China on the part of the neighbouring peoples' (邻国民间的对华无知令人震惊). The article says, 'The history of the border war compiled by

Among the Hindus, 'atma' is absolutely overpowered by 'paramatma/the supreme soul'. This idea was spread in China to become the culture of 'sacrificing the micro-self for the macro-self' (*xisheng xiaowo wei dawo*牺牲小我为大我). Both Chinese and Indian cultures denigrate 'atmagraha/ego-clinging' to 'put oneself in the other's situation'. This greatly impressed me during my sojourn in India. People talk about the 'argumentative Indians'. I think they tend to abrasively speak out their minds while listening to others seriously. After an acrimonious debate they remain friends and reach a consensus. In China, we see some people being apparently modest but really not. That they don't argue does not mean they are humble and receptive to others' opinions—only refraining from disagreeable expressions. There are Chinese intellectuals who become such bigots after a stint in the U.S. universities. They are heavily infected by the bad habit of American egotism and become overweening. They despise the scholars form the developing countries, and are especially impudent to the traditional wisdom sans Westernization. Every time I see them I am reminded by the 'pseudo-foreign-devil' (假洋鬼子) of Lu Xun's (鲁迅) novel 'The True Story of Ah Q' （阿Q正传）.

Tan Chung and I and some Indian friends formed a gang. Not only we met regularly every week to discuss China and Sino-Indian relations, but also we socialized intimately. Before arriving in India I had never entered the kitchen to do any cooking. Socializing in the Indian society made me a renowned chef of Chinese cuisine. Actually, I was a fake. I had no time to learn cuisine. I only picked up a few tricks from the Chinese restaurants and overseas Chinese homes plus my own innovations. My fame was also created by the 'superstition' of my Indian friends who believed a Chinese housewife must be a good chef of Chinese food. They had few chances of eating genuine Chinese food, and I tried to delight their appetite. Those who had eaten my food advertised my cooking, and often people would ask for an invitation to dine in my house. Of course, it was always a two-way traffic. We were often invited to the parties of Indian friends as well.

About the superstition that all Chinese must be good cooks, I am reminded of an episode. In the 1980s, I obtained a grant to go to China to collect information and materials for a project. When I came back after a month, I heard from an evening gathering people praising Tan Chung as a good cook. I was puzzled that what had gone wrong with my husband who had never even made a cup of tea for himself. It so happened that when he was alone and feeling bored at home, he often went to a close friend, Giri Deshingkar's place for chitchat. One day, suddenly, Deshingkar proposed that Tan Chung cook a meal for a dozen people and Tan Chung accepted the challenge. Deshingkar, then, called many friends to his house for dinner. Tan Chung opened the kitchen cupboard and found it stacked with tinned food from China along with packets of dry mushrooms, tree-fungi, shrimps, and scallops. Deshingkar did not consume them or did not know how to cook them. Tan Chung of ideology. Later, Tan Chung became the Head of Department and also took up teaching of history courses (then he joined Jawaharlal Nehru University). I became the only Chinese among full-time Chinese language teachers. Afterwards, research courses of M. Phill and Ph. D started, and the researchers who had completed the language courses continued to come to me for reading Chinese language materials. Colleagues of the University who undertook research on China also came to me for consultation. I became a walking encyclopaedia of Chinese language and also a tour guide of Chinese civilization.

The University built the Arts Faculty Extension for four departments. The second floor was occupied by the Department of Linguistics and Chinese Studies (then expanded into Chinese and Japanese Studies). The Department of Linguistics had very few teachers and students hence we got most of the rooms. I was allotted a fairly spacious room which I used as office-cum-classroom (as I was teaching only the higher language classes and research students with very few students, the space was sufficient). Every day, as soon as I entered my room I would be fully engaged without a moment's rest. In between my classes there would be people for consultation. I ordered tea to my room, and chatted with Indian intellectual elite on Chinese language and Sino-Indian relations. The intellectual activities in my room aimed at promoting understanding of, and empathy and sympathy for China on the part of Indian friends. This continued from 1971 to 1997 at my retirement.

What an ingenious thing the Chinese script is! Non-alphabetic, playing with the strokes. It is not only the visual of the sound-symbols of Chinese language, but also ideographic marks of Chinese culture. Indians find them difficult to learn initially, but feel them interesting after learning. When I taught the visual '仁' to the students, I pointed out that it was a combination of '二/two' and '人/human-being' which was a statement that the society was essentially of two persons: oneself and the other. I went a step further to introduce to them the ideas of Confucius and Mencius on '*tui ji ji ren* (推己及人)/put oneself in the other's situation', '*ji suobuyu wu shiyu ren* (己所不欲勿施于人)/do not do unto others what you don't want done to you', '*ji yu li er li ren* (己欲立而立人)/stand others up if you want to stand up', and '*ji yu da er da ren* (己欲达而达人)/make others prosper if you want to prosper'. After such teaching, my students developed an appreciation for Chinese civilization. On many occasions, they quoted corresponding Indian sayings to match the Chinese. My Chinese classes became a dialogue between the civilizations of China and India.

Eastern civilizations they are: Chinese and Indian—applauding harmony but not power-pursuit, and the collective but not individualism. Indians don't emphasize on 'atma'. Yu-lan Fung (冯友兰) had an in-depth understanding of Indian civilization by saying that Buddhism commended 'dharmagraha/truth-clinging' and disparaged 'atmagraha/ego-clinging' in his *A History of Chinese Philosophy*.

daughter-in-law, I had to fulfil the duty of a good daughter-in-law, wife and mother. I also taught Chinese in Delhi University for 33 years, contributing my mite to the Chindia synergy of this family.

Having been respected by Tagore, Tan Yun-shan was a monument on the campus of Visva-Bharati at Santiniketan in West Bengal. I was welcomed passionately and became the focus of attention. Famous musical expert, Indira Devi, niece of Tagore, christened me with an Indian name 'Subbha' (meaning good woman). I became well-known on the campus as 'Subhadi/good sister', 'Subhaboudi/good sister-in-law' and 'Subhama/good mother' instantly. Tan Yun-shan's closest Indian friend, Mr. Anil Kumar Chanda who had been Tagore's secretary and a professor of Visva-Bharati before Independence, and a deputy minister of the Republic of India met us often as we lived in New Delhi. He and Madam Chanda treated Tan Chung and me as their son and daughter-in-law. Every time when Madam Chanda saw me she would warmly call me 'Subhama/good mother' (in affectionate Bengali tradition the mother-in-law would address the daughter-in-law as 'ma') and hug me. I never had such an experience in China. My heart melted, and I regarded myself a member of the joint-family of India.

India needed my expertise on Chinese language and my perceptual knowledge of growing up in China. The Department of East Asian Studies of Delhi University is going to celebrate its golden jubilee in 2014. It will look back to the initial stage of establishment. In the Autumn of 1964, after obtaining a grant from the Ford Foundation, Delhi University decided to start the Chinese studies programme. It established the 'Centre for Chinese Studies' even before the Ministry of Education approved the programme and placed the 'Centre' in the Department of Buddhist Studies. Then there came the approval from the Ministry, but the Head of the Department was yet to be appointed, a number of the faculty members were under training in the U.S.A. The 'Centre' was placed under the direct administration of the Dean of the Faculty of Arts. Actually, the 'Centre' had only one Chinese language programme with two teachers: Tan Chung and I.

Fifty years have passed like a wink. I remember how we started the part-time Chinese language courses. (Initially, we were assisted by short-term visiting teachers sent by the Ford Foundation.) We had a lot of students and a start with a bang. Many under-graduate students of the University joined because in the Civil Services' entrance examinations there was a paper of foreign languages in which Chinese was an option. And taking the Chinese paper could score higher marks than other papers—hence higher chances of getting into the government. Many students got through and became members of IAS (Indian Administrative Services) and IFS (Indian Foreign Services). The most famous among them is Shivshankar Menon who was the Indian Ambassador to China, Foreign Secretary, and National Security Adviser of India. Many left-leaning students also joined the course because

Part III
One Endeared Family within Four Seas

One Intimate Family for China and India: Sharing the 'Rich-and-Strong' Dream

Ishu Huang 黄绮淑

Born and brought up in Shanghai, she was teaching Chinese language in India where she had a 45 year sojourn from 1955 to 1999. She had had a brief experience as a Chinese language announcer in the All India Radios before she started teaching Chinese language in Delhi University in 1964. She retired in 1997 as a 'Reader' (Associate Professor). One of the founders of the Institute of Chinese Studies of India, she still remains a life-long researcher of the Institute. She has translated literature from Indian languages into Chinese and published in Chinese language newspapers. Hundreds of her comments on world affairs have appeared in *Lianhe Zaobao* (the major Chinese language daily newspaper of Singapore) and other papers and journal of Hong Kong. She has been highly respected in India as many high-ranking government officers and ambassadors had been taught by her.

'Both sides of the Taiwan Strait are in one intimate family', this utterance of Chairman Xi Jinping during his meeting with the Taiwan friendship delegation led by the Honorary President of Kuomintang, Mr. Lien Chan, on February 18, 2014 in Beijing have created reverberations on Mainland China and Taiwan. I now paraphrase them to talk about my first motherland China and second motherland India—one intimate family for China and India who should share the 'rich-and-strong' dream.

In the 1980s I and Tan Chung visited China after 30 years. People were surprised that we had made India our permanent home. 'How could you live in India for so long?' For many Chinese, India was unfamiliar, perhaps unfriendly to China, they were perplexed that as a Chinese I could regard India as my 'home'.

I went to India in 1955. After living there for 45 years I settled down at Chicago in 1999. Tan Chung is my husband, and Tan Yun-shan, my father-in-law. The Tan family was one thoroughly integrated into the Indian society. Being the eldest

161

Four seas to One Family:
Overseas Chinese and Chinese dream

Since time immemorial this has been the description of the Chinese who uprooted themselves from their homeland. Today, after the Reforms and Open-up, it is a changed picture. Those who study abroad are labeled 'gold-plating', and those who do work and business abroad 'gold rush'. Yet, there is the feeling of 'The outside world is wonderful and the outside world is impossible.' (外面的世界很精彩，外面的世界很无奈) In the advent of the 21st century, especially the duration of the great rejuvenation of the Chinese nation, China's interconnection and interaction with the outside world are expanding increasingly, so also the people's mobility. Besides short-term trips and conferences, innumerable people among the 1.3 billion China are going abroad to do studying, jobs and business to realize their own 'Chinese dream'. Our motherland is having rapid economic growth, our wallets are getting fatter, and our spine straightened and stronger. However, the globe isn't a village yet and there are linguistic, cultural, customs and institutional hurdles to be crossed. When we arrive in a new environment where the institutional network of our motherland cannot reach, we miss our homeland, our hometown and our near and dear.

> My humble standing,
> It doesn't mean
> I am short of affection
> For my nation.
> (位卑未敢忘忧国)

These words of Lu You (陆游) encourage me to sustain my dedication to mobilizing the overseas Chinese and Chinese scientists and their families to join our Friendship Society. I wish to build it into an exemplary model of cooperation for the overseas Chinese so that all of us can live happily, making all four seas on earth our homeland.

My Chinese dream is the eternal good neighborliness between China and Japan that are separated only by a strip of water. My Chinese dream is that China and Japan are interconnected in their respective dreams, Chinese love Japan and Japanese love China. My Chinese dream is that peoples of China, Japan and the world concentrate their attention to social concord and ecological harmony. My Chinese dream is that I, the 'micro-self' is me, and the world, the 'macro-self' is also me, that all individuals, families, societies, nations and the globe *bury their hatchets and live in peace and happiness. My Chinese dream is: reality is the dream and dream is the reality…Perhaps* I've written too much. O! My mother, my son and my benediction!

Part III
One Endeared Family within Four Seas

In this than last Spring,
Who's there to share my joy?
(聚散苦匆匆，此恨无穷。今年花胜去年红。可惜明年花更好，知与谁同？)

I was always seized by the sentiments of these lines from Song poet Ouyang Xiu (欧阳修). I received the postcard you designed from Taipei which seems to convey the same sentiments. Looking at the picture of the three of you with Building 510 at your back, the logo of our society in the middle and the other nostalgic visuals, I could not hold my tears. The loss of such a talented friend by our Society, the years we worked together, and the sadness of separation between Mainland and Taiwan…! Fortunately there is internet and we can chat over it after our children go to sleep. Also there is the moon ship designed by you just like a Noah's Ark for the members of the Friendship Society which makes everyone feel safe. There is the little flame inside the ship which is the flame inside your heart and the hearts of all members of the Society that shines upon our future path…..

Many thanks to you for what you've done for the Friendship Society. Wish all the family a happy Spring Festival! Wish you god speed!

Your sincerely,
Zhang Siqi

My XiaoMiu and my Friendship Society in Takezono, Tsukuba, this is a common yet uncommon story. It reflects the imperishable bonds of Chinese wherever they are—the bonds deeper than the sea. It reflects such a national soil that is segregated from the outside world by the ferocious sea waves. All this and more… My heart fly back to my motherland which I haven't returned for a long time, and to my Alma mater—that campus by the side of Weiming Lake where we the youthful and patronizing intellectuals liked to harangue commentaries on politics. Is it the Chinese dream that is twanging the guitar in the hearts of the people? Who says that I don't have my Chinese dream? True my dream has shed its youthful windward flippancy, it is still a dandelion with solid roots and blooms happily with its pretty little yellow flowers, watching the kids dancing with the wind with great satisfaction.

O! Footprint of the wanderer
That's the mixture
Of blood and tears.
(游子的脚印，血泪斑斑)

celebrating the Lantern Festival, bidding farewell to friends who were returning to China, and a special parent-toddler get-together.

The housewives who burrow themselves day and night in household chores and baby-care found the get-togethers a chance to relax. With microphone in hand, they vied with each other to narrate their dreams, their realization of illusion and reality, and their embarrassing experiences in Japan in the stranger-society and alien language and culture environment. At first, everybody was in a jovial mood and laughing mirthfully. Then, someone talked about the lonely life of herself and her child, and wished there always be night and there would never be dawn. Then, the speaker's voice disappeared and tears rolled out among the listeners. You were the one who walked to the speaker and gave her a tissue paper. And then you took over the mike and told us about your own stories. When you first arrived and were at a loss you joined our Friendship Society and enjoyed the warmth of the compatriots from the Mainland. You confessed that your earlier misconception about the disunity of the mainland Chinese had disappeared. You discovered the 'new mainland Chinese' (新大陆人) who were keen to share each other's experience in living and in studies. You said your friend from Taiwan staying in Sendai had the same discovery. Your intervention had such a great impact on the crowd that I proposed you should lead a group of parents and toddlers in the Friendship Society so that we could meet at regular or irregular intervals in order to make more friends and create an atmosphere of an affectionate Chinese family for our children.

On the afternoon of March 11, 2011 when you and your daughter, I and my son, and some other Chinese friends had a mini-party on the small square under the Building 511, there erupted the strongest earthquake of Japanese history. The sky became dark at once, and there was violent wind and sand storm. Aftershocks followed up. The buildings around us wobbled with loud clacking of doors and windows. People cried in panic. All of us who had never experienced it before did not know what to do. We stood in the center of the square and formed a little circle shoulder to shoulder and hand in hand. A few days later, there arrived a radiomimetic cloud from Fukushima which terrified us once more. In such chaos, you left for Taiwan while most of us returned to mainland China without even bidding each other goodbye.

After I returned to Takezono and resumed activities around Building 510, I took the kids to the park where we used to have our moon ship fun. We were no longer having you in our midst, many of our mutual friends also left Tsukuba forever.

> Reunion and parting
> Always in a wink!
> Flowers more enchanting

Part III
One Endeared Family within Four Seas

your report on the entire process of how the inspiration of the Moon ship had crystallized into the final picture I was shocked that with apparent fragile looks you were such a person of hardy resolve and execution. The logo astutely used the colors of yellow and black won the appreciation of members of the Society, reminding us the majestic Yellow River and its fertile soil.

I always thought the gigantic motive force behind your selfless service was from Taiwan. I still remembered your answer that you were the only representative of Taiwan when I asked you why you always contributed so much to the Friendship Society and always worked against the clock. I must let you know what really happened. Because of your joining the Friendship Society changed its name several times. We adopted the name 'Friendship Cooperation Society of Takezono, Tsukuba' (筑波竹园友好互助会) finally to make the society not belonging exclusively to the mainland or Taiwan or any part of China. Here you see a society of the people from the mainland to make its name suiting you—our compatriot from Taiwan. By the way, after you left another member from Taiwan joined. A pretty young lady who is a researcher. She told me that her membership benefited her for learning how to make dumplings from the friends of mainland China.

You played the major role in organizing the 2011 Spring Festival gala evening of the Friendship Society and worked very hard. You surveyed every corner of the venue repeatedly before planning how to organize the celebration. (I can't keep a secret from you that President Liu Xuefeng complained to me after the event that you were too fastidious and he had to ask the building manager to open the hall several times for you. But, this is just between you and me.) After a thorough inspection of the venue, you and your husband turned the searchlight onto the marketplaces of Tsukuba for buying materials which could be in keeping with Chinese customs for the celebration of the Spring Festival. You kept a tight control over all those in charge of various programs to avoid any mishap. Tell you the truth, all of us from mainland China learned a lot from you especially your heightened sense of responsibility which had been neglected by us.

I was always wondering whether you had worked so hard for a good image of Taiwan or just giving the best account of yourself. In fact, the gala evening of the 2011 Spring Festival under your charge has been the best and obtained maximum praise for Taiwan. It attracted many Chinese and non-Chinese and the venue was packed. After food many non-Chinese mobbed you with questions about Chinese art. The most interesting thing was everybody took home the paper cutting of the logo you designed and decorated their doors and windows for the Spring Festival.

As the Chinese say all good things must come to an end. Being women, we always like to extend the festivity. Indeed, on the Lantern Festival we had a get-together again in Ninomiya House. We redecorated the place by making use of the left-over materials of the Spring Festival and held a function for three purposes:

ascended the stage with husband and daughter and a huge bag of moon ships there was prolonged ovation from the crowd with thunderous applause and whistling. You were so pretty and people were expecting the moon ships. But, after you opened the bag and put the boats made of palm leaves row upon row on the table, there was great disappointment. Where was the moon ship that was advertised in the photo? Such simple boats made of palm leaves, could they float on water? At that time, host Li Hongfang and her family guided all of us to fit the candle and chrysanthemum on the boats. Then, we followed the host and walked in formation to the lake of the Kinrin Park carefully holding our moon ship in hand.

That evening the moon was shrouded in dark clouds and the air was cold with wind. Insects rustled in the grass. The branches of weeping cherries moved up and down. All of us walked silently lest the solemnity and serenity got spoiled.

The lake was 200 meters in length and 40–50 meters in width—a place frequented by us with kids. No one else was there, and the water rippled to greet us. We lit the candles and silently said our prayers, and sent our boats to the water. One, two, three….more and more moon ships going, the lake was suddenly lit and the crowd got excited. Everyone wished his or her moon ship surge to the front.

Li Hongfang the host and her family led the chorus of 'Moon Ship':

> O! Moon ship, Moon ship,
> You enter my cradle
> With mother's lullaby.
> The moonlight flickers, so gentle
> Like mother's round eyes
> Offer me a smile.
> ……

O! Moon ship, on the moon-lit evening of Mid-Autumn Festival, please carry our greetings and benedictions to our near and dear in the Mother Land, please bless everyone of us, old and young, with safety and harmony, please translate our dreams into reality.

The moon ship has kindled the fervor in our hearts which were long suppressed. The song of 'Moon ship' revealed our inner affection. All of us blushed with joy, and our eyes glistened. In the society of Japan, so somber and grave, we had seldom gotten into such effusive mood. All participants expressed our wishes to keep this program as a regular feature for the Mid-Autumn Festival evening of the Friendship Society. I, then, asked you to design a logo for the Friendship Society and everyone clapped in approval.

You showed us a specimen of the logo after the Friendship Society organized a photography exhibition by Li Mao on a very cold wintry afternoon. After hearing

Chinese in addition to the affectionate cooperation and mutual help between people from the Mainland and Taiwan.

January 13, 2014

Dear Xiaomiu,

How are you doing?

Once again, the Spring Festival is coming and the Friendship Society is preparing for its 5th Spring Festival evening. I worry who can be entrusted to take charge of decorating the venue. Had you been here my worry would not have been there as you had always done such a good job and created the boisterous and gay atmosphere with high standard and enrichment. After your departure all activities of the Friendship Society lost the thrill and glitter you used to create. The new hands in charge don't have your grasp of the spirit of the Friendship Society and come to the expectations of various age groups. The input of the 'old people' like me lacks the same talent and devotion as shown by you.

Remembering your devotion evokes my unbounded admiration. Can you recall the meeting of preparatory committee for the Mid-Autumn Festival of 2010 when I mooted the suggestion about an additional Moon Ship program for the kids? I suggested that we sing in chorus the song of Moon Ship and put some boats into the pond of the park. Everyone liked the idea. Then, we started to wonder from where to get the moon ship. We heard you murmur that you had made it before, and would give it a try. I was at once relieved and entrusted the task to you and assigned two persons to help you.

This was the first time that we worked together but I didn't know your style at all. Two days passed, I saw no movement. I asked your helpers privately what's going on. Their reply was you didn't seem to need their help at all. Hearing that I began to doubt whether you could manage as you had to take care of your child and cook for your family. I worried that such an excellent proposal of mine might be in vain. Surprisingly, at about 2 or 3 o'clock a.m. on the third day all the members of the preparatory committee received the photo of the moon ship sent by your husband. You could not imagine the surprising excitement as soon as I saw it which was exceedingly beautiful, exactly what I had expected. I began to cite the line of Cui Tu's (崔涂) poem that 'a single candle lit an out-of-towner along' (孤烛异乡人). A small flat boat gave people a feeling of loneliness and melancholy. But a candle at the bows created warmth and the purple chrysanthemum at the stern added a romantic touch. The photo was so beautiful that it was loved by all and has since been used by the Friendship Society website on the main page till date.

The 2010 Mid-Autumn Festival evening get-together went on very well. We had the long waited moon-cakes from Mainland China. People could not wait to join in the program of moon ship after eating the moon cakes. I remember when you acclimatized in living in the country. Others are from the Mainland, Taiwan, Hong Kong and other countries and regions to pursue post-Ph. D. research knowing only English, no Japanese. They are in the age of marriage and parenting, many with their parents and kids and facing difficulties and complicities in housing, visa, medical care and education.

In June 2010, residents of Building 510 in Tsukuba Science City where there was a concentration of overseas Chinese took initiative in organizing the 'Friendship Cooperation Society of Takezono, Tsukuba' (hereafter the 'Friendship Society') along with its website and group mailbox. It is a little difficult to count the exact number of its members, but 160 people are listed in the group mailbox. Most of the listed members represent a family of three plus. Family members are very active in the activities of the Friendship Society.

The Friendship Society has been very active since its inception. During traditional Chinese festivals and important Chinese national holidays it has organized various kinds of get-together, eating dumplings, moon cakes and so on. On Japanese holidays it has organized excursions, tree planting, barbecue, fruit-picking, sightseeing trips, skiing, and so on.

The Friendship Society has also carried out specific activities for the needy. It has organized talks for the researchers who wanted to return China. For example, in December 2013, the Friendship Society and The Tokyo Office of the Department of Economics and Trade of Shenzhen City organized a New Year party which was reported by Xinhuanet.com. It held photo shows and saloons for those who like photography. It has started Japanese language classes for the new comers. It has organized talks and discussions for pregnant women and new mothers. All these activities are aimed at sharing information and experience among members of the Chinese community, promoting mutual help, heightening fellow-Chinese affinity, strengthening unity, and relieving mental tension and nostalgia.

Liu Xuefeng is the president of the Friendship Society and Zhang Siqi its vice president. Yabe Takeshi, our Japanese friend is its consultant. Xiaomiu, who came from Taiwan, has made the moon ship[1] and designed the logo for the Friendly Society.

The letter below addressed to Xiaomiu may reflect the early activities of the Friendship Society as well as the spirit of unity and fraternity among fellow-

---

1 The 'Moon Ship' is originated from the Chinese custom of lighting lamps to add glitter to the moonshine on the night of Mid-Autumn Festival. In Hubei, Hunan and Guangdong, people make tiny towers by piling up broken tile pieces and light a lamp on top of it. In Jiangsu and Zhejiang, people make tiny boats and light lamps in it. They float on water to decorate the reflection of the moon and, in addition, some boats have the crescent moon shape, thus the name of 'Moon Ship (月亮船)' is wide spread.

The Moon Ship with Hopes and Dreams

Zhang Siqi 张四齐

From her ancestral home in Tongcheng County of Hubei Province, she had many years of higher education and post-Ph.D research in Beijing (mainly in the China Institute of Contemporary International Relations and Peking University). She is still a Chinese citizen after settling down in Japan since 2008. With her experience in promoting Sino-Indian friendship and understanding, she has dedicated herself to the people-to-people contacts between the Chinese and Japanese communities as well as solidarity and mutual help among the overseas Chinese in Japan. She founded the 'Friendship Cooperation Society of Takezono' at Tsukuba which is a well-known 'science city' of Japan.

'I, now a white-head,
My tears soaked in sorrow
For dear motherland
They would not fall
Onto the neighbouring hill.'
– Liu Kuzhuang (刘克庄)

The nation of Japan is very singular. This nation encloses itself with a fence made of laws, culture, language and social groups to keep the foreigners out. Foreigners, whether from the USA, Europe or Asia, always feel they are aliens and can't be integrated into this society. For us, Chinese, the feeling of alienation is all the more acute because of historical problems and the contemporary estrangement of political relations between the two countries though we are supposed to 'share the language and ethnicity' (同文同种). Our feeling of homelessness and all-adrift generate a strong desire to interact and connect with fellow countrymen.

Tsukuba Science City is a cluster of more than 60% of Japanese scientific institutions with a concentration of young Chinese researchers numbering nearly 2,000. Some of them have obtained the doctorate degree from Japan and courses to master and doctoral students on rhetoric and communication. I helped launch a speech communication program in the School of Communication and Journalism at the university and set a scholarship for students of this major. In 2008, I published a Chinese textbook *Introduction to Speech Communication* for this major (Published by Tsinghua University). In addition, I have given lectures introducing Western rhetorical studies at Beihang University, Harbin Institute of Technology, and the Chinese People's Institute of Foreign Affairs. It is my dream that before long Chinese universities will graduate students with political vision and rhetorical eloquence to impress the world.

In sum, as a rhetorical scholar living overseas, I sincerely wish China is strong; Chinese culture is rejuvenated, and Chinese people live a happy life. This is the dream of several generations of Chinese people. It inspires us to do better and stimulates us to strive for improvement, whether it is in a small scale or for a lofty goal. Chinese civilization has offered us rich resources and Chinese culture is our spiritual home. Being a professor of rhetoric, I feel I have the knowledge and privilege to make a contribution to China's rhetorical education. Max Weber said well, 'Man would not have attained the possible unless time and again he had reached out for the impossible' (Weber, 1958, 128). China has created the economic miracle and achieved the impossible since 1980s. Chinese dream as envisioned by President Xi will be realized if we truly enhance Chinese spirit and gather China's strength.

References:

Becker, Carl.(1986). Reason for lack of argumentation and debate in the far east. *International Journal of Intercultural Relations*. 10, 75–92.

Foucault, Michel. (1969). *The archaeology of knowledge*. Trans. A. M. Sheridan Smith. New York: Random House.

Kelman, Herbert C. (1965). From dystopia to utopia: An analysis of Huxley's Island. In Richard Farson (Ed.) *Science and human affairs*. Palo Alto: Science & Behavior Books.

Mao, Zedong. (1967). *Selected works of Mao Tse-Tung*, Vol. III. Beijing: Foreign Language Press.

Murphy, James. (1983). *A synoptic history of classical rhetoric*. Davis, CA: Hermograras Press.

Oliver, Robert. (1971). *Communication and culture in ancient India and China*. New York: Syracuse, N.Y.: Syracuse University Press.

Weber, Max.(1958). Politics as a vocation. In Hans Gerth and C. Wright Mills, (Eds.) *From Max Weber*: *Essays in Sociology*. New York: Oxford University Press.

improve the way they talk in the public domain. By blending both wisdom and eloquence, their speeches would be more interesting and effective to foreign and domestic audiences. Chinese official language has been influenced by that of the Soviet Union to some degree. Its sentence structure tends to be long, rigid, and complex; its vocabulary appears to be abstract, vague, and banal. Public speeches in political contexts are filled with formulaic and jargons, having lost their appeals and persuasive effectiveness in the modern world.

We need to reform the way government officials talk. Our Chinese culture has rich resources in linguistic expressions and rhetorical devices. During the Spring-Autumn and Warring States period, many schools of thought contended for philosophical ideas; scholars wrote books and travelled to different states. They embodied the highest level of Chinese wisdom and eloquence and demonstrated the charm and magic of Chinese language. Chinese history recorded many eloquent and powerful speakers. Just in the history of modern China, Liang Qichao, Sun Yat-sen, and Mao Zedong are well-known effective speakers. They awakened the Chinese consciousness, mobilized masses, transformed Chinese people's thought, and pushed Chinese history forward.

Mao Zedong, one of the greatest leaders in the 20th century and the founder of the People's Republic of China, is a rhetorical genius. His use of language in his speeches and writings is simple, colorful, and metaphorical. He has made numerous references to Chinese classical texts and employed rhetorical techniques such as analogies, maxims, narratives, rational argument, emotional appeals, moral appeals in presenting his arguments and persuading his target audience. By doing so, he won the support of Chinese people and admiration of the third world. Mao Zedong once said we must have a cultural army and use pen as well as gun to defeat our enemy. He disliked 'eight-legged writing' calling it 'foot-binding of a slattern, long as well as smelly' (Mao, Vol. III., p. 56).

In the recent speeches by President Xi Jinping, I have noticed some similarities between Xi and Mao in their rhetorical styles. In many of his speeches, President Xi used metaphors, testimonies, narratives, deductive and inductive reasoning to explicate his foreign policy and expectations for party members. 'Chinese dream' is a good use of metaphor that is easy to understand and relatable for the audience. It is far more effective than the slogan of 'Three Represents' and 'Scientific View of Development' coined by previous leaders. If we want to enhance Chinese spirit and gather China's strength, we must explore and employ our rhetorical resources and speak more vividly, explicitly, and effectively. The way our national leaders and government officials talk represents China's image and symbolizes colorfulness of Chinese culture.

In order to realize my Chinese dream, I used my summer and winter school breaks to teach in Xiamen University from 2005 to 2008. I taught a total of six demonstrated to the West the Chinese humor and Chinese art of living. They are my role models! My biggest wish is to enhance Chinese spirit and continue to present China to the world. By using English language and my scholarly training, I can disseminate and explain Chinese wisdom, knowledge, and experiences in the area of rhetoric and communication. My goal is to promote the understanding and positive communication between China and the world, reducing stereotypes and misperceptions on China from the West.

I have been teaching in the College of Communication, DePaul University for twenty-two years. I have taught over twenty courses over these years. I created four of these courses on the topics of Asian culture and communication and Asian American experiences. A course I teach every year is Intercultural Communication. I was born and grew up in China and received some education in the U.S. I have experiences and perspectives of living in both cultures. I have the privilege to be a bridge person of the two cultures. It is my life-long mission to contribute to world peace by teaching these courses, a small way but has its significance.

American students know very little about China and Chinese culture. American media mostly have negative reports on China. In the eye of American students, China is an authoritarian society; people have no freedom and human rights even though their material life is much better. The image of Chinese officials is formal, rigid, and boring. They do not know how to express themselves to engage the audience; their communication style is too vague and implicit. Some Chinese cultural practices such as gift-giving, debt in human relationship, and interfering other people's business are incomprehensible to them.

In my classes, I try hard to present China with multiple perspectives, introduce historical contexts and cultural elements, explain cultural habits and practices to my American students. I carefully prepare my teaching materials, presenting evidence to illustrate my points. For example, some students did not understand China's one-child policy. I explained to them the harm of overpopulation in China and in the world and how much this was a cultural sacrifice for Chinese people as traditionally Chinese family valued having more children. I explained to them that this policy was only temporary.

Chinese culture is a collectivistic culture, emphasizing filial piety to parents, human connection, loyalty to friends while American culture is an individualistic culture, valuing personal freedom and choice. Human relationship is based more on social contract and law rather than human feelings. The two cultures can complement each other and learn from one another. In this global world, nations and cultures need to respect and understand each other for the peace and prosperity of humanity.

My current Chinese dream is to help improve the image of Chinese leaders and China's political rhetoric. I wish our national leaders and government officials will

Part III
One Endeared Family within Four Seas

system. Chinese '*youshui* (游说)' (traveling persuaders) engaged in similar rhetorical activities as Greek sophists. While the Daoist notions of '*wuwei* (无为)' (nonaction) and '*buzheng* (不争)' (noncontention) are in contrast with the Greek values for winning and argumentation, both traditions share many similarities. Both traditions emphasize the moral character of speakers; both traditions have theories on the power of symbols on human perception and psychology in the process of persuasion; both traditions recognize the persuasive functions of emotional appeals and rational arguments. I was impressed and fascinated by Chinese rhetorical tradition and very proud of it. I found myself a new subject of study: comparative rhetoric of the East and West.

From my intensive reading and careful studying, I noticed that Chinese rhetorical concepts and theories are embedded in Chinese philosophical, ethical, literary, and logical texts. My task was to identify, classify, and analyze rhetoric from these texts, particularly from the texts of Confucianism, Daoism, Mohism, Legalism, and the School of Ming. I took on this formidable task to codify Chinese rhetoric. In the summer of 1991, I defended my dissertation and received my doctoral degree in Rhetoric and Communication. I spent next few years revising, expanding, and fine-tuning my dissertation into a book. In 1998, I completed the book and published it by the University of South Carolina Press under the title: *Rhetoric in Ancient China, Fifth to Third Century B. C. E.: A Comparison with Greek Rhetoric*. Because the book filled a missing puzzle on the history of rhetoric, I won the James A. Winans-Herbert A. Wichelns Memorial Award for Distinguished Scholarship in Rhetoric and Public Address from the National Communication Association in 1999. The book has been cited numerous times in research throughout the world and used as a textbook on Chinese language, culture, and rhetorical studies in the U.S.

I have lived in the United States for twenty-seven years. I completely agree that a strong China has profound impact on overseas Chinese. The impact is not just in material terms, but in cultural terms as well. Chinese people can have a lot of money, but may still not be given the respect it deserves in the world. The deeply rooted image and perception of a 'sick Asian man' and 'crazy communist' take time to unpack. To gain respect culturally and to be treated equally, works still need to be done to introduce Chinese rich cultural tradition and the contribution Chinese civilization has made to the world to the Western audience. Prominent scholars such as Koh Hong-being, Tan Yun-shan, and Lin Yutang all made significant contribution introducing Chinese culture to the West. In his *The Spirit of the Chinese People* first published in 1914 , Koh used three words to describe the Chinese spirits: deep, broad, and simple that Westerners can learn from. He also first translated Chinese classics *The Analects*, *The Middle Way*, and *Great Learning* into English. While living in India, Professor Tan dedicated his whole life introducing Chinese religion, language, and culture to the world through his English writing. Lin Yutang the Chinese spirit, and uniting China's strength. China has achieved remarkable success in economic development in the past thirty years, which has impressed the world. It is undeniable that Chinese people stood up in Mao Zedong's era and have become well-off in the post-Mao era. However, because of the negative effect of 'Orientalism' and 'Cold War' mentality, the world, particularly the Western world still has many misunderstandings about China. When I first came to the U.S., I noticed that even our American professors believed that all Chinese students in the U.S. are Communist Party members. Some of my American classmates even thought Chinese men were still wearing queues of Qing dynasty. On one occasion, a classmate lost his notebook; another classmate said 'It must be lost in China'. Later I learned it is a set-phrase to mean you can never find it if something gets lost in China as China is such a mysterious place. Seeing all this, I was determined to introduce Chinese rhetoric to the West. I wanted to make a little bit contribution to rejuvenating Chinese culture.

I was growing up during the Chinese Cultural Revolution (1966–1976). The school virtually stopped in the early period of this culturally destructive movement. We did not learn Chinese classics, nor had training in classical Chinese language. There were no Chinese books in the library of the University of Oregon. At this time, I purchased a TV show series called 'Journey to the West' (西游记) and watched it together with my daughter. The lyrics in the show 'May I ask where the path is? It is where you take your first step' (敢问路在何方，路在脚下) inspired me and boosted my confidence of taking on this project. President Xi has referenced a line from the *Book of History* (尚书), one of the Chinese classics in some of his speeches. It reads 'One must have determination in order to achieve a grand goal; one must work hard in order to succeed.' (功崇惟志，业广惟勤) This was exactly what I must do: setting up a big goal and working hard to achieve it. I decided on my dissertation topic to be 'Recovering the Past: Identification of Chinese Senses of *Bian* (辩) and A Comparison of *Bian 10* (辩) to Greek Senses of Rhetoric in the Fifth and Third Centuries B.C.E.' I purchased books of Chinese classics from China; I found a tutor to help me with classical Chinese language; and I began to read and take notes of Chinese classics, including the *Book of History* (尚书), the *Book of Odes* (诗经), the *Analects* (论语), *Mencius* (孟子), *Laozi* (老子), *Zhuangzi* (庄子), *Mozi* (墨子), *Hanfeizi* (韩非子), the *Spring and Autumn of Lu* (吕氏春秋), *Records of Historian* (史记), *Discourse of the States* (国语), *Zuo Commentaries* (左传), *Intrigues, Strategies of Gui Guzi* (战国策) etc. I discovered from reading these books that China has a rich and vibrant rhetorical tradition. Chinese philosophers such as Confucius, Laozi, and Mozi have written about and conceptualized rhetoric and communication. Confucius and Mencius share similar ideas with Plato on ethics; the School of Ming and Greek sophists have the same interests on the relationship between language and perception; the logical formula of Mohism is similar to Aristotelian logical

Part III
One Endeared Family within Four Seas

When I was in my second year of the doctoral program, I realized there was no coverage of Chinese rhetoric and rhetorical practices in American textbooks on the history of rhetoric. A very small number of American scholars had written about Chinese rhetoric, but no one seemed to pay much attention to their works. Moreover, some American rhetorical scholars are ignorant and have bias toward Chinese rhetorical tradition, claiming that rhetoric is the property of the West and China does not have a history of rhetoric (Murphy, 1983). Some scholars have concluded that Eastern rhetoric is unsystematic, incomplete, lacking theoretical foundation, and logical components. Thus, Eastern rhetoric and Western rhetoric are not comparable and they are mutually exclusive (e.g. Becker, 1986; Oliver, 1971). My nerve was poked when I was reading these negative and ethnocentric evaluations of Eastern rhetoric imposed by Western scholars. I began to ask myself, 'Is that possible that China, with its 5,000 years of history, never produced rhetorical theories and never had rhetorical practices?' I could not believe it. But 'what can I do to change Western scholars' bias and misunderstanding of Chinese rhetoric?'

Foucault (1969) contends that discourse formation shapes knowledge, power, and history. When the contribution of a civilization is denied and wiped out from history, and legitimized by academic discourse, its image and status in the world will decline and disappear; its voice will not be heard. This is the reason why Western hegemony is so powerful and controlling in how we see the world today. Being a Chinese, I felt I had the obligation to correct the bias Western scholars held on Chinese rhetorical tradition. I felt the responsibility to teach them the richness of Chinese civilization. I wanted to challenge Western perceptions of China. I wanted to carry on the torch of Chinese culture. Now when I flash back to think about this self-imposed mission, this is my Chinese dream.

Herbert Kelman, a prominent social psychologist has said, 'There is often much we can learn about the nature of a society and its dominant values by examining the dreams that it has produced'. (1956, p. 168) Dreaming is not reality, but what people dream has a great deal to do with how they shape reality. President Xi Jinping's proposal of 'Chinese dream' aims at building a strong nation, rejuvenating Chinese culture, and bringing happiness to Chinese people.[1] The approaches to reaching these goals consist of taking the Chinese path, enhancing

---

1 The Chinese term 'Zhongguo (中国)' has been politicized. Many of the Chinese descendants from Taiwan, Hong Kong, and other Southeast Asian countries do not called themselves 'Zhongguo ren (中国人)' which is a term they use to refer to Chinese people from Mainland China. They call themselves by their regional or national identity to distinguish themselves from Chinese people from Mainland China. I suggest using the term 'Zhonghua (中华)' to replace 'Zhongguo' in political leaders' speeches so that Chinese people outside Mainland China can identify and resonate with.

Dreaming between Civilizations: Rhetoric and Communication

Xing Lu 吕 行

Born and grew up in China, she received her doctoral degree from the University of Oregon in Rhetoric and Communication. She has been teaching at DePaul University since 1992 in the areas of rhetoric, intercultural communication, Asian and Asian American Studies. Her first book, *Rhetoric in Ancient China* (The University of South Carolina Press, 1998) won the James A. Winans-Herbert A. Wichelns Memorial Award for Distinguished Scholarship in Rhetoric and Public Address. Subsequently, she published *Rhetoric of Chinese Cultural Revolution* (The University of South Carolina Press, 2004), *Introduction to Speech Communication* (Tsinghua University Press 2009, in Chinese) in addition to two co-edited volumes on Chinese communication studies and over 30 peer-reviewed articles and book chapters on rhetoric and intercultural communication.

I was accepted to the doctoral program in Rhetoric and Communication by the University of Oregon in the USA in 1987. This golden opportunity opened a new door of knowledge for me. I was impressed by the history and practice of rhetoric and argumentation in ancient Greek and Roman time periods. I was fascinated by rhetorical theories formulated by Plato, Aristotle, Cicero, and Quintilian. I admired those rhetorical scholars and their works in the West since the time of ancient Greece. I was intellectually attracted to Western rhetorical studies, including ethical, emotional, and logical appeals in the process of persuasion. I am convinced that Socratic dialogue as a means to explore truth and oratories in addressing political and social issues is the best approaches to both private and public communication. I love Western rhetoric so much that when I visited Rome in 2013, I stood in front of the half-burned podium where Cicero delivered his speeches in Forum, imagining how he argued against his political opponents and won him the name of the most fearsome and awesome orator-statesman in Roman history. However, his eloquence offended Mark Anthony who ordered Cicero to be killed with his tongue being cut off.

a long process, in which childrearing style or parental influence plays a decisive role. Quality early childhood programs can produce only half of their promises if parental support is not in place. Parents need education in order to become more effective parents. For the Chinese dream to become a reality, preschool education must educate young children and their parents.

Early childhood is the most critical phase of human development. The early childhood years offer an unparalleled opportunity to educate children and bring out the best in each of them. Studies have shown again and again that investments in quality early education can produce a rate of return to society that is significantly higher than returns on many stock market investments and traditional economic development projects. For example, for every $1 invested in providing access to quality early care and education programs for disadvantaged children, additional 94 cents is generated. Such investments are long-term, requiring a clear vision, meaningful policies, substantial funding, public support, great patience, and concerted effort from all involved. The endeavor is challenging given the population of China and the vast differences in economic development across the nation. However, the effort offers the surest way to make the Chinese Dream real.

As a Fulbright Senior Scholar in Education, I have traveled to many countries to learn about different early childhood education and child care systems. I am proud to say that some of the Chinese child care programs can be ranked at the top internationally, both in terms of hardware and software. Such top programs are rare and a large proportion of Chinese young children experience mediocre to low quality care. Of critical importance to ensure that every children receive quality early care experience includes the stronger provision of teacher professional development that meets high training standards, the better education of parents for strengthening children's learning and development, and greater attention to the wellbeing of high-needs children.

To ensure quality early child care programs for all Chinese children is my dream and can become the shared dream of the nation. Progress toward the Dream will be determined by the support we offer to our nation's young people. If we can empower millions of children to pursue their dreams, to achieve their full potential, and to create the brighter futures they deserve, we will not be far away from the realization of the Chinese Dream.

told me that questioning and arguing was also the way she was brought up. 'We argued so much at home when I grew up. Anything—assumptions, facts, theories, statements, or hypotheses, could be challenged and debated. That was so fun.' This approach to childrearing style is seldom heard or seen among Chinese families.

A professional habit, I love observing child and adult interactions. In Chicago, I live 10 minutes from the Laboratory Schools of the University of Chicago. I encounter parents and children walking to and from school on a daily basis. Regardless of their age, most, American children carry their own school bags. One time, I saw a tall, strong father walking ahead with his preschool son walking behind him. The boy could not walk standing up straight because the bag he carried was so heavy. His father expected him to carry the bag and did not seem concerned that it was so heavy. The parents of one of my son's friends are medical doctors at the University of Chicago's Hospital. For several summers, the father took his two teenage boys to visit the border area between America and Canada. The three of them camped in the wilderness, carrying not only their bags but also a canoe. They walked miles each day and camped for a couple of weeks. I admire this father giving his sons such an exciting experience, filled with discovery and challenges. In that moment, I feel ashamed of my inferiority.

In sharp contrast to these scenarios are my experiences with Chinese parents of young children. For the last four years, I worked one month per year in the East China Normal University. Also, my apartment was about a 10-minute walk to a preschool affiliated with the University. Every morning I saw parents and grandparents walking to school with their young children. Based on my informal survey, more than 70% of the adults carried the young child's back pack. In the child care center, the teachers told me that certain types of large motor activities planned for outdoors were eliminated because parents were so concerned for their children's physical safety. These seemingly trivial incidents can have significant consequences for the development of the child. Over-protective Chinese parents take away opportunities for young children to develop strong bodies and to persist when faced with a challenge.

Many Chinese students study aboard nowadays. Based on my own experience and anecdotes from my colleagues who are teaching in American universities, most of the Chinese students work hard and earn good grades. A large portion of them however tend to be rather self-centered, irresponsible, and lacking in social skills and interest in helping others, to name a few of the undesirable character types observed. It is important to point out that these expressions of character are not in-born traits. Rather, they have developed over the years through inappropriate education, particularly through misguided childrearing styles.

The Ministry of Education in China has advocated character education for quite awhile. The effects are unfortunately lamentable. Character development is has an external evaluator who gauges the efficacy of our work. I talk to my external evaluators on a weekly basis to ensure that program implementation and evaluation are going smoothly. Compare to my Chinese colleagues, I have received significant more support in my service of PD. With this rich support, my PD program produces significant change in teachers' teaching and students' learning.

The single most important determinant of what children learn is what teachers know. For teachers to be effective in their interactions with children, ongoing PD is a necessity. Teacher professional development is a specialized domain of expertise; so is early childhood education. To get the job done and done well, training is a necessity. Specialists are needed. Thoughtful planning must precede implementation. Clearly, the delivery of PD will require a concerted effort, including funding at all levels from the central government to local school districts. This funding is an investment that will pay dividends. When competent teachers interact with young children, our classrooms and schools are more likely to succeed in helping prepare qualified citizens to join with others in achieving the Chinese Dream.

Parents are a child's first teachers. During the early childhood years, a child spends most of his time with his parents. Parental values, beliefs, attitudes, habits, and patterns of interaction implicitly and explicitly influence childrearing styles and the way the child grows. Good parenting that promotes the development of a well-rounded child is as indispensible as air and water are to the growth of a plant.

Chinese are known for their strong emphasis on education and learning. The practice of learning, however, frequently focuses on the acquisition of factual knowledge and the mastery of certain technique skills. These skills include knowing the Chinese characters, counting numbers, reciting Chinese traditional poems, and playing a music instrument. Many Chinese parents value such educational practice, because factual knowledge and concrete skills are observable and easy to measure. This may allow parents to showcase how smart their child is, but it does little to help young children become critical and innovative thinkers, the kind off thinkers who are essential for realization of the Chinese Dream.

Many Chinese admire Jewish people for their achievements. Like Chinese, the Jewish culture is also known for highly valuing education and learning. Unlike Chinese, Jewish parents pay more attention to critical thinking skills in fostering the development of young minds. A couple of my personal experiences illustrate this point. My mentor, a German Jew and a recipient of the MacArthur genius award, attributed his achievements in part to the questions his parents asked him on a daily basis when he was growing up. He recalled, 'When I came home from school, one of the first things my parents asked me was what kind of questions my teachers asked today, and what kind of questions I asked my teachers today.' One of my former Jewish doctoral fellow students, now a distinguished professor, in designing national professional development (PD) programs for preschool teachers organized by the Teacher Development Bureau in China's Ministry of Education. The major challenges I have experienced in this endeavor include: (1) PD is too infrequent; (2) the duration of PD is too short; (3) PD participants are usually limited to lead teachers; (4) the PD content does not always meet the diverse needs of the teacher participants; (5) there is little follow-up after the initial PD; (6) the quality of the PD varies enormously; (7) support for the PD trainers is minimal, and (8) no effective evaluation of PD is in place. Without addressing these challenges, the efficacy of PD for preschool teachers rests on a weak foundation. This important national initiative, though well intentioned, is at high risk.

I have been planning and delivering PD to early childhood teachers in the U.S. for more than 20 years. Research indicates that effective PD has several common features that relate to teacher change, content, format, and timeframe. First, teacher change is a dynamic, multi-dimensional process involving teachers' belief systems, teaching knowledge, and classroom practice. The PD that focuses on one area without simultaneously attending to the other two is less effective in producing teacher change. Secondly, PD content has its greatest impact when it aligns with classroom-based teaching practice. Content needs to be specific, curriculum related, and include useful tools and resources for teachers. One size does not fit all. Teachers with varying degrees of expertise need differentiated PD experiences. Teachers who work with different populations of children also have different PD needs. In terms of format, PD needs to be interactive; that is, hands-on and minds engaged. Teachers learn when they actively participate in the training while being challenged to think critically and problem solve. Last, for PD to be effective, it must be ongoing with extensive follow-up. A one shot, cursory workshop cannot produce lasting effects on teacher change.

Let me give a personal example to show the support that PD trainers need in order to provide quality services to teachers. I am a recipient of a prestigious Investing in Innovation (i3) grant from the U.S. Department of Education (DOE). One of the grant goals is to support innovations in teacher professional development. To ensure that the PD we, the trainers, provide to teachers is high quality, the DOE offered us a variety of training techniques and resources over the years. For example, we met twice a year in Washington D.C. to learn about trends and emerging knowledge in the field, to become acquainted with new federal education policies, to discuss challenges and identify approaches to addressing them, and to share information and practices that have proven to be effective. In addition, the i3 grantees have a shared website where numerous resources are available. Each grantee is also assigned a program officer and connected to a technical assistance team who provides individualized support and guidance. The DOE does not evaluate our work directly. Rather, each of the i3 grantees and talking about their surroundings than they learn by sitting together for hours, trying to memorize lines that have little to do with their interests or their lives.

When asked about the biggest challenges the center faced, the director of the center said, 'behavioral problems', namely, children who didn't sit still and listen attentively. If the director were trained in child development, she would know that the experiences young children are having in her center are developmentally inappropriate as are her expectations. No wonder young children have 'behavioral problems.' When asked about children's attachment issues, since many of the children in the center are 'stay behind' kids, the response was surprise. 'No such problem, because these children have their grandparents or relatives taking care of them.' The lack of even the most basic understanding of young children's social and emotional needs results in negligence and misaligned practice.

My experience in another rural preschool setting was even more difficult to witness. A teacher led the class in singing a popular song, 'Black Cat Police Officer.' However, she used the song to humiliate a five-year-old boy for unacceptable behavior. The teacher asked all of the children to pretend to be the black cat police officer and point their fingers at the boy while singing, 'You are to be punished! You are to be punished!' The little boy squatted in a corner and covered his face with his hands. When questioning the teacher about her approach, she was proud to claim, 'This is the most effective way to change his behavior!' Yes, it was effective in sending the message to the boy that 'you are not liked by the class'. The research has clearly shown that this kind of punitive approach is not effective in altering a child's behavior. Further, bullying and humiliation affect the child's mental health. The damage to the child's self-esteem and self-image can be lasting.

Receiving a good education and being treated with respect are basic human rights of every citizen in our modern society. A child should never be discriminated against because of the family she or he was born into. If our society pays too little attention to the most needy children, we will suffer when they grow up. They may become anti-social and they will not be prepared for the job demands of the 21st century. The Chinese Dream is not the dream of the elite. For all Chinese to have a dream and for that dream to become the reality, we must start when children begin to tell us their dreams in the early years of their lives, and we must not forget the disadvantaged children who have the least and need the most.

Teacher effectiveness is a fundamental factor in determining the quality of a child's education. Yet, many Chinese preschool teachers are not well-equipped to work effectively with young children. This is particularly true in China's rural areas, where a large percentage of preschool teachers have no or minimal credentials. Necessary for these teachers' professional development is the provision of in-service training or on job training, which is problematic at the moment.

Serving as consultant to the United Nations Children's Fund, I have participated from brain research and field studies clearly indicate the critical importance of high quality early childhood programs. When well-designed, they can produce positive, long-lasting effects on physical health, social-emotional wellbeing, language development, and cognitive functioning that extend well into adulthood. Longitudinal studies show that quality early care and education programs can also help to reduce crime, promote academic achievement, and raise earnings. In fact, research shows that a high-quality early education is one of the best investments a society can make in a child's life.

The Chinese government understands the critical importance of quality child care. Its ten-year strategic plan, beginning in 2010 set the goal that by 2020, the nation will ensure access to one-year of universal preschool education. Further, two to three years of universal early care should be the goal in the more developed areas. While applauding the attention that the government is giving to preschool education, it is important to point out that the funding largely focuses on the initial stage of program development, such as construction and personnel hiring. Without buildings and staff, there can be no programs. Yet, buildings and personnel do not necessarily guarantee high quality programs. For Chinese society to invest in quality early childhood programs for all children, three areas require special attention: serving high needs children, teacher professional development, and parent education. I will briefly discuss each one below.

High-needs children in China refer primarily to children who live in poor or less-developed geographic areas. Some of them are also 'stay behind' or 'latch-key' kids, meaning that their migrant worker parents have no choice but to leave them behind either at home alone or with relatives or grandparents. These children often lack the basics necessary for healthy development such as balanced nutrition and human affection. Adequate intellectual stimulation is often unattainable. Sadly, the voices speaking for these high needs children are so weak and infrequently that society's attention to this population has remained minimal.

Working with the Ministry of Education in China, I had opportunities to visit preschool settings in poor rural areas. Many of these visits were heartbreaking experiences. In one rural preschool, for example, more than forty 3–5 year olds sat on benches lined up in rows. The room was very dark because it had a low ceiling and small windows. Lights were not turned on because there was no money to pay for electricity. A teacher was leading the children in recitation of a nursery rhyme. Some children followed the teacher, others looked around, and some fell asleep. Outside of the classroom door, there was a weekly schedule full of 30– to 40–minute classes on math, language, writing, drawing, and singing. I question the extent to which such practices are contributing to the development of young children. Young children need to learn by doing or through play. In rural areas where space is not an issue, children can learn so much more by exploring, observing, experimenting,

My Chinese Dream: High Quality Early Childhood Programs for All

Jie-Qi Chen 陈杰琦

Graduated from Beijing Normal University in 1982, she is Professor of Child Development at Erikson Institute in Chicago where she also serves as the director of Ph.D. program, the executive director of the International Initiatives, and the principal investigator of Early Math Collaborative. Her areas of interest include cognitive development, early math education, teacher professional development, classroom assessment, educational implications of multiple intelligences theory, and educational reform. She is frequently invited for talks and lectures about early education internationally, has published eight books in English and Chinese and many scholarly articles. As a consultant to UNICEF, she participated in the evaluation effort of China's national teacher training project.

The essence of the 'Chinese dream' is sustained economic prosperity, healthy growth, and a harmonious society for the country and its citizens. To realize this dream, education is the key. No nation can achieve its lofty goal of significant advancement without educating a critical mass of its citizens. Early childhood education comes first and is the foundation of the educational system. High quality early childhood programs, accessible to all Chinese young children, is my Chinese dream.

Early childhood education refers to the care and education of children from zero to age seven or eight. I have been studying, researching, and teaching in this field for 40 years. In 1978, I was among the first group of college students who majored in early education in China. Prior to 1978, the field had been relatively inactive for 30 years. College major in early education was in fact discontinued following the breakdown of diplomatic relations with the Soviet Union. As time passed, only a few understood the field. We were frequently questioned by curious friends and relatives, 'Why does babysitting need a college degree?'

This question is rarely raised in contemporary society. Convergent evidence

States and help to promote Chinese language study in universities across the region. That is the best reward to me and my colleagues.

With the hard work of Chinese language students and their instructors, the Chinese Bridge speech contest has become more and more established since its birth in 2002. It attracts the attention of thousands of Chinese language students each year. Every July, Chinese language students and their friends around the world look forward to watching the live coverage of the Chinese Bridge speech contest on TV. After three rounds of contests, contestants receive medals based on their performance, but each one of them is named a Chinese Cultural Ambassador to their own home country. While in China, contestants not only participate in the contest, but also travel in China with their local hosts. They get to live in the homes of ordinary Chinese people and make friends with them. All the contestants go home with true knowledge of China and the friendship of the Chinese people. Traveling over the Chinese Bridge, these contestants help to build a common understanding between the Chinese people and the people of the world.

Because people speak different languages and have different cultures, we did not succeed in building the Tower of Babel and did not have opportunity to meet with the Lord and hear his teachings in person. But today, we have successfully built the Chinese Bridge to link the Chinese people with the people of the world. Over the Chinese Bridge, students from all over the world are coming to China to learn Chinese and further their understanding of China, while the Chinese people also have the opportunity to learn other languages and understand the world better. As one of the many ordinary Chinese language teachers, my dream is to help to build, maintain, and strengthen the Chinese Bridge so that it can help more students to learn Chinese and understand China. This is my Chinese dream.

May the Chinese Bridge be solid and strong in building friendship between the Chinese people and the people of the world! May all the Chinese dreams of the Chinese people, at home or abroad, be realized soon!

asked to participate in the Chinese Bridge Speech Contest in China, so *Hanban* requested someone in the Midwest conduct a preliminary Chinese Bridge contest to screen and select the best representatives to go to China.

To answer the call from Hanban and to meet the needs of Chinese language students, the Chinese Language Program in Northwestern University started to organize the Midwest Chinese Speech Contest in 2004. Chinese language students in the Midwest participate in the contest enthusiastically. Every year, 60 students from over 20 universities in the nine states of the Midwest come to compete.

In addition to selecting two students to send to China to participate in the Chinese Bridge speech contest, we also take the opportunity to promote Chinese language education in universities across the Midwest. For this reason, we encourage all levels of Chinese students to come and participate in the Midwest Speech Contest. Students are divided into six groups based on the level of their current Chinese class. Elementary Chinese students compete in the 1st Year Group, Intermediate students compete in the 2nd Year Group, Intermediate/Advanced students compete in the 3rd Year Group, and Advanced students compete in the 4th Year Group. Heritage learners compete in another two separate heritage groups. In this way, all students have a chance to compete fairly with groups of their own level.

Each contestant presents a five-minute prepared speech in front of an audience and a group of judges. Contestants also participate in a talent show. They may sing a Chinese song, dance a Chinese dance, or do anything that demonstrates their understanding of Chinese art or culture. Based on their pronunciation, intonation, structure, content, and presentation of the speech, as well their talent show performance, a panel of five judges evaluates each contestant in the group. Out of a total possible score of 60 points, the speech is worth 50 points while talent show is worth 10. The scores from each of the five judges are averaged to determine the final score of the contestant. The judges line up the contestants of each group according to their scores and decide which contestants receive gold, silver, or bronze medals for that group.

Finally, the top two contestants in the highest group, the 4th Year Group, are selected to go to China to compete in the Chinese Bridge Contest. In the past ten years, 12 students from Northwestern University, the University of Chicago, the University of Minnesota, and the University of Wisconsin have won the opportunity to travel to China and compete on behalf of the United States. The students sent from the Midwest have always done well in the Chinese Bridge contest in China, but more importantly, these students have broadened their horizons through seeing the real China. They have made friends with the local Chinese people, and become acquainted with Chinese language students from other parts of the world. They bring honor home to the Midwest in the United roller or chopping knife, only his skillful stretching. When he presented the two-foot long noodles, the audience gave him a big round of applause. More than ten years have gone by since that day. I trust that Kavson has entertained a lot of friends with his hand-made noodles. His noodles must have awakened many people's interest in China.

In response to the promotion of Chinese Bridge, President Obama launched a '100,000 Strong Initiative' in November 2009. He is planning to send 100,000 American students to study Chinese in China over the next few years. China was very happy to support the initiative and immediately promised 10,000 scholarships to American students who wish to come to study in China. Hu Jintao, then president of China, personally talked to Chinese entrepreneurs and invited them to contribute to the scholarship fund. Seeing the great importance and significance of this initiative, many Chinese companies responded enthusiastically. In the past two years, they have donated millions of dollars to support the '100,000 Strong Initiative' and sponsored hundreds of American students who came to study in China. Among the many companies in China, Wanxiang Corporation has stood out and made special contributions to the '100,000 Strong Initiative'. Based in Hangzhou, China, Wanxiang Corporation has sponsored 100 Wangxiang Fellowship students from the Chicago area in the past two years. 40 of these came from high schools in the Chicago Public School System, 30 from Northwestern University, and 30 from the University of Chicago. China happily accepted these students and provided the best studying and living conditions possible for them. In the summer of 2012, President Hu Jintao even invited the high school students to Beijing and met them at Zhongnanhai. The joint efforts between China and the United States in advocating study abroad in China greatly promoted the interests of Chinese language education and enthusiasm in participating in Chinese Bridge speech contests across the United States.

The Midwest plays an important role in developing and promoting Chinese language study in the United States. Richard M. Daley, former mayor of Chicago, is a strong advocate for developing the U.S.–China relationship and promoting Chinese language study in the region. The Education Department of the Consulate General of the People's Republic of China also supports any school that needs help to open a Chinese language program. *Hanban* also provides support, sends volunteers as teachers, provides teaching materials, and sponsors local Chinese Bridge speech contests. Thanks to their strong support, there has been a big surge in Chinese language education in the Midwest. More and more elementary, middle, and high schools have started to include Chinese in their curricula. These pre-college Chinese language programs have prepared many students for college study. Enrollment in Chinese classes has been rising for many years in American colleges as well. Chinese language students in many colleges in the Midwest have

At the beginning of the summer program, I arrange a dinner at a restaurant for the language partners to meet with our students for the first time. To help them to get to know each other, I prepare 40 questions in both English and Chinese. Each pair of students has to ask each other these questions. While eating and talking, the students quickly become friends. I also arrange gatherings on the 4th of July (America's Independence Day) and on the 7th of July on the lunar calendar (Chinese Valentine's Day). My American students and their Chinese language partners also meet frequently on other occasions. The Chinese language partners help our students get to know China while my American students help the Chinese students get to know the United States. In this way, a bridge between American and Chinese students is built. Through this bridge, some Chinese students come to United States to study and some American students return to China to study or work. 13 years ago, I did not have a name for this bridge. Today, it has a name. It is the famous 'Chinese Bridge'.

In order to promote deeper cultural exchange and to encourage more students in the world to study Chinese, the National Leadership Group for Promoting Chinese Language, better known as *Hanban* (汉办), started the Chinese Bridge, the World Chinese Speech Contest. Each year since 2002, the Chinese Bridge Speech Contest brings one hundred Chinese language students from all over the world to China in July. These 100 contestants are the best Chinese language students selected from universities in their countries or regions in the world. In the contest, each student presents a five-minute speech. Judges evaluate their pronunciation, intonation, grammar, and vocabulary, as well as the structure of their speech. Judges also ask them questions about Chinese language and culture. On top of that, the 100 contestants also present their Chinese talents, such as Chinese calligraphy, painting, songs, dances, operas, playing musical instruments, or even performing skits.

I was fortunate enough to serve as a judge for the first Chinese Bridge contest in 2002 in Beijing and met many great Chinese language students from all over the world. They all had been learning Chinese diligently and had just crossed the Chinese Bridge to come to China. They demonstrated their great achievements in learning Chinese through speeches, answering questions, and demonstrating their talents. Kavson Yiu, a student from Northwestern University, not only presented a great speech, but also shocked the audience and judges with his talent show performance. While other contestants demonstrated their skills in fine arts like singing and dancing, Kavson demonstrated his newly learned skill—making noodles. In front of the camera on the stage on CCTV, other contestants were writing Chinese characters with brushes or playing songs with traditional Chinese musical instruments, but Kavson was making and stretching dough. In no time, Kavson produced two pounds of long noodles from the dough without using a faith.

David was touched by Dali's misfortune and his positive attitude towards life. They became friends from then on. David came to visit Dali and Lanlan every two days. David played with Lanlan and taught her English. Dali taught David how to cook pancakes and David taught Dali how to play guitar.

Dali was a good teacher and David quickly learned how to cook pancakes. Customers warmly called Dali 'Big Brother Pancake', and David 'Younger Brother Pancake'. Whenever the two cooked and sold pancakes together on the streets in Beijing, it was a huge hit. They could always bring in a lot of customers. In their busiest day, they cooked and sold over 800 pancakes. They were exhausted by the end of the day, but they were very happy. They knew that they had made enough money for Lanlan to see her doctor again.

Dali was also a good student and took well to learning guitar. He seemed to have some talent with music. David and Dali often sang songs and played guitar together on street corners and attracted a lot of people. They became so popular that last August, Beijing TV featured them in an episode of the show 'Beijinger'. In February of 2014, Dali and David sang songs and played guitar on the famous 'Starlet Road' program on China Central TV. Their music entertained millions of people and their story of friendship moved millions more in both China and the United States.

From his Chinese friend Dali, David learned how to face misfortunes and deal with difficulties. To David, this is something more valuable than anything else. With this kind of mindset, he will remain strong and hopeful on his long road in life.

From Dali, David also learned how to cook Chinese pancakes. David is planning to participate in the America Midwest Chinese Speech Contest this year at Purdue University. His topic is 'Brother Pancake'. For the talent show, David plans to sing a Chinese song and cook Chinese pancakes. Through this performance, people will not only enjoy his singing and guitar playing, but also his freshly cooked pancakes.

In order to help my American students to quickly become immersed in the life of the Chinese people, I secure a Chinese language partner for each of my American students. All the language partners are students from Tsinghua University (清华大学) or Peking University (北京大学). These young people become friends in no time. The Chinese language partners bring my students to their classrooms, their dormitories, and their extracurricular activities. They even bring our students into their homes to visit their parents in other parts of China. In return, our American students introduce their Chinese friends to American life. They help their Chinese friends with their English and introduce them to the procedures for applying to American universities. They also invite their partners to visit them in the United States. These pairs of students learn from each other and help each other as friends.

Part III
One Endeared Family within Four Seas

He wanted to buy some lunch when he heard someone singing and smelled something good in a small alley nearby. Following the song and the smell of food, David walked ahead and found a pancake stand. A middle aged Chinese man was cooking pancakes there and some customers were waiting for their food. It was a hot day and cooking in front of a burning stove made it even hotter, but that did not seem to bother the man. He was working swiftly and happily, singing as he cooked, as if to entertain his customers as well as himself. The customers lost their usual impatience. They waited for their pancakes while enjoying the good smell and the singing. Out of curiosity, David joined the line.

When it was David's turn, the man asked:

> 'How many would you like to have?'
> 'Just one.'
> 'How many eggs would you like to have?'
> 'Two, please.'
> 'Spicy or plain?'
> 'Spicy, please.'

While talking, the man never stopped working on David's pancake. He elegantly poured some soft flour paste onto the hot pan. With a gentle scrape, he made a perfectly circular, extremely thin pancake. Then he skillfully cracked two eggs in one hand and deftly added them onto the pancake. After adding some salt, pepper and spices, he tossed the whole pancake into the air. It flipped over and landed neatly on the hot pan. In two minutes, David received a freshly cooked pancake in his hand. He took a hearty bite. It was delicious. The outside was crispy and crunchy while the inside was tender and soft. It just happened that no other customers were waiting behind him, so David chatted with the man and found out about his life.

The man is called Zhou Dali. He was a peasant from the Chinese province of Inner Mongolia. He and his wife had a young daughter, Lanlan, who had cancer. To give her proper medical treatment, Dali and his family came to Beijing. Lanlan was only five years old, but she had already endured four major operations and many rounds of chemotherapy. Her treatment cost all the family's savings. Dali had to work like crazy to pay the medical bills. He worked on two full-time jobs. During the day, Dali sold pancakes on the street in Beijing, and at night he worked as a security guard for a school. The family lived a simple life, even by Chinese standards. They ate the simplest food and lived in a shabby place, but Dali never complained and never gave up hope. He had faith that life would become better eventually. Whenever he had a minute off from work, he took care of Lanlan and sang songs for her. His songs kept Lanlan happy and kept him going ahead with mountains, and raced horses on the grasslands in Inner Mongolia.

In addition to traveling, students have also served as volunteers in Chinese communities during the two months they are in China. They have worked in solar panel factories in Baoding, and cooked and served meals to seniors in a nursing home. They have donated toys and taught children English on visits to an orphanage. They have also volunteered in rural community clinics and helped doctors to take care of patients.

While in China, students have also conducted all kinds of social research according to their interests. Past projects have included:

> Interning in stock exchange markets and writing a report on the psychology of Chinese investors. Interviewing taxi drivers and writing a report on the development of transportation in Beijing.

Shadowing homeless people and writing a report analyzing the patterns of charity of the people on the streets.

Helping street vendors to sell their wares and writing a report on people's shopping behavior.

Helping vendors cook snacks to sell and writing a report on people's eating habits.

Following and observing *Chengguan* (城管) (urban adminstration) and writing a report on the way they conduct their business to keep the city in order.

Some Chinese American students even joined a group of migrant workers and worked for a couple of days on a construction site. They moved bricks and poured concrete, ate the same food as the workers, and slept in the same tent at night. They learned the true hardship of the life of people at the bottom of society by working and living with these migrant workers in Beijing. Through this kind of ethnographic research, observation, and participation, students get a chance to talk to true Chinese people from different walks of life. After studying in China, my students have become more mature and more appreciative for what they have in the U.S. Having seen and experienced China themselves, they grow to love the China they see and the Chinese people they meet. They won't be easily influenced by negative portrayals of China in the American media.

Many of my students have also made friends with local Chinese people. From their Chinese friends, they learn something that they cannot learn from their classrooms either in China or in the U.S. The following is a story of friendship between my student David Harris and his Chinese friend 'Brother Pancake' Zhou Dali.

One day last summer in Beijing, David was hanging out in Houhai, a popular tourist spot in Beijing. It was almost noon and David was already hot and hungry.

from their parents, their reading and writing skills are typically less developed. They may have attended weekend Chinese schools during childhood, but these schools often leave students with important gaps in their knowledge. I served as a principle of a Sunday Chinese school for eight years, so I know from experience that these heritage students need more formal training when they enter college. For these reasons, we train them to give speeches in Chinese, help them to increase their vocabulary, and teach them to write Chinese papers. Through readings and writing, they improve their Chinese and identify more with the Chinese culture.

Besides the language courses, Northwestern University also offers Chinese cultural courses through various departments, including literature, history, philosophy, religion, art, and political science. More and more students want to learn about China and show interest in these courses. To learn Chinese and Chinese culture well, students need to go to China and be immersed in the environment, especially when they reach the intermediate or advanced level. This is much like the case of the Tang dynasty Buddhist Master, Reverend Xuanzang, who went to India to study Buddhism. Reverend Xuanzang was convinced that only in India could he learn authentic advanced Buddhism. For American students, only in China can they reach a new level of proficiency. Therefore, we established Northwestern Summer in Beijing Programs for students to travel to China and study.

Every summer from mid-June to mid-August, I bring an average of 50 Chinese language students to China to study for two months, first at Tsinghua University from 2000 to 2010, and then at Peking University from 2011 until present. In the morning, students take Chinese classes taught by local professors. For lunch, they eat together with local students in student cafeterias. In the afternoon, students take cultural courses in English. These courses include Chinese history, political economy, public health, traditional Chinese medicine, environmental protection, and green energy technology. In the evening, students may visit restaurants in Beijing with their newly made friends, prepare for the next day's lessons, or attend extracurricular activities on campus with the local students. During the weekends, we go to visit historical or scenic spots like the Great Wall, the Forbidden City, the Summer Palace, the Ming Tombs, the Qing Tombs, Confucius Temple, Lama Temple, Laoshe Tea House, Beihai Park, Jingshan Park, Pearl Market, and the Temple of Heaven. We also go to see Peking opera and acrobatic shows in evenings.

During a long weekend break in mid-July, students travel out of Beijing to see other parts of China and experience different cultures of the Chinese people. We have been to Huangshan, One-Thousand-Islet Lakes, Hangzhou, Shanghai, Xi'an, Guilin, Chongqing, Inner Mongolia, Changsha, Taishan, Qufu, Jiuzhaigou, and Hainan. We have watched the sunrise on Yellow Mountain, and the sunset on the Three Gorges on the Yangtze River. We have collected wild Chinese herbs in the topics.

2.Organizing and expanding study abroad programs in China and bringing more American students to China to interact with Chinese people and learn about Chinese culture.

3.Organizing local Chinese Bridge speech contests every year in the Midwest and selecting the best students to represent the U.S. in Chinese Bridge, the World Chinese Speech Contest in China. These Chinese Bridge speech contests will encourage more American students to study Chinese.

Since 1993, I have been teaching and promoting Chinese at Northwestern University. When I first arrived, the Chinese program had only three instructors and 60 students. Today, the program has ten instructors and over 300 students, 60% of which are regular learners and 40% of which are heritage learners. The term 'heritage learners' refers to students who were born into Chinese American families. Based on their different needs, we offer four levels of Chinese language courses to regular learners and another four to heritage learners. Students in elementary and intermediate level classes meet five hours per week while students in intermediate-advanced and advanced classes meet three or four hours per week.

In the 1st year Chinese class for regular learners, we train students the basic skills of listening and speaking. We pay special attention to their tones and pronunciation, correcting any problems in order to make sure that all our students master the four tones before moving to the next level. In the 2nd year, we train students to develop the habit of thinking in Chinese and to speak Chinese with the grammatical structures they have learned. Through interactive methods, we help students to master the basic structures of Chinese and increase their vocabulary. We also show short video clips to allow students to get a taste of authentic Chinese. We train them in all the four areas of listening, speaking, reading, and writing. In the 3rd year, we help students to develop a feeling for the Chinese language through authentic materials from Chinese novels, plays, newspaper articles, and movies. Students discuss these readings or movies in class, and then write papers based on their findings. Their papers are meticulously corrected by their instructors before they deliver them for the second round. In the 4th year, students are introduced to classical Chinese literature ranging from the Book of Odes, to Tang and Song dynasty poems, to Yuan dynasty dramas, to Ming and Qing dynasty novels. Students discuss these works and write their reflections on the readings. At this stage, they are trained to pay special attention to the elegance of the style of their writings. On the whole, through four years of training, students will go from zero to advanced level in the areas of listening, speaking, reading, and writing. This creates a solid foundation for them to build on in the future.

For the heritage learners, we have a separate curriculum based on their unique needs. Even though these students have already learned to speak Chinese at home communicated easily and the project progressed quickly. In no time, the base of the tower was completed and it grew higher and higher into the heavens. People were so delighted, because very soon they would be able to see the Lord and talk to him in person.

The efforts of the people on Earth startled the Lord. He was afraid that once the tower was completed, people would bother him with their trivial issues on a daily basis. To protect his peace of mind, the Lord devised a strategy to confuse people so that they could not complete the tower. He changed their one common tongue into hundreds of other languages. From then on, people of each country could only speak their own language and were unable to understand what the people of other countries were talking about. Without a common language, hostility and suspicion grew between these fractured groups and the project was abandoned. Finally people left the half-finished tower and let it remain there for centuries. The tower was named the Tower of Babel because of the confusion experienced when nations heard each other's speech as incomprehensible babble.

This story teaches us that confusion, misunderstanding, hostility, and even war can arise if people do not understand each other's language. Today there is a population of over seven billion people in the world speaking over 5,600 languages. It is a daunting task for people of the world to learn foreign languages and understand foreign cultures.

Among all the languages used in the world today, Chinese and English are two of the most widely spoken languages. Approximately 1,200,000,000 people speak Chinese while 1,400,000,000 people speak English as their mother tongue. In order to function as global citizens, many people are learning these two languages. In China, 100,000,000 are learning English and in the United States, 100,000 people are learning Chinese. Many people in these two countries teach these languages as a profession. I am one of these language teachers.

After graduating from Beijing Foreign Language School in 1976, I became an English language teacher and taught English for 12 years in China before I came to the United States. Since receiving my Ph.D. in Education from the University of Oregon in 1992, I have been teaching Chinese as a foreign language in the United States. Looking back at those years, I can proudly say that I have taught many Chinese people English and sent them out into the world and have taught many American people Chinese and sent them to China. My current dream in the United States is to teach more people Chinese so that they can gain a better understanding of China. This is my Chinese dream.

Specifically, my Chinese dream has the following three parts:

> 1.Promoting Chinese studies and expanding the Chinese language program. Offering more courses on Chinese language and culture to encourage more Americans to learn about these

My Chinese Bridge And My Chinese Dream

Licheng Gu 顾利程

Born and raised in Beijing, he received his B.A. at Beijng No. 2 Foreign Language Institute, an M.A. from Canberra College of Advanced Education, and his Ph. D. from the University of Oregon. He is Professor of Chinese in the Department of Asian Languages and Cultures at Northwestern University, Chicago. He also serves as field director of Northwestern's China Summer Program. His publications cover both language pedagogy and Chinese American history. He is the author of two books, Learning Chinese Characters through Pictures and Learning Chinese with Lulu and Maomao.

A bridge can help you travel from one side of a river to the other without danger of shipwreck in bad weather. A dream is a great ambition in your life. Step by step, you work for it diligently, without giving up under any circumstances. As a Chinese American, my bridge is the Chinese Bridge, the official name for the World College Student Chinese Speech Contest. My dream is to contribute to building a Chinese Bridge between Chinese and American students. Over the Chinese Bridge, I hope the Chinese and American people can communicate effectively through cultural exchange, foreign trade, and economic development. I hope the Chinese Bridge will help to strengthen the mutual trust and understanding between China and the United States so that a friendly relationship can develop between the two countries.

In the story of the Tower of Babel in the Bible, all of humanity shared one common language and culture. There was no confusion and no misunderstanding among the peoples of the world. These people lived a happy life, but they wanted to see the Lord in heaven with their own eyes and listen to His words with their own ears. They decided to build a tower which could take them from the earth all the way to the heavens. They drew the blue prints, divided their jobs, and started their great endeavor. Speaking the same language, the people of different countries of sorrow' onto the Land of Bliss. The greatest 'dream' of my father and me in between the two great civilizations is such a 'dream of grand harmony'.

Tan Yun-shan made a 'Sino-Indian motto' for himself, his family, and his students with these eight characters: '*lide liyan* (立德立言)' (cultivate one's virtue and speech) and '*jiuren jiushi* (救人救世)' (rescue humans and the world). The motto's first half came from the millennial 'Three Immortals' (三不朽) teaching of China, taught from emperors down to commoners. The motto's second half came from the Indian 'Bodhisattva spirit' which has been disseminated to China. I was disciplined by these eight characters since boyhood. Although never exemplary of them, I was always inspired by them wherever I would be. Indeed, I sincerely wish the 'Chinese dream' not to be a narrow-minded, national dream, a 'dream of hegemony'. It would be like erring in the proverbial folly of the Eastern Lady (东施) mimicking the sick looks of the Western Lady (西施). Rather, I wish the 'Chinese dream' to be a 'Bodhisattva dream', rescuing humans and the world.

of Tagore in the past. Chinese academia, once again, are translating Tagore works directly from Bengali into Chinese and have started publishing a new *Complete Works of Tagore*. When this is done, Chinese will surpass English as the greatest foreign language to display Tagore's literature while the Indian spirit of 'Satyam, Shivam, Sundaram' glitters brilliantly in the language of China.

In 1921, the poet, Guo Moruo (郭沫若), returned from Japan to China. When his boat entered River Huangpu and he sighted the motherland he so sorely missed, he instantly rhymed the 'Huangpu jiangkou' (黄浦江口/at the Huangpu estuary'). He exclaimed: 'O, the village of peace, the country of my parents!' (平和之乡哟！我的父母之邦！) This 'village of peace/*Santiniketan*' of Tagore who was his cynosure broke the boundary between China and India. '*Santi*/peace' is the soul of Indian civilization just as '*he wei gui* (和为贵)' (peace is precious) is the soul of Chinese civilization. Today, these three glittering golden characters of '*he wei gui*' are like Lady Chang'e (嫦娥) fleeing the earth to the moon. When she stands on the 'bright moon' and sees the earth so mired in the viciousness of 'nation-states', how could she be attracted to return?! In the 'Chinese dream' there are various plans of probing and landing on the moon in the name of 'Chang'e' in addition to an unannounced Chinese-landing-on-the-moon project. How nice if, on one hand, there would be a Chinese landing on the moon while on the other, inviting '*he wei gui*' back to earth. That would make the 'Chinese dream' even more perfect. It would also mean the realization of the 'Indian dream'.

The ancestors of a large number of overseas Chinese left their homes because of disturbances and insecurity. Tens of millions of overseas Chinese who are most sensitive to chaos and violence cherish the 'peace dream' as their greatest aspiration. Harmony and conflict are like the *yin* and *yang* of human life. The 'Chinese dream' should vigorously carry forward the 'Chinese spirit', travel on the 'Chinese road', and radiate towards the world, making the *yang* of harmony overwhelming the *yin* of chaos. In this way, the 'Chinese dream' will inevitably unite the two 'civilization-states' of China and India, transforming the world into a comity pervaded by family warmth and affection.

The Tang poet, Liu Changqing (刘长卿) once noted: 'No reason for wind and frost any harm to things inflict, see how Heaven and Earth love humans without sentiments!' (风霜何事偏伤物，天地无情亦爱人) The 'Chinese dream' is the manifestation that Heaven and Earth love humanity, that government loves people. The 'Chinese dream' is a 'world dream'. For millennia China has been such a universe where 'Heaven shrouds without selfishness, Earth carries without selfishness, and the sun and moon shine without selfishness' (天无私覆，地无私载，日月无私照). China is also a universe for the Great Tao to prevail, and whatever is there it is for the public good. China is also a universe where Empathy is supreme, and the Bodhisattvas ferry every being from the '*duhkha-sagar*/sea

Beijing's Commercial Press published the Chinese version; the English version became Volume III, Part 6 of the series on 'History of Science, Philosophy and Culture in Indian Civilization'. All this has marked my odyssey for realizing the 'Chinese dream', the 'Indian dream' and the 'dream of Grand Harmony between China and India', following in the footsteps of my father, Tan Yun-shan.

For 45 years while teaching and researching in India, I daily interacted with Indian intellectual elites. I was moved by the interconnectivity and reverberation between the two great civilizations of China and India. Even today, I continue to be exalted by Indian friends to unearth from Chinese civilization knowledge that has long been forsaken and forgotten. They have supported my advocacy of the 'geo-civilizational paradigm'. It promotes understanding and friendship between China and India so that we can remould the present world order from the venomous smoke of the theory of a 'clash of civilizations'. With the pursuit of the dreams of '*Vasudhaiva kutumbakam*/the world is like one family' by India and '*Tianxia datong* (天下大同)' (grand harmony all under Heaven) by China, we see the millennial 'dream' of the 'Himalaya Sphere'. It has brought us a bright spot of human evolution that the two ancient civilizations of China and India have not turned into ruins today.

Not only have Chinese and Indian civilizations survived their long history, but also the total population and wealth of the two were ahead of the rest of the world before the 18th century, comprising about 40–50% of the world. Today, both countries are relishing the dream of 'making the country rich and strong'. China aims to have a larger economy than America's by 2030 while India wishes to become 'the second China' by then—a topic aired by the 'Global Public Square' programme on CNN on 29 December 2013. An additional aspect of the dream of 'making India rich and strong' is to regain India's and China's historical proportion of population and wealth to 40–50% of the world's total. This is the 'Indian dream' and also the 'Chinese dream'. In the 'Indian dream' there is the 'Chinese dream', and in the 'Chinese dream' there is the 'Indian dream'. Therefore, realizing the 'Chinese dream' is to realize the 'Indian dream'—the embodiment of the Chan/Zen culture of 'I in you and you in me (你中有我，我中有你)'.

Every Hindu chants 'Satyam, Shivam, Sundaram' in his/her daily prayer. This idea travelled to China more than a millennium ago, first translated as '*zhen shan miaose* (真善妙色)', then into '*zhen shan mei* (真善美)' (truth, goodness, beauty). Sharing this ideal signifies the fusion of the 'Indian dream' and the 'Chinese dream'. Tagore's literature and culture exemplify the realization of the 'Satyam, Shivam, Sundaram' dream in modern times. Tagore received the Nobel Prize for Literature a hundred years ago. Since then, there have been many upsurges of 'Tagore fever' among the literary and cultural circles in China. Tagore was essentially a Bengali writer. China had already brought out the *Complete Works* experience, full of ideals and sentiments.

As China never ceases to revamp itself, it remains constantly in the limelight of international attention. The ruling elites of India regard China as the most important country, and evince the greatest interest in and concern for China's development. Colleagues and I at Delhi University and Jawaharlal Nehru University formed a small collective of 'China experts', meeting regularly every week to discuss the events of China from the 1960s onwards with not infrequent participation from government officials. For several years, we met at the office of the Founder-Director of the Institute for Defence Studies and Analyses, Mr. Krishnaswamy Subrahmanyam (late father of Ambassador Subrahmanyam Jaishankar, former Indian Ambassador for China, then, USA, and currently the Foreign Secretary, i.e., the overall in-charge of Indian Foreign Service). The small collective converted itself into the Institute of Chinese Studies (ICS). From the 1990s onwards, it was backed financially by the Ministry of External Affairs, Government of India.

My wife, Ishu Huang, and I are the founding members of this small collective that has regarded China and India as one family. Only one among our initial friends, Professor Manoranjan Mohanty, President of the ICS, survives. Others have left our world. Not only did we live like brothers and sisters, but we maintained our camaraderie mentally and spiritually—all firmly committed to close unity between the two great civilizations of China and India. Each of us individually published articles in Indian newspapers and journals to form the mainstream of Indian opinions on China. Our late lamented friend, Mira Sinha Bhattacharjea, focussed on the border dispute between China and India. She proposed a 'political solution' as early as the 1970s. Both governments have now accepted this proposition.

In 1994, the Indian Ministry of External Affairs invited me to guest-edit a special issue on 'India and China' for its journal, *Indian Horizons*, to mark the 40th anniversary of the Panchsheel (Five Principles of Peaceful Coexistence) Agreement. I produced a fat book of 555 pages which brought out reprinted versions twice, amounting to a total of 9000 copies and distributed all over the world by Indian embassies and other government institutions. In the 1990s, I organized a conference on 'India and China Looking at Each Other' at the Indira Gandhi National Centre for the Arts, and brought out a volume titled *Across the Himalayan Gap: An Indian Quest for Understanding China*. Later, other friends and I brought out the English version of the book in Chinese edited by Zhang Minqiu (张敏秋), entitled '*Kuayue Ximalaya zhang'ai: Zhongguo xunqiu liaojie Yindu* (跨越喜马拉雅障碍：中国寻求了解印度/*Across the Himalayan Gap: A Chinese Quest for Understanding India*). I also co-authored a book with my good friend, Geng Yinzeng (耿引曾) of Peking University, on *India and China: Twenty Centuries of Civilizational Interaction and Vibrations*.

away at Bodhgaya in 1983 before completing his last tour de force. Throughout his life, he devoted his research and writing to materializing Tagore's ideal of 'Grand Harmony between China and India'. He dedicated his life selflessly to the 'civilizational dream of China', 'civilizational dream of India', and the 'dream of Grand Harmony between China and India'.

As the eldest son of Tan Yun-shan, I was born in Batu Pahat, Malaysia. My parents carried me, a two-month old baby, to India to pay homage to Tagore at Visva-Bharati. Tagore honoured me with the Indian name 'Asoka', and I went back to Batu Pahat after a two-week stay. I returned to China at the age of two and grew up there. I went to India in 1955 to reunite with my parents and younger brothers and sisters. I lived and worked in India until the summer of 1999 when I settled in Chicago. Although I never did have the chance to use my Indian name, 'Asoka', my entire career has navigated along the trajectory predetermined by this name. A contemporary of Qin Emperor Shihuangdi, Ashoka was a powerful champion of the Buddhist movement that united the two back-to-back sisters of the Himalaya Sphere—Chinese and Indian civilizations. As Tan Yun-shan was the crystallization of these two civilizations, 'Asoka' epitomizes the gene I have inherited from my father.

Arriving in India, I began to teach Chinese language from 1958 until 1994. At age 65, I retired from the Indian universities. The ancient adage of '*jiaoxue xiangzhang* (教学相长)' (teaching and learning from one another) has impacted me profoundly. Being a teacher in India (mainly teaching Chinese language with a near ten-year interval taking up additional teaching in history), I found pride in and enjoyed myself as a radiator of Chinese civilization intimately interconnecting with thousands of young and affectionate radiators who wanted to understand Chinese civilization. This made me 'evergreen'. I was regarded as a relative, even a parent, by some pupils. Parents often called upon me at the university to counsel their children; or, they would consult me about their children's potential marriage partners. I felt like I was becoming a part of Indian society. My instructions melted lots of 'non-understandings' or 'misunderstandings' about China. I was able to subtly expand their affection for me onto China.

Twice did Chairman Mao Zedong observe that India was 'a great nation/country' and Indians were 'very good/great people'. The first time was in 1951, when he attended the National Day reception at the Indian Embassy; then, in 1970, on the 'May Day' when he shook the hand of Brajesh Mishra, Charge d'Affaires of India. This was exactly what I felt when I lived in India. For 80–odd years, the two generations, father and I, and all members of our family, have loved China and India. We felt both Chinese and Indian—never conscious of the differences and distances between these two nations and countries. 'Grand Harmony between China and India' was never a hollow phrase for father and me. It was a real living hill flown from India to China). In the vicinity, there have been shrines of '*Shang Tianzhu* (上天竺)' (Upper Heavenly India), '*Zhong Tianzhu* (中天竺)' (Middle Heavenly India), and '*Xia Tianzhu* (下天竺)' (Lower Heavenly India). There are, thus, Indian territories on the Chinese map symbolizing Sino-Indian friendship. For a thousand years or so, no one has objected to this.

We have such a moving story of a 'hill flown from India to China' in ancient history. Modern-day Tan Yun-shan tried his level best to create a 'Sino-Indian Cultural Society' (中印学会) to help establish 'Cheena-Bhavana' in Visva-Bharati and enabled China to return the love India had given to her. 'Cheena-Bhavana' was like the 'hill flown back from China to India' (飞回峰). The two—the Hangzhou 'hill flown from India to China' and 'Cheena-Bhavana', the 'hill flown back from China to India', have composed a symphony of civilizational reverberations.

On the one hand, there was Tan Yun-shan's dream of 'Grand Harmony between China and India'. He never wavered in his firm belief of China and India as 'fraternal countries'. On the other hand, our world has been hoodwinked by the 'geopolitical paradigm' of 'nation-states'. The Westphalian regime is pushing Sino-Indian relations towards competition and emphasis on defence as well as mutual rivalry. After the Sino-Indian border war of 1962, the Indian public regarded the Chinese as foes. There is a story of Tan Wen, the elder daughter of Tan Yun-shan, who was most loyal to India and most dedicated to Tagore. She once met her Ph.D. supervisor with a group of guests. While introducing her, the supervisor remarked: 'She is different from those [Chinese] bad guys'. She was deeply hurt by it and her conviction in Tagore's 'racial-blindness' was shattered.

However, the millennial 'civilization-state' tradition of China and India is indestructibly eternal. Two weeks after the border war, Jawaharlal Nehru, the Indian Prime Minister, presided over the convocation of Visva-Bharati. The moment he saw Tan Yun-shan, the never-wavering believer of 'Sino-Indian fraternity', sitting erectly in the audience, the anger within Nehru against China disappeared. He threw out his official address. In his actual speech, he never said a word hostile to China, but used Tan Yun-shan and 'Cheena-Bhavana' as reference to reiterate that India was 'not at war with China's culture or the greatness of China'. Hearing this, Tan Yun-shan broke into tears.

After his death, Tan Yun-shan was eulogized as the 'modern Xuanzang'. There were commonalities and dissimilarities between him and the renowned pilgrim of the 7th–century. Like a great swan, Xuanzang toured India and flew back to China to preach and translate the scriptures (the 'Great Swan Pagoda (大雁塔)' in Xi'an (西安) today is his insignia). Tan Yun-shan flew to India in 1928. First he nestled in Tagore's 'World-meeting-in-bird's-nest University' and gathered a flock of Chinese birds to make it truly an 'International University'. After retirement, he wanted to build a 'World Buddhist Academy' at Bodhgaya in India. Unfortunately he passed

Part III
One Endeared Family within Four Seas

'*Vasudhaiva kutumbakam*/the world is like one family' is the core idea of Indian civilization. Tagore named his school 'Visva-Bharati', meaning 'where the whole world meets in one nest'. The Chinese now call it '*guoji daxue* (国际大学)' (international university) but its name should have been 'World-meeting-in-a-bird's-nest University'. In 1920, Tagore wrote to Chinese writer, Xu Dishan (许地山):

> 'For us there is but one country—the world. We have but one nation, that is Man.'

These words echoed well with the 'Political Report' of the 18th Congress of the Communist Party of China of 2012. It says: 'There is only one globe for the humanity'. Tagore's letter also mentions that in Visva-Bharati there was no 'illusion of geographical barriers'. No sooner had Tan Yun-shan arrived in Visva-Bharati than he equated Tagore's ideal with the thought of '*datong* (大同)' (grand harmony) from Chinese tradition, and decided to contribute his efforts to the realization of Tagore's dream of '*Zhong-Yin datong* (中印大同)' (Sino-Indian Grand Harmony).

Fired up by Tagore's dream, Tan Yun-shan went to work. He knew that Tagore was keen on establishing a 'Cheena-Bhavana' (Chinese institution) within Visva-Bharati. Tan shuttled between India and China to form the 'Sino-Indian Cultural Society' (*Zhong-Yin xuehui* (中印学会)). Funds and books were collected and 'Cheena-Bhavana' was established in 1937. Tagore said with great excitement when he inaugurated 'Cheena-Bhavana':

> 'This is indeed a great day for me, a day long looked for, when I should be able to redeem, on behalf of our people, an ancient pledge implicit in our past, the pledge to maintain the intercourse of culture and friendship between our people and the people of China, ...'

This was Tagore's acknowledgement of Tan Yun-shan's help in realizing his dream of the 'World meeting in my bird's-nest University'. It also revived his dream of 'the intercourse of culture and friendship between our people and the people of China'. Tan Yun-shan became the Founder-Director of 'Cheena-Bhavana' from 1937 until his retirement in 1967.

The two great civilizations of China and India are back-to-back sisters within the Himalaya Sphere. When they interacted with each other, there was no 'illusion of geographical barriers' as Tagore observed—virtually boundary-blind. During the twenties of the 4th century, an eminent monk from India, Huili (慧理) (Matiyukti), arrived at the hill beside the West Lake of Hangzhou. He observed with excitement that the hill was the *Gridhrakuti* (Hill of the Sacred Eagle) of 'Madhyadesa' (Bihar) that had flown to Hangzhou. The locals believed him and built the 'Monastery Lingyinsi' (灵隐寺), meaning 'the Indian *Gridhra*/Sacred Eagle coming to rest in this temple', and the hill acquired the name of 'Feilaifeng (飞来峰)' (meaning the and study, and return to the country with revolutionary theories to 'revitalize China'. But financing for travel to Europe was difficult. So he started for Southeast Asia first and took upon himself the assignment of helping the Chinese overseas community run newspapers and schools. After reaching the 'South Seas (南洋)' (Southeast Asia), however, he met with the great Indian writer, Rabindranath Tagore, in Singapore in 1927. And he changed his life's journey entirely. He never made it to Europe, nor did he see the motherland of Communist revolution, the Soviet Union as he had longed to.

Carrying the mud of Chaling (茶陵), his village from Hunan (湖南), in his bones, Tan Yun-shan was filled with resolve the moment he left the Gate of China. He published an article '*Chidaoshangde husheng: zhiyi* (赤道上的呼声：致意)' (The Appeal on the Equator) in the *Lat Pau* dated 13 November 1925. He wrote:

> 'All ambitious youths must unite to make this cold world warm with our burning passion to elevate this decadent world to the high morality to which we hold for ourselves.'

Tan Yun-shan was a typical Chinese who sought after and was entranced by dreams.

A famous French writer, Romain Rolland, described India as the only 'place on the face of the earth where all the dreams of living men have found a home from the very earliest days when man began the dream of existence'. To my mind, India is the motherland of 'dream culture'. The first great dream of humanity was the one that gave birth to the Buddha. The first great dream of China's was not Confucius' dream of the Duke of Zhou (周公). (In Section 7 of the Analects (论语), Confucius lamented that he had missed dreaming of the Duke of Zhou for a long time.) Rather, it was Han Emperor Ming's (汉明帝) dream of a golden Buddha flying over his palace. The Indian dream of the birth of Buddha resulted in Buddhism disseminating in China while Han Emperor Ming's dream of the golden Buddha symbolized China's welcoming Buddhism in all walks of life from the Emperor down. These two great dreams made the dream culture thrive in China.

Tan Yun-shan could recite Buddhist sutras from boyhood. When he was studying in school he admired the two great men of modern India: Gandhi and Tagore. Between the two good friends, Gandhi named Tagore '*Gurudeva*' while Tagore named Gandhi '*Mahatma*'. Gandhi was the icon of Indian independence and national rejuvenation while Tagore initiated the modern Indian Renaissance. In 1924, Tagore visited China to give lectures. It was the time when Tan Yun-shan left the country, and he just missed seeing the great poet. In 1927, when Tagore was lecturing in Southeast Asia, Tan Yun-shan got to Tagore's hotel in Singapore to pay his respects. The two took to each other at first sight. Tagore invited Tan Yun-shan to his Visva-Bharati to teach, and Tan went the winter of the following year.

For A World of Grand Harmony: A Chinese Dream from Two Generations

Tan Chung 谭 中

Born in 1929, taught in Indian universities for four decades, was Head of Department of Chinese and Japanese Studies in Delhi University during 1971–78, Chairman of Centre for Afro-Asian Languages, and Chairman of Centre for East Asian Languages of Jawaharlal Nehru University during the 1980s and early 1990s until retirement in 1994; was Professor-Consultant and head of East Asia section of Indira Gandhi National Centre for the Arts from 1990 to 1999. Was the founder-chairman of Institute of Chinese Studies, Delhi (1990–2003). Settled at Chicago from 1999 till date. He won the Indian civilian award Padma Bhushan in 2010, and was the second Chinese scholar (after Ji Xianlin) winning this honour. He was awarded the highest honorary degree, Deshikottama, by Visva-Bharati (the university founded by Tagore) in 2013, and was the fourth Chinese scholar to win the honour after Zhou Enlai, Tan Yun-shan, and Wu Baihui.

'Alone I embark on a long journey to a foreign country, my bosom friends, how hard it'll be for me to part with thee?!...Woe faces our country, and as for our village, we cannot even mention! It falls on our shoulders to rebuild them...We must work for the good of humanity, but work as well to rebuild the village and the country...As we encounter calamity, our responsibility is great. Let us spare no efforts in undertaking it.'

My father, Tan Yun-shan, wrote these words at age 26 on 15 May 1924. It was entitled '*Changsha linbie zeng Chaling xueshe zhuyou* (长沙临别赠茶陵学社诸友')' (Parting words for friends of the Chaling Association before leaving Changsha). It appeared in the '*Xingguang*' (星光) Supplementary No. 23, in *Lat Pau* (叻报), 28 December 1925. While sharing the dream of 'making China rich and strong and reinvigorating the Chinese nation' with Mao Zedong who was his senior school-mate at First Normal School in Changsha, Tan Yun-shan was thinking of following the footsteps of Li Fuchun (李富春) and Cai Chang (蔡畅) to go to France to work

Four seas to One Family:
Overseas Chinese and Chinese dream

Part III
One Endeared Family within Four Seas

by both sides. Practice in parliamentary procedures may help foster a tolerance of diversity, and promote time-saving as well as practical communication ways.

China's future will be affected by many long-and short-term factors. Touching the rocks would help navigating across a river, but is not helpful for guiding across an ocean. That requires the vision, expertise, research, communication, and genuine cooperation of many more people. Hence, I need to dream big: I dream about not only having more Chinese dreaming about the future, but also an extension of natural love and sense of responsibility (practice Ren), clarification of goals and improvement of means (respect De), getting more fingers that can turn things into gold (think scientifically), and practice effective efficient communication skills (adopt parliamentary procedures). Ren and De are traditional cultural elements already existing, proven effective by the Zhou leadership and Confucius) and need only some refinement. If the Chinese could integrate these traditional virtues with science and parliamentary procedures (elements proven effective as the West overtook China with them), the journey to actualize their collective dreams would be a solid one.

questions and debate with authoritarianism and mystification, etc.

With rigorous definitions, the Westerners employ logic and probability as the basis for inference. They also tend to make judgments based on empirical testification. Whereas, the Chinese lacking of the habit in using rigorous definitions has become a cultural DNA that hinders their logical thinking (for instance, the lack of documentation about the changing definitions of measurement units. Even if there were some records, inconsistencies are plenty and rarely challenged by scholars). Other than Mozi and the School of Logicians, traditional Chinese scholars often twist the notion of their vocabularies at will, to the point that some adopted others' without explicit declaration. With shaky terms, the thinking process lacks discipline. No wonder the Chinese prefer analogy to logic when making speculations. They are also very careless about treating necessary and sufficient conditions.

The direction of logical inference is set off by the preposition statement. If it is wrong, logic could mislead the inference farther away. A common problem among many Chinese writers is to substitute objective/real situations with subjective/desirable statements. They would often start from a desirable rather than the real condition (such as vilify opponents' motivation, over-or under-estimate opponents' ability). They also tend to treat the current conditions as what should be the condition, employ pre-conceptions in decision making, characterize something 'desirable' or 'may happen' as something 'must be' or 'will definitely be' happening.

Another problem stems from the employment of a narrow perspective (such as following only that of the teacher's). Many Chinese students are not used to analyze and integrate issues from multiple perspectives (including that of the competitors'). A university practice in China that restricts change of major subject of study has reinforced the traditional authority of the mentors. While a single perspective is conducive to maintain consensus, the price is the suffocation of debates and innovation.

Aside from close-door self-improvement and secret recipe, the traditional Chinese discussion style also hinders communication. Being overly concerned with modesty and tactfulness often leads to indirect and ambiguous expression of views. The habit of modesty however has not been able to overcome the framework of hierarchical communication, which neither treats equally opinions from people of different status, nor encourage different opinions. Often, the 'us-them' dualistic mentality lowers the expectation that people disagreeing on one topic could agree on another. A dispute encountered during negotiation, especially when it is publicized, tend to be interpreted as a watershed marking no change on either side's stand. The response would turn to attacks of the other side's background and motivation, rather than calm exploration and analysis of anything acceptable

First, the goals must be defined. A goal should be conceived against a specific context of time and space. Existing goals need not be retained. New goals must be clearly defined. All means should be highly efficient.

This set of De Improvement is no different from the principle and procedures of modern management. Its biggest difference from the Confucian 'adherence to discipline even in a private setting' and from the traditional business practice of guarding family secret lies in its clearly defined procedures and independence from secrecy. The reasons that Western Civilization overtook Chinese in the past several centuries can be found in its adaptation of scientific elements that include procedural operation, standardization, logic, openness, empirical testification, and probabilistic inference, as well as parliamentary procedures which filter and blend diverse opinions into consensus that mobilizes collective actions.

The Respect of De is complimentary with the Anglo-American professionalism. Occupational groups in the West establish their reputation with standardized training and self-disciplined service procedures. They rely upon legislative procedures to monopolize business and fight for their interest, but insist on defining the content and liability of their practice (for instance, the medical society advocates for saving every patient without considering the cost to the patient, family, other patients, and society). Such a scheme of limited liability protects more of the practitioners than the overall benefit of the customers and all others affected.

People who respect De could learn from professional practice about systematic training and the principle of equal treatment for all customers. Yet the targets and means of professionalism are restricted by formal rules. Training and service require plenty of resources, and preclude wide participation. Whereas, the goals and means for Respect De can be determined by an individual, without the need for formalization. It does not always require resources for training and practice. People who practice Ren, while in accordance with their individual hierarchy, would not ignore others whom could be indirectly affected. Currently, professional ethics has become a key concern in medicine, business management, engineering, and law, etc. Yet the focus is on individual practitioners. The interest of the whole profession is still their utmost concern. If the American Medical Society adopts the principle of Ren, it would reconsider whether a huge amount of health care cost (which is far higher than the patient-population ratio) should be spent on patients dying within one month.

There are many obstacles hindering the Chinese way of thinking. The more frequent obstacles include: the belief that things are forever changing leading to the avoidance of definitions which could distort the dynamics of the changing world; overreliance of analogies that preempts the use of logic; taking into account of multiple variables at the expense of focusing on clear-cut causal relationships; ambiguous and causal explanations; assertion despite ignorance; snapping support actively initiated under complex social structures.

Modern societies are even more complex than any patrilineal hierarchical society. People nowadays have to constantly leap into different roles expected from various structures. Patrilineal hierarchical rules alone is far from adequate in guiding life beyond the kinship. On the other end, the Western way of treating everybody as absolutely equal, while seemingly simple and easily adoptable, is too general to handle subtle relationships. It is very hard to balance the demand from all sorts of structures and to handle daily interactions among all sorts of roles in a measured way. No wonder there so many delicate and exceptional cases left for Western literature, movies, and psycho-analysts to explore and explain. In comparison to these two sets of principles, Confucius' establishment of the principle of Ren is most appropriate to provide tailor-made guidance for personalized interactions.

With such an understanding, I de-couple the essence of Ren from the patrilineal hierarchy, return Ren to 'a universally applicable passion and sense of responsibility'. There is no need for a Ren-relationship to be restricted to the ascribed kinship network. As long as a person can develop a genuine passion with others, whether they are relatives, friends, neighbors, colleagues, or anyone with a naturally evolved feeling, both sides can initiate and develop a relationship filled with mutual love and support.

Recent Western democracies place too much emphasis on means like election and winning benefit through voting. They forget about defining the goals, and pay little attention to the price paid by the losing side and those who do not vote (including the future generations). Such an incomplete sense of responsibility cannot sustain. If China could promote Ren, help voters understand that civil responsibility does not stop at voting, but includes ensuring long-term benefits for the whole population and the environment; and help the tourists understand that their duties do not stop at spending money, but includes respecting local culture and living conditions, then it will become a country respected by the world.

Relative to the impractical idea of loving everyone the same way, 'Ren' requires only a naturally evolved relationship of love and responsibility. While the practice of Ren follows a hierarchy of priorities, it extends to everyone and everything. The target of Ren is no longer limited to the Chinese, citizens of China, people from the same hometown, members of the same tribe, or family members. Accepting such a notion of Ren, the Chinese people could minimize conflicts with the family and neighbors and workplace, reduce resentment caused by regional and income discrepancy within their country, and avoid hatred and hostility aboard.

Once the target of concern is identified, concrete actions can proceed to match the goals and improve the means. Here are a few examples that each Chinese could do for each level of targets:

Improvement of De should take the whole conceptual structure into account.

laws and cases are accumulated before enforcing order. The Confucian approach to reduce persecution through education could still be an effective and efficient strategy. What should be taught? Instead of rapidly enacting countless rules and regulations, the most efficient approach seems to be to promote love. There are many ways to teach love. Confucius's treatment of the notion of 'Ren (仁)' is a most simple and feasible approach. Unfortunately, the essence of Confucius' 'Ren' has long been twisted.

The fault does not lie in various interpretations of 'Ren (仁)'. Most of these interpretation are shallow and superficial, incomplete and abstract. 'Ren' has been referred to a general sense of love, a partial treatment in accordance with bloodline hierarchy, the highest virtue, or the sum of all virtues. This term is also entangled with several other terms of morality. So much confusion has been generated that it has almost become an unusable behavior guideline. No wonder some people suggest not to use the term again. In my opinion, however, if we go back to Confucius' original idea, we will find a simple and workable concept.

The main concern of Confucius was the disorder that caused people's suffering during the Spring and Autumn Period. The political system built be the Duke of Zhou on a patrilineal network with the oldest son from the first wife inheriting family authority. There were over two centuries of estrangement, compounding internal coups and external invasions. Confucius' solution was to restore order by instilling a genuine passion and sense of responsibility into the system. The kind of 'genuine passion and sense of responsibility' he proposed was not something artificial or imaginary, but a natural and genuine loving relationship between brothers (called 'Ren' or brotherly love) still being practiced in his matrilineal community. Believing that the patrilineal structure represents the future despite short-term difficulties, Confucius intended to enrich it with the brotherly love inspired from his matrilineal community, but without heralding its source. Later Confucians either did not know or refused to accept the source and meaning of such brotherly love. They insisted to tie Ren to the patrilineal hierarchy, thereby restricted the application of Ren to other social relationships.

Confucius did not transplant Ren in a broad stroke. The social functions and structure of a patrilineal hierarchical society are much more complex than those in a matrilineal community. The brotherly Ren is inadequate if directly applied to other kinds of relationship. As recorded in the *Analects*, Confucius presented multiple ways about the practice of Ren under various concrete situations specific to the relationship between the interacting individuals. He did not unconditionally accept the patrilineal leadership system either, as he recognized more about its problems than the Duke of Zhou. The 'Ren' proposed by Confucius therefore includes not only the passion and unconditional responsibility naturally evolved from an ascribed relationship in a simple society, but also the affinity and mutual improve the respective means. While seemingly abstract, such an approach in fact could rely upon three components already in existence: the notion of "Ren" as originally introduced by Confucius, the scientific attitude and parliamentary procedures developed in the West. Blending these three components together and promote their wider application, the "Chiness Dreams" will have a better chance of getting continuously constructed and actualized.

Each goal of 'De' has its own target. The target was the tribe in the period when De represented a sign, was the state when De represented benevolent rule, and was oneself/the extended family/the feudal lord/ the world as seen by the king when De represented virtue. Today, the world extends much farther beyond the kings' horizon, the state has become a modern political system, both affect the individual more directly and deeply. The extended family is weakened. Between the family/clan and the state, there are now many more human aggregates and organizations which were completely absent in the Confucian spectrum of concerns. The relationship within and among these levels of structures are much more complex. How to deal with such relationships? The Western principles include: treating each individual person equally, the rights of individual entities cannot be impinged, individuals are free to participate in politics or not to (other than paying taxes, people do not have to pay any attention to public affairs, esp. those pertaining to the well-being of the competitors), people can fight for benefits through election or collective actions. Aided by money and national power, citizens can enjoy extra treatment or consumption inside and outside of the country. Is this a desirable and sustainable way of life? Can and should China follow suit, without modification?

Regardless of how much Western culture they have been exposed to, there are quite a few of Chinese, whether as residents of a country or as tourists, sometimes behave in a way that raises eyebrows. They jump the queue, spit at anywhere when they feel needed to, litter public facilities, pocket excessive supplies, pinch fruits and vegetables too hard when picking, submit fake certificates, exaggerate skills, commit plagiarism, apply for citizenship but do not take part in local affairs, evade taxes, apply for benefits even though they are over-qualified, ... etc. Such behaviors have become the basis for being labeled as 'Ugly Chinese' overseas. Within China, there are wide and frequent reports of inappropriate behaviors. Should such behaviors be regarded only as a natural evolvement during rapid socio-economic transition? A sense of urgency is due to develop new social norms for the future.

Recognition of individual rights is now a main trend globally. It is becoming harder and harder for a country today to prevent misbehaviors using laws and regulations alone. The Western legal system is not only expensive to operate, but also take time to develop. The volume of Western laws and cases have been accumulated for several centuries. Developing countries cannot wait until enough took on the notion of virtue, an internalizable attribute. As such, the term 'De' has evolved from a concrete, externally observable sign to a macroscopic policy, then internalized into personal virtue. Yet, the Confucian notion of self-improvement has never been separated from the collective well-being,

Throughout the changing process from an anthropological notion (identity sign), to political (benevolent rule) and ethical / psychological (virtue), the term 'De' has maintained an everlasting core notion and conceptual structure — an appropriate means/tools/reliance to accomplish one's goal. Goals can be different (victory, ruling, maintain a virtuous living and facilitate virtuous politics). 'Respect De' (敬德) means continuous clarification of goals and improvement of the means relative to each goal (to win over consensus, implement benevolent rule, extend personal improvement to the caring of the world).

As the Chinese society has expanded beyond recognition since the unification of the Qin Dynasty, the opportunities of participation in political and administrative affairs have not increased accordingly. As a result, the link between self-improvement has weakened and the Confucian call for serving the world has become too high-sounding. For over two millennia, the relationship between means and collective goals has become less direct for most people. Without the clear and direct guidance from goals, efforts to improve the means has become relaxed. The disconnection between public goals and means has been extended to the De pertaining to personal improvement. To this date, while the Chinese people are willing to work hard, they are not particularly accustomed to defining their goals. Too often they even forget about or escape from defining their goals. It would be hard to evaluate means without the pre-defined goal. 'Respect De' becomes lip service. The large number of Chinese idioms and vocabularies critical of the de-coupling of means from ends (such as 'chasing after minor things at the expense of the main goal', 'buying the box instead of the pearl', formalism, 'pretending but not really doing something that matters', etc.) provide ample evidence of the Chinese self-consciousness of the disconnect between their means and goals.

Therefore, the most urgent task at this historic juncture is to pull closer the goals/objectives and tangible undertakings so as re-vitalize the attitude of 'Respect De'. Everybody works harder on everything each of us could do. The objectives worth striving for could be one's mental and physical health, interpersonal relationships, study, career, and all sorts of collective undertaking. Since 'Respect De' could evolve from 'Respect Sign', 'Respect Policy', 'Respect Virtue', it could also be extended to 'Respect One-self', 'Respect Others', 'Respect Study', 'Respect One's Business', and 'Respect the Collective'. Such attitudes can be summed up into a term 'Respect Living'. Accordingly, the term 'De' can be appropriately regarded as a verb—'To Respect' . The strategy for Respect Living is to constantly review the approach in the identification and clarification of goals, as well as to continuously the established procedures and culture in the USA for establishing new initiatives, however, the Civil Rights Movement was able to push for legislative, judicial, and executive means, along with efforts via schools, churches, and the media, to sanction and prevent civil rights violation. Such actions are later applied and promoted to other under-privileged groups and other countries.

Constructive dreams for China are much more complex than rebellious dreams since they deal with larger scopes, involve more dreamers, and their common expectations seem harder to be blended together. For a long time in China, most processes for the development of new initiatives have been a result of executive decisions rather than being processed through legislative procedures. Whereas expedient, aggressive decisions could bring about instant results, the ranges of success rates and the costs fluctuate widely. The role of dissident intellectuals is generally limited to criticism. Most dissenting responses from the public are expressed in terms of emotional swears. The whole society has not got used to raising and discussing new ideas in detailed, practical terms. The Chinese people are still not accustomed to finding common dreams, interpreting and communicating dreams together. The process of translating and refining vague dreams into consensus and operational procedures is often ignored.

People have all kinds of dreams. How to gather and turn their mutual expectations into energy for common actions? Given the longevity and widespread of their civilization, the Chinese people must have accumulated plenty of experiences. One way to trace their experiences is to review the evolution of a core concept called 'De (德)'. 'De' as 'virtue' is but a later notion. In the frequently found clause of 'same mind and same De' (同心同德) in pre-Qin classics, the term 'De' means 'a sign' (德徵). Signs were simply what people wear. Warriors of the same tribe wore a same sign on the battlefield. They shared the same mind, and therefore could be counted on to fight together. The term 'same De' (同德) was also applied to the same residence or the same customs. Whichever sign chosen to be the identifier, people having the same sign were believed to share the same goal, and can be relied upon for protection and victory.

By the end of the Shang Dynasty, the notion of De was further extended from a concrete, externally identifiable sign to a political call of 'benevolent rule' (德政). To legitimize why a small tribe like the Zhou could and should replace the powerful Shang as leader of the Central Plain, the Zhou leaders advertised their benevolent ruling style in contrast to the tyrant Shang ruler. The abstract notion of 'benevolent rule' hence became the reason Heaven/God changed its mind and let Zhou replace Shang. To make sure that Heaven/God does not change its mind again, the Zhou leaders urged their off-springs to learn about benevolent rule, to constantly love their subjects, and to refrain from an excessive lifestyle. Later, when Confucius extended education, a privilege of the aristocrats, to the commoners, the term 'De' suffer, and civil wars may break out. If the Chinese people treasure such a rare legacy of scale and superiority, they must understand, objectively, their strength and weakness, so as to devise sustainable strategies for future development. My beautiful dream about China is to see more and more Chinese concerned about its sustainable development, dream about its better future, and learn about how to rationally explore, communicate, and cooperate in order to achieve their common dreams.

Dreams neither directly reflect reality, nor present themselves along rigid definitions and logic. In the past, people sought help for guidance through dream interpretation. But a same dream could be interpreted very differently. So are dreams today, despite the relatively scientific approach of psychoanalysts. Some dreams are too individual and should be kept in private, some could hit a common cord that may lead to common action. For instance, Dr. Martin Luther King's dream struck a concordance very rapidly and bonded the hope of African and other Americans to fight for equal rights. This sort of individual dreams might have already been taken place widely, all is needed for them to interact is communication. Collective dreams therefore could lead to the release of huge social force. Yet, current scientific ability of various national strategy designers within and cross individual countries is not necessarily better than that of the psychoanalysts.

There are two types of collective dreams. One type is the 'rebellious dreams' which share a specific target but tend to defer attention to concrete goals. Such collective dreams are relatively easy to gather forces, and are more likely reliant upon force as the means of solution. Yet, even with victory, due to the lack of discussion over new directions and inadequate consensus, the new operation could not avoid the interference from the military and intelligence units for at least several decades. Military rule and torture will dominate, social and economic operation could easily fall back to the previous orbit. This mode of changes could easily be found in China's past.

Another type is the 'constructive dreams' which heralds a new way of business. It tends to encounter more disagreement in various stages and takes longer to reach consensus. Hopefully, the more concordance and flexibility the common platform attained, the more likely violence can be avoided. The Second Feudal Design in the beginning of the Zhou Dynasty and the several attempts of major reformation in Northern Song are rare examples of large collective dreams that had a chance of getting implemented. The implementation of these dreams, nonetheless, had the support from the top or the military.

A classical case of a rebellious dream initiated from the grass root and succeeded without widespread bloodshed was Dr. King's Dream. The call of the movement is simple enough to draw together the rebellious spirit among black folks, even though there could have been more discussions on what to construct. Aided by

The Chinese Pursuit of Common Dreams

—New Approaches for Concerns, Reasoning, and Communication

Tom Chung 钟伦纳

He is Executive Director of China Initiatives at the University of Cincinnati's. He was Research Associate Professor at the UC Department of Family Medicine, Executive Director of the Cincinnati Foundation for Research and Education, Research Director of the Massachusetts Executive Office of Elder Affairs, Director of Greater Cincinnati Chinese Chamber of Commerce, and on part-time basis, Founding Director of the Tufts University Institute for Leadership and International Perspective and Founder of Asian American Research & Training. For over 20 years, he has participated in the research, evaluation, legislation, and planning of elder care policies. He has wide social activities including being the President of the Cincinnati Association of Rational Thought. His publications in Chinese include books and poems on Chinese history and culture, Chinese societies inside and outside of China, the American society, social research methods, and parliamentary procedures. He has also written articles on the societies and culture of Hong Kong, China, and western countries for magazines and newspapers in the USA, Hong Kong, Taiwan, and Mainland China.

Whether out of individual or collective concerns, there are beautiful dreams and nightmares. My nightmare about China is the possible break out of big chaos. World history shows that there have only been a few civilizations that could maintain a strong state for long. Given the huge population size, diverse environment, and recent rapid changes, it would be hard to avoid internal or external conflicts. China encountered chaos in the past, when it was much stronger than other countries and was blessed with a strong sense of belonging. Today, even a smaller enemy possesses a strong destructive force, a small internal unrest could also light up a large spark. Even though China would not be conquered or broken into pieces like the Middle East, its development would be smothered, its people

Guo Fenglian (郭凤莲), Lu Guanqiu (鲁冠球), Liang Wengen (梁稳根), Wang Jianlin (王健林) and so on. There are innumerable 'villages of moderate prosperity' (小康村) that have amassed billions of *renminbi* and made every villager rich. This is the significant symbol of China coming out of 2.0 development and entering the 3.0 version. Such a 'Chinese dream' is beyond imagination and worthy of emulation by other countries.

I am a staunch follower of 'Evolution' and firmly believe that 3.0 would be superior to 2.0, just as 2.0 had been far superior to 1.0. Thomas Friedman, the famous *New York Times* columnist, wrote in his column on 31 July 2014 that we now have two worlds, the 'world of order' and the 'world of disorder'. China, America, EU, India, Japan and countries of Southeast Asian are in the 'world of order' with things looking up. They are the specimens of 3.0. We shall have the American, EU, Indian, Japanese, Southeast Asian versions of 3.0 development. Each will have its own idiosyncrasies. The Chinese idiosyncrasy for its 'Chinese economic entity' (中华经济体) will be development with millennial wisdom. Domestically, the present Chinese leadership led by Xi Jinping and Li Keqiang will pursue a policy of people-intimacy, frugality, and anti-corruption. Internationally, it will try to establish a 'new great power relationship' with America, Russia, and the EU, in addition to creating a 'common destiny with surrounding countries.' All this shows the road-map towards 3.0 development.

The 'Chinese dream' that is being avidly talked about consists of two 'centenary ideals': (1) when the CPC celebrates its centenary in 2021, China aims to achieve a nation-wide level of 'moderate prosperity'; (2) when the People's Republic of China celebrates its centenary in 2049, China hopes to become a *real* 'strong power' in the world: that is, an up-graded version of 'Chinese power.' When China returns to the center stage of world politics, it is not returning to the 1.0 version of a 'regime of rites from the Celestial Dynasty' (天朝礼治体系), nor is it to replace the Number One position of the US in 2.0 development, using the traditional notion of 'kingly way' (*wangdao*王道) to swap with the American 'hegemonic way' (*badao*霸道). Rather, it is to create a world of 'common destiny' in which the prevailing spirit is '**you-in-me and I-in-you**" (你中有我、我中有你).

modernization through 'self-strengthening' (自强).

I have always advocated that the four economic entities of mainland China, Taiwan, Hong Kong, and Macau intensify their intercourse with the countries of Southeast Asia in which overseas Chinese concentrate. Today, Chairman Xi Jinping has conceived the construction of 'a common destiny with neighboring countries.' It has my whole-hearted support. Chairman Xi's idea of 'constructing the Silk Road economic belt and a 21st–century Marine Silk Road' (see www.21cbh.com jingji.21cbh.com › 宏观 › 中国政经) has been my thinking for many years. The "Chinese community" I proposed twenty odd years ago can now play a critical role in Xi Jinping's 'common destiny with neighboring countries'.

On further inquiry, I discovered that as early as December 2012, Xi Jinping had said to some foreign guests that 'China's cause is **win-win cooperation with all countries. The world is increasingly becoming a common destiny of "you-in-me and I-in-you"**' (*Renmin Ribao*人民日报/**People's Daily**, 6 December 2012: 1). This '**you-in-me and I-in-you**' (你中有我、我中有你) comes from Chan/Zen Buddhism—a traditional spirit of Chinese civilization (or 'Chindia'). This shows that when China is coming out of 2.0 development and entering the 3.0 version, it is carrying forward the spirit of 'Chinese/Chindia civilization.' Xi has added that 'a country must allow others to develop in order to develop itself, it must allow others to feel secure in order to make itself secure, and must allow others to prosper in order to make itself prosper' (*www.ssbgzzs.com* ‹时事报告刊 › 国际大势). This is the spirit of internationalism that greatly expands beyond 2.0 development manipulated by the geopolitical paradigm. This is what I mean by up-grading 'Chinese power'.

Readers might feel that the Chan/Zen discourse of '**you-in-me and I-in-you**' ill-fits my seemingly unilinear presentation of development as 1.0 => 2.0 => 3.0. I admit that this rendition has been inspired by Western commentators to whom evolution is unilinear. However, readers should have discovered by now how much I treasure the Chinese conception of time and space to which Buddhism has made a substantial contribution. I am with the 7th–century Tang poet, Wang Bo (王勃) who observed that 'in this universe with the Heaven so unbounded and Earth so impenetrable, I feel the infinity of the Creator' (天高地迥，觉宇宙之无穷.) We can highlight China, but not isolate it from the universe. It is the infinite universe that makes us feel we are in a world of 'common destiny'.

The world is watching China's advocacy of 'socialism with Chinese characteristics'. It has transcended the debate between 'socialism' and 'capitalism', and filled up the gap between 'capitalism' and 'socialism'. It is beyond doubt that the CPC is a party firmly rooted in socialism. It is also beyond doubt that China is relying on the capitalist 'market economy' for development. There are now thousands of "red entrepreneurs" like Wu Renbao (吴仁宝), Wu Xie'en (吴协恩),

Indian capital back for investment. Indian descendants abroad who played an important role in the world information technology revolution contributed greatly to India's becoming a software superpower and the 'office of the world'. All this demonstrates a reverberative effect between the 'Chinese dream' and the 'Indian dream'.

In 1980, I proposed the idea of a 'common Chinese community'(中国人共同体) and a 'Chinese economic collaborative system' (中华经济协作系统). My forceful advocacy in the last twenty odd years has earned the support of many scholars in China and abroad. I am glad to see from 'www.china.com' an article written by Professor Cao Xiaoheng (曹小衡), Vice-Director of the Institute of Taiwan Economic Studies of Nankai University (南开大学) entitled '*Haixia liang'an jingji yitihuade xuanze yu dingwei* (海峡两岸经济一体化的选择与定位)' (The choice and categorization of integratization of the economy of mainland China and Taiwan) in which the author mentions the World Bank's emulating my catigorization by describing the four economic entities of mainland, Taiwan, Hong Kong and Macau as a 'Chinese economic region' in 1993. (www.china.com.cn/chinese/TCC/haixia/50151.htm)

After the third plenum of the 11th CPC Party Central Committee, there has been fervent feedback from overseas Chinese in the reform and opening-up process to construct and develop the ancestral land, and enhance the posterity of the Yellow Emperor (黄帝) and Sun God (炎帝) within and outside China. This 'Chinese economy' all over the world is interacting with the 'Chinese economy' of the four economic entities of mainland China, Taiwan, Hong Kong, and Macau. It constitutes what I call an 'economic China' (经济中华). Through the organization of 'Hong Kong AP21', I jointly sponsored international conferences on the 'Eurasian continental bridge' (欧亚大陆桥) with the Academies of Social Sciences of Sichuan, Yunnan, Chongqing, and Guizhou. We sought to promote contacts between southwest China and Southeast Asia, South Asia, and Central Asia. I am happy to see that the 'Kunming initiative' (昆明倡议) was mentioned in the 'Joint Statement' issued in New Delhi in May 2013 and signed by Chinese Premier Li Keqiang and Indian Prime Minister Mammohan Singh. The Kunming initiative aims to establish a 'China-India-Myanmar-Bangladesh economic corridor' (中印缅孟经济走廊), as formulated by the two Presidents of the Yunnan Academy of Social Sciences, Professors He Yaohua (何耀华) and Ren Jia (任佳).

From 1980 to 2009, not only Hong Kong but also Macau returned to the ancestral land, and animosity between the mainland and Taiwan changed to pacifism. The posterity of the Yellow Emperor and the Sun God, all over the world, carries forward the spirit of 'fours seas to one family' (四海一家).

From 2010 onwards, China will come out of 2.0 development and enter the 3.0 version. The 'Chinese dream' today is far richer than the second wave of

Part II
Chinese Dream and the World

From 1980–2009, China pursued the 'Deng Xiaoping model'. It shifted decisively from 'politics in command' to 'economics in command'. Deng's slogan of 'poverty is not socialism' overpowered the Gang of Four's 'preference of socialist weeds to capitalist paddy'. There was massive construction of infrastructure with a trend toward 'building a nest for the phoenix' (筑巢引凤) and 'building roads for prosperity'. The 'phoenix' symbolized foreign investment while 'building the nest' meant building infrastructure, the secret to success in post-Mao China. Industrial development diversified and foreign investment came from Taiwan, Hong Kong, Macau, and overseas Chinese. Private enterprises were encouraged. An atmosphere of ease grew between government authorities and ordinary folks. China's interactions with the outside world intensified, transforming from an inaccessible to accessible country.

Special economic zones (SEZs) emerged. Shenzhen and Zhuhai were established to take advantage of their vicinity to Hong Kong and Macau, respectively. This was Deng's great invention. When taking up residence at Shatin in the New Territory of Hong Kong, I saw with my own eyes the emergence of the world's busiest transportation artery: trucks carrying goods from the production centers of Guangdong to the piers of Hong Kong to distribute to the entire world. China became the 'factory of the world' after joining the World Trade Organization (WTO). This was what the 'far-from-the-madding crowd peach-blossom land' (世外桃源) version of Chinese civilization could not have dreamed of a millennium ago. People-to-people contacts between the mainland and Taiwan, Hong Kong, Macau, and foreign countries were booming. Compatriots from Taiwan, Hong Kong, and Macau freely participated in various social developments in mainland China. These improvements in relations between the mainland and Taiwan, Hong Kong, Macau were due, also, to a thaw in Sino-American relations. The Chinese government announced the 'nine recommendations of Ye Jianying' (叶九条) and the return of Hong Kong and Macau to China to practice the principle of 'one country two systems', which also applied to Taiwan. Institutions like CEPA (Mainland and Hong Kong Closer Economic Partnership Arrangement) and ECFA (Economic Cooperation Framework Agreement) were created.

International observers, especially Indian friends, have noted that the Chinese developmental model of reform and opening-up succeeded in absorbing huge foreign investments to enable rapid industrial development. A large part of it came from overseas Chinese (including compatriots from Taiwan, Hong Kong, and Macau). Involved was the ethnic factor that 'blood is thicker than water' (血浓于水) and the political factor of 'one China' (一个中华). Overseas Indians also possessed huge stocks of capital but they were not as forthcoming as their Chinese counterparts in investing in the ancestral land (*zuguo*祖国). Later, India emulated China in implementing reform and opening-up, and sought to attract overseas

Beijing in 1992, especially on the Chinese cultural influence on Korea and Liuqiu/Ryukyu/Okinawa. A temporary harmony and tranquility could be obtained and considered an "order." This was a gigantic construction. Before the 19th–century, on the eve of the rise and expansion of Western colonialism and imperialism, the Asian continent could maintain its regional order mainly because of this Chinese imperial center. Its philosophy, norms, and governance based on rites stabilized the region.

The bad side was that the 'Chinese empire/civilization' and its 'regime of rites from the Celestial Dynasty' could not respond effectively and promptly to the challenges of the West. After this order suffered defeat and humiliation from the Opium War, it could not protect its communities domestically or internationally, thereby losing efficacy, rationality, and legality.

From 1840 onwards, China sought to emulate the developmental paradigms of various countries. Due to internal and external troubles, China's modernization could not take off for a prolonged period. Only with the establishment of the People's Republic of China in 1949 did we see China making progress. We may describe the three rungs of China's 30–year development for modernization as a zigzag course in pursuit of a Chinese dream, paying heavy tuition fees to mistakes, and maintaining its forward march by rectifying deviations time and again.

From 1950 to 1979, China pursued the 'Mao Zedong model'. It tried to replicate the 'Soviet model' with the slogan: 'Today's Soviet Union is tomorrow's China'. However, Mao was a man deeply rooted in Chinese tradition and did not like being led by the nose by Moscow. He could not 'sovietize' China. Internally, the new China pursued high-speed constructions of agriculture, industry and defense with forceful Party-Government leadership, highlighting ideology and organizing mass movements. The government tightly controlled social institutions and people's lives, interfering in individuals' biological, psychological, demographic, physical, and spiritual developments. Impatience for success accounted for mass movements like the Great Leap Forward and its slogan of 'the entire nation makes steel' (全民炼钢), and so on, violating a natural rhythm to economic development, exploiting natural resources, and destroying ecological systems. These movements, in effect, killed the goose that lays the golden eggs, resulting in natural calamities.

China's foreign policy also gravitated towards extremism. First, there was the policy of 'leaning to one side' (一边倒) which aligned China with the Soviet Union against the US. Later, foreign policy shifted to the strategy of 'one line alliance'(一条线) which aligned China with the US against the Soviet Union. There was the promotion of contact with Hong Kong and Macau, but continued hostility against Taiwan. Great power rivalries restricted China's usual connections with overseas Chinese while the countries of Southeast Asia retained strong anti-communist and anti-China sentiments.

are on the move. What the Chinese could not dream of for millennia is a reality today. We know the American professor of Indian descent at Harvard University, Tarun Khanna, and his book, *Billions of Entrepreneurs* (2007) with *How China and India Are Reshaping Their Futures—and Yours*, as its subtitle. I think these are not overstatements. People of China and India vie with one another to get rich and become entrepreneurs, thus the world is bound to add 'billions of entrepreneurs', and the future of the entire world is bound to change. In this way, the realization of the Chinese dream is to enhance the spiritual and material power of China. Putting it in geopolitical parlance, it is to create an up-graded version of 'Chinese power'.

Since October 2013, I have been collaborating with Professor Wu Xinbo (武心波), Vice-Dean of the Academy of International Relations and Foreign Services of the Foreign Language University of Shanghai and Professor Zhou Feng (周峰) of the Communist Party of China's (CPC) Party School of Guangdong Province to pursue the conception of creating a 3.0 version of development. I divide global development into three phases: 1.0 from 500–1500, 2.0 from 1500–1999, and 3.0 from 2000–2499. It is for the sake of convenience that I start the periodization from 1500. The date symbolized the beginning of modernization of the Western world, and China's reaching an advanced stage in economic development during the Ming Dynasty (明朝). I take 500 years for the duration of a 'version' according to the progression of world evolution. The 500 years of '2.0' version were surely much more advanced than the previous 500 years. This '2.0' version of the world was also an epoch of earth-shaking changes with unprecedented fision and fusion between the old and new, between the East and West civilizations. I create the category of '3.0' version (2000–2499) in order to expand my insight and imagination for the future world.

According to my analysis, the US entered 2.0 development during the Civil War and has retained this position *par excellence* for more than a century. For the future, the US has to enter 3.0 development to stay young, vibrant, and competitive. We can also say that the European Union (EU) is entering 3.0 development. Japan is in the same situation. The newly-born Republic of India relies on its construction of a great civilization-state to show how it's entering 3.0 development.

Returning to China's development, the Chinese did a very bad job in the past in transiting from 1.0 development to the 2.0 one. I have categorized the millennial development of Chinese civilization as a 'regime of rites from the Celestial Dynasty' (天朝礼治体系). The good side was that this regime could handle contradictions between the 'four worlds': i.e., the 'inner world' of the individual, the 'social world' across individuals, the 'natural world' between humans and other beings, and the cosmos. I have discussed this in details in my 3–volume book '*Tianchao lizhi tixi yanjiu* (天朝礼治体系研究)' (Studies on the regime of rites from the Celestial Dynasty) published by the Press of the Chinese Renmin University,

Revolution challenged both the American and Soviet models of development. Mao Zedong thought seemed to provide a brand-new developmental paradigm.

At the international forum on China's development model in London, we also focused on India's development. Most of the participants, except the Indian scholars, viewed India's independence in a disparaging light, regarding it as a peaceful transition that would not transcend the Western paradigm and would not allow India to march forward in stride from a complex history and reality.

Looking back after half a century, the mindset of those days was rather naïve. In comparison, we have a more complicated world today. The two only billion-size countries of China and India with millennial-old histories and substantially new potential are showing their similar but different 'Chinese dream' and 'Indian dream'. Similarly, when we discuss the 'Chinese dream' today, we must not see it like a 'frog in the well'. Rather, we should delve into its warp and woof by placing it a larger, worldly context. China and India today are providing two different models for the world. Of course, they have great potential to complement and supplement one another. History shows us how.

In my long tenure of teaching at Hong Kong Baptist College/University (1972–2002), I spent half a year as a visiting professor at the Graduate School of Asia Pacific Studies at Waseda University in Japan, courtesy of Professor Lim Hua Sing (林华生). Professor Lim and I jointly taught a course titled, 'Greater China and its Economies' (经济中华). It covered the four different economic entities of mainland China, Taiwan, Hong Kong, and Macau as well as the economic networks of the global Chinese communities and their interconnections. The topic of a Chinese dream was part of this course. Later, Dr. Liu Chak Wan (廖泽云) of Macau University of Science and Technology invited me to create and head the Institute for Sustainable Development (MUST-ISUS). This was a four-year assignment (2002–2006). Teaching as well as administering required that I read a lot of books and journals on 'Macau studies'. It deepened my understanding of China's policy of 'one country two systems' (一国两制) for Hong Kong and Macau.

For several decades, I have been comparing the Chinese and Indian development paradigms and felt the 'Indian dream' was as great as the 'American dream' and the 'Chinese dream'. These three dreams add up to an important part of the history of human civilization.

According to Mencius, economic development combines the 'celestial seasons' (天时) with 'terrestrial resources' (地利) and 'human harmony' (人和), of which the last is the most important. In my view, the 'Chinese dream' and 'Indian dream' are important because these countries have approximately one third of the globe's population. In the past, India was number one in the world in railway transportation, and every day millions of people used to travel by train. Now, China has surpassed India. On important holidays hundreds of millions of people

Upgrading 'Chinese Power': The Chinese Dream that Creates a 'Common Destiny' for the World

Huang Chih-lien 黄枝连

Born in Malaya and having his primary and high school education there, he moved to New Asia College, Hong Kong and joined the East Asia Program at Harvard University for his further studies. He returned to the Chinese University of Hong Kong to start his teaching in Chinese and Western social thought and social development. He went to Nanyang University, Singapore, conducting teaching and field study of the history of Southeast Asia in Southeast Asia. He returned to Hong Kong Baptist College and taught there for about thirty years. He specialized in the teaching and research on Pax Sinica and future of China. He has written about twenty books relating to the subjects. He has just finished a book *On the Future History of the Chinese Civilization* and plan to write another one *On the Future History of the American Civilization*. He is the founding president of the Hong Kong Society of Asia & Pacific 21.

In Autumn 1964, I returned to Hong Kong after studying at Harvard University. I started teaching at Chung Chi College, Chinese University of Hong Kong, which had just been established. Before preparing my lectures, I had to read deeply of the works of Chinese thinkers from the end of the Ming Dynasty up to the founding of New China. This gave me a chance to survey the Chinese dream of modern times. Soon after, I went to London to participate in an international forum on China's 'Maoist' developmental model. I presented a paper on 'The Chinese Development Model and Mao's Mass Line'. It contained a study of the Chinese Dream from the Maoist perspective. Mao was the greatest dreamer Chinese history has ever seen. In my paper, I was infected by his grand vision for China. This paper turned out to be my first study of the Chinese dream.

Because of China's Cultural Revolution and the movement against the Vietnam War during the 1960s, a large number of young scholars in the Western world were quite left-leaning. This affected my thinking as well. We felt that the Cultural and while superficially advocating virtue, not force, actually pursuing force, not virtue, differing nothing with Europe in yesteryears' (我邦自秦以来，闭关自守，压民之力极重，名为尚德不尚力，其实尚力不尚德，与欧洲昔日情形无异)[1]. These observations reflect Zheng Guanying's viewing the Chinese civilization which he had ardently loved with the same perspective like Sun Yat-sen and other revolutionaries.

With five millennia of civilization and wisdom, we Chinese should have enough cultural confidence and creative spirit to tackle our problems. The convictions and principles beginning from the essay on '*datong*' in addition to the observations of Zheng Guanying and Sun Yat-sen should be our guide.

'I ride my dream into historical times' (words of Li Bai (李白), Tang Dynasty). 'I ride the iron horse to recover the frozen country' (words of Lu You (陆游), Song Dynasty). The Chinese dream! Indeed, where shall I be when I wake from my dream? On the shores of hanging willows, the gentle breeze of dawn with the parting moon?

Our country still needs several generations with exuberant cultural confidence and an open mind to absorb the modern culture and strive together with the nations that would treat us as equals to live the Chinese dream and realize the rejuvenation of the great Chinese nation.

I wish China all the best!

---

1 Ibid, p. 174.

living its dream. The US is dispatching its forces to the Pacific, meddling in Asian affairs, gathering its tiny cohorts to encircle China, wishing to impede China with quarrels on territorial waters as well as scrambles for energy resources. In the face of a US-Japan alliance, China and Russia are drawing closer. Asia is swathed by war clouds. Swift winds signal an incoming storm. Before China can live its sweet dream there is the possibility of a nightmare of stormy passage and sand storm.

I am glad to report that in 2012 when we observed the 'Zheng Guanying Week' at Macau, celebrating the 170th birth anniversary of Zhong Guanying and the 120th anniversary of the composition of Zheng's classic *Shengshi weiyan* (盛世危言) (Cautions for a Booming Era). We drew 130 scholars from China and abroad to discuss the importance of carrying forward Zheng Guanying's dream of a prosperous and strong China. Sun Yat-sen and Zheng Guanying were praised as the 'two great men' (双伟人). This was the first series of public activities after the renovation of the 'Zheng Guanying Mansion' (郑家大屋) at Macau. Ten years before that (in 2002) we, the Association For Macau Historical And Cultural Heritage Protection and the Macau Association of Historical Studies, observed the previous 'Zheng Guanying Week' on which occasion we brought out Zheng Guanying's writings which had been out of print.[1]

Zheng Guanying observed: 'the Westerners have no understanding with the grand truth, only obsessed with one extreme' (西人不知大道，囿于一偏)[2]. Again, 'when we gather together all the talent and sagacity of China to comprehend the vicissitudes of times in the country and abroad, showing the new and different, in good time there will emerge from the four hundred million Chinese those who could surpass peoples of all over the world' (若合天下之才智聪明，以穷中外古今之变故，标新领异，日就月将，我中国四万万之华民，必有　出九州万国之上者)[3]. In his 'Letter to Mr. Pan Lanshi "on convening parliament in order to unite to rescue the country"' (《致潘兰史征君"论开国会以合群救国"书》), Zheng Guanying observes: 'our country has accumulated her weakness for several thousand years' (我国积弱数千年)[4]. His chapter 'On the ruler/(原君)' (189–196) not only condemns the 'despotism of Qin' (嬴秦之暴), but also describes 'our rulers installed by Heaven specifically for the sake of butchered the people' (天之立君，专为鱼肉斯民) in China 'from the Han and Tang dynasties onwards' (汉唐以降)[5]. He adds: 'Since Qin Dynasty our country has been pursuing a close-door policy that has heavily oppressed the people,

---

1 Xia Dongyuan 夏东元 (ed), *Zheng Guanying wenxuan* (郑观应文选) (*Selected Works of Zheng Guanying*), Macau: the Association For Macau Historical And Cultural Heritage Protection (澳门历史文物关注会) and the Macau Association of Historical Studies (澳门历史学会), 2002.
2 Ibid, p. 157.
3 Ibid, p. 351.
4 Ibid, p. 196.
13 Ibid, pp. 189–196.

After the United Nations (UN) was established, a plaque bearing the handwritten copy of the essay on '*datong*' by Sun Yat-sen was installed in front of the building.

The ideas of democracy and a world of grand harmony enshrined in '*datong*' are also incorporated in 'The Universal Declaration of Human Rights'. When it was drafted in 1948 by the committee led by Madame Eleanor Roosevelt, Vice-Chairman Peng Chung Chang (张彭春) of China took the initiative in incorporating these ideas. Thus, we see the noble spirit of respecting the human rights not an exclusive patent of the West. China's age-old culture has a share as well.

Based on the tripartite system of the separation of powers of the West, Sun Yat-sen advanced a theory of Chinese constitutionalism called '*wuquan xianfa lun* (五权宪法论)' (Constitution of Five Powers). It incorporated the Chinese Imperial Examination system with the 'power to exam' (考试权). It also incorporated the traditional notion of 'censorial power' (监察权) to prevent graft and malpractices by officials. We see that to this end the new Chinese leadership is prescribing a heavy dose of censorial medicine to cure the bureaucracy of special privileges and unjust distribution as China gets richer. The gravest corruption is in education.

A huge pile of thorny problems sits before China today. The society is weak in finding stability and balance, the traditional power-money nexus is hard to break. There is the top-down rage in seeking gains and profit sans considerations of morality. Social crisis is lurking at various corners.

The silver lining lies in the Chinese ruling party's thunderbolt-like anti-graft campaigns against corruption, abuse of governing power, monopolist tendency, and the *killing-the-goose-for-golden-eggs* mode of development, in addition to anti-terror and anti-violence moves. The leadership keeps a cool head in realizing that though China's GDP is the world's Number Two, its per capita GDP is at the tail end of the world's 100 richest countries. The regional development opportunities are imbalanced while income disparity is as far apart as heaven and earth.

As a matter of fact, China is only a middle-ranking developed country of moderate prosperity. The ranking of per capita GDP in 2013 was: the largest economy of US$ 16.2 trillion, i.e., the U.S.A., ranked the 11th place while China with 9.1 trillion ranked 86th. It is estimated that China's per capita GDP could increase nearly 7 times from 2011 to 2060, from US$8,387 to $60,000, still trailing the US.

Beginning from the Industrial Revolution, Great Britain spent 150 years to double its per capita GDP from US$1,300 to 2,600. 120 years after that the US spent about 1/3 of the time (53 years) to achieve the same. It took China only (only 12 years) 1/10 of the time Britain had and 1/3 of the time America had taken to raise per capita GDP from US$1,300 to $2,600. We are optimistic that China can raise its per capita GDP from the present US$8,400 to over $10,000 in seven years or so.

Being a 'peerless' superpower, America would not feel at ease to see China

When we reminisce, we find Sun Yat-sen's 'Chinese dream' from a hundred odd years ago so loveable. This prominent dreamer and great man has made indelible contribution to the Chinese nation in overthrowing the imperial system, in advancing China towards modern civilization, and in ushering in the fight for the dream for revitalizing China and creating a rich and strong China.

After a century of struggle, China became a Republic then a People's Republic. For the last six decades, mainland China has gone through stormy and life-and-death struggles, driving past the phase of universalizing poverty and eating from the 'big pot', as well as the phase of Reform and Opening-up and allowing a part of the people to get rich first. Today, the economy is developed, and the country rich and strong. What next? It is easier to share poverty than prosperity. How do we make China enter the status of universal moderate prosperity? Can Chinese society share its wealth? When we confront such a thorny problem concerning the fate of the country and people's livelihood, let us remember Sun Yat-sen.

Sun's favorite calligraphy for friends are the words '*bo ai* (博爱)' (universal love) and '*tianxia weigong* (天下为公)' (Justice under Heaven). The phrase '*tianxia weigong*' is enshrined in the essay on '*datong* (大同)' (Grand Harmony) in *Liji* (礼记) (Book of Rites). The section on '*Liyun* (礼运)' (The Operation of *Li*) reads:

> When the great Tao (道) prevails, all under Heaven are for the public good. People elect the sagacious as leaders and entrust responsibility on the capable persons. They advocate faith and cultivate harmony. Hence people extend their affection beyond the narrow confines of their own parents and children. All the old live a fruitful life until the end. All the young grow up in full bloom. All widowers, widows, orphans, and issueless, as well as disabled are taken care of. The male grows into an independent householder. The female grows into the family of her in-laws. It is a pity that money litters on the ground, yet no one keeps a private treasury. It is a pity that more energy does not come out from the bodies, yet no one works only for his/her own good. Thus we see no conspiracies and machinations, nor break-ins, nor robbery, nor violence, nor sabotage. People don't close and lock their doors. This is the state of grand harmony.

This essay on '*datong*' is the world's first on democracy and socialism. It mentions democratic elections, a society of trust, social welfare, universal education and employment, highlighting the utopia of a world of grand harmony. It is the quintessence of Confucian teaching that has an imprint on the inner soul of the posterity of the Yellow Emperor and the Sun God. It has been vigorously recited for two odd millennia. It is the origin of the 'Chinese dream'. We see in the Chinese race an innate dreamer of socialist idealism. '*Datong*' accentuates 'advocating faith and cultivating harmony', starting from people-to-people social structures and extended to a peaceful international relationship. It contributes to peace for all of humanity.

The patriotic emotions and constructive opinions of *Shengshi weiyan* also impacted the mind of the teenage Mao Zedong (毛泽东) several decades later. Here we see the making of a second-wave, self-strengthening Chinese dreamer who had the audacity of 'haranguing commentaries on universal politics' (指点江山) and 'striking at the waves in mid-stream' (中流击水).That is what we all are familiar with.

Sun Yat-sen concluded that it was the Manchu administration that had led to the decay of China. He advocated 'driving away the Tatars, reviving China, establishing the republic, and distributing land rights equally' . As the son of a farmer of the Xiangshan area, he had profound sentiments towards the land. He was the earliest to raise the issue of redistribution of land ownership, thinking it of primary importance to the people's livelihood. The three principles of '*minsheng* (民生)' (people's livelihood), '*minzu* (民族)' (nationalism), and '*minquan* (民权)' (democracy) wove his dream of revitalizing China.

Of course, after he lived in England, and more so in the US, the prosperity of countries with an advanced culture influenced Sun Yat-sen's 'American dream' as well. As a dreamer to save China with revolution, Sun Yat-sen pursued a course for eternal prosperity for the Chinese nation, and resolved to convert his 'American dream' into the 'Chinese dream'.

Good at campaigning, Sun Yat-sen became a dreamer-cum-revolutionary. He was so confident when the twilight of the 20th–century dawned on the land of China. Seven years away from the victory of the 1911 Revolution in August 1904 and on the eve of the tenth anniversary of the Revive China Society, he gave a talk on 'The Real Solution to China's Problems'. In it, he described his grand 'Chinese dream':

> Once we realize the great goal of renewing China not only will the twilight of a new era dawn on our beautiful country, but also the entire humanity will share a brighter future. Universal peace will follow the birth of a new China. A grand venue that no one has dreamt of before will open to the socioeconomic activities of the civilized world.
>
> It is entirely our own responsibility to save China. However, as this problem is connected with the interest of the world in recent times, we have to appeal to the people of the civilized world universally, especially to the American people, for moral sympathy and material support so that we can succeed, our movement will be facilitated, unnecessary sacrifices will be avoided, and the misunderstanding and interference of the world powers will be prevented. (*The Collected Works of Dr. Sun Yat-sen*, 孙中山全集, I: 255).

Sun Yat-sen also observed: 'The selfless people of the entire world will gradually understand that the revitalization of a country which is one fourth of the world's population is the beatitude for humanity' (*The Collected Works of Dr. Sun Yat-sen*, I: 319).

for a Booming Era) for suggesting ways and means of getting China rich and strong, especially highlighting the role of all talents of the country by giving their best account.

Unfortunately, the corrupt Manchu government over a century ago could not embark on this road.

Sun Yat-sen rose after Zheng Guanying. He wrote about the Macau connection to his dream of revitalizing and saving China when he recounted the episode of his 'being kidnapped in London' (伦敦被难记):

> I went to Macau to know a political movement aimed at transforming China. Its name was *xing Zhong hui* (兴中会, Revive China Society) which felt China's political system not suitable for the times, and wanted to resort to peaceful means with an approach of gradualism, appealing to the imperial court to adopt a new system. The most important was to replace the decadent autocracy with a constitutional government. I was greatly impressed and became a member of the Party, hoping that it would work for the good of the country and welfare of the people. China had enough of its stupor. If there was no reform top-down it would be hopeless. This was why there was the establishment of the Revive China Society.

That was the time when Japanese troops were approaching Beijing. Our Party saw it as an opportunity while the imperial court was hesitant to repress the new party lest it lost the hearts and minds of the people. The news about the Party was not reported (to the Empress Dowager). After the Sino-Japanese War and the conclusion of peace, the imperial court issued an edict admonishing the petitioners and forbidding further memorials for reform.

Our Party was shocked and realized the futility of peaceful means. However, the desire for new politics was gathering momentum, and we were gradually moving away from pacifism towards relative militancy. Our comrades were all over the country. Those in high society were disillusioned by the corruption and arrogance of the military that was a total wreck in fighting foreign aggressors. There was increasing dissatisfaction among the people while the most emotional ones were determined to overthrow (the bad government) to bring change (to the country).

In 1879, the 13-year-old Sun Yat-sen went from Macau to study in Hawaii (which was yet to become a state in the United States). 'It was the first time that I saw the marvelous steamer, the expansive ocean which made me admire Western thought, and dream of the universe'. Even as a teenager, he wrote about the awakening dream of rescuing his country. China was too backward. In the same location of the estuary of the Pearl River, foreign-ruled Macau and Hong Kong were far more orderly than the Chinese homeland. This unfavourable contrast was quite a revelation, creating a hole in the dark house of the Chinese Empire that made light penetrating inside possible.

Four seas to One Family:
Overseas Chinese and Chinese dream

> For sixty years since China established trade relations with all countries the world has been on the move. However, how many people can discuss conservatism and reform, westernization and maritime defence, past and present, temporary solution and fundamental cure? Sunzi taught us about knowing one's own strength and the enemy's being the sure way to victory. It is a minor advice that can do a major job. Though I am not a talent…I feel that the solution for the crisis and the way for getting China rich and strong lie not only in having a strong army and navy, but also in having a parliament uniting the country and having adequate education. We must establish new schools, expand academies, sharpen technology and perfect civil examinations so that all talents of the country can give their best account. We must develop agriculture and irrigation, and transform poor soil into fertile field so that we get optimal benefit from terrestrial resources. We must build railways, install telephone lines, reduce taxation, and protect commerce so that we get maximum flow of goods.

The idea of 'having a parliament uniting the country and having adequate education' (议院上下同心、教养得法) was democratic politics in a nutshell, and the Chinese dream of Zheng Guanying.

Zheng Guanying firmly believed in 'without being rich the country cannot become strong, without being strong it cannot remain rich.' He vigorously advocated 'commercial war being the essential while soldierly war being the trifle' (商战为本，兵战为末). He was China's earliest constitutionalist who thought industry could save China. Let us see how he described his life-long quest for his Chinese dream for a rich and strong country more than a hundred years ago.

During a mid-Autumn festival evening in 1909, on the 15th anniversary of China's defeat in the first Sino-Japanese War, the 68–year–old Zheng Guanying wrote his famous essay on how to make China rich and strong, all the while enjoying the full moon:

> When a country wants to defend itself from foreign aggression it must strengthen itself. When a country wants to strengthen itself it must enrich itself. The prerequisite of enriching a country lies in revitalizing industry and commerce, and the prerequisite of revitalizing industry and commerce lies in the emphasis on education, establishment of the Constitution, heightening morality, and reforming politics. Constitution is the foundation of the country. Morality is the root of scholarship. Education is the resource of human talents. Politics determines the rise and fall of enterprise. If politics is not reformed, enterprise cannot prosper.

We still feel the excitement of this observation when we read it after a hundred years. It seems to have been written especially for China today.

The dream of our forebears will not be forgotten by their posterity.

I still remember Premier Wen Jiabao's (温家宝) visit to Macau in November 2010. In his speech, he praised Zheng Guanying's *Shengshi weiyan* (盛世危言) (Cautions politics. Constitution is the foundation of the country. Morality is the root of scholarship. Education is the resource of human talents. Politics determines the rise and fall of enterprise. If politics is not reformed, the enterprise cannot prosper.

Zheng Guanying (郑观应), 'Preface' of Shengshi weiyan houpian (盛世危言后篇, Supplement to Cautions for a Booming Era, 1909)

What is a dream? A dream is the awakening of the inner consciousness of the people. There is the age-old Chinese saying of '*ri you suosi, ye you suomeng*' (日有所思，夜有所梦). That is: in daytime we think, at night we dream.

What is the 'Chinese dream'? It is a dream for revitalizing China into a rich and strong country, and a dream for a secure, healthy, and happy life for the people. It is a rational quest for an ideal life.

As a sleeping lion for a century, China woke up from its stupor, gained its freedom and independence, and several generations have struggled hard for a hundred years to make it a top-ranking economy and a great political power on its own feet. Now wakened, China has regained its majestic outlook and is rising peacefully.

During the modern period, when the setting-sun of the Chinese imperial system went down and China started its stupor, two intellectuals arose from Xiangshan (香山) and established a mentor-disciple relationship in Macau. One was Zheng Guanying (郑观应, 1842–1922)who started to write his classic *Shengshi weiyan* (盛世危言) (Cautions for a Booming Era) on the eve of the first Sino-Japanese War (1894–95) to wake up the *booming-era* stupor of the imperial dynasty and show the road-map to his countrymen who had lost their direction. The other was Sun Yat-sen (孙中山, 1866–1925)who started traveling from place to place to mobilize his countrymen and became the pioneer of the Chinese revolutionary movement, opening a new chapter of Chinese history.

People of Xiangshan (香山) area on the coast of Lingding Sea (伶仃) ('Lintin' of the British East India Company records) at the estuary of the Pearl River were deeply impacted by the maritime powers. They had a reputation for 'leading the tide and daring to act before everyone else' (得风气之先，敢为天下先). They were intellectuals conversant in Chinese as well as foreign thoughts, having the deepest insight into the modern world while maintaining full confidence in traditional culture.

Zheng Guanying was a businessman by profession while a political thinker at heart. He had no ambitions for any political career, but devoted himself to the study of the ways and means to make China rich and strong. He completed his book, *Shengshi weiyan* in 1892 in the Zheng family mansion in Macau. In the 'Preface' to the first edition, he wrote:

Four seas to One Family:
Overseas Chinese and Chinese dream

Twilight of a New Era Dawns on Beautiful China

—The 'Chinese dream' from Zheng Guanying to date

Zheng Guoqiang 郑国强

Born in March, 1947 at Macau as a member of the extended clan of Zheng Guanying (郑观应), he also shares his ancestral home with Dr. Sun Yat-sen (孙中山)—the two early dreamers of modern China. He has half a century experience in the mass media of Macau since 1966, having worked with the *Macau Daily* (澳门日报), *Citizens' Daily* (市民日报) as editor at various levels. He is now the President and CEO of Macao Global Culture Communication Co., Ltd., of the Association For Macau Historical And Cultural Heritage Protection, and of Macau Television Transmission Association. He is also the Vice-President of Macau Scholars League as well as the Culture Media Association of Macau. He is also one of the leaders of the Centre for Zheng Guanying Studies and the Macau Association of Historical Studies dedicating himself to the protection of historical monuments and the popularization of Zheng Guanying's theories.

Once we realize the great goal of renewing China not only the twilight of the new era will dawn on our beautiful country, but also the entire humanity will share a brighter future. Universal peace will follow the birth of a new China. A grand venue that no one has dreamt of before will open to the socioeconomic activities of the civilized world.

—Sun Yat-sen, '*Zhongguo wentide zhen jiejue*' (中国问题的真解决, 'The Real Solution to China's Problems,' 1904)

When a country wants to defend itself from foreign aggression it must strengthen itself. When a country wants to strengthen itself it must enrich itself. The prerequisite of enriching a country lies in revitalizing industry and commerce, and the prerequisite of revitalizing industry and commerce lies in the emphasis on education, establishment of the Constitution, heightening morality, and reforming understand Marxism. The first generation of Chinese Marxists 'sinicized' Marxism, and successfully became ruling party mandated by the Chinese people.

In a period that heralds the Renaissance of the Sinic civilization, I hope contemporary Chinese Marxists will be able to comprehensively understand the core essence of Marxism, and effectively integrate them with Chinese dialectic thinking, to further the sinic-ization of Marxism. Through this, the socialist spirit behind Chinese philosophies and ethics can be theoretically grounded and developed, paving the way for the Chinese people to achieve the goals of two 'one hundred years' set out in the 18th National Congress of the Communist Party of China, and bring the Sinic civilization to new heights.

As an overseas Chinese—a descendant of the Sinic Civilization, this is my greatest Chinese dream at this very moment.

The development of science has changed the way we think over the past 300 years, often turning supposedly logical and rational thinking on its head. With increasing decline in the societal, political, financial, environmental and all other aspects of the global climate over the last 10 years, we need to start redefining what has become overly familiar to us before the 21st century, including 'rational' Western notions of freedom, democracy, human rights, and other social 'norms'.

In this period where China is recognized as the second largest economic power in the world, we need to look again to the civilizations of the Axial Age, and with the traditional Chinese ethics of inclusivism and tolerance, bring to fruition this great opportunity to harmonize Eastern and Western civilizations.

In summary, as we work towards the revival of the Sinic civilization in this critical period, if aspects of traditional Chinese philosophies can integrate with scientific advances discovered over the past 300 years, I am confident we will have the theoretical basis to forward a model of socio-cultural governance that differs from the West. These philosophies that are rationally-developed with strong ethnic characteristics may provide alterative solutions to the urgent social, political, economic and cultural problems we have in contemporary society.

In fact, as early as 1954, Einstein had reflected and made projections based on the philosophies developed since the Renaissance, Reformation and the Enlightenment. He said, 'The religion of the future will be a cosmic religion. Buddhism has the characteristics of what would be expected in a cosmic religion for the future: it transcends a personal God, avoids dogmas and theology; it covers both the natural & spiritual, and it is based on a religious sense aspiring from the experience of all things, natural and spiritual, as a meaningful unity. Buddhism answers this description. If there is any religion that would cope with modern scientific needs, it would be Buddhism.'

Friedrich Engels in his *Dialectics of Nature* also said, 'Dialectical thought, precisely because it presupposes investigation of the nature of concepts, is only possible for man, and for him only at a comparatively high stage of development, as it was with the Buddhists and Greeks'.

Influenced by Max Weber's *The Protestant Ethic and the Spirit of Capitalism*, Confucian Capitalism was in vogue in the 1980s, but after the Asian financial crisis, interest in Confucianism died down. But now, socialist China's GDP has already surpassed the U.S., becoming the core engine of the world's economy. Marxism, like thoughts from the Axial Age, will make a comeback, for 'whenever a social development faces critical problems or come to a crucial turning point, we will pay closer attention to the influence of Marxist thoughts'.

At the close of 2012, the head of China's Central Compilation and Translation Bureau told reporters that they were editing the 'Complete Works of Karl Marx and Friedrich Engels' with reference to historical findings, in order to comprehensively period in China, India and the Occident, to develop philosophies behind the major religions of today; and that in period of cultural renaissance, we have to look back to the Axial Age for inspiration.

Jaspers' observation highlights that influential thoughts developed during the Axial Age remains the foundation for philosophical debates of today, and demonstrates the systematicity of spiritual development in the current age. When he became aware of the laws of 'conditioning cause (缘起论)' under the Bodhi tree, Śākyamuni Buddha states: 'It is amazing that there is no being who is not fully endowed with the Tathāgata's wisdom. It is only due to false conceptualization that wisdom is not attained'. This indicates that both realms of matter and consciousness can be conquered and verified objectively and systematically.

Human history is one where scientific technologies continually transform the physical world and advance our material wealth; but in the process also cause catastrophic damage to our natural environment, and erode humanity's intrinsic spiritual and moral values, leading us away from the model of an enlightened 'noble savage' to become savage intellectual beings instead.

Since the formulation of calculus by Gottfried Wilhelm von Leibniz and Sir Isaac Newton in the 17th century, we have entered into an era where the emic studies of phenomenology, 'impermanence', 'instantaneous change' are given emphasis. Coming to the 19th century, Schopenhauer's philosophy of the Will provided the theoretical foundation and a realist perspective to the laws of causality, hence pulling Buddhism back from its metaphysical and transcendent form to its existential roots.

Entering into the 20th century, Einstein's General Theory of Relativity offered the possibility of warping space and time, and hence a scientific basis for the 'beginning-less' world-view of Buddhism. In this, there is an option for us to break free from the mythical confines of creationism and doomsday. Quantum physics and its uncertainty principle turned our attention to the role of the observer or 'self' as crucially involved in or the determiner in all things. Or in the words of Buddha, 'In the heavens above and (earth) beneath I alone am the honoured one'.

Into the 21st century, especially its first 20 odd years, the Hubble Space Telescope was carried into orbit, and man no longer needed complex mathematical calculations or esoteric discourse, but could for the first time through naked eyes gaze into our ever-changing universe since its proposed inception 13.7 billion years ago.

In September 2010, Stephen Hawking provides additional basis from theoretical physics for the Buddhist concept of Dependent Origination with his Model Dependent Realism. These scientific advances will gradually break down the mystical veil that obscures religious cosmology, theology, and other metaphysical disciplines; thereby bringing more credibility to these ideologies.

of the classical style of writing) under the pen name 'Learning Ren' (学任), and model his works after Liang Qichao (or Rengong)'s (梁启超号任公) 'Xin Min Ti' writing style. Fortunately Mao's teacher Mr. Yuan Jieliu (or Yuan Zhongqian) found out about this and ridiculed his essay to be like those of 'a news reporter', and criticized Liang's essay to be incoherent.

Mr. Yuan's incisive critique of the 'Xin Min Ti' prompted the astute Mao to 'change my writing style, study the writings of Han Yu, and learn the classical genre'. Mao later said 'Fortunately I had Master Big Beard Yuan, which is why I'm still able to adequately pen a piece of classical style essay'. And hence China did not lose a great poet in Mao Zedong.

Mao's rumination on being fortunate in his ability write in the classical, is worthwhile noting for those literati who devote themselves to the promotion and revival of a Sinic civilization. How many college students in China today are able to 'adequately pen a piece of classical style essay'?

It was during that time that Buddhism, lead by Master Taixu (太虚), evolved a 'Buddhism for Human Life (人生佛教)' to 'Buddhism for the Masses (群众的佛教)'; and in the absence of China's influence, together with the efforts of overseas Buddhist communities, developed the philosophy of 'Humanistic Buddhism (人间佛教)'. This opens another pathway towards understanding the wisdom of Buddhism, the sophistication of the Sinic civilization, and illuminates another chapter in the religious civilizations of the world.

In another fortuitous turn of fate, the German philosopher Arthur Schopenhauer interpreted the ancient wisdom of Indian Buddhist doctrines using European philosophical traditions on the Will. In his dissertation 'On the Fourfold Root of the Principle of Sufficient Reason', he states that 'nothing is without a ground or reason. It is a powerful and controversial philosophical principle stipulating that everything must have a reason or cause.'

In Buddhist nomenclature, this is Dependent Origination, or the existence of everything is dependent on other causes and conditions. Buddhism is about using the conditional existence of things to recognize the reality of 'emptiness' in the existence of being. In that moment of recognition, the true nature of being is revealed. In explicating the phylogenesis of phenomena, there is not only philosophical and logical truth, but more importantly, also the perspicacity of Karmic moral truth. In this sense, all roads lead to Rome when we're looking at the pinnacle of Eastern or Western intellectual civilization, and mutual harmonization can be attained.

The Axial Age, or Axial Period, is a term coined by German philosopher Karl Theodor Jaspers to describe the appearance of Socrates, Confucius, Laozi, Śākyamuni Buddha (Siddhārtha Gautama) within a relatively short period of history. He pointed out that revolutionary thinkers emerged within this short time to Apple founder Steve Jobs, began their eastward-looking journey by seeking the truth through Zen. From my conversation with a new generation of American Zen practitioners, they have integrated technology with the practice of Zen Buddhism, and initiated their own style of Zen meditation.

As Americans increasingly detach themselves from the church, these new believers have labeled themselves as 'nones' (I translated this word as 'nan shi' 赧士), which means the absence of guilt for not attending church. I believe that following former American President Carter's article *'Losing My Religion for Equality'* in 2009, this feeling of guilt will continue to dissipate.

According to a report in the New York Times (22 December 2012) citing survey results from the Pew Research Center: since 2008, American 'nones' have risen from 16% of the population to 20% in 2012, increasing at a rate of about 3–million per year, thereby becoming the second largest population of atheist after China.

Some churches, such as the Fourth Church of Christ in Colorado where I visited, have been remodeled as Zen centers, due to the dwindling number of church-goers. Such cases of churches turning into Zen meditation centers are not uncommon around the US. The most famous being the Garrison Institute in New York, which was previously the Monastery of Mary Immaculate.

An impact of globalization is the interesting phenomenon of the Chinese being highly interested in Western religions, while the 'West' pursues Zen Buddhism. With help of modern technology and neuroscience, Americans have made the practice of Zen more scientific, technologically advanced, modernized, accessible, measurable and practical, leading to the exponential growth of Zen practitioners in the West.

The above observations has made me optimistic that a great opportunity has presented itself, for the harmonization of eastern and western civilization through the propagation of Buddhism culture in tandem with technological advances. This would be constructive as a form of East-West cultural exchange and particularly beneficial for the huge communities of Buddhism practitioners in Hong Kong, Macau, Taiwan, and other regions in East Asia and the Indo-China Peninsula.

Such opportunities for cultural exchanges and harmonization can be traced back in history. Positive examples would be how, Mouzi (牟子), a governor and scholar in the Eastern Han Dynasty, integrated the wisdom of ancient India in Buddhist doctrines with Confucian and Taoist thoughts, and established the Zen School of Chinese Buddhism. This form of sinicized Han Buddhism spread throughout Eastern Asia, and influenced the development of Neo-Confucianism.

Negative examples would be how Chinese traditional culture was trampled upon in the face of exclusionary predisposition of other 'Western' cultures during the May Fourth Movement in 1919. For instance, Mao Zedong in his early year would indulged in the Plain Language (bai hua 白话) style of writing (instead developments in China. At that time, I dreamt of a China that could surpass Britain and America, that the Chinese people could be seen as equals among other nations, and that overseas Chinese would not be persecuted together with our culture.

In my university freshman year, Professor Xie lectured on Marxist economic principles in the last lecture of his course on Agricultural Economy. After the class, I immediately bought a copy of 'Das Kapital' by Karl Marx to read. I went to Canada for my further studies, which provided me with further opportunities to learn about and understand contemporary China. It was then that I decided to transform my dream to reality—I would go to China to gain firsthand experience of the tumultuous land that I often dreamt of.

I backpacked my way in China over more than ten coastal cities in two months. I also retrieved my grandmother's remaining deposits in the Bank of China (Xiamen branch), and distributed them to two distant uncles in Xiamen. During my travels, I saw the signs of a crumbling economy and impoverished country. As a guest invited home by a common Guangzhou citizen to have a meal, I saw him stir-frying vegetable with water instead of oil.

I spent 8 RMB (chinese dollar) on a bottle of Maotai (茅台) in a scarcely seen state-run shop. Although I had brought along the national ration tickets (liang piao 粮票), I used foreign exchange currency (wai hui juan 外汇卷); and as I normally had meals in the hotel, I rarely had the chance to use the tickets. I noticed that the Friendship Shops primarily sold daily consumables often seen in foreign countries, but did not allowed local Chinese to enter.

There was a notice at the Badaling section of the Great Wall that said: No entry for Foreigners. Although I had a 'Chinese Travel Pass' (中国人通行证) with me, the armed People's Liberation Army soldier there knew I was a 'foreigner' with a single glance. At the end of my travels, I dreamt of how China might soon be modernized and prosperous.

After completing my master in Canada, China had entered into a new era of economic reforms. After having experienced the commercial world for over 20 years, I left it without regret nor yearning. In the year 2002, after I sent my daughter for her undergraduate studies in Peking University, I returned to my roots and continued the legacy of my grandmother by studying the grand and noble thoughts of Chinese Buddhism and its culture.

Besides attending and giving various lessons, practicing Zen, and publishing papers, I also participate in international cultural forums, seminars and Buddhism conferences in Singapore, China, US, Hong Kong. Particularly in the US, I came into contact with many 'Buddhist Geeks', and personally seen the vibrant development of Buddhism websites and Zen meditative centers springing up around the country. Buddhism has become an upcoming trend in the religious practices of America.

Since the 1950s, America's Beat Generation such as the famous poet Gary Synder following discussion on the religious cultures between East and West will have such a distinction in mind. Readers are asked to take note of this.

Without such a distinction, an effective dialogue between Eastern and Western civilization is untenable. Even if such a dialogue took place, the result would inevitably be each side holding on to their own terms of reference, or simply reducing all forms of religion to be about guiding people to do good, or talking about some abstract concepts, such as 'universal love', 'conscience', 'peace', 'equality', 'human rights', etc., that do not actually engage both religious cultures.

The West have long upheld these abstract concepts to be 'universal values', thereby controlling the discourse on civilization, religion and 'universal values' in a form of western cultural hegemony.

To revive the Sinic civilization, we must first regain the ability to re-examine premises and the discourse on religious civilization and universal values, and not to engage each other on pre-established terms. What we should not do is to equate Confucius, Lord Laozi and Buddha as alternatives to Jehovah, Jesus, etc. Or to compare pragmatic concepts such as the benevolence (ren仁) of Confucius, Non-socialized action (wu mei无为) of Laozi, and great compassion of the Buddha with abstractions such as 'For God so loved the world'.

What's worse is that after the establishment of the People Republic of China in 1949, feudalism and colonialism were severely denounced without any critical reflection on traditional Chinese culture, resulting in thoughtless reverence of Western thoughts in the mass media of China today, much to the angst of overseas Chinese. This will not only obscure the understandings of Christians and believers of other religions, but also work against a renaissance of Sinic civilization.

In the mid-fifties of the last century, my uncle attended the first Guangzhou Import and Export Goods Expo as a member of a team coordinated by Mr. Chen Jiageng (陈嘉庚), on the invitation from Prime Minister Zhou Enlai. My clan hence became the first importer of Proprietary Chinese Medicine (Zhong cheng yao (中成药)) in Singapore and Malaysia. I remembered that as a child, I often had to go to the warehouse to handle shattered medicine bottles due to shipping, resulting in cuts on my fingers. My first impression of China was thus formed.

I received a Chinese education since young. During that period of time, incidents discriminating the overseas Chinese were frequent. Just as China was on its path towards reformation and its open door policy, the only overseas Chinese university was ordered to shut down, all Chinese schools were anglicized overnight, and the use of our mother tongue (Chinese regional 'dialects') was systematically penalized. It seems that Chinese culture was being persecuted.

During my secondary school, China was engulfed in political turmoil. I often listened to the Xianmen dialect news broadcast from the Central People Broadcasting with my elders during dinner time, united in our concern with a Malaysian citizen, and now am a Singaporean citizen. But the one identity that remained constant despite the changing political climate was the Chinese blood that flowed in my veins, identifying me as a descendant of Sinic Civilization (huan xia zi men (华夏子民).

My grandmother never went to school but could chant Buddhist sūtras. My parents also did not receive much education, and were not well versed in Confucianism. We considered ourselves as descendants of Sinic Civilization because we had ancestral shrines at home and altars for the worship of Buddhas and noble bodhisattvas. We celebrate all traditional Chinese festivals. The rituals and ceremonies our family practiced during birth, birthday, marriage, funeral, etc. are all centred on Confucius, Lord Laozi, the Buddha, Yellow Emperor (黄帝). We also had rituals to appease the ghostly world (Yulan / Ullambana Feast (盂兰胜会)) and to venerate different local deities including General Guanyu关帝爷 and goddess Mazu (妈祖).

These gods and deities were brought over with reverence by overseas Chinese when they left their ancestral homes to travel over long distances to settle in a foreign land. The veneration of these same gods as those honoured by mainland Chinese form a culture that ties Chinese diasporas with their Motherland, like blood that flows through the umbilical cord. The contiguity of a Sinic Civilization depends on the veneration and cultural practices developed around the three pillars of Confucianism, Buddhism and Taoism, embodied by the burning incense sticks at the altars.

In September 2010, famous theoretical physicists Stephen Williams Hawking and Leonard Mlodinow co-wrote and published *The Grand Design*. I translated the book title as *Da yin yuan* ((大因缘) meaning great causes and conditions). This book offered a 'Model of Dependent Realism', to explain the origins of universe and life without the design of a 'Creator'. 'There is no picture- or theory-independent concept of reality. The idea that a physical theory or world picture is a model and a set of rules that connect the elements of the model to observations.' Furthermore, the book paved a way for religion to be understood from a scientific perspective.

Western religions have predominantly been about an omniscient, omnipresent and supreme Creator. Moreover, religion is seen as an interpretation of phenomena, and not an explanation of phenomena. Clearly, this differs greatly from the Eastern religious perspective.

Confucianism states 'Four Seasons successively occur, and all things are created'. Laozi explains the transformation of Dao as 'The Dao begets one; one begets two; two begets three; three begets the myriad creatures'. Buddhists offer a powerful theory—Dependent Origination, all subject to causes and conditions. Karma theory plays a fundamental role in human behaviors. All three doctrines above have one thing in common: that there are no creator for the universe and the world. My

My Chinese Dream

—A great opportunity to harmonize Eastern and Western Civilizations

Lin Mingya 林明雅

Born in Singapore and spent over 20 years running a business in the Greater China region, he is currently a senior researcher at the Singapore Buddhist Federation. Prior to his current role, he used to teach Buddhism Ecology at the Buddhist College of Singapore and History of Buddhism in China and Buddhist Studies at the Singapore Buddhist Federation. He has a Bachelor of Economics from Nanyang University in Singapore and Masters in Economics from York University in Canada.

Dreams are complex and myriad things. Unlike animals, Man can dream, and also interpret and analyze their dreams. This was how primitive religions were first developed. The ancient Egyptians deal with dreams through different rituals and ceremonies. Expecting to get inspirations from gods, they went to Incubation Temple to make dreams, and have them analyzed by priests in order to avoid of disasters and to create good fortune. Religious culture has developed hand in hand with other human civilized cultures. In Karl Marx's words, 'Religion is the general theory and outline for whole world, consisting of everything'.

The first Chinese dictionary, (entitled) Shuo wen jie zi (说文解字) in Eastern Han Dynasty by Xu Shen (许慎), lists 'Zong'(宗) as 'to respect ghosts and spirits of ancestors'; and 'jiao' (教) as 'to educate, cultivate and instruct'.

However, influenced by Western religious studies, the Chinese term "zong jiao" is now simply used as a translation for 'religion'.

I was born in 1948, three years after World War II. My grandparents emigrated to Singapore from Xiamen, China. My grandmother was a vegetarian throughout her life and a devout Buddhist. I am a third generation overseas Chinese. I was born as a British colonial subject, which later transitioned into a Malayan citizen, then

Part II
Chinese Dream and the World

China that will not try so hard to be Chinese.

And within the new internationalised China itself? A resurgence, I hope, of philosophy and poetry; less emphasis on material luxuries. There was a great Tang age. I am told my family histories on both my father and mother's sides stretch back to the Tang. It was a golden age, and I am proud of that golden age. However, all nations have their golden ages. The European Renaissance was one in which the artists discovered how to paint perspective - how to depict what the eye saw of closeness and distance and those points of observation in between. Being able to look back with perspective and being able to look forward with perspective are qualities to be shared by all cultures and civilizations. A China that could do that? Discuss that with others—America as well as Africa? Bring something special to the table but share in the eating of all foods? That's maturity. Well, I could be proud of that.

because I thought the Chinese diaspora did not represent what I already knew of Chinese history and culture. No one could talk about the philosophers and mystics I encountered in my endless reading. So, on the basis of my reading of Chinese philosophy and mysticism, what kind of China would I like to see? What is my Chinese fantasy? What would give me hope in China?

III

There are strange similarities between Taoist sages and Persian poets. Both pretend to be drunk all the time - but they are both drunk and using drunkenness as a metaphor for abandoning the cares of the world. By that I think they meant the over-careful ordering of the world into strict ideologies and forms of formal organisation. The sages never abandoned the world. They had to eat, buy alcohol, and acquire the boats or oxen upon which they explored the world. But they did not need an anchor in the world. They did not feel committed to one central place. For them, the Middle Kingdom, the Central Kingdom, would have had no meaning. When they went out into the world they were not afraid—for they went out with good humour and acceptance of whatever it was they would meet. They had no stereotypes.

Once there was a Taoist sage who fell in love with the ocean. The ocean could take him to many new lands. The trip, travelling on the ocean, was a pleasure in itself. He had no boat. He had a sword. Perhaps in the new lands he encountered he was some kind of peacekeeper. He didn't care whether he lived or died in these new lands. But, before he reached each new landfall, he would balance on his sword and surf the ocean - laughing his head off - and going where the waves and wind seemed to take him. His hair blew in the wind. He was always in gentle conversation with the dolphins and the great albatrosses. They would guide him from below and above. This being 'one with nature' is in fact a method. It allowed him to sail across all seas. If he was a peacekeeper in the new lands, his sword was far too rusty from the ocean to be used as a weapon. So when men came for him, he would smile—and they would take out chopsticks.

I do not think for one moment that a nation can live like this. The ethics of Confucius must come into play somewhere. But I think a nation can learn to relax like this. To be sure about itself in a relaxed way like this. To take the world by a storm of relaxed interaction.

It should also plant many trees in Africa and in China itself.

The China of my fantasy, of my hopeful future, is a China that does not try so hard. That recognises the great differences and individualities of the world—including Africa and all 54 states within a continent that could swallow China three times over. I want a truly internationalist China. One that understands the international. I could live in a China like that. But that means I fantasise about a hardened up quickly.

But, three years before, I had gone to Beijing to advise on the Darfur issue. Many American film stars had been accusing the Chinese of being wicked by not denouncing President Bashir of Sudan, of being interested only in buying his oil, and not caring whether he killed his own people. I was greeted by many senior people who expressed amazement that China was being accused in this way. 'What can we possibly do?' they asked. 'You make me ashamed,' I said. 'The Chinese can do much. It doesn't have to be in public. But the President can express strong words in private to his Sudanese counterpart. Of all countries, it is China who has leverage on this issue.' I addressed a conference and repeated some of these words. 'The Chinese say they are helping Africa. This is true. But it also helps many bad Presidents. And many Chinese businessmen are corrupt and, above all, racist. Once, liberation soldiers would tell me of their gratitude to the Chinese. Now, in Africa, I am ashamed to be Chinese.'

II

The China of today is better than the China of yesterday and of any previous time. Although there are great limitations, people have more prosperity and freedom than at any time of Chinese history. It is secure from the imperial incursions of the nineteenth and twentieth centuries. Once again, it leads the world in many scientific and technological fields. Chinese musicians and artists are much admired and two Chinese authors have recently won the Nobel Prize for Literature. The balance between normally cautious state affairs and a more liberal world order will become even more difficult in the years ahead. I do not wish to say how China should approach this balance. I do want to say that, whatever it does, China must learn to understand the world better.

Chinese diplomats live isolated lives in embassy compounds and, when they take part in public occasions, read official speeches. They do not interact with their audiences. Chinese English-language television news channels still produce reports that are favourable to the Chinese Government. In this, they are worse than the BBC, CNN, Al Jazeera, and even the Iranian Press TV. Only Russia Today has a similar sense of bias in its news programmes. A mature country doesn't need to do that—because a mature country knows that the watching world doesn't believe what is broadcast. The watching world would be much more impressed if Chinese television was sometimes critical of China. It would then seem that the country is mature, self-reflective, and honest. And not afraid to show this side of itself to the world.

But I would also like the country to feel free enough to recapture some of the best parts of its past. By that I mean its philosophy and poetry.

When I decided, as a child in New Zealand, to abandon being Chinese, that was or weapons of our own. I have maintained this as a practice ever since, and will not travel with an armed escort or carry arms myself. But I have had more guns pointed at my heart and head than most people have had hot breakfasts. My liaison level was at Lieutenant Colonel rank, and when I met the Lt. Colonels of Robert Mugabe's army they carried more than arms. Seeing I was Chinese, they took out chopsticks. They said, 'your people came to help us in our hour of need, no one else did, so today we will eat as your people eat.' At that moment, I felt very proud to be Chinese.

There have been 33 years of African adventures since then, and some in the Middle East and other parts of the world as well. In Africa, the most momentous were in the early 1980s, as part of the reconstruction of Uganda after the disastrous rule of Amin—huge parts of the country were devastated; in the early 1990s, in both Eritrea and Ethiopia, after the fall of the Stalinist dictator, Mengistu - and, again, I saw endless death and destruction; in the early 2000s as, once again, Zimbabwe fell apart; in 2010, in South Sudan as another destroyed country edged its way towards a troubled independence; and, more recently, I have been working with the Libyan effort to reconstruct a country that simply refuses to be reconstructed. In that time, there have also been many negotiations. I took part in the Trilateral Dialogue between high-level African, American and Chinese delegations on trade with Africa. The Chinese were amazed I sat with the Africans. And I was involved, albeit as a minor player, in the first and last negotiations (1984 and 1989) to free Nelson Mandela. But there was an interesting episode in South Sudan.

I had been deployed to Lakes Province, and instructed to seek shelter in Rumbek, then still a town filled with violence. But the liberation movement had started there and so observation of the elections in that area was symbolically important. But I had been given a very inexperienced team to lead. They shouldn't have been there. There was no shelter to be had and a curfew was about to be imposed on the town. Just as the sun was setting, I found a collection of UN peacekeeping camps. One camp was occupied by Canadian and Ukrainean soldiers. One was occupied by Kenyan soldiers. And one was occupied by Chinese soldiers. 'Would you have a floor where my people can sleep tonight?' Fortunately, the Ukraineans had some floor space. I didn't even bother to ask the Chinese. You, my readers, know as well as I do what the answer would have been. But I awoke at 5am the next morning and went out to watch the soldiers exercise. The Chinese were out running—and they looked at me as if an alien from outer space had suddenly arrived in their midst. I was wearing a very grubby white shirt. I was unshaven. My hair was blowing as the sun rose. I must have looked like something out of a kung fu movie. I looked back at the soldiers staring at me. Too many were tubby. They didn't look like frontline soldiers to me. And they weren't. In Sudan, the Chinese soldiers were backup technical troops. For the troubles ahead I hope they toughened up and wash very much. I used a bath for the first time when I was seven, when my family also was able to move to the new suburbs of wooden houses with bathrooms but no flushing toilets. But I could go to school. I studied ferociously. I realised I had to speak English better than my white classmates. And I deliberately stopped speaking Chinese. It wasn't even proper Chinese, was what I thought. Not even proper Cantonese. I wanted to be a successful New Zealander—until, shortly afterwards, for reasons I have never understood, I started having nightly dreams about Europe and Africa. Cypress trees in Umbria. I had no idea that they were Cypress trees in Umbria until as an adult I went there and saw trees and hills just like in my dreams. As for Africa, the dreams were of poverty - and this poverty was also brown. When, in 1960, *Life* magazine, weeks after the event (it took six weeks for each copy to reach New Zealand), carried the famous photo of the Sharpeville massacre in South Africa, covering two of its large pages with this one photo of white policemen shooting and beating black people, I was outraged. I was 13, and I knew I was going to Africa. I was going to be the New Zealander who left New Zealand. My teachers had already taught me to speak like an Englishman. I was going to go to the great universities in Europe, under green trees, and then go to Africa.

But, before then, I studied and I wrote. By my early 20s I had become nationally known as a poet and an intellectual. I had my own small publishing house. And, since it was the late 1960s and early 1970s, I demonstrated and fought in the streets against the Vietnam war, against links with Apartheid South Africa, basically against anything that oppressed other people. My friends and I occupied the American consulate. We were thrown into police cells and made a stand in the courts. We were not afraid, and the university's law professors came to help us. In 1973, when I had been elected the national student president, I helped lead the way for New Zealand to recognise the People's Republic of China—and the days of attachment to the government in Taiwan faded away, even among the Chinese. I had long hair, I wore long silk scarves and long coats and long boots, and looked like a 17th century English highwayman. I had notorious affairs with many beautiful women, but none of them was Chinese. Foreign scholars studied what I had done for their PhD theses from Berkeley: taking integration by storm. I became a successful newspaper editor and then, at 27, left New Zealand and I have never lived there again. I refused even to visit for ten years and, by then, I was a veteran of the great adventures of modern African history.

These adventures began in the last days of Rhodesia, from January to March 1980, as it made the fraught journey to independence as Zimbabwe. I was part of the implementation of the peace treaty between the warring factions, monitoring the ceasefire, the electoral process, and the behaviour of many soldiers (who kept their arms) from four recognised armies. We travelled without protection be a ship evacuating New Zealand soldiers. The refugees had no idea where New Zealand was. However, my mother's recent ancestors had been gold miners in the far away country - and there were stories of discrimination by white communities, and other stories of the wild Maori warriors. But at least the new country was not engulfed by war.

Sure enough, when they landed there was discrimination. There were even laws against Chinese people. The two families arranged a marriage between my father and mother when they were teenagers. I was the first born, and they were only 18. In 1949, the Labour Party was in power in New Zealand, and it said that, with the Communist victory in China, the Chinese refugees could stay. Until the second wave of Chinese migrants and refugees from Vietnam in the 1970s, and the wave of Chinese from Hong Kong afterwards, the first generation of Chinese in New Zealand voted Labour as a rock-solid electoral 'thank you'. But there were no Chinese MPs, no Chinese Knights, no Chinese in any public office. The discriminatory laws were repealed, but to grow up Chinese in New Zealand was to grow up as a tolerated outcast. But you knew you were an outcast. And the refugees lived for many years in poverty. My first memories were of poverty. Somehow, everything was coloured brown. I just remembered everything in brown. I think that was when I came to love trees. Trees were brown but, on top, the leaves were green. In the leaves were birds. The birds loved to sing. So my first memories of loveliness were green leaves and birds. Even now, as I wander Africa, I am always looking for birds.

To be fair to the white New Zealanders, they were recovering from World War Two, where the small country had lost a greater percentage of young men that any other Allied nation. Rationing of foodstuffs was still practised in my first years. The white population was also poor. Good manners were practised but in a rough and raw way. New suburbs sprang up around Auckland, where the young war veterans built their own houses from timber. There were often no sewage facilities and night-soil collectors were as common in New Zealand as in a third world country. In many ways, it was in fact a developing country, or a redeveloping one, and it didn't have time to waste on integrating Chinese refugees.

The Chinese population was also spread out in the suburbs. It would congregate in the very small China Town in the central street called Greys Avenue. In fact, China Town was basically two restaurants and two Chinese grocery shops. As a Sunday treat, my family would eat at one of the restaurants. It was called the Chungking - after the Kuomintang capital in the war against the Japanese. And that was the key unifying factor among the Chinese in New Zealand: they voted Labour but they also supported the Nationalist regime in Taiwan. If their New Zealand hosts were rough and ready, so were they. Everyone spoke countryside Cantonese, spat in the streets, and had no high cultural habits. No one seemed to

Part I
My Trail Trodden by My Feet

Sailing All the Seas Balanced on a Sword

Stephen Chan 斯蒂芬·陈

He has been twice Dean at the School of Oriental & African Studies in the University of London, and has held Honorary and Visiting Professorships at many universities internationally. In 2010 the Queen awarded him the OBE(Order of the British Empire) 'for services to Africa and higher education'; and the International Studies Association awarded him the title 'Eminent Scholar'. Stephen has published 29 academic books, 5 volumes of poetry and 2 novels. He was an international civil servant and is still asked to participate in diplomatic work on a regular basis. However, he also conducts a slum and ghetto-based martial arts and education project in several African cities which has served to develop many hundreds of young people. In his youth he was a rock'n roll guitarist and fashion model and was recently brought out of 'retirement' to model Savile Row suits for a national photographic campaign.

I

I do not have a Chinese dream. I have a Chinese fantasy. I have no past in China. I have a hope for the future China. When I visit China I feel misunderstood—as someone who looks Chinese, but also Japanese, so people whisper behind my back that I am surely Japanese and to be scorned; someone with long hair like a rock star, not like a professor; someone who is 'sort of Chinese', who should try harder to understand and fit into the new China. All I want is for the new China to understand the outside world from which I come. Where I come from I can look and speak as I like. I do not have to fit into a stereotype. I feel China looks at the world in stereotypes. Across the many seas of the world there are no stereotypes.

I was born in 1949, the year of the Revolution. My parents had come as children to New Zealand. They were refugees of the war in China against Japan. My mother remembered fleeing across fields of dead bodies and watching her own mother bribe Chinese soldiers for safe passage. My father's family fled in the second-to-last ship to escape Hong Kong harbour before it fell to the Japanese. It just happened to fuels, heavy metal ions, and pesticides all have similar long-lasting and cross-generational effects. Recognizing the huge challenges in China in controlling air pollution, we cannot underestimate the adverse health effects of PM2.5, diesel exhaust particles, and polycyclic aromatic hydrocarbons on childhood and adult asthma, cardiovascular diseases, stroke, cancer and dementia-related disease in its population.

China has the capital and the technological base to significantly contribute to these technological advancements for its people. In fact, it must do it as the health care costs and the economic cost of health for this huge population would not allow the contrary. I hope China can become a leader of and a collaborative partner with these advancements. For millions of years, human health and environment have been inseparable. When the two are in sync, prosperity happens. The contrary invites suffering.

My biggest Chinese Dream is to see China become a respectable and responsible 'superpower.' That is, it helps improve the life of people in China and in the world. As a scientist, I tend to look at things inductively. I would start from learning about individual problems and find out if there are any systematic connections among the problems. The role of the scientist is to observe, question, and interpret before coming up with suggestions for solutions, and anticipate what could be the intended and unintended effects of the proposed solutions. I believe if every scientist worked this way, all societies, China and the whole world included, would be able to make rational decisions.

As environmental scientists, we hope ordinary citizens can breathe clean air, consume safe food and water, and live a healthy lifestyle. Yes, getting higher wages and accumulating more wealth is a popular dream, but hopefully not at the expense of one's health and that of future generations. While the government is trying to increase productivity and feed those who suffer from malnutrition, individual citizens who have benefited from economic growth should start working on their long-term well-being and responsibilities: eating less, exercising more, reducing unnecessary consumption, and preserving the environment. Failure to do that, given the sheer size of China's population and consumption, can accelerate the depletion of natural resources in China and the world.

and Antiandrogens for NIEHS, and the National Toxicology Program. I received numerous teaching and research awards including the National Science Foundation Career Advancement Award for Women in Science, the Women in Urology Award for Excellence in Urologic Research in 2007, a recognition from the 127th General Assembly of the Ohio Senate for uncovering a fetus as a potential origin of prostate cancer, and the 2013 Prostate Cancer Foundation Mentor of Excellence Award.

The academic circle in many American universities is filled with all races. For all these years in America, I have often been identified as a Chinese scholar from the Mainland or Taiwan. My lab is almost like a United Nations, even though there are more Chinese. I am also regularly interacting with scholars from both sides of the Taiwan Strait. More and more scholars are coming from China nowadays; many have returned and become very successful. I received plenty of support in my early career from many generous scholars from Taiwan. They went out of their way to help young Chinese faculty develop their career. To keep this tradition going, I have been helping Chinese scholars in many ways: helping them write grant proposals, establishing collaborations, enlarging their network, nominating them to responsible positions, supporting their candidacy in selection committees, and promoting them to leadership positions.

Yet, despite such exceptional academic and administrative accomplishments, as an Asian woman, I have continuously been challenged with being marginalized and by-passed in various stages of my career. One of my American Dreams is that Asian Americans will be fairly treated in the US society.

Today, modern medicine is becoming capable of precisely identifying all the variations in one's DNA using a technology called the next-generation sequencing to enable better prediction, prevention, diagnosis, and prescription for the right treatment. As the director of the Center of Environmental Genetics and with over 150 members in the Center,we focus on understanding how a person's genetic environment interaction will affect the risk of disease development and health outcome. This line of research is particularly important for China as its economic development also ushers in unprecedented environmental pollution problems.

I hope China could strike a balance between economic growth and conservation of its environment as 1.2 billion people's health is at risk. Current handling of water, air, soil, and heavy metal will have long lasting impacts on future generations. My research has showed that through a process called 'epigenetics,' disease risk and health outcomes can be determined as early as during and before conception. The detrimental effects can also be passed through generations. For example, our findings clearly demonstrated that in utero or perinatal exposure to the endocrine disrupting chemical, Bisphenol A, increased the risk of prostate and breast cancer in adult life and this impact may last for more than three generations. Other pollutants such as those released from incomplete combustion of fossil submissive Asian American woman to one who would speak up, lead by action, voice concerns, and implement solutions.

As my research became more clinical and translational, I moved over to head up the Translational Studies and Urological Studies programs in the Surgery Department of the University of Massachusetts Medical Center. Soon after being appointed as Vice Chair of Research in the Department, my service was sought after by many institutions. I accepted an offer from the UC Medical Center to become chair of its Department of Environmental Health, one of the top departments in the country. It has about 50 full-time faculty members and over 250 graduate students, along with medical fellows and professionals for training in biostatistics, bioinformatics, epidemiology, molecular toxicology, occupational safety and medicine, industrial hygiene, public health, and environmental genetics. Each year we have received over $20 million in research funding and have published about 200 papers. I continue to be blessed with multiple research grants, including a NIH-funded Center for Environmental Genetics that involves over 100 scientists.

I have served on advisory boards at various universities and national grant review sections, I have routinely chaired or served on the Expert Advisory Panel of various programs at dozens of institutions including those organized by Johns Hopkins University, University of Pennsylvania, UC-Berkeley, MD Anderson Cancer Center, and the University of Michigan. Outside of the USA, I have chaired or served on research grant application review committees/panels in the United Kingdom, Canada, Israel, Taiwan, and Hong Kong.

I am also a regular editor for several journals and an ad hoc reviewer for dozens of journals. I have been active in the professional networks, including being the Chair-Elect of the Hormonal Carcinogenesis Gordon Research Conference, Chair-elect of the Society for Basic Urologic Research, member of the American Urology Association, Endocrinology Society, Prostate Cancer Research Program, Society of Toxicology, and the American Association for Cancer Research. I have organized many national and international conferences and have been the chair or keynote speaker in these conferences. I was also honored to be the Speaker of the 2002 National Institute of Environmental Sciences Annual Speaker Series and the Inaugural Speaker of the California Environmental Protection Agency Speaker Series.

I have been active in frontier scientific activities such as chairing the National Toxicology Program Subcommittee to Review High Throughput Technology Application in Roadmap Initiatives, and serving on the National Academies of Sciences Standing Committee on Use of Emerging Science for Environmental Health Decisions. I have regularly chaired scientific review and policy committees for several National Institutes of Health and the Department of Defense, including the Office of Dietary Supplements, the Sub-committee on Androgens

Cultural Revolution in China. I started thinking about how our deeply rooted Chinese culture of modesty and the lack of training in communicating have prevented us from speaking up. I admired those who did stand up, and began to dream about Chinese as people who could express themselves, get their ideas heard, and put into action their visions. Meanwhile, there was nothing I could do or any channel I could communicate through, until I studied hard enough to get into one of the best universities in Asia—the University of Hong Kong (HKU).

My fate changed when my parents decided against the traditional notion that women need not learn much, that their daughter should go to college. There is another Chinese tradition that intellectuals should be socially conscious. I participated in various student activities and visited major cities as well as smaller towns in the mainland and Taiwan. I also spent a summer in Pity Me (in northeast England, a small and really poor town by Western standards) and backpacked around major cities in Europe. I was so impressed by the train stations in Europe and hoped China one day would have such an advanced transportation system. Through many contrasting experiences, my understanding of China at that point was that it needs drastic modernization in order to bring people's life up to Western levels. In addition to internal changes, China would also need a tremendous amount of outside investment in finance, science and technology; indeed, so much that few people could even dream about.

Like many overseas scholars, learning 'Western' science and technology was one way we could better serve China, our country of residence, and the rest of the world. Such a dream has stayed with me over the years and become a driving force to help me overcome all challenges in pursuit of excellence and leadership so that I could contribute more.

In 1974, I received the Most Outstanding Graduate of the Year Award and won a full scholarship toward a Ph.D. degree at HKU. I worked very hard and finished the doctoral requirements in three years, only to face the reality that, especially for a female, there was little chance of pursuing an academic career without further training abroad. I set off for postdoctoral training at Boston University, thinking that in a year or two I could return with a faculty position waiting. Instead, I got an offer from Tufts University, a consistently-ranked top–30 university in the US. While there, I worked 14 hours/day, 7 days/week for 18 years. Fortunately, my academic career took off.

I started getting federal research funding continuously. I was among the most junior faculty invited to review federal grant proposals and journal articles. After a relatively short period of time, Tufts promoted me to full professor and then to an Associate Dean of Research, Graduate Studies and Continuous Education. While at Tufts, I was lucky enough to learn from a cadre of influential women leaders. Their mentorship and fellowship transformed me from a stereotypically

My Life and Dream about Environmental Health

Ho Shuk—mei 何淑薇

Shuk-mei Ho, Ph. D. , is currently the Schmidlapp G. Jacob Endowed Chair/ Chairperson of the Department of Environmental Health and Associate Dean for Basic Research at the University of Cincinnati College (UC) of Medicine. She is also the Director of the Center of Environmental Genetics, a National Institute of Environmental Health Sciences funded Center at UC. In addition, she is recently appointed Director of the Cincinnati Cancer Center formed by the UC College of Medicine, UC Health, and Cincinnati Children's Hospital Medical Center (its pediatric cancer is currently ranked #1 in the USA). This Center of 1,000 cancer research and patient care professionals aims at generating innovative scientific discoveries that can be translated to improve the quality of cancer care and prevention in the region, the USA and the world. She is internationally known for her contributions in prostate carcinogenesis, estrogen action, early origin of complex diseases including asthma and cancer, and as a mediator of gene and environment interaction. Her seminal work on the epigenetic reprogramming effects of bisphenol A raised public health concerns and policy changes in the country.

Growing up in colonial Hong Kong, I always had a complex view of China and being Chinese. China as a country was vague in my young mind while being Chinese was always a source of pride that was often challenged by the news and history. While our teachers and parents always taught us to be a good person, they never linked 'goodness' with politics. Like most students in Hong Kong, I had little understanding of politics and the history of China. Our Chinese history curriculum stopped at the end of the Qing Dynasty. Complacency was viewed as a virtue and a means to get ahead especially for a young female. We did not dream much. We were just told that the harder you worked, the more you can help. But how?

Even though I graduated at the top of my high school class and was the head prefect, I did not treasure the opportunity to express my thoughts. That is, until I was chosen to deliver the Founder's Day speech. It was a time when frequent upheavals broke out over social injustice in Hong Kong and triggered by the

the invader's devil dream and ultimately built a new China in 1949.

With no serious cultural arts initiated by a ruling government for cultivation of social resources, how could its citizenry think creatively in science and technology, and breakthrough the boundaries for outsourcing manufactory? Over the past twenty years, China has been benefited by a jump-started economic metaphor of the twenty-first century—As it was characterized by Thomas Friedman, *The world is Flat*, under which China has been providing services for a vast and diverse volume of outsourcing and offshoring business that are financially manipulated by the Western powers via economic globalization. It has turned China's manufacturing industry into an assembly line of blood/sweat factory across the globe. Today China's GDP ranks as the world's second largest economy. At the same time, a previously well-ordered socialist state now experiences floods of crime like prostitution, gambling, drugs and racketeering; it has directly speeded up the rise of lust and concubine cultures. Erotic night-club show arts have even been included for higher-education curriculum in college. By social function, this kind of popularly-demanded lust show just reflects an immediate crisis of a structuralized corruption syndrome, a collapse of civic sense and sensibility. Prior to President Xi Jin Ping's rise to political power in 2013, who would, and could denounce this kind of cultural crisis and social syndrome in China? Urgently it is time to clean house, to reactivate the legacy of traditional values and to tune-up judicial ethics!

At this juncture, we all have an indispensable stream of dream for President Xi— We eagerly dream that his governing administration shall be able to clear up the organized crime of a nationwide corruption bureaucracy with a new generation of spiritual soldiers; revitalize the judicial system for justice and equality that safeguards civic liberty; lead to a new phase of civilian discipline and serious cultural arts grounded on a functional civic infrastructure over the Straits.

BLOOD & FLESH ON WINGS OF THE NINE DRAGONS—
MUSKETEER'S DREAM TO GREAT WALL BY WAGONS
(炎黄子孙，同舟共济，全民并肩劈荆斩棘，圆了凌宵好梦豪情!)

may brace....   let's praise....

boy braces,   joy praises,
frameless on eye,   blameless in mind,
rejuvenation mindful,   emancipation touchful
wires to pierce on a click,   off-fear from peace make,
silence concertizes a bitter smile,   resilience vitalizes rubble of tile,
calm de weeping rain under pillow,   storm ripping pain above arc de sorrow,
brass choral thumbs ring off star-night,   grass in green curve hums onto moonlight.

A SONATINA THEMED ON STARLIGHT

Footstep on ink score of tones over sonority of storm,
across the boundary.
Down to new century,
blink out core of cones beyond a conformity of norm.
Ink-brushing strokes of starlight,
foot onto one single sight,
root upon the bingo right,
night after night,
time in life runs tight,
long way trumpet a morning bright.
No touchy notes can express:
Keyboard inside nourish heart,
keys touching nudely hard,
with no rest, to theme my best!

Back in October 1983, I had a private meeting with distinguished composer Ting Xin-De (丁善德) in Hong Kong, then Vice President of the Shanghai Music Conservatory. Our conversation was published by the *Mingpao Monthly* under the title 'Listening to Serious Music Requires a High Level of Scholarship' (欣赏严肃音乐 必须要有高度文化水平). Since the May Fourth Movement of 1919, which motivated a mass intellectual movement, serious cultural arts have made a vital contribution to the rise of a national spirit in modern China. Adoption of vernacular language and integration of westernized medium have inspired innovations over a broad spectrum of serious cultures in literature, music, fine arts, and films. For eight years during the Sino-Japanese War, being empowered by the patriotic song 'Volunteer Soldier's March' (义勇军进行曲), tens of millions of Chinese soldiers and civilian defended their town and country by sacrificing their blood and flesh in front of Japan's catastrophic gun powder. That kind of unforeseen spirit burst off by a norm of tonal rhyming. Residing at a cross-roads of multiple cultures and disciplines in the capital of the United States, I struggled to form a serial structure in composing my own English poems that I had absorbed from the twelve tone technique for atonal music. In a letter from John H Reid, Chief Judge of Tom Howard Poetry Contest, Mr. Reid complimented that 'This is to confirm that "A Fugue of Tone Rhyming" by Wing-chi Chan was Highly Commended in the 2009 Tom Howard Poetry Contest for Verse In All Styles and Genres.'

BALLET SHADOW MESMERIZED BY SYMPHONY STAR BRIGHT

婵娟弄影清

Poetized under a keyboard of moonlight,
Let's tone along rhyming river with wine.
best not to miss any ballet shadow on sky.
Mesmerized by symphony of star bright,

Let's paddle toward the torrent, over thy tempest
of the spring evil king.
for musketeer to sing.
Bet nightingale will wing-kiss upon my naked chest

(韻遊江月一樽倾　何负婵娟弄影清
逆水行舟秋煞过　披襟还赋燕歌声)

APPASSIONATA ARIA ON PRAISING …

moonlight thumbs onto thee pillow,	river belted by curve of green grass,
star-night hums with no choral,	strings melted on winds and brass,
drums ring off arc de sorrow,	sonic shaped beyond tone row,
concertizing your resilience,	makes peace off from fear,
along a vitalized silence,	a click pierced to wire,
for thou rejuvenation,	for thy emancipation,
being blameless,	to be frameless,
resonant joy,	dissonant boy.

steps on weeping rain and storm,	behind the ripping pain but calm,
under mindful dedication,	upon touchful motivation,
by thine bitter smile,	along thy rubble of tile,
mind beyond harm,	touch with no arm,

Four seas to One Family:
Overseas Chinese and Chinese dream

stone flown to bits by bombs,
a land in blood weeping—
The rupture.

Seven weeks,
thousands of hundreds,
even many minor, females,
a page of devil lines recalled—
Raped under chilled katana by a gang of killers.
The female-homed samurais'
Male defoamed in volunteer.

Being shaped shielded agenda bang for healers,
stage for de civil signs scored—
junior/senior, not only males,
thousands of millions,
seventy years.

Weep,
with peers,
underground passion of rings,
pain never make past saddened alone,
moon's cold long badly atoned a country,
emotion of the rape harked by map wrapping,
year 2007 torched against sin under global integrity.
Hear heaven's vocal sincerity torching with dignity,
a nation to shape among marks of gap lapping,
wound's old song sadly toned each entry,
an ever main pick for a heartened tone,
extra-sound of lotion on strings,
with no fears—
A rip.

Dears, thou unrested—
Let hearing renew: Tone to heal, stone peeled, thy tear sealed.
Dears, be rested.

Alongside my career as an arts administrator and linguist in Washington, composing classical Chinese poems has been melodizing my life since June 1989. For thousands of years, classical Chinese poetry composition has been regulated to become a US permanent resident. Twenty-two years later, that musician was honored with a prestigious Pulitzer Award.

At the Memorial Concert for the 70th Anniversary of the Nanking (Nanjing) Massacre in 2007, I was appointed the choral conductor, bringing a team of twelve American vocalists to participate in the event. Heading toward the Concert, we, the American team, arrived in Nanjing on 11th December at 1 am after a bus trip of five hours from Shanghai Airport. I got the score on the same day at noon. Our twelve American singer teammates listened to the local orchestra (comprised of additional players from Korea, Russia, Hong Kong, Singapore, Macao and Taipei) and the choir's second rehearsal at 1pm under Maestro Mu Hai Tang's baton. I waited until 4 pm to coach the first rehearsal for our American singer team—from reciting the romanized Chinese lyrics to running through the score and practicing by parts. I was completely relieved by 5:30 pm when we finished our first but only rehearsal. By that time, I knew we would be ready! Suddenly the accompanist student from Beijing pointed to our tenor teammate and said, 'I got your DVD.' At that moment, I realized that Thomas Young, a faculty member from Sarah Lawrence College, came to sing with the local choir for this memorial concert without telling his soloist status as one of America's three best known tenors. The first concert performed nicely on the 12th . By 13th of December, everybody voiced out fully on the stage. Together with Tang on the podium, I, as the choir conductor, thanked with tears to the audience's roaring, standing ovation. Returning to the hotel, I was not able to sleep; my ears echoed with the very first song that I learned from my father (who worked for The Flying Tigers) — 'Defense of the Yellow River'. I drafted a poem and eventually expanded it into a two-stanza 'Mass'.

MASS FOR NANKING'S 1937

Stanza I

The butcher—
hands on bone flipping,
boned through like combs,
every single park bloodied by gun,
knifed to cave after cave of wounding,
a Messiah's frame, mad overturned thunder,
12–13–1937 for Japan in years of our memorization,
irrelevant pen it mini-civilized, a year off civilization,
of an Emperor's name, a flag turned blunder,
life under wave over wave of pounding,
below a darkened and wrinkle sun,

surplus for a reserve fund—What a triumph! A few weeks prior the Orchestra's departure for China, I received a call from Ms. Lo Ai Mei (乐爱妹) (Mrs. Yang Jiechi), secretary to Ambassador Han Xu (韩叙), requesting me to present a party for the Orchestra members and the Ambassador, so he could greet the students, staff and parents. It was a time China just deported an American reporter due to some unknown issues. I made phone calls round the clock to the media circle in Washington and emphasized a point that the Orchestra simultaneously had been invited, on this tour, by both Taiwan and Communist China—Something could happen! Within a few days, I kicked off a press conference. To a big crowd of television and media reporters, Ambassador Han charismatically praised the young people acting as good-faith cultural envoys between the two nations. A historic paradox came up two nights before the event, Lee Ching Ping (李庆平), then Cultural Director of Taiwan's Coordinated Council of North American Affairs, asked me to let him sit next to Ambassador Han at the press conference. Relations across the Straits were still chilly at time. I replied to Lee, 'Please make your own decision on whether to come. I personally have no problem having you present there.' He did not come to the conference but six years later, serving as Deputy General Secretary for Taiwan's Straits Exchange Foundation (海基会), Lee played a key role in facilitating the first official meeting between the Communist and KMT Party leaders in Singapore in 1992, stoning a mutually recognized One-China-Over-the-Straits landmark. A new era has begun for communications across the Straits!

Immediately after our concert performed in Beijing, US Ambassador Winston Lord invited the Orchestra for dinner at his official residence. Dan Sutherland, Washington Post's Beijing correspondent, asked me why the audience was hysterically screaming at the moment I announced that the Orchestra would play Beethoven's Symphony No. 5, the Fate Symphony. I explained that "During the Cultural Revolution, the ruling government ignorantly purged Beethoven and all kinds of Western culture; meanwhile Western-trained scholars had been barbarically tortured. Now they are officially liberated from their sad fate of persecution!" In 1988, the National Endowment of the Arts (NEA) appointed me as a panel judge to pay on-site visits to a community-based orchestra in New York's Chinatown. Visiting their facility and listening to their rehearsals on-site, I reminded the orchestra's Executive Director, who was a no-paid volunteer, that I tended to give my best recommendation to the NEA panel for the orchestra's artistic/managerial merits if they provided me supplement materials regarding the social demographics and immigration history of Chinatown as an inner-city community in New York city, along with a revised budget that was to be itemized with its in-kind-support revenue earned from a team of volunteer staff. This Chinatown orchestra got the grant, as it had been so well deserved, and used it to employ and sponsor their Artistic Director, an emerging musician-immigrant,

Fallen Petals" (花落知多少) was commissioned and premiered by the Louisville Symphony. It crystallized his decade-long study in America and portrayed a bitter and passionate passage between life and death in China under Japan's war crimes. Chou's highly-acclaimed orchestral work marked a monumental achievement for Chinese composers in the West—American musicologist Gilbert Chase praised Chou as 'a really profound "meeting of East and West"—on the philosophical, aesthetic, and technical levels—[which] has rarely been achieved. Perhaps it required a composer from the East, but one with thorough mastery of Western musical traditions and techniques, to accomplish this creative synthesis. Such a composer is Chou Wen-chung.'

Being the first Chinese scholar in the position for Associate Dean of Fine Arts and Music Department Chair at an Ivy-League university, Wen-Chung also was the first Asian composer who has been honored to be a member of the American Academy of Arts and Letters. For sixteen years, he served as one of the Board Officers of the National Committee on United States-China Relations. Furthermore, he volunteered his administrative services and lectured for hundreds of academic and professional events throughout Europe, Asia and America. It was at Wen-Chung's recommendation in 1977 that the spacecraft Voyager of NASA included a recording of an ancient Chinese qin-zither music, 'Water Flow' (流水) for the Golden Record, a space station project of Music from the Earth. He also founded the US-China Arts Exchange Center at Columbia University in 1978, which was the most significant source of serious arts exported from America to China immediately after the Cultural Revolution. Through Wen-chung and the Center, Arthur Miller, Isaac Stern, and many other American artists were introduced to a tremendously affectionate reception from a new generation of serious arts learners in China.

Five years later, my American dream materialized. As Development Director, I took the Washington Youth Symphony Orchestra on a successful concert tour to China in 1986. For this task, 108 staff and students performed and visited Qingdao, Jinan, Beijing, Shanghai, Hong Kong, Taipei, Kaohsiung and Tainan, while many students had never even left their hometowns. At first, my American supervisor sought to gain financial support from then-Mayor Marion Barry, but it was in vain. So I lunched with a lady staff member of the Mayor's Office and was tipped to prepare a letter signed by ten students from the Orchestra, addressed to the wife of Mayor Barry. The letter pointed out that the underserved students' financial limitation did not allow them to sell raffle tickets to cover the tour costs. Soon Mayor Barry allocated $50,000 from the Escheat Fund and endorsed an official letter for all corporate businesses in the District of Columbia that had ties with China trade to support these under-privileged kids. With these efforts, we were able to bring a full orchestra of students with a team of staff and chaperones for a month-long concert tour in China, plus making three hundred thousand dollars hometown) in 1923. His family tree could be traced back to Chou (Zhou) Dun Yi (周敦颐), a Neo-Confucian thinker of the Song Dynasty. His father Chou Miao (周淼), who joined the 1911 Revolution, once pulled out a pistol, barrel to barrel, in confrontation with a Japanese colonel when he (Chou) represented the Northern China Government to negotiate with Japan in taking back Tsing Tao city then occupied by Japan. Soon after the Marco Polo Bridge Incident on 7 July 1937, the Chou family moved from Nanking (Nanjing) to the French-governed territory in Shanghai. At time Chou Miao, Assistant Minister for General Services of the Interior Ministry, followed the ruling government to withdraw from province to province. Wen-Chung's eldest brother (文晋) had already left to pursue his studies at the Massachusetts Institute of Technology, and later became a distinguished scientist in designing war jets for the Allied Forces during World War II and inter-continental ballistic for the United States after the War. In early 1938, the three younger sons of the Chou family caught typhoid through Japan's biological warfare. Wen-Cheng (文正), the youngest, recovered with no harm. Sadly, Wen-Chung's second eldest brother Wen-Ho (文禾), who was the most talented one with music in the family, who had self-taught string instruments and had been a concert master for the Nanking High School Orchestra, lost his life. Wen-Chung was diagnosed by Dr. Lu Jin Wen (陆锦文), who had studied medicine in America, as being at critical status. By accident, a nurse dropped alcohol on the floor and caused a fire. Wen-Chung did not have the strength to move away. At such a moment fighting for life, he rolled down from his bed to other side of the floor. And by miracle, he said goodbye to the death ghost after heavy vomiting.

Japan occupied the French Concession of Shanghai right after the Pearl River Incident in 1941. Even though being a teenager at the time, Wen-Chung refused to be a servile subject for the invaders. His mother Madame Chou Fu Shou Xian (周富守贤) sold a large number of family items to pay for Wen-Chung's escape with a group of adults via Zhejiang to Hunan and then to Gwei Lin of Guangxi, dodging lines and lines of Japanese barricades and witnessing barbaric rapes and killings. Another deep wound to the Chou family at time: Wen-Chung's aunt was brutally killed by the uncivilized. A nun at Qing Liang Temple in Chang Zhou, she had saved the lives of many wounded guerrillas and refused to divulge their whereabouts to the Japanese. In less than two years since Wen-Chung started college at Guangxi University, Gwei Lin city was lost to Japan's military occupation. Wen-Chung escaped again by the last train for Chonqqing while witnessing millions to flee Japan's bombs.

Japan finally surrendered in 1945. Yale University awarded Wen-Chung a full scholarship to study architecture. Two weeks upon his arrival in Boston, Wen-Chung decided to turn down his Yale scholarship and transferred to the New England Music Conservatory. Ten years later, his orchestral triolet "And the a month later. Emotions fueled our days and nights! Fearing that Mao's wife, Jiang Qing, would take over the throne, a few peers and I came together to start a student movement emphasizing on Premier Zhou and the then-denounced Deng Xiaoping's pragmatic policy on culture and economy. We had no political support from any government agency but rushed to submit a list of twelve representatives for a student government ten minutes before the deadline. Through a legitimate election, our list of candidates was elected by a majority over the unexpected defeat of Maoist-backed opponents.

In early November 1977, our cabinet successfully presented a University Open Day, receiving over two hundred thousand citizens to tour various facilities of the campus. At night, an open-air banquet of 2,000 seats was monumentally programmed at the University Million Square. A week later, the Vice-Chancellor-Designate Prof. Ma Lin (马临) advised me to present a Chinese University 15th Anniversary Ball, to be attended by members of the diplomatic corps, on December 30. A remarkable black-tie party for 2000 guests was then presented at the elite Hong Kong Convention Center. Then Colony Secretary Sir Dennis Roberts and major international diplomats sat at the head table, along with television and mass media providing on-site coverage. Vice-Chancellor Choh Ming Lee (李卓敏) and I both gave high-profile opening speeches insisting that the University's four-year undergraduate curriculum not to be cut into three years by the colonial government. The then-pro-colony South China Morning Post and other key Chinese newspapers critically covered the issue next day.

Ten years later, however, the colonial bureaucracy cut all subsidized undergraduate colleges into a three-year curriculum prior to Hong Kong's handover to China in 1997. This conspiracy in shrinking higher education laid the foundation for an unnecessary booming of college graduates after 1997. The reduced curriculum resulted in endless infrastructural turbulence, setting back the goal of cultivating citizenry. Reviewing campus newspapers published by college students in the 1970s, it is shocking to find that a large number of young undergraduates during this period of time, with a rare sense of dignity, had already outmatched the highest levels of thinking of today's academia both in mainland China and Taiwan. A tragic academic setback!

Pursuing another personal dream in life, I went abroad and worked on my master's thesis on Chinese American legendary composer Chou Wen-Chung (周文中) at Northern Illinois University in 1980. On a New Year's Eve, I hitched a ride with a fellow student and arrived in New York under a shower of snow flurries. Knocking on Prof. Chou Wen-Chung's office at Columbia University subsequently led to a generous invitation to join his family for a New Year Eve's dinner, and a second visit to his residence in Soho on the following night.

Prof. Chou, a native of Jiangsu Changzhou, was born in Qufu (Confucius' grass under a slogan: 'Honor for Doing Labor Work'. Cool—The excited crowd of students screamed and applauded the Dean's charismatic action that had been orchestrated with gongs and drums sounding over the lotus lake! One night, I told my Ying Lam Hall classmates that the colonial police CID agents slipped into our campus without any special warrants issued by the court for an entry to the University. These college boys declared to organize their martial arts team members to defend the college's autonomy. What a musketeer spirit!

The 1970s was a time full of dreams among Hong Kong college youth. Over waves of propaganda on 'Purges of Lin Biao (Mao Zedong's designated successor) and Confucius (批林批孔)' promoted by the Communist China, intellectually it was not a pool of calm water within the academic community in Britain's last colony. On one side, there was a political doctrine in place for 'to extend our vision to the world, learn about the motherland, care about Hong Kong society and fight for student rights' (放眼世界, 认识祖国, 关心社会, 争取同学权益). On the other side, it was a vigorous time with high spirits to continue the Chinese intellectual legacy of searching for truth and values from different angles and positions (吾将上下而求索). Students in the field of humanities and social sciences generally reacted against the Cultural Revolution's disastrous ideology (文革浩劫) on mainland China; anti-Maoist opinions were passionately circulated inside the campus (坚持反逆流的言论). So precious were the young people's idealistic passion! I took my summer break to finish an analysis of Brahms' Symphony No.1 and several other classics, including the Book of Music in Sima Qian's *Shi Ji* (史记), i.e., 'Annotation on Music Chapters of History Books' (历代乐律志校释), Emperor Kang Xi's 'Orthodox Interpretation of Music' (律吕正义), Xi Kang's 'No Determinant for Joy or Sad Inside Music' (声无哀乐论), Mao Tse-tung's (Mao Zedong) 'Selected Works', *Communist Manifesto* and so on. I also covered various publications by modern sinologists like Qian Binsi (钱宾四), Wang Jianmin (王健民), Li Dingyi (李定一), Fei Xiaotong (费孝通), Lao Siguang (劳思光), Yang Yinliu (杨阴浏), Mai Xiaoxia (麦啸霞), Ouyang Yuqian (欧阳予倩), and so on. When I took an elective on culture, I chose Plato's 'Republic'. In addition, cohorts came together, after class, to share and argue on noted articles for Chinese affairs that encompassed opinions by both the doves and hawks, like Li Yizhe's 'Big-characters Post' (李一哲的大字报), 'Whither China?' (中国往何处去) by Yang Xiaokai (杨小凯), and 'On the Bourgeois Legal Authorities' (论资产阶级法权) by Zhang Chunqiao (张春桥)—A sonata of proud notes!

Amidst this fervor, Premier Chou En-lai (Zhou Enlai) passed away in January 1976. That night, as the television broadcasted his funeral services, every dorm lobby was packed with weeping students; everybody was painfully worried about what would happen next. Eight months later, in September, Mao Zedong died. However, the dramatic arrest of the Gang of Four was not announced until

Part I
My Trail Trodden by My Feet

Let Blood/Flesh on Wings of a Waked-up Dragon

—*Musketeer's Dream Fly to Great Wall by Wagon!*[1]

Chan Wing-Chi 陈咏智

A Washington-based poet and musician, he has been committing himself as an arts practitioner for the global communities. During his tenure as Development Director for the Washington, DC Youth Symphony Orchestra, he had raised multi –millions of funds to operate the Orchestra's international tours to Europe and Asia. His artistic advisory spectrum has been crossing over the ocean, including serving as consultants for US National Endowment for the Arts, New Jersey and South Carolina Arts Commissions, D.C. Mayor's Office, Jiangsu Provincial Performing Arts Group and China National Symphony, as well as adjunct professor of music at Green Mountain College in Vermont and Shenyang Conservatory of Music in China. He presented academic papers on music and culture to various higher education institutions: Columbia University, Kingston Polytechnic University in London, Tenri in Japan, Hong Kong University, Pennsylvania State University, University of District of Columbia, US Library of Congress, to name a few. For the past eight years, he has been spearheading to score his mind of conceptual art, minimalism and pointillism music with synchronization profile and tonal rhyming perception in composing English poetry.

In 2007, Chan, he took a team of twelve American vocalists to participate in a Memorial Concert for the 70th Anniversary of Nanking Massacre that vocalists included Thomas Young, who has been praised as one of the best three American tenors today.

One of my biggest childhood dreams was fulfilled when I eventually passed my college matriculation exam and was admitted to The Chinese University of Hong Kong in 1973. At the freshman orientation camp, Dean Madame Lu Wai Hing (庐慧卿) dressed like a janitor and, at 65, led students to dig soil by hand and to re-set the

---
1 I am indebted to Professors L.H.M. Ling and Tan Chung's esteemed advice in preparing this article.

the world, it seems only the Nordic countries have both freedom and equality, but they also pay a high cost in terms of heavy taxation and prices.

To conclude, my 'Chinese dream' was in part shaped by my father's example. He lived at a time when China was weak and powerless. His 'Chinese dream' was modest: to protect China's cultural heritage and to manifest its greatness to the rest of the world. Living the life of an exile and refugee, he tried to work tirelessly on one project after another. My 'Chinese dream' went through different phases. As China became stronger, my dream(s) also changed. Because of my sufferings during the Japanese invasion as a child, uppermost in my mind was the question 'what can I do to help China'? In that regard, my position was quite similar to that of many post-Holocaust Jews who ask the question of what they can do to help Israel. When I was a teenager, I had idealism and enthusiasm for sacrifice. As a middle-aged faculty member, I could only offer some advice but little more. I was more a bystander and witness of the enormous changes in China, yet I marveled at how much old habits remained. Now that I am a retiree in my 70's, I am primarily concerned with my own interests. I read books on China, but I also read books on the Middle East, Southeast Asia, and even Africa. My 'Chinese dream' consists of what I would like China both to become and not to become. In other words, my dream is for China to acquire the desirable qualities and to rid of the undesirable ones. Ultimately, I would like to see a China that is prosperous, democratic, peaceful, and respected in our time and future.

expenditures can become a self-fulfilling prophesy in going to war. I for one would like to see more funding for education, medical care, and the needs of the poor. Wars create future enemies and solve no territorial issues. I always remember what my father said about peace: 'if we can keep peace for fifty years, China will be strong.' Perhaps one means to develop friendly relations with China's neighbors and potential foes is to use Chinese tourists as good-will ambassadors. I have noticed their growing numbers in such places as Thailand, Sri Lanka, and Nepal in my recent travels. Their behavior and demeanor will be of utmost importance and will have a direct impact on whether China will be respected or ridiculed.

My current 'Chinese dream' involves greater development of the Chinese people as 'new citizens' with civic virtues and responsibilities. Just over a hundred years ago, the thoughtful Liang Qichao spoke of transforming the Chinese character. The 'new citizen' should be thinking less of his/her family and more of the nation and society. He/she should get rid of bad habits such as smoking and gambling, wasteful weddings and mournings. My recent travel experience in China gave me examples where civic virtues are needed. Car drivers have little concern for pedestrians' rights as they cross the pedestrians' white lines while the pedestrians for their part walk against red lights. Another example is the frequent occurrence of motorbikes and the new quiet electric bikes that often navigate on pedestrians' walk-ways. Again, many young, healthy riders on buses do not yield their seats to seniors. The Chinese public should stress civil virtues of courtesy and the Public Security Bureau should punish the transgressors.

It is easy to say that China should have 'democracy' and 'human rights'. But what does 'democracy' really mean—is it freedom or is it equality? Of course, both are important and we want both. China need not to copy the Western style of democracy where business interests can often buy elections. As the use of the internet spreads in China, it is increasingly difficult for the government to block and censor. As China's middle class expands and as the masses make gains in education, they are bound to become more politically vocal. It is the task of the Chinese Communist Party to enlist China's best and brightest 'new citizens' as well as to guard itself against nepotism and corruption. I agree with the priority of 'social stability', which seems now increasingly at risk: Uighurs' armed attacks, Tibetans' immolation, workers' demonstrations, not to mention disasters unleashed by earthquakes, flooding, and smog skies. In foreign affairs, China is faced with a rearmed Japan intent to flex its muscles, unfriendly neighbors such as the Philippines and Vietnam, and above all a suspicious U.S. now intent on 'rebalancing Asia', i.e. containing China. With low poll numbers for the Kuomintang in Taiwan, it is entirely possible that the pro-independence People's Progress Party may win the presidency in two years' time. This may not be the right moment to inaugurate Western-style 'democracy' in China, as much as I wish for them. As I look around

Chinese still suffer from various degrees of discrimination and volatile violence. It has become my 'Chinese dream' that these Chinese abroad be allowed to live in peace. They should not be cast as villains and sacrificial lambs in any outburst of anti-Chinese riots in the future.

Now that I am retired, what are some of my current "Chinese dreams" in the 2010's? Rapid and reckless industrialization have created polluted rivers/lakes and near poisonous air in urban cities. One of my dreams would want to reduce the pollution by restricting auto traffic and closing delinquent polluters. There should be greater expansion of public mass transportation as well as environment-friendly paths for bicycling and jogging. Accident-prone mines should be closed and the use of solar energy increased. More trees and more public parks should cover urban areas.

I have inherited my father's interest in China's border areas, especially Xinjiang. Over the years I have traveled to Xinjiang four times, Tibet once, Inner Mongolia three times, and the Mongolia Republic twice. It is my 'Chinese dream' to see harmony and peace between the Han majority and the various minorities or nationalities. Han settlers in these border areas should learn the local languages, customs, as well as the minorities' religious beliefs and practices. Chinese universities should offer courses in Uighur, Tibetan, Mongolian and other minority languages and literature as electives just as they offer English, German, or Russian languages and literature. In fact, it is my 'Chinese dream' to see some day an Uighur or a Tibetan becoming China's Energy Minister or Foreign Minister.

It is also my 'Chinese dream' to see the gap between China's rich and poor narrowed. On the top are the beneficiaries of the modern market economy, the corrupt officials, and their business associates; at the bottom is a floating population of laborers and seamstresses from the countryside. For the urban poor and for many living in rural areas, health care and education are at a premium. For most urban dwellers, the cost of medical services and drugs as well as education has skyrocketed in recent years. Added to the average family's financial burden is the care for China's elderly. Because of the one-child policy, there needs to be a major expansion of senior care centers. Moreover, the retirees should have the option of engaging in socially beneficial activities besides playing bridge and mahjong.

As China becomes militarily stronger and economically crowned as no. 2 in the world, there bounds to be counter forces that see China a threat as well as a rival competitor. How to maintain friends and keep enemies at bay? There are no easy answers. There is a great temptation to use force as a solution. Some countries such as the U.S., as noted by President Dwight D. Eisenhower, have a military-industrial complex. Despite the U.S. Executive Branch's best efforts to economize the military with a downsized budget, legislators in Congress time and again would undercut such cost-saving efforts. China should not follow such an example. Military a semester at the latter institution. During this period I was able to know Beijing and the Chinese people in greater depth. I was better able to adapt myself to their lifestyle, including riding the bicycle to some spots around campus. It so happened that a close neighbor was a member of the People's Political Consultative Conference. He asked me what I would have him propose during the Conference deliberations. I remember three very simple proposals I gave him, which might constitute my 'Chinese dream' at the time: speed trains, cutting down on smoking, extending service hours by eliminating the noon rest between 11:30am and 2pm. As of my last trip to China a year ago, I was glad to ride on a speed train; I did find less smoking, at least in public places. Although some institutions still have long lunch breaks, I did find some others without such a break.

Another 'Chinese dream' of mine during the 1980's was to bridge the gap between intellectuals on the Mainland and those on Taiwan. In the early 1980's such scholarly exchanges were highly suspect and extremely rare. A turning point came at the annual meeting of the Association for Asian Studies in 1981 on the seventieth anniversary of the Revolution of 1911 when historians from both sides of the Taiwan Strait sat on the same table to discuss its significance. A few years later, at the University of Illinois-Champaign Urbana, we discussed the significance of the Xian Incident of 1936. Both events were sponsored by the Historical Society for the Twentieth Century China in North America. I was new to the society, which was basically located in the New York City area and drew its members from Columbia, City College, where Professor Tong Te-kong (唐德剛) was a prime mover. I became the society's Secretary and succeeded Professor Tong as its President in 1989.

It was during my tenure as President of the society that tensions within a fast-changing China culminated into the Tiananmen Incident. It was my job to sponsor a session to discuss this incident in a joint meeting with the American Historical Association. We tried to keep the discussion at a scholarly and dispassionate level amidst the emotions the incident evoked. There was no question that at that juncture, many scholars of the American New Left who had sympathized with the PRC turned to become its severest critics. Since the study of Chinese politics became increasingly polemical, I found it more useful and rewarding to study the Chinese Diaspora as a field of research.

Overseas Chinese in Southeast Asia in particular appealed to me for study. Many of them fulfilled their 'Chinese dream' by moving abroad and becoming fabulously rich. While some have assimilated to local culture, others have remained staunchly Chinese in language and culture. It is also interesting to study their host countries be they Islamic in the case of Indonesia, Malaysia, and Brunei, or Buddhist in the case of Thailand, Myanmar, Cambodia, and Laos, or Christian in the case of the Philippines, or Communist in the case of Vietnam. Over the years, I managed to visit all these Southeast Asian countries. Despite their economic power, overseas supplemented my budget by working on weekend evenings at the Eliot House library. I could not say I had a 'Chinese dream', but I was sufficiently concerned with China by reading Chinese newspapers at the Harvard-Yenching Library then at Boyleston Hall. My main concern at the time was that the Chinese Mainland was becoming a Soviet satellite and Soviet advisers were big brothers who controlled China. In 1956, I entered an essay contest with the topic of 'Tradition and Change in Asia,' where I emphasized the fact that we could use tradition to legitimize change, the importance of legal protection, as well as the goals of freedom and equality under the rubric of 'democracy.' I won the third prize as a college sophomore, while the winners of the first and second prizes were Ph.D. candidates. I remember when Khrushchev's denunciation of Stalin first became known in the West, I became very excited and dashed off a letter to the pro-Mainland Chinese newspaper *Huaqiao ribao* (华侨日报, *Overseas Chinese Daily News*) urging its editor to publish the denunciation in Chinese. Although the newspaper never followed my request, Chairman Mao unleashed the 'Hundred Flowers Blossom, Hundred Schools Contend' Movement shortly thereafter. I think I caught the contagious fever that democracy was at hand, and that it was time for us to return to China. Since my choice of a vocation (and even a major) was still unsettled, going back to China was all the more tempting. Exacerbating my situation was that while some of my well-to-do classmates were taking breaks on long trips to favored vacation spots, I was working at the minimum wage of 65c per hour on weekends. Selfishly and unselfishly, my 'Chinese dream' was to serve China. One 'dream' in particular was for China's steel production to reach its targeted goal of 18 million tons per year. So much for my 'Chinese dream' in the 1950's.

While my first return to China did not materialize until 1978, my "Chinese Dreams" during my teaching career in Ohio in the 1980's took different forms. After the Nixon thaw and as the Cultural Revolution wound down, my dream to see China became a reality. The train ride from Hong Kong to Guangzhou was filled with martial music as well as music from Albania. After reaching Beijing, I was able to see my many relatives, but only at the Overseas Hotel (华侨大厦) where we stayed. There was hardly any street traffic and stores closed early around 5pm. The streets were deserted and dark at night. Our relatives needed coupons for rice, vegetable oil, and a host of other necessities, and we helped them to buy a few things at the Friendship Store. Still, after clearance from the Beijing Public Security Bureau, we did get permission to visit a number of cities and towns such as Xian, Nanjing, Shanghai, Nanchang, Jiujiang with Mt. Lu, and Guilin. Although we were often greeted as curiosities, many of the people we met around the country seemed genuine and friendly. They seem not interested in material wealth.

In 1982 after my institution, Wright State University, signed a sister-relationship agreement with Beijing Normal University (北京师范大学), I was able to spend

Continental Europe. When he died in 1965, he left uncompleted a bibliography on Chinese art and archaeology. Fortunately, this work was completed by Professor Harrie A. Vanderstappen of the University of Chicago and published as "The T. L. Yuan Bibliography of Western Writings on Chinese Art and Archaeology," and published by Mansell in 1975.

What was my father's dream or dreams? During a walk from our home to the Library of Congress, he confided in me that what China needed was peace: 'if we can keep peace for fifty years, China will be strong', I remember him saying. Indeed, from about 1840 until the time of his death, there was no decade in which China did not have a war or a rebellion/revolution. I think it was also his 'dream' to show the greatness of Chinese culture, its permanent value, and to increase its appreciation by the rest of the world as well as by the Chinese people themselves. I am also sure that he would have wanted to go to China to see his relatives and former friends, a wish his death in 1965 was to cut short.

As for my 'Chinese dream', I would like to break it into three stages of my life: 1. during my college years in the 1950's, 2. during my teaching career in the 1980's, and 3. in my retirement years in the 2010's. I came to the U.S. at the age of 11 in 1949 not knowing a word of English. But I had already read several Western novels in translation such as *The Three Musketeers*, *Sherlock Holmes*, and *Uncle Tom's Cabin*. When I was in China, I loved the Chinese classics such as *Sanguo yanyi* (三国演义)(*Romance of the Three Kingdoms*), *Xiyouji* (西游记) (*Pilgrimage to the West*), *Qixia wuyi* (七侠五义) (*Seven Heroes and Five Righteous Men*), and *Shuihuzhuan* (水浒传) (*Outlaws of the Marsh*). It was only after arriving in Washington and living close to the Library of Congress that I started reading Chinese modern fiction by such authors as Ba Jin (巴金), Lao She (老舍), Mao Dun (茅盾). They conveyed to me the conflicts between the old and the new, the tensions within the clannish family, and the deprivations of the industrial worker within the Chinese capitalist order. By the time I entered Harvard in 1954, I prided myself on my knowledge of China and Chinese culture and saw no need to take courses with the eminent historian of modern China, Professor John K. Fairbank. My 'Chinese dream' then was to gain knowledge not obtainable in China.

During my first two years at Harvard, I was torn in my choice of a vocation: to be a scientist/engineer which would be more job friendly or to be a historian. For a time, I was a major in History of Science so I could be in both camps. Having taken courses in Physics and Geology as well as a History course, I decided to major in History. In my sophomore year, I took a course in the History of Modern India then taught by Professor Daniel Ingalls, a Sanskrit scholar, a course on Imperial Russia by Professor Robert Wolff, as well as a course on the Ottoman Empire offered jointly by three Professors, Richard Frye, William Langer, and Speros Vryonis. Although I had a Harvard scholarship, I still needed money from home and I

My father had an early interest in locating China's 'lost' rare books and treasures abroad. As early as 1927, he researched the 'Yongle dadian' (永乐大典) located in Japan—a monumental collection of Chinese rare books which were dispersed when the British and French troops took Beijing in 1860. He subsequently published an inventory of the various Yongle dadian scattered at major libraries around the world. Under his prodding, his assistant Wang Zhongmin (王重民) went to the Library of Congress as well as European libraries to catalogue rare books, especially ancient Buddhist manuscripts from the Dunhuang Caves. My father moved the National Library's rare books and manuscripts to China's interior and later to the U.S., just in time before Japan's occupation of Beijing.

Another dimension of my father's 'Chinese dream' was his desire to understand the depth and sophistication of Western knowledge of China, i.e. Western Sinology. When we left China for the U.S. in 1949, my father was already 54. He had a family of five with two college-age children and one still in the sixth grade, myself. Before he found a more permanent position at the Library of Congress, he was for several years living on grants and temporary jobs. Life was not easy and we all learned to be frugal. But during those early years of our American stay, he was devoted to a grand project: to compile a comprehensive bibliography of all Western books on China between the 1920's and the 1950's. He was single-minded in his dedication to this work, which contained some 18,000 books and monographs in English, French, German, and Portuguese. And he did the job by hand before there were computers. The work, entitled 'China in Western Literature' (802 pages), was published by Yale University Far Eastern Publications in 1958. What was particularly unusual in such a bibliography was the listing of the authors' year of birth, and in the case of Chinese authors, their names in Chinese as well as their westernized names. Subsequently, he also published a bibliography of Russian works on China, which is particularly valuable for their coverage of Mongolia and Xinjiang as well as Sino-Russian relations.

After my father accepted a relatively minor position at the Library of Congress, he was tireless In continuing work on many worthy projects. Perhaps it was his 'dream' to aggrandize Chinese 'brain power'. At a time when many Chinese-Americans were in the laundry and restaurant business, he decided to embark on a compilation of doctorate holders in the U.S. from the first recipient in 1905 to 1960. I remember him coming home from work looking a bit tired, but right after dinner, he would start working on this project. The result was 'A Guide to Doctoral Dissertations by Chinese Students in America 1905 –1960', published in 1961. In all, 2,789 dissertations are listed with their authors' names in both Western and Chinese forms, their year of birth, the names of the degree institutions, as well as the dates of the doctorate. Not content with the U.S. recipients, my father went on to complete doctorate dissertations by Chinese students in Britain and in foreign troops parading in the streets of his native city. Graduating from Peking University in 1916 in the same class as Fu Sinian (傅斯年), he received a scholarship to study History at Columbia University in 1920. He told me that one of his favorite courses was that of Carlton Hayes, the eminent historian of nationalism. During the Washington Conference in 1921–22, my father served as secretary to Huang Fu (黄郛) and also interned during the summers at the Library of Congress. After receiving his B.A. degree from Columbia in 1922, he decided to devote his career to a field which had very few professionals in China at the time, that of library science. So at the age of 28, he received a B.L.S. degree from the New York State Library School in Albany, founded by Melville Dewey of the 'Dewey Classification System' fame. He proceeded to England for a year's study at the University of London Institute of Historical Research before returning to China in 1924 to become the librarian of Guangdong University (now Sun Yat-sen (中山) University) in Guangzhou, then the hotbed of revolution in China.

As I look back on my father's career, I see his 'Chinese dream' reflected in several dimensions. First of all, he was concerned with the professional preservation and management of China's cultural assets such as libraries and museums. At the age of 30 in 1925, he became the librarian and professor of bibliography at Peking University, and thus was a friend of Li Dazhao (李大钊). When the Peking Metropolitan Library was reorganized in 1926, Liang Qichao (梁启超) was named its Director and my father its librarian. After this library merged with the old National Library to form the National Library of Peiping (currently the National Library of China (中国国家图书馆) in 1929, Cai Yuanpei (蔡元培) was named its Director and my father its Vice Director. Since Cai was a pivotal figure in a number of cultural and educational institutions, including being the President of the Academia Sinica, he left the administration of the National Library largely in my father's hands.

While my father played a role in the creation of the National Palace Museum, it was his work at the National Library that was his most important legacy. He helped to design and construct a new Sino-Western library building at the side of Beihai Park. He inaugurated the compilation of union catalogues, serial lists, photo-duplication service, interlibrary loan, and exchange of materials with foreign countries. Above all, he had the foresight to foster a younger generation of scholars and bibliophiles as interns and researchers at the National Library and dispatch some of them abroad for advanced training. There is a long list of beneficiaries from this program: Wang Zhongmin (王重民), the great bibliographer, Xiang Da (向达), the great historian of East-West contacts, Tan Qixiang (谭其骧), the great scholar of historical geography, Sun Kaidi (孙楷弟), the great literary critic, Xie Guozhen (谢国桢), the great Ming-Qing historian, Zhao Wanli (赵万里), the great rare books specialist, and Fu Zhenlun (傅振伦), the great antiquarian among others.

My 'Chinese dream', My Father's Heritage

Tsing YUAN 袁 清

Arrived in the U.S. in 1949 at the age of 11, majored in History at Harvard College, George Washington University, and the University of Pennsylvania, where he received Ph.D. in 1969. Taught at Swarthmore College and Wright State University, and was one time Chair of the History Department. Also taught at Beijing Normal University, Ohio State University, and lectured at Nankai, Fudan, Zhongshan, and several other universities. Published articles on Ming-Qing history, Central Asia, the Chinese Diaspora, and Sino-Japanese Relations. Served as President of the Historical Society of Twentieth Century China in North America, 1989–90 succeeding Professor Te-kong Tong.

What is my 'Chinese dream'? Are there several "Chinese Dreams"? I am thinking back to the time when I had my first 'Chinese dream'. I was very small and my family was fleeing from the Japanese invasion of China's interior. My dream at that time was that China must be strong and that any such invasion must not be repeated. I was born in Beijing (then Peiping) two weeks after the Marco Polo Bridge Incident. My father Tung-li Yuan (袁同礼) was on the Japanese blacklist as he was head of the National Beiping Library, so he decided to leave Beijing for the south even before my birth. At six months, I left Japan-occupied Beijing with the rest of my family, led by my mother, for the Chinese hinterland. What followed were the war years of privation, hardship, and our struggle for survival until V-J Day in 1945. Before dealing with my 'Chinese dream' in different stages, I need to dwell briefly on what I imagine as my father's 'Chinese dream' and its influence on me.

I would not presume to speak for my father regarding his 'Chinese dream'. But as a student of History, I think it probably involves the dream of a strong China. Born in Beijing in 1895, he must have witnessed the 8–Powers' occupation of Beijing in 1900 as a child. He must have felt the shame and humiliation of seeing

Part I
My Trail Trodden by My Feet

concern about India strengthened my determination to work for the popularization of the cultures of China and India and interactions between China and India.

The 'India' conceived by my parents through the friendship of Uncle Jin was rather pedantic, but the innumerable letters and photos sent by me from India created a sense of reality, imagination and hope in their minds. I always wanted to fetch my parents to India to live their dreams, but my wish was not fulfilled.

After father passed away, I took mother to India to visit the renowned Ajanta and Ellora caves, my octogenarian (85) mother received homage from the Indian people and the pilgrims.

Having done archaeological studies for many years in India, I feel that I should offer my knowledge to the public and let them know India's great civilization. It was for this purpose that I wrote Art of the Hindu Pantheon. I wrote in the Foreword:

> I dedicate this book to my dear father, Professor Zhu Xihou (朱锡侯), a founder of the Department of Psychology at Hangzhou University (杭州大) now Zhejiang University (浙江大学). He had obtained a double PhD in France from the fields of Biology and Psychology. He was a founder of the Chinese Association of Biology and the Chinese Association of Psychology. He was a poet, writer and translator, and a bosom friend of the famous scholar of India studies at Peking University, Professor Jin Kemu. He loved Indian culture and art and was looking forward to visiting India. He passed away without fulfilling this wish.
>
> Dear father, you left us without a chance of coming here. I wish that you can see through your daughter's book what you had wanted to see. You left us without a chance of coming here. How I wish you would become the Kalkin of *rani ki vav* and return to the world on the white horse![1] I am looking forward to reunion with you, father, you who gave me life, dream, personality and wisdom!

In two odd decades, I have done my best to study and popularize Indian culture and art. I did so with the expectation of making Chinese people understand more of this our great neighbor and appreciate an ancient civilization with the same antiquity as ours. May the great civilizations of China and India eternally interconnect and intermingle, eternally prosperous!

---

1 'Kalki' (meaning 'Eternity', or 'White Horse', or 'Destroyer of Filth') is the final incarnation of Vishnu.

(师范大学) and Foreign Language University(外国语大学), from Shenzhen University (深圳大学) to Peking University (北京大学), I talked about the *rani ki vav*, the Indian marriage ceremony, the Sanchi Stupa, the footprint of the Buddha and so on, hoping to infuse young students with the information and inspiration I had gained from India to broaden their vision and make them look at the world from various perspectives. Many diplomats were encouraged by me to come out of their cocoons to gain an in-depth understanding of India, appreciating India's brilliant culture, loving India's refined art, feeling the beauty which conceals depth beneath the surface, perceiving the true historical culture which is elaborately designed but somewhat beyond normal comprehension.

In my childhood, my parents always talked about their friend Mr. Jin Kemu (金克木). At the beginning of the Anti-Japanese War period, my father went to France to study while Mr. Jin Kemu went to India. My parents maintained correspondence with Mr. Jin when Eurasia was burning with the fire of World War II.

When Uncle Jin knew I was in India, he sent me a long letter with earnest guidance. He wrote : « Your first feeling about India would be its sharp contrasts. » Indeed, many who have visited India have been puzzled by the scene of poverty on the streets as well as the insurpassable complexity. They either eschew comments or abuse their critique, resulting in their ignoring the creation of spiritual and material wealth for the world by this great civilization.

In July 1995, I wrote in my diary :

> Day before yesterday, I reopened Uncle Jin's book, *Tianzhu jiushi*(天竺旧事, *Reminiscence of Heavenly India*), I discovered that on the opening page there was the autograph of Uncle Jin Kemu presenting the book to my father and me, signed '1986.' Ten years after that I added my own remarks, reading : I read Uncle Jin's *Tianzhu jiushi* and read again to my father, I was deeply touched. I have been to many of the places he described. But due to the lapse of such a long time I could not trace the pure and simple folkways recorded in the book. The book narrates the moving story of the Chinese monk who lived in an improvised structure on a tree and was famously known as the *Niaochao chanshi* (鸟巢禅师, Chan master in a bird's nest). This reminds me of Reverend Yuqing (玉清法师) whom I met at Sarnath. At the age of nine, he walked from the Kumbum Monastery (塔尔寺) of Qinghai (青海) Province to India with a group, and became a disabled person due to frostbite. For those who were devoted to Buddhadharma to have their pilgrimage from China to India, how many could end as a success story like Xuanzang ?

Every time I returned to China I made it a point to visit the residence of Uncle Jin at Wexiuyuan (蔚秀园, Weixiu Park) and chat with him. Uncle Jin was always concerned about what had happened in India and inquired about its details, about the development and changes of the places in India where he had stayed. His years along with 280 plus unpublished pictures. I worked at the computer for 15–16 hours a day for the book, and got an acute attack of glaucoma which led to a sudden, total loss of eyesight.

A revelation from the study of *rani ki vav* is: The pantheon epitomizes the world. The world is vast, but also petty, especially today. The world is exactly like this underground palace built by Rani Udayamati—it is tiny but also huge.

This is the first scholarly work of Indian archaeology written in Chinese covering history, archaeology, religion, architecture, legend, iconography, and folklore, providing a tool of research for many readers. It has been welcomed by many experts. The Secretary General of the Chinese Association of Dunhuang and Turpan Studies (中国敦煌吐鲁番学), Mr. Chai Jianhong (柴剑虹), wrote to me that he thought the work could promote studies of Dunhuang and Central Asia. Famous India expert from Shenzhen University(深圳大学), Professor Yu Longyu (郁龙余), thought it was a great contribution by introducing India's art to 1.3 billion Chinese. Dr. Cai Feng(蔡枫) of the Academy of International Cultural Intercourse at Shenzhen University wished there could be greater publicity for the book so more Chinese could understand Indian culture and correct the misconception that Indian art meant only Buddhist art. Yang Fuxue (杨富学), a professor at the Dunhuang Academy (敦煌研究院), said he used the book when he taught master's and doctoral classes on Indian culture.

Much as there was millennial cultural intercourse between China and India, today the general knowledge of Chinese people on India is rather superficial. They know little beyond the transmission of Buddhism to China from India. I have tried my best to popularize the great culture and magnificent art of India, carrying on cultural exchanges between China and India. The publication of the book has been widely reported by the media of China and other countries. The Indian media has called me the 'modern Xuanzang'. The Indian Ambassador for France inaugurated my exhibit of the *rani ki vav*. When the Indian government celebrated the 55th anniversary of India-China diplomatic ties, I was the only special invitee representing Chinese people in the event.

In 2012, a volume one of my academic works in English and French(its English title is *The Fantastic Beings of Ancient India, from 2500BC to 6th century AD* and its French title is *Les Êtres fantastiques de l'inde ancienne, De 2500 av.J.-C. au 6ème Siècle*') was out, published by Franco-Indian Research, Mumbai. It covers the study of 3000 years from the Indus Valley Civilization to the Gupta Dynasty. It solves many historical controversies by showing detailed archaeological evidences, and has been appreciated by the academic circles of Indian archaeological studies and French studies on Asian art and archaeology.

I have lectured on Indian culture and art organized by universities in China, from the Vocational University of Suzhou(苏州职业大学) to Tianjin's Normal University

India has abundant historical sites. The head of our Indian cultural institution, Mr. M. Postel, discovered an abandoned temple from 9th–century Rajasthan. The institution had collaborated with the Archaeological Survey of India for many years in surveying and studying the site and discovered in it an architectural masterpiece with high value in historical art. One day, I accompanied Mr. Postel and the Indian art historian, Dr. K. Mankodi, to the excavation site. We saw four pairs of deities just excavated perfectly unimpaired after more than a millennium. Everyone was excited and wanted to take a picture. The government official allowed only one person to photograph them. As I had been a university professor teaching photography, I was nominated on the spot for the job. Unexpectedly, the photos I took on site and its idols were put to good use later.

In order to appeal for restoration of this historical site and make the public aware of its importance, I organized a photo exhibit at the Museé Asiatica at Biarrits, France. It received good coverage and support from the media. Six months later the unearthed idols were stolen, and we were shocked by the bad news. We spent months to track the world sales of Indian artifacts and discovered that they were sold to an antique shop in the US. I rushed to Paris to contact the Indian Embassy. I was the only person who photographed these idols at the site, and my photos served as evidence about the stolen goods. Joint operations of the Indian government and Interpol ensued and the stolen artifacts were returned to India.

The *rani ki vav* (the queen's stepwell) in the town of Sidhpur near Patan in Gujarat was discovered by Mr. Postel in the 1950s. The excavation of *rani ki vav* was a great archaeological excavation of the 20th century. In order to photograph the art masterpieces from over a thousand years ago, I descended to the ancient well 30 metres below by climbing over the pump's water pipe. I had to lie in the muddy water, or hang in the air, putting the stand of my camera on the beam of the ancient well. I visited the site again and again over 18 years to study and photograph, and could claim to know every detail of the stepwell. Yet, there was always a new discovery of its contents and secrets with every visit. I always felt flabbergasted every time I stood before it. My study of *rani ki vav* not only makes me feel overpowered by the vicissitudes of time and the monument's greatness, but it also gives me a sense of good fortune and mission: Good fortune that I can witness this miracle after a millennium, and a sense of mission that I must try my level best to popularize it among people.

In order that the readers of China and the world know this historical miracle, and in order that more and more people share my joy of seeing this world miracle, I spent several years to write and publish *Yindujiao wanshendian yishu—Yindu wanghoujing tanmi* (印度教万神殿艺术——印度王后井探秘) (*Art of the Hindu Pantheon: Explore the Mystery of the Rani Ki Vav of India*). The book encompasses my archaeological studies and understanding of Indian historical culture for 20 country of most complicated languages and scripts. There are fifteen languages printed on India's currency notes. When I held my exhibits, many Indians came and chatted with me in the gallery from dawn to dusk. They liked my paintings, and the calligraphed poems on the paintings. Many carried notebooks and copied them out. Later, I printed out the English translations of these poems and placed them at the exhibit. A thick pile in the morning vanished in the evening. I had to place a fresh pile the next day.

In order to study the Bastar Folk Art, I lived among various tribes in the Indian jungles to study their totemic signs and lifestyles. I looked at thousand-year-old obscure steles to peep into the largely forgotten past. In order to study Buddhist art, I retraced the footsteps of the Buddha and paid homage to and studied the historical monuments of Sakyamuni. In order to understand the mystic religious activities in the hills of Kerala, I sacrificed sleep on many nights, waiting from dusk to dawn to shoot the march of the sacred fire.

The study of iconography of the Indian religious art drove me to surviving yet forgotten temples and historical sites: e.g., Khajuraho, Odisha, Gujarat, Rajasthan, Tamil. I visited and studied several hundreds of ancient Indian temples, and studied several tens of temples from the 1st–19th centuries across the length and breadth of India, photographed innumerable first-hand materials, sketched several hundred legendary animals, drew the complicated maps of a few scores of temples.

While proof-reading my book, I travelled by suburban trains as much as possible to save time on the road. The trains of Mumbai were extremely crowded during office rush hours with people hanging from the doors as we see on television. I had to buy a first class ticket to avoid the crowd. First-class seats were not much different than the ordinary second-class ones—the same hard benches—but with a huge difference in fare.

There were many computers in the editors' room at the publisher's, making blocks for various books and pictures. At a casual glance, I could tell the names of the deities on the monitors. There were 330 million deities in the Hindu pantheon. Some of the major deities like Shiva and Vishnu had a thousand names. The editors were surprised that I could name so many deities, even the obscure ones. Gradually, they exclaimed: 'You know more than us.' When my work was over, they felt sorry that I was leaving, 'We look forward to working with you for a longer period,' they said. For a foreigner who knew their religion and culture, there was abundant friendship and respect.

I participated in several archaeological, anthropological, religious and iconographical research and photograph projects and became a member of an Indian cultural institution. In 1997, my doctoral dissertation on Indian art obtained the highest evaluation and I was awarded the Ph. D. degree by Sorbonne University, Paris.

My 'Chinese dream': Eternal Prosperity for the Great Civilizations of China and India

Zhu Xintian 朱新天

In 1990, as the lone Chinese participant in the excavation and photography of the great historical site, *rani ki vav* (the queen's stepwell), which had been created a thousand years ago, I was amazed by the great civilization and unrivalled art of India.

India is a bewildering country. One is always aroused and puzzled by her long sustained yet ambivalent history, her extremely complex yet closely knit religious institutions, her unrivalled wisdom and philosophical thought, her magnificent temple and palace architecture, her exquisite sculptures and paintings, her rich and colorful languages and scripts, and her kaleidoscopic folklore. She makes people stimulated, mystified and perplexed. I have met lots of people, including foreign diplomats, who have sojourned to and in India for years. Whenever people talked about India's religious art, the array of gods and goddesses and the visual features of avatars of Indian deities, they were at once blanketed by a thick haze without a clear clue. This is India! I feel Indian history, culture and mythology as a vast encyclopaedia which cannot be completely comprehended by people who study it.

In order to understand Indian folklore, I braved torrential rain to be immersed waist-deep in the sea from noon to midnight to photograph the grandeur of the *ganesha chaturthi* (festival of Ganesh, the deity with the elephant head), which is the greatest red letter day in western India. I carried a plastic bag with three cameras on my back and mixed with the devoted worshippers, singing hymns and praying together with them as well as receiving *bindi*, the auspicious mark on my forehead by the priest and sharing the *prasāda* (food first offered to the deity and, then, consumed by the worshippers)…People hugged me and took group photographs with me and shouted *hindi-chini bhai bhai* (Indians and Chinese are brothers).

I had numerous exhibits of my personal paintings at various galleries to introduce Chinese traditional painting, calligraphy, poetry and philosophy to Indian masses. When these exhibits were reported in the press, I could not recognize it was about me as my name was rendered unrecognizable. India is a dedicated ourselves to the neglect of our own well-being. Mr. Postel still works and studies for the museum though he is an octogenarian of 88. He compiled four museum albums with his rich knowledge and experience. He provided more than 150 valuable exhibits free of charge for the large scale exhibition of 'Journey to the Himalaya' (*Voyage dans l'Himalaya*) under the auspices of the Municipality of Biarritz, and compiled the album for it.

In 2000, my paper, 'On the Similarities between Modern Western Painting Trends and Chinese Traditional Painting Ideas' (*Shilun Xifang xiandaipai huihua sichao yu Zhongguo chuantong huihua lilunde gongxing*, 试论西方现代派绘画思潮与中国传统绘画理论的共性) won the 'thesis gold' of the 'world academic contribution prize' awarded by four Chinese associations : Chinese Center for International Famous Academia (中国国际名人学术研究中心), Chinese Association for Famous Personalities in the Cultural Field (中国文化名人联合会), Chinese Foundation of Love for International Famous Personalities (中国国际名人爱心基金会), and the Evaluation Committee of World Academic Contribution Prize (世界学术贡献奖评审委员会). In 2005, *China Pictoria* devoted four pages to my contribution to China's culutral intercourse with foreign countries. In 2007, L'etoile Europeenne du Devouement Civil et Militaire of France awarded me the Etoile Européennee du Dévouemment Civil et Militaire La Médaille d'Honneur échelong (European Star for Civil and Military Devotion Gold Medal Category). In 2008, the Societe Nationale des Beaux-Arts (National Association of Artists) awarded me a silver prize (*Medaille d'Argent de peinture*) at an exhibition in the Louvre Museum. I treat all this as humanity's encouragement for me.

In my childhood, I was fond of quoting the Chinese translation of the talented Russian writer, Vassiliev Mikhail Lermontov. He said life was not just a tiny candle, but a shining torch. I wish my life can become a rainbow, and my museum can become a painting brush so that the beautiful picture of human civilization can be painted forever and ever…

Westerners understand the culture and art of China and Asia. We cannot expect every French school to organize students to go to China to see the artifacts of the Han Dynasty. But, history teaching without viewing historical materials is an idle exercise. Our museum is recognized by the government as a venue for children and teenagers for visual enrichment. The cultural activities of our museum have been appreciated and supported by the French ministries of education and culture. They have been applauded by local residents, visitors, and experts around the world.

Every time when I lectured in China I was asked by the media about collections in world museums. Discussions always touched upon the topic of 'what's hot' (*re* 热) like 'patrioritc fever' (*aiguo re* 爱国热) or 'collection fever' (*shoucang re*, 收藏热). In my opinion, such 'heat' or 'fever' is unhealthy. The 'collection fever' has led to an intensification of greed for artifacts on the part of many people, and also led to illegal excavation of historical sites and acitives of fakery and counterfeit.

In July, 2013, four thugs of an international gang raided our museum and took away some ancient Chinese jade pieces. I tried to stop them and had a brutal fight with them. I was beaten to the floor several times and dragged by the hair and thrown from the four-storey platform to the ground. Till the time of writing I have yet to recover from my serious injury. But, I kept on fighting them until they fled. When I was struggling with one of the thugs, two of them entered the exhibition hall, broke the cases that exhibited the ancient jade and took away ten odd pieces. The crime remains unsolved. This was an international crime induced by 'collection fever'. According to the police, some so-called art collectors of China hired international gangsters to rob foreign art museums of famous valuable artifacts (making them 'return home'). Chinese art pieces of several British museums were similarly taken away. Afterwards, I received messages of consolation from known and unknown friends all over the world. Their advice : even if the artifacts are priceless they won't be more valuable than life, and I should not have risked my life for them. I feel grateful for their concern. Actually, when I saw a gun aimed at my chest, I never thought of the value of the art pieces, nor about my own life. My only thought was to prevent the robbers from entering the museum, not to allow the thugs to get what they wanted.

Artifacts are the assets of human civilization, the evidence of human history, and both the spiritual and material treasures of peoples of the world. It is our duty to preserve them and pass them down to future generations. Whatever rich collections an art collector can amass, he/she can only be a 'traveller' in history. The art collector can do it for his/her passion, not greed. There is a moral red line for an art collector. By crossing the line, he/she would become a villain for thousands of years.

For running this museum, for the cultural intercourse between the East and West, and for popularizing culture and art of China and Asia in the West, we have that the participants have to be inspired by characterization and skill as well as the culture, art, philosophy, and religion of Asia, and internalize it in their creation. The event not only enhances the interactions and friendship between Chinese and foreign artists, but even deepens the understanding on Asian culture and art on the part of Western artists. The year 2014 marks the golden jubilee of diplomatic relations between China and France, and I titled the event 'Rencontre avec la Chine'. China became the source of participants, and a number of excellent works were produced. Several years ago, this event obtained the support of the municipal government, and we began to have a thousand more Euros for awarding excellent artists.

In the last 15 years over a thousand artists of various countries have participated in this event with ardent love for Asian culture and art. The number of Chinese artists has also constantly increased. I have held more than a hundred exhibits and talks. Apart from introducing Chinese culture and art through my own works, I have also invited artists from China and other countries to exhibit, demonstrate, and lecture. We have exhibited Chinese paper cuttings, Chinese pottery, famous works of Chinese painters, embroidery and textiles of China, India and Thailand, Chinese paintings by French artists, porcelain of traditional Chinese style made by French and Japanese artisits, Japanese flower cutting made by French artists, Vietnam folk painting influenced by China, portraits of Indian maharajas, copper-plate painting about Chinese folklore by British artists of the 19th century, bronze sculpture by Indian tribals, as well as photographs of scenery and people of China, Tibet, India, Nepal, and the Himalaya region. I selected some rare sites and monuments from the photographs I took in India and other Asian countries to hold exhibits to introduce the great history and culture of China and Asia to viewers in the West. These included the mystic Angkor Wat, sacrificial ceremonies in the holy city of Varanasi, Hong Kong, villages inside Indian cities, mass celebrations of the Ganesh Festival, Indian marriage ceremonies, traces of Sakyamuni, the exploration of the Queen's Stepwell of India, a new Angkor Wat—Atru. The Indian Ambassador to France came specially to Biarrits to inaugurate my exhibits.

After years of running a museum my feeling is that education ranks higher among the tasks of a museologist than collecting, preserving, and exhibiting. Several years ago, the French customs handed over to us some smuggled Chinese and Japanese ivory sculptures. I instantly organized an exhibition for them along with some 'vegetable ivory' sculptures to show that the latter were by no means inferior as works of art so that people should not butcher the elephants.

Right now, the curriculum prescribed by the French government makes compulsory courses for students to study the Han Dynasty of China and the Gupta Dynasty of India. It so happens that the exhibits of our museum can provide supplementary materials that the textbooks cannot. It has been my dream to make

Four seas to One Family:
Overseas Chinese and Chinese dream

The artifacts of our museum are from various countries and regions, and different historical periods and cultural backgrounds. They are from China, Chinese Tibet, Nepal, India, Myanmar, Indonesia, Japan, and Kampuchea. We also have artifacts from the tribes of the Himalayan region and India. We have ornaments, miniature paintings, and commemorative stamps. The range of their antiquity is over several thousand years. The complexity of the artifacts created a complex task of exhibiting them. I had to highlight the idiosyncrasy of the art pieces as well as the cultures of the countries and regions to which they belonged, but also create a harmonious ambience for the exhibition hall. From an educational perspective, I must exhibit them in accordance with their historical, geographical, cultural and religious backgrounds so that the viewers not only see the art pieces, but also comprehensively understand the affinity of the respective pieces with human civilization.

My approach was original, breaking the conventional adoption of the off-white or ivory color in the display among world museums to adopt various colors from the rainbow. I decorated the walls of various halls to highlight what a specific color symbolized. For instance, I used red to decorate the halls of the Chinese exhibits, and the saffron, the color worn by lamas, for the Tibetan hall. I moderated cold colors with mystical colors for the Himalayan region. Besides the walls, I considered the harmony of colors for the boards, cases, stands and so on. With these specific modes of exhibition, I created a cultural and religious ambience for viewers. Innumerable viewers have expressed to me their feeling of gaining knowledge in addition to an experience of purification of the heart, freeing themselves from the madding crowd where material lust and greed were rampant. They felt this museum not only the venue of learning and research, but also an ideal place for spiritual cultivation. Many thought a visit to the museum a world tour. The color schemes I invented have been adopted by several museums in France.

In 2000, Museé Asiatica (which is situated in the historical cultural city, Biarrits, on the Atlanta coast in southwest France) formally opened. It became one of the three most famous museums with ancient Asian artifacts in Europe—along with the British Museum of London and the Guimet Museum of Paris. I became the first Chinese to set up a museum of Eastern art in the West.

It was difficult to create this museum, running it is even more so. The museum is now running, but my work still continues. I wish to make this museum a bridge between Eastern and Western cultures. Besides Paris, there is no full scale and typical museum of Asian art in the entire southwest of Europe, from western France to Spain, Portugal, up to Greece and Italy.

Every year, I organize 'Rencontre avec l'Asie'—painting, sculpture and photograph exhibition and competition highlighting Asia. I make it a prerequisite

Nouvelles d'Europe (欧洲时报) that 'The new era of popularizing Chinese culture and art has arrived!'

In 1989, I obtained my master's degree from Université de Paris VIII by submitting my dissertation *Etudes Comparatives sur l'Ecole de Yangzhou de la peinture chinoise et l'Ecole impressionniste française* (中国扬州画派与法国印象派的比较研究), and continued to study for my doctoral degree.

In 1990, I was the only Chinese participating in the excavation and photography of the thousand-year-old great Indian historical site of 'the queen's stepwell' (*rani ki vav*). In 1992, I discontinued my half-completed doctoral dissertation as well as my discipline and speciality to pursue the Ph D course of the Sorbonne campus of Paris University and continued with my archaeological work and research on the ancient art in India. In 1997, my doctoral dissertation defense was highly evaluated and I obtained the PhD degree from Sorbonne University.

In 1998, I started the work of creating Museé Asiatica at Biarritz in France, the first museum of art of the East in France (as well as in the entire Western world). I had to transform the abandoned premise of an old workshop for high tech in an art palace. The architecture did not provide space according to the needs of our artifacts, and budget constraints prevented me from making the exhibition cases according to the specifications of a normal art museum. We bought some replaced cases from the Guimet Museum and the Louvre of Paris, the latter of which were more than a hundred years old.

The exhibits of Museé Asiatica are mainly the personal collection of Dr. Michel Postel, famous art collector and expert in art history and archaeology. He is an ardent lover of the East, has studied Indian history, culture and art with several publications. He spent his lifetime savings in collecting artifacts from the East, buying them from antique markets and auctions in the West. He did this not for his private enjoyment, but to create this Museé Asiatica with his own funds so that he can display this cultural treasure to the public and let viewers from all over the world appreciate this precious legacy of human civilization, to understand the East, to love the civilizations of Asia, and to gain inspiration, information and wisdom from these artifacts, and enrich their living philosophy from the perspectives of Eastern philosophical thoughts and conceptions.

What we did initially was to dismantle the hundreds of optic cables and the huge air-condition fittings (weighing several tens of tons) from the old workshop. Then, I started working with my hands to create frames for the Tibetan Thangkas, special stands for Chinese snuff bottles, and miniature Buddha statues from Tibet, special exhibition cases for Indian jewels, and exhibition devices for stamps, for the weapons of the Moghals, and furniture from a Manchu palace…I became the carpenter, painter, fitter, mechanic, and the one doing manufacturing, sewing, and renovating, all rolled in one.

Four seas to One Family: Overseas Chinese and Chinese dream

I am a painter. My dream is to knit a rainbow with my own brush. My ideal is to construct a bridge between the East and the West. The rainbow is no mirage to me, but a fantasy after having studied and absorbed East-West culture and art. It is the spiritual symbol of my sojourn and penetration into Eurasian civilizations. I wish to pave a highway with my life to make the culture and art of China and Asia extend to the world, and make the quintessence of Western civilization extend into China.

In the early years of the 1980s, as a teacher in the Department of Cultural Heritage and Museology at Hangzhou University (杭州大学), I participated in seminars under the auspices of the Chinese Association of Museums (中国博物馆协会) and was a founding-member of the Chinese Association of Museum Art Display (中国博物馆陈列艺术协会).The museum display in China had rather poor facilities those days. They put artefacts inside cases for the public to view without elaborate lighting equipment. I cherished the dream of transforming Chinese museums into magnificent art palaces of Chinese civilization. With such motivation and helped by my father's friend, renowned expert in the studies of *Dream of the Red Chamber* (*Honglou meng*, 红楼梦), Professor Li Zhihua (李治华), I went to France as a self-financing scholar to study museum displays at the Ecole Nationale Supérieure des Arts-decoratifs à Paris (the national institution for decorative art in Paris) in 1986.

After nearly three decades, I have worked hard to spread Chinese art in the West. I have held exhibitions and talks at galleries, universities, and cultural centers in Paris, Mulhouse, Limoges, Biarritz, Anglet, and Bayonne in France, Geneva in Switzerland, Berlin, Hamburg and Nuremberg in Germany, Vienna in Austria, and New Delhi, Mumbai, Ahmedabad in India, popularizing Chinese culture, art, and philosophy. I have also published articles in various newspapers and journals, and seminars in China and other countries, not only introducing China to the West, but also introducing the culture and art of the world to China.

At the beginning of 1987, I had my maiden exhibition-cum-talk on Chinese painting and calligraphy abroad under the auspices of Librairie Les Herbes Sauvages, Paris. There were sufficient press announcements and a record registered audience. Unexpectedly, a few days before the lecture my over-fatigued body collapsed over the ten-odd-storey-high stairs of the Paris metro while carrying two big bags of research materials, and suffered a fracture in the right ankle. I was carried to the talk on the back of a fellow-student. In the course of the talk, which took over two hours, I stood on my slightly injured left leg while resting my right leg on a bench, talking and demonstrating. While the talk was successful, I nearly collapsed at the end of it. On April 5, 1987, *China Youth Daily* (*Zhongguo qingnian bao*, 中国青年报) carried my article, 'I Wish to Create a Rainbow with My Watercolors' (*Yuan sa danqing hua caihong*, 愿撒丹青化彩虹). In 1988, after receiving a one hundred plus delegation of calligraphers from Taiwan, I declared in the

Wish I Were a Rainbow: The First Chinese to Set up a Museum of Eastern Art in the West

Zhu Xintian 朱新天

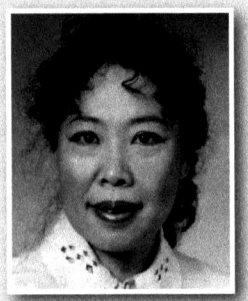

Born in 1951, she was a painter and photographer, teaching history in Hangzhou University (杭州大学). In 1986, she went to France for higher studies and obtained the Master of Art degree from the 8th campus of the University of Paris. In 1990, she was appointed a researcher of the Indian cultural institution and engaged in the Indian archaeological excavation. She obtained the Ph. D. degree from the University of Paris in 1997, and founded the Museé Asiatica (Museum of Aisan Art) at Biarritz in France along with the famous archaeologist and artifacts-owner, Dr. M. Postel. She is now the Deputy Director of the Museum. Her major publications are: a) the book on ancient indian art tiled *The Fantastic Beings of Ancient India, from 2500BC to 6th century AD* in English along with its French edition titled *Les Êtres fantastiques de l'inde ancienne, De 2500 av.J.-C. au 6ème Siècle*'; b) a book in Chinese titled *Yindujiao wanshendian yishu—Yindu wanghoujing tanmi*（印度教万神殿艺术——印度王后井探秘）(Art of the Hindu Pantheon: Explore the Mystery of the Rani Ki Vav of India).

To me, the rainbow is the most gorgeous image that Nature has gifted to humanity. It is a melody of peace in the wake of an orchestra of storms. The rainbow is the crystallization of sunshine and mist, and it gathers innumerable 'vital elements' of the universe to reflect a seven-color magnificent dreamland under the sun. The rainbow is like the most splendid arch in the cavernous blue sky, and it displays the flamboyance of the 'grand-mega-universe' (*daqian shijie*, 大千世界) or *mahasaha*sra-*lokadhatu*). The rainbow is like a bridge across time and space, standing aloof above everything on earth, lining up mountains and rivers. The rainbow epitomizes expectations and imaginations, and its serenity and magnificence carve out a romantic ideal for the future. The rainbow is also a bridge to the heart, and, like the colorful brush in the painter's hand, constructs a mystic road between Heaven and Earth, enabling various races to interconnect with each other by transcending all regional and linguistic barriers and to understand each other…

of art. There has always been 'instruments made of strings, bamboo, metal, and stone' (丝竹金石) to create effects that 'please the ear, move the heart, and stir the entrails' (感心动耳，荡气回肠), hence the development of music. All this is for the purpose of enjoying 'the good and the beautiful' (美) for oneself and for others. This is culture: literature, art, and music. There are no borders of country, race, language, or religion. It is for humanity to create a world of grand harmony. Wherever there are Chinese people there is the manifestation of Chinese culture. This is the real meaning of 'wherever I am, China is'.

We all know that after suffering for over a century of domestic disturbances and foreign aggressions, China became impoverished and backward and Chinese culture declined. Old China was ridiculed as a country of 'opium addicts' and 'the sick man of Asia'. Since 1949, China has been overburdened by restoration and rejuvenation. There is still a long way ahead for the revival of Chinese culture. Various ugly phenomena have spilled overseas. According to recent reports, some Chinese have discarded their self-respect totally in France and Spain and soiled the reputation and dignity of China and Chinese people. All kinds of uncouth behavior by Chinese nouveau riche while touring foreign countries have been exposed. If this is the kind of 'wherever I am, China is' that takes place, the 'Chinese dream' will turn into a nightmare and will never materialize. Therefore, when we advocate the 'Chinese dream' we should first advocate the revival of Chinese culture. We should advocate 'the true, good, and beautiful' (*zhen, shan, mei*, 真善美, *satyam, shivam, sundaram*) and eliminate the 'false, evil, and ugly' (*jia, e, chou*, 假恶丑).

The ultimate realization of the 'Chinese dream' must come from the approbation of the majority of people all over the world. Overseas Chinese are the natural bridges between the 'Chinese dream' and dreams from other countries. We depend on overseas Chinese to make the vast majority of the world people know and support the 'Chinese dream'. The 'Chinese dream' of overseas Chinese is the nearest to the world, and their "world dream" is the closest to China. Overseas Chinese, especially overseas Chinese scholars, are the most important source of connection for China with the world and promote the progress of the world. One hundred years ago, overseas Chinese all over the world gave great support to the Revolution of 1911 in China. Dr. Sun Yat-sen (孙中山) regarded them as 'the mothers of the revolution'. Today, overseas Chinese are still a great, indispensable resource for realizing the 'Chinese dream'.

his typical Gallic countenance. On the evenings of 6–7 January 2010, the couple delivered two lectures at Shenzhen University, respectively, on the topics of 'The Queen's Stepwell of India' and 'Indian Weddings' which were warmly received.

There is a Chinese saying: 'the fragrance of plum blossoms comes from a severe winter' (梅花香自苦寒来). This was how Dr. Zhu achieved her accomplishments amidst adverse conditions from childhood till her sojourn in Paris. She epitomizes the perseverance of the "Chinese dream." This reminds me of an observation by Rabindranath Tagore, the great Indian writer and first non-white Nobel laureate in Literature a century ago:

The lamp of ancient Greece is extinct in the land where it was first lighted, the power of Rome lies dead and buried under the ruins of its vast empire. But the civilization, whose basis is society and the spiritual ideal of man, is still a living thing in China and in India. Though it may look feeble and small, judged by the standard of the mechanical power of modern days, yet like small seeds it still contains life and will sprout and grow, and spread its beneficent branches, producing flowers and fruits when its time comes and showers of grace descend upon it from heaven.

Tagore spoke these words in a speech at Tokyo Imperial University in 1916. At that time, the Chinese sociopolitical, economic and cultural conditions were "feeble and small" judging by 'the standard of mechanical power in modern days'. However, what I saw in Vienna in 1993, let alone today, was that Chinese culture had 'sprouted and grown, and spread its beneficent branches, been producing flowers and fruits,' even abroad. I sincerely admire Tagore's vision.

The stories of Li Xiangting, Li Zhihua, Guan Yuqian, Zhu Xintian and many many other overseas Chinese not mentioned in this article are the best testimony to the 'Chinese dream' of 'wherever I am, China is'. In other words, wherever there are overseas Chinese, there is Chinese culture and there is the echo of the 'Chinese dream'. China was there when international intellectuals got together in Vienna to listen to the *jiuxiao huanpei guqin*'s 'peerless music under the Heaven'. China was there when French people read Li Zhihua's translation of *Dream of the Red Chamber*. China was there when Guan Yuqian did research and propounded on his theories in Germany. And China was there when Zhu Xintian runs the Museé Asiatica in Biarritz.

Now, people all over China, even the entire world, are talking about the 'Chinese dream'. This shows that China is peaceful and prosperous and the Chinese people are doing well. It also demonstrates the Chinese people's entreaty to the world. Since ancient times, Chinese culture has had its practice of '*qi*/spirit realizing *zhi*/vision' (气以实志), and 'from *zhi*/vision to *yan*/expression' (志以定言), hence the development of literature. There has always been 'the red-and-blue brush' (丹青之笔) to capture 'the wonder of Nature's creation' (造化之功), hence the development

2009, I received Dr. Zhu Xiantian's book, *The Queen's Stepwell of India*, from Mumbai, India. After reading her book from cover to cover I was excited and wrote to her highlighting three things: 1) 'You are the savior of Indian art', 2) 'you are the glory of the Zhu family', and 3) 'you are the pride of all my friends'.

I had a completely new understanding of Dr. Zhu and her husband after reading her book and other materials she sent me. Michel Postel was a member of the French Resistance, a fighter in General De Gaulle's anti-German Army, and a pilot in the American Air Force. He received the Legion of Honour (Chevalier) for his bravery. In 1949, he started a pharmaceutical company in India and started learning Indian culture. He accumulated a fortune for six odd decades, a part of which he donated to India's health care while spending the other part buying Asian (including Indian) artifacts. In 1970, he set up the Indian Culture Institute in Mumbai. In 1999, he spent all his money to establish the Museé Asiatica at Biarritz in France. Museé Asiatica now shares a similar reputation to the British Museum and the Guimet Museum in Paris as the three leading art museums in Europe. After decades of field investigation and empirical research, Michel Postel published more than a dozen academic books and became a world famous specialist in the history of South Asian art.

Born in a scholarly family in Hangzhou (杭州), Dr. Zhu Xintian is a famous painter and photographer. In 1986, then a teacher at the Department of Cultural Heritage and Musicology in Hangzhou University (杭州大学), she went to France for further study and completed a master's degree of comparative fine arts at the Université de Paris VIII and gained her doctorate in Far Eastern arts and archaeology from the Sorbonne, Université de Paris. A series of her papers and books have been highly praised by international academic circles. Her doctoral dissertation, *Vyala Motifs in Indian Art*, and M.A. thesis, *Comparative Studies on the Chinese Yangzhou School of Painting and French Impressionism*, have been regarded as masterpieces in the study of Indian art and comparative study of Chinese and French art. She devoted nearly 20 years to study and inform the public about the Queen's Stepwell of India. In January 2009, the obscure Queen's Stepwell was eventually known by the world and listed as a World Heritage by the UNESCO.

Based on the above information about this couple, I submitted a proposal to the authorities of Shenzhen University to invite them to deliver lectures and award them Honorary Professorships. Being in the forefront of reform and opening-up, the President of the University, Professor Zhang Bigong (章必功) green-lighted the process to the Director of Human Resources, Mr. Wang Entang (王恩堂). President Zhang invited Dr. Zhu Xintian and her husband, Mr. Michel Postel, to visit the University in January 2010. On January 6, 2010, I met the couple at the Shekou (蛇口) Port, Shenzhen and said to them, 'This is our third handshake'. When Dr. Zhu translated my words into French to her husband, a soft smile appeared on fleet invaded Yongtai Bay (永泰湾) from Fuzhou (福州), his father led the county's security forces to fight against them while they were landing. Yongtai is very close to Minjiang (闽江), my wife's hometown. Therefore, I always remembered Guan Yuqian and his story.

Not long ago, I suddenly saw Guan Yuqian in a program on Phoenix TV. He was analyzing German opinions of the latest developments in Ukraine. At once, I called my wife to see the program and told her that the scholar in the red coat was Guan Yuqian whose father fought against Japanese invaders in Yongtai. My wife said that there was a county magistrate whose family name was probably 'Guan' (管) who had been popular among the people as she was told by her father. I was wondering whether there was any mix-up between the two homophones. I checked on the Internet and discovered that it was indeed so. Guan Yuqian's father, Guan Xibin (关锡斌), was a member of the Chinese Communist Party (CCP) and a descendant of Guan Tianpei (关天培), the famous anti-British general during the Opium War. In the early years post-Liberation, Guan Yuqian was a Russian-language interpreter for Soviet advisors. No wonder he was so familiar with Ukraine on the Phoenix TV program! I guess there must be quite a number of overseas Chinese who, like Guan Yuqian, have had a connection with China's post-Opium War wake-up and development. They are the seeds of the 'Chinese dream' being sown all over the world.

I also got to know Dr. Zhu Xintian (朱新天) and her French husband, Mr. Michel Postel, also at the 1993 conference. On the afternoon of 29 July, we took a bus to the Vienna Woods to have dinner after visiting Österreichisches Parlament, Rathaus Wien, and sightseeing around the city. In downtown Vienna, I saw old palatial buildings everywhere, in the hilly suburbs it was an unending forest. I felt as though I was coming to Xiangshan (香山), a suburb of Beijing. We had dinner at the Happy Farm Restaurant. Hanging on the walls were carriage wheels and the driver's clothes and other decorations. We had typical native food. While eating, I was talking with Mr. Xu Xueqiang (许学强), professor at Sun Yat-sen University (中山大学) and Director of the Department of Higher Education in Guangdong (广东) Province, and his student Dr. Chen Zhenxiong (陈镇雄). Dr. Zhu Xintian waved at me and asked me to share a table with her and her husband. She asked for more food and we started talking about everything under the sun. Very soon, our topic turned to Indian culture. She asked me about Professor Jin Kemu (金克木) and told me that Professor Jin was a good friend of her father's.

My second handshake with this couple occurred in Shenzhen at the end of the 20th–century. A Chinese company wanted to import a drug for diabetes produced by Michel Postel's pharmaceutical firm. They agreed to negotiate the deal at Shenzhen. My wife, Zheng Yilin (郑亦麟), accompanied me to call on them at their hotel. We stayed in touch for quite a while but it suddenly stopped. In November surrounded by children and grandchildren. The proudest thing in Li Zhihua's life was devoting 27 years in translating into French the famous Chinese classical novel, *Dream of the Red Chamber* (*Honglou meng*, 红楼梦). The subjects of Li Zhihua's doctoral dissertation were 'Studies on Chinese Yuan Dynasty Opera' and 'French Translations of Chinese Yuan Dynasty Opera.' It was his mastery in translating ancient Chinese literature that drew the attention of Mr. Etiemble, Chairman of the Editorial Board of the Oriental Knowledge Series, under the auspices of United Nations Educational, Scientific, and Cultural Organization (UNESCO). Etiemble then persuaded Li Zhihua to translate *Dream of the Red Chamber* into French. Li Zhihua's 27 years of hard work, from 1954 to 1981, yielded a marvelous translation of this great masterpiece, one of four Chinese classical novels. Jacqueline was not only his first reader, but constantly helped him polish the translation. Therefore, Li Zhihua's French translation of *Dream of the Red Chamber* is elegant in expression, profound in message, and easy to read. It has been well received by the French readership. The book is sheepskin-bound and now a part of the famous series of 'Bibliothèque de la Pléiade'. The UNESCO office and the Chinese Embassy in France jointly hosted a cocktail reception to launch this book. Sales of the book run to tens of thousands of copies a year, a record of its kind. For this, Li Zhihua was awarded the 'Ordre des Arts et des Lettres' (Officier) by the Cultural Ministry of the government of France.

In September, 2002, the National Museum of Modern Chinese Literature, Beijing, created a 'Li Zhihua-Jacqueline collection' as the repository of hand-written manuscripts from the French translation of *Dream of the Red Chamber*, as well as the decades-long correspondences of Li Zhihua with his parents, relatives, and friends which he had donated to the Museum. That done, he felt happy and said, 'It marks the return to my root culturally'.

When Chairman Xi Jinping (习近平) visited France in April, 2014, he paid special tribute to the 99-year-old Li Zhihua. It was a sensational news. I believe Li Zhihua is the most successful example of a Chinese scholar living his 'Chinese dream' by devoting all his life to creating a significant chapter in the history of Sino-French cultural exchange and eventually staging a return to his cultural roots.

At the 1993 conference, Dr. Guan Yuqian (关愚谦) from Germany also created a deep impression on me. His paper, 'China's Economic Reforms through European Eyes', showed sharp views and refreshing insights. Actually, we first met not at the conference, but at the bus station. I had arrived early and stayed for a while at the bus station as there was plenty of time to register for the conference. I sat on a bench and saw him: a tall man lying on the bench opposite me with a German newspaper covering his face. Then we met again at the conference. In our subsequent chat, he told me that his father was the Magistrate of Yongtai County (永泰县) in Fujian (福建) Province during the Anti-Japanese War. When the Japanese in the annual exhibit of Chinese artists under the auspices of the Beijing Branch of the Chinese Artists Association. He also held personal exhibitions of his paintings at the Chinese Art Gallery of the University of London in 1989. In 1991, he lectured on 'The Shared Beauty of the Dot and Line between Chinese Painting and *Guqin* Music' at Victoria University, Wellington, New Zealand. He is listed in the *Dictionary of Chinese Artists* (*Zhongguoyishujia cidian*, 中国艺术家辞典), *The Famous Figures of the Contemporary Arts Circles in China* (*Zhongguo dangdai yishujie mingren lu*, 中国当代艺术界名人录) (1993). He also figures in *Outstanding Intellectuals of the 20th Century* (1999) compiled by the International Biographical Centre of Cambridge University, England. He won the Gold medal awarded by "Chinese Art Across the World" for his landscape painting, 'High Mountains and Flowing Waters in My Dream' (*gaoshan liushui rumeng ping*, 高山流水入梦频) in 1999.

During our chat, Professor Li told me that his performances were well received in Europe and he was often asked by people to stay on (that is, to not return to China). But, he said, his heart remained in China even when in Europe. Even though many Western people loved the *guqin* music, he said, China was still its homeland. Only in China could the audience truly understand his music.

I returned to China after the conference and lost contact with Professor Li. One year (I can't remember which), I saw Professor Li on Chinese TV. He had the same elegant look of a Confucian scholar, still playing the music of 'High Mountains and Flowing Waters' on the *jiuxiao huanpei guqin*, though with a few more grey hairs, but charmingly so, and definitely with more disciples and fans. After that, I saw him a few more times again on TV with his *guqin*. I know for certain that Li Xiangting and his *jiuxiao huanpei guqin*, playing 'peerless music under the heavens', accompanies the 'Chinese dream' in reverberating in the heart of his audiences, in China and overseas alike, making decades seem like a day.

At the 1993 conference, the other person who impressed me most was an overseas Chinese scholar: the translator, Li Zhihua (李治华) and his French wife Ya Ge (雅歌, Jacqueline). Li Zhihua was the first speaker after the Opening Ceremony. His paper was on 'The History and Significance of the Spread of Chinese Literature in France'. At that time, he was entering his 80s, with a head full of silver hair but with bountiful energy. A great ovation arose when he walked onto the stage. A Chinese scholar by my side told me that Professor Li was the most prestigious Chinese scholar in France.

Li Zhihua was born in 1915 in Beijing. He studied in a Sino-French University in Lyons, France, after graduating from the Sino-French University of Beijing when he was 22 years old. His French classmate at the time, 20–year–old Jacqueline, offered to be his partner in class and helped him improve his French. Soon, this pair of 'Golden Boy and Jade Girl' fell into the proverbial River of Love. They have had a marvelous marriage, weathering thick and thin for seven decades, now

'Chinese dream' overseas.

My mind flies back to the summer of 1993. I attended the Seventh International Conference in picturesque Vienna on 'East and West: A Cultural Comparison', at the invitation of the Association of Chinese Scholars in Europe (ACSE). Vienna, the capital of Austria, that renowned royal city of the Austro-Hungarian Empire, was admirably beautiful and majestic. It was at this conference that I had the opportunity to speak with some overseas Chinese and felt that the 'Chinese dream' had spread all over the world.

At the opening session on the morning of 26 July, Professor Li Xiangting (李祥霆) played the Chinese *guqin* (古琴). Professor Kaminski Gred, President of the Austria-China Friendship Association, followed with a keynote speech. I had the good fortune to meet with the world-famous Professor Li. He was the Number One *guqin* player in the world and *guru* to more than 400 disciples from all over the world since the 1960s.

China is not just a country but also, more significantly, a millennial civilization. The instrument played by Professor Li named *jiuxiao huanpei* ('jewel from nine heavens', 九霄环佩) was a product of the Kaiyuan (开元) Era of the Tang Dynasty during the 8th century; it had been handed down for 1300 years. Households across China know the *jiuxiao huanpei guqin* as an instrument of 'peerless music under the heavens' (天下第一声音). I chatted with Professor Li during the break. I asked him how he could manage taking this *guqin*, a national treasure, out of the country. He said that the customs officers had very limited knowledge about the national treasure. When he claimed that it was his personal instrument they allowed him to carry it to England (he was then a visiting scholar for an English university). I asked when he might return to China, he gave an uncertain answer.

I witnessed how Professor Li played the *jiuxiao huanpei*. Creating 'peerless music under the heavens,' he resonated with the foreign audience in Vienna. Wearing the traditional Chinese shirt, Li looked like an elegant Confucian scholar. He blended tension with ease, his melody leading the audience to the lofty mountains in one moment, as if lifting all of us to the summit of Mount Tai (泰山), then to flowing water in another moment, as if making all of us swim in Yangzi River. All of us were immersed in his music. Some European professors were especially moved by the elegance of classical Chinese music. They sighed and exclaimed with appreciation. They repeated requested encores. During the entire conference, Professor Li performed several rounds and played Chinese classic songs including the renowned 'three stanzas from the "Song of the Gate of Yang",' (*yangguan sandie*, 阳关三叠). What impressed me most was that Professor Li could play on whatever topic or poem posed to him. He won warm applause and admiration from the entire audience.

Actually, Li Xiangting is a painter as well as musician. In 1988, he participated

Wherever I Am, China Is: The 'Chinese dream' Overseas[1]

> Yu Longyu 郁龙余
>
>
>
> Born in Shanghai in 1946, he is Professor and Director of the Centre for Indian Studies, Shenzhen University. He completed his studies in the Department of Oriental Language and Literature, Peking University, majoring in Hindi, and began to teach Hindi at Peking University after graduation in March, 1970. He moved to the Shenzhen University in 1984 as a professor and has been there ever since having, successively, held the positions as Director of the Department of Chinese Culture and Mass Communication, Dean of the College of Arts, Chairman of the Board of Studies at the College of Arts, Deputy Director of the Department of International Culture, etc. Concurrently, he was member of the Board of Studies and Guest Professor at the Center for Oriental Literature, Peking University, Vice-President of the Chinese Association of Indian Literary Research, Vice-President of the Chinese Association of Oriental Literatures, member of the Standing Committee of the Chinese Association of Comparative Literature, member of the Standing Committee of the Chinese Association of South-Asian Studies, and Vice-President of the Chinese Association for the Studies of History of China's External Contacts, etc. He has published more than 80 academic articles in the journals of China and abroad. He has edited more than 20 books including *Fandian yu Huazhang: Yindu zuojia yu Zhongguo wenhua* (梵典与华章：印度作家与中国文化) (Sculptures of Brahma and classics of Zhonghua: Indian weiters and Chinese culture) which won a grade-II prize from the Ministry of Education of Chinese government.

I am not an overseas Chinese. However, Professor Tan Chung and I are fellow-members of the "Four Seas to One Family" club, and it gives me great pleasure to contribute to his book, *Overseas Chinese and the 'Chinese dream'*. My daughter, Yu Xiu, suggested a topic. She gave me a quote from the great German writer, Thomas Mann: '*Wo ich bin, ist Deutschland*' ('wherever I am, Germany is'). By changing only one word—'China' for 'Germany'—I use 'wherever I am, China is' to depict the

---

1 Translated into English by Wang Bi (王璧)

> except what has been marked
> by your toes.

The poet was talking to me. My poetic instinct echoes his words with my own aria of the lotus. I see the old weeping willow waiving its branches, watching every step of my odyssey. I see the lotus flirters her skirts, and the pearls on the lotus leaves—what are they doing, kissing or inquiring?

Like the lotus, I grew up from the perilous mud. I printed my feet from my homeland at Xiamen to the foot of Mount Yan of Beijing, further to the capital of the US, teaching Spanish languages and literature, singing my little arias.

Dreaming is a hard job, living the dream is even harder. I have my dream, and the dream melts into musical notes, and the harp plays a cacophony—like the lone lotus struggling inside the lake with its root trudging in the mud, searching…

I wish good luck to all my friends, old and new, known and unknown, in their quest for serenity and tranquility, when they are trudging in the mud, shedding fragrance all the way.

Team, got into Stanford University with a full scholarship. She nominated me for *Who's Who Among America's Teachers*. It was an incredible honor. The students in my classes know that their Asian Spanish teacher is strict and demanding. They know that they have to work hard to live up to my expectations, but they can learn from me in one year what they cannot elsewhere. I tried to implement what my Chinese ancestors taught me: 'True knowledge consists of teaching what you really know and admitting what you do not.' Also: 'The teacher and the student complement each other.'

Last year, when many of my AP Spanish Literature students made constant grammar mistakes, confusing gender, number and some literary terms, I was furious. Out of a teacher's desperation, I corrected all their mistakes and worded them into a Spanish poem of surrealist style. Next day when I presented my forty verse long poem as a gift to my students, they laughed until they cried amidst amusement and humiliation. They appreciated my humor, my poetry, and my love for them. I treat my students with love and respect, and my students give me their love and trust too.

In September 2014, I gave a presentation to a group of noted Chinese American scholars and professionals in the Washington area on the topic of 'Magical Realism and Garcia Márquez, a Colombian Writer and Nobel Laureate.' My mastery of Spanish literature and my Chinese translation of García Marquez's fiction created a deep impact among the learned audience. I have come to feel that perhaps my understanding of Latin American literature is even deeper than that of Western scholars because I come from the East, from a country of five millennia of civilization, and I have the poets Qu Yuan (屈原), Li Bai (李白), Du Fu (杜甫) and others in my blood. I have, in my lifetime, been so often moved into tears by their poetic lines.

Along my long journey as a Chinese immigrant in the United States, these famous lines of Spanish verse constantly ring in my ears:

> Caminante, son tus huellas
> el camino, y nada mas;
> caminante, no hay camino;
> se hace camino al andar.

These internationally known lines convey what the Castilian poet, Antonio Machado, wished to tell:

> Traveler, your footprint
> is your road, and nothing else.
> Traveler, there is not any road

University, and taught Chinese students about Li Bai, Du Fu or *The Dream of the Red Chamber*.

Thanks to my accumulated knowledge plus hard work, I sailed smoothly through this seemingly untenable reality, and completed the semester with a lot of love and respect from my Latino students. They invited me to their homes and even tried to organize a protest when they found out that the university could not renew my contract due to a budget crunch. Although I had already received an offer for a tenure-track position at a private university in Alabama, I was very touched all the same. This first success in teaching and the love and trust from my Hispanic students encouraged me constantly during my long teaching career afterwards.

Since the beginning, my Chinese face has marked me and I have encountered a layer of prejudice wherever I went during my teaching career. Uninformed students always walked into my classroom with an automatic impression that I am a Chinese language teacher. I remember at a national Spanish oral proficiency workshop, the moderator, upon seeing me walking into the room, reminded everyone very politely that the meeting was not an ESOL workshop and it would be conducted completely in Spanish. Responding to his remark I calmly introduced myself and put forward my opinion about the subject in elegant chaste Spanish, and immediately won the respect of the moderator. I could see that everyone was stunned and impressed. Such a scenario has happened many times, but with my confidence, dignity, tolerance and patience, little by little, I gained respect and a reputation among my colleagues. I consider it not just defending my personal dignity, but the dignity of overseas Chinese scholars as well.

I realize that the best vindication for any teacher to be respected and loved by the students is to have both a solid command of his/her subject and to treat the students with empathy, compassion, and patience. In the US, authority or honorifics on a business card matter less than a person's character. In 1992, I presented my paper about Benito Pérez Galdós at the Northeast Modern Language Association Annual Convention. Later, I served as the secretary and president of Galdós panels. I also went to Prince Edward Island in Canada to present my paper on the Cervantes novel at the XXVII Congress of the Canadian Congress of Hispanics. As the only Asian in these national and international conferences, where did I get the courage and enthusiasm to present these papers? It was my dream — the dream that has never been extinguished even during the worst times of my life, the dream that energized me with knowledge and confidence.

During the years of my teaching career, more than once, students have tried to change their schedule in order to switch into my Spanish class. In 2003, one student of mine, who was an excellent student and a gymnast for the American National

Spanish class. Some of my graduate classmates were actually university professors back in Latin America. They came to Stony Brook for the express purpose of receiving their Ph.D. in order to continue teaching in their country. Some of them carried in their suitcases an already finished PhD thesis when arriving in the US. Stony Brook was just a place that would allow them to obtain a terminal degree. In comparison with them, I felt like Cinderella.

I was fearless or, perhaps, unable to fear. I did not have a word for 'retreat' in the dictionary of my life. Whenever I think of the days of being deprived of the right of study, of living without opening a book, crying without tears at the day-care job, I considered Stony Brook a godsend. Notably I was the only Chinese in the crowd chasing a PhD degree in Spanish Literature. I had no alternative but to advance against the currents, no matter what the sacrifice.

After my first semester, it was time for the PhD qualifying examination, a great hurdle in US doctoral studies. The scope of the exam included five books from different subjects, from philosophy to novels to poetry. Two of the books, *Fábula de Polifemoy Galatea* (*Fable of Polyphemus and Galatea*, 1613) and *Soledades* (*Solitudes*, 1613), were so complex and enigmatic that they had scared away thousands of Spanish readers in the past. I studied them day and night for a month and passed the exam, while some of my classmates were unlucky and failed. In the following three years of intensive study, I read, wrote, and breathed Hispanic literature. It was ridiculously difficult, but I accumulated, at unbelievable speed, knowledge about Hispanic literature and culture, and started to gain self-confidence. My fellow graduate students and professors gave me lots of respect and support as I was the only Asian student in the PhD program. Several professors gave me as gifts their autographed books. I remember that, in our upper level seminar about Cervantes, my professor was so impressed with my final term paper that he asked me to revise it for publication—a very treasurable gesture from a world famous scholar.

Three years of intensive study flew by. It led to another big exam, the most challenging one toward the dissertation: the PhD Comprehensive Exam. In order to pass this exam I had to read 150 titles of literary works as well as their critiques. The exam lasted for three days, about eighteen hours in total. It was with tremendous pride that I passed the exam successfully. I was appointed by the SUNY College at Old Westbury as their Instructor to teach a second year Spanish class and Survey of Latin American Literature. While I was very proud to become part of the faculty in an American university, I was naturally nervous because all the thirty something students of the Literature course were native Spanish speakers. They came from Hispanic families in the US and spoke perfectly in at least two languages. The fact that I was teaching them Don Quijote, Spanish Baroque, or the Golden Age was like an American professor who flew over to Beijing, landed on the campus of Beijing literature in Chinese. What a daring and ambitious proclamation from a novice!

Longing for a completely new life filled with various dreams, I boarded the airplane with a ticket that cost me five times my annual salary in China. I left Beijing and landed in New York to start my PhD program at the State University of New York at Stony Brook. Used to being the best at Beijing's Institute of Foreign Languages, the best language university in China, perhaps, even in Asia, I naively assumed I would be peerless in my Spanish studies in the US. After reaching New York, I discovered immediately that the Spanish courses in China were 30-50 years behind those in US universities.

In the 1980s, SUNY Stony Brook's Department of Hispanic Languages and Literature was one of the best in the country. It had an impressive array of faculty members. The director of the graduate program, for example, was a former Cuban ambassador in Fidel Castro's administration.

Many young graduates from Spain and around the world came to Stony Brook to study with these leading figures in the field of Hispanic Literature. Not only did the professors offer a variety of seminars and graduate courses, but they also brought other famous scholars from all over the world to be our visiting professors for one or two semesters. I felt extremely fortunate to be part of this graduate program. However, the impressive array of famous professors in addition to the outstanding scholars among my classmates created immense pressures on me — the odd one out from China. I shudder even today, more than twenty years later, when I remember those days and nights of excruciating hard work in order not to cut a sorry figure for myself and for my country.

When I think of how foreign languages were taught in China, I regret that there was concentration only on memorization and articulation as well as sentence structures. The students who grow up in the Chinese education system usually have a solid foundation in the language with accurate pronunciation and sensitivity to syntax. A foreign language full of human experience should have been an interesting subject to study, but it was taught like mathematics in China. The classes were conducted like military drills and the students were on high alert with tension, all human flavor gone with the wind.

In an American classroom, life is not easy but there is always fun and laughter. Though I had had first-class foreign language training in China, I found my appreciation of Spanish literature rather poor, equivalent to that of a junior high school student in the US. In my undergraduate studies, we read little literature, just some newspaper articles and a couple of short stories written by Latin American revolutionary authors. Now in a world-class Hispanic literature study, I had to take a gigantic leap from junior high to graduate studies.

Every week, each of my three graduate courses assigned me a book to read. Some spanned over a thousand pages. Meanwhile, I was an instructor for a sophomore above the white clouds in the big, blue sky. We studied 15 hours or more a day, and reading rooms in the library was packed to capacity — we had to fight for our seats with master strategies. Materially, we were poor, but the sky was the limit in our spiritual life. We had inflated hopes for anything we wanted and for living our dreams. My dream world was made of color and music, poetry and fantasy.

Those were the days when we dared to dream. A peer wanted to translate the Chinese masterpiece, *Hong Lou Meng* (红楼梦, *Dream of the Red Chamber*) into Spanish. Others wished to become first-rate diplomats. Still someone else wanted to compile a Chinese encyclopedia of Spanish language and literature. I was the youngest in the class, timid and quiet, but I also bore lofty aspirations within. I wished to become a first rate Chinese expert of Hispanic language and literature.

During those four years of my undergraduate study, the only entertainment that we students could enjoy was a weekly outdoor movie. I still remember that, at dusk, the college would hang a big piece of white fabric tied with ropes as a screen in the center of the playground. During summer, a gentle breeze swept the ground with cool air and the stars twinkled in the sky. We had a perfect romantic outdoor cinema. Sometimes, a strong gale blew and the pretty faces of the film stars on the screen got funny distorting images. In winter, we wrapped our bodies and faces with cotton-padded clothes and headgears and scarves, leaving only the eyes uncovered. When the temperature dropped to below 30 degrees Fahrenheit, everyone seemed frozen into an ice cube. No sooner had the romantic dialogue or kissing scene of the movie ended than the entire audience would stomp its fee in unison. The thundering stomping echoed the heartbeats of those young men and women, who had cried and laughed sincerely with the heroes and heroines of the movie. I have lost count of how many of them have become prominent personalities in their respective careers — as ambassadors, ministers, academics, and poets!

I had the good fortune to become a member of new China's first-generation of degree-holder in Spanish. After graduation, I obtained a job as a full-time translator for the Foreign Language Press in Beijing. It was a good job that would provide a comfortable and worry-free living, but I was neither comfortable nor worry-free. The dream deep in my heart made me restless. I studied for one year and passed a rigorous entrance examination for a Master's program in Latin American Literature at my alma mater. I took classes with Professor Liu Xiaopei who had been the chairperson of the department and had returned from his study from Chile. I also studied under a visiting Professor, Norman Cortes, a famous scholar from the Universidad de Valparaiso in Chile. After two years of rigorous study, I applied for a PhD program in the US and received acceptances from six universities with a full scholarship. I wrote in my statement of purpose that my dream was to pursue an advanced study of Latin American literature and write a history of Hispanic

University) originated from the Yan'an Foreign Language School. It was administered directly under the jurisdiction of the Ministry of Foreign Affairs for many years due to its crucial and sensitive role in training Chinese diplomats. Only after 1980, two years after I joined, was it transferred to the Ministry of Education. The School was the last bastion of the revolutionary traditions of the 1940s.

In the years of 'Reform and Opening-up' in the 1980s, female students at Chinese universities vied with one another to make themselves colorful and pretty. However, the girls in this conservative revolutionary bastion of Foreign Languages were frugally dressed and without make-up. They resembled the cadres of Yan'an caves. An iron rule was political studies on Saturday afternoons. All students had to abide by a rigid timetable for work and rest.

Every morning, when the dorm's hallway bell rang, we all rushed out of our warm beds and doubled down to the cold central field. Each class had a 'leader' who religiously took attendance. After being assured that no one was absent, we ran as a group around the campus, a distance of about one mile. After this routine morning exercise, we rushed back upstairs to the public bathroom to cleanse our sleepy faces with freezing water. Then, we dashed down again to the courtyard with textbooks in hand for our morning pronunciation drill. For four years, we never broke this morning routine, rain or shine or snow. Each of us had our favorite corner to drill our tongues — the edge of an abandoned swimming pool or the side of a basketball court. The sound of more than twenty foreign languages reverberated throughout the campus. Small wonder that every graduate from our university has acquired a perfect accent in one's respective foreign language.

After the morning pronunciation drill, we all proceeded to the student dining hall for breakfast. In the first year, we had no choice about our meals. Breakfast was a bowl of hot yellowish soup of corn meal, a steamed corn bun of the same color, and several slices of salty pickles. For lunch, we were served with rice topped with vegetables mixed with pork. Dinner had a monotonous dish with Chinese cabbage boiled in soy sauce and bean noodles — all with poor taste and nutrition. The monthly charge was 15 yuan (about 2 US dollars). The big dining hall had only rows of long tables without benches. We had to eat while standing, training ourselves for fast dining in military style. We had a few yuan for pocket money. However meager this might be, we tried to save some money to shop for our favorite books. Sometimes, we asked friends for loans to buy new arrivals which we wanted to read and had to skip a few meals to pay back the loan without any regret.

I was ecstatic to be liberated from the prison-like daycare job for the stoic lifestyle of the Beijing Institute of Foreign Languages. We all wore a small metal badge engraved with the name of our institution. It was a symbol of our pride, confidence, and rosy future. Our self-image was so inflated. It was as if we lived and fetched water from wells. We lived as if in a military camp. The day began at 6am with hard, physical labor and continued until 10pm with political study sessions of Community Party newspapers and documents.

I remember vividly one particular task. The kindergarten was pursuing self-sufficiency according to official guidelines. The authorities decided to raise pigs and we had to build a big pigpen from scratch. In order to use what was left from the abandoned hospital where the day-care center was situated, we demolished a mortuary and carried every single stone pillar to the top of a hill. Each pillar weighed around a ton and it took six people using large bamboo poles to carry it. I was so tiny and not tall enough to bear the same weight as my older and stronger colleagues. I could not keep up with their sturdy steps. I felt the pillars bearing down on me like a mountain on my fragile shoulders. To this day, the experience of that pulverizing drudgery has left a deep scar on my heart, following me around the world. This scar, however, has turned out to be the source of a strong determination and undaunted spirit in my life and career.

Hardship never erased my childhood dream. In 1977, the Chinese government decided to resume the nationwide college matriculation examinations to enroll university freshmen purely by academic merits to replace the on-going system of selecting college students totally based on the political status of their families which had been introduced for many years. Strangely, the news came to me like a cruel joke. With only six years of basic rudimentary education, how could I expect to get through the entrance examinations? I was instantly reduced to defeatism and escapism, and bought a train ticket to visit my father's home village in Shandong to run away from reality. The day before my departure, my engineer maternal uncle came home from a business trip. Furiously, he tore up my train ticket, filled out the application forms for me, and forced me to appear in the entrance examinations. I complied with uncle's instructions and applied for studying the Spanish language although I could not even tell the number of alphabetical letters in the language. In fact, I was no different from millions of Chinese of my age. If only I could go to college, I wished fervently, I would not even mind becoming a veterinarian and hang around asses.

For three days, I braved the torrential winter rains with a broken umbrella to reach the examination hall six times and without any escort, not even an encouraging smile from a bystander. It turned out that my scores were exceedingly high, and I was admitted to the Department of Spanish and Portuguese languages at the Beijing Institute of Foreign Languages. At the age of nineteen, with this incredible bit of luck and an utter lack of confidence, I rode a train for 48 hours to the capital of China to live my dream with a four-year college study in tow.

The Beijing Institute of Foreign Languages (now the Beijing Foreign Studies tiny Asian female.

In the US, the second largest group of immigrants is Hispanic, making up 17% of the population. Millions of people speak fluent Spanish which is becoming the second most important language in the US. I have taught Spanish for over twenty years to students from various ethnicities, including second-generation, Latino immigrant families or teenage immigrants. For both, Spanish is their native and daily language. For the past eight years, I have been teaching also a third-year Spanish literature course at the college level in suburban Washington D.C. Many of my students come from families of elite professionals or high-ranking diplomats with a Latino affinity.

These young boys and girls follow my guided tour in the vast spectrum of Latin American literature every year. We memorize together the poems of Pablo Neruda and mingle our tears over the melancholic romances of Garcia Lorca's 'Gitanos' (gypsies). Little do they realize their tri-lingual professor is the first female recipient of a doctoral degree in Latin American literature among 1.3 billion Chinese — the person who emigrated to the US 28 years ago and, beneath her genteel smile, lies the trail of a long, twist-and-turn adventure of inter-continental passage from Xiamen in southern China to Beijing, to New York, then Washington.

I was an only child and granddaughter of a traditional Chinese family eager to shower affection for its 'pearl-in-the-palm.'[1] Those were happy days, full of childhood dreams. However, when I started first grade, a totally unexpected political turmoil consumed China — the so-called Cultural Revolution. My grandparents who helped my sick mother to raise me were humiliated and tortured due to their capitalist background and 'counter-revolutionary' status. I was a silent victim-cum-witness to those catastrophic years of my homeland.

Thanks to several of my talented uncles and aunts who loved music and literature, I was able to spend my early years listening to classical music and reading Chinese literary masterpieces. From those songs and verses, I envisioned a dream of learning more and more to become erudite one day and to be able to teach literature at a university. Due to my diligence and gifts, I finished my elementary education in four years. I went on to middle school for two years as this had been cut short in China due to so-called 'educational reforms.' After completing middle school, I could not brook the mediocre education any longer. To escape 'rustification' in rural areas, I dropped out of high school at age 16 and took up a job as a day-care teacher at a boarding school for kindergarteners.

There was no heart-warming music or color in my life anymore, only babies crying and dirty linens. Aside from teaching toddlers and preschoolers, I also bathed them, hand-washed their clothes in frigid water, grew vegetables, fed pigs,

---

1 This is a Chinese phrase similar in meaning to 'apple of her [parent's] eye.'

Daring to Dream in the United States: An Aria Sung by a Spanish Professor of Chinese Origin[1]

Xuhua Liang 梁旭华

She was born on the scenic island in the southern China: Xiamen (Amoy), Fujian. During the political turmoil of Chinese Cultural Revolution, her mother passed away. Raised by her grandparents, she was deeply influenced by her uncles and their love for traditional Chinese literature. Even though she only had six years of basic education, she qualified the all-China examinations for higher education with a high grade in 1977 and gained admission to the most prestigious language university in China: Beijing Foreign Language Institute (today the Beijing Foreign Studies University). After she graduated with a Bachelor of Arts in Spanish, she worked as a full time translator at the Foreign Languages Press, Beijing. She passed the national examination for the master program of Latin American literature and rejoined her Alma Mater. Two years later, she received a full scholarship to study Latin American literature at the State University of New York at Stony Brook. There she received her Master's and Ph.D. in Latin American Literature.

During her twenty eight years in the U.S., she has devoted herself completely to teaching Spanish language and literature. She has taught at different state universities and private colleges to American and international students. She moved from New York to Bethesda near Washington D. C., where she has been teaching Spanish language and university Spanish literature courses.

For more than twenty years, often when I am about to roll-call for the first lesson of Spanish Literature during the Fall semester, the classroom door suddenly swings open — tardy students, one after another, storm in and feel so embarrassed when they see me in the teacher's seat. Turning back as quickly as they rush in, thinking they have crashed into a Chinese language class, they hear a genteel female voice beckoning them in chaste Spanish: 'Yes, this is your Spanish class…' Never have these young American people imagined that their Spanish professor would be a

---

[1] For writing this essay, I am indebted to my beloved daughter, Zhi Fan Chang, with whom I share many of my dreams, one after another.

Part I
My Trail Trodden by My Feet

the knowledge they receive from one source, whether Chinese or Western, and draw—even if partially, incrementally, or experimentally—on multiple traditions from multiple sites and see what results. For China, many of our contributors have emphasized, this means learning (or re-learning) the wisdom of how to live *in* the world, as one among many, rather than as a mighty Phoenix, perched high above and away from all others. Perhaps, in this way, we could all experience a rebirth for ourselves, for China, and for the world.

L.H.M. Ling (凌焕铭)
December 2014
New York, USA

Introduction II

Professor Tan's offer to co-edit this volume came as a delightful surprise and deep honor. I had met Professor Tan only once before, when he gave a talk at The New School and I had served as his moderator. The occasion happened to fall, quite by coincidence, on Professor Tan's eightieth birthday. Yet, I feel in retrospect, we were the ones celebrating a birth that day. At one point in the discussion, an especially aggressive member of the audience, a man in his 40s, challenged Professor Tan's ability to conduct 'proper historical analysis' due to some contention regarding an empirical fact. *He must have been trained in Germany!*, I thought testily. Instead, Professor Tan answered gently: 'We may disagree but I don't question your identity as a historian, why do you question mine?'

This encounter revealed a distinction in knowledge *and* politics. Professor Tan did not respond with the usual verbal jousting, so common in academic debates, to throw off a younger member in the audience who, in turn, sought to upset the older, more established speaker with a tricky question. Quite the contrary, Professor Tan personified and marshaled the wisdom of two ancient civilizations—Indian and Chinese—to reframe the question to the questioner: that is, can we *talk* without you trying to show you are superior and I am inferior, or *vice versa*? Yet this is precisely the kind of wisdom that has been marginalized by the West after five centuries of colonialism and imperialism. And many cultural heirs to India and China have internalized this Western-centric way of thinking as much as their counterparts in the West. Indeed, the aggressive questioner himself was originally from China.

This volume aims to build on the insight from that day. And it does so precisely by voicing 'the Chinese Other' within a context of 'the Western Self'. (Almost all of our contributors are Chinese who live and work in North America or Europe.) In focusing on this cultural-ethnic bridge called overseas Chinese, our volume achieves two goals at the same time: (1) it disrupts the binary of Self vs Other (exemplified by Kipling's *White Man's Burden*) by showing that a vibrant 'middle' exists, even though some overseas Chinese, like the aggressive questioner mentioned above, may think and act in ways that have left Chinese civilization far behind; and (2) in accessing the dreams of overseas Chinese, we see how identities and experiences are never pristine. Instead, they overlap, mix, and co-create given simultaneous histories of struggle and triumph, sorrow and joy, old-home-sickness and new-home-making. From this 'middle', *all* Chinese could learn to interrogate more you give away to others the more you will possess' (既以与人己愈多), then the nightmare of the past will not recur, and the 'Chinese dream' will be truly a sweet dream.

Readers can discover from our book that there is an ardent wish in every essay for living the 'Chinese dream'. The articles also offer criticisms on the various stages of Chinese development and on certain unsavoury Chinese phenomena. These are from the bottom of our hearts for the reference of Chinese government and people.

Dear readers! Our book is a collection of essays that reflects the various opinions of the authors. I am a co-editor, not their spokesman. What I can do is to offer their ardent words from the bottom of their hearts. If these words are laudable they are here for your appreciation. If these words are improper, they are here for your criticism and correction.

Tan Chung (谭中)
November, 2014
Chicago, USA

Should not these also become the inspiration of our 'Chinese dream' today?

All the Chinese in China and overseas are the posterity of the legendary Yellow Emperor (黄帝) and Sun God (炎帝). The 'Chinese dream' of the Chinese in China is more profound than that of overseas Chinese while the 'Chinese dream' of the overseas Chinese is more comprehensive than that of the Chinese in China. We have, in the last section of our book, a symposium on 'Chinese dream' jointly participated by the Chinese in China and the overseas Chinese. Professor Wang Yiwei, an expert in international relations of the Renmin University of China, initiated the discussion by his discourse on *Transform the 'Chinese dream' into a world dream*' in which he quotes the Song Dynasty scholar, Zhang Zai's (张载):

> Develop a heart for Heaven and Earth,
> Ensure life for all people,
> Continue the forgotten wisdom of past sages,
> Establish peace for all eternity.
> (为天地立心，为生民立命，为往圣继绝学，为万世开太平)

Wang thinks that these are the inspirations of today's 'Chinese dream'.

Just when I wrote these words I saw an article in *The Pioneer*[1] dated June 23, 2014 authored by Mr. Balbir Punj, member of the Rajya Sabha[2] and the newly elected Vice President of the BJP (Bharatiya Janata Party). The article advocates that India should strike an alliance with Russia, China, America, U.K., Europe, Bangladesh, Thailand, Indonesia and so on to face the challenge of the 'Islamic State of Iraq and Syria'(ISIS) which is also called the 'Islamic State of Iraq and Revan'(ISIR). It is very clear to us overseas Chinese that the entire world is in an Era of Peace. The US would not want to fight war with China, Japan would not want to fight war with China, Vietnam would not want to fight war with China and India would not want to fight war with China. And no other country would want to fight war with China except the ISIS/ISIR which vows to turn Xinjiang into the Empire of Eastern Turkistan. If China really rises 'peacefully', not pursuing power, nor hegemony, properly tackling and resolving the problems and disputes with other countries; meanwhile in economic development and international trade avoiding the single-minded '*dui wo shengcai* (对我生财)/fortune to come only my way', observing the principles of 'win-win' and 'sharing prosperity', even adhering to what Laozi taught: 'the more you work for others the richer you are' (既以为人己愈有) and 'the

---

1 The English newspaper published from New Delhi which is supposed to be the mouthorgan of the Bharatiya Janata Party (BJP) which is currently the ruling party of India.

2 The upper house of Indian parliament.

and external aggressions and there was no sign of the 'beautiful country', and 'the twilight of the new era'. However, the observations of Sun Yat-sen injected the 'Chinese dream' into the minds of the people who began to wait for the 'birth of a new China'. On October 1, 1949, Mao Zedong spoke with his heavy Xiangtan (湘潭) accent: 'the Chinese people have stood up'. That was, indeed, a historic moment. Gone is the sad plight of China of being aggressed upon by foreign powers after the 'birth of a new China'. What I had experienced in my boyhood—'We haven't erased the national shame,/To our anger, there's no end.'—can only be witnessed in historical movies. Today, I am afraid that the 'Chinese dream' of our young generations in China for 'rejuvenating China' is rather different from the perceptual knowledge of the older generations like us.

I hear some young Chinese feel boring about 'qiali (起来)/rise', 'qiali (起来)/rise' of the National Anthem! I remember being a student of the primary school in the 1930s and so fond of singing this song which was titled the 'Marching song of the volunteers' (义勇军进行曲). In 1959, when I heard from the radio (no television then) that Rong Guotuan (容国团) won the singles international champion of table-tennis when I was teaching in India, the sound of the 'Marching song of the volunteers' (义勇军进行曲) me exhilarated. Tears burst out, and I sang in my heart: 'Up! We who refuse to be slaves!' and 'we unite, thousands into one, brave the enemy fire, march forward!' In the 1970s, suddenly, these words were replaced by 'we, generation after generation, hold high the banner of Mao Zedong, advance!' by Hua Guofeng (华国锋) and others. Being shocked and depressed, I no longer felt it was my national anthem. (Fortunately, the revised wording was rejected by the third plenum of the eleventh Party congress.) All this shows that no one can tamper with the historical background of the 'Chinese dream'. Today, when we talk about the 'Chinese dream', we must not sever it from its historical background.

Then, there is the problem about sorting out the historical background of the 'Chinese dream' which had a millennial duration. I have alluded to Li Bai's dreaming of:

> How I wish that
> I have
> The magic sword
> In my hand
> To slay the triton
> Across the ocean!
> I shall ride the wind
> And break the waves,
> My sail charges ahead
> Into the blue spread.

Spanish language and literature who has the black hair and yellow skin. Our book glitters with her story of success through arduous efforts. Zhu Xintian (朱新天), the first overseas Chinese to create a museum of Eastern art in the Western world, has a long story to tell. She has authored two excellent articles for our book. All the twenty articles of our book have their excellent stories that await the readers' perusal to realize the richness of the 'Chinese dream' of overseas Chinese and savour China's spirit culture.

Liang Xuhua has unique experiences in the US. Her black hair and yellow skin constantly cause misunderstanding for her life and career as an expert of Spanish language and literature. When she is in the teacher's seat in the Spanish classroom of an American university, tardy students storm in to think they must have crashed into a wrong class. When she is joining a high-lever seminar of Spanish literature, American experts are shocked to think she must have crashed into a wrong conference. However, ultimately this overseas Chinese has gained the confidence of the American community of Spanish teachers, and has been passionately welcomed into the American club of experts on Spanish literature. How we hope all overseas Chinese create the loveable and respectable *black-hair-and-yellow-skin* image like Liang Xuhua. Unfortunately that is not to be.

We have to remember 'there is always internal disorder and external treachery' from time immemorial. We always have good guys and bad guys among overseas Chinese. Some Chinese live overseas to bring blasphemy to the name of China and some even betray the forbears of their ethnicity. However, the overwhelming majority of overseas Chinese holds up the banner of Chinese civilization and help the motherland confirm its image of 'peaceful rise'. Many authors of our book have their achievements overseas. The achievement of Prof./Dr./Ms. Ho Shuk-mei (何淑薇) in medicine and medical research is to be noted and appreciated. The article of Professor Wing-Chi Chan (陈永智) is a moving account on two internationally famous musicians—that of Prof. Chou Wen-chung (周文中) and himself. There is also the achievement of Professor Li Zhihua (李治华), the translator of the classic '*Honglou meng* (红楼梦)/The red-chamber dream' into French being highlighted in Yu Longyu's article. Unexpectedly, our book has transcended its original aim of 'overseas Chinese and the 'Chinese dream' and turned out to become an account of the success stories of Chinese in their strife for living the 'Chinese dream' abroad.

The article of Mr. Zheng Guoqiang (郑国强), President of the Association concerned with Macau's history and heritage, helps us trace the genesis of 'Chinese dream' in modern times by highlighting the two pioneers, Zheng Guanying (郑观应) and Sun Yat-sen (孙中山) and their ideals. Sun Yat-sen was confident a hundred odd years ago that 'the twilight of the new era will dawn on our beautiful country' and 'universal peace will follow the birth of a new China'. I was born a quarter of a century after Sun Yat-sen had said this. China was plagued by internal strives

University, and Professor Hu Chang-tu (胡昌度), renowned expert on education of Columbia University. Professor Tong Te-kong initially had some grievances against the People's Republic of China. However, he was often insulted publicly by white Americans who would cry 'Johnny' (which carried the same derogatory connotation as 'Nigger'). One day, he had reached the limit of his toleration, and went to confront his tormentors face-to-face and said loudly: 'Johnny has the atom bomb now!' Those who were insulting him melted away timidly.

Hu Chang-tu (who is more senior than an octogenarian now and I wish him long life) told me that those who went from China to study in the US in the 1940s were all social creams, and they worked diligently in their studies, adding Ph D to their Master's degree from US universities. In the early years of the 1950s they had all the impressive academic qualifications but no job. Many went into the 'three *guans* (三馆)' the Chinese Americans were famous for—'*Zhongcanguan* (中餐馆)/Chinese restaurant', '*xiyiguan* (洗衣馆)/dry-cleaner', and '*tushuguan* (图书馆)/library'. Getting a teaching post in the university was as difficult as going to Heaven. Then, there was the rise of the People's Republic of China and especially the Korean War. The Americans realized how tough it was to tackle China, and strengthened the Chinese studies at their level best. Many Chinese scholars began to find good jobs in the universities. They all cried 'Long live Chairman Mao' from their heart whether they were pro- or anti-communist. These two illustrations vividly tell that overseas Chinese depend upon the backing of the motherland for good life, and that overseas Chinese have a personal interest in living the 'Chinese dream'.

We overseas Chinese easily see the rationality that 'there is only one globe for the humanity'. On the one hand, the earth is increasingly becoming flatter, and distances shrinking beyond recognition. On the other hand, the size, weight, fame and responsibility of China are growing larger and larger in comparison with other countries. Overseas Chinese are reflecting China in a nutshell. 'Wherever I go it is China' is an excellent topic thought out by young overseas Chinese, Ms Yu Xiu (郁秀) for our book. Her father, stalwart academician, Professor Yu Longyu (郁龙余) of Shenzhen University, composed the article for our book to add glitter to it. The article says: 'China is a "country", but more of a millennia-old civilization.' Every overseas Chinese is the representative of this millennial civilization. The overseas Chinese have contributed greatly to China's 'making friends all over the world'.

I must highlight two authors of our book who grew up in the People's Republic of China with great ambitions and ultimately giving a good account of themselves abroad, bringing credit to their motherland. Liang Xuhua (梁旭华) who was reared up by her maternal grandparents benefited in her childhood from her talented music and literature-loving uncles and aunts and inherited the wisdom and aspirations and ideals of the millennial Chinese civilization. She surprised the American community of Spanish teaching and research as the lone expert of

noble priests from Chang'an
set out in groups of hundreds,
not even ten of them return.
Posterity cannot imagine
how hard the pioneers had been.

'Set out in groups of hundreds, not even ten of them return', thus are we informed by Yijing about the undaunted spirit of the ancient pilgrims. Liang Qichao called this the ancient Chinese movement of going abroad to study. The overwhelming majority of the authors of our book are the modern participants of such a study movement—hence the successors of the ancient pilgrims. They have been living the 'Chinese dream'. It is the 'Chinese dream' to land them in the situation of 'fours seas to one family'. Readers can learn from their discourses of the 'Chinese dream' blending perceptual and conceptual knowledge.

Readers can see how closely connected are the existence and circumstances of the overseas Chinese with the development and vicissitudes of China. Professor Lin Mingya, a Buddhist expert of Singapore writes: 'I am a third generation overseas Chinese'. He describes 'the goals of two "one hundred years" set out in the 18th National Congress of the Communist Party of China' as those which can 'bring the Sinic civilization to new heights' and 'my greatest 'Chinese dream' at this very moment'—the dream of 'a descendant of the Sinic Civilization'.

Among our authors we also have the second generation of the Chinese who have created careers overseas. Professor Yuan Tsing (袁清) starts with the 'Chinese dream' of his father (famous librarian and expert of library science, Yuan Tongli (袁同礼) and, then, moves onto his own 'Chinese dream'. His autobiographic narrative movingly presents a part of the story of the two generations striving for a career in the U.S.A., and a part of the entire story of the 'Chinese dream'. My own article opens with 'Alone I embark on a long journey to a foreign country' written by my father, Tan Yun-shan (谭云山) in 1924 when he left the country. He earned the reputation of the 'modern Xuanzang', actually his last sojourn in China was in 1959 as a specially invited member of the Chinese People's Political Consultative Conference. He had no chance to visit China till he was recalled by Lord Buddha from a Chinese temple at Bodhgaya in Bihar State in India.

When I was appointed a lecturer in Chinese language by Delhi University and participated in the establishment of a Department of Chinese Studies being aided by the Ford Foundation during mid–1960s, I had the opportunity of meeting and chatting with two scholars sent by the Ford Foundation to help and guide our work—two senior overseas Chinese who had left China to study in the US during the 1940s, i.e., Professor Tong Te-kong (唐德刚), late famous historian-cum-writer, former Chairman of the Department of East Asian Studies of New York City strong', and 'a universal moderate prosperous society', and have our real 'Chinese dream'.

We bring out this book not to present an authoritative discourse on 'Chinese dream' because 'Chinese dream' is not a political theory, and discussing it is not a special privilege for anyone. The 'Chinese dream' does not form the ideas of one particular school hence impossible for any 'hundred schools contending'. Today, we have Chinese theoretical authorities merrily discuss 'Chinese dream', we also have Chinese common people merrily discuss 'Chinese dream'. We have Chinese within and outside China merrily discuss 'Chinese dream', we also have foreigners merrily discuss 'Chinese dream' internationally. When we, overseas Chinese, quietly watch foreigners merrily discuss 'Chinese dream', we laugh at their scratching the boot in order to stop an itch of the foot. Nevertheless, we concede that foreigners have the same right as the overseas Chinese to merrily discuss 'Chinese dream' and arrive at this or that, rational or ridiculous conclusions. Similarly, experts and intellectual elites in China might feel that we overseas Chinese cannot merrily discuss 'Chinese dream' as deeply and relevantly as they can, but they should concede to us overseas Chinese the right to merrily discuss the 'Chinese dream' and arrive at this or that, rational or ridiculous conclusions.

However, there is a basic difference between the foreigners' merrily discussing the 'Chinese dream' for the fun of it and our discussing it in this book. We want to talk about ourselves through discussing the 'Chinese dream', and we want to discuss the 'Chinese dream' through talking about ourselves. Had there not been the 'Chinese dream' there would not have been us the overseas Chinese. Had there not been us the overseas Chinese the 'Chinese dream' would not have been so sweet.

Readers will see this sentence in Zhang Siqi's article in our book: '"O! Footprint of the wanderer/That's the mixture/Of blood and tears." Since time immemorial this has been the description of the Chinese who uprooted themselves from their homeland.' Karl Marx described that every sleeper of the American transcontinental railroad symbolized a corpse of the Chinese migration workers. Whenever people discuss the overseas Chinese, their tearful stories inevitably overwhelm our minds. However, in Chinese history we also had ancients who cherished noble ideals and wanted to '*qiufa* (求法)' (in search of Buddha-dharma) and '*qujing* (取经)' (get the authentic Buddhist scriptures) from India. Reverend Yijing (义净), the renowned Chinese pilgrim who went to India to get the authentic Buddhist scriptures in the 7th century wrote:

> During the period from Jin
> to the Southern and Northern regimes,
> in addition to our Dynasty Tang,

end up in Li Bai's bosom and mind. No wonder a spectacular picture was woven between his living reality and his ambit of imagination! Listen:

> How I wish that
> I have
> The magic sword
> In my hand
> To slay the triton
> Across the ocean!
> (安得倚天剑，跨海斩长鲸)

> I shall ride the wind
> And break the waves,
> My sail charges ahead
> Into the blue spread.
> (长风破浪会有时，直挂云帆济沧海)

In our times, we have our living conditions many times richer than Li Bai's. Our imagination of 'Chinese dream' is also kaleidoscopically gorgeous and variable. We must realize that the speedy roads, speedy railway, motor vehicles, trains, airplanes, space ships, moon-landing gadgets, computers, cell phones and internet, and so forth we now live with are what Li Bai could not have dreamt of. We must also realize that none of these modern gadgets is China's invention hence China has to live the modern life by emulating foreign countries. We must also realize that the countries that have invented these gadgets don't have Li Bai. They don't have Li Bai's imaginations of:

> Falling from Heaven,
> The Yellow River
> Travels to the Eastern Ocean,
> Journeying the *li*s of ten thousand
> Ending in my bosom.

Thus, when we discuss the 'Chinese dream' today, we must respond to what Li Bai had wanted: with the 'magic sword' in hand to 'slay the triton across the ocean' so that our minds are not wallowed in the mire of the worldly vulgarity of the speedy roads, speedy railway, motor vehicles, trains, airplanes, space ships, moon-landing gadgets, computers, cell phones, internet and so on, and lose the millennial civilizational wisdom of China. Only in this way can we have Chinese characteristics when we dream of 'rejuvenating China', making China 'rich and

常在我心头环绕。
只因为耻辱未雪，愤恨难消，
四万万同胞啊，
洒着你的热血去除强暴)

This was a sad song. It suppressed the 'Chinese dream' and let its clarion call vibrate at the bottom of people's heart. I often took this song to the school singing competitions. When I sang it, I was streaming with sweat as my blood was boiling. A teacher saw it and told me: 'Take it easy!' But, I simply could not sing it calmly. Now, when we compare this song with the words of Kipling's *The White Man's Burden* quoted above, we see the excitement of different times and different countries.

When the 'Chinese dream' was calling people to shed their blood, even sacrifice their lives, millions of patriots fell to enable China to stand up. We the overseas Chinese stood as witnesses to this historical process although we did not join the fray. Today, people discuss the 'Chinese dream' emotionally in China. Through this book, we overseas Chinese get into the thick of this discussion. In China, the Chinese have their 'blood boiling'. Outside China, the Chinese also have their 'blood boiling'. Innumerable 'blood boiling' within and outside China surge like 'ripples in the river, waves in the ocean', always marching forward with the times.

> Falling from Heaven,
> The Yellow River
> Travels to the Eastern Ocean,
> Journeying *lis*[1] of ten thousand
> Gushing into my bosom.
> (黄河落天走东海，
> 万里写入胸怀间)

These words of famous Chinese poet, Li Bai (李白), constantly remind us that whether the 'blood is boiling' within or outside China, we have the excitement of Yellow River 'falling from Heaven' and 'travelling to the Eastern Ocean' in our bosoms, it is the crystallization of millennial civilizational wisdom, and the reverberation between the 'civilization-state' of China and the world of humanity. A thousand odd years ago Li Bai had his 'Chinese dream'. The picturesque landscape of China, the unbounded vast country, the adages of the sages and philosophers, the romanticism of the poets, the destiny of the state, the personal experience in society, the vicissitudes of times, and ups-and-downs in life, they all

---

[1] A '*li* (里)' is a Chinese measurement of distance roughly equivalent to half a kilometer.

Part I
My Trail Trodden by My Feet

Introduction I

> Take up the White Man's burden—
> Send forth the best ye breed—
> Go send your sons to exile
> To serve your captives' need.

These words were the opening shot of British poet, Rudyard Kipling's masterpiece, *The White Man's Burden*, which was the outcry of the dream of the West for the conquest of the world. The poem was composed in 1899, and in the year I was born (1929), it became the golden part of the first edition of *Rudyard Kipling's Verse Definitive Edition* published by Doubleday of New York. This verse was universally hailed as the soul of the Era of Imperialism. However, the world hegemony of Great Britain was in the process of meltdown in the rising sun of the 'American dream'. What about the 'Chinese dream'? China was the infamous 'sick man of East Asia' and it would be a laughing stock to talk about the 'Chinese dream'. When I was three, I saw the ferocious Japanese soldiers at Zhabei(闸北) in Shanghai. Later, I grew up like a refugee of the Japanese aggression at my home province, Hunan(湖南). Never had I heard anyone talking about the 'Chinese dream'. Yet, I was daily nurtured by patriotic songs. Even before I was a teenager I fell in love with a song the first stanza reads (my translation):

> My blood boiling,
> My blood boiling,
> Like ripples in the river,
> Waves in the ocean,
> Around my heart gyrating.
> We haven't
> Erased the nation's shame,
> Our fury burns unending.
> O, my fellow-countrymen,
> Four hundred millions of them!
> Go shed your boiling blood
> Drive your tormenters back home.
> (热血滔滔，热血滔滔，
> 像江里的浪，海里的涛，

Dreaming between Civilizations: Rhetoric and Communication　/146
The Moon Ship with Hopes and Dreams　/153
One Intimate Family for China and India: Sharing the 'Rich-and-Strong' Dream　/161

Part IV　Symposium I: Transform the Chinese Dream into a World Dream　/169

Transform the 'Chinese dream' into a World Dream　/171

Part V　Symposium II: Delving into All Aspects of the 'Chinese dream'　/199

The 'Chinese dream': In Comparison with the American Dream　/201
The 'Chinese dream'　/208

Contents

Introduction I /1

Introduction II /11

Part I The Trail Trod by My Feet /13

Daring to Dream in the United States: An Aria Sung by a Spanish Professor of Chinese Origin /15
Wherever I Am, China Is: The 'Chinese dream' Overseas /25
Wish I Were a Rainbow: The First Chinese to Set up a Museum of Eastern Art in the West /33
My 'Chinese dream': Eternal Prosperity for the Great Civilizations of China and India /40
My 'Chinese dream', My Father's Heritage /46
Let Blood/Flesh on Wings of a Waked-up Dragon /55
My Life and Dream about Environmental Health /66
Sailing All the Seas Balanced on a Sword /71

Part II Chinese Dream and the World 79

My Chinese Dream /81
Twilight of a New Era Dawns on Beautiful China /90
Upgrading 'Chinese Power': The Chinese Dream that Creates a 'Common Destiny' for the World /99
The Chinese Pursuit of Common Dreams /107

Part III One Endeared Family within Four Seas /117

For A World of Grand Harmony: A Chinese Dream from Two Generations /119
My Chinese Bridge And My Chinese Dream /128
My Chinese Dream: High Quality Early Childhood Programs for All /139

Four seas to One Family

Overseas Chinese and the Chinese Dream

Edited by Tan Chung & L.H.M. Ling